CLUVERIUS

v.

THE COMMONWEALTH

Virginia's Murder Trial of the Century

A Novel Based on True Characters and Events

By D. N. Wilson

Copyright © 2019 D. N. Wilson

All rights reserved

ISBN-9781072961116

Print Edition 8.25.19

TABLE of CONTENTS

A Note from the Author	*vii*
Acknowledgements...	*ix*
Chapter 1 ... Boulware v. Lumpkin	*p.11*
Chapter 2 ... The Body...	*p.18*
Chapter 3 ... Bath to Richmond	*p.24*
Chapter 4 ... So Do Wait for Me...	*p.27*
Chapter 5 ... Well, Lead Me to the Body	*p.30*
Chapter 6 ... The Demure Marse Robert	*p.34*
Chapter 7 ... Investigating Old Marshall	*p.39*
Chapter 8 ... Insubordination	*p.44*
Chapter 9 ... Canvassing the Area	*p.52*
Chapter 10 ... Are We Friends?	*p.57*
Chapter 11 ... The Autopsy	*p.64*
Chapter 12 ... Sunday Morning	*p.68*
Chapter 13 ... Not Enough Meat	*p.70*
Chapter 14 ... Captain Billy	*p.75*
Chapter 15 ... The Lady in Room 21	*p.81*
Chapter 16 ... It's Lillie Madison	*p.87*
Chapter 17 ... The One-Legged Man	*p.94*
Chapter 18 ... Things Are Going to Change	*p.101*
Chapter 19 ... It Had to be Done	*p.106*
Chapter 20 ... Private Detective	*p.113*
Chapter 21 ... Merton and Cluverius	*p.122*
Chapter 22 ... Mayo's Bridge	*p.128*
Chapter 23 ... American Cincinnatus	*p.132*
Chapter 24 ... The Proud Mrs. Tunstall	*p.136*
Chapter 25 ... Under Arrest	*p.141*
Chapter 26 ... The Prisoner Escapes	*p.146*
Chapter 27 ... You Will Not Forsake Me	*p.149*
Chapter 28 ... Arraignment	*p.151*
Chapter 29 ... The Horn Has Blowed for Dress Parade	*p.160*
Chapter 30 ... A Loser's Bet	*p.167*
Chapter 31 ... The Marshall House	*p.174*
Chapter 32 ... Opening Day	*p.179*
Chapter 33 ... John Brown's Body	*p.191*
Chapter 34 ... Heed Your Own Advice	*p.203*
Chapter 35 ... A Satchel and a Watch-Key	*p.212*
Chapter 36 ... Burn It	*p.220*
Chapter 37 ... Benny Havens, Oh!	*p.226*

Chapter 38...	He Certainly Resembles the Man	p.237
Chapter 39...	Sergeant Haight.	p.245
Chapter 40...	Mad King Ludwig.	p.251
Chapter 41...	The Seduction of Miss Madison.	p.256
Chapter 42...	On the Delaware.	p.265
Chapter 43...	Sic Semper Tyrannus.	p.273
Chapter 44...	A Storm is Coming	p.276
Chapter 45...	We Do What They Want.	p.285
Chapter 46...	Twenty-One Days in May	p.297
Chapter 47...	Better Than Being a Defendant	p.306
Chapter 48...	The 6th of January	p.314
Chapter 49...	Cluverius, Inc.	p.322
Chapter 50...	He Looks Scared	p.325
Chapter 51...	The Prosecution Rests	p.328
Chapter 52...	Loose Ends	p.339
Chapter 53...	The Defiant Mrs. Tunstall.	p.341
Chapter 54...	The Difference Between Doctors and Lawyers.	p.350
Chapter 55...	Who's the Bigger Man?	p.358
Chapter 56...	Welcome to Fendallsburg	p.370
Chapter 57...	Keys to the Case.	p.378
Chapter 58...	So, Be It.	p.385
Chapter 59...	Debt Collection	p.391
Chapter 60...	The Dark Mantle of Midnight.	p.395
Chapter 61...	What He Deserves	p.402
Chapter 62...	Step Forward, Mr. Cluverius	p.412
Chapter 63...	Give Them Their Waterloo	p.420
Chapter 64...	Appomattox to New York	p.426
Chapter 65...	The Readjusters	p.436
Chapter 66...	Small Compensation.	p.440
Chapter 67...	The Fight for His Life	p.445
Chapter 68...	Mud Splattering in the Homestretch	p.456
Chapter 69...	Mugwumps and Warhorses	p.462
Chapter 70...	A Riot in Baltimore	p.468
Chapter 71...	The Right to Testify	p.479
Chapter 72...	Toddies at The Willard	p.482
Chapter 73...	Incoming Fire from All Directions	p.487
Chapter 74...	Coming Over to Your Side	p.501
Chapter 75...	All's for the Best	p.509
Epilogue		p.516
Appendix		p.526
Bibliography/Notes		p. 528/537

A Note from the Author

There can be little doubt that *The Commonwealth of Virginia v. Thomas J. Cluverius* was Virginia's "Trial of the 19th Century". The crime and the events leading up to it were multi-faceted, leading the observer in many intriguing directions. The investigation was equally complex, yet was conducted with such meticulous rigor, that it could rival any investigation of the present day, albeit without the tools of modern forensics and surveillance. Investigators were able to identify the unknown victim and place the suspect under arrest within five days of the crime. The trial was exhaustive and truly Herculean in scope, considering that the proceedings commenced a mere fifty-five days after the arrest. The prosecution brought forth an astounding eighty-three witnesses while the defense provided an additional sixty-one. The verdict was entered twenty-three days after the trial commenced. Packed within those eighty-three days is a tale which contains all of the elements of a great story; forbidden love, sex, murder (perhaps multiple murders), lasciviousness, lying, cheating, witness-tampering, corruption; all juxtaposed with honor, duty, perseverance, loyalty, and an adherence to the law. And, all the while, a voracious local and national press closely followed the proceedings; blasting sensational headlines and commentary across the country on daily basis.

Richmond at this time was a city just twenty years removed from the catastrophic consequences of the Civil War. It was a city which had come quite some distance from the desperate days of 1865, but was still on the mend; still grappling, as all of the South was, with its post bellum identity. This understanding led me to consider the story in the context of Virginia's long history – a history replete with victories and losses, achievement and failure, morality and immorality. The story, for me, became about the omnipresent contradictions of human nature. It clearly illustrates the observation often attributed to Mark Twain, "History doesn't repeat itself, but often rhymes." The conflicts and choices which these men and women of the 19th century faced still reverberate through our own times; war and peace, law and order, the role of the Federal Government, sectionalism, social mores, matters of race, equality, freedom of the press, sensationalized journalism (media), political corruption, police corruption, and personal corruption - just to name a few. It is said that our precious Republic can be lost in a generation or two if we fail to teach and understand, within proper context, the struggles which have persisted since our founding and those oft-times imperfect attempts to address them; efforts which continually renew and, at times, redefine the "American Experiment". The similarity between issues and experiences Americans of the 19th century faced and those which we face today should not be ignored. Nor should the remedies employed by these 19th century Americans be ignored. There is wisdom to be found in both their successes and failures; just as there will be for future generations to find in our own.

As I drilled-down deeper into some of the personalities involved with this matter, it occurred to me that their conduct was certainly influenced and informed by the events which preceded them. It was Governor Fitzhugh Lee, a critical player in the ultimate resolution of the Cluverius case, who drew my particular interest. Lee's story has largely gone unsung as the centuries have turned. His exceptional life-experience, coupled with the power of his indefatigable personality, made him one of the shining characters of 19th century Virginia. Much can be learned from a man whose life spanned an era in American history which presented a direct threat, perhaps rivaled only by the Revolution itself, to the survival of its people. Fitzhugh Lee not only witnessed the destruction and rebuilding of a nation, but actively participated in each, first by bravely waging war on the Union and then, after honorably accepting defeat, by humbly crossing the fault lines and boldly bridging the chasm.

Although I have conducted a substantial amount of independent historical research on the trial and other historical figures and events which I have incorporated into the story, this work is, first and foremost, a novel. The preponderance of the information and events is somewhat accurate, but, in the interest of cohesion, I have consolidated, blended, truncated, and simplified several of the events and characters. For example, my story features only thirty-five witnesses for the prosecution (as opposed to the aforementioned eighty-three). As another example, the lead prosecuting attorney's final argument lasted an inconceivable nine hours. My rendition of his oratory is, thankfully, far shorter. I have also embellished and dramatized events, altered some timelines, and introduced entirely fictional characters and events; all with the goal of moving the story forward and illustrating the themes therein. This said, I have attached detailed endnotes to help "separate fact from fiction" for those readers who may be interested in such things. I have also included a bibliography to help any interested reader consult my sources for an even more in-depth analysis. Lastly, I have clearly drawn some inflammatory inferences regarding the actions and intent of Thomas J. Cluverius and others involved with the matter which cannot be proven. These are my own opinions and theories. However, they do largely coincide with the findings of the court and the historical record.

Acknowledgements

First and foremost, I would like to acknowledge my parents. In addition to being wonderful parents, they always took great care to expose my sister and me to Virginia history. In particular, my mother has ingrained in me a love for historical anecdotes. She has been a great sounding-board for my ideas throughout the process. It's often the smaller stories in history which provide context for understanding the bigger picture.

It could be said that I have been marinating in Virginia history from the beginning. I was raised in Old Town Alexandria, Virginia, spent my college years in Colonial Williamsburg, Virginia, and have lived my entire adult life in Arlington, Virginia. The idea that so many of the formative episodes of my state and country occurred in my "back yard" has always intrigued me. Not a day goes by when I don't pass by a place of historical significance and think about the people who lived and worked there; literally setting the course of American events.

I also need to acknowledge a longtime family friend, Fitzhugh Lee Rhea Opie. Mr. Opie was a true student of Civil War history, most particularly of his great grandfather, General Fitzhugh Lee. We had several discussions about his distinguished family through the years. Shortly before his death, he gave me some of his research on the Cluverius Trial and some related documents. These items formed the basis of the information which would grow into this novel. Subsequent to Mr. Opie's death in 2000, I began to read through the information and was naturally quite intrigued by the subject-matter. By 2002 I decided that I needed to try to put pen to paper and get this amazing tale out to the public. I wrote most of the first half of the book at that time; but alas, the joyful demands of a family business and raising a young family of my own took precedent. By 2004 I had stopped researching and writing, but the idea that one day I would return to and complete the story never left my mind. In 2018, my family now grown, I dove back into the project. Of course, I have found that during my hiatus, others had re-discovered the story of the Cluverius Trial. Several books and articles have been written on the subject in recent years. I have purposely avoided reading these works, choosing instead to rely upon, as much as possible, primary sources for my information. I did not want my thoughts, reactions, and ideas to be influenced by the research of my contemporaries. Although I have fictionalized events and characters in the story, I have also tried to stay true to the broad elements of the case and the personalities involved. Admittedly, some are depicted more accurately than others. I have tried, to some extent, to "set the record straight" in the "Epilogue" and "Notes" sections of the book.

I have listed over 140 different sources (the large majority being primary sources) which informed this story. Certainly, the story could be approached from a purely historical perspective. An author could probably fill three volumes if he or she chose to dig deeply into each of the incidents and individuals which arose from the proceedings. In many ways, my work only scratches the surface. I chose to weave the story into a novel, a format which I hope will hold the interest of the reader and still provide some informative historical context and perspective to the times and places in which it all transpired. I felt that a pure, straight recitation of the facts, though full of information, may not hold the attention of a casual reader. Not all readers are historians; but almost all readers like to be entertained (and maybe learn a thing or two along the way).

As stated, I have consulted many different sources. This most definitely would not have been possible for me were it not for the internet, in general, and the site Newspaperarchive.com, in particular. That site has been an invaluable tool; allowing me to search, access, and organize nearly 200 newspaper articles from all over the country relating to the subject matter.

Many thanks to Rachel at Old Town Editions in Alexandria, Virginia for all of her help with the cover design.

Lastly, I would like to thank a couple of friends of mine, Michael and Dave; two fellow "volleyball dads" who have indulged me by energetically discussing the topics which have arisen with the writing of the book; both from content and technical perspectives. I have often thought that, other than my own mother, these may be the only two people to actually read the book!

Chapter 1   *Boulware v. Lumpkin*

More than a dozen people in King William County Courthouse rose to their feet. Judge John D. Foster reemerged from his chamber following a midday recess and approached the bench. Every other Wednesday civil cases were brought before the court. Most of these hearings regarded simple disputes, usually of a business nature. With few variations, these cases were heard and ruled upon within the same day. At 12:50 PM, on March 18, 1885, Judge Foster firmly struck his gavel.

"Please, come to order." the judge bellowed. "Plaintiff's counsel, you may begin your closing remarks. But, gentlemen, please avoid extraneous argument. This court has a great deal of business to address and over-extended oratory will not advance your case."

The plaintiff's attorney stepped in front of his table and collected his thoughts. The short boyish lawyer cleared his throat and quickly wiped his brow, then his upper lip, before making his first closing argument before the indomitable Judge Foster.

"Your honor. The record shows that on November 1, 1883, Mr. Samuel Boulware of Gloucester County, the plaintiff, legally deeded two hundred seven acres located in this jurisdiction, King William County, complete with improvements thereon, to the defendant, Mrs. Annabelle Lumpkin. The Deed was recorded among the land records of this county. Also brought forth is clear evidence of a debt. The defendant verbally agreed to purchase the aforementioned acreage from the plaintiff for an amount equal to $3,300.00. Both the plaintiff and the defendant have confirmed this fact; and the real estate solicitor, Mr. William Fleet, has corroborated it. The defendant willfully paid $100 cash toward this amount at the time of sale and willfully executed a Note for $3,200.00, payable in ten equal annual installments plus applicable interest. The defendant has acknowledged this indebtedness and has acknowledged that she has not made the first payment due November 1, 1884. The original Note has been submitted to the court as evidence for the debt. Despite the defendant's flat refusal to pay as agreed, defendant has continued to occupy the property and has made no effort to satisfy the plaintiff."

"The plaintiff entered this agreement in good faith. The terms of the indebtedness, as expressed in the Note, have clearly been breached by the defendant with impunity. Per the motion for judgment and the bill of indebtedness filed with the court, the plaintiff hereby requests that this court affirm the debt and enter a summary judgment against the defendant for the amounts outstanding per the terms of the Note plus all court costs and plaintiff's reasonable attorney fees. Plaintiff requests that such judgment be in a form recordable with the County Clerk's Office in this jurisdiction and any other jurisdiction within the Commonwealth, in order to secure the debt and grant the plaintiff an avenue for remedy. Thank you, your honor."

The young plaintiff's counsel smiled slightly at the judge and returned to his seat assured that he had put forth a very convincing argument on behalf of his client.

The defendant's counsel stood and walked toward the small pulpit in front of the judge. He was a tall, brash, clean-shaven young man with a head full of wavy dark brown hair. He subtly manipulated a small golden chain that dangled from his watch chain. He rubbed the end of the short chain between his left forefinger and thumb as he stood before the judge and offered his final defense.

"Your honor, my client, the defendant, Mrs. Annabelle Lumpkin, agreed to purchase two hundred seven acres from Mr. Samuel Boulware in October, 1883. The sale was finalized November 1, 1883. The original recorded Deed of that date has been submitted into evidence. It is my client's contention that although the sale was finalized and a Note was signed for a portion of the sales price, the terms of the verbal agreement, which initially bound the transaction, have been severely breached by the plaintiff, and therefore, in effect, have voided the terms of the Note. The plaintiff made inaccurate representations regarding the condition of the property at the time of sale. As a result, my client has been forced to burden many unexpected costs to repair the property, placing upon her undue financial stress. This unfortunate burden has served only to exacerbate her already tenuous medical conditions, including, among other afflictions, a weak heart and pellagra. This court has heard the testimony of Mrs. Lumpkin's carpenter, Mr. Curtis Roane, describing just how extensive the deterioration is and how costly it will be to fully restore. My client has already spent $200 making necessary repairs. As the court has been made aware, these repairs are wholly inadequate and she stands to spend much more than that to make the premises habitable by basic standards. We have heard testimony stating that the plaintiff never revealed the poor state of the property to my client. The court also has in its possession a copy of the letter my client wrote to the plaintiff in October, 1884, describing in detail the misrepresented condition of the property. It is my client's contention that these misrepresentations constitute a breach of the verbal sales contract."

The defendant's counsel locked eyes with Judge Foster and sensed the judge's patience was wearing thin. Wisely, the quick-thinking young attorney abbreviated his remaining comments and brought his defense to a conclusion. "It is incumbent upon the plaintiff to remedy this breach, your honor. Until such time this remedy is complete, the defendant is under no obligation to adhere to the terms of the Note; a Note that was signed under false pretenses. It is incumbent upon this court to deny the plaintiff's plea for judgment and to use the authority of the court to cancel the Note. Thank you, your honor."

The defendant's attorney stepped away and the plaintiff's attorney rose for his final comments.

"Your honor; the Note which has been submitted into evidence is indeed valid. It was executed willfully by the defendant and represents a valid debt associated with a legal arms-length transaction. If the court were to invalidate the Note, as the defendant's counsel suggests, it would deal a serious setback to our civil system. We cannot set a precedent whereby a legal note is invalidated simply because the debtor decides it should be invalidated. This would encourage irresponsible and dishonest conduct of business and would lead to the unraveling of business agreements throughout the Commonwealth. The plaintiff humbly submits that this court uphold the indebtedness and, in fact, further validate it by securing it with a lawful court sanctioned judgment. Thank you, your honor."

Judge Foster looked at his watch. "This court will recess while I deliberate. I will return and render a decision in one half hour – that's at 1:35. I expect all interested parties to be here at that time." The gavel came down again and all rose to their feet as the distinguished judge retired once again to his chamber.

Samuel Boulware stood from the plaintiff's table and anxiously walked to the large window to his right. He put his hands in his trouser pockets and gazed silently outside. Boulware was a widower nearing seventy years of age. He was a tobacco farmer in Gloucester County. His aunt left him the 207-acre farm in King William County upon her death in 1880. She had no children of her own, so she left the property to the only son of her only sibling. Boulware allowed his own son and his new bride live and work on the farm. The young couple was just settling in to begin a family of their own when a typhoid epidemic struck their part of the county, taking the two newlyweds, among dozens of others, within a few weeks. Following this tragedy, Boulware vacillated for a couple years concerning his interest in the property until he ultimately decided to sell.

On the opposite side of the room, the defendant, Annabelle Lumpkin remained seated. She leaned and whispered to her attorney. Though seemingly frail and, at times, introverted, she sat back with arrogance as she removed the shawl from around her head, revealing a face of a woman aged well beyond her years. Annabelle Lumpkin was only forty-two years of age at this time. Many would have guessed she was sixty-two. She had already been married four times and was the mother of three children, all of which had been given up for adoption. Annabelle's first husband died nearly twenty-five years prior from injuries received from a freak farm accident. Her second husband died during the War. Her third husband, after losing his employment, left her and went west. His whereabouts were unknown. Her fourth and final husband died from an apparent self-inflicted gunshot wound six years prior. During and subsequent to her last two marriages, Annabelle had become very adept at confidence gaming. She swindled a string of unsuspecting individuals over the many years; usually single men, by winning their trust and seizing their money or possessions. She rarely maintained a fixed address, thereby becoming known throughout the region as "Suitcase Annie". She had been prosecuted a few times for her unscrupulous acts, but was convicted only once before and never served more than a week or two in jail.

Judge John D. Foster re-entered the courtroom at 1:35 PM. He nodded at the bailiff and sat in his tall-backed chair. He placed his spectacles on his face and thumped the gavel. "Order in the court. Order in the court." he projected. The litigants and the few observers in the court quieted quickly and waited for the judge to render his verdict.

"This case is an interesting study in very poor business practice. One of the central questions of this matter revolves around the validity of this Note." The judge held the Note up and waved it toward the courtroom. "Well, I see no reason to try to dance around that question." He held the Note in front of his face and smartly ripped it in two. A collective gasp came from the court. Mr. Boulware deflated in his chair in catatonic despair. The only hope he had of getting his money was just destroyed. By contrast, Mrs. Lumpkin sat forward and opened her eyes widely in jubilant disbelief. She rubbed her soiled bony hands together in anticipation of complete exoneration.

The judge looked up at Suitcase Annie and sensing her teeming delight he said, "Now, dear Mrs. Lumpkin, this is really no occasion to gloat. In my years on this bench I have found that justice can at times be best achieved when there is neither a clear victor nor a clearly vanquished. This is one of those times." He picked up the Deed to the two hundred seven acres granting her ownership and likewise tore it in two. Suitcase Annie's expression made a rapid three-stage metamorphosis as the judge served his full-baked verdict. From pure satisfaction to surprised discomfort to unbearable indigestion, her demeanor soured as the judicial force-feeding became less and less palatable.

"You see, my friends...", continued the judge, "This transaction was fatally flawed from the outset. There was no written contract and no reliable third-party witnesses to the terms of your so-called verbal contract. Therefore, in the judgment of this court, there never was a lawful agreement. If there was no lawful agreement, then the property could never have been lawfully deeded and a note of indebtedness could not have been lawfully executed. An unlawful contract, written or verbal, invalidates any and all documents and agreements which claim derivation from such contract. Therefore, Mr. Boulware has always been the lawful owner of the property and Mrs. Lumpkin is under no obligation to pay the indebtedness."

"Now, it is my understanding that Mrs. Lumpkin has paid a total of $300.00 relative to her extended stay in the property. She paid Mr. Boulware $100.00 on November 1, 1883 and she has paid for $200.00 of physical improvements to Mr. Boulware's property. She has also lived in the property nearly 17 months. In the judgment of this court, this $300, which has accrued to the benefit of Mr. Boulware, shall be deemed as rent paid by Mrs. Lumpkin to live on the property at a fair rate of $25.00 per month. Therefore, by my arithmetical calculations, it would appear that Mrs. Lumpkin has paid 12 months of rent. However, she has lived in the property for nearly 17 months. Mr. Boulware; as her landlord, under the laws of Virginia, you may require her eviction. Be reminded, Mr. Boulware, that the property taxes are delinquent. You, as the owner throughout, are responsible for all of them, including any penalty. I urge you to visit the Clerk's Office after these proceedings and remedy such. Now, regarding the back rent owed by Mrs. Lumpkin, you are not required to accept any further payment by her, even if it is enough to bring her rent current. If you so wish, I will order her to vacate the premises within a reasonable period of no less than thirty days. How do you answer?"

Mr. Boulware looked at his attorney, then across the room at Mrs. Lumpkin. With vengeful delight he clearly stated, "I want her off my property as soon as possible".

"Very well, sir", said the judge. "It is my order that, in light of the fact that she is now nothing more than a trespasser, Mrs. Lumpkin must vacate the property by May 1 of this year or face a court ordered eviction on May 2. In other words, Annie... Pack your suitcase!" The courtroom erupted in laughter. The bailiff turned bright red trying to suppress his hysteria.

The judge banged his gavel three times. "Enough! Enough! Order, please!", he shouted.

"Now, Mr. Boulware; a word of advice to you. If you want to sell the farm, please make appropriate repairs; or at least make a comprehensive list of the deficiencies. Secondly, demand that the potential purchaser present a written contract in proper form. Ask your attorney to review it before you sign it. Lastly, if you decide to take a note for some part of the sales price, secure it with a recorded trust deed. Your attorney can help you there, as well. Case dismissed!", the judge pounded his gavel one last time then turned to have a private joke with the bailiff.

Suitcase Annie glared at her attorney. "Damn you, Cluverius! You told me you have never lost a case!"

"I still have not, Mrs. Lumpkin. You don't have to pay the Note!", said the young attorney.

"Yes, but now I've got to move off the premises! I've lost my house and it's all your fault!"

"Mrs. Lumpkin. The only thing you have lost is the free ride you sought at the expense of Mr. Boulware."

"You are fired! This will be your last case, but it won't be your last trial! I will make sure of that!", she screeched as a frothy white wad of saliva collected in one corner of her mouth. Thomas J. Cluverius looked into her cold left eye as it pierced through him with bewitching credibility. "You are doomed!", she insisted like a crazed prophet. "Everyone responsible for this is doomed!". The volatile woman clutched her shawl around her and bounded with surprising speed up the center aisle of the courtroom. She flung open the doors to the courtroom with impressive force, loudly cursing her failed attorney every step of the way.

Thomas Judson Cluverius
(Library of Virginia Archives, Richmond)

The draft created by the old hag's hasty departure blew some of Cluverius' papers off the table. As he knelt down to retrieve them, he noticed that all the eyes in the room were trained upon him. He shrugged his shoulders and blushed a little as he crammed the papers in a file folder and latched his brief case. He reached for his hat and nodded to Mr. Boulware and the opposing counsel as he walked silently to the back of the courtroom and exited. (1.1)

The mid-afternoon sun poured down on Cluverius as he entered the walled green public space outside the doors of the King William County Courthouse. He turned and looked back at the impressive brick courthouse structure, pausing briefly as he lost himself in the hypnotic beauty of the Flemish bond brickwork. Feeling strangely sentimental and sensitive to his surroundings, Cluverius filled his lungs to capacity with the fresh mid-March spring air and filled his ears with the nimble melody of the busy songbirds and their honeybee accompaniment. The brick arched piazza cradled the common lawn and the chimneys stretched toward the heavens. It was a scene that was purely Virginian, a serenity of such proportion as is only occasionally attained when architecture and craftsmanship are carefully integrated with the beauty of the natural countryside, rendering a pleasing scene reminiscent of mankind's never-ending quest to incorporate its own best attempts at perfection with the flawless order of the Creator.

The young attorney turned to his right and focused on a smaller but equally well-built building in the complex which housed the Clerk's Office. His first instinct was to immediately file an appeal to Judge Foster's decision, but then he smiled self-deprecatingly as he remembered that he'd just been fired by his client. Cluverius held his head up as he exited the grounds, turned to his left, and walked fifty yards straight ahead where his horse was stabled. Cluverius rolled his suit jacket and fastened it, along with his briefcase, to the saddle. After mounting old *Cornbread*, he adjusted his new black derby squarely on his head, pulled the ends of his suit vest down, and rode east from the small hamlet toward the Mattaponi River, which separated King William County from his home county of King & Queen. He rode two miles before boarding a flat ferry barge which crossed the river using a system of ropes and pulleys. The next run across was scheduled for 3:30 PM, so Cluverius tied *Cornbread* off at one end of the barge and sat himself down near the opposite end, leaning against the split wood rail. He sat upright and looked above, watching the treetops lazily sway in the breeze. He then looked down at some healing scratches on his right hand. The young man gently ran his left hand fingertips across the scratches, bringing some relief to the very low grade pain. He was thankful to have the recent stressful days and weeks behind him. The thought of returning home for a few quiet days was very welcome.

Cluverius passed through the front door of Aunt Jane Tunstall's house a few minutes before 7PM. He had been living with his elderly widowed aunt near Little Plymouth for over nine years. Aunt Jane's husband, Samuel Tunstall, had passed just a few months after Thomas and his brother Willie had come to stay with her. She paid for their schooling including Thomas' two years at Richmond College. Although she experienced some mental lapses, Jane Tunstall was quite independent and her health was generally strong. Aunt Jane's home was in good proximity to King & Queen County Courthouse and Cluverius' law firm employer.

The Tunstall home was a classic frame center hall farm house dating to the colonial era. The clapboards were wide, milled from the enormous pine trees found in the virgin forests of the colonial Old Dominion. The windows were tall with six over six panes. A large room flanked each side of the center hall, which ran from front to back the entire depth of the home and featured a wonderful wide staircase with a hand-carved newel post and delicately complimentary spindles running alongside the ascending the stair treads. There were four large bedrooms upstairs. Out back, there stood a kitchen building, an outhouse, two coops, a tool shed, a large corn crib, and a large barn. The house was situated on over three hundred acres of rich farmland. In addition, Mrs. Tunstall had inherited, through the death of her husband, over one thousand additional acres of farmland throughout the county. She leased all of the land out to tenant farmers, providing her with a large, and wholly unused, income. The house was in generally good condition, but Aunt Jane's age was diminishing her standards for upkeep and young Cluverius' burgeoning career left him little time to attend to such matters.

It struck T.J. Cluverius as odd that Aunt Jane was not on the front porch to greet him that evening. She generally enjoyed watching the sunset, particularly on a warm day. "Aunt Jane?", Cluverius called out as he opened the parlor double doors. "Aunt Jane?", he said again as he pushed through the doors and found Aunt Jane, his brother Willie, and three other men seated in the parlor. He sensed the seriousness in the room as his Aunt looked at him in regretful despair. "Aunt Jane, Willie… What is the matter?"

The three men stood as one. The man on the right was familiar to Cluverius. He stepped forward and said, "Mr. Cluverius… I am Deputy Sheriff Oliver. These men are Captain Epps and Officer Robbins of the Richmond Police." (1.2)

Chapter 2   *The Body*

The James River remained a symbol of prosperity and freedom for those who had inhabited the area from time immemorial, stretching its watery fingers back through the heart of Old Virginia and holding in its grip the history of a nation. The City of Richmond stood firmly at the fall line, at the economic head of the river, at the governing head of the Commonwealth of Virginia, and at the cultural head of Southern Society. Post bellum Richmond was in the midst of a renewal. It was often slow and riddled with complications, but despite the far-reaching destruction of the War, Richmond had successfully reconstituted and now embodied a uniquely glorious combination of Southern American tradition and Victorian style.

Lysander W. Rose was up early this morning. He was up early every morning. The Old Marshall Reservoir was a lifeline for the City of Richmond and although his task as its keeper was quite mundane, he purposefully and faithfully performed a thorough inspection of the facility each morning. The middle-aged keeper finished his cup of coffee and put on his coat. As he swung open the door to the office, he struck a match and lit his first pipe of the day. Wally Trainham stayed behind in the reservoir house, huddled over his warm cup. Not much was said between them. It was the middle of March and winter had passed, but the dampness of early spring still proved uncomfortable, particularly before sunlight. Rose rubbed and flexed his right knee. He hoped his morning inspection would loosen it a bit.

Rose checked his watch and it was just before 6:30 AM. He looked out to his left and saw Lucas getting an early start on repairing the stop-valve. Rose thought to himself, "Hope he gets it right, this time." He walked off in that direction, to the north side of the facility. The sun was just beginning to break that morning. Low-hanging cloud cover sat off to the east, the tail end of a weather system that had moved through overnight. The bottom half was glowing with color, resembling a determined school of salmon struggling upstream against an icy steel blue current passing above. Only the strong ones complete the perilous journey to spawn. Ironically, the very water, which sustains them in life, renders the mere continuation of the species an arduous undertaking.

It dawned upon Rose that he had seen skies like this with some frequency during the War. He had served as a junior officer aboard the C.S.S. Torch, where he gained invaluable technical experience with handling large industrial equipment and in managing men. After the War, Rose was discharged from the disbanded Confederate Navy and returned to Richmond. He owned and operated several businesses in Richmond, including a small life insurance company, a dry goods store, and the Virginia Nursery and Wine Company, to moderate success. He also invested in real estate. Speculative land investments led to cash management problems which resulted in the foreclosure of several properties. This, in turn, left him responsible for a great deal of unsecured debt and subsequent judgments which served to infect all of his operations. It culminated for Rose in a humiliating personal bankruptcy in August, 1877. In 1878, Rose was able to gain employment with the municipal water service of Richmond. He worked in various capacities with the water company and at several different facilities. (2.1)

Rose was named the superintendent of the Old Reservoir two-and-one-half years prior. At the outset, his mission was to oversee the refurbishing, modernization, and upgrading of the reservoir, but setbacks in the City's budget were delaying what was rapidly becoming a critical need. Rose had heard rumors that new studies were recommending the closure of the Old Reservoir and the construction of a new facility further west of the city. He had no idea what that would mean for him, but he had a pretty good understanding of why the City repeatedly came up with the money to fund engineering and cost study after cost study, but never seemed to have any money for the facility itself and the people who actually make things work. Richmond was governed by Union occupation administrators for many years following the War. This created an influx of Northern opportunists who sought to exercise a new leverage over Southern commerce. These carpetbaggers, usually of the professional class, were consistently granted preferential consideration, particularly regarding government contracting and services. Natives of Richmond, such as Rose, were often left with the scraps of a difficult, thankless, but noble, labor.

Rose stopped to talk with Lucas. Lucas was installing a new stem, washer, and handle for the valve. The parts had just come in the day before, having been weeks on order with the mechanics at the iron works.

"How's it look, Lucas?" as he peered over the chest high fence which surrounded the reservoir. He could lean just far enough to catch a glimpse of Lucas.

"I think this'll work, jus' fine, Mr. Rose." as he struggled turning his large plumber's wrench. "Once I get this c'roded ol' pieces off 'n clean it out 'n oil it, it oughta work much better." He stopped briefly and looked up at Rose. Rose tipped his hat, exhaled some smoke from between his teeth clenched his pipe, and moved on.

Rose continued to the north for a few yards and then began turning east around the reservoir. This track eventually turned him southward where he reached a point directly across the reservoir from the reservoir house. The sun was just breaking enough where he could see the gray figure of Trainham standing outside the house door. The flicker of Trainham's cigarette intensified with each puff, then toned down again.

"That man is of little use," thought Rose. He had seen men like Trainham through his entire life. Trainham thought he understood the world well beyond his years. Men such as this live as if they have everything and if they ever come realize that they do not have everything, they also tragically come to understand that they have wasted what few things they really did have; and now have nothing. Rose doubted that Trainham would ever have such a capacity, or even the desire, to understand himself.

Trainham had been working at the facility for nearly two years. He was in charge of keeping the grounds; cutting grass, trimming trees, cleaning up refuse. He was also responsible for cleaning out the drainage intakes and outlets in the reservoir. In addition, Trainham was required to take water samples per the schedule provided by the Richmond Water Works and deliver these samples to the agency for proper analysis. Trainham was not particularly inspired by any of these tasks and did only the minimum required to justify his employment. Rose never felt obliged to offer him any pay raise. Deep down, Rose hoped this strategy would induce Trainham to seek employment elsewhere, but to this point, he had failed to create the desired effect. The lack of advancement seemed not to bother Trainham. As long as he had enough money to frequent his favored bars and bawdy houses, Trainham appeared content. (2.2)

Trainham stood opposing Rose on the west side of the reservoir and cast an equally harsh judgment. "That man must lead the most boring existence on the planet", he thought. Two times every day he watched the old horse chug around the reservoir billowing stale smoke rendered from his cheap pipe tobacco. The predictability of Rose's efforts sickened the young man. "He'll be doing the same thing twenty years from now". Trainham liked to have a good time and at age twenty-nine and as of yet, unmarried, he remained confident that another opportunity would come along for him. When that high-speed locomotive came his direction, he intended to have his ticket punched. Trainham just knew the world had more to offer him than water works; he planned to leave that work in the dull, if capable, hands of men such as Rose.

Rose could go no further south on this side of the reservoir. A patch of trees, bushes, undergrowth, briars, and thickets, thirty or forty yards thick, cut him off. So, as he did every morning and every evening, he doubled back. As he passed Lucas once again, he heard his heavy breathing interrupted only by an occasional grunt when excessive effort was being put forth. Then he heard the clang of a dropped wrench and muted cursing. He smiled as he pictured Lucas hard at work.

R.G. Lucas was reliable, honest, and quite resourceful when it came to repairs. He was the boss workman on site and was probably the single most valuable figure in the continued operation of the deteriorating and somewhat inefficient facility. Parts for the reservoir's antiquated system were very difficult to come by as much of the equipment in place had been hand crafted by machinists long ago, so were almost never calibrated nor of a scale compatible with the machine-made assembly line replacement parts and equipment now produced by modern factories. Although this newer and far more productive system was well-entrenched in the factories and facilities of the North, and it's value was certainly well understood by operators in the South, the general lack of a factory infrastructure in the South, and more importantly, the lack of money in the Commonwealth's coffers to build new factories or to upgrade and purchase modern equipment, precluded men like Rose and Lucas from having the best available tools and devices at their disposal.

As Rose passed by the office, William Hutcheson was just showing up for work. He was a young man of seventeen and Rose had already determined that he had a good mind and a decent heart. However, like most teenage boys, Hutcheson liked to sleep, which often made him late for work. Hutcheson made up for this with equal frequency by being the last one to leave the facility, excepting, of course, Mr. Rose.

"Hutcheson, good morning. Go get a cup of coffee, leave your lunch and coat in the office and get down there and help Lucas with Valve Number 2."

"Yes, Mr. Rose."

Trainham had finished his cigarette and was heading over toward the pump house to clear some of the debris that had fallen around it during the previous night's inclement weather. Rose continued on toward the south end of the reservoir. A few steps onto the walkway around the southern embankment of the reservoir Rose discovered a woman's garnet-colored glove. It sat like a small pool of blood amongst some scuffmark disturbances on the damp clay pathway. He reflexively picked the glove up and put it in his trouser pocket. A yard or two ahead, lay part of a broken shoestring. It curled back upon itself forming a noose-like loop. The end opposite the loop was frayed and the individual strands stretched and recoiled, as if separated by a forceful violent shock. Rose was curious and at this early hour, safe to say, confused. He walked toward the fence on the edge of the embankment and saw more footprints. Rose looked over the fence and down into the water.

"Oh, my Lord..." he said lowly to himself.

"Lucas..." Rose muttered; then he found his voice and yelled, "Lucas!", shattering the silence of the cool dawn. "Lucas! Come over here! Lucas, come quick!", waving him over emphatically.

Lucas shot up the opposite embankment and leapt the fence. He raced around the reservoir at top speed. Rose just stood there still. He had not seen anything this disturbing since the War. He was entering a tunnel of focus and instinctively knew to remain calm and rational. "What's the matter, Mr. Rose?" said a concerned but potentially annoyed Lucas.

"Look...", and he pointed directly below.

"Oh, Mr. Rose, Mr. Rose... What is that? What's happened here?"

Hutcheson was following behind. Rose yelled out to him, "Hutcheson, grab that long pole over by the house and bring it over, quick!".

Hutcheson responded and immediately hustled the eighteen-foot wood pole over to his bosses. Rose carefully reached a long pole over the picket fence and into the reservoir below. He lifted the edge of what appeared to be a woman's dress. As he raised it the men gasped in horror as a leg was exposed.

"My Lawd" said Lucas, "What are we gonna do?"

"Lucas, you run over to the Penitentiary and get them to call for the police. The rest of you men, stay here. Don't do anything! I'm going to get the coroner."

Rose ran faster and harder than he'd run in years, probably since he was a boy. His mind was moving just as quickly, but at the same time he was absolutely dumbfounded at what he had just discovered. He bolted up one street and down another, completely oblivious to the arthritic condition of his knee. Richmond was just awakening from its late winter slumber and wasn't sure what to make of Rose. Most people he passed looked at him curiously, but he dared not stop to explain. He knew a crowd at this point would not be helpful. He turned onto Main Street and spotted the horse drawn trolley a few blocks ahead. Instinct took over and the cramp forming in his side disappeared as he sprinted for the car with renewed resolve. He finally caught up with the tug horse trolley and leapt aboard. He paid the fare and tried to regain some composure. Rose pulled a handkerchief from his hip pocket and wiped his brow. There were three other passengers aboard. Two of them looked at him quizzically, the third was too involved in the morning newspaper to notice Rose. Rose was out of place and all present, excepting the gentleman reading his paper, were well aware of it. A common working man riding a tug horse trolley into the City center on this day and at this hour was most uncommon. The three others were all dressed in expensive clothing; Rose was dressed somewhat less impressively. No words needed to be exchanged. In well-mannered Victorian Richmond, a queer look and a simple understanding of one's position in society spoke for everyone.

Rose smiled rather self-consciously at the onlookers and simply said in a low tone, "I'm late." The two inquisitors, a mother and her daughter, were notably unimpressed. They were too dignified to sneer, but a subtle roll of mother's eyes and a quick clenching of her daughter's hand, drawing the girl tightly against mother's side conveyed the message. The third, a middle-aged man, read his paper and expressed no concern.

After eight blocks, Rose, having caught his breath, could no longer contain his anxiety. He jumped off the trolley and started running again. Two blocks further up Main he turned north on 9th Street and blazed past the Henry Clay Monument. He rounded the corner at Capitol Street and made a quick left up 10th and bounded onward to the next intersection at Broad Street. There he stopped and entered the Richmond Coroner's Office. It was only 8AM when he dashed to the 2nd Floor. He could hear his blood coursing through his veins as he knocked gently on the office door of Dr. William H. Taylor.

"Come in.", was the muffled reply.

Rose stepped in. The office was dark due to lack of morning sunlight. To the right was a tall narrow table with a microscope, Petrie dishes, and beakers. A Bunsen burner sat at one end and was unlit. Two or three stools sat around the table. The entire right-hand wall was lined with eight-foot glass front cases, like those one would see in an apothecary. In them were chemicals, solutions, tissue samples, and all manner of medical supplies and materiel. On the back wall, near the right corner was a sink. The smell of formaldehyde was overwhelming, but in light of the urgent circumstances, Rose barely took note.

"Dr. Taylor?" said Rose as he looked at the back of a thin balding gentleman standing at his desk and gazing out the adjacent window. The old man spun around and squinted hard in the voice's direction.

"Yes sir, and you are?"

"My name is... Rose. Excuse me doctor, but I've run quite a distance. I am the superintendent over at the reservoir and we have a problem. There's a dead woman in the reservoir and we need immediate help."

"Do you know who she is?" the doctor said as he felt around for his spectacles.

"No sir, we don't.", still breathless, "All I've seen is a leg and a dress in the water on the edge of the reservoir. I told my men not to touch it until I got you." At this point, Rose's eyes cut to his left thru the doorway and into the adjoining room. There he saw a gurney with a cadaver. A bright white sheet was draped over the body, covering all but the left leg. It was a small leg, undoubtedly the leg of a woman. Rose clenched his eyes shut and turned his head toward the floor.

"Are you alright?" asked Dr. Taylor.

"Yes, sir, I think so."

Well, good work this morning, uh, Rose, is it?"

"Yes sir"

"Well, Mr. Rose," said Taylor. "I've got to get some things together and I'll be right over. Have you contacted the Police Department?"

"Yes sir, I sent one of my men to notify them."

"Very good. You head back to the reservoir and don't do anything else."

"Thank you, sir. Yes, sir". With that, Rose retreated from the office and turned back toward the reservoir. His mind was still racing, now more than ever. He walked to try and calm himself down. He thought about how this could be. Where would this person have come from? When could this have happened? He had performed his last inspection of the entire facility yesterday evening just before dark and had seen nothing unusual. Why would any person, much less a woman, be in that area? (2.3)

Chapter 3   ***Bath to Richmond***

Miss Fannie Lillian Madison boarded the Thursday noon train in Bath County. The Chesapeake and Ohio Railroad was bound east for Richmond. She presented her ticket to the conductor. He punched the ticket, took her brown canvas bag and placed it in the luggage rack above the seating. As she slid into a seat next to a window, her stomach pressed against the backrest of the seat in front of her. She slowly lowered herself and leaned back, straightened her legs, and emitted a sigh. She removed her black straw hat and veil and sat them carefully on the seat next to her. The young woman re-wrapped her red knitted shawl around her shoulders. She was a rather short young woman and from this somewhat reclined position, she couldn't see too much outside on the station platform. She soon adjusted her position, sitting more upright, but leaning on her hip in the direction of the window.

"That's better" she mumbled to herself.

Fannie Lillian Madison
(Library of Virginia Archives, Richmond,)

Lillie, as she was called, had been teaching school that year. She looked out the window at the station and she heard the whistle blow signifying the train would soon be leaving. It reminded her of the school bell she was so accustomed to now. She thought how excited many of her students would be to be taking a train ride to the city. She thought about their laughter, about their inquisitive natures. Oh, how Lillie truly enjoyed their company. She marveled at how, just a few short years ago, she was one of them. But now, at age 20, things were very different. Life was no longer so carefree.

Lillie had received a letter in the mail just a few days earlier. It had come bearing the name of her dearest schoolmate, Laura Curtis. Lillie pulled the letter from her pocket and read once again the plea for help written in that very familiar penmanship:

Richmond, VA, March 9, 1885

My Dear Lillie, It is on business of sad importance I must write you to-day, as you know, both mama and Aunt Mary have been in wretched health for a long time, and both have been getting worse for some time, and the doctors say if Aunt Mary doesn't leave here, and soon, she cannot stand it long; so they advise papa to take her to Old Point, in order that she can take those sun-baths, which are proving so beneficial to consumptives. But she *will not agree to go unless I go with her, which of course is out of the question, as mama is too ill for me to leave her, so we have been trying to persuade her to let someone else accompany her. So, at last, she agrees that if we can get you to come down and go with her, she will consent to go. Of course we told her you were teaching, but she begged we would try to get you with her just as company for her, as her nurse will go with her, who has been waiting on her all the time. She says the reason she wants you to be with her is on account of your being so quiet and gentle in your manners when you were visiting us, and she is so nervous she could not bear to have some one with her who is not so gentle and kind. She told me to beg you please to grant her this request, as it was her last resort for momentary relief of her sufferings, as of course, we know she can never be well. My dear Lillie, imagine how it is with me, my dear mama and aunt both so sick. Mama is rapidly declining, I think, and aunt worse, I think; but if she can get to Old Point we hope she will get better. She will only stay there one week, as in that time the doctors think she will be better, if it will benefit her at all, Lillie, please come. Ask Mrs. Dickinson, I say, please excuse you under these sad circumstances, just for a week, and she will do it, I know, as you wrote me she was so good and kind. Papa wishes me to say to you, if you will come and go with aunt, he will never forget your kindness, and, besides, he will pay all of your expenses and $2 per day for every day you are with her. He is such a devoted brother to her he would do anything in his power. Lillie, don't get any dresses for the purpose, as you and I wear the same clothes, and as we wanted, if possible, to attend the exposition, I have made up alot of new clothes for that purpose, but, of course, now we can't go, but we were in hopes mama and aunt would get better, so we could go, but we have given it out now. Now, dear Lillie, we are in hopes of seeing you soon. If you will accompany aunt, come Thursday (12), either on mail or express; we shall send to meet you and please, dear Lillie, do not disappoint us, for you know there is nothing I would not do for you. If aunt should get too ill, we will telegraph to you, so you will get it before time for you to start the 12th. If you will ask the lady you teach for to excuse you for just a short time, she will do it I know. All send much love; aunt is very nervous to-day.*

Ever your loving schoolmate,

Laura M. Curtis

(3.1)

The young teacher was so relieved that Mrs. Dickinson let her take a short leave from the school. Lillie hurt so terribly for the letter's author. She hoped and prayed that somehow, this trip would change everything for her. At that moment, the conductor approached Lillie and asked if she needed anything. She smiled and replied, "No sir, thank you."

"Well, Miss …"

"Yes sir, it's Lillie... Lillian Madison".

"Will someone be meeting you at the station, Miss Madison? We may be getting in rather late."

Lillie took note that the conductor was tall, very pleasant in appearance, and extremely considerate. She also noted that he had a gold wedding band on his finger. "Yes, sir, I expect some ladies to meet me either tonight at the station, or perhaps tomorrow, at the American Hotel, where I will be staying."

"Very good. Do you have family in Richmond?

"Well, yes, but I'm actually going to visit friends. Just for a short time."

"Well then, we'll just have to speed up this train so you have more time with your friends.", he grinned.

"Oh, that would be wonderful. Maybe it will get going so fast the cars will run off the track and kill me!"

Lillie put her palms together and spastically slid the top one off in an almost morbid delight. Her eyes briefly caught fire in anticipation until she quickly regained her composure. The conductor, rather taken aback by this strange remark, decided to end the conversation. With an uneasy smile he tipped his cap and said, "Well, if you need anything further, Miss Madison, please let me know." (3.2)

"Thank you, sir; I shall."

After some time watching the Virginia countryside pass by, Lillie stood briefly and reached into the overhead luggage rack. She struggled to pull down her satchel and a gentleman from across the row quickly came to her aid. He helped her lower the satchel. From it she took a wooden box. She asked the gentleman to place the satchel back above. He gladly complied. Lillie thanked the stranger, smiled, and returned to her seat. She sat the small box next to her on the seat and opened it. Inside was her needlepoint. She had completed about two thirds of this particular project and the result was increasingly pleasing to her. Her hope was to complete the project in its entirety by the end of her trip. It was a depiction of a colorful songbird derived from an old oriental folk tale. The lovely full-feathered creature was in the process of thrusting itself upon the long thorn of a rose bush. The wings were gloriously akimbo and the beak was wide open, releasing a song of the highest quality and resonance. The brilliantly red and black song bird had long pursued the most pure of notes; something so natural, so clear, and nearing perfection; the type of performance one could only hope to produce once, if ever at all. Tragically, in order to give birth to such a crescendo, this bird must painfully pay with its own life.

Chapter 4   *...So Do Wait for Me*

The train pulled into the station and it was very late. Lillie awoke from an uncomfortable nap as the mighty engine came to a complete halt. "Richmond Station...", announced the conductor. "Last stop.... No trains leaving the station until 7AM."

The weary passengers began to disembark. By the time Lillie had struggled to her feet, in which she had lost feeling during her uneasy upright slumber, the conductor stood before her with her brown canvas bag. "Have I got the right bag? Those are your initials, Miss Madison?"

"Yes sir, thank you"

"Alright, you have a nice stay in Richmond."

"Thank you", she quickly picked up her still unfinished needlepoint and the wooden box from the seat and placed them in the bag.

Lillie lowered herself carefully down onto the platform. There was a lighted clock at the station that read 2:35 AM. Lillie rubbed her sore eyes and walked alone eight-and-one-half blocks to the American Hotel. Prior to the War, the American Hotel was one of the more popular hotels in all of Richmond. Though not as luxurious as some of the competition, it was very well located and always provided crisp service, clean rooms, and a charming atmosphere. It reached five full Georgian stories into the air and its footprint occupied about 1/8 of the block.

During the War, like many businesses in Richmond, the hotel fell upon difficult times. Extenuating circumstances, impatient creditors, and rampant inflation put incredible economic pressures on the business. It changed hands four times between 1864 and 1872, each time being sold at a further discount and all the while slipping a little further into disrepair. By 1875, it had hit rock bottom and was nothing more than a bawdy house, and a poor one at that. In 1880, a new group of young Richmond professional speculators recognized the potential of the stately old building just blocks from two train stations and across the street from Capitol Square. It was bought once more at a distressed sale, but unlike previous efforts, this time, the investors had a vision and were well-capitalized. They immediately breathed new life into the tired structure and hired a competent management staff. By the time Lillie was checking in, The American Hotel was recognized throughout the City as prime evidence that the middle class was on the way back in Virginia and that the City had gotten rid of not only one more piece of blight, but had, in fact, brought forth a jewel, albeit of the more affordable semi-precious variety.

Lillie wearily signed the hotel registry and was assigned Room 21 by the skeleton night staff. Within ten minutes she was asleep once more. (4.1)

Lillie slept on her back. At first, she had no dreams, but as 10AM approached, a dream began to materialize. She was walking alone in a place she did not recognize. There were sounds of people and activity nearby, but she saw nothing. There was grass and a few trees, but no people. Then she saw a young man in the distance. As he approached, it became clear that she did not know him, yet physically, she recognized him. It was her cousin Tommie, at least it was his face, but yet it clearly was not Tommie. As is often the case with dreams, complete nonsense passes for clarity. On a certain level, she knew this man looked exactly like Tommie, but she never really questioned it. He was a complete stranger to her. The man came nearer. She smiled at him. Suddenly she felt a burning in her throat, an uncomfortable and vile churning. She could feel something coming up her esophagus. She dropped to her knees hands over her mouth and looked up at the man, who stood silently by. He had a look of contentment and the beginnings of a smile. She was confused. Lillie wondered if he would do anything, would he even acknowledge her obvious distress? Suddenly a black mud like substance flowed uncontrollably out of her mouth. It drained out of her and down the front of her dress like an open water valve. She gasped for air and looked upward again only to see the man calmly put his index finger to his lips. He turned and walked away, checking his timepiece. She tried to reach out to him and ask for help, but he paid no mind.

The fit abruptly ended. Lillie's eyes popped open and there she was in Room 21. She covered her mouth and winced as she swallowed, feeling the burn in her throat. The acid reflux she had been experiencing in recent months was creeping up on her again.

"Oh, this terrible heartburn", she thought, "I can't tolerate this much longer." She got up from her bed and poured water from the pitcher on the dresser. She took two gulps. It did little to bring relief.

The young woman instantly forgot about the dream as her attention turned to the matter of food. After all, she had eaten little since boarding the train yesterday afternoon. She called for room service and placed a breakfast order.

By 11:00AM Lillie was finishing up her meal when a knock came at the door. It was a young colored boy employed by the hotel.

"Here's a letter for you, ma'am; it was just delivered by messenger". He handed her a note. Lillie opened the note and became very excited. She quickly read it and ran to the desk in the corner and scribbled out a reply:

I will be there as soon as possible; so do wait for me.

She folded the note and placed it in a cream-colored envelope. As she wrote a name on the envelope she asked, "Is the messenger waiting for a reply?"

"I thinks so, ma'am."

"Good, go return this to the messenger right away.", she instructed the boy.

"Yes ma'am, right 'way ma'am." She handed him the letter and two pennies for his trouble. He nodded his head and disappeared down the hall.

Lillie rushed about getting ready. She put on her dark dress, washed her face, and quickly brushed her hair. Her pulse was racing as she thought to herself, "Oh thank goodness, he has come. Now this can finally be settled." She anxiously wrapped herself in her red shawl, put on her black hat, and was out the door and down the stairs within minutes of receiving the message. She walked briskly through the lobby and out the front door of the American Hotel.

She looked directly across the street and there, in a doorway covered by an awning, talking to another gentleman, stood T. J. Cluverius. (4.2)

Chapter 5 *Well, Lead Me to the Body*

Dr. William H. Taylor arrived at the Old Marshall Reservoir by 10AM. L.W. Rose was waiting there alongside a few other reservoir employees.

"Good morning gentlemen. It would appear we've got a full day ahead of us."

The men stood silently by, still somewhat in shock over what was happening.

"Have the police arrived, yet?", asked Taylor

"No, sir," said Rose.

"Very good. Well, lead me to the body." He reached in his breast pocket and put on his thick spectacles. He picked up his examiner's case and followed Rose and the others in the direction of the reservoir.

Taylor was a very bright and organized man. He had been a practicing medical examiner for many years and was very well known and respected in the field. Taylor was born and raised in Richmond. He was among the first graduating class of the Medical College of Virginia and throughout his long professional life, Taylor had attained such esteem and notoriety among his colleagues as is reserved for but only a few. He had, at one time or another, practiced every medical procedure from miraculous child birthing to brutal battlefield surgery. He considered himself lucky to be able to serve humanity in such a fashion. However, the one aspect of medicine that most intrigued him was not trying to save a life but rather trying to determine what caused the end of one. To Dr. Taylor, this was the ultimate value and calling of a medical researcher. He felt that to successfully care for the living, doctors must first fully understand the dead. One could sense the seriousness with which he approached his profession, but one could also see that, as a man who never married and lived alone, he had certain eccentricities, as well. He removed his notebook from his case and a pencil from his coat pocket. He made an entry: (5.1)

14 March, 1885
8AM - Mr. Rose, reservoir superintendent, advises of possible dead body in reservoir, probably female

10AM - Arrive at reservoir to begin analysis - Superintendent Rose and others to assist.

The old man moved slowly, but purposefully. As he neared the south end of the embankment, he crouched and looked out across what lay in the immediate foreground, much the way an Indian tracker would. He shielded his eyes from the still emerging sun as he carefully studied the top of the embankment. Taylor softly ran his fingers across his white mustache as he cast his eyes downward; and then, deeply concentrating, turned his attention to his notebook.

On walkway top of embankment to the South saw many shoe tracks and scuff marks. Soil is soft here. Light rain and snow last evening.
Tracks are fresh and are in area covering width of path for a stretch of six to eight feet. Tracks are numerous and confused.
Two tracks of broad heels near picket fence facing reservoir. These are probably male tracks.

Taylor lifted his head to have another look. There was complete silence, but everyone knew there was a great deal happening. The energy surrounding the area was intense. Rose's ears rung with the sounds of deafening anticipation and apprehension.

Other footprints are much smaller and appear to be female.

Taylor stood and walked over to the fence that separated the pathway from the embankment that sloped to the reservoir below. He looked down on the water with such focus as it seemed he was wearing blinders and earplugs. Now standing still, he checked his pocket watch and returned back to his notebook.

10:15AM - Picket fence encircles reservoir. Fence approximately 3 and 1/2 feet high. Pickets are sharp and extend approximately 4 inches above top rail.

Stone embankment rather steep and conditions slippery. Body face down in water near edge of reservoir just below disturbed area. Arms are forward in front of head.

"Mr. Rose, could we get the body from the reservoir?"

"Of course, sir. Hutcheson, Trainham; Come with me."

The three men carefully climbed the picket fence and traversed the embankment to the water's edge. The coroner watched every move.

Reservoir near edge is about 18 inches deep. The floor appears very soft and silty. The men's feet sink 8 to 10 inches when walking along this part.

Men lift the body from the water. Cadaver hauled up the embankment face up. Fully clothed young adult female.

By then, Lucas had returned with an officer from the Richmond Police.

"Dr. Taylor. I'm Officer Walton." the young man said. His eyes were wide open, as he was as nervous as the rest, excepting the experienced doctor. "I'm here to assist in any way I can. I have sent another officer to the station and he will arrange for a detective and more men. They should be here soon."

"Very good, officer." replied Taylor. "You and this man help the others pass the body over the fence."

In the course of a few moments, all were back over the fence, including the deceased.

"Mr. Rose, if you and the other men would be so kind as to remove the body to the reservoir house. That would be a far more dignified location for making an initial observation and identification."

"Yes sir, Dr. Taylor."

"But wait a moment..." interjected the doctor. He walked over to the body, which lay horizontal facing the sky in the hands of the five men. Taylor took off one of the woman's shoes and took it over to the disturbed track-ridden area. Once again, he stooped and dropped on one knee. He slowly leaned forward with the shoe and placed it directly in one of the smaller tracks. He then lifted it and placed it in another a few feet ahead. He put the shoe on the ground and opened his notebook once more.

Removed left shoe and was able to match it to female footprints near embankment.

Lucas could not contain himself any longer, "Dr. Taylor, 'scuse me for askin', but do you think this here woman's been kilt?"

"Well, I don't know yet, but it's certainly a possibility. I will, however, do everything in my power to determine the exact truth."

"Oh, dear Lawd, Doctor, I don't like this."

"I know son, I know."

10:45 - Female body removed to reservoir office.

The men placed the body face up on a large rectangular table. Taylor removed a measuring tape from his coroner's case. He gently adjusted the head to a straightened position and in good Victorian taste, closed the cadaver's mouth. With that, the body suddenly reacquired some humanity, and from the looks of her fine and delicate features, an angelic humanity.

Age 20 to 25 years. Covered in mud. Approximately 4 feet 11 inches in height. Hair still pinned up.

He lifted her right arm and tried to pry open the fingers of her hand with his.

Hands tightly clenched with mud still in them.

He walked around the table to the other side of the body.

Blue Jersey has small tear inside left arm. Black skirt has some small rents. No jewelry.

Stiffening of the joints and muscles indicate death occurred at least six hours earlier. Exact time of death undetermined as of now.

  Taylor ran his hand along the deceased's abdomen, pressing inward intermittently. He suddenly stopped and looked worriedly toward the horrified yet solemn group of reservoir workers, "Oh, my God. Do any of you recognize this woman?"

  To a man, the answer was, "No".

  "It is very well you do not.", said the Dr. in a morbidly concerned manner. He wiped his brow, took a deep breath, and made another entry in his notebook.

Dead female in advanced stage of pregnancy, perhaps 8th month.

Chapter 6   *The Demure Marse Robert*

Lillie Madison's pulse quickened as she left the American Hotel and started toward the street curb. T. J. Cluverius shook hands with the man standing beside him. The man turned his back and disappeared into a doorway behind Cluverius. At that moment, Lillie called out and extended her hand in the air, "Tommie! Cousin Tommie!"

Cluverius rushed toward her. He met her in the gutter on his side of the street. A light mist was falling as he wrapped his right arm around her and quickly ushered her to the area under the shadowy awning.

"Hello, dear Lillie" said Cluverius softly.

"Oh Tommie! I have missed you!" said the excited girl.

"Alright... Alright... Lillie." begged Cluverius, trying to calm her. He clutched her tightly. Her head pressed against his long grey overcoat just below his chest. He could feel her round but firm stomach against his hip. Cluverius' eyes darted all around the street as he smiled to mask some nervousness. "Let's walk this way. There are too many people we may know in this part of town", as he pointed toward the James River. Lillie would have followed him anywhere. The sound of his voice was hypnotic.

Cluverius adjusted his slouch hat, pulling it down over his brow. Lillie clung tightly to his arm.

"Tommie, I approve of the new mustache. It looks very distinguished."

"Well, thank you, Lillie. I quite agree." as he stroked the thin band of light brown hair on his upper lip.   (6.1)

"Was there any problem getting away?", the young woman asked.

"No, none at all.", replied Cluverius. "One case I have been handling concluded yesterday before noon. The judge will deliberate and render a decision Monday or Tuesday. I think his decision will favor my client. I will not need to appear in court again until Wednesday. That will be in King William."

'That is wonderful, Tommie! I always knew you would become one of the best lawyers in the county."

"Yes, Lillie, things are going well."

"Did you tell Aunt Jane where you were going?", she asked.

"No, I just told her I would be away for a few days. Since her rheumatism has flared, she hasn't had the energy to meddle."

They shared a brief laugh at the expense of their elderly relative and continued making their way southwesterly along the James River. They passed by the legendary Tredegar Iron Works and on a little further until they reached the footbridge heading over to Belle Isle, which was a large island in the middle of the channel which throughout Richmond's history had been everything from an Indian encampment to an industrial complex to a Civil War Prison. The young couple walked out on the footbridge and paused midway to look upon the river.

"How about you, Lillie? Did you have any difficulty getting away from school?"

"No. I showed Mrs. Dickinson the letter and she made no issue of it. It worked perfectly."

"That's very good.", said Cluverius

"I do like Richmond.", said Lillie. "The memories it has for us will always be dear to my heart." She stretched onto her toes and leaned over to look straight down below at the current.

"Yes", said Tommie as he reached his hand behind her beneath her shawl. He gave her a playful jolt, as if he were going push her over the rail. She flinched and let out a brief shriek, followed by a laugh. He then slid his hand a little further down and squeezed her rear end with relish. "Lillie, my memories of Richmond are fond, as well." He smiled devilishly as he drew her near, pinned her against the rail, and whispered in her ear.

"Why, Cousin Tommie!" she blurted as she pushed the scoundrel away playfully. Cluverius backed away and brushed lightly against a passing gentleman. Lillie put her hand to her mouth with a schoolgirl's embarrassment. Tommie met eyes with the strange gentlemen and nodded his head. The young man grabbed Lillie's arm and led her onward to Belle Island.

Belle Isle was a curious mix of untamed wilderness and industrial development. Some parts of the island looked just as John Smith would have found them, while other parts were churning with industry. The sounds of machinery, the smell of smoke and chemicals, and the voices of men at work coming from the center of the island pierced the wildly pristine visuals of the shoreline.

The couple walked toward the center of the island. Old Dominion Nail Works was busy with activity that Friday morning. Steam and smoke were belching from the chimneys atop the single level brick structure. The misty air transformed to a light rain as the couple toured the area. The drops intensified and the two wanderers sought shelter by entering the factory. The heat met them like an invisible wall as they crossed the threshold into the facility. They passed a number of work men, each conducting a simple but vital task in the line of production.

"How is Pa?", asked Lillie. Pa was Lillie's maternal grandfather and uncle to Tommie.

Cluverius, watching a puddler pour molten iron into a vat as part of the metallurgic purification process, responded, "He is quite well. I heard he did have a bout with a fever this winter, but evidently, all is well. I have not seen him since you and I were last there."

"And your brother?"

"Willie has not changed. He still is having trouble keeping work. He still drinks too much. He is devoted to the family and I care greatly for him; but I'm concerned that he will always be a burden to us all.

"Does he have any marital prospect?"

"Are you teasing? Cousin, he has little desire to marry. And who would have him? This *is* Willie we are speaking of." The two had another laugh. They continued their tour of the facility, walking deeper into the building toward the firing room.

"How about you, Tommie?"

"What?"

"Have you the desire to marry?"

"Oh, Lillie, you *know* that I do."

At that moment a burly colored man briskly cut between the two carrying a large pan of hot iron to feed the nail mill. He was breathing heavily and rhythmically as he struggled onward with the fiery load. His upper lip would fill with air, then suddenly deflate. The negro worker lightly bumped into each of them as he passed, but since his load was hot and quite heavy, and as his focused exertion was intense, he was unable to utter any mannerly plea. He walked a few more feet beyond Cluverius and Lillie before he sat the pan down in a controlled but heavy manner. The muscular man then wiped his brow and looked back at the young couple. He smiled slightly and nodded his head offering his belated request for pardon. Cluverius and the young woman replied in kind.

Changing the subject, Cluverius said, "Lillie, why don't we go visit our friend, Nellie."

"Now, Tommie...", in thinly veiled honorable resistance.

"Lillie, our time together will be brief. I think we should take full advantage."

She smiled slyly at Cluverius' persistence and, after a brief second thought, readily capitulated.

"Yes, we really should visit Nellie before we have to leave. I always enjoy spending time at Nellie's." She gripped Cluverius' hand and led him from the factory.

Cluverius and Lillie discreetly made their way from Belle Isle across the bridge to 15th Street, where they turned north. At 15th and Main Street Cluverius stopped. He grabbed Lillie's arm and pulled her to the side up against the Planter's Bank Building. "Lillie, you stay right here. I need to run in the bank and get some money." Cluverius disappeared into the bank. A couple of minutes later he re-emerged. With a wry smile he said, "For Nellie!"

Lillie knew exactly what he meant. She bit her lip to mute her devilish smile and grabbed Tommie's arm, "Let's go!", she squealed.

The couple rushed north another block, stopped and ducked into the vestibule of a dingy three-story brick building that sat next to Walnut Alley. They slowly opened the door and walked into the front room of Nellie's. The front room was a cigar store, but anyone who knew of Nellie Goss, knew that Nellie's real business was run out of the next room. Cluverius and Lillie quietly passed through the front room into the back room bawdy house. It was nearing 1PM. Nellie's was usually quiet at this hour and this day was no different. The shades were drawn and the gas lamps were dim. There were a few vagrants and haggard prostitutes seated at the tables near the bar area.

"Is Nellie here?", Cluverius asked one of the men.

Saying nothing, the man pointed over his shoulder toward the doorway to Nellie's private quarters. The man almost sneered in suspicious disapproval of the professional class couple and then turned his attention back to his unsavory circle of friends.

"Thank you, sir."

Cluverius and Lillie walked over and knocked lightly on the door. Within moments they heard footsteps approaching from the other side. The door opened and there stood Nellie, owner and proprietor.

She squinted to make out the faces in the low light. "Yes, what is it?"

"Well..." Cluverius cleared his throat. "My wife and I would like to rent a room."

"Your wife, eh?", asked the weathered madam with a chuckle. "It's amazing how many men bring their *wives* here!" as she put her hands on her hips. She raised her voice and announced, "Nellie's is a very popular family destination, right Fogelman?"

Laughter burst out at the table and the seated man agreed, "Right, Nellie! Must be the fine food you serve!"

Cluverius and Lillie shrunk with the increasing attention. Nellie continued, "Now, all rooms here rent by the hour. It's a dollar for the first hour. Judgin' by the age of this boy, I should prob'ly charge by the minute! Am I right, Mildred?" The group howled again and the overly painted Mildred nodded in hysteric affirmation.

"Here, take Room 7; the *Lee Suite*. It's on the third floor. I just changed the bed linens... three or four weeks ago!" The humorous old harlot bent over with a raspy hacking laugh, slapping her thigh, and stomping her foot. The rest broke into veritable applause. Nellie collected herself. She could sense that maybe she'd carried her bemusements too far.

"It's alright boy, don't take no offense. Everyone here likes to laugh at one 'nother. Here's the key." She reached back inside the doorway to her quarters and lifted a key off the rack.

"It's quite alright, madam. You realize, we have been here before."

"You have?" She took a step closer to eyeball the pair.

"Yes, about two months ago."

"I don't remember..." she paused. "Hell, I was probably drunk!" She laughed; the room laughed; even Cluverius and Lillie laughed. "Speakin' of that, where's my bottle, Fogelman!?"

Cluverius handed Nellie a dollar and led Lillie up the creaky stairwell to the third floor. He put the key in the lock of Room 7, and with some effort, turned the key and opened it up. The room was very small with a single bed covered by an old patchwork quilt. It was against the wall opposite the doorway under the window. There was a small braid rug on the floor, a simple dresser on the left wall with a mirror hung above. A single picture of General Robert E. Lee hung on the right-hand wall. Lee's expression was stoic, as always. It was not judgmental, but like everything about him, it evoked the essence of piety and leadership by example. Lee's piercing eyes followed the young couple as they entered the room.

Cluverius immediately seized his prey in a powerful kiss. He removed her shawl and quickly began to loosen her blouse. As they spun in a tight circle of anxious physical lust, her eyes opened and met directly with Lee's. She stopped and beckoned Cluverius to do something about the picture.

"General Lee should really not be subjected to our animal indiscretions, Tommie." Cluverius fully understood her concern. He turned and reverently lifted the picture from the wall. He crossed the room and carefully placed Lee in the top drawer of the dresser as if he were placing the Body of Christ in a Holy Sepulcher.

"Better?" he asked as he turned back around. There, just removing her last undergarment, stood a nude Lillie Madison. Her form had changed dramatically since their last encounter, but that did little to curb Cluverius' hormonal overdrive. He removed his gray overcoat and hastily moved to extinguish his lit desire. (6.2)

Chapter 7   *Investigating Old Marshall*

Detective Jack Wren arrived at the Old Reservoir with five officers of the Richmond Police just past 11AM the morning of March 14. He methodically trudged up the south embankment toward a small group of men gathered there. He recognized Jackson Bolton of the City Engineer's Office and bid him good morning. Officer Walton had just come back from the reservoir house with Hutcheson and Lucas. Trainham had come over to the site, as well. The five uniformed officers stayed below awaiting instruction.

"What have we got, here?" Wren grunted at Officer Walton.

"Well, sir, it appears we have a dead body. A young woman about twenty years. Dr. Taylor is inspecting the corpse over in the reservoir house."

"Where was she found?". The short and stocky Wren squinted at the officer.

"Right below us down there in the reservoir. She was face down. By the appearances up here, it seems there may have been a struggle, sir." Walton anxiously pointed to the path. "There are some tracks on the path over there, sir. "

Wren and Walton walked about ten yards further and there, Wren knelt and picked up the piece of shoestring. He placed it in his right coat pocket and reached almost simultaneously into his left coat pocket, removing a small leather-bound notebook and a pencil. He entered his first notation regarding the investigation.

14 Mar '85 11am

Old Reservoir. Body Female found at south end in water. Path above has signs of struggle. Collected part of a shoestring, origin unknown.

"Alright Walton," Wren looked up from his notes, "I want you to take those five officers down there and do a complete search of the area. I want you to try and determine how this woman gained access to the reservoir property and, in the event someone was with her, how they got back out." The detective stood with one hand on his hip and pointed west toward the Clark Spring property. "Inspect that fence line and the complete perimeter and alongside the road out there. Collect anything you think may be of interest and if you find anything that cannot be moved, send for me. You will find me here or in the reservoir house, which we will establish as our forward investigative office. Report back to me by 2 this afternoon."

Wren was a competent young detective with a very direct manner and a quick temper. He was, however, rather sensitive to any criticism of himself, a weakness that many sensed and some exploited.

Wren pushed his brown bowler back on his head, put his hands in his trouser pockets, and looked down to gather his thoughts. He realized the gravity of this situation and reminded himself that, at a minimum, a thorough, methodical, and careful investigation would be required. At that moment a hand came down firmly on his shoulder and shook him from his trance. It was the hand of Jackson Bolton. Wren and Bolton had been friendly acquaintances going back to their school boy days in Petersburg, Virginia. They also served together in the Confederate Artillery during the War. Wren was a water boy and helped ration gunpowder amongst the batteries which defended Petersburg from the Union siege of 1864-65. Bolton, nearly four years older, was part of Battery Team 29, usually performing ramming duties on an 8-inch canon.

"Well, old friend, this really is a tragedy.", said Bolton.

"Yes, Jackson, it is… But we'll find out what happened and if someone out there is responsible for this, we will find them."

Bolton saw the determination in Wren's face and knew Wren meant what he said. Bolton assured Wren that, as an administrative representative of the Civil Engineers Office, the operating authority of the old reservoir, the full and complete cooperation of the Civil Engineer's Office with regard to this case would be at Wren's full disposal.

"Thank you, Jackson. If I need anything from your office, I know I can rely upon you. For now, I don't see what that may be other than your permission for full access to this site."

"Absolutely." said Bolton, "Take whatever time is needed. I will instruct Rose and the men here to fully cooperate."

"That is appreciated", returned Wren, as he touched two fingers to his bowler in a casual salute. "If you will excuse me, I need to go inspect the body."

"Good luck, Jack; and do not hesitate to contact me if you need further assistance."

Officer Walton was less than two years removed from his Police Academy training. Having been entrusted with organizing the initial search, he frantically tried to recall site and evidential search procedures. On the one hand, it was fortunate that events such as this were quite rare in Richmond, but by contrast, it was quite unfortunate that when such an event did occur, there were not a great deal of experienced investigators available. Eagerness was in full supply, but experience was scarce. Walton had never been involved with a criminal search of this magnitude nor importance. Most of his early career was spent as a beat officer. Despite his lack of experience, Walton fully recognized that this was an opportunity to elevate himself and he intended to try in earnest to professionally complete the task at hand. He resigned to himself to the approach that where academic investigative procedure abandoned him, he would substitute his own instinct and logic. He was nervous, but at the same time, was confident that he could direct the search with comprehensive dispatch.

"Jones; you, Stewart, and Keller go walk the fence line to the north and west. Look for any items of clothing, or signs of a struggle, or weapons… anything that may have pertinence. Aborghast and Wilkins, you begin searching the south and east."

Detective Wren entered the reservoir house and in a small back room encountered the macabre scene of Dr. Taylor and the deceased. The late morning sun provided plenty of light for the initial inspection and attempts at identification.

"Dr. Taylor, I am Detective Jack Wren. I will be handling the investigation."

"Yes, Detective, that is fine." Taylor had seen many detectives come and go over the years. It was not so much that he was dismissive, but he was more interested in an efficient autopsy and identification than stroking the ego of any detective. So, he got right to the point.

"We have a young unidentified woman here, between twenty and twenty-five years. I cannot determine at this early state how she died, but I can tell you she is in an advanced stage of pregnancy."

Detective Wren exhaled audibly through his nose, as if receiving an unexpected jolt. Wren looked down upon the muddied face. She was so young and quite pretty. Despite the encrusted translucence of the aged panes, the sunlight broke through the window with resolute clarity and bounced radiantly off her brassy but soiled hair, creating a halo effect. She now appeared comfortably at rest, but the state and condition of her body and clothing indicated her demise was anything but peaceful.

"It is my recommendation, Detective, that we transfer the corpse to my office, where I can perform a complete evaluation. After the examination, I propose we transfer the body to the morgue where we can invite the public to come view the deceased and hopefully obtain a positive identification."

"Yes, Doctor, I concur. That would be best. I will arrange for the transfer to your office immediately."

At that moment, a clerk of the Coroner's Office burst into the reservoir house. "Dr. Taylor! Dr Taylor!" a youthful voice beckoned.

"In here." responded Taylor. Through the door walked John Bellows, Taylor's clerk and another man, Joseph Mountcastle. Bellows was carrying a brown canvas bag with leather straps.

"Dr. Taylor, this man works at the C&O wharf and he and some other men there found this satchel floating in the river. It's full of women's clothing. I thought there could be some connection. He handed the bag to the doctor who stepped over closer to the light of the window and held the bag closer to his eyes. (7.1)

"Well, Detective, here is a lead. The initials on this bag are F. L. M… Perhaps this belongs to the deceased." Taylor handed the bag to Detective Wren; he then turned to Bellows.

"The deceased appears to be about your age, Bellows. Do you recognize her? Do you know any young women with those initials?"

"No, Doctor, I don't think I know her." Bellows, rather taken aback at what he was suddenly involved with thought for a moment. "I did go to primary school with a girl named Fannie Mays. Her family runs a small butcher's shop downtown. I don't believe this is her, but it has been some time since I have seen her. I'm not even sure if she lives in Richmond anymore."

"There's another lead for you, Detective. A name of a local young woman of similar age to the deceased with initials matching those on this mysterious satchel."

Wren was becoming a bit annoyed with the old man, but out of respect for his elder and in light of Taylor's impeccable reputation as a professional, he held his angst in check.

"Thank you, sir", said Wren. I will pursue these matters." He turned to leave the room when Taylor stopped him once more.

"But Detective Wren, before you leave. Perhaps we should take some of the items from out of the satchel and make certain that they would fit the deceased. Then you could have stronger reason to believe the bag is indeed hers."

Wren shut his eyes and rolled them in his head as he clenched his teeth. He briefly decompressed and followed, once again, the suggestion of the old sage.
The men removed the items from the bag. There was a tan alpaca dress, a bone white blouse, a pair of black stockings and some undergarments. The blouse had some initials written on the inside of the collar. The letters were quite blotted and smudged, but appeared to be "F.L.M." or perhaps, "T.L.M.". Also, there was a small wooden cigar box. Water was slowly seeping through the box bottom. Detective Wren slowly opened the box and there, submerged face-down in about an inch and one half of river water, was the left-unfinished songbird needlepoint.

Mountcastle explained to Detective Wren that he and two other employees at the wharf had spotted the bag floating in the river early this morning. Mountcastle himself rescued it from the shoreline. They removed the contents and spread them out to let them dry a bit, then put them all back in the satchel. Then, Mountcastle's foreman, Mr. Redwood, instructed Mountacastle to deliver this suspicious bag to the Coroner.

"Are you certain that you put all of the contents back in the bag?"

"Yes sir, Detective, everything we found is in there."

At this same moment, Dr. Taylor was laying out the alpaca dress on top of the body. "This appears to be the right size for this woman. However, I cannot definitively say it belongs to her. Detective, do you have any further suggestions? Is there anything else we should look for before you move on?"

Wren was beginning to wise up a bit. "Yes, Dr. Taylor, there is. Surely you have already thought of this, but we should check the clothing on the deceased for matching initials."

"Ah, very good Detective; let us do just that." With that the doctor playfully winked at the young detective, as if he had decided to remove his foot from his neck. Taylor asked all but Wren to leave the room, as he was going to undress the body and decorum prohibited him from allowing any unnecessary audience for such a process. After all, Taylor was a gentleman and always discreetly sensitive to the privacy of a woman, even a dead one. He and Wren carefully undressed the body and inspected each clothing article for initials or a name. No other identification was found to further support a link between the deceased and the satchel.

Wren noted this, as well as other information, in his booklet.

Canvas satchel brought to Dr. Taylor by Mr. Mountcastle of C&O wharf. Bag found in river near wharf this morning with woman's clothing and sewing items inside. Bag has initials F.L.M. and same appear on collar of blouse in bag. Clothing appears to be the correct size for the deceased. No initials found on clothing worn by the deceased. Mr. Bellows of Coroner's office mentions existence of Richmond woman of this approximate age named Fannie Mays. Family owns a butcher shop downtown.

Taylor then pulled a loose pure white gown from his bag and dressed the body. He asked Wren to arrange the transfer to the morgue for a complete autopsy. Detective Wren asked the doctor to leave the satchel, its contents, and all of the deceased's clothing there in the reservoir house. It was now official evidence and would be held in police custody. (7.2)

Chapter 8   ***Insubordination***

Detective Wren walked outside. He lit a cigar and stood looking out over the Old Reservoir. The midday sun was bright and warming. Off to the south he caught an occasional glimpse of some of the young officers scouring the fence line. To the north, he saw Officer Walton talking with Peter J. Burton, of the *Richmond Dispatch*.

"My God…" Wren muttered to himself. Wren rushed directly over to short circuit the conversation. Like any good reporter, Burton always had at least one informant within the police department who alerted him to any breaking news. He had been reporting the police beat for four or five years with the *Dispatch* and had quite a reputation for covering the story and, when the circumstances allowed it, portraying police ineptitude. Some argued that Burton habitually sensationalized the news and regularly smeared the police force in a vindictive and counter-productive manner. Others saw his aggressive reporting as an effective antidote to over-reaching police authority.

Burton saw Wren approaching. He turned from his conversation with Walton and smiled, "Well, Detective Wren, how are you? I haven't had the pleasure of covering one of your investigations since the F&M Bank Robbery. Have you apprehended the perpetrator, yet? Is the department still investigating that one, or has it been relegated to the voluminous inactive file?"

"Still open.", Wren curtly replied.

Wren was seething. There was nothing worse than an over-bearing reporter, but Wren understood he had little to gain by giving his nemesis the satisfaction of spontaneous retaliation. It took a great deal of personal will for a man of Wren's temperament to exercise such constraint, but this was a lesson hard-learned for Wren; and one not to be forgotten.

In 1863, when Wren and his cousin Will Rollings had volunteered for duty, the War seemed like a wonderful adventure. Wren and Rollings both felt compelled and honored to fight for their state and the Confederate cause. They had grown up in a family where military service was quite important. Wren's father had served with distinction in the Mexican War and the boys' common grandfather was a decorated veteran of the War of 1812. As a small boy, Wren planned to break new ground in his family's military record and attend The Virginia Military Institute. His dream was to become an officer, perhaps a general officer. The outbreak of War and the threat to his hometown of Petersburg delayed that prospect.

By the spring of 1864, the Confederate Army was rather depleted, not only in weapons and supplies, but also in leadership, particularly at the junior officer level. The War had taken a desperate toll on battlefield officers forcing numerous battlefield promotions. This produced an officer corps that was inexperienced and often psychologically ill-equipped to deal with the destruction and decay surrounding them. Captain Christian R. Morse commanded Wren's Artillery Regiment. Morse was a recent graduate of the Virginia Military Institute where he focused his studies upon artillery operations and tactics. The pressures on the young officer far exceeded anything he had envisioned while a cadet, certainly beyond anything he should have expected as a twenty-two-year-old in such desperate times. In search of comfort, Morse drank regularly. He was not particular about his brand; he could not afford to be. As was the case with most luxuries, good alcohol was a scarcity in battle-torn Virginia. Occasionally, he was able to get some wine, or perhaps some sour mash whiskey; but usually, he relied upon moonshine to relieve his anxieties. Partly due to his own youth and immaturity and partly due to his taste for the drink, it was clear, that although Morse had the respect of his subordinates with regard to technical military matters, he completely failed to live up to the standards of an officer and a gentleman. Deep down Morse knew this himself, but chose to deflect his self-disappointment by projecting his anger upon others, particularly upon those whom he perceived as weak, vulnerable, and in no position to fight back.

At sixteen, Private Wren was overweight but physically immature compared to others his age. He worked as hard as any of the boys in the Artillery Regiment, but his size made him a little slow and somewhat awkward. Morse took notice of this and out of pure mean-spiritedness, often spotlighted Wren for criticism and ridicule. Despite his youth and vulnerability, Wren maintained a rather dignified facade through all of the embarrassments, but sometimes at night, while others were asleep, he reluctantly shed tears and stubbornly sought revenge, if only in the far reaches of his imagination.

On September 16, 1864, Confederate forces were heavily entrenched in defensive earthworks on three sides of Petersburg. The fierce battle the previous June had ended in stalemate and the Union offensive had become a siege. There was no immediate threat of a frontal assault, but the dark blue specter was looming. The men kept busy cleaning their equipment, reinforcing the earthworks, and drilling for the inevitable onslaught to come as Grant's Army relentlessly amassed deadly forces; pushing tremendous amounts of men and materiel further south and west. Wren was attached to Battery 29 positioned along the Dimmock Line of Defense about one-and- one-half miles south of Petersburg just west of the Jerusalem Plank Road. The Union line facing him was just a mile in front. The tedious existence seemed, at times, unbearable; but most of these men had endured the hardships of battle and knew that tedium was far preferable.

That afternoon, Wren was passing out hardtack rations and goober peas to his battery mates. Captain Morse and two lieutenants were seated at a table outside a tent nearby under the auspices that they were discussing some logistical matters. Morse had been drinking hard that day, having just procured a few bottles of decent whiskey. His fellow officers joined in, but Morse, as always, consumed much more than anyone else.

Wren crouched down to allow a reclining soldier reach into his satchel of peanuts for a helping. As his knees bent and spread apart, the seat of his pants suddenly split revealing two raw white ham hocks.

Morse, positioned about forty feet away, but with a perfect view of the unsavory scene, spit his entire mouthful of whiskey across the table top and exploded in a loud howling laughter. He stood choking for a breath in coughing hysterics and pointed at the lowly private. Immediately all eyes cut to Wren and the group uproar became deafening. Men from all over the camp poked their heads from their tents, sat up from their resting spots, and rushed toward the scene as the din of hoots and rebel yells echoed through the encampment. It could have been a fight, perhaps over a card game gone bad; or some sort of accident; whatever it was, it was something worth investigating.

Within seconds there were thirty or forty men standing there, laughing, pointing, and mocking. Wren was absolutely crushed. His face flushed, he dropped his satchel and reached to secure his deteriorated ill-fitting pants. He was lost in a sea of faces, each distinctively laughing, but creating a singular orchestrated movement which so shamed and embarrassed the befuddled Wren that he simply froze in his spot, lowered his head, and endured the seemingly endless castigations of the sophomoric mob.

Then, from the pot of ebullient faces emerged a particularly virulent yet happily vengeful face. One face, which should not have even been a pinch of salt in such a distasteful stew much less the primary ingredient.

"Well, fat boy, as your superior, I order you to remove that disgraceful uniform."

"But, sir…"

"Do not question my authority, private. Remove the uniform. Now!" Morse slightly lost his balance but caught himself.

Wren was reeling. The haranguing and intimidation were intense. The men stood around, still laughing. In utter disgrace, Wren slipped out of the tattered pants and humbly stood half naked before his audience.

"Now turn around and bend over"

Wren looked up at Morse in complete confusion and amazement. His eyes began to well with tears.

"You heard my order; now follow it!"

The other men stood by, though they were becoming increasingly quiet as they witnessed the bizarre scene and wondered what was next.

Wren sheepishly turned his back to Morse and warily bent over at the waist. Morse then reared back and forcefully placed the heel of his boot directly in Wren's rump, sending the young overweight boy lunging forward and awkwardly sending him into a face first sprawl toward a large puddle of mud.

Morse spun around in the direction his men and raised his arms in gladiatorial victory. Some men cheered while others cringed, unsure what to make of their officer.

"Look at the little pig private in his muddy pen! Bring me my bottle, Richards!"

Morse arrogantly shouted.

Wren gathered himself in the mud puddle. His fear suddenly turned to rage. His angry mud-covered hand located a rock. He clenched it in his fist, scrambled to his feet, turned and threw the rock with all his might at the back of Morse. The rock landed squarely behind Morse's right ear knocking him forward into a drunken heap.

Morse was quickly back on his feet. "You, insubordinate bastard, you will pay!" The belligerent captain removed his sword and scabbard from his belt and rushed the boy. Morse landed two quick blows to Wren's shoulder and back with the broad side of scabbard-covered sword. Wren collapsed in a fetal ball as a number of men rushed in to stop the beating. Lieutenant Richards grabbed Morse's right arm and managed to pry the sword and scabbard from his hand. Two other Lieutenants and Sergeant Amos further restrained the enraged Captain and escorted him away to his tent.

Corporal Jackson Bolton and Cousin Will emerged from the crowd and came to Wren's aid.

"Wren, are you alright? Come with me back to my tent. I've some pants you can borrow and you need to be cleaned up.", whispered Bolton.

Once inside the tent Wren put on the pants so charitably offered by Bolton. They were a bit snug in the waist, so Wren left the top button unbuttoned. He rolled up the cuffs to accommodate his short limbs and gingerly sat on a small trunk. He slowly twisted to his left and lifted his muddy shirt and revealed a large red welt which was quickly turning purple. It covered a swath about six or seven inches across the back of his rib cage, where Morse had landed the most severe blow.

Will grimaced at the sight and said, "Cousin, I believe you'll be sore for some days.

Wren nodded and then stretched his collar to reveal a lesser but still painful bruise forming on top of his left shoulder.

"I couldn't help myself, Will. When he pushed me over and everyone was laughing, I could not contain myself any further. What do you think will become of me?"

"I don't know, cousin. Striking and officer is a very serious offense. I just do not know. But, if I can help you, I will."

"But Will, my father; he will never forgive me. The shame I will bring him and the family; the shame I have brought upon you; I cannot bear it."

"Come now, Wren; your father will not be mad.", said Bolton, trying to give some comfort to the beaten young private.

"Oh, Jackson, you do not know my father. He gave his left leg and part of his left hand for the army in Mexico. He nearly bled to death. He cares for the military more than me. He would support any punishment placed upon me and would probably seek to worsen it." Wren's imagination began to speed away and he soon became chilled at the prospect not of a long prison sentence, nor even a firing squad; but rather, the disappointment, condemnation, and estrangement of his father and family.

"Dear cousin, do not think for a moment I feel any shame because of what you have done. You are not the only one who would like to get at Morse. I, for one, will be forever thankful that you found the courage to stand up to that dog. You will always be held in esteem by this member of your family."

"Thank you, Will. That means a great deal to me, but you must understand that my father will not see it that way."

"Yes, cousin, it is unfortunate; from what I know of uncle, you are probably right."

The sun was setting and Wren returned to the tent he shared with Cousin Will and two other privates to rest. Will brought him a plate of food and a lukewarm cup of black coffee. Wren was exhausted and after finishing his plate of food, he laid down on is worn blanket and fell asleep.

Just after dawn, Wren received a message to report to Major John Angle's tent immediately. Major Angle was the regiment's commander and was therefore charged with investigating the incident. Lieutenant Richards reported the incident to Major Angle the prior evening with great reluctance. He preferred to just let the matter rest, but Sergeant Amos pressured the young lieutenant. Amos was concerned that other enlisted men in the regiment, for whom he was directly responsible, may incur the wrath of the drunken and unpredictable Captain Morse. Richards knew in his heart what was right; even though the pangs of loyalty he generally felt for other officers made this action very discomforting for himself; even though such action would, in all likelihood, prove quite unpopular among his officer colleagues; and, even though, potentially, this action may inflict irreparable damage to his own reputation and ambitions within the Confederate Army.

Wren was shaking as he entered Major Angle's tent.

"Private Jack Wren, reporting, sir."

"Yes, Private Wren.", the tent was dark that early morning with a small oil lamp casting shadows upon the stern bespectacled face of Major Angle. Angle understood perfectly well that he had the legal authority to put Wren in prison for many years. Perhaps more importantly, the Major also understood that at this desperate breaking point in the conflict, a prison sentence for this boy was akin to a dismal death sentence. Angle had seen many young men perish. The once hospitable South had become very hostile to young men. He did not want to unnecessarily contribute to that condition. The Major kept his eyes directed down toward his dimly lit desktop. Angle considered Wren's action a serious breach of conduct and there must be a consequence. No offense against any of his officers, warranted or not, could stand unpunished. Wren noticed a slight quiver in Major Angle's hand as he passed papers across his desk but the Major's voice was deep and unwavering.

"It is my understanding that there was an incident in camp yesterday. Your involvement reportedly included some serious misconduct and insubordinate actions toward an officer. This is a very serious charge and if I choose to pursue the matter by recommending a court martial, it will lead to a conviction and you will undoubtedly spend an extended amount of time in prison. This recommendation, however, may also bring some disgrace upon others involved, your regiment, and the Confederate Army as a whole."

Wren was becoming a bit frantic. His arm pits wear dripping as his anxiety increased.

"It is for this reason, and because you are a mere boy of sixteen, that I require the following. You will turn in your weapon. You will leave the regiment immediately and return home to your family. You will speak of this no more with any member of the regiment and will spend the duration of the War at home, until such time you reach the age of eighteen, when, should the Cause require your renewed participation, you will be eligible to re-enlist in the Confederate Army. I will expunge all records of your service, as if you were never here. You now may go." The Major brushed his hand in the direction of the tent entrance as if swatting an insignificant house fly out the door. The fly had not been gone but for an instant and Major Angle had dropped the entire matter and was never to think of it again.

Wren was certainly relieved, but also quite confused. As he walked quickly through the camp toward his tent to collect his things, he began to reflect upon what had just transpired. He was increasingly dejected, demeaned, and rapidly feeling disenchantment toward the army, particularly its officers. Wren had put forth as honest an effort as anyone who believed in the Confederacy and he felt betrayed that there would be no official record of his service. As a young boy, he was not capable of really explaining these feelings, even to himself. He knew he had been wronged yet it would be many years before he would acquire the maturity to fully comprehend and express the genesis of these feelings. An entire year of thankless, but dedicated, effort would ultimately leave no mark on the official record because of a brief, albeit understandable, act of revenge. Wren had secured for himself some modicum of personal dignity and pride by standing up to the bullying officer, but the cost was historical anonymity and a disgraceful scourge upon his proud military family. He vowed to himself that he would never again let his temper cost him, in a single instant, the dignity and honor his family had built over generations.

Wren quietly rolled his few personal belongings up in his blanket and slung it over his shoulder. He quietly crept to the other side of the tent and shook Will awake.

"Will, come outside" he whispered. Will wrapped his filthy blanket around his shoulders and stepped out into the cool Fall air.

"What is it, cousin?"

"I'm leaving."

"You can't desert!", interjected Will concernedly.

"No, no, Will, I'm not deserting. I've been ordered to leave by Major Angle. I am going home. For me, the fighting is over. I'm not supposed to talk about what happened to anyone."

"Good Lord, cousin. So, they aren't going to court martial you?"

"No", said Wren with a tearful smile. "But, I won't be back. I will go visit your mother when I get home and tell her you are well. I will see you when the War's over, right?". Wren was becoming emotional, for now he feared for his cousin's life. They had signed up together and Wren had always assumed the two would return home in victory together. Wren was finding it hard to look his cousin in the eye. The boy felt guilty to be leaving his favored cousin behind to face alone the dangers of combat, but in contrast, Wren was profoundly jealous that honor and dignity would be there for his cousin, but had coldly abandoned him.

"Yes, cousin, we will visit when the War's over." The two young men shook hands and Wren quickly turned to shield his quivering breakdown. He walked away, never once turning back. Will stood in the dampness and watched Wren disappear into the obscurity of the camp, knowing there was a chance they would never see one another again, but believing a reunion was far more likely. Wren mistakenly felt the embarrassment of a boy at the tearful farewell, but Will rightly knew, tears or not, he was proud of his cousin and looked forward to seeing him again and, if necessary, rectifying any misunderstanding regarding Wren's conduct in the Confederate Army which may arise between Wren and Wren's father.

Wren walked alone northward toward Petersburg. He looked around at the landscape and thought to himself how much it had changed. Almost every tree had been felled, either to construct fortress breastworks or as an unintended casualty of battle. Once lush crop fields were now denuded and strewn with litter and refuse. Broken wagon wheels, burned out carriages, empty barrels, boxes, and junkyard items of all sorts were scattered over the entire countryside.

Wren heard the thunder of approaching hooves. He looked up and saw a silhouette of six or seven horses with riders moving quickly as one. He stepped off to the side of the road and watched the party pass. Leading the group was one of the Confederacy's many gallant generals. Wren had seen the general once before. He had a glorious long dark beard and blazing blue eyes. The general was young, but most assuredly in command. It was Major General Fitzhugh Lee, nephew of Marse Robert, with his staff. Wren watched the horsemen resolutely disappear in the direction of the front line. He was inspired at the site, but he soon remembered that his orders were no longer to stand and fight, but to return home.

The matter of Captain Morse's abusive behavior was never again addressed by the Confederate Army. However, less than seven months later, poetic justice, as heavy-handed and permanent as it may have been, was served upon Morse in the form of an exploding Union shell. However, like these scales of justice, the scales of injustice, were balanced just hours later, when Cousin Will Rollings, age eighteen, was cut down in a maelstrom of mini balls as Grant's inexhaustible forces overran the depleted defenses of Petersburg. The Old South was fitfully breathing its last and was irreversibly passing from a lucid, if tumultuous, reality into the foggy realm of legend, remembrance, and nostalgia.

It was just a few weeks prior to that final Union assault on Petersburg that Wren and his family fled to Richmond, hoping against all hope that the heroes in gray could mount a final stand against the Northern aggressors. (8.1)

Chapter 9   *Canvassing the Area*

Peter J. Burton of the *Richmond Dispatch* glibly asked, "Well, Wren, what is going on here? I understand a woman's body has been found, eh? Is it murder? Any comment?"

"No, Burton. I can't have you following my men around while they are trying to conduct this investigation. I will answer your questions later. But, for now, I must insist that you leave the premises. If you refuse to leave, I will have you removed. If you resist, I will have you arrested and charged with interference in a police investigation."

Burton smiled wryly. "Yes, Detective Wren, I will do as you say. But, I assure you, I will pursue this story and will be watching your every move."

Wren puffed on his cigar. "You do your job, Burton, and I will do mine."

Burton walked away toward the reservoir entrance. Once he was safely out of earshot, Wren turned to Walton.

"What are you holding?"

"A hat, sir." Walton handed a woman's black hat. "I found it on the floor inside the old dead house on the Clark Spring property."

Wren checked his watch and got his notebook out:

14 Mar '85 - 1:15pm - Woman's black hat found by Walton in the dead house on Clark Spring property on Ashland St adjacent to Old Reservoir. Hat is in good condition.

Wren looked closely at the hat and returned to his notebook.

Red wool lint on hat. Some sand on inside.

"Walton, take me over and show me exactly where this was found."

As Wren and Walton approached the doorway to the old dead house, Officer Aborghast and another man came rushing toward them from the field behind the house. In his hands were the other garnet glove and a woman's veil.

"Mr. Archer here, the keeper of this property, found these down there by the fence." Aborghast turned and pointed toward the fence which separated the Clark Spring property from the reservoir. "They were just laying there in the grass."

"Good work", said Walton. "I found a hat inside this building I was just showing the detective."

The four men entered the old dead house. About fifteen years prior, there had been a deadly outbreak of small pox in Richmond. The epidemic grew to such proportion that the Clark Spring property had been designated for use as a quarantine hospital site, temporarily housing many of the afflicted. The unfortunate who succumbed to the disease were stored in the old house on the property until they were deemed safe for burial. This house of suffering came to be known throughout Richmond as the "dead house".

There was a large hole in the roof and many birds had taken up residence, resulting in a most unappealing floor cover. The dank air and muted moans of the wind seeped through the weathered clapboards and coldly gripped the senses of all who entered, echoing the legacy of suffering which still haunted this place. Until the generation who so clearly remembered had passed, this unholy stigma would carry the burden of the melancholy memory of the hundreds of innocents who perished.

Walton pointed to a spot on the floor just inside the door and a few feet to the right, directly below a window. Wren opened his notebook.

Hat found inside dead house under right front window. Bottom sash of window missing and open to the elements.

The three men went back outside. Wilkins, Jones, Stewart, and Keller were standing nearby awaiting their next task.

"Have you men found anything of interest?", said Walton in a loud voice.

"No sir." said one of them.

Walton looked at Wren, who said to him, "Tell them to canvass the area and find out if anyone heard or saw anything. Send them out in a six or seven block radius to question the residents."

Walton repeated the instruction to the men and sent the four of them in different directions.

"Mr. Archer. Please show us where you found the glove and veil."

Archer led Wren, Walton, and Aborghast about seventy-five yards down the fence line. He stopped and indicated the spot where he had found the two items of apparel. Wren looked at the fence, back toward Ashland Street, then back at the fence again. The wood plank fence was as dilapidated as the dead house. Wren noticed that one of the nearby planks slightly overlapped the one next to it. He went over and grabbed the edge, finding that it had broken loose from the bottom of the frame and swung freely on the nail which attached it to the top frame. He pushed the plank to one side, crouched a bit and took a look through to the other side.

"Boys'ev bin goin' in an' outta this hera fence hole fah yea's, 'tective." said Archer. Wren immediately recognized the accent of a Dinwiddie native, a rural community southwest of Petersburg. Archer turned his head downward to the left and jettisoned a thick brown gelatinous mouthful of tobacco juice. He smiled at the detective exposing just a few coated yellow teeth. "I see 'em almos' evry day."

"Do you live on this property, Archer?"

"Yessa, I do. Lived hera more 'n ten yea's. Right ova' der, in de small hoose."

"Did you see anyone yesterday evening, or last night?"

"No sa, not las' night. I do sleep awful heavy, 'speshly on Fridee night." He smiled again slipping his tongue through the gap where his front teeth once were and further salted the expression with a wink.

"Yes, Archer, I understand. Thank you for your help."

Detective Wren made an entry in his booklet.

Woman's veil and garnet glove found on Clark Spring property by E.J. Archer, keeper of the CS property approximately seventy-five yards from Ashland St along the fence line between CS property and Reservoir. Fence board nearby is loose, providing access to and from Reservoir.

"Walton, we need a wagon to transfer the corpse to the morgue and I need a bag for all of this evidence that is mounting. Please arrange for these things and meet me at the reservoir house by 4 o'clock."

"Yes, sir. I will send Aborghast."

"Very good."

Wren walked slowly back around the block to the reservoir entrance. He was beginning to pull the evidence together in his mind and although he had some suspicions, he was careful to withhold judgment until he had investigated further. He walked onto the reservoir property and went straight to the place on the eastern fence line directly opposite the position where the veil and garnet glove were found. There, Jackson Bolton approached and watched silently as Wren located the loose plank. Bolton noticed that there were footprints similar to those earlier discovered up on top the embankment leading from that position along the fence directly toward the embankment. He pointed these out to Detective Wren. In his booklet Wren wrote:

Two sets of footprints discovered on Old Reservoir property running from loose plank on fence between Reservoir and CS property and leading to steps up to south embankment of reservoir. Appear to match footprints cited earlier on top of embankment. One set is smaller and apparently female. Other set is larger with wide flat heel, apparently male. Footprints are side by side along a small pathway worn from this position in fence to embankment steps.

Wren re-lit his cigar and perched outside the reservoir house door. Rose came out of the office to talk with the detective. After a day of unusual activity around the reservoir, it had suddenly become quite tranquil. Rose had sent the other employees home early to their families, or in the case of Trainham, his bawdy house.

"G'afternoon Detective. I'm Rose, superintendent here."

"Yes, Mr. Rose."

"I have something here for you. I picked this up this morning and you should have it." Rose pulled a red woman's glove from his pocket. "I found that up on the embankment just before I saw the girl's body in the water. I've been carrying it around in my pocket; I don't know why…"

That's fine, Mr. Rose. Thank you. This is an important piece of evidence. We found it's mate on the Clark Spring property."

"I am still shocked by what has happened here. I'm not sure what to make of it.", said Rose.

"I feel the same way, Mr. Rose. The death of this young girl, no matter how it happened, is truly a tragedy. I am mournful for her family, and we do not even know who they are. The worst part is that her family probably thinks everything is alright. If you think we feel horror, can you imagine what they will feel once they hear the news?"

There was a conversational lull. "Well Mr. Rose, why don't you go home, too? It has been a very difficult day."

"Oh, I can't, Detective. I am responsible for the Reservoir and must stay until after dark."

"I understand fully, Mr. Rose."

Officer Walton returned with the men who had been scouring the neighborhood. He was holding a red wool shawl. He explained to Detective Wren that Officer Stewart interviewed, among others, Mr. J. W. Dunstan, who lived about one quarter mile up Reservoir Street. Mr. Dunstan had found a red wool shawl draped over his front wall at 6 am this morning and had no knowledge of its owner.

Red woman's glove found by Mr. Rose this morning on south embankment. Appears to be a match for glove found on Clark Spring property by Archer. Red shawl found early this morning by Mr. J.W. Dunstan hanging on the wall of his property approx. ½ mile from reservoir on Reservoir St. Turned over to Officer Stewart.

"Excellent work, men.", said a proud and commanding Wren. "Officer Aborghast should be returning soon with a litter. Once we have delivered the deceased to the

Coroner's Office, you men are free to go. If you have been on duty beyond your allotted shift, inform your superior. If you need any verification in that regard from me, I will be happy to provide it." After a pause, Wren added, "And men, regarding Burton of the *Dispatch;* none of you are to speak one word to him, nor to any other newsman, regarding this investigation. We cannot have our investigation compromised by any corroboration of any fact, theory, or suspicion regarding this matter until we have determined for ourselves if there was any foul play. And, if there was foul play, I do not want anything divulged to the press until we have apprehended the culprit. If Burton has any questions, refer him only to me. Is that understood?"

"Yes sir, absolutely", interjected Walton. "These men will adhere to your instructions." All of the men nodded and grunted in acknowledgement. (9.1)

Chapter 10 *Are We Friends?*

Lillie Madison and T. J. Cluverius got dressed. After pulling up his pants, the young man dutifully walked over to the dresser and resurrected Marse Robert from his temporary tomb. He carefully re-hung the picture in its sacred spot on Nellie's wall.

"I think it's safe for General Lee to be out, now.", said a smirking Cluverius.

Cluverius felt like his demons had been temporarily exorcised and Lillie just felt awkward anxiety. As she draped her red shawl around her shoulders and sat on the edge of the rumpled bed, she mustered up some courage and asked,

"Tommie... Have you thought more about our circumstances?"

He was silent for a moment. Then he said, "Lillie, I'm not sure what to do. I am very confused by this. I thought we had agreed that our union would be impossible for many reasons. I plan to marry Nolie and you were to marry Edward."

"Yes, I know that is what we talked about. But, you don't love Nolie and I don't love Edward. On top of that, Edward is concerned with taking responsibility for the child." She began to get emotional. "I love you, Tommie... and I always have. All I've ever wished for was to be with you."

Cluverius sat beside her and turned her shoulders toward him. He held her head against his chest. He closed his eyes, rolling them up into his head as he calculated his next move. Cluverius' thoughts clearly revolved around how to get away from this woman and the disastrous situation. Cluverius continued to hold Lillie close, though his level of disgust for her was escalating. He was repulsed by her presence and now, since he had gotten what he needed, he wished she would just disappear. Cluverius was also well aware of the problems it would present for him back home if he were to simply scorn her.

"Lillie, you've told no one else in the family about your condition, have you?"

"No, Tommie. No one knows."

"Lillie, you have to consider marrying Edward. You must! We could not bear the shame within the family if they knew about us!" Cluverius stopped himself from going further. As a lawyer, he understood that when emotion starts creeping into an argument, mistakes are usually the result. He told himself he needed some time to think more clearly about how to handle Lillie before poorly chosen words led to an irrational outcome.

As Lillie cried into his coat, Cluverius tried to comfort her. "Listen, Lillie; I think you are very weary. I need to attend to some business in town. Let me take you back to the hotel, where you can rest." He reached beneath his coat and took out his watch. It was

1:45 PM. He continued, "I will come call for you this evening by 8 o'clock. We can talk more about this. Do not go anywhere; just stay in the hotel. We don't want anyone to recognize you, remember?" She nodded. "Do not worry, Lillie. I will come up with a solution which will serve well. I just need to take care of a few things first."

He cupped her wet cheeks in his hand and kissed her on the forehead. "Come, now. You can rely upon me." he softly whispered.

She nodded her head and wiped her tears on her shawl. "I know you will, Tommie. I have always believed in you." Lillie flinched and held her side as the baby kicked.

The young couple crept back down the stairwell. Cluverius left Lillie at the front door while he returned the key. Nellie was now seated at the table with the others.

"Thank you, madam."

"Hope you enjoyed your stay.", said the incorrigible Nellie.

"Yes, we did; thank you and good day." Cluverius quickly turned and walked toward the door. He grabbed Lillie's elbow and led her out the door.

As he reached to shut the door behind him, he heard Nellie exclaim, "Another satisfied customer! Please come again!". He closed the door in the face of laughter.

The five-block walk seemed like ten. Each felt like nary a word could be fit in amongst all the tension. Cluverius saw Lillie to the entrance of the American Hotel. He reassured her that he would return for her by 8 o'clock that evening. She entered the hotel lobby and turned right into the dining room.

Cluverius continued west on Main Street. He was walking slowly with his head down, intermittently putting his thumb and index finger together under his nose and separating them along the path formed by his mustache. His armpits were dripping as he loosened his collar to let in some air. Suddenly, he came to an abrupt and inspirational stop. He completely reversed direction and began walking again, this time at a more hurried and purposeful pace. Cluverius marched back past the American Hotel looking directly ahead.

Lillie was seated in the hotel dining room perusing the menu when she caught a glimpse of the familiar figure passing by the front window. She was curious, but unconcerned. She was very hungry and focused on placing her order.

Less than five minutes later, Cluverius peeked his head through the front door of Nellie's. Three of the original four were seated at the table. One of the men was now gone.

"Back again, stranger?", asked Fogelman.

"Um, yes, is Nellie still here?" said Cluverius trying to avoid ridicule.

Fogelman pointed again over his shoulder, just as before. Cluverius walked nervously over and rapped on Nellie's door with trepidation. Once again, he heard her quick footsteps approaching from the other side. The door opened and there was Nellie standing in a silk robe that barely covered her large but sagging breasts.

"You again? I give you young ones credit, you don't last long, but you come back quick!"

Cluverius was not amused. His thoughts were very far from idle tawdry chatter.

"Miss Nellie… I have a very serious problem and need your recommendation." He was holding his hands together in an almost prayerful manner.

"So, what is it?"

"May I step inside? I prefer to not discuss this in front of the others."

"Alright, come on in."

Cluverius' brow was wet and his face was chalky. He stepped into Nellie's quarters and closed the door behind him. He leaned back against the door.

"Nellie, you know that woman I was here with earlier?"

"Yeah, your wife." she goaded.

"Well, uh, yes…" he muttered with a chilled hesitancy. "She is carrying a child and cannot any longer. She needs to terminate the pregnancy; for her own good health. I am hopeful that you may know someone who performs this practice."

"Glad to see you think so highly of me." She put her hands on her hips, further exposing her breasts. "Hell, who'em I kiddin'?… Of course, I know someone. Go see Rachel McDonald. She lives over on Jacquelin Street, over on the other side o' Hollywood. She'll take care o' things."

"What is the house number?"

"Hell, I don' know. It's the secon' house from the corner; east of Washin'ton Street on the riva' side."

"Is she reliable?"

"She's been doin' this for years, boy. Jus' tell 'er I sent ya."

"Thank you." Cluverius smiled and then started to turn toward the door. He stopped and said, "Oh, Miss Nellie, one more thing; if you would be so good not to mention this to anyone. It's very sensitive."

"I'll take it to my grave.", pledged Nellie.

A loud voice from the back room startled Cluverius. "Nellie, where the hell are ya? I'm getting' a little bored back here!"

"Shush, Harry; I'll be there in a moment!"

"Do I owe you anything, Nellie?"

"Naah... just come back 'n see me." she waved him off and escorted him through the door.

Cluverius quickly walked a half block south to Main Street. He turned right and walked straight ahead about two blocks until the tug horse trolley came up from behind. He boarded, paid the fare to the driver, and stood near the back. The trolley rolled past the Capitol and stopped two blocks later. The sight of Mozart Hall marquee two blocks up 7th Street jogged his memory. Cluverius looked at his watch. He jumped off the trolley and walked toward the ticket office in front of the Mozart Theater. He bought a ticket for the 2:30 Dime Museum production of *Chimes of Normandy*, entered the theater, and chose a seat on the floor level about five rows from the rear near the center aisle. The orchestra was finishing its warm-up as the last patrons were taking their seats. Cluverius removed his hat as he stood and looked around the theater. It was as if he were trying to see someone in the crowd; or perhaps he wanted someone to see him. As the overhead lights dimmed and the stage lighting came up, he sat, deeply exhaled, and lost himself in the music.

Mozart Hall, Richmond, Virginia

T.J. Cluverius exited the theater just after 4 o'clock before the show had concluded. The sound of the orchestra was snuffed out as the large theater doors closed behind him. The temperature had noticeably dropped over the last hour, casting an ominous pale on the early Spring afternoon. He flipped the collar of his grey overcoat up, protecting his neck and chin from the biting wind. Once again, he boarded the west-bound tug-horse trolley but this time stayed aboard for seventeen blocks until reaching the end of the line at the head of Reservoir Street. The trolley driver pulled up on the reins and Cluverius leapt from the running board. His mind raced as he considered his circumstances and what must be done to alleviate them. He turned south on Reservoir and followed it to Wallace Street, where he was to turn west once again. Cluverius turned on to Jacquelin

Street just after 4:25 pm. Near the end of the next block sat Rachel McDonald's house. Cluverius was the only person on the street. He heard only the sound of his own footsteps as he neared his destination. His time at the theater enabled him to sharpen his focus and crystallize his plan.

Rachel McDonald's two-story frame house was in serious disrepair. The gutter hanging over her front porch was pulling away, causing the downspout it fed to buckle and bend in an unnatural position. The roof shingles were old and frayed, like a layer of wet worn wool draped atop the peeling wood structure. Cluverius knocked firmly on the door. The door cracked open and a woman's voice said, "Yes, who are you?"

"Madam, I have come at the recommendation of Nellie… uh…. I don't know her last name; but she runs a house behind the cigar store on 15th Street."

"Yes, I know her - Nellie Goss."

"Yes, well, she told me you could help me with a certain problem." said an anguished Cluverius.

"What kind of problem?" said the voice.

"Madam, may I come in? The topic is private and sensitive."

"Well, I suppose." She closed the door and opened the chain lock, then opened the door again. "Come in."

Cluverius stepped inside and removed his hat. Cluverius immediately felt a little uneasy as the woman's eyes opened wide, scanning downward from his head to his toes and back up again, scrutinizing his impressive and youthful figure. She put her forefinger between her teeth and clenched it lightly. Then removing it, she said in a rather enticing manner.

"And, why, sir, did you come here?" She ran her finger tips deftly up and down along her breast bone while she coyly awaited a response.

Cluverius was surprised by her suggestive body language. He swallowed and tried to focus on his response; all the while noticing that, although this woman was more than twenty years his senior, and despite the fact that she was poorly dressed and in need of a hairbrush, she retained a curiously natural, but sophisticated, attractiveness; as well as a physical interest in him which was undeniable.

"Well, madam…", he paused. "I am seeking to help my dear cousin. She has found herself in a rather undignified predicament."

The middle-aged woman interrupted him, "Why don't you come into the parlor and tell me all about it. Would you like some tea?"

"Oh, no madam. I wish to be brief and not take up much of your time."

"I have no other appointment today. Please, come in.". She lightly touched his arm and guided him to the right toward a seating area arranged in front of a small fireplace. From the surroundings, it appeared that at one time, many years before, Rachel, or at least her family, had some status in society. This status had somewhat deteriorated; in concert with the high quality, but rather decrepit and outdated, home furnishings.

"I will take your hat and coat." Cluverius reluctantly removed his coat and handed it to her along with his hat. She placed the items on a straight back chair which was positioned against the small triangular wall beneath the banister. He politely followed her lead into the parlor.

He sat on a small chair on one side of the fire and she sat herself on the matching loveseat opposite him. Rachel McDonald sat back in the seat, laying her right arm across the back and continuing to softly stroke her subtly heaving chest and neck with her other hand. She looked intently upon him. Cluverius was seated upright with his knees apart. His elbows rest upon his thighs as his clasped hands were suspended between his knees.

"Please continue, dear man." as she drank in his beauty.

"You see, my cousin is with child and has no husband. I am trying to help her and, alas, she has come to such a desperate point that she requires certain services which I am told you are willing to perform. I was hoping I could arrange an appointment on her behalf with you as soon as possible. Her time in Richmond is very limited."

"Now, dear man, you understand what you are asking me to do is beyond the law? I am certainly able to do such a procedure, but you must understand the risk I would be taking. I do not know what you are expecting, but the incentive for me must be, um, substantial."

"Well, madam, what would be the cost?", asked Cluverius bracing himself.

"Well, that all depends...", she said as she sat forward and looked directly at the handsome young Cluverius. "That depends on whether or not I am doing this for a *friend*. Are we *friends*?", she asked him.

Cluverius thought he understood what she was saying, but in his uncertainty, he did not wish to make an offensive conclusion. Rachel stood and came over to the seated Cluverius. She put her right foot up on the edge of his chair and grabbed his hand, quickly forcing it up under her skirt. She cupped her other hand under his chin and lifted his head up. His eyes met hers as she repeated, "Are we, *friends*?"

Cluverius' involuntary tongue thrust covered his upper lip; then he smiled with an incontrovertible understanding. "Yes, we *are* friends.", he said. Rachel turned and led the young man up the stairs to her bed chamber.

Twenty minutes later Cluverius emerged from Rachel's bedroom. He stood at the top of the stairs and spoke back through the door. "There is no need for you to see me out, my dear. I will bring my cousin here after 9 o'clock as we agreed."

He took a few steps down the stairs when he heard her speak. "Oh, dear man, I forgot to ask your name. I make a habit of knowing all my friends' names."

"Merton, my dear; T. J. Merton.", he convincingly called back in her direction. Cluverius made his way briskly down the remaining stairs, plucked his hat and coat from the hallway chair, and continued straight out the door with no further hesitation. (10.1)

Chapter 11   ***The Autopsy***

Dr. William H. Taylor arrived at his office just after dawn on Sunday, March 15. Most other city employees were home. Taylor figured Sunday was as good a day as any to conduct the post mortem examination of the young woman. In fact, it was probably better as he would not have the distractions of the official workday.

Taylor placed his medical case on the floor next to his desk and removed his coat. He hung it on the coat stand nearby and began to roll up his sleeves.

The office door opened and John Bellows, Taylor's assistant appeared. His hair was disheveled and his shirt only half tucked in and buttoned incorrectly. Even with Taylor's questionable eyesight, it was clear the lad was up much earlier than he would have liked.

"I know you have little taste for alcohol, Bellows, so why do you look in such poor condition this morning?"

"Yes, doctor, I know. I was up very late reading. I have a very important test tomorrow morning."

"That is right; your entrance examination at the Medical College; you must forgive me, but it had slipped my mind. Are you prepared?"

"I am not sure, doctor. I fear I will have another late night ahead of me."

"Well, boy; I always felt that if I did not command all of the material by midnight or 1 o'clock, I would let fate make the final determination. I believe that it is better to have a rested and clear recollection of the few facts you command, rather than a blurred and cursory understanding of but a few more facts. In other words, my boy, get enough rest and let clear thinking guide you where your rote memory cannot. Swing on to it." (11.1)

Bellows knew there was real wisdom in those words somewhere, but he was so tired he could not ponder it for long.

"I won't keep you here late today.", said Taylor. "I need you to help me bring the body up to the examination room and then move it back to the ground floor once again after I have completed the autopsy. You are welcome to witness the examination, but if you prefer to take a nap, that will be fine."

"Thank you, doctor."

After helping Taylor retrieve the body and prepare for the examination, Bellows returned downstairs to lay down on a vacant gurney in the cadaver room. It was cold, so Bellows left his coat on. He slipped under the thin sheet and lay perfectly prone on his back between Mr. Hubert L. Gibson, who had collapsed suddenly and died while gardening

Saturday morning; and Mrs. Velma Howard, who had taken very ill after her evening meal Thursday, fell into a comatose state, and expired Friday afternoon. The coroner and his assistant had another busy week ahead of them; in this field of endeavor, there was an endless supply of work. Bellows quickly fell asleep.

Taylor opened the shades on the examination room windows, letting in the bright morning. He removed the sheet covering the deceased. The doctor put on his large white examination apron. He placed a new medical file on the small stand beside the examination table and opened it to a pre-printed form. Taylor put on his eyeglasses and began to fill in the blanks.

Date of Examination:	*15 Mar 1885*
Time of Examination:	*7:20AM*
Examination Procedure:	*Post Mortem Autopsy*
Place of Examination:	*City of Richmond Coroner's Office*
Name of Examiner:	*William H. Taylor, M.E.*
Subject Name:	*Unknown*
Subject Gender:	*Female*
Subject Age:	*20 - 25 years*
Subject Height:	*4 feet 11 inches*
Subject Weight:	*120 pounds (approx)*
Date of Death:	*March 13 or 14, 1885*
Time of Death:	*Betwn 9pm -13 Mar and 1am - 14 Mar*
Cause of Death:	*Drowning*

Notes: Subject found in Old Marshall Reservoir, Richmond, on morning of March 14, 1885. Subject was face down in water's edge. Preliminary examination revealed subject to be in 7th or 8th month of pregnancy.

Body completely intact. Decomposition at time of examination is minimal.

Taylor moved closer to the body and softly pressed around the skull, feeling for any wounds or fractures

Skull is intact. One large bruise approx. two inches wide directly above right eye near temple. No breaks in the skin in this area. Light scratches on right eyelid and on forehead. Another lighter bruise just below the bottom lip. Area beneath lower lip is slightly discolored in even distribution across two-and-one-half inch span. There is light blood vessel breakage on interior of lower lip.

The deceased retains fourteen lower teeth and thirteen upper teeth. First molar on the right side is missing and based upon condition of the gum, was removed at least thirty days prior to death. All teeth appear normal and of adequate condition.

Taylor put down his pencil and retrieved his cranial saw. The doctor placed a small metal tub on the floor beneath the deceased's head as it hung slightly over the edge of the examination table. He carefully cut around the top of the skull near the hairline and exposed the interior. As the blood drained into the tub, the doctor carefully rinsed the surface. He repeatedly filled a large sponge with water in a five-gallon bucket and carefully squeezed it over the soft wrinkled tissue. Taylor painstakingly cut the connective tissues on the outer layer of the brain and dislodged the mass from the cranial cavity. He held the loosened brain in his left hand as he reached in with his large surgical scissors and snipped the stretched stem, releasing the object from its final tether. The old doctor placed the brain in a large steel pan and rinsed it a few more times, wiped his hands dry on a towel, and picked up the pencil.

No fractures inside skull. Brain appears normal and fully developed. On left top surface of brain an effusion one inch in diameter is observed.

Dr. Taylor re-attached the top of the skull with sutures. He moved alongside the table to examine the torso and internal organs. Other than the pregnancy, there were no other notable exterior abnormalities. There was no unusual bruising, no scratches, no cuts. The old man steadily made an incision from the sternum down to the lower abdomen. Dr. Taylor first performed the unenviable procedure of removing the fetus and placenta. He tried to keep is thoughts and observances clinical, but he could not avoid letting some emotional frustration creep in as he withdrew the perfectly formed unborn male and his ruby red nutritional source from his loving sanctuary. For a brief moment, as he looked upon the cherubically innocent face, this was not a fetus, but a child. Taylor quickly reacquired his detached professionalism. He cut the umbilical cord, then measured the length and weight of the fetus. Taylor then unceremoniously placed the unborn and placenta in a canvas sack, carried it to the corner of the examination room and left it there to await disposal.

The cadaver's rib cage was already widened by the advanced pregnancy, so with the fetus now removed, Taylor found the other organs he was interested in examining easily accessible. He removed the lungs and placed them in a pan. He then removed the stomach and placed it beside. Experience told the doctor that the heart, liver, spleen, and intestines were immaterial to his inquest, so he felt them and observed them for any irregularities and left them for the embalmer. Dr. Taylor sewed up the incision and respectfully covered the entire body with a sheet. He picked up the tray of harvested organs and moved them to another smaller table for close inspection.

After nearly thirty minutes of scrutiny, Taylor washed his hands, dried them, and recorded his findings.

Exterior of torso and extremities in excellent condition. No signs of bruising nor lacerations. There is some light elongated scarring from lower abdomen up to navel, due to rapid stretching of skin associated with advanced pregnancy.

Male fetus was well--formed and appeared normal. Weight - 4 pounds 11 ounces; 15 inches in length. Placenta was normal.

No signs of internal injury nor bleeding. All organs appear of normal size, location, and outer appearance.

Lungs are normal size. There is unnatural redness on the interior lining and some small amounts of frothy water.

Stomach retains ten ounces of undigested food. Appears to be chicken or duck, green string beans and bread. No presence of the frothy water observed in the lungs. Otherwise, stomach appears normal and healthy

Taylor read through his notations and then offered his medical opinion on the cause of death.

The body was first examined at the Reservoir by this Examiner at 11 am on March 14, 1885. At that time this Examiner noted that based upon stiffness of the body and its general condition, it appeared the body had been dead for at least six hours prior to the examination. The presence of undigested food in the stomach indicates that the death probably occurred sometime before midnight on March 13, 1885. Assuming the victim ate her last meal sometime between 6 pm and 8 pm on March 13, 1885, this level of digestion would be consistent with food in the living and functioning stomach for a period of two to four hours.

The existence of the deep bruise above the right eye, coupled with the effused blood located on the left top of the brain, it is clear that a heavy blow was sustained.

The light bruising under the lower lip may have been caused by external pressure. The time of this bruising cannot be medically determined. It may have happened in conjunction with the bruising above the eye, or it may have happened sometime prior under completely different circumstances.

It is the Medical Examiner's opinion that the cause of death was drowning. It appears that the victim was knocked unconscious, but not killed, by a blunt blow to the head above the right eye and upon falling in the water in an unconscious state, was unable to breathe, thus causing distress in the lungs and accounting for the redness observed there. Though a large amount of water would generally be found in the lungs of a drowning victim, it is likely that the reduced breathing rate of the unconscious victim accounts for the reduced, but clear, presence of the frothy water in the lungs. It should be noted that at the initial inspection of the body, this Examiner noted that the victim's hands were clenched with mud inside them, lending further support to the idea that the victim entered the water in a living but somewhat incapacitated state and expired in the water.

In summation, the victim most likely received a solid blow to the head, then entered the water where she drowned sometime before midnight on March 13, 1885.

William H. Taylor, M.E.   15 March 1885   10:12 am
(11.2)

Chapter 12   **Sunday Morning**

By Sunday morning, news of the death of the mysterious young woman was rapidly spreading through the city. The *Dispatch* had officially broken the story in the Sunday morning paper.

The Richmond Dispatch
March 15, 1885

Woman's Body Found

City of Richmond, A young woman's body was found early the morning of March 14 floating in the shallow edge near the south end of the Old Marshall Reservoir. Mr. Walter Trainham, an employee of the reservoir was among those who made the grisly discovery and immediately reported the finding to local authorities. The victim appears to be aged twenty to twenty-five. Mr. Trainham indicated that, in his opinion, this was a murderous deed. There are reports that there were signs of a struggle at the site as well as two sets of footprints, one appearing to be those of a woman, presumably the deceased, and another set belonging to a man, presumably the perpetrator.

Many articles of female clothing were found at the reservoir and on adjacent properties. Mr. A. J. Archer, the caretaker of the old small pox dead house property, located a glove and veil and turned it over to the investigators. He also said a woman's hat was found inside the dead house. It is Mr. Archer's belief that the victim and her attacker accessed the reservoir through a hole in the fence between the dead house property and the reservoir.

Joseph Mountcastle, an employee at the wharf of the Chesapeake & Ohio Railroad found a satchel full of women's clothes floating on the banks of the river more than a mile below Mayo's Bridge. According to Mountcastle, the satchel bore the initials "F.L.M." and may belong to the victim. He turned the satchel over to officials.

The Richmond Dispatch Offices

More than a half dozen police officers and City of Richmond officials were seen on site. Dr. William H. Taylor, Coroner, took possession of the body and is examining it. According to Dr. Taylor, the body will be transported to the morgue after his examination. There, it shall remain until the woman can be identified. At the Coroner's request, anyone who may be able to identify the body is asked to come to the morgue at the Old Almshouse after Sunday church services, when the body will be displayed for identification.

The official investigation is being headed by Detective Jack Wren of the Richmond Police.

Detective Wren refused comment on the matter. It should be noted that Detective Wren headed the investigation of the Farmers and Merchants Bank Robbery last year. That investigation is unsolved and, according to Detective Wren, remains an open investigation. (12.1)

Wren threw down his Sunday *Dispatch* on his dining table. "Well, it's quite obvious how Burton spent his Saturday evening." he said to his wife. "Did you read this?", picking the paper back up with one hand and quickly and repeatedly poking it with the index finger of his opposing hand. He then threw it back down in smoldering disgust.

"Oh dear, stop worrying about that man. It is a waste to do so", said Madeline.

"I know, but he is so unfair. The way he mischaracterizes everything the police force does is criminal in itself."

"Jack, you must do what *you* know is best and cannot be concerned with what *he* does with the truth. His credibility is fleeting. Yours is not. Even if most people never understand what is the truth, God will. That is when that reporter will have to answer for all of his scurrilous tricks."

All at once Wren began decompressing. Madeline's sweet but sensible voice always seemed to trigger the release valve. "You are a wise woman, my dear. I will do what is right. Where are the boys?", looking at his watch. "We need to be off for church."

"In the front; they are dressed and ready."

"Very good." Wren tightened his tie to his throat and picked up his bowler. Madeline straightened her large hat in front of the mirror near the front door. She opened her matching parasol as she stepped out onto the front porch. At the bottom of the porch steps, she crouched and plucked a small purple crocus. She turned back up the porch steps and met Wren as he closed the front door. She smiled and placed the small bloom in his lapel. She gently pressed the lapel back against his shoulder softly saying, "There now." with granite reassurance. Wren fell in love all over again as her brown eyes cut upward and met his. "Thank you, dear."

Jack, Jr. and Edward were waiting impatiently near the front gate. They were playing tag, sure to soil their good clothes at any moment unless diverted. "Let's go, men." said Wren. The boys immediately obeyed at the sound of their father's voice and dutifully fell into line. The young family marched east on Grove Avenue toward Lombardy Street. Church was just a few blocks away. The bright morning in the company of the people he loved most inspired honest introspection and welcomed redemption. (12.2)

Chapter 13   *Not Enough Meat*

Nineteen-year old Fannie Mays and her father arrived a few minutes late for church Sunday morning. It was an unusual occurrence for the Mays family, but a problem had arisen regarding a pork shipment to the butcher shop and it took some time for Mr. Mays to sort it out. As they opened the heavy doors the opening prayer was being said by Reverend Jenkins. A few turned to look. Then more turned. Old Widow Sanford's eyes reacted with horrid surprise as Fannie quietly sat in the pew across from her. Others smiled when they saw her. Fannie looked with confusion at her father as eyes continued to turn their direction, usually followed by a hand-shielded whisper to the next person. Fannie shrugged her shoulders as she and her father looked at one another. She mouthed the words, "I don't know" to her father. They both smiled uneasily, Mr. Mays nodding his head to those he recognized. Politeness ordered that the parishioners not stare too long, so most turned their attention back toward the pulpit. Fannie wondered what could be the matter. She knew that being late was never good form, but she was stunned that on this particular occasion, it created such unwanted attention. She silently asked herself, "Is this a feast day? She answered. "No." She could not imagine why such importance had been placed upon her and her father's late entrance.

News traveled fast within the congregation. That morning prior to church, rumors and speculation were spreading about the death of the mysterious young girl reported in the newspaper. As always, Old Widow Sanford was right in the thick of it. She usually arrived fifteen minutes before the 9am service to indulge herself in a little tawdry gossip before a good cleansing. This morning she arrived twenty minutes early.

Widow Sanford sat on the bench under the dogwood tree out in front of The Monumental Church. After three or four minutes, Mr. and Mrs. James Lavery arrived alongside Mr. Francis B. Johnson, a widower, and his spinster sister Anna. The ladies sat beside their friend and the gentlemen broke off and stood at the base of the church steps to talk of more dignified matters.

"Have I some news for you two." She was very excited but at the same time, noticeably concerned.

"What is it, Ellen?" said the spinster.

"Yes, what?" chimed Mrs. Lavery.

"Well, my nephew Charles heard something dreadful. I'm sure you read the story of the girl found in the reservoir."

"Yes, yes; absolutely horrible!" said Miss Johnson.

"A tragedy; poor thing." added Mrs. Lavery

"Yes, well Charles tells me he knows a man who works at the C&O wharf; and evidently, someone there found some clothing items belonging to the girl. And her name was on one of them. It was young Fannie Mays!"

"No, it cannot be!" exclaimed Mrs. Lavery. "You mean the Fannie Mays of the Mays who attend our church? The butcher's daughter?".

"Yes, it is true. I heard the Coroner's Office even confirmed it." Widow Sanford clutched each of their hands tightly for dramatic effect.

"Oh, that is terrible. Does the family know?"

"I would assume so", said Widow Sanford "What a shock, it is. I was thinking of going to their shop after services to express my condolences, but then I would feel obligated to buy some meat; and quite frankly, I've never been satisfied with the Mays cuts; they always leave too much fat, not enough meat."

"Yes, yes, I agree; too much fat. Oh, but this is awful."

By the time the bells rang to call in the flock, the information had disseminated through them like a contagion. One parishioner refuted the claim, stating she had just seen Fannie the previous day on Main Street, but to no avail. The rumor had gained tremendous momentum and nothing short of Fannie's physical appearance would thwart it, though for some, even that may not have been persuasive enough.

The Monumental Church, Broad Street, Richmond

After the service, the Reverend dismissed the congregation. The crowd immediately broke into conversation and turned toward the rear of the church. The Mays, both quite self-conscious by this point, moved toward the doors as the organ music started and drowned out the hum of the crowd. Outside, Mrs. Alice Gruden, a friend of the Mays, ran up and hugged the bewildered father and daughter.

"What is this all about?" asked Mr. Mays.

"We all had heard Fannie was dead!"

"What?" said Mr. Mays.

"Yes, everyone thought she was the girl found in the reservoir."

"Ridiculous." said Mr. Mays, not amused.

Dozens then descended upon the two Mays expressing relief and thanks that the story was unfounded.

"They even said the Coroner confirmed her death!" shouted one man above the crowd.

Mr. Mays' annoyance mutated into anger. "That's preposterous! Come now, Fannie, we've got to make this right!" He grabbed his daughter's hand, broke through the ring of well-wishers, and rushed in the direction of Capitol Square and the Coroner's Office.

Old Widow Sanford observed from a distance. A part of her was happy that the Mays girl was safe, but another was very disappointed that the best piece of local information she had unearthed in many years had turned out to be false. In any event, she had no plans to ever patronize the Mays Butcher Shop. "Too much fat, not enough meat", she repeated to herself.

Mays marched forward at a determined pace, gripping his daughter's hand. Fannie was having trouble keeping up, particularly in her Sunday dress and shoes. Every third or fourth step for her was a double one and although they were not running, she was starting to experience some labored breathing. Seven-and-one-half blocks later Mr. Mays burst through the door of the Coroner's Office and lunged toward the room on the right. He stuck his head in the door, and the room was empty. He backed out and turned to his daughter and said, "Try that one, Fannie." pointing to the door on the opposite side of the hall.

Fannie walked over and pushed open the door to the cadaver room. She stepped through and right in front of her were three sets of feet. The two pairs on either side were bare and the middle pair had brown shoes.

She let out a shriek, realizing she was now in the midst of the dead. In reaction, the middle cadaver's left leg jerked and it sat straight up with eyes popped wide open. She screamed louder again; the ashen cadaver screamed right back at her. Mr. Mays came in and Fannie rushed to his open arms. He led his daughter out into the hall and tried to calm her.

John Bellows warily stepped into the hallway. Fannie was crying into her father's coat.

"What is wrong with you!?" said a stern Mr. Mays. "You scared this girl half to death! What are you doing in there!? What kind of people sleep with the dead!?"

"I'm terribly sorry.", said a stunned Bellows, "I assist the Coroner and was, uh, just taking a nap. I know it looks rather odd, but I guess you get used to the bodies after a while. Once again, sir, I'm very sorry. Miss, please accept my apology."

Fannie had gathered her emotions and turned from her father's breast. Suddenly her face brightened, "John Bellows? Is that you?" she wiped her tear dampened cheek and snorted to control her running nose.

"Yes." replied a guarded Bellows.

"It's me, Fannie. Fannie Mays. We went to school together! Remember?"

"Oh, Fannie. Yes, I remember." He smiled, "How are you?"

"Well," said Fannie, having reacquired her sense of humor, "other than recently being pronounced dead by the Coroner's Office and having heart failure at the sight of you, I am just fine."

"What?" asked Bellows.

"It is being spread all over town that the Coroner's Office said the dead girl from the reservoir is my Fannie." Mr. Mays aggressively interjected.

Bellows could see that Mr. Mays was volatile and impulsive. The young man's instincts told him that the last thing he should do is let it be known that it was he who first brought up Fannie's name in connection with the investigation.

"That is complete rumor, Mr. Mays. I assure Dr. Taylor did no such thing. That girl remains unidentified. As a matter of fact, Dr. Taylor is upstairs performing an autopsy on the girl now. I will inform him that any insinuation the girl in question is your Fannie is utterly false. You have my word."

"Good, then we have an understanding. Thank you. Let's go home, Fannie"

"Good bye, John", said Fannie. "So nice to see you again."

"Yes, Fannie, it is nice. Perhaps next time it will be under more ordinary circumstances. Thank you for understanding."

Mr. Mays and Fannie disappeared through the door. Bellows went upstairs to check in on Dr. Taylor.

"Dr. Taylor, said Bellows, "Do you remember the woman whose name I mentioned yesterday? Fannie Mays?"

"Yes, the one about the age of the deceased and with the same initials."

"That's correct, sir. Well, the body is not her. Fannie came here just now. She was with her father and he was enraged to hear that his daughter's name was being bandied around town. He heard you, well I mean your office, had confirmed her identity."

"Oh, dear."

"But I explained to him that this was certainly not the case."

"Oh, good."

"He seems like a very temperamental man, doctor."

"I have no children, but I certainly can understand his concern."

"Well, doctor, I think my explanation was satisfactory to him."

"Good boy, Bellows. We need to take this body over to the morgue. I expect visitors there soon."

The men transferred the body onto a litter, carried it downstairs, and out the rear entrance of the building. It was then loaded into a covered wagon.

"Bellows, you harness the horse, I am going to get my case."

"Yes, doctor."

It was 11:30 AM when the wagon pulled up to the morgue at the far north end of the city. It was located in the City Almshouse next door to the City Hospital and across the street was Shockoe Hill Cemetery. Most church services were ending and based upon the plea published in the *Dispatch,* Taylor and Bellows were hopeful the woman's identity would soon be confirmed. (13.1)

Chapter 14   *Captain Billy*

By noon there was a line stretching one-and-one-half blocks westward on Hill Street from the door of the Old Almshouse. An event that by all standards of decorum should have remained a solemn civic duty quickly acquired a circus atmosphere consumed by gossip, innuendo, and reckless speculation. Some were there in the honest hope that they could identify the body. Most were there with little hope of actually knowing the woman, but rather with a morbidly innate curiosity and an insatiable calling to be a witness to history if and when the body was identified. (14.1)

After viewing the body and exiting the Old Almshouse, most loitered in the street to discuss the situation. Groups formed up and down the street, usually divided by gender; invariably, by class. The carriage park adjacent to the hospital was filled with more than a dozen carriages. Many of the most privileged class had turned out after church to participate in the spectacle. Bank presidents, attorneys, wealthy entrepreneurs, philanthropists, and old-money inheritance cases alike were spellbound by the incident.

Professional men tended to congregate on the sidewalks or curbside smoking pipes and expensive cigars as they marveled at the scene before them. The gents were in tastefully well-made suits and their thoughts on the matter were equally tailored. Their conversations were quiet and reserved, with only an occasional expression of controlled emotion.

The working-class men typically gathered in the middle of the brick-paved avenue, smoking cigars and chewing tobacco. Though most were in their Sunday best, the lack of a tailored fit and the absence of fine accessories was a distinctive moniker. Their comments were often crassly boisterous and distasteful. A slap on a friend's shoulder followed by a hoot and a howl was commonplace.

The society ladies overtly shielded their eyes and ears from the working-class chortling, often pulling their veils tightly around their heads as they passed by the loutish men. However, more than a few could not contain themselves from casting a quick, and hopefully unseen, glance in the direction of the lower class and straining to hear but a small titillating snippet of tripe which those of the lower class were so prone to publicly verbalize and which those of the upper class thought of with ashamed frequency but dared never to utter. The overheard remarks were scandalous and displayed poor breeding, but that did nothing to diminish the private delight they engendered in the staid and, in instances such as this, envious upper echelons of Southern society. The ladies in their lovely hats and dresses sought the shade of the trees which sprinkled the street. A fair complexion was mandatory and even the March midday sun was a threat to the perceived status of a lady. Their groupings were much smaller than the men's, usually exclusive cliques of three or four which allowed the discussions to remain in discreet whispered tones.

The lower-class women were far more reserved and tactful than their sons and husbands. But they were far more comfortable and less intimidated by the carnival-like surroundings sprouting up in the streets than society ladies. They were uninhibited by the midday sunlight and although the size of their groups and the volume of their opinions paled in comparison to the men, these farm yard hens were much more inclined to make public proclamations than their upper-class counterparts.

    This death of the mysterious young woman had sparked the interest of nearly the entire population of Richmond. For the most part, it mattered not from which class or family one came, this was an incident, and perhaps a crime, which transcended class interests and appealed directly to basic human interests. The negro population, however, remained on the outside looking in. Though news of the incident had penetrated their neighborhoods, most blacks understood that they were better off viewing this matter from a distance. Any attempt to get a closer look at the situation in this segregated society would only bring unwarranted scrutiny and scapegoating upon themselves, particularly since the victim was a young white woman. This was one of the few occasions in Richmond society when the population, save the negro population, came together as equally concerned parties and, although it still wrought some discomfort and provoked disdain for some involved, social protocol was softened and, in some cases, completely discarded in the cause of finding an answer to this mystery.

    Detective Jack Wren arrived at the morgue about 1pm. He had seen his family back home after church and then left them, promising to be no more than a few hours. Sundays were usually his day to enjoy time with his boys, but the unusual urgency attached to this tragedy took precedent. Wren's first stop was at Mays' Butcher Shop. The reception from Mr. Mays was as cold as the beef hanging in his locker and when Fannie herself appeared before the detective, that road officially reached a dead end. He wrote in his notebook:

15 March, 1885

    Visited Mays Butcher shop to find out if Fannie Mays may be missing. Miss Mays appeared and has been ruled out as the victim.

    The detective then made his way toward the Old Almshouse. Wren was there first to interview any who may identify the dead woman. But secondly, and perhaps more importantly, he was there to try and develop a lead on any possible killer. Wren understood that suicide was feasible and the most expedient possibility, but his instincts told him to keep looking in all directions. He walked down Hill Street carefully observing the crowd. It had occurred to him that the public viewing of the victim may provide an irresistible opportunity for the killer, if indeed there were one, to resurface and see what the nefarious action had wrought. Wren pictured a potential murderer as a man, between the age of twenty and fifty, and probably of the middle or lower class. He also felt the killer would likely have previous offenses. A perpetrator may feel safe mixed anonymously amongst a crowd and would certainly feel pride, if not outright hubris, at the spectacle he had created. Wren noted that most people conversing outside the morgue had formed distinct groups. He decided to focus on those who stayed to themselves and were watching from a distance, or perhaps those who appeared to briefly engage one party and then move to another.

Wren stopped briefly and leaned against the Shockoe Hill Cemetery wrought iron fence across the street from the Almshouse. He lit a cigar and watched. It wasn't long before "Captain" Billy Pierce appeared like an apparition along Hill Street. He was wearing a long black overcoat with holes in the elbows and dark grey trousers that were too long, or perhaps, so large around the waist that they hung too low on him. Pierce's heels trampled the trouser cuffs, reducing them to tatters and strands. The tall and thin man dragged himself slowly up the street, like a marionette which had all but the single string connected to the nape of his neck cut loose. Pierce was a well-known vagrant in the City of Richmond. He had spent many nights in the City Jail, usually for drunkenness, but occasionally for loitering, petty thievery and; on a few rare occasions, assault and battery. On one occasion, more than ten years earlier, he had nearly beaten a man to death in a bar room dispute. He also was known to get rough with prostitutes.

On particularly raucous nights, provocative conversation and doubtful chiding challenged Pierce to recount his supposed escapades as "Captain" of a Confederate blockade runner during the War. His tales had swashbuckling appeal, but based upon Pierce's quirky unreliability and downtrodden appearance, few believed a word of them. Invariably, his stories climaxed with Pierce embarrassingly on table top, lifting his empty inverted whiskey bottle thunderously slurring orders to his men. "Tack Starboard! Silence the engines! Starboard turn forty-five degrees!". It seemed to observers like the disturbed old man was fitfully shouting in the throes of a nightmare.

Pierce grew up in a proud seafaring family in Savannah. He served on his father's merchant ship from the age of thirteen and by age twenty-five had become 2nd mate on an English merchant ship. Pierce made many beneficial journeys from the Eastern seaboard to England on to the West Indies and back again, prospering from the trade with Britain and her possessions which was vitally important to the burgeoning democracy of the United States and gaining invaluable experience as a sailor and unofficial ambassador. During this period, he also found a wife and fathered two fine boys, future men of the sea.

By the time the War began, Pierce was commanding his own vessel. The tacit, moral, and intellectual support by Britain for the Confederate Cause and the Union's aversion to giving the great European power any reason to officially join forces with the rebels provided ships of English ownership a distinct advantage in navigating the political waters of the blockaded South. Pierce, a Southerner who happened to be affiliated with a British vessel, suddenly became a very important man in the shadowy world of running guns and other contraband. He became a legend to those in the game, but this status brought not only acclaim and riches, but a secret bounty. Union politicians and military leaders understood that forcibly boarding an English ship amounted to an attack on England herself, so they waited covertly and patiently to close in upon their adversary. The political cost of overt or ill-timed action would probably exceed the entire value of Pierce's contraband.

Pierce was crafty and difficult to locate, but Union counter forces calculated that eventually, he would make a mistake. As with most aspects of the War, time and attrition proved favorable to the Northern aggressors. One night in November, 1863, Pierce came discreetly ashore in Charleston. After arranging for a weapons delivery for the following January, he visited a few bars; and then, a few more. Before Pierce knew it, he was in a card game and losing badly. As his losses mounted, his frustrations grew and the whiskey began to talk. After a careless outburst and a few more hours burrowing his way through his bottle, Pierce was unconscious. He awoke on the bar room floor before dawn, clumsily made his way to his feet, and meandered through town toward Charleston Harbor. His head was pounding. The suffering captain approached the dock where his ship was at rest. A man appeared and asked him the time. It was first light. As Pierce unguardedly fumbled in his pocket for his watch, a blow struck his head from behind. A canvas sack was thrown over his head and he was tossed over the side of the dock and into a row boat. Four men leapt into the small craft. Two worked feverishly to untie and push off, while the other two, with equal intensity, securely bound Pierce's arms and legs for the journey to a Union vessel clandestinely anchored a mile offshore.

Perhaps more damaging to the Confederate cause than Pierce's capture was the information found in his possession. In his jacket was a sealed envelope Pierce was transporting to Wilmington, North Carolina. The wax seal bore the image of a snake, an indication that this was correspondence between participants in the Copperhead Movement. It was a cryptic hand-written message from a prominent New York banker promising to divert 10,000 British Pounds Sterling to covert Confederate bank accounts domiciled in Bermuda. The funds were to finance an arms shipment for an impending early Spring rebel insurgency in southern Ohio. Pierce's captors were able to get a general idea of the subversive operation from their initial analysis of the letter, but the coding prevented them from identifying the names of the operators involved.

After a series of interrogations and beatings, Union inquisitors determined that Pierce was not likely to divulge any further information; if in fact, he even knew what he was delivering. They plied him with whiskey and after some very difficult hours, his demeanor changed suddenly and he wove them a glorious tapestry of fact, lie, accurate information, feasible disinformation, pure conjecture, and irrational absurdity. They held him for six more days with little food and water before frustratingly abandoning their efforts and transferring the most unreliable informant to a Union prison in Elmira, New York. It was there that Pierce would spend the miserable duration of the War.

Pierce's Wilmington contact was quickly identified by Union spies and captured. After some rough treatment, he agreed to cooperate with the counterinsurgency. This ultimately led to the dismantling of the conspiracy, costing the lives of the banker and many of the Copperhead operatives in Ohio.

Six months after the War, Pierce was unceremoniously released and told to go home. Weeks later he reached his home near Savannah to find it vacant and completely ransacked. His wife and young boys were nowhere to be found. A neighbor informed him that his family had disappeared during Sherman's fiery assault and had not been seen since. Pierce was never able to find even the first clue as to their fate, and after a month's long fruitless search of the town, resigned himself to the fact that he may never see them again. His deep sadness and desperation plunged to abject depression. Pierce had lost his family, his ship, his country; all that remained was perhaps a shred of dignity; but in this state, he saw little cause to maintain even that. Pierce had no desire to return to the sea and was simply not fit for any other career. He turned to a life in the streets, working an occasional odd job, but more often living off of whatever he salvaged from garbage or what he derived from the charity of others. By the time Pierce arrived in Richmond in 1870, his spirit was irreparably broken. Flickers of his relevance only surfaced on occasion as a drunken side-effect, but these moments were fleeting and though entertaining, were ultimately attributed to delusion rather than historical record. Although the lonesome vagrant boasted regularly of his seafaring exploits, he never once uttered a word about his family nor the mysterious end they met. Not even exorbitant amounts of alcohol could lend access to that scar-ridden chamber of his darkly dejected heart.

Wren did not seriously consider Pierce a suspect, as Pierce was nearing sixty years of age and had not been involved in any significant violence for some time. Still, Wren decided to talk to Pierce. If nothing else, Pierce may be able to lead him to other suspects.

Wren approached Pierce from behind "Well, Captain Billy, what leads you to this part of the city?", asked a sarcastic Wren as he beheld Pierce's matted and tangled long grey beard.

A bit startled, Pierce returned, "Oh, most likely the same thing that brings you here, detective. Good afternoon, by the way." with equal sarcasm.

"Yes, for most of us, it is a good afternoon; one to be thankful we're here to enjoy. How have you been spending your day, Captain?"

"Understand something, Wren; I'm no old fool and I'm not interested in talking nonsense with you. I know exactly what you're looking for. Unfortunately, I'm not going to be of much help. I came here to see if by chance I know the dead woman and to get supper at the almshouse. That is all." Wren could see the clear steeliness of Pierce's eyes darting from his obscured dirty facade.

"Now, Captain, there is no need for contrariness. I am sure you have nothing to hide. That said, I am certain there must have been discussion of this matter in your circle of associates. What have you heard?"

"Nothing.", he paused and glanced at the doubtful detective, "Well, some men were talking about it last night at Nellie's, but that is all I heard. Then, this morning, I heard the body was goin' to be here to view today."

"What did these men say, exactly?"

"Well, I don't know word for word, but one man; I've seen him around before; he said he saw the body when they took it from the water."

"Who was this man?" asked the detective.

"I don't know his name, but like I said, he's at Nellie's regular. He was talking to

Fogelman and a few others."

"Ah, Cyrus Fogelman. Just another good citizen of Richmond."

"We all have our stories, don't we, detective? I suspect there are things in your past that could have changed the way things turned out for you, aren't there? Even though you are young enough to be my son, detective, you should be old enough to understand that every man has weaknesses; especially the ones like you who think they don't."

Wren's expression remained unchanged, but privately he shuddered with recognition. He felt exposed and humiliated as the truth from the perceptive vagrant rang in his ears. He did not want to hear any more.

"Good day, Captain."

Pierce nodded in acknowledgement, but offered no salutation. (14.2)

Chapter 15   *The Lady in Room 21*

A young man in a long grey coat entered the Davis Hotel at 8:05 pm on March 13. The night clerk looked up from his desk as the man removed his hat and approached.

"Good evening, Mr. Cluverius. May I help you?"

"Yes. Has a young gentleman come to find me this evening? We were to meet at Mozart Hall."

"No sir", replied the clerk. "I have not seen such a gentleman."

"Thank you." Cluverius turned and left the hotel.

That same young man entered the American Hotel at 8:20 pm on March 13. Once again, he was greeted by a night clerk.

"Good evening sir. May I be of assistance?"

"Yes." said the stranger. "I would like to see the woman in Room 21."

"Do you have a calling card, sir? I can have the porter deliver it to Room 21." The man reached into his coat pocket and pulled out his card. The clerk read the name on the card and beckoned the porter.

"Yessuh?", responded the porter as he approached the desk.

"Tyler, please show Mr. Johnson to the parlor, then deliver his card to Room 21."

"Yessuh, right away, suh." replied the porter.

A few minutes passed before the porter returned to the parlor. He explained that the lady in Room 21 was not in her room. Cluverius was visibly annoyed. He did not want to be late for the appointment. Just as the porter was turning to leave, Cluverius saw Lillie and a tall white-haired man entering the hotel lobby through the ladies' entrance. The older man stopped the porter and asked if he could get the young lady a room. The porter escorted the two of them into the parlor, where Cluverius stood discreetly off to one side near the window. Lillie's initial reaction upon seeing Cluverius standing there was to greet him, but he signaled her with a quick baring of his gritted teeth and a head shake not to let on that she knew him while the old man was there. Cluverius flipped the collar of his overcoat up around his cheeks and deftly slipped past them and out the parlor doorway. He turned down the hallway to the right, hoping to exit the building undetected. Near a side door adjacent to the service stairs at the end of the hall, Cluverius encountered the night clerk. The clerk looked quizzically at Cluverius.

"I don't think that is the woman I wanted to see.", explained Cluverius. "The young lady I wanted to see went to school with my sister."

The clerk was a little confused, but having experienced many confusing circumstances as a night clerk at a busy hotel, he pressed no further.

"That is fine, Mr. Johnson. Is there anything else I can help you with?"

The American Hotel, Richmond, Virginia

"No, sir. Thank you and good night." Cluverius walked through the side door and into the dark alleyway outside.

As the night clerk walked back behind the registration desk, he noticed that the hotel porter was waiting for him.

"Uh, Missa Dillard, suh?"

"Yes, Tyler?"

"Dat ol' gent'man in da parlor has axed fo' a room fo' dat young lady wif him."

The night clerk stretched forward to see the woman.

"She's already registered here, Tyler? That woman's in Room 21."

"Oh... Alright, suh. I sho' am a little confooz'd." The porter returned to the parlor and approached the old gentleman.

"Da young lady has a room, suh.", explained the porter.

"Very good. Please show her to it. I must be on my way."

"Thank you for your time with me, Mr. Chiles.", said Lillie. "I will see you out." Lillie took the old gentleman's arm and began leading him toward the lobby.

"But ma'am...", the porter interjected, "Dar was anuva gent'man here jus' a few moments ago. He was lookin' for da lady in Room 21. I don' know where he gone now, but he was here. I thought you should know dis."

"Thank you, porter; but there must be some mistake." The porter shrugged and turned back toward the front desk. He picked up someone's suitcase and carried it down the back hall toward the service steps.

Lillie escorted the old gentleman to the door and then turned quickly back toward the main stairwell.

"Madam, please wait!", said the night clerk. "Please allow me to escort you to your room."

"Very well.", said Lillie not wanting to arouse any more suspicion. A lady should never walk to her room alone.

As they neared the top of the stairs, the night clerk said, "When that young man came in, he wanted to see you. Then, I saw him later and he said he did not want to see you. He said he wanted to see the lady who went to school with his sister. This seems very odd, madam?"

"Do you know where that gentleman went?", asked Lillie. "He was supposed to come after me this morning", groping for an expedient and plausible answer for the clerk's questions.

"No, madam." The night clerk waited, but the young girl's vacant expression made it clear that her thoughts were truly elsewhere and that no further explanation would be forthcoming. Out of mannerly consideration, he did not question his patron any further. He opened the door to Room 21 for her and bid her good night.

Fifteen minutes later, Cluverius re-entered the American Hotel and stood restlessly near the main staircase. The night clerk approached him.

"Sir, the young lady in Room 21 wants to see you. She says you were to call for her this morning."

"Where is she?" said Cluverius. He was slightly out of breath. His eyes darted nervously around the lobby, never stopping on any place for more than a second.

"In her room.", said the night clerk as he grew ever-more uncomfortable with the couple's unusual behavior.

"Show me to the parlor, and please bring her to me."

"Yes, sir." The night clerk escorted Cluverius once again into the parlor. The clerk stopped and whispered instructions to Tyler. A few minutes later, Tyler brought Lillie Madison to the parlor. Cluverius grabbed Lillie's hand and whisked her across the parlor to the far side. He sat her down in an over-stuffed wing chair. He knelt on one knee before her, clasping both of her hands in his own.

Cluverius looked very seriously into her eyes and began speaking in hushed tones, "Lillie, what were you doing with that man?"

"Mr. Chiles? Why, I just met..."

"What were you doing with him!?"

"Oh, heavens, Tommie!", sensing his angry tone, "I just met him while I was out walking. We were just watching the birds in Capitol Square. The time got away from me and he was very kind to offer to walk me to the hotel. He seemed a bit lonely and I wasn't sure how to find the hotel again, so I obliged."

"Did you tell him who you were?", as he tightened his clutch on her hands.

"No, Tommie."

"You told him nothing about us?", ratcheting tighter.

"No, Tommie... Our conversation never became personal...We just talked about birds... Tommie, you're hurting my hands!"

Cluverius loosened his grip and heavily sighed to regain his composure.

"I am sorry, Lillie; but now you can see why I wanted to avoid him. We cannot afford to let anyone who knows the family see us together. In fact, I have been thinking about this. Under no circumstances do we want Aunt Jane to know we have been together. If you write a letter to Aunt Jane telling of your trip to Old Point to visit Laura's sick aunt and date it March 14th, I will have proof that we were not together for this entire weekend."

"But Tommie, why do you need a letter? Wouldn't Aunt Jane believe you if you told her we were not together?", asked Lillie.

"Well, maybe... But you know Aunt Jane. She is very suspicious and distrustful. She gets worse with every year. If she thinks I am lying, she would throw me out. I just want something I can show her if someone claims to have seen us together. It would protect you, as well."

"Alright, I understand... Yes, it would be good to have that just in case."

Cluverius got up and went over to the writing desk in the parlor. He pulled a blank sheet of paper from the drawer.

"Come over here and sit, Lillie. I will spell out what to tell her." Lillie walked over to the desk, sat down, and waited for Cluverius' dictation.

Richmond, March 14th, 1885

My Dear Aunt Jane,

I will drop you a few hurried lines this morning, as I want to go with a friend of mine on quite an unexpected little trip. As the weather is too bad up in the mountains either for me or the children to attend regularly, we thought proper to suspend for awhile, and so a friend of mine wants to go to Old Point for awhile and will pay all my expenses if I will go to be company for her. She is a nice and good lady, and it will be a nice little trip for me. Don't you think so? I have not time to say more, as it will be time to start soon. We came down on the train this morning. Love to all, and tell Tommie I will write to him real soon; but they must not count letters with me. You all need not write until you hear from me again. I will write as soon as I can. As I am in such a hurry I must stop. Love for all and lots for your dear self.

I remain, as always, yours,

Lillie   (15.1)

"That's good.", said Cluverius. He took the note and folded it into an envelope. Now, Lillie, just write the address. Lillie wrote the address on the envelope and handed it to Tommie.

"Now, Lillie... About this child..."

"Yes, Tommie?", Lillie sat forward in her chair in anticipation. and listened intently.

"Well, I've thought about it and I think we need to make preparations. Obviously, I want to help you through this and we need to be as discreet as possible. But, I know we need help. I have found a midwife here in Richmond who will help with the birth. When the time draws nearer, we need to be back here in Richmond and she will help us. No one else need know about this. I met with the woman this afternoon and she would like to meet you and make a preliminary assessment of your condition. We are to meet her tonight." He looked at his watch. "We're supposed to be there now! We should be going. She's out on the west end of town."

Lillie was unsure where Cluverius was going with this.

"Tommie, will we marry?"

Cluverius crouched down to her eye level and smiled. "Yes, Lillie, we will. But I just can't say when that will be, Lillie. I would like to, but there are other things I need to take care of before we can fully plan for that." He put his hands on the side of her face.

His fingers reached behind her ears and he gently scratched the back of her head. "My first priority is to make sure that you get through the pregnancy with no problems and with no detection. After that, we can plan for our future."

This was not exactly the commitment Lillie was hoping for, but it was enough. She looked at him and she believed him. "Alright, Tommie…"

"Good, my dear.", said Cluverius. "Why don't you spend the night at my hotel tonight?"

"Thomas Cluverius!", exclaimed Lillie, putting her hands on her broadened hips.

"Well, dear girl. I just thought we should take full advantage of our fleeting moments. Besides, if we are to become man and wife, would it not be wise to get acquainted with one another's, well, personal habits?"

"Tommie, you are a scoundrel!", said an excited Lillie. "But, that's what I love about you! I will run get my bag and be right back!" Lillie beamed with fairy tale bliss and Cluverius smiled back at her. She bound out of the parlor and toward the stairs. The night clerk started to make a gesture to escort her, but before he could get a word out, she had disappeared up the stairs.

Cluverius sank heavily into the wing chair and buried his head in his hands. He was weary of these complications. After a brief moment of anxiety, he drew once again on his innate self-confidence. Cluverius reassured himself that he could make it all work out to his satisfaction. No more than two minutes passed before Cluverius heard a lighthearted Lillie coming back down the stairs. He popped onto his feet and moved to meet her in the lobby. She handed him her satchel and announced, "I'm ready!"

As they passed through the hotel lobby, Cluverius stopped at the registration desk and purchased a postage stamp. He wet it and put it on the letter to Aunt Jane. The couple continued out the hotel entrance to Main Street. They stood briefly under the large gas lamp in front of the hotel. The wind was swirling as a cold front continued through the city. An occasional flurry could be seen as they passed through the glow of the gas lamp. The sound of clunking hooves gave notice that the west bound tug horse trolley was approaching. The trolley stopped near 15th and Main Streets in front of the American Hotel. (15.2) Cluverius dropped the letter in the mail box near the front door of the hotel. He grabbed Lillie's arm led her aboard.

The couple sat near the back as the trolley methodically cut through the darkness, tracing the route Cluverius had taken just hours earlier. Lillie pressed up against Cluverius and sought warmth and protection under his long, left arm. She clenched her red shawl tightly around her head and shoulders as she burrowed into his side, shielding herself from the damp wintry wind. Within a few minutes the security and comfort of Cluverius' presence, coupled with the soothing rhythmic solitary sound of the horse hooves meeting the street, lulled young Lillie into a restful slumber.

Chapter 16   *It's Lillie Madison*

Melanie Dunstan was in line nearing the entrance to the Almshouse just before 2pm on Sunday. She had first heard the news of the mysterious death the prior evening. One of her cousins had come calling to inform her and her parents of the incident and of the red shawl, which purportedly belonged to the deceased, being found on the wall of her uncle's home near the reservoir.

Melanie and her neighbor Lizzie Thomas were, like many, quite intrigued with the matter. After services, the two young women left their homes on Church Hill and walked toward the north end of town. Melanie's mother was too ill for the walk and her father had little interest in affairs such as this. Lizzie's parents too were not interested in such activity.

"Lizzie, it shouldn't be much longer."

"I hope you're right, Mellie. I can't believe how many are here. Surely, someone will recognize the body."

The clamorous surroundings were energizing. This was a most atypical Sunday in Richmond. Melanie and Lizzie moved through the crowded doorway and turned to their left. There were six or seven people still ahead of them in line. John Bellows was standing at the door. He was metering people into a room in groups of ten. To this point, though some had expressed some slight recognition, no one had been able to positively identify the body.

A group of ten exited the room single file. One gentleman emerged looking down and shaking his head. An older woman was beginning to cry, but most were just silently dumbfounded. Melanie and Lizzie held hands as Bellows counted them among the next group. Bellows held open the swinging door and the small group entered. The temperature dropped ten degrees as she crossed the threshold into the realm of the dead, but to the apprehensive and spooked Melanie, it seemed more like thirty degrees. Mr. Miles Trowbridge, Esq. first approached the gurney. Dr. Taylor calmly withdrew the sheet which obscured the deceased's face. Trowbridge pulled his handkerchief to his nose and mouth as he leaned over to study the visage more closely. She was greenish gray and in the peculiar light of the morgue, her hair looked like tarnished gold. The black thread sutures in her scalp caught his eye and he swallowed hard. Trowbridge shook his head and turned away.

Mr. John McLeish, a teller at the First National Bank of Richmond, and his new bride reverently approached the body. Mrs. McLeish turned into her husband's arms and he held her close.

"No, we don't know her." McLeish whispered softly to Dr. Taylor.

Taylor nodded and the couple stepped aside.

Mrs. Alice Hawkins, a destitute woman from the west end who took in laundry to make ends meet, then stepped toward the body. She had visited the Almshouse many times since the unexpected death of her husband. Alice had three young children at home and relied heavily upon charity for clothing and food. She gazed downward at the dead woman's face and was devastated to see the tragic youthfulness of the victim. Poor Alice clutched her tattered shawl closer to her throat as she recounted her own blessings, crossed herself, and offered a brief silent prayer for the pitiful soul before her. Alice understood that as difficult as her own circumstances were, hope for her future still remained; but for the deceased, whom she recognized only on as a similarly troubled young woman, all earthly hope was lost. She slowly reached out her long dry hand and lightly touched the forehead of the deceased. It was cold and clammy. A few strands of the brittle hair became entangled in her worn fingers and easily broke away as she lifted her hand. Alice closed her eyes, emitted a grievous sigh, and backed away from the ghastly scene.

Melanie and Lizzie confronted the body together. Their hands were tightly intertwined, each turning cold blue.

Melanie looked down at the face and felt the hair on the back of her neck rise. It felt as a though a cold and evil hand was slowly descending upon the top of her head and wrapping its long icy fingers around her to the tips of each ear. Her eyes began to roll as she released Lizzie's hand and staggered backward a half step. Lizzie looked at her friend and braced her hands behind the small of Mellie's back, preventing a fall. Melanie gathered herself and breathlessly said, "I know her."

Dr. Taylor, sensing this was no act, rushed to Melanie's side. "Her name, miss… Do you know her name?"

Melanie closed her eyes tightly and put her hands up to her cheeks and mouth. Through her fingers she said. "It's Lillie Madison… I know her relatives here in Richmond. They live just down the street from me! How can this be?"

The small group gathered in the room then burst into conversation. Dr. Taylor encouraged them to leave the room and continue their conversations outside. He instructed Bellows to make it known that and identification had been made and that if anyone outside knew a "Lillie Madison", they were to come forward. Bellows raced out to the street and made the announcement. Many shrugged their shoulders and looked at one another. No one came forward except for Detective Wren followed closely by a group of three mischievous boys. Wren approached Bellows in the doorway.

"Good day, Mr. Bellows; Detective Jack Wren."

"Yes detective."

"So, we have an identification?"

"Yes sir, we do. Another young lady has identified the body."

"Well, I would like to speak with her."

At that point the three boys tried to slip past the distracted Bellows and into the morgue.

"Where are you going? Do you boys know Lillie Madison?", asked Bellows.

"No sir, we don't.", said one of them. "We just want to see the body".

"Absolutely not!", interjected a scornful Wren. "This is not a side show attraction here; you young men should be ashamed. Now be on your way!"

The boys laughed to one another at the reaction. Wren squinted at them as he lifted his coat lapel and exposed a shiny police badge. "I think you should be on your way", said Wren in a lower but more authoritative manner. The humor quickly disappeared from the boys faces and they sheepishly crossed the street to continue surveying the scene at a safer distance.

"Thank you, detective. It is hard to believe we were once like them."

"I don't remember ever being that way.", said Wren.

Bellows was a bit confused by the statement, but chose not to pursue it with any more levity. There were more serious matters to address.

"Come this way, detective, I'll take you in to meet with the young lady." Bellows closed and locked the doors to the Almshouse behind them, then led Wren into the morgue.

Dr. Taylor had gotten a chair for Melanie. Lizzie knelt beside her holding her hand.

Notebook and pencil in hand, Wren removed his bowler, placed it on a small table near the door, and introduced himself. "Miss, I am Detective Wren of the Richmond Police. I understand you know the dead woman. First, may I have your name?" His intensity and stern voice immediately put the young girl on the defensive.

"I... am Melanie Dunstan."

"And, where do you live?"

"On Church Hill, on, on Grace Street."

"What is the name of the dead woman?"

"Lillie Madison, sir.", said a trembling Melanie.

Dr. Taylor tried some comforting words, "Now, miss, please do not be scared. The detective is here to help this poor woman."

"How do you know Miss Madison?", asked the intimidating Wren.

"She used to visit her aunt, Mary Rutherford, who lives three houses from me. She would come for occasional visits. I first met her years ago. You see, Mrs. Rutherford and my mother are friends."

"Did Miss Madison live in Richmond?"

"No detective, she lived in King and Queen County. She came to Richmond only once or twice a year."

Wren paused and made an entry in his notebook.

15 March, 1885 2:10pm

Body of deceased identified at almshouse by Ms. Melanie Dunstan of Richmond. She identifies the body as Lillie Madison of King and Queen County. Says Miss Madison occasionally visited her aunt, Mary Rutherford, of Church Hill neighborhood.

Melanie and Lizzie sat still, waiting for the next uncomfortable query. Wren filled his upper lip with air, then let it out abruptly before his next questions. He seemed agitated, almost volatile and bullying.

"Was she staying with her aunt on this visit? Did you see her before today?"

"No sir, I don't believe she was. My mother visited Mrs. Rutherford just yesterday and made no mention of seeing Lillie. I assume if Lillie were staying there, her aunt would have invited me to visit, as well. I have not seen Lillie since, well, it was probably last Fall, maybe October; yes, I think it was October."

Wren tilted his head further downward toward Lizzie. "How about you, miss; did you know Miss Madison?"

"Oh, no, detective. Honestly, I have never seen her before. I will swear to that."

Trying to soothe the obviously innocent, but understandably paranoid young girl, Dr. Taylor chuckled and interjected, "Now, dear girl, that won't be necessary."

The sensitive detective cut him off. "Doctor, please refrain. This girl's legal testimony may indeed be required."

The doctor chuckled again. "Yes, yes, detective." he said as he slightly raised both hands and ducked his head gesturing a surrender.

"Thank you, ladies." said a commanding Wren. "You are free to leave. If I need anything further, Miss Dunstan, where can you be reached?" The detective made another entry as Melanie recited her home address.

Melanie Dunstan
2206 E. Grace Street

He further noted:

Miss Dunstan had not seen the deceased Miss Madison since October last before this day. (16.1)

The young ladies departed the Almshouse and melted into the crowd in the street. Wren put his notebook in his side pocket and checked the time. He was anxious to get back home for a few hours with his boys.

"Thank you for your services, Dr. Taylor. You have been of great help in this investigation."

"Thank you, detective; but I am just doing what is required of me."

Turning a bit surly, Wren muttered, "Yes, and I hope that is *all* you will continue to do."

"What, sir, do you mean by that?", asked the suddenly guarded doctor.

"Well, doctor, I am a bit irritated that you have spoken so extensively with Mr. Burton of *The Dispatch.* It is a counterproductive for the investigation for you to inform him of your findings, particularly at this early stage. His reckless speculations may sell newspapers, but they do not solve crimes. With all due respect, I hope you will not continue to speak with him."

"Detective Wren; I understand your concern and perhaps, your embarrassment. However, it is my job to make medical determinations of the causes of death for poor souls like Miss Madison. My findings are always intended for the public record. I am not an alienist and draw no conclusions unless the physical evidence allows for it. My job is not to protect any police investigation nor any members of the police department from public scrutiny. I am wholeheartedly willing to work with you to answer this mystery. In fact, I am wholeheartedly willing to work with Mr. Burton to answer this mystery. Finding the truth behind the death of Miss Madison is what matters here. Protecting professional reputations at the expense of a timely truth is of little consequence to me. I hope this is all clear for you now. I will not place any limit on your associations, so it would be appreciated if you would extend me the same amount of consideration!"

Wren was visibly frustrated by the doctor's obstinacy, but he acquiesced to the doctor's tenured authority. He closed his eyes and controlled his ill temper. Wren understood that a protracted conflict with the influential doctor would not accrue to his long-term benefit so he chose wisely not to press the matter any further.

"Yes, doctor. I meant no offense. It was my hope that you would see things my way, but it is certain you do not. I respect your view and I will not bring this matter before you again. Good day, sir."

"Good day, detective."

Wren placed his hat on his head and left the Almshouse. The crowds in the street had thinned little. In fact, it appeared to have grown. Forty-five feet to the right of the Almshouse entrance stood Melanie and Lizzie. A small crowd had formed behind the two young women as they stood speaking with Peter Burton.

Wren's frustration was becoming so complete that even he was beginning to see warped humor in it. "My albatross...", he said to himself under his breath.

Burton saw the detective storming toward him and cut off his interview with Melanie and Lizzie. "I think that will be all, ladies. If I need to speak with you again, I can contact you at home, right Miss Dunstan?"

"Yes, Mr. Burton."

"Thank you and good day." said Burton as he looked away from the young ladies and directly at the fast-approaching Wren. The girls turned into the crowd and Burton stepped toward Wren to meet him head on.

"Burton, you won't give it up, will you?" said the terse detective.

"Now, detective, you know I have a job to do... I understand the body is one Lillie Madison of King and Queen County."

"That's correct."

"Any suspects at this time?"

"Burton, this investigation is being conducted as a suicide. We have no compelling evidence to consider it anything else."

"Is that right, Detective Wren? I thought there was a great deal of evidence already collected."

"It is currently being investigated as a suicide, Burton. For you to insist otherwise is folly."

"Perhaps, detective. I know you are quite familiar with folly." smiled Burton knowingly.

Wren was beginning lose control. Burton could see the blood rushing to his face. Wren hesitated and looked around him. There stood at least a dozen people; silent with gaping mouths; all waiting for the conflict to heighten. Wren stepped up close to Burton. He threateningly pulled a fist back, then released his index finger and put it firmly in the taller Burton's chest as he looked up the nostrils of his adversary. Burton could feel the little pit bull's hot breath under his chin as Wren said firmly in repressed tone. "You better be careful, Burton."

"Is that a threat, Detective?" asked Burton he took a quick step back.

"Just be careful, Burton."

Wren pushed through the crowd and marched down the street away from the Almshouse. He hated himself for acting as he did. He despised himself for not being able to control his outbursts. He loathed himself for giving the impression to many that he deserved such disrespectful treatment. He was well aware of this character flaw, but he had no idea how to correct it. At the moment, Wren felt helpless. He understood his effectiveness as an investigator was being compromised by his personal shortcoming; he was vulnerable. Wren was committed to his work; he just was not sure others believed he was up to it.

Chapter 17   The One-Legged Man

Detective Wren moved at a hurried pace to separate himself from the scene at the Almshouse. He was quite angry, leaning forward seemingly with purpose but really with no sense of direction. He passed the west side of the cemetery and within minutes was three blocks further south at Duval Street. His mind was busy, but there was no coherence, no logic. In the fog of a thinly veiled rage he walked on, not even knowing why he did nor where he was heading. Like a rabid hound he aimlessly wandered in dazed and desperate need of relief.

Wren's mood and circumstances reminded him of a time earlier in life, when he felt equally alone and misunderstood. His stride slowed as his mind drifted back to his long walk home from the battlefield outside Petersburg to his hometown 10 miles north and west of Petersburg up the Appomattox River at Wesley Chapel.

He passed through Petersburg from the south that Fall morning in 1864 with little more than the dirty clothes on his back, his worn shoes, and a blanket. He was nervously ashamed of his unceremonious dismissal and was not looking upon the reunion with his family, particularly his father, with joyous anticipation. Even though he was never more than a mile or two away, it had been over one year since he had set foot in the town limits. The last year had not been kind to Petersburg. Shortages, inflation, and the specter of destruction at the hands of invading Union forces created a depressed, but edgy atmosphere. Many shops on Market Street were boarded up, closed tightly either out of sheer terror of the impending plunder or lack of general business. Trash was piling up in the streets, courtesy of the tens of thousands soldiers of The Army of Northern Virginia who had maneuvered in and out of town over the last few months, setting up encampments, breaking them down, then returning again; all part of the military game of chess being played by Lee and Grant. The smell of gunpowder, horse manure, and general filth created an unwelcome odor in town. Petersburg was no longer the town Wren thought he knew. It was like a strange parallel version of itself; wholly recognizable, but monstrously different.

Wren crossed the bridge at the northwest end of Petersburg over the Appomattox River into Chesterfield County. He looked back toward the town witnessing a flurry of activity at a railroad depot. A delivery of 12-pound Napoleon canon was being off-loaded to bolster the defense of Petersburg. The canon were fresh off the production lines of Tredegar Iron Works to the north in Richmond. The fall of the Ducktown Copper Mines of Chattanooga, Tennessee into enemy hands in 1863 had brought a devastating halt to the production of the preferred bronze 12-pounders, but by this time the resourceful men of Tredegar had developed an effective iron substitute. Wren could sense the urgency and desperation in the men's voices as they scurried about the flat cars trying to streamline the logistics of transporting the heavy defensive weaponry closer to the fight.

Wren entered Chesterfield County and picked up the River Road. He headed west about seven more miles to the crossroads hamlet of Wesley Chapel. The Wren home sat in a cluster of similar homes on a lane which extended from River Road to the north. As he approached the small brick two story structure, the boy turned and walked uneasily up the side yard toward the small kitchen building in the rear. He saw smoke coming from the kitchen chimney, a sign that his mother was preparing the midday meal for Wren's father and young brother, Thomas. He saw the glow of the fire through the kitchen window as he gently turned the knob. There his mother stood with her back to him, stoking the small fire under the bread oven. She was a short woman with a plump figure. She was always well-groomed before the War and this, at least, had not changed.

"Tell your father I will be there in a moment, Thomas.", never turning her head. "Thomas... Thomas?" she turned around and beheld her eldest son in disbelief.

"Jack... Oh dear Lord, Jack! You are home!" She rubbed her eye and began to tear. "Oh, Jack... you're home! Are you hurt?" She lunged across the small space and grabbed each shoulder, clutching her beloved to her chest. "Are you alright?"

"Yes, mother, I am well.", noticing that he was now taller than she.

"How did you get here? You haven't deserted, have you?"

"No ma'am, I have not deserted."

"Oh, good... But why?"

"Well, mother, it will probably bring you shame, but I was told to leave. They don't want me anymore. I... lost my temper. I struck an officer."

"No, Jack! It cannot be! How could you do something like that?"

"It's difficult to explain, mother, but I assure you I had good reason. The army just did not see it that way."

"Did they send you to prison? No mother, no... It just happened yesterday and the colonel told me this morning to leave and go home immediately and not to re-enlist for at least two years. What will I tell father?"

"Oh, poor Jack, I don't know. You know how he wanted you to perform admirably. I don't know if he will understand, but we must try and make him."

"Mother..." Jack interrupted. "The bread."

"Oh, dear!", said Mrs. Wren. She rushed back over to the small oven and removed the somewhat browned, but not yet burned, bread.

"It isn't going to be a pleasant day for your father. He doesn't like even slightly over-baked bread. Jack, I am glad to have you home. I have worried so these many months."

"I am glad to see you, too, mother. I only wish I were coming home with honor."

"Jack, dear. You know the truth. You are a good boy and would never perform unfaithfully. You cannot control others' thoughts about you, even your father's. In the end, the Lord will know and it is only his approval with which you need to concern yourself."

Wren nodded. The words were comforting for the boy and enhanced his devotion to his mother. However, they did little to cool the fiery maelstrom Wren was sure to endure in the presence of his father.

Wren and his mother slipped into the side door of the home and crossed the hallway into the dining room. There sat Josiah Wren at the head of the small dining table awaiting breakfast. His crutch was leaning against the sideboard. Despite his amputation, Josiah Wren remained a very impressive figure. He was tall, thin, and broad shouldered. He had a wonderful swathe of thick wavy hair that was once black, but now salt and pepper. He maintained the thick burly mustache he had first grown as a Master Sergeant in the Mexican War nearly twenty years earlier. The damage caused by Josiah's wounds went well beyond the physical. Although Josiah took some sanctuary in the fact that his wounds were received under very honorable circumstances, he was increasingly frustrated and embarrassed over the years by his disability and the constraints it placed upon him as a provider for his family. The wounds forced him to leave the army much earlier than he expected, leaving the old sergeant with a sense of guilt that he was unable to fully perform his duty. No amount of recognition could satisfy the innate desire he felt to serve and protect his homeland. Family wealth insured that Josiah was economically independent, but he never felt comfortable receiving help from others of any sort, even something as simple as a helping hand up a flight of stairs. He viewed pity and charity as an affront; something which further weakened one's character and resolve rather than propping them up.

Josiah's own father had distinguished himself as a military man during the War of 1812. Richard Wren served with a volunteer force made up of 103 Petersburg men under General William Henry Harrison. Josiah had grown up hearing tales of the great "Cockade City" Company, a name bestowed upon the town and those brave patriots from there by none other than the very grateful President James Madison. The company's exploits at Fort Meigs helped recapture the northwest from British invaders and became legend in Petersburg. Nearly every boy in town grew up with a detailed understanding, albeit a rather glorified one, of the steely honor and iron-clad sacrifice their forefathers forged on the field of battle. The Wren family had built a reputation for selfless military service over many generations. Everyone in the area recognized their steadfast courage and knew that no Wren would ever shy from a fight; particularly one where it was a duty to serve and honor was at stake.

Jack followed his mother through the doorway and Mr. Wren immediately popped up on his single leg and nearly smiled as he said, "Boy, you're home."

"Yes sir, I am."

Mr. Wren detected some nervousness in young Wren's response.

"What's wrong, boy? Why are you home now? I hear the Yankees are bearing down for a big fight now."

"Yes sir, I have heard the same. I was ordered home."

"What?", Mr. Wren's mouth hung wide open and he shifted his weight on his one foot to get better balanced.

"Yes sir, I am sure you will not find it satisfactory, but I was ordered home for the duration of the War.", Jack quickly stated.

"For what reason?"

"Well, sir, I committed an insubordinate act. They probably could have imprisoned me, but, on account of my age, the colonel discharged me and told me not to return for at least two years."

Mr. Wren turned his back on his son.

"Then you must leave here, too. If you are not worthy of serving in the fight, you are not worthy of taking refuge in my house. This is an absolute disgrace!"

"But, Josiah…"

"Enough, Mary! Do not defend this boy!"

"But, Josiah, you don't even know what happened..."

He cut her off again, "And I do not want to know. The facts of the incident are irrelevant. The only relevant fact is that this boy has besmirched the good name and record of this family. I will not tolerate that and I certainly will not reward it by allowing him to stay in my presence for even one night."

Mary was beginning to get angry. "This is your son, Josiah, not some anonymous private!"

"No son of mine would act this way, Mary… And you should be equally ashamed of him. Your family bears a stellar record military service, as well! Men of our family have served with honor alongside the men of Petersburg in every war on this continent! That chain will not be broken in this time when our town and our country most need us!"

"But Josiah, he's a boy."

"That is the truth… He's definitely no man! Take him from my sight!" thundered Josiah.

Jack stood there knowing this would happen, yet still completely unprepared to confront the assault. He rushed out of the house and ran down the street. He turned toward the Appomattox River and disappeared down the rocky embankment into the misty Fall air hovering over the river's edge.

"Look what you've done!" pleaded Mary.

"I am not finished. This has to be made right."

Josiah Wren got his crutch and moved through the front living room into the foyer and made his way up the stairs. He passed young Thomas coming down and made not even the slightest gesture of recognition of the boy. Mary began to cry as Thomas, only eight years of age, began to worry.

"What's wrong, Mama?"

"Oh, Thomas, you shouldn't worry. It will be alright. Jack came home and has had an argument with your father."

"Jack's home!", his little brown eyes were afire. "Where is he?"

"He's run out, but he'll be back."

"Oh, Mama, that is wonderful news!"

"Yes, it is.", softly stroking the top of Thomas' head. "Come with me to the kitchen and I'll serve your breakfast out there. It's probably best that we leave your father to himself for awhile."

About thirty minutes later, Josiah Wren came down the stairs dressed in his full Mexican War U.S. Army uniform. He sat down quietly in the living room leaning his crutch against the fireplace mantle. He looked around at all the nice items Mary had acquired over the years. The lovely sofa; the gold leaf mirror. He thought to himself how wonderful an eye for color and placement his wife had. He was proud of the home they had established, but it wasn't enough. He reached over and picked up a small brass birdcage from the end table. He reached to the underside and gave the key three or four turns. All of a sudden, the little blackbird inside sprung to life, rotating its head from side to side; fluttering its tail up and down; and chirping gleefully at Master Sergeant Wren. He placed the cage back down and sat back as the bird slowly but steadily wore himself down until the final half note and partial turn of the head signaled the finish. The damaged but vigorous fifty-four year old thought how all lives come to an end at some point, it's just a matter of how many turns of the key you are given. Josiah rose and placed his crutch under his arm.

Mary carefully entered the room to see Josiah standing there, sword and scabbard in one hand and crutch in the other. His pistol belt was on and the gun was loaded.

"What are you doing, Josiah?"

"I'm leaving… for the War. I can't allow the last military act of a Wren remain the dishonorable discharge of my own son. This will not stand."

"But, Josiah… You… can't…" looking at the space where his leg should have been.

"Of course, I can, Mary…And, I will. I know my tunic is the wrong color, but it will have to do. I will do my duty and Jack's, as well. I am sorry dear, but this must be done. You will not stand in my way."

"What about the boys? What about Thomas?"

"I am certain that should I never return, they will be safe in your hands, my dear. I must go." He kissed her on the forehead, hobbled out the side door, and around to the small back yard where the old plough horse was tethered. He saddled, bridled, and awkwardly mounted the beast. The old warrior steadied himself in the saddle, put on his faded kepis, glanced down at the stripes on his sleeve, and proudly rode out of the yard.

Mary ran to the front door. She watched him disappear around the corner toward the south. She was absolutely shocked at how in such a short time, she had gotten a son back and lost a husband. She couldn't muster the strength in her voice to yell good bye as he left. She was lost, but hoped that Jack would soon return to find her.

Jack did return later that afternoon. He, his mother, and young Thomas would never see Josiah again. Years later Jack heard an account of his father's fate. Josiah roamed the Confederate lines for days before finding a home in Fort Gregg, which defended the southwestern point of the Dimmock Line. He understood that due to his handicap, he would be most useful in a contained defensive position rather than out on an open battlefield. The old sergeant spent more than seven months doing whatever he could to help the cause and to re-establish the honor of the Wren name.

On April 2, 1865, Federal troops launched a vicious attack on Fort Gregg. Wave after wave of Union men assaulted the structure, each rush being repelled by the hardened Confederates hold up inside. Finally, it became a continuous Union attack. It was said that the men in the fort fought like demons. After more than one hour of fierce bombardment and a full-bore frontal assault, the Yanks finally broke through the fortress breastworks. Intense hand to hand fighting ensued within the fort for more than twenty-five minutes. Men lost all sense of reason and were driven purely by the blinding urge to kill. Bayonets, knives, rifle butts, fists; any means to deliver a deadly blow was employed. Josiah Wren fought valiantly but Union numbers and determination were too great to resist. He emptied his revolver taking down two or three, then managed to club down another with his crutch before being knocked off his single leg and slaughtered by a blunt blow to the head and half a dozen bayonet strikes. By 3PM that afternoon, after two hours of violence, the fort was plundered. Only a few Confederates survived and none of them would ever forget the valor of the old one-legged man.

Seven days prior to the calamitous assault on Fort Gregg, Jack, his mother, and young Thomas evacuated their home near Petersburg and withdrew to Richmond to live with cousins. Seven days *after* the assault, General Robert E. Lee surrendered the Army of Northern Virginia to General Grant at Appomattox. (17.1)

Chapter 18   Things Are Going to Change

Detective Wren turned onto East Clay Street. East Clay was indicative of a Richmond slowly but steadily on the mend. A smattering of small but stylish homes were springing up on vacant lots. A few older houses were being renovated and updated to modern standards. Picket fences and Victorian gingerbread were in ample supply, lending a warm and inviting feeling to the neighborhood. Young children's voices provided a lovely score for the hopeful serenity of the Spring afternoon scenery. Wren slowed his pace as he passed a group of six or seven boys kicking a can in the street. He stopped and watched as the boys jockeyed for position, quickly accelerated in one direction only to completely stop and dash in another. One danced tantalizingly behind a street light with the battered can, then faked a movement one way, kicked the can another, and bolted after it. Hats were flying off, shoes were scuffed and occasionally, a knee was bruised or skinned. It reminded him of his boyhood before the War, playing games of a similar carefree nature with cousin Will and other boys. As he watched the boys at play he noted that the competition was intense, but the game was always fair. It struck Wren that fairness is often safer in the hands of children. Maturity, life experience, and knowledge don't ensure fairness; in fact, in the adult street game, fairness is often ignored or even discarded.

Wren's focus had completely changed by the time the game was finally put on hold by the call of a mother to come home. The detective realized he was no longer angry, in fact, he had involuntarily cracked a smile. He put his hands in his trouser pockets and continued east on East Clay Street to 12th Street. There he turned south toward Capitol Square. Detective Wren crossed Broad Street. City Hall was to his left. Straight ahead, 12th Street jogged to the east and met 13th Street just in front of the Governor's Mansion. Wren stopped and looked through a tall heavy iron fence at the old beauty. He was proud to be a Virginian. As the detective stood still, gazing at the majesty of the mansion's columns, a short round figure of a man appeared in the doorway. The portly gentleman shook hands with Governor William E. Cameron, placed his hat on his graying head, and walked down the front path leading to the street. As the man drew near Wren was able to see the face shaded by a felt hat and immediately recognized him. He knew this man; well, at least he had seen him twice before. It had been more than twenty years since Wren had last laid eyes upon him. General Fitzhugh Lee was older, much heavier, but no less impressive a figure. On foot rather than horseback, he passed more slowly, allowing the opportunity for a brief greeting. A gentlemanly "Good afternoon" and a slight tip of the cap was the extent of their exchange. Wren was a bit surprised to discover that he and Lee were about the same height, no more than five-and-one-half feet. Wren almost made mention of seeing Lee those many years before near Petersburg, but then thought better of it. He was sure that a man of Lee's status and popularity ran across admirers often and probably had his fill of overzealous well-wishers trying to place themselves in the annals of history beside him. This was a poor assumption on Wren's part as Lee was not the type of character who sought to monopolize the spotlight for himself. Neither was he so self-absorbed that he would ever discount what was of importance to others. The General's delight was founded in the events and circumstances themselves, not the people who took credit for making them happen. He always enjoyed recounting shared memories and experiences with people of all sorts, no matter how insignificant the recollections may have seemed when measured against his exemplary experience. To a man of his people like Lee, all memories were significant.

Lee was visiting Governor Cameron this Sunday afternoon to discuss a host of issues. Though Lee had never been elected to office, he was deeply involved in continuing Reconstruction efforts. He was not a politician per se, but a tireless advocate for the Commonwealth who was heavily relied upon within Virginia politics to turn ideas into action.

After the brief encounter, Wren looked at his watch. It was getting late and he turned westward on Main Street toward home.

Wren walked through the front door of his home just after 5PM. His long walk had cooled his fiery temper. The smile on Madeline's understanding face as he walked into the parlor snuffed the last embers of his frustration. Madeline had changed from her Sunday best into her house gown, but to Wren, she was just as lovely and presentable.

"Hello, dear; sorry I was gone so long."

"Oh, Jack, that's fine. How did it go? Did anyone recognize the body?"

"Yes. Yes, a young woman from Church Hill identified the body. She said the dead woman is from King and Queen County. The dead woman has relations here in Richmond and visited on occasion."

"Well, that is good news.", said Madeline. "You've done good work."

"Well, I suppose so.", then, trying to accept the compliment more gracefully, Wren added, "Thank you, my dear. We are making progress." He then tempered the statement with a return to humility, "But, tomorrow will be a full day. There remains a great deal of unanswered questions."

"You will sort it all out, Jack. You will…"

Wren smiled at Madeline. "The boys?"

"Out in the yard. I'll call them in for dinner, soon. You go wash yourself and relax for a spell before dinner."

"Thank you, dear." Wren hung his hat on the rack in the foyer and walked up the long staircase to his bedroom. He removed his suit coat, loosened his tie, and sat in the comfortable wing chair near the front bedroom window. He cracked open the bottom sash to let in some of the cool evening air. He lit his pipe and sat looking out the window. He took a puff, then rested the pipe on an ashtray. Wren laid his head back against the chair back and before he knew it, he dozed off. Fifteen or twenty minutes later he woke himself as he emitted a strange sound somewhere between a snore and a sigh. He closed his eyes for a few moments more. He was roused once more by the stampede of four feet tearing up the stairway. The boys had been called in to wash for dinner. He heard them giggle and shout as they poured some water from the pitcher in their room and washed themselves in the large bowl on the dresser between their beds.

Detective Wren stood from his chair and straightened his shirt and tie. He walked out into the upstairs hall and caught a glimpse of the boys flicking sprays of water on one another. They were each double fisted; plunging their little hands into the basin and pulling them out sopping wet, franticly flicking their fingers open in the direction of the other while simultaneously ducking to guard against the incoming spray.

"Boys… Boys! That is quite enough! You'll soak the entire room! Your mother will not be pleased." Wren was trying to mask a smile and maintain his authoritative demeanor. Jack, Jr., the older and more perceptive of the two sensed his father's disingenuousness. He turned and flicked a full handful of water on his father.

"Why, you… You've got some nerve!", cried Wren as he started to laugh. The father ducked down and moved in grabbing each of the hellions in an arm and plucking them off their feet. He secured each of them like sacks of flour under his arms and bolted for the stairs. The entire way down, he dug his strong thumbs and fingers into their little ribs, causing them to laugh and scream in tortured delight. He put them down in the dining room as Madeline appeared from the kitchen with a platter full of lamb and potatoes. It smelled positively glorious.

Madeline gave a disapproving glare at the three rambunctious males and softly requested that they quiet down and take their seats. The detective found it nearly as difficult as the young boys to recapture his composure. He took a deep breath and said, "Alright boys, mother would like us to settle down. She is absolutely right. It is time for dinner and playtime has ended. No, more outbursts." Edward snickered. "Did you hear me, Edward?", Wren pointed at the boy and it became clear that it was time to cease and desist.

"Yes, father."

The three men sat as Madeline circled the table dishing out the meal. Lamb, potatoes, string beans, and fresh-baked carrot bread. The boys loved Madeline's carrot bread. Another family favorite was Madeline's mint jelly, always a welcome compliment to lamb. There was an ample supply in a small bowl near the center of the table.

"This is a fine-looking meal, mother", said the endearing elder son helping himself to a gob of the jelly.

"Thank you, Jack.", said the pleased mother as she took her seat. "But please leave some jelly for the rest of us."

"Edward, I believe it is your turn to say the blessing.", said father.

"Yes sir." Edward cleared his throat, put his hands together, and, with a slight lisp, said.

"Dear Lord, dank you for the food. Dank you for muver and fawver. Dank you for my bruver, too. Amen."

"Very nice, Edward.", said Madeline

"Yes, well done." Wren silently realized how thankful and blessed he truly was. His troubles with the investigation and his conflict with Burton now seemed unimportant and hundreds of miles away.

After the meal, Madeline brought out tea to Jack. Jack, Jr. and Edward were sent upstairs to look at their books and ready themselves for bed. At 8 o'clock Madeline tucked the boys in their beds and turned out the gas light. She came back downstairs and joined Jack in the parlor for a few quiet hours in front of the fire.

Jack read while Madeline made sewing repairs to the boys' clothes. She sewed up holes in their socks, sewed buttons on their shirts and patches on their trousers. After a while, Madeline broke the silence.

"Jack, dear... There is something I want to tell you." She sounded very serious.

"What Madeline? Is something the matter?"

"Well, there's no problem, but things are going to change around here."

"Whatever do you mean, dear?"

"Jack, I am pregnant." she just blurted it out.

Jack was completely flabbergasted. "You mean?". He dropped his book into his lap and sat forward on his chair.

"Yes, Jack..."

"Oh, my...", said the shocked family man. "That is... absolutely wonderful!"

"You are pleased?", asked Madeline.

"Of course, dear. How else would I be?". He sat back again.

"Well, I was worried that you may feel it would be too much."

"Never.", said Wren.

"Maybe it will be a girl.", Madeline hypothesized as the firelight skipped around her face.

Wren was not even remotely considering that possibility. In his mind, all babies were male. "Yes, perhaps it will...", said an unsure Wren. He thought about how different a daughter would be, the entirely different set of challenges raising a daughter would present. It scared him a bit, but the more he pondered the idea, the more comfortable he became with it. After a few moments, he found himself hoping it would be a girl.

"A girl would be a blessing.", he said.

Chapter 19　　　　　　*It Had to be Done*

      Cluverius gently shook Lillie as the tug horse trolley came to a stop at the southern end of Monroe Park. It was very dark and although the snowfall had intensified, there was no accumulation. Cluverius leapt down onto the wet pavement and turned to help the groggy Lillie. He held her hand as they stepped up on the sidewalk at the corner of Beach and West Main Streets. Cluverius turned to pay the trolley driver, "Where is Reservoir Street?"

      The driver lifted his hand and pointed to an intersection a quarter of a block down Beach Street. "Right there."

      "What is that building?", Cluverius continued.

      "That would be Morton's Flower Garden.", replied the driver with a slight Irish brogue.

      "And that's the Reservoir right beside?"

      "Yes, sir; that's the Reservoir."

      "Thank you, driver." (19.1)

      After a few more steps Cluverius stopped under the dim light of a gas street lamp. He handed Lillie the small satchel and pulled his watch out from under his coat. It was 9:35 PM.

      "Come now, Lillie. The midwife is this way." He interlocked Lillie's arm in his own and led her down West Main Street. The street was dark and empty. The wind rustled the trees and the wet snow continued to fall. The couple turned left on Reservoir Street where they passed a gentleman coming from the other direction. In the obscure darkness, Cluverius stopped the man to confirm that the street they were on was Reservoir Street. The man replied in the affirmative. Even though he had just checked his own watch, Cluverius asked the stranger if he knew the time.

      The man pulled out his watch and strained to read it in the darkness. "I cannot see it clearly, but I just checked my watch a few minutes ago. I believe it's nearly 9:40, sir", the man informed them. Cluverius and Lillie thanked the lone gentleman and continued on.

      "I know that man but he doesn't know me.", Cluverius said to Lillie in a lowered voice.

      "From where?", Lillie asked.

      "Don't worry, I'll explain later. We are late." (19.2)

Within five minutes, Cluverius and Lillie were at Rachel McDonald's front door. Cluverius lightly knocked with one knuckle. The door opened slightly. Cluverius removed his hat.

"Miss McDonald... It is T.J. Merton. I am here with my cousin to see you."

"Yes, I've been expecting you."

Rachel McDonald opened the door and invited the couple in. She immediately closed the door behind them.

"May I have your coats; and the bag?" Lillie removed her shawl and hat. Cluverius took off his overcoat and slouch hat. They handed the items to Miss McDonald. She hung the garments in a narrow wardrobe in the entry hall and placed the satchel on the ladder-backed chair near the stairwell.

"Please, go in.", she smiled as she encouraged the couple toward the parlor. Lillie walked in first with Cluverius behind her. Rachel McDonald followed him. She reached out and quickly put her hand on his back side as she said, "I so enjoyed meeting with you this afternoon, Mr. Merton. I hope that I can serve your needs."

Cluverius understood her double meaning, but he was initially too preoccupied to reply in similarly playful code. "Yes, Miss McDonald.". As the words crossed his lips the scent of her perfume awakened his basic senses. He noticed that the temptress looked very presentable this evening. She was wearing a nice light blue blouse with a complimentary floral skirt. Her hair was brushed and pinned up. She had applied some deep red lipstick and just the right amount of makeup. She appeared ten years younger than she had earlier that day and despite the pressures and importance of the matter at hand, Cluverius found himself drifting into a lustful fantasy involving this maturely titillating and alluring woman.

"Well, why don't we dispense with such formal names. I prefer to be called Rachel. How may I address the two of you?"

"I am Lillie.", Lillie turned to cue Cluverius. He was silently caught in his daydream. Lillie nudged him gently.

"Yes, uh, my name is Thomas."

"Very well; that is much better!", said the quirky midwife.

Lillie was a little surprised by Rachel's oddity, but she was quite intrigued and was somewhat refreshed by the midwife's unorthodox and confidently eccentric manner. After a brief but awkward silence, Rachel continued.

"Shall we go into the back room where we can get started?"

"Yes, absolutely." said Cluverius.

Lillie was suddenly nervous as the weightiness of her responsibility suddenly fell upon her. She grabbed Cluverius' hand tightly as she moved to follow Rachel. In the back room, there were three wall-mounted gas lamps. Rachel turned them up to provide maximum lighting. There was a table in the middle of the room. A white bed sheet was draped over it. A small buffet table sat against the wall. On top of it were some bottles of various shapes and sizes, a wash bowl, some towels, and rudimentary medical instruments.

"Please sit up on the table and un-tuck your blouse, Lillie." Lillie lifted herself up onto the table top and complied. She sat at one end with her short legs hanging down from the edge.

Rachel walked over and began feeling Lillie's mid-section. She probed with both hands along the lower abdomen of the young woman.

"Definitely eight months, or more, but the head is still up.", she said. "I generally don't like to do this so late in the term; but it can be done. I've done it before."

Lillie turned quickly and looked with puzzlement at Cluverius. Her mouth opened slightly as her brow crinkled in wonderment.

"Well, dear. This can be a little painful. Would you like to numb yourself with whiskey, or, if you prefer, I can administer some chloroform; but that usually requires more time to overcome than the effects."

"What are you talking about!", said Lillie. "Tommie? What is this all about?" Suddenly it began to ring clear. "No... No Tommie! No!", she began to shout and moved to get down from the table.

"Now Lillie, wait a moment!", pleaded Cluverius. "This is the only way to handle this..."

"Tommie... You lied to me! You said I would have the baby and we would get married!" Cluverius moved over to control her. He put a hand on each of her shoulders and tried to immobilize her.

"Lillie...Stop Lillie! This is the way it *must* be!", he shook her. "There is no other choice! You *must* do this!"

"No! ... No! Tommie, I won't do this!", she began to struggle to free herself from his grip.

"Damn it, Lillie! You *will* do this!", ordered Cluverius. "Otherwise, I will kill you!" Rachel stepped away and stood speechless against the wall.

"You will do no such thing!", cried Lillie. "If you or that butcher woman lay a hand on me, I will go to the police! In fact, I will go there anyway. This is wrong! I will not do this!" She moved in the direction of the doorway.

Cluverius lunged back toward Lillie to silence her. She lashed out pushing him away. She tried to kick him, but missed. Cluverius maneuvered around her and clamped her down in a bear hug. He forcibly covered her mouth with his hand, attempting to quiet the flailing young woman. She reached her hand up and dug her fingernails into the back of his hand. Cluverius quickly entered a state of frustrated rage. He charged the maniacally possessed woman across the room, maintaining his strong hold, and with the full force of his weight, rammed her forehead into the door jamb. Her body immediately became limp and as he let go, she fell directly to the floor.

Cluverius looked over at Rachel, who stood by in horrified disbelief.

"This is not what I expected, Thomas.", Rachel breathlessly spoke. "Did you not tell her why she came here?"

"Well… not exactly. She thought we were here for a preliminary examination and that you would handle the delivery when that time became apparent."

"My God! What are we to do now?"

Cluverius straightened his shirt. He ran his fingers through his hair. He took a deep breath.

In a very matter-of-fact and unemotional manner Cluverius stated, "We must find a permanent solution."

"What are you suggesting? You told me she is your cousin!"

"She is my cousin…", he replied. Rachel was surprised but devilishly intrigued with the man's tawdry nature.

Cluverius continued, "I don't see any other alternative, Rachel. I know this woman. She will not let this rest. It will ruin my life and yours. Listen, no one even knows I am here in Richmond with her. No one knows she is here. I made sure of it. You are the only one who knows this much."

It was odd to Rachel, but suddenly this young man had become so self-assured, so confident, so in control of a situation which seemed, just a few moments ago, uncontrollable. It was as if he had experienced some sort of revelation. Now that a clear course had finally presented itself, he had complete faith in its viability and strangely, she in him.

"So, what do you want me to do?", asked Rachel.

"Get some of that chloroform and give it to her. I don't want her to awaken. We'll take her over to the reservoir and drown her. Everyone will believe it was an accident, or suicide."

"Oh, Thomas ..."

"It will be fine, Rachel. Just give her the chloroform." Rachel went over to the table and put some chloroform on a rag. She then went over to Lillie, stooped down, and held the rag over her nose and mouth. Cluverius rushed into the front hall and put on his hat and coat. He grabbed Lillie's garments and returned to the back room.

"Go get a coat, Rachel." Rachel left the room and quickly returned wearing her coat. "You carry these things.", Cluverius pointed to Lillie's things. "I will take care of her. Make sure you bring some of that chloroform with you." He bent down and lifted Lillie up and over one shoulder. They slipped out the back door and quietly made their way from the back yard to the street. They crept along Jacqueline Street and turned right on Randolph. Two blocks further they turned left onto Ashland Street and hurried a half block further to the north side of the Marshall Reservoir. Cluverius, was growing a little weary, but like a stubborn pack mule, he kept on. "We'll get into the reservoir through a hole in the fence next to that vacant field on the other side.", he whispered to Rachel.
Rachel nodded and followed Cluverius.

About seventy-five yards from Ashland Street, Cluverius sat Lillie down on the grass. In the dark Cluverius felt along the fence until he found a loose plank. He carefully moved the plank to one side, trying to minimize any noise. He crouched down and crawled through the hole. On all fours, Cluverius reached back through the opening and grabbed hold of Lillie's rubbery arms. He pulled the body completely through before assisting Rachel. Once inside, Cluverius picked up Lillie and once again slung her over his shoulder. He and Rachel walked side by side toward the southern embankment of the reservoir. They trudged up the embankment stairway. Once on top, Cluverius once again laid his burden down. He took some deep breaths. Rachel was agonizingly unnerved. "Thomas, what now? We must get on with this. I am afraid someone will see us."

"Stop worrying, Rachel. We're almost finished." The words had barely left Cluverius' lips when Lillie's eyes popped open and she let out a frightful shriek.

Rachel shook to her core. Cluverius dove atop Lillie and tried to muffle the screams. "Give me the rag! Give me the damned chloroform!", he implored Rachel. Rachel fumbled through her coat pocket. She frantically opened the bottle and dumped the remaining chloroform on the rag.

Lillie freed her mouth long enough to make one last appeal. "Oh Lord!", she cried. Rachel swiftly handed the chloroform rag to Cluverius. He forced it over Lillie's nose and mouth. After a few fitful seconds, Lillie was once again unconscious.

"Hold that over her nose for thirty more seconds.", instructed Rachel. "Make sure she has a good dose."

After a long thirty seconds, Cluverius pulled the rag away, reached toward Rachel to give it to her, and said, "Alright... Let's get this over with." He stood and picked up Lillie. Rachel stood by to help him. As she neared his foot came down upon her untied shoelace. She lifted her foot quickly to step toward the short picket fence atop the embankment which encircled the reservoir. The shoes string snapped, but in her anxiously focused state, she did not take note. The two hoisted Lillie's still body above the fence and with one mighty coordinated effort, they thrust Lillie feet first over the fence. The body tumbled in the darkness down a steep grade until it plunged into the shallow water at the reservoir's edge. Cluverius looked over the fence, squinting through the blackness to see down into the water. Lillie was face down and appeared motionless.

"I am sure she will sink to the bottom.", whispered Cluverius. "Collect all of the clothing; we cannot leave anything to be found."

Cluverius and Rachel scrambled to pick up the loose articles of clothing. Rachel stuffed the chloroform bottle and the rag back in her coat pocket. In the darkness and their desperate haste, one of Lillie's garnet gloves fell silently to the ground atop the embankment.

The two shadowy figures rushed down the embankment toward the hole in the fence. As Cluverius forced his way back through the opening, his watch chain became entangled. Sensing a slight snag, he stopped awkwardly in the darkness. The subsequent sound of a distant barking dog startled him and he continued through the opening, prying a link in the chain loose. Rachel was anxiously pressing from behind in panting desperation, furiously trying to get away from the scene as quickly as possible. Cluverius paused and stood in the shadows along the fence. He extended his arm to slow Rachel, "We have to dispose of these things." Rachel nodded. He grabbed Lillie's veil from Rachel and stashed it against the fence. Unbeknownst to both, the other garnet glove was wrapped in the veil. Cluverius then motioned Rachel to follow him toward the dimly lit Ashland Street. They slowly emerged from the shadows, making certain no one was in the area. Cluverius then took Rachel's hand and led her east on Ashland toward Reservoir Street. They passed an abandoned old frame house. Cluverius saw that one of the first story windows was broken out, so he quickly let go of Rachel's hand and whisked over to the window. He tossed Lillie's hat through the window and scampered back to the sidewalk.

The paranoid couple turned north on Reservoir Street. They walked stealthily onward, staying on the darker side of the eerily still street, attempting to remain invisible. Near the intersection of Reservoir and Taylor Streets, Cluverius took the last article of Lillie's clothing from Rachel's arms and tossed it up in the air toward a high wall near the sidewalk. The fraying ends of the red knit shawl hung like running drips of blood suspended in time over the ten-foot wall.

Cluverius and Rachel turned left on Taylor Street and circled back to the south down Washington Street until they reached Rachel's house on Jacqueline Street. They slipped up the side of the house and entered from the rear yard.

Rachel trembled as she sat down in the parlor. "Thomas, what have we done?"

"Rachel, my dear, it had to be done."

"What if we are caught?"

"We will not be caught. As I explained, no one even knows Lillie came here. If she is ever found, she will probably never even be identified. You cannot worry. It is her own fault. She would not listen to reason. She was a dumb, pig-headed girl. She never understood what was good for her!" Sensing Rachel's surfacing weakness, Cluverius continued, "I know that you are quite different. You certainly understand what is good for you, *don't you?*"

Rachel was chilled by Cluverius' veiled threat. She looked at him and saw a madman. But almost inexplicably, she felt a great amount of loyalty to him. Perhaps it was predominantly fear that engendered this sudden loyalty, but also, deep in the far reaches of her soul, she was perversely energized by his wickedness. Rachel had acquired more emotional sustenance in the short time she had known Thomas than she had gained from any man in her life. The attraction was instinctive, undeniable, and for her, increasingly insatiable. She could not bear to lose him.

"Where will you go? When will I see you again, Thomas?"

"I have to go home for a short while, Rachel. I will be back to see you; perhaps in two weeks or a month." He could see by her expression that his promises were having the desired effect. "I care deeply for you and appreciate what you have done on my behalf. You must know this. I just need to take care of some things and then I shall be back for you, dear."

Cluverius stood and approached her. He put his hands on her shoulders and guided her gently out of her seat onto her feet. He bent over and kissed her. She was sorrowful yet full of hope. Cluverius walked into the foyer and picked up Lillie's satchel from the chair. He placed his hat on his head and smiled at Rachel. He opened the front door and disappeared. (19.3)

Chapter 20   *Private Detective*

Detective Jack Wren arrived early at Police Headquarters Monday morning. He was anxious to continue his investigation but wanted some time to organize his thoughts free of distraction. Wren's desk sat at the back of the large room on the second floor. The walls were a dull, dingy grey. The plaster, particularly on the water-damaged ceiling, was in need of repair. The windows were large but obscured by the build-up of dirt and dried condensation. The worn floor squeaked and moaned as Wren walked across the threshold. There were a half-dozen desks in the "*Pig Pen*" as the detectives liked to call their office. Most of the desks certainly belonged in a *Pig Pen*, but Wren's decidedly did not. It was organized and by comparison pleasing, but only in a Spartan sense. There were so few items on his desktop that a casual observer could have mistook it for unoccupied. On its top was a pristine blotter, an ink well, and a pen holder; nothing more. All other items belonging to Wren were in their assigned place either neatly in a drawer or in one of the file cabinets that flanked his desk. The file cabinet to the right housed the closed case files while the one on the opposite side was for open cases.

Wren was the first man in the *Pig Pen* that morning. He opened the Venetian blinds along the eastern wall to let in a flood of morning sunshine. The detective walked over to a table centered on that same wall and selected a blank evidence form from one of the piles sitting there. He turned and went to his desk, sat the blank to one side, and withdrew a lined notepad from the right side drawer. He began to collect his thoughts.

March 16, 1885

1. Tag and catalogue evidence collected.

2. Request a copy of the Autopsy Report from Taylor

3. Locate and inform family of the deceased - Madisons of King & Queen Co.

4. Interview Mrs. Rutherford of Church Hill

5. Perform secondary search of reservoir and surrounds

Wren pulled a large canvas evidence bag from beneath his desk. One by one, he removed each item, placed an identification tag on it, and entered a corresponding description onto a form for the official investigation file. He catalogued the evidence according to where it was found. Wren assigned the case number "8557-3". The first two digits indicated the year ("85"). The second two digits were his badge number ("57"), and the last digit ("3") represented the third new case Wren had opened this particular year.

Case Evidence Catalogue
City of Richmond
Police Department

Case #   *8557 - 3 Death of Woman believed to be Lillian Madison of King & Queen Co., Virginia*

Date of Investigation   *14 March 1885*

Date Evidence Catalogued   *16 March 1885*

Filing Officer   *Detective Jack Wren*

Exhibit(s) A 5 items worn by deceased when discovered in water at the south end of the Marshall Reservoir on 14 March

     A1 - Black skirt
     A2 - Blue Jersey
     A3 - Pair of black woman's lace up shoes (laces intact)
     A4 - Pair of black stockings
     A5 - 6 hairpins

Exhibit(s) B 2 items located atop southern embankment Of Old Marshall Reservoir. Collected 14 March

     B1 - Garnet Woman's Glove (Left)
     B2 - Part of shoestring (approx. 2 1/2 inches in length)

Exhibit(s) C 1 item located inside old deadhouse on Clark Spring property (near Ashland Street) under open window. Collected 14 March

     C1 - Woman's Black Hat with red lint inside

Exhibit(s) D 2 items found on western fence line between Clark Spring property and Marshall Reservoir near hole in fence approx. 75 yards from Ashland Street. Collected 14 March

     D1 - Garnet Woman's Glove (Right - matches Exhibit B1)
     D2 - Woman's Veil

Exhibit(s) E 1 item located by Mr. J. W. Dunstan on wall of his property ½ mile north of Marshall Reservoir on Reservoir Street. Collected 14 March

 E1 - Red Wool Shawl (matches lint on Exhibit C1)

<u>Exhibit(s) F</u> Canvas bag with contents found floating in James River near C&O Railroad Wharves 3 ½ miles from Marshall Reservoir. Collected 14 March

 F1 - Brown Canvas bad with straps. Initials on bag "F.L.M."
 F2 - Long black skirt
 F3 - Bone white blouse (initials written on collar are "F.L.M.")
 F4 - Pair of black stockings
 F5 - Woman's undergarments
 F6 - Wood Cigar Box. Needlepoint of bird, 6 small spools of thread, and 2 needles contained within

  Detective Wren wrote his initials next to each Exhibit entry and placed the paper in a file folder. He placed the file off to one side of his desk. He then carefully returned each item to the evidence bag and put it, for the time being, underneath his desk.

  Wren pulled a clean sheet of Police Department Letterhead from his file drawer and wrote the following.

16 Mar 1885

Dr. William H. Taylor, M.E.
City of Richmond Coroner's Office

Dear Dr. Taylor:

  The Richmond Police request a complete copy of the report regarding the autopsy examination performed by your office of the young woman identified in your presence as Lillian Madison of King & Queen County. This request is in conjunction with our investigation regarding her demise. Please forward said report to my attention at Police Headquarters. Your efforts and cooperation are appreciated.

Respectfully,
Richmond Department of Police

Jack Wren
Detective

  The detective sealed the letter in an envelope and addressed it to Taylor. He placed the letter in the outgoing mail box near the door of the *pig pen* and returned to his desk. He placed a notation in the file that he had made such request of Dr. Taylor.

Wren tore a blank sheet of paper from his notepad. He jotted down a draft telegraph message.

16 Mar 1885

To: Sheriff's Office
King & Queen Co, Virginia

From: Detective Jack Wren, Richmond Police

Dear Sheriff:

Please be advised that a young woman was found dead in a reservoir within the Richmond City limits on 14 March. She has been preliminarily identified as Lillian Madison of King and Queen Co. Please inform nearest relatives and request that someone who knew Miss Madison come immediately to Richmond to positively identify the deceased and, if appropriate, collect her remains. Please advise when to expect their arrival.

Respectfully,
Richmond Police
Detective Jack Wren

He folded the paper and put it the side pocket of his coat.

Wren walked down the hall past the stairwell to the back room of the building where coffee was brewing. He poured a cup and took a sip. It was hot, but that was about the only thing good to be said about it. The detective quickly reached for some sugar cubes to blunt the bitterness. He tasted it again. "Not much better..."; but Wren kept the cup anyway and returned upstairs.

Just before reaching the doorway to the *Pig Pen*, Wren stopped to sip once more from his coffee cup. Just inside the doorway, but out of his view, he overheard a man speaking softly but with audible conviction.

"Hanson, stop concerning yourself with this!", said the man in a sternly hushed manner. "If you stay quiet, nothing more will come of it... But, I assure you, if a time comes when some of us require your support, you *will* give it. Otherwise, you will fall by whatever means necessary!"

Hanson's response was even more muted. Wren strained to hear what Hanson was saying. He could only decipher part of it; something about "having to find a way out of this" and "feeling pressured".

Wren was surprised by what he heard. Hanson was a respected veteran detective.

The conversation ended abruptly. The other man rushed from the *Pig Pen* and breezed past Wren without more than a quick look and a grunt.

It was Sergeant Charles Deuring, one of the least likeable and certainly one of the most corrupt officers on the force. He was a fifteen-year veteran of the Richmond Police and regularly accepted bribes. His activities were well-known by his superiors, but they often chose to ignore the shortcomings of some of their officers in order to keep the ranks at minimally acceptable levels. The longer Deuring served, the more difficult it became to quash his ongoing immoral conduct. He managed to corrupt and compromise enough of his fellow officers in key positions, such as Hanson, to insulate himself from retribution. Deuring's abuses were not contained to blackmail and illegal payoffs alone. When the opportunity presented itself, the large, intimidating officer relished the opportunity to apply coercive force; sometimes verbal, but frequently, physical; taking full unabated advantage of his authority as a man with a badge.

Wren stepped into the *Pig Pen* and nodded good morning at Hanson. Hanson was clumsily rearranging items on his desk, seemingly trying to distract himself from what just happened. Wren sensed Hanson's nervous discomfort but gave no indication of what he had just overheard. Wren sat quietly at his desk. He checked his watch. It was 8:52 AM.

A few minutes passed before Lieutenant Grimes entered the *Pig Pen*. Grimes was an officer in the Internal Affairs Division of the force, working directly under Police Chief Justice D. C. Richardson. Chief Richardson had been elected five years earlier with a vow to reform the tired Richmond force. Internal Affairs was formed by Richardson and charged with uprooting department corruption, inefficiency, and abuses. He was a tough but fair administrator who refused to tolerate illicit behavior within the force. Many procedural changes had been made during Richardson's tenure; but it now appeared that cost-savings and personnel changes were also on his agenda.

Grimes approached Hanson and quietly asked the detective to leave with him. Hanson looked concerned and although he turned his head in Wren's direction, he avoided making eye contact. Hanson put on his jacket and the two turned to leave the room. As Grimes passed, he leaned over Wren's desk and uttered with complete lack of emotion, "Chief would like to see you in his office at 9:30."

Wren visibly shook when the words registered. "What could this be about?", he thought to himself. "I've been doing my job". Wren sat in silence for the next thirty minutes, trying to imagine what was coming next. He checked his watch and it was 9:28. He took a deep breath and stood to go face the unknown.

Wren walked down the hall and up one flight of stairs to the Chief's office. Wren followed with some trepidation. He passed by a smirking Peter Burton of the *Richmond Dispatch* in the doorway as he entered Chief Richardson's office. The Chief looked up from his paperwork, "Be seated, Detective Wren."

Wren sat in the wood chair opposite Richardson's imposing desk. Sensing a presence, he turned and looked back over his left shoulder as he shifted his weight and spotted Lieutenant Grimes.

"Wren, have you read the *Dispatch* this morning?"

"No, Chief. I haven't."

"Well, Mr. Burton, has been following your investigation of the Madison girl. Needless to say, he has been quite critical. I am not sure all of his criticism is unwarranted. Read this…"

The Chief handed Grimes the newspaper. Grimes stepped around the desk and presented it to Wren.

The Richmond Dispatch
March 16, 1885

Woman's Body Identified; Police Call It Suicide

A large crowd gathered at the Old Almshouse yesterday after church services. The Coroner's Office was displaying the body of a young woman found floating in the Old Marshall Reservoir early the morning of 13 March. The furor raised throughout the City by this tragedy has been astonishing. This reporter remembers no other incident which has so quickly ignited the attention and concern of the citizenry.

Hundreds filed through in groups of ten to view the cadaver. After some time, a young girl of the Church Hill area recognized the body as that of Lillian Madison of King & Queen County. The girl, Melanie Dunstan, said the deceased visited relatives in Richmond periodically and that she herself had met Miss Madison on a few occasions.

Dr. William Taylor, M.E., who conducted the viewing, confirmed that Miss Dunstan did positively identify the deceased as Lillian Madison. Detective Wren, of the Richmond Police lent further confirmation of the woman's identity. Dr. Taylor affirmed that the deceased is approximately twenty years of age and was within a month of giving birth. Dr. Taylor also stated that the victim had a large bruise above her eye but the cause of death was drowning. He stated that, based purely on the medical facts, he could not rule out either suicide or homicide.

Detective Wren of the Richmond Police insists this matter is being investigated as a suicide. He says there is no evidence to suggest otherwise. As reported in a previous article in this publication, this would seem not to be the case. There were signs of a struggle at the site as well as two sets of footprints, one appearing to be those of a woman, presumably the deceased, and another set belonging to a man, presumably the perpetrator.

Many pieces of female clothing were found at the reservoir and on adjacent properties including; a matching pair of women's gloves, a veil, a woman's hat, and wool shawl In addition, a satchel full of women's clothes floating on the banks of the river more than a mile below Mayo's Bridge near the Chesapeake & Ohio Railroad wharves . The satchel bore the initials "F.L.M." and may belong to the victim. Mrs. Mary Rutherford, the aunt of the deceased, confirmed that the deceased's first name was Fannie (Fannie Lillian Madison), thus matching the victim with the initials on the satchel. Mrs. Rutherford stated that she had not seen Miss Madison in many months and knew of no reason why she would be in Richmond nor who else the young woman would be staying with. Mrs. Rutherford said no one from the Police had contacted her about this case.

When asked if homicide were a possibility, Detective Wren flatly refused to comment. It appears very likely that there is a killer among us and the department seems unwilling to examine this probability. It is curious that this department purposely fails to publicly address such fundamental questions and even seems to deny the questions exist. (20.1)

Wren's complexion exposed his embarrassment and frustration.

"Chief Richardson, I'm not sure what you are trying to ask me…"

The Chief cut him off. "Wren, on top of this unflattering portrayal of your, and by extension, the department's, performance thus far in this investigation, Mr. Burton has brought to our attention a piece of physical evidence gathered from the site of the incident… by a twelve-year-old boy!" The Chief was obviously annoyed. "This was found caught in the fence between the Reservoir and the Clark Spring property. Some boys were going through the fence and found it hanging right there yesterday morning." The Chief held up a gold watch key with a damaged ring upon it. A blinding little burst penetrated Wren's eye as the twisting and dangling key caught a ray of sunlight. "How you missed it is difficult to excuse."

After a brief silence, the Chief spoke again. "Wren, now listen…" The Chief sat more upright in his chair and folded his hand s together on his desktop. The watch key was between his intertwined fingers. "I have reviewed your record. I think you are an honest and forthright man.... I don't like doing this, but the department cannot afford to have an investigation led by the press and twelve-year-old boys. It looks bad when a reporter, like Burton, here, is collecting evidence and interviewing witnesses before the lead detective."

"Are you dismissing me from the force, Chief?" Wren's left hand quivered in his lap. He put it between his clenched knees to stabilize it.

"Well Wren, in all honesty… normally, I would just let this go with a warning. But these are not normal times. You see, it really would not matter now how fine or poor your performance has been. Powers that be have determined that the Richmond Police no longer need the services of *any* detectives. Going forward we will operate with our standard force. I'm afraid all of you out there in the *Pig Pen* will need to move on. And this is effective immediately. Captain Epps will be taking over the investigation from this point forward. Thank you for your service, but this is the way it must be. Please turn over all of your files and records to Epps and then clear your desk."

Wren was devastated. His mind went blank as he tried to understand what just occurred. He slowly stood and turned toward the door.

"And Wren, please send Ferguson up here to talk to me. He's next. Thank you."

Wren saw Burton still lingering out in the hall. "I won't forget this, Burton..." growled Wren as he moved toward the stairwell.

"I am certain I won't either.", returned the glib Burton.

As Wren descended the stairs, Burton slipped back into the Chief's office.

"Burton, you've won this round.", said Chief Richardson. "You've embarrassed and undermined the department. But believe me, once I get this department righted, you will not be able to influence it any further. I hope it is worth your petty games; because the worm will turn, my reporter friend... The worm will turn..."

The defensive Burton replied. "Sir, I sincerely hope you are able to 'right the department'. It is exactly the type of ineffectiveness as displayed by men like Wren that I wish to do something about. My goal is no different than your own, Chief. It is my job to bring attention to these inadequacies and I'm a little surprised that you feel so threatened. I hope there isn't something else you're trying to obscure by directing your frustrations at me, Chief." Burton cracked his familiar wry smile.

"Your goal is very different from mine, Mr. Burton. I want to build up the department, you seek only to tear it down. You are not a native Southerner. The War is long over, Burton; and, as long as men like you continue to sow the seeds of vengeance through manipulation and by undermining the South's right to self-rule, the longer it will take Southerners to fully come back to the Union. I will not engage any further in this senseless discussion. There is no point in giving you any further statement nor opinion that you can recklessly mischaracterize and use against the department. I thank you for bringing in this important piece of evidence to the department, but I condemn your underhanded self-serving methods. Good day, sir. Escort Mr. Burton to the sidewalk, Lieutenant Grimes."

"I am certain we will meet again, Chief Richardson."

"Yes, I too, am certain, Mr. Burton."

Lt. Grimes escorted Burton out of the police precinct without uttering a word. The Lieutenant returned to the Chief's office within a few minutes.

"Lieutenant...Take this watch key down to Epps and tell him to expect Wren to deliver the other case information."

"Yes, sir."

"And Grimes, I want you to keep an eye on Burton. Use whatever means you can within the law, but find *something* on him. The department needs to be prepared. I'm not interested in ruining him, but… I want it to be clear to him that if he wants to act unfairly in the future, it will cost him."

"Yes, sir."

Detective Wren's anger grew as he marched the hallway back toward the *Pig Pen*. But, he consciously changed course and converted that anger to resolve. Upon returning to his desk he took his copy of the Richmond City Directory out of his left-hand drawer. "R, R, R…" he quietly repeated to himself. He found one listing of *"Rutherford, M."* with an address on North Jefferson Street. "Not it…", he thought. There were no other Rutherfords beginning with *"M"*. "Must be under the husband's name." he postulated. There were four other Rutherfords in the directory, the one under *"Mr. and Mrs. William A."* caught his eye; *2214 East Grace.*

"That's got to be it!"

Wren's thoughts then drifted to his family and the baby on the way. His resolve stiffened. From that moment he was no longer Detective Jack Wren, but rather Private Detective Jack Wren. A forlorn Detective Hanson was still clearing his own desk in the opposite corner of the room.

"Detective Hanson… It appears I will be leaving with you this morning. I have a proposition." (20.2)

Chapter 21 *Merton and Cluverius*

Church Hill was the oldest residential area in Richmond. It was an architecturally eclectic neighborhood with structures that spanned from the Georgian colonial roots of the City through the present day. It lay just to the north of Police Headquarters a short but uphill walk for the two men. The morning sunlight was brilliant and little shade was found on the west side of the street. Though the sidewalks were lined with trees, most were plantings dating back ten years or less. Nearly all of the mature trees on Church Hill had been cut down during the War; primarily consumed for fuel during the last bitter winter of '64 and '65. As they walked, Wren briefly outlined the day's mission.

Within minutes the men were near the corner of 28th Street and Venable Street at the door of Mary Rutherford. Wren stepped forward and firmly knocked. Any elderly woman in all black came to the door.

"Mrs. Rutherford?", gently asked the detective as he removed his bowler.

She nodded.

"I am Detective Jack Wren. This is Detective Hanson." Hanson tipped his hat, removed it, and then held it under his arm.

"Good day, gentlemen." she was looking beyond the men toward the street.

"We would like to ask you a few questions."

Her eyes cut to meet the detective's. "Yes, about Lillie... I know.", she said.

"Yes, Madam. May we come in for a moment?"

"I would prefer you did not." said the cautiously reclusive old lady.

Wren was a bit surprised by this response, but he understood the quirkiness that often accompanies age.

"That's fine, madam. We will keep our visit brief. Well, I assume you knew Miss Lillie Madison?"

"Yes, she was my niece."

"What was her full name, Mrs. Rutherford?"

"Fannie Lillian Madison."

"Yes, well I also assume you have heard what has happened?"

"Yes, detective.", her lip quivered.

"When was the last time you saw your niece?"

"I have not seen her since last October. She did write a lovely letter to me at Christmas.", she began to get more emotional.

Wren and Hanson looked at one another and were increasingly uncomfortable questioning the distraught old lady.

"So, she was not here in your home recently?"

"No."

"You did not know she was here in Richmond recently?"

Mrs. Rutherford shook her head.

"Do you know where she would have been staying if not here? Are there any other relatives in Richmond?"

She shook her head again and wiped her red and watery eyes.

"Do you have any idea why she would come to Richmond and not tell you?"

"No… I cannot talk any more… I am tired of answering questions from strangers about this…", she sighed, then sobbed, then closed the door.

Wren was able to squeeze in a clipped "Thank you" just before the door shut. He had planned to ask Mrs. Rutherford to identify the body, but after this meeting and taking into account her fragile state of mind, he was hopeful it would not be necessary.

Then men quietly descended from the porch and stood briefly on the sidewalk.

"What now, detective?" asked Hanson.

"Well, Hanson… It is my belief that if she was not staying with her aunt and we know of no other relatives in town; we should look at the local hotels. We need to check the registries and see if we can find where this poor girl spent her final hours."

Hanson nodded in agreement.

Wren and Hanson entered the Davis Hotel near the corner of 15th and Franklin Streets. It was an old five story brick building with a rather shabby appearance. The window sills needed painting. The weather-beaten glazing peeled away from the mullions like banana skin. The front lobby was dank and musty, long overdue for a thorough cleaning. As the morning sunlight cut across the floor, Wren could see the thick dust particles whimsically sputtering as the air drafts ceaselessly, but randomly, circulated through the structure. The small sofa near the registration desk was covered in a burnt orange crushed velvet fabric. The upholstery on the arms was nearly worn through and the seat had a mixture of stains, cigar burns, and small splits in the fabric caused by excessive fatigue. The feet were heavily scratched, having felt the heels of many shoes. The Davis Hotel had been family owned and operated for nearly forty years. At one time it was a decent working-class establishment, but the War and subsequent hard times had rendered it little more than a flop house.

The two men approached the registration desk and called reservedly through the open doorway behind the desk. A short bald man appeared from the doorway. He was wearing a white under shirt and blue trousers. His suspenders were off his shoulders and dangling from his waist.

"Good morning gentlemen. Can I help you?" The man smiled.

"Yes, we are with concerning an investigation. I am Detective Wren and this is Detective Hanson."

"Is there a problem, gentlemen?" said the hotel man, rather nervously.

"May I ask your name, sir?", asked Wren.

"Vashon... Bruce Vashon."

"Mr. Vashon; do you regularly work here?"

"Yes sir. Been here about four years."

"Well, we are looking for someone we thought may have been staying here last Friday night. A young woman. May we see your registry?"

"Would she have been staying here for the entire night?", asked the man. The detectives looked bewildered. "Well, what I mean, detective, is, that, well...". Vashon looked up at the ceiling as he groped for the right words. "Any women that stay here usually do so for a very short-term basis. And, they are usually not the one's paying. Do you understand what I mean?"

"I think we get your meaning, sir." Hanson couldn't help but smile a bit. Wren, ever serious, continued, "Yes, this woman would have been staying here for all of Friday night and perhaps, the night before."

"Well, Detective, I am quite certain that all female visitors over the weekend were not here for a full rental period."

"Your registry... Mr. Vashon", the detective reminded the man.

"Um... Well..." he hesitated and looked downward at the desktop, "We do not keep a registry... there is no need, you see..." Vashon deftly slid a book on the shelf below the desktop further back on the shelf and completely out of view. Neither Wren nor Hanson saw the evasive maneuver.

"Yes, I see... Very well." Wren looked down at the beetle laden carpet and paused. Then, looking back at Vashon he said, "Did anyone leave without paying their bill this weekend?"

"No, Detective. You see, I collect the charge before I let anyone have a room. That way, there are no problems.

"Um... Yes, Mr. Vashon. I think we understand. Well, thank you for your help. We may be back."

"Yes, Detective. Many men of the police department have come back here more than once." Wren wasn't amused. He grunted, turned and tapped Hanson on the arm, then left the hotel. Hanson followed him out. Vashon was a little embarrassed at his own comment. The top of his head turned red as he silently waved to the backs of the detectives. His statement was awkward and not exactly as intended, but nonetheless, it was accurate.

When they reached the street, Wren stopped.

"Hanson, he wasn't referring to you in there, was he?"

"Oh no, Jack. I assure you I do not get involved with that sort of activity."

"Very good; I didn't think you would be, but I have been fooled before."

Hanson was not sure whether there was an element of humor in Wren's words, or not. He chose not to pursue the conversation.

Wren and Hanson continued four blocks west and turned one block north to Main Street. The American Hotel was situated on the north side of the street, midway between 11th and 10th Streets.

The men felt much more comfortable in the recently refurbished surroundings of "The American". Wren was seen frequently around the hotel. A barber shop occupied some space in the building's basement. Detective Wren was a regular customer. The detectives approached the polished front desk. Standing there was Joseph Dodson, the morning clerk at the hotel.

"Good morning, Detective. Are you here for a shave? The shop should be open."

"No, not today Mr. Dodson. I'm actually here for business."

"What can I do for you, sir?"

"Well, sir; Detective Hanson and I would like to take a look at your registry for this past week. May we?"

"Of course, Detective." Dodson reached over to the edge of the desk counter and slid the large registry book in front of them. He flipped back through the pages. "What dates would you like to see, Detective?"

"Oh, maybe beginning with last Thursday, the 12th. Has anyone left the hotel without paying in recent days, sir?"

"May I look at the registry, Detective?" Wren spun the book around 180 degrees. Dodson ran his finger down the list. "Yes, I knew there was one…" Dodson spun the book back again and pointed to a name. "This person here. He registered late Thursday night; well, actually, early Friday morning, and never checked out."

Wren read the name, **"F.L. Merton"**. Under residence was simply written **"Virginia"**.

"You said '*he*'; so, this person was definitely a man?"

"I am not sure. The person was in Room 21. Maybe Henry will recall." Dodson stepped away from the desk and poked his head through the doorway to the office. "Henry? Henry? You back here?"

"Yessuh" came a brisk and simple reply.

"Henry, please step out here for a moment."

A young negro boy emerged from the office. "Gentlemen, this is Henry Hunt. He works here. Henry, do you remember who stayed in Room 21 last Thursday and Friday?"

"Yessuh. 'Twas a woman.", answered the boy.

Wren stepped in. "Did you speak with this woman? How old was she?"

"Yessuh, I gone to her room Fridee morn an' gived 'er a messige. She give me one back, but the mess'ger was gone by den. I give it to Missuh Dodson… I believes she was twenty, maybe twenty-five year. But, she ain't no taller 'en me, 'tective."

"Who sent her the first message?"

"Don' know, suh"

"What happened to that message, Mr. Dodson?"

"Well, later that day, when nobody had come for it, I think… Yes, I opened it and read it… And then I tore it and threw it in the trash!"

Dodson quickly stepped out from behind the counter and rushed over to the small waste can in the corner. He lifted it up onto the counter. He pulled out a few pieces of paper, some crumpled, some torn. He found an envelope and four pieces of a note. Detective Wren put the pieces of the note back together on top of the clerk's counter.

"Is this the note?", asked Wren.

"Yes, I believe that's it, Detective", said Dodson.

Wren read the message. Hanson and Dodson each strained to read it, too.

I will be there as soon as possible; so do wait for me.

Wren then pieced the envelope together. Scrawled on the front was the addressee:

T. J. Cluverius

Wren's heart was beating quickly, but he kept a calm demeanor. "May I have this note and envelope?"

"Well, of course, detective. But what is this all about?"

"Sir, I am sure you have heard of the girl found in the Reservoir?"

"Yes, detective?"

"It would seem that the mysterious woman who left your establishment without paying may be that girl."

"Hanson. please write down the name and address of every person registered here for Thursday and Friday past. Then, please go to the Exchange Hotel and The Ballard House and do the same. Look particularly for these names, "*Merton and Cluverius*". I need to prepare to speak with the Commonwealth's Attorney tomorrow. Come meet me at my house after you've completed the assignment."

Torn Note Retrieved from the American Hotel Wastebasket

"Understood, Jack."

Chapter 22 *Mayo's Bridge*

Cluverius stopped and briefly looked at his watch under the street lamp near the intersection of Reservoir Street and West Main. It was 11:10 PM on Friday night, March 13, 1885. The tug horse trolley had stopped operating at 10:00 PM. The wind blew in fitful bursts through the trees and a steady sleet continued to fall. Cluverius walked toward Monroe Park and turned south on Belvidere Street. At the Penitentiary, he turned left and followed the lonely thoroughfare around to Byrd Street. He continued eastward along the back end of Tredegar Iron Works toward the center of the city.

The adrenaline coursing through Cluverius produced diverging emotions. He clutched the handles of Lillie's brown satchel tightly. He walked quickly enough that his breathing became slightly labored as he recounted in his mind the bizarre events which had just transpired. Cluverius was feeling relief and liberation, with only brief interruptions of paranoia and fear. The ponderous responsibility of Lillie and her bastard offspring were no longer a burden, but completing the necessary steps and ensuring his alibi curbed his jubilation. He was anxious to escape Richmond and return to the safety of his law practice and the life of wealth and leisure he had envisioned for himself and his fiancé, Nolie Bray. He knew there would be questions and concerns from the family once it was discovered that Lillie was missing from far away Bath County, but he was confident that she would never be found nor, at a minimum, identified. Each time uncertainty pierced his confidence, the young lawyer reminded himself that even if her identity were somehow confirmed, neither his scandalous relationship with her nor his presence in Richmond at the time of her death could be proven.

He arrived at the Davis Hotel just prior to midnight. Cluverius approached the front desk. He saw the glow of a gas lamp spilling through the cracked office door. He beckoned softly as he leaned over the desk.

"Hello… Good evening?"

After a few moments Mark Davis, proprietor, emerged eating an apple.

"Good evening, Mr. Cluverius.", Davis said with a mouth-full of apple.

"Oh, hello Mr. Davis. Sorry to disturb you, this evening; but I need you to call my room at 5 o'clock."

"My goodness, man. That is a beastly hour for me to get up!"

"I am truly sorry for the inconvenience, but I have to get up the York River Road to West Point and catch the boat up the Mattaponi."

"Aww… Very well… I'll call at 5." Davis reached into his coat pocket and pulled out another apple. "Would you like an apple, Mr. Cluverius? On the house!"

"Why yes, that would be nice. Thank you, sir." Davis tossed the apple across the front desk. "Are we all square with regard to the bill?", Cluverius asked.

He pulled out his registry and thumbed through it. "Yes; you owe three dollars for last night and tonight."

T.J. Cluverius placed his satchel on the floor near his feet, pulled three dollars from his wallet, and handed it to Davis. "Did a gentleman ever call here for me tonight?" asked Cluverius. "I was supposed to meet him at Mozart Hall for a concert. He never made it."

"No. Nobody came in here looking for you.", replied Davis.

"Very good. I just wanted to confirm that. Oh, but one more thing, sir. Can you have a bottle of whiskey brought up to my room?"

"Yes, I'll have Curtis run it up. You can pay for it when he gets there." Mr. Davis handed Cluverius the key to his room and returned back to the hotel office.

Cluverius stepped quietly up to third floor. He entered his shabby little room and threw the satchel on the single disheveled bed. He removed his coat and hat, casting them beside the satchel. Cluverius exhaled sharply and pulled the lone wooden chair over toward the window. The chair moaned under his weight as he sat down and gazed out onto the street below. There was little activity on Franklin Street at this hour. The gas street lamps provided just enough light to witness an occasional blurred silhouette, usually a rat, scampering up, down, or across the street. The room was stuffy, so Cluverius cracked the window, letting in a cool stream of damp stormy air. He loosened his collar and tried to calm himself. He turned the back of the chair toward the window sill and straddled the seat, supporting his forearms on the top of the chair back. He softly ran the fingers of his left hand across the back of his scratched right hand. The blood from the nail marks left by Lillie had already coagulated; and the light rubbing soothed the low-grade itching as the healing process began.

Cluverius laid his head down upon his hands as his mind began to race. He briefly closed his eyes. The haunting image of Lillie's final shrieking expression kept entering his thoughts. In the depths of his imagination, he watched himself force the chloroform-laced rag over her gaping mouth. He wondered if he'd gone too far and if his desperation would be his undoing. A sudden knock at the door temporarily spared him from the self-inflicted torture of his own doubts. He spun out of the chair and answered the door.

"'Nevenin' suh.."

"Yes, thank you… How much do I owe you?"

"Haff dolla', suh."

Cluverius reached in his pocket and pulled out some coins. He leaned toward the hall gas lamp and counted out fifty-five cents.

"Very well." Cluverius handed the negro boy the money and the boy handed him a bottle of whiskey.

The boy's eyes widened as he looked in his hand. "Much obliged, suh! Yessuh."

"Good night." said Cluverius as he smiled faintly. He closed the door and the young boy left.

Cluverius found a well-used tin cup on the small table in the corner of his room. He wiped it clean of dust with his fingers. After setting it back on the table, he uncorked the full whiskey bottle and poured his first cup. He returned to his seat straddling the chair and facing out the window. He took a mouthful and cringed as his eyes began to water. He forced himself to swallow the burning elixir in anticipation of its numbing effect.

After two more cups, the alcohol began to take hold. The troubled man's agitation became apparent when he heard some footsteps in the hall outside his door. He rose quickly and stepped gingerly over to the door to listen. He heard a man's whisper and his senses heightened. Cluverius clenched his fist as he strained to hear further. He knew it was unlikely that someone had witnessed his dastardly act and already tracked him, but his paranoia was increasing with each restless hour he spent in Richmond. He was relieved to hear a woman giggle as the door across the hall opened and quickly shut.

Cluverius sat on the bed and took another large gulp from his cup. He laid back and put his arm over his eyes. He wanted to sleep but could not control the urge to recount his actions and to plot an undetectable flight. After some restless moments Cluverius resigned himself to the idea that he would never be able to get the rest he needed until he was safely home. He rose to his feet and poured one more cup. He looked at his watch as he swished a mouthful of whiskey around his teeth. It was just past 2AM. He quickly packed his small suitcase with the few clothing articles he brought. Cluverius re-corked the whiskey bottle and packed it, as well. He placed the battered tin cup in alongside the bottle and latched the suitcase. With his coat and hat back on, he picked up the suitcase in one hand and Lillie's satchel in the other. He cautiously opened the door to the hall and crept lightly down the stairs. The young traveler laid the room key on the registration desk and left the hotel without further notice.

Although Cluverius walked briskly, he treaded lightly; fully cognizant of the echoes of his own footsteps as he headed anxiously south on 15th Street toward the river. 15th Street ended at the Kanawha Canal. Cluverius turned to his right and crossed one block over to 14th Street. There, he turned south once again a walked straight ahead toward Mayo's Bridge. Mayo's Bridge was the furthest downstream crossing of the James within Richmond's city limits. The bridge spanned Mayo's Island, a sliver of land which sat mid-channel at the eastern end of a small splintered archipelago. The current of the James River scattered as it forced its way through the shards of land and rock, producing a sieve-like effect; but melded back as one just below the bridge. Cluverius walked across to a point on the bridge beyond the island below and about two thirds of the way to the Manchester side of the river. In obscure solitude he cast Lillie's satchel over the bridge. The bag quickly disappeared from his view as it hurtled into the black rushing abyss. Cluverius was relieved when the faint sound of the satchel touching down in the current reached his ears. Slowly a resolution was coming into his view. The only thing that remained was to return home and embrace his alibi.

Chapter 23   ***American Cincinnatus***

Detective Jack Wren quietly entered the Commonwealth's Attorney office in Richmond. He approached the desk of the young clerk sitting in the front office. Wren placed his brief case down near his feet.

"Good morning, sir. I am Detective Jack Wren. I would like to speak with Mr. Charles Meredith."

"Good morning, sir. I believe he is in his office. I will tell him you are here." The young man rose to his feet and disappeared through the large paneled double doors to the right side of the office.

Wren walked over to the large windows on the left, opposite the double doors. He had come to present all of the evidence he had collected with regard to the demise of Lillie Madison to those charged with conducting any potential prosecution. He would also present a bill for his services subsequent to his dismissal from the Richmond Police. Wren placed his hands in his trouser pockets and looked out at the seat of power. To his left was a vacant lot where Richmond City Hall once stood. A beautiful structure with massive Doric columns and a symmetrical dome, it fell prey to an urban renewal panic that took hold of the City subsequent to the deadly 1870 collapse of an entire floor in the State Capitol Building. The Capitol, which stood just across the street from City Hall, had been granted priority and was completely refurbished, in all its Roman-inspired Jeffersonian white glory, during the renewal period. By the time it became apparent that, unlike the Capitol, the City Hall was indeed structurally sound, it was too late to halt its destruction. A new City Hall plan was well underway in 1885; but whether the new structure would match the majesty of the original was still in question. Just beyond the Capitol was a partial view of The Governor's Mansion. In the foreground of Wren's view was a statue of the Great Washington on horseback; with right arm and forefinger extended, more than fifty feet above the fray, he was still directing his countrymen toward their destiny.

On November 2, 1857, the *Waiborg* entered the large locks of the James River and the Kanawha Canal, dropped anchor, and moored in the Port of Richmond. Multiple tarps covered a massive crated treasure which had taken more than ten years to finally arrive at its destination. Captain D. F. Lund and one of his junior officers walked down the gang plank and were greeted by a young civil engineer.

"Captain Lund. Welcome to Richmond, sir. I am Charles Dimmock. I am an engineer and I am at your service."

The junior officer turned to his captain and relayed the message in Dutch. After a response to his subordinate, Captain Lund smiled. The young officer replied, "Uh, ya Mr.

Dimmock. Ve are glad to be here. Our passage has gone vell. Our large concern now is giving der cargo to you… um, take it off da boot. This is quite difficult."

"Yes, gentlemen. I am aware of such difficulties. With your help and patience, we shall be successful. I am told the sculptor has travelled with you. I would like to speak with him."

The young officer looked uneasily at Dimmock and then transmitted his request to the captain. The captain nodded to his man and said, "Vertel het hem."

"Um.. Mr. Dimmock. Ve have, um, uh, information. Der artist, Mr. Crawford? He has died before ve leave Amsterdam. He vas qvite ill."

Dimmock's eyes widened as he felt even more responsibility to complete the project successfully fall upon his shoulders. "Good Lord, that is unexpected. I believe he was a young man."

In 1834, at age twenty, Thomas Crawford left his home in New York for Rome to hone his skills as a sculptor. By the late 1840's, he had gained notoriety with several masterful works which combined Classical Antiquity with Renaissance Humanism. This, of course, was the perfect combination of styles to represent a burgeoning American democracy intellectually and physically founded by the sons of Virginia; the primary laboratory for the grand experiment to combine the power of conquest with the rights of the individual.

Crawford sculpted the main statue of Washington which was to sit atop the fifty-foot stone plinth awaiting it in Capitol Square. Inside that massive plinth was a single burial chamber. Although Washington had directed that his remains be laid to rest at his beloved Mt. Vernon, Richmond City officials had long-hoped that circumstances would somehow change and that Virginia's first son, indeed the Nation's first son, would someday come to rest in Richmond. This burial transfer was not to be; but the arrival of the impressive bronze would provide some consolation for a public that idolized the man. Crawford was also commissioned to complete six additional statues to surround the base of the memorial; permanently standing guard for Washington and the ideals of The Revolution. At the base would stand prominent Virginians Andrew Lewis, George Mason, Thomas Jefferson, Patrick Henry, Thomas Nelson, Jr., and John Marshall; each symbolizing a critical element in the revolutionary formula which begat a lasting republican solution.

Charles Dimmock and Captain Lund oversaw the precarious unloading of the eighteen-ton crate from the ship. Word had spread of the arrival throughout Richmond, attracting a crowd of hundreds of onlookers. Dimmock was surprised by the size and weight of the shipment. As the large dockside cranes slowly lowered the crate onto the flat wagon near the end of 23rd Street, Dimmock became more concerned. The sides of the crate overhung the sides of the cart by three feet on either side. It overhung the front and rear by nearly six feet on each end. A four-horse team awaited harnessing to the ten-wheeled wagon. After consulting with the Board of Commissioners the decision was made that a six-horse team was required.

Dozens of men, many sons and grandsons of Continental Army veterans, came forward and volunteered to pull the cargo themselves to the final destination approximately fifteen blocks away. The crowd became agitated with pride and excitement. As the vigor heightened in the crowd Dimmock stepped upon a platform near the dock.

Statue of Washington, Richmond Capitol (Library of Congress)

"Citizens of Richmond. I am Charles Dimmock, the engineer tasked with erecting the statue on the Capitol grounds. The Board of Commissioners and I are deeply thankful for your interest in completing this project. We understand your desire to deliver General Washington in place. And, we want to do that as soon as possible. But, we must do so with great care so as to not damage this important piece of art and of our heritage. We ask that you all remain patient while we make accommodations for a larger team of horses to pull the wagon."

"We can do it! You don't need horses!", came shouts from the crowd.

"Please gentlemen.", pleaded Dimmock as he raised his hands in the air. "The hour is growing late and darkness will prohibit any more progress today. We will begin again at 9 o'clock tomorrow morning."

The crowd was disappointed but peacefully dispersed. The next morning the horse team was in place and the hulking crate slowly started making its way up 23rd Street. The crowd assembled to witness the undertaking numbered over three hundred. It took nearly thirty minutes to move a mere block and one half. Workmen from Dimmock's staff removed several low-hanging branches crossing over the street as the horses trudged forward. The wagon took a slow wide turn left on to Main Street. The crowd numbers continued to grow as the horses struggled to move the behemoth. Four hours later, the cargo had reached the intersection of 17th and Main. The horses were exhausted, many frothing at the mouth with legs beginning to buckle. Dimmock was distraught. He ordered fresh horses be brought immediately. As his men began to unharness the horses the crowd began to roar. Men quickly discarded their coats and rushed toward the container. Dimmock tried to stop the crowd, but with "one patriotic impulse, the populace seized the ropes and began to draw the vehicle and its load up Main Street". (23.1) Over four hundred men joined in and the shipment began to move with surprising dispatch west on Main Street.

Less than one hour later they had covered more than nine blocks when, once again, progress came to a halt at 10th and Main Streets. There was just one more block before they were to make a final right turn on to 9th Street very near the statue's final destination. At the 10th Street intersection Main Street narrowed significantly. Larger trees further obstructed the pass as their roots encroached into the gutter. Progress stalled for ten minutes before several men appeared with axes, saws, and pry bars. Dimmock grasped his forehead in sheer terror as men scaled the sides of the giant crate and began pulling off the sides. This was an impromptu community effort like few had ever witnessed. Dimmock faithfully summoned the grace of God to see things through. Several trees were felled to cheers and quickly dragged by groups of inspired free men to the side. From Washington's heavenly perspective this much have looked like a Continental Army of ants bravely and relentlessly bringing their national treasure home. Forty-five minutes later the path was clear for the furious but mindful final push forward.

For the following two months Charles Dimmock and his team carefully constructed a derrick crane to lift the precious cargo into its ultimate position. Over two thousand watched as another seven hours was spent completing an effort worthy of the American Cincinnatus. The statue was set and immediately covered with a large black tarp. One month later, on Washington's 126th birthday, the statue was formally revealed to a throng of thousands and duly dedicated to Virginia's first hero. (23.2)

Detective Wren chuckled to himself as he recalled the old joke that Washington's pointed finger was actually directing us toward the State Penitentiary ten blocks to the Southwest; a self-deprecating interpretation by a citizenry that fully understood its inferiority to a man of such character and accomplishment. Wren's smile evaporated as he expanded and personalized the symbolism; mentally continuing in that same direction a few more blocks he came upon the Old Marshall Reservoir. The large paneled door re-opened.

"Detective Wren; Mr. Meredith will see you now."

Chapter 24   *The Proud Mrs. Tunstall*

Captain Charles H. Epps and Officer Logan S. Robbins of the Richmond Police Department followed John L. Oliver, Deputy Sheriff of King & Queen County, onto the front steps of Jane Tunstall's porch. They knocked gently on the door. A large colored woman came to the door.

"Yessum?", she said.

"Deputy Oliver spoke with discretion. "Hello. I am Deputy Oliver. Is Mr. Thomas Cluverius here?"

"No suh."

"How about Mrs. Tunstall? Is she here?"

"Yessum."

"May we speak with her?"

The woman looked guardedly at the three suited gentlemen. "Yessum, folla me, gents." She opened the door and guided the three men into the parlor.

The gentlemen stood, hats in hands, in the parlor and waited nearly five minutes for Mrs. Tunstall to emerge from the rear of the house and greet the unexpected visitors.

"Good day, gentlemen. Sorry for the delay. How may I help you?"

No sooner had the words crossed her lips than the colored woman reappeared in the front hall and looked anxiously into the parlor at Mrs. Tunstall.

"'Scuse me, gentlemen. Yes, Maybelle. What is it?"

"Ise gots to run out fo' awhile, Ms. Tunstall. I be back befo' suppa."

"Oh, very well. Go, Maybelle..." said the old woman with a bit of impatience as she waved off her servant.

"Yessum.", said Maybelle as she placed her hat on her head and walked quickly out the door.

Mrs. Tunstall visited a brief time with the men before offering them a cool drink. Captain Epps obliged, but the other two declined, stating that they preferred to indulge in a smoke, with Mrs. Tunstall's permission, on her front porch.

"Why, of course, gentlemen! You are my guests!", exclaimed the delighted old woman.

Captain Epps sat quietly in the large wing chair in Mrs. Tunstall's parlor. Officer Robbins and Deputy Oliver stood out on the front porch smoking cigars. Epps heard women whispering in the rear of the home. He strained to hear the conversation, which was intermittently sprinkled with light laughter. Within ten minutes Mrs. Tunstall returned with a tall glass of water and handed it to Captain Epps.

"I see you are admiring my husband's grandfather. Did you know him?", she said as she pointed to the oil portrait hanging above the fireplace.

"No ma'am. I did not have the honor.", said Epps graciously. He understood that of course such a meeting was an impossibility, seeing how Mrs. Tunstall was nearing seventy years of age herself and he was just past thirty.

"Oh, Mr. Epps, he was a wonderful man! He was a credit to this county. Never was there a man who more perfectly combined honesty, integrity, and intellect. My nephew, Tommie, is very much the same."

"Er, yes ma'am, Mrs. Tunstall.", agreed Epps, being far too polite to argue with a lady.

Epps looked up at the portrait of the handsome young Zachariah Shackleford. He noted the man's confident expression, somewhat cold, yet very engaged. "That's an impressive portrait, Mrs. Tunstall."

"Yes, it is, Mr. Epps.", as she swelled with pride. "It is a Charles Willson Peale, you understand."

"Oh, very good, ma'am.", Epps had no idea of whom she spoke, but he was bright enough to understand that he should. "He is one I admire!".

"Ah, yes, Mr. Epps, Peale was tremendously talented, but always busy. He studied under Benjamin West, you realize." The energized old art lover gazed up toward the painting. "You can see that the face is very detailed and well composed, while the hands are rather flat and crudely formed. That is because Mr. Peale always traveled with at least one apprentice. He, the Master, would paint the face and neck, then leave an apprentice to complete the body, hands, and background." She moved her hand through the air placing wistful brushstrokes on an invisible canvas.

"I did not know that. That, is very interesting, Mrs. Tunstall." Epps looked toward the old widow and saw the youthful delight in her eyes.

The old lady became still and placed her fingers on her chin, pensively beholding, as she had hundreds of times before, the classic artwork. "I never tire of looking at this portrait, Mr. Epps. I suppose that is what separates a masterpiece from the others."

"Quite right, Mrs. Tunstall. Quite right." Epps was still wondering who Mrs. Tunstall had been talking to in the other room. "Is anyone else here, Mrs. Tunstall?"

"Well, er, well…", she looked from one side of the room to the other. "Well, Maybelle left, right?"

"Yes, ma'am, she did."

"Well, then there's no one else."

"No other women here?", the Captain asked again.

Mrs. Tunstall shook her head distinctly, "No, sir."

Epps was a bit disturbed by the old woman's unusual behavior, but he was also quite intrigued and, to some degree, sympathetic.

At that moment a tall man burst through the front door and rushed into the parlor.

"Aunt Jane! What is happening here? Where is Tommie?", he demanded breathlessly.

"Willie! What are you doing here?"

"Maybelle came and got me. Who are these men?"

"Why… This nice gentleman is Mr. Epps."

"Why is he here, Aunt Jane?", said Willie.

Aunt Jane paused and thought to herself. She glanced down, then back up at Willie. "Well, I don't know? Willie, dear boy; you need to shave your face."

Willie completely ignored his aunt's recommendation. "Alright, then I'll ask you, sir." Willie stepped close to Epps and adamantly asked, "Why are you here?"

Epps took half a step back from the intrusive man. "Sir, I am Captain Epps of the Richmond Police Department. These men are Officer Robbins of the Richmond P.D. and Deputy Oliver of your county Sheriff's Department. We have come to question Mr. Thomas J. Cluverius in connection with the death of a young woman."

"Oh, that's it, Willie! They wanted to talk with Tommie so I just invited them to stay until he got home.", said the accommodating old woman.

Willie looked with confused disgust at his aunt. "What's this about? What woman?"

"The woman has been identified as Fannie Lillian Madison. She was found drowned in a reservoir in Richmond. Some of her family members have positively identified her. We need to speak with Mr. Cluverius about her. We think he may be able to answer some questions for us."

Willie Cluverius' combative posture quickly retreated as the words became clear.

"Lillie's dead?", he asked.

"Yes, sir."

"No! It's not possible!"

"I'm afraid so. And what is your name, sir."

"Willie… William Cluverius", the distraught man rubbed his brow and raked his hand across the top of his head. "I am his brother."

"Were you aware that Miss Madison was in Richmond this week past?"

"No."

"Were you aware your brother was in Richmond at the same time?"

"No… No, you can't believe he had any involvement with this! Not Tommie! He loved Lillie! Oh, Aunt Jane!" Willie Cluverius collapsed into the chair under the front window of the parlor and buried his head in his hands.

Epps stepped back in to control of the conversation. "When will your brother be home?"

"I don't know… Maybe in an hour or two. He had a trial in King William today."

"A trial?", asked Epps.

"Yes, he practices law."

"I see.", said Epps. "We would like to wait until his return and interview him; if that is acceptable to you and your aunt."

Willie was suspicious and fearful, but deferential. "Yes, that will be fine." He looked at Aunt Jane for reassurance. She nodded her head slightly and looked Willie in the eye.

"Yes, we will all wait here calmly for Tommie.", she said as she reached out and squeezed Willie's hand.

Few words were exchanged while the next hour passed. Maybelle had returned and was out in the kitchen preparing an evening meal. Aunt Jane, Willie, and the three law men sat quietly but with great apprehension awaiting the arrival of Thomas J. Cluverius.

Chapter 25   *Under Arrest*

It struck T.J. Cluverius as odd that Aunt Jane was not on the front porch to greet him that evening. She generally enjoyed watching the sunset, particularly on warm days. "Aunt Jane?", Cluverius called out as he opened the parlor double doors. "Aunt Jane?", he said again as he pushed through the doors and found Aunt Jane, his brother Willie, and three other men seated in the parlor. He sensed the seriousness in the room as his Aunt looked at him in regretful despair. "Aunt Jane, Willie... What is the matter?"

The three men stood as one. The man on the right looked familiar to Cluverius. He stepped forward and said, "Mr. Cluverius... I am Deputy Sheriff Oliver. These men are Captain Epps and Officer Robbins of the Richmond Police."

Captain Epps leaned forward. "Mr. Cluverius... We are placing you under arrest for murder."

Cluverius stood quiet for a moment. He looked down at his feet, then coolly lifted his head. "Perhaps you gentlemen could stay for supper?"

Everyone was stunned at the suspect's odd reaction, but Epps, sensing the cunning of the suspect and fully aware of the suspect's legal training, set himself upon the task of studying Thomas Cluverius' every move, every word; seeking to detect any evidence of guilt, either implied or overt.

"Well, yes.", said Epps, "I am sure we are all in need of a meal. But afterwards, we must request that you, Mr. Cluverius, accompany us back to Richmond."

"Yes, gentlemen. Let us go into the dining room. Aunt Jane, is Maybelle ready to serve?"

"I will go find out, dear. You and Willie escort these gentlemen into the dining room.", said the old woman.

The men seated themselves around the large dining table in the room across the front hall from the parlor. Thomas Cluverius boldly moved to the head of the table. Willie sat to his right. "Aunt Jane will sit here.", he said pointing to the seat on his right. "Gentlemen, please sit.", he graciously requested, waving his extended arm with palm turned upward once across the table top in the direction opposite his seat.

After the disturbance of five chairs moving upward, backward, and to the sides had subsided, an awkward silence endured until T.J. Cluverius spoke.

"What evidence do you have against me?", Cluverius bluntly asked Officer Robbins.

"I cannot say, sir. We are authorized only to place you under arrest and bring you to Richmond."

"I should like to know, sir…" said T.J. Cluverius, "so that I may know what line of defense to prepare."

"Mr. Cluverius…", said Epps, "this is not the appropriate time to address such questions. As a lawyer you know that it is well for us not to say anything of these matters until we come upon the witness stand. We can read you the warrant."

"That would be fine, Captain Epps."

"Robbins, please read the warrant.", ordered Epps

"Yes, sir." Robbins reached into the breast pocket of his suit jacket and pulled out a single folded piece of paper. He stood and walked over toward the window to make use of the last few minutes of remaining daylight. Maybelle entered the room from the opposite end with a large tray full of food. She sat the tray on a nearby buffet table and rushed to light the candles on the table top. Mrs. Tunstall followed her in and set place settings for the three extra guests.

Robbins cleared his throat.

By order of the Honorable David C. Richardson, Police Chief Justice of the City of Richmond, Virginia, a warrant for the arrest of Thomas Judson Cluverius, of King & Queen County, Virginia is hereby issued in connection with the murder of Fannie Lillian Madison, of King & Queen County, Virginia. This warrant authorizes all Commonwealth and/or local law enforcement authorities to act in the apprehension, arrest, and confinement of said individual and to deliver said individual to the City Jail of Richmond with dispatch, where said individual shall be confined until lawful arraignment.

"I was there, but I did not see her while I was in Richmond", the suspect clearly stated. "It will be easy enough to prove where I was. Every place I went to I met somebody that knew me."

Willie Cluverius' concerned expression was well understood by his younger brother. Tommie grabbed his older brother by the arm just above the elbow. "Willie; everything will be alright.", he said softly. "I am going to need your help and support, but I will get through this."

Willie closed his lips tightly and nodded, gathering his emotions and letting his younger brother lead.

"Gentlemen.", Thomas J. Cluverius announced, "There is no reason why such matters should spoil a very good meal." He smiled in the direction of Maybelle, who stood catatonically near the buffet table. "Let us eat, and then afterwards, I shall collect my things and go with you. But first, let us offer thanks to our Lord." Cluverius lowered his head, keeping a firm clutch on the arm of his brother. He reached out his opposite hand and gripped Aunt Jane's hand as it lay flat on the tablecloth. Captain Epps noted four or five small marks on the back of Cluverius' hand as it rested atop his aunt's. They were raised and pink, as if the scabs had fallen or been pulled away, but the tender skin beneath had yet to fully heal. "Dear Lord and Provider.", Cluverius began. "We offer our gratitude for the fine food which sustains our bodies. Without this, we would be unable to seek the food that nourishes our souls and brings us closer to your blessings. We offer our prayers for all of our loved ones, most particularly at this time, for dear cousin Lillie, whom we have just learned has entered your sacred kingdom." Tommie raised his head and opened one eye. Directly across he beheld Captain Epps sitting judgmentally back in his chair with arms crossed, staring intently back at him. Cluverius slowly closed the eye, lowered his head, and concluded his offering. "Please, dear Lord, keep Lillie near your side and grant all of us guidance in our eternal search for truth. Thy will be done. Amen."

"Very inspiring, Mr. Cluverius.", said Captain Epps.

"Tommie often speaks at church, Captain Epps. He is very faithful to the Almighty's teachings.", interjected Aunt Jane.

"Yes, ma'am.", simply replied Epps, seeking not to antagonize his gracious elderly hostess by exposing his cynicism.

Epps looked down at his plate and found a succulent Cornish game hen, fresh green beans in butter, and crispy Yorkshire pudding. Maybelle placed a large pitcher of water on the table alongside a bowl full of steamy biscuits.

"This meal is tremendous, Mrs. Tunstall.", said Captain Epps.

"The credit belongs solely with Maybelle, Captain. She is a blessing on this household."

Maybelle dipped her head in understated gratitude. "Thankya', Ms. Tunstall. Ise goin' back to da kitchun, now. If anythin' else is requied, jes' lemme' hear it."

"Very well, Maybelle; thank you.", said Mrs. Tunstall. Maybelle left the group to enjoy their supper.

Thomas J. Cluverius ate very quickly. He devoured every morsel on his plate within minutes and swallowed three glasses of water before anyone else had finished one. He stood abruptly and tugged with both hands on the ends of his suit vest. Officer Robbins and Captain Epps looked at one another as they each noted the short gold chain dangling from the watch chain that draped the suspect's vest. There was nothing attached to the end of the short chain and the final link appeared slightly sprung.

"Well, if you gentlemen will excuse me for a few moments, I will go to my room and collect a bag." Cluverius calmly walked into the front hall and up the staircase. After a few moments, Epps became uneasy and told Officer Robbins to follow the suspect upstairs. Robbins nodded and walked directly up the staircase. There were four doorways leading from the upstairs center hallway. Three were open, but the one in the back, left corner of the hall was fully shut. Robbins crept quietly to the door and leaned his head close to listen. He felt the vibration of pacing footsteps emanating from the floor system that ran under the door and into the hall. Suddenly the door opened and Robbins was nose to nose with Thomas J. Cluverius.

"Officer Robbins…were you looking for me?", taunted the suspect.

"Yes, Mr. Cluverius. The hour is getting late and the Captain asked me to inform you that we all must leave."

"Yes, Officer. I have gathered a few items and have a few others to gather downstairs. Then, I shall be ready.", Cluverius said with confidence.

The two men descended the stairway. Thomas Cluverius walked immediately into the parlor. He reached into a small desk in the corner of and removed five dollars from a small metal cash box. He then turned toward a bookcase against the wall. He searched the shelf second from the top. He rustled through some note booklets until he found one with some blank pages. The suspect tore the pages from the book and picked up a pencil. He quickly stuffed all of the items into his satchel. Officer Robbins had stopped alongside Captain Epps and Deputy Oliver as they gathered in the front hall and thanked Mrs. Tunstall for her hospitality. Willie walked past them into the parlor and found Tommie crouching near the wall opposite his desk warming his hands over a heating grate. Willie crouched beside him. "Say something, Willie.", Tommie whispered. Willie looked at him quizzically. "Say something, and say it loud enough for them to hear." Tommie began feverishly loosening his watch-key chain from his watch guard chain.

"Tommie, Aunt Jane and I will look after things here. We will arrange all your affairs, as necessary. Is there anything you would like me to…", Willie truncated his question as he heard footsteps behind him.

"It is time to leave, Mr. Cluverius.", said Officer Robbins.

"Yes, I understand.", said Tommie as he rose to his feet with the watch-key chain hidden in his closed left fist. Tommie looked at Robbins and Robbins at him. "I will need to get my coat."

Thomas Cluverius reached for his gray overcoat and slouch hat hanging on a coat stand in the hallway. Before placing the slouch hat on his head, he hesitated and turned back toward the coat stand. He switched the worn slouch hat for his brother's black Derby. "I'll wear this one, the other has a hole in it." The suspect picked up his small bag and strode toward Aunt Jane's front door. The old woman started to tear as he bravely passed. He stopped and kissed her on the cheek. "I will be home soon, Aunt Jane. Do not worry." He clasped her hand in his and then quickly let go. Willie was already out on the front porch when Tommie crossed the threshold into the evening darkness. Tommie stopped and turned to his brother. He wrapped both arms around Willie and as he buried his chin in Willie's shoulder, he whispered softly into Willie's ear. "Look in my hat. Hide what's in there." Tommie stepped back, putting a firm reassuring grip on each of Willie's shoulders.

"Tommie, I will be in Richmond to see you tomorrow. This is all a mistake, brother. I won't leave you."

"Alright, Willie. Very well. Go to Pollard and Evans. They will know what to do. Take care of Aunt Jane; I'm afraid she will need you more than I in the coming days."

Willie nodded his head, then quickly embraced his brother once more. Tommie and his three escorts descended the front stoop into the yard. They walked about twenty yards from the house to the edge of the drive way before pausing. Deputy Oliver disappeared behind the house into the rear yard. Captain Epps turned to Officer Robbins. "Restrain the prisoner, Robbins.",

"Yes, Captain."

Cluverius looked with irritation at his captors as Robbins removed the heavy metal shackles from his coat and placed them securely around the suspect's wrists. "This is not necessary, Captain Epps.", protested Cluverius. "I am going with you under my own volition."

"I understand, Mr. Cluverius;", explained Epps, "But this is the procedure and I will not deviate from it; even in the presence of a cooperative prisoner like yourself."

"Very well, Captain. Kindly stand in front of me so my aunt does not bear witness to this indignity.", said Cluverius as he invisibly seethed at the thought of being treated as a common prisoner.

Epps signaled to Robbins and the officer deftly shifted his position, obstructing Aunt Jane's view of the prisoner. Within a few moments, Deputy Oliver guided the small horse-drawn wagon around the home and pulled up alongside the three men. He held the reigns firmly while Epps and Robbins each took one of Cluverius' arms and supported him as he climbed into the wagon. The two law men climbed aboard and seated themselves one beside the prisoner and the other directly across. With one snap of the reigns, the horse started toward the road, which lay about forty more yards down the drive way.

"Did you see Miss Madison when you were in Richmond?", Epps asked directly.

"I no more saw Miss Madison than Deputy Oliver did.", Cluverius snapped.

The carriage turned right at the trees that lined the dirt road and rolled toward King & Queen County Jail. (25.1)

Chapter 26   ***The Prisoner Escapes***

    Thomas J. Cluverius woke early his first morning in custody. It had been a restless and uncomfortable evening in the King & Queen County Jail. He slid his tongue across his front teeth trying in vain to spread moisture through his dry stale mouth. The young man stood and looked through the dim dawning light at the bars of his cell. There were three cells in the block. In the cell to his right slept Captain Epps. To his left, snoring loudly, was Officer Robbins. Cluverius pressed his face against the bars and strained to peek down the hallway to the right toward the sheriff's office. The door to the office was half open and Cluverius could see a pair of socked feet hanging over the end of a cot in the office. He pushed firmly on the door to his cell and to his utter surprise, the door popped open and glided away from him. He quickly grabbed hold of both the cold iron bars of the door and his inner jubilation before either resulted in a disturbance capable of awakening the three lawmen.

    The thin knotty pine boards squeaked only slightly as the barefooted Cluverius traversed the floor. Calmly, he closed each of the adjoining cell doors. A large golden key appeared before him on the opposite wall. He lifted it gingerly from the hook and, with the steadiness of surgeon, the resourceful young Cluverius inserted the key into each of the well-greased locks and turned them, effortlessly throwing the heavy bolt on each. He tip-toed toward the office. Once inside the office he quietly closed the door. A large nightstick was leaning against the deputy's desk. He gripped the club and turned toward Deputy Oliver, who soundly slept on his back with his arms stretched out. The enterprising prisoner delivered two sharp blows to Oliver's head, rendering the deputy helpless. Cluverius' mind raced quickly as his plan fell into place. On the floor beside the cot were a pair of shackles connected by a long, forged metal chain. Cluverius quickly snapped one cuff around Oliver's wrist and then fed the other underneath the cot. The chain was of perfect length to allow Cluverius just enough room to secure the opposite cuff on Oliver's other wrist, binding the comatose deputy tightly to his bed. Cluverius paused briefly while he admired his own genius.

    Cluverius remembered his clothes. He carefully opened the office door. Epps and Robbins remained in undisturbed slumber. Cluverius quickly re-entered his cell, collected his boots, hat, and coat. Once again, he left the cell with barely a sound and scurried down the hall, through the office, and out of the jail. He put on his boots and scampered over to the hitching post near the roadside. The only horse there was a wonderful creature - a large black thoroughbred of racing quality. Cluverius' luck was running high as he looked down at the ground and spotted a red wool horse blanket and a brightly polished saddle. Within seconds Cluverius saddled the horse and leapt confidently aboard clutching the reigns and assuming full control. The great animal burst with breathtaking ease from the scene. As horse and rider bolted down the road, Cluverius heard a waning call from the jail.

    "Mr. Cluverius... Mr. Cluverius!"

    Cluverius smiled wryly as he made his brash escape. He closed his eyes tightly as the morning air freshened his face. He opened them again and the horse suddenly pulled to a stop. Cluverius dismounted and looked with puzzlement back toward the jail.

"Mr. Cluverius... Mr. Cluverius...", the man's voice hauntingly drew near. He looked back toward the horse. The horse was gone, but there stood Lillie Madison in a black dress and red wool shawl. There was a large contusion above her right eye and her expression carried the weight of confused betrayal. She reached out her trembling hand and pointed at Cluverius as if identifying him for someone. Her mouth spoke, but he could not hear. The phantom girl's expression changed to enraged damnation, as her brows pinched down toward her nose. With one hand on her swollen stomach, she spoke again, this time slower than before. Cluverius still could not hear her, but he read her lips and her chilling message was clear. "Murderer... Murderer..."

"Mr. Cluverius...", he heard the man's voice again. "Mr. Cluverius!"

"Wake up, Mr. Cluverius!", insisted Epps. The prisoner opened his eyes and looked upon his captor outside the iron bars of his cell. "We need to start for Richmond, Mr. Cluverius. Please get dressed while I get you some water and a biscuit."

Cluverius was horrified but stiffly maintained his composure. He sat up slowly and buried his face in his hands. The distraught prisoner rubbed his temples in a tight circular motion as he focused his thoughts. He exhaled deeply and mumbled to himself. As if he had thrown a switch, the prisoner's demeanor changed instantly. His expression became confident, erudite in its assuredness. He stood and promptly tucked in his shirt. He sat once again on the edge of the cot and put on his boots. He picked up his vest which hung over the back of the single wood chair in the cell and began to whistle as he slung it around his back and buttoned it in front of him. Cluverius formed a comb with his right hand and ran it straight back across the top of his head, clearing a few clumps from his eyes. (26.1)

Epps and Robbins appeared outside his cell. "Here's a biscuit and water, Mr. Cluverius.", said Officer Robbins. Robbins handed him a small tin cup of water and the single biscuit through the bars.

"After you eat it, we will be leaving." Epps began to turn back toward the office then stopped suddenly. He tapped Robbins in the midsection with his knuckle as he addressed the prisoner. "Where is that piece of chain, Mr. Cluverius?"

"What chain?", Cluverius quickly responded.

"The small piece that hung from your watch chain, sir.", said Epps

"There was none there." declared Cluverius.

Captain Epps pursed his lips and tilted his head with doubt. "Now, Mr. Cluverius, don't tell me that! Officer Robbins and I both saw you wearing a gold watch chain yesterday evening with another small piece of chain hanging from it. Where is that piece? I will go back and search your aunt's house, if necessary. If Robbins and I have to tear her house apart, we will do so. Where is it, Mr. Cluverius?" The Captain glared at Cluverius.

The prisoner bit halfway through the stale biscuit to buy himself more time to think. He chewed and swallowed steadily, enjoying the impatient suspicion of his captors. He then gulped some water before coolly answering.

"I left it for my brother."

"When?", said Epps

"Last night." answered Cluverius.

"I am certain I saw you wearing it last night on our way here, Mr. Cluverius." Epps purposely made the erroneous statement hoping to elicit a similar inaccuracy from the captive.

"You most certainly did not, Captain." said Cluverius sharply. "Why? Do you want it?"

"Yes", said Epps flatly.

"There is no need to go back and disturb my Aunt… I will get it for you."

"Very well, Mr. Cluverius. If it is not in my possession within two days, I will do whatever necessary to find it." The words only posed a threat, Epps piercing eyes confirmed it.

"I said, I will get it for you!" snarled Cluverius. (26.2)

Chapter 27   *You Will Not Forsake Me*

Willie Cluverius was escorted to the cell in the Richmond City Jail where Tommie was being held. The cell was dark and damp. The bare brick walls did little to amplify the small amount of sunlight that came through the high iron-barred window on the side wall. Tommie stood as the heavy cell door swung open and his devoted brother rushed in. Willie was overcome with emotion at the sight of his brother. He clutched Tommie tightly.

"My God, Tommie! I'm lost! What shall we do?"

"Shh… Willie", Tommie whispered. "It will be alright. I will not spend the rest of my life in this cell and I am relying on you to help me. You must get control of yourself and your actions. We will defeat this."

Willie was awestruck by his brother's courage. He always knew Tommie was strong-willed and graceful under pressure, but this was more than he could have imagined.

"Sit; sit down, Willie. We need to talk… discreetly…", Tommie lowered his voice even more. Willie sat on the cot's edge and Tommie pulled a worn wooden chair from the corner. "Did you speak with Pollard?"

"Yes, Tommie. He'll be here tomorrow morning, first thing."

"Good. I am going to need him then."

"What is happening tomorrow?", asked Willie.

"They'll take me to court and they will read the charges against me.", said Tommie solemnly.

"They're wrong, Tommie!", Willie's voice began to rise.

"I know… I know, Willie. You must stay quiet. Did you get the chain out of my hat like I asked?"

"Yes, Tommie. I have it right here.", Willie reached into his pocket.

"No… No Willie! Don't get it out now! Get rid of it.", demanded Tommie.

"What?", said a confused Willie, "It's just a little chain. Why?"

Tommie stood and crouched in front of his brother. He grabbed both shoulders and looked directly into his eyes. "Willie… You must listen. You and I both know I had no involvement with Lillie's death. But, to convince everyone else, I may need to ask you to do some things for me. I don't know what they may be nor when it will be necessary, but when I do, you have to promise me that you will follow my instructions without hesitation. My life may depend upon this… You will not forsake me, will you?"

"Tommie… Of course not. I will do whatever you ask.", said Willie.

"Very well. First, destroy that chain; but bring me another one."

"What?"

"Willie. I thought you understood…"

"I'm sorry, Tommie."

"Find another chain that is similar but clearly different. Then, bring it to me; No! Bring it to Pollard; he will know how best to deliver it to the police. But, under no circumstances are you to let the chain you have here fall into the police's hands. I need this done by tomorrow. Do you understand?"

"Yes, brother."

"Thank you, Willie. Now go. I will see you tomorrow."

Willie stood and moved toward the cell door. He paused and turned back toward his brother. "You know, Tommie… There's a large crowd out there waiting to see you. The streets of this town are flooded with talk of Thomas Cluverius."

"Is that right?" asked Tommie with curiosity bordering on pride, "I never would have thought that."

Chapter 28   Arraignment

Dr. James Beale picked up a copy of the *Richmond Dispatch* from a newsstand as he walked down Bank Street past Capitol Square. He paused to read the top story:

Richmond Dispatch

March 20, 1885

Richmond Police took a drastic turn in their investigation into the mysterious death of Lillian Madison of King and Queen County. Miss Madison's body was found in the Old Reservoir on the morning of March 14. Initially, the police investigated it as a suicide, but recent evidence of foul play has come to light which implicates Thomas J. Cluverius, also of King and Queen County.

Captain Charles Epps of the Richmond Police, who has replaced Detective Jack Wren in the investigation, placed Cluverius under arrest at the home of his aunt the evening of March 18. The prisoner was transported to the Richmond City Jail where he awaits due process. Although Cluverius has acknowledged that he was in Richmond at the time of the incident, he denies any involvement with the crime. He says he was in Richmond for purposes of business and had no knowledge of Miss Madison's whereabouts.

A critical piece of evidence is a gold watch key found near the body at the Old Reservoir which investigators believe belongs to Cluverius. It is said that he is known to wear a watch chain with a small key hanging from it. The arresting officers confirm that they saw Cluverius wearing the watch chain at the time of his arrest. There was a smaller piece of chain dangling from the watch chain but no key at the end. By the time they reached Richmond, Cluverius no longer possessed the chain. He claimed he left it at his aunt's home.

There has been much speculation upon the motive of the suspect. A trunk containing Miss Madison's personal belongings has been shipped from Bath County, where she was working as a schoolteacher for the last six months, and is now in the possession of the Richmond Police. It is said to contain some evidence of a very personal nature which would indicate a strange and intimate relationship between the deceased and the murder suspect. Miss Madison was approximately eight months pregnant at the time of her death.

It has been said that Cluverius has visited Richmond on many occasions over the last several months. It is believed that Miss Madison had come to the City on other occasions, as well. One clerk at the Exchange Hotel claimed to have seen Cluverius in January. The clerk says the man he saw had a light mustache and light hair. He also said Cluverius was wearing a light-colored overcoat and a black slouch hat. Cluverius denies ever seeing the clerk and says he was not in Richmond at that time. (28.1)

Fifteen minutes later, Dr. Beale entered the cell block at the Richmond City Jail unannounced. It was 7:45 AM and the prisoner in cell number four still slept. Officer Sweeney opened the cell door and Dr. Beale walked directly in and sat his medical case on the chair beside the drowsy inmate.

"Mr. Cluverius; I am Dr. Beale. I am here to perform a physical examination."

The young prisoner slowly cracked open his eyes. He was in no mood for cooperation; he rarely was during his first waking moments. Beale stepped back and crossed his arms, waiting for the prisoner to get up. After a few moments, Beale's patience was thinning.

"Mr. Cluverius; I have other duties to perform this morning. I prefer not to get too far behind schedule."

Cluverius was surprised at the forcefulness in the doctor's voice. Beale was not much older than he and his patronizing tone was irksome.

"Remove your shirt, sir.", ordered the doctor. Cluverius exhaled loudly through his nostrils in bullish protest, but then began to unbutton his shirt.

"I am sorry this is such an inconvenience for you, Mr. Cluverius; but such is the life of a criminal."

"Doctor, I resent that inference. My innocence will be proven.", declared Cluverius.

"Yes, Mr. Cluverius; I am certain you will bring forth a formidable defense."

Though tempted to retaliate, Cluverius controlled his impetuous instincts. "Just perform the examination, doctor. That is your charge. There is little use to be found by indulging your unprofessional comments."

The doctor smiled, but he wasn't happy. Dr. Beale had been performing routine physical examinations on City prisoners for nearly six months. It was a grudging economic necessity for the struggling young doctor. He hoped to be in a position to stop performing this duty within the next three months as he found most of the in-mates to be unsavory characters. It was not a physical aversion he held for the prisoners, but a moral one. From what he had learned about the alleged nefarious deeds of Mr. Cluverius, he could barely contain his contempt.

Dr. Beale performed a cursory examination of Cluverius, noting his heart rate was slow and his body temperature normal. He asked the seated prisoner to extend his hands. Dr. Beale saw five small marks on the back of his right hand. The left hand quivered slightly. The doctor firmly grabbed hold of Cluverius' hands and told him to squeeze. Cluverius clamped down, exerting slightly more strength with his right hand but in a force consistent with a man of his age and size.

"Let go.", said the doctor curtly. "Where did you get those marks on your hand?"

"Oh... I scraped it on a fence a few days ago."

Beale pulled the hand closer to his eyes, then nodded. The doctor reached into his case and pulled out a tongue depressor. "Open.", said Beale flatly. "Turn toward the window." Dr. Beale looked down Cluverius' throat. Everything was normal. Beale then inspected the prisoner's scalp for fleas or lice. Finding the prisoner clean of bodily pestilence, the doctor packed his stethoscope and the used tongue depressor in his bag. He turned without further comment toward the cell door and beckoned the guard. (28.2)

Cluverius sat quietly on his cot until 8:30 AM, when his morning meal was brought to him. The meal consisted of a single piece of bread, a small bowl of corn chowder, and a cup of water. The chowder was cold and coagulated, but the prisoner was famished. Within thirty seconds he had devoured the entire ration.

The young suspect stood and belched as he waited. Oddly, the after taste was more pleasing than the initial one. To and fro, he paced across the nine-foot cell. Occasionally he stopped and listened near the window. The morning birds and insects, combined with the muted sounds of gathering human voices was curious to him. At 9:35am Henry R. Pollard appeared at his cell.

"Thomas.", he said softly. Cluverius' head spun quickly toward the cell door.

"Henry! What a relief!" Cluverius smiled for the first time since his incarceration.

Officer Sweeney opened the cell and let Pollard in. The two shook hands. Pollard removed his overcoat, folded it once, and laid it over the back of the wood chair. "Thomas, what has happened? Willie told me you had been arrested for the murder of the Madison girl. He said you are to appear before the Police Chief this morning. I am here to accompany you."

"Yes, it is true, Henry. They think I did it. They claim I killed my own cousin. You saw me that morning. You will help me prove innocence."

Pollard could sense the seriousness in Cluverius' voice, but was puzzled by the man's calmness. His client and friend looked tired, his complexion ashen; yet he seemed unusually confident and resolute for a man facing such a burden.

"Thomas, you understand as well as anyone else that we need to construct an alibi. You need to show where you were that day, who you saw, what you did."

"Yes, Henry... I know. I know."

"Thomas, there are attorneys with far more experience in this area than myself. My first advice is that we contact someone to lead your defense. I am glad to participate, but I don't think I'm fully equipped to take the lead on something of this nature."

"I appreciate your candor, Henry. Whom do you suggest?"

"I believe Bev Crump may be best suited.", said Pollard.

"Absolutely, Henry. I trust your judgment. Of course, Crump's reputation is exceptional."

"Yes, but with Crump, you must understand that it is Crump, and Crump alone, who will make the decisions. He will demand full control of your defense, Thomas."

"Very well. Whatever is necessary." said Cluverius by rote affirmation.

Pollard nodded but was hardly reassured. He did not feel like he had gotten through to his colleague. He knew Cluverius possessed an ego typical of young lawyers and lawyers make most difficult clients. Pollard glanced down at his watch. "We're to be over in the police court in twenty minutes, Thomas."

Thomas J. Cluverius and his attorney, H.R. Pollard emerged from side entrance the City Jail and quickly crossed the street toward Pollard's carriage. A crowd of more than fifty had formed in front of the jail that morning, all seeking to get a look at such a man as could coldly ravage and kill a young innocent woman. A young man saw the pair moving quickly toward the carriage. "There he is! It's Cluverius!", the man shouted as he pointed one half block down the street. Like a wave the crowd turned and flooded down the street. Cluverius' hands were shackled in front of him. Following closely behind was a single police officer, armed with nothing more than a club. Pollard and the police escort rushed Cluverius up into the carriage before climbing aboard themselves and securing the carriage door just before the first hungry hands of the crowd befell the carriage. The driver sat motionless as the crowd surrounded the carriage. "Did you kill her? Are you innocent? Were you lovers?" The questions were persistent, frank, and to some degree, rather offensive. The speculation in the newspapers had lit an uncontrollable voyeuristic fire in the hearts and minds of the Richmond citizenry. The ghastly deed was shocking and difficult to believe, but with each emerging tawdry detail and scandalous rumor, the public's ravenous addiction for information exponentially heightened and decorum was proportionately cast aside. "Be gone! Away from the carriage!", Pollard scolded and waved them away.

The single horse tethered to the carriage was becoming a bit uneasy with the pressing crowd. The driver was unable to direct the old mare with enough precision to break through the howling citizenry. The portly little man tried to descend from the driver's seat, but the crowd was too dense and he feared for his safety. A mounted officer appeared and broke through the crowd. The officer made his way alongside the rocking carriage and reached down and grabbed the bit of the nervous mare. He pulled her forward, forcing a part in the ever-growing throng of fanatical observers. Free of the crushing thrill-seekers, the mounted policeman let go of the bit. The driver snapped the reigns and the horse responded with a quick jolt, leaving behind a gang even hungrier than before.

Cluverius' senses were aroused by the attention. To most, this form of celebrity would have been unflattering and unwanted; but, within Cluverius, it engendered a sense of excitement and power that was strangely intoxicating. He remained silently aloof, but in his heart, he was relishing the scene without the slightest degree of shame nor embarrassment.

"What is wrong with those people? Have they no better way to spend their time?", asked Pollard rhetorically.

"It's alright, Henry. They don't bother me. Don't allow them to bother you.", said Cluverius.

Pollard turned to see the crowd pursuing the carriage. He reached up and knocked on the carriage ceiling. "Driver, quicken the pace!", he ordered.

A muffled "Yes, sir." was heard followed by a quick "Heyaa" and a snap of the reigns. The carriage sped up and within a few seconds the driver pulled up to a complete stop at the Richmond Police Station.

T.J. Cluverius and H.R. Pollard exited the carriage quickly and bolted for the door of the station. A young man was standing at the top of the steps; "Mr. Cluverius! Tommie!", he called.

"Bagby!", Cluverius called back as he went to the man and shook his hand.

"I saw you at the Mozart Hall on the 13th, Tommie. I was there, too."

"Was it the evening or the night performance when you saw me?", Cluverius asked.

Bagby looked at Cluverius with some confusion, "Why, Tommie; it was the evening performance."

"That is good." Cluverius turned to Pollard. "Henry Pollard; meet Thomas Bagby. Please speak with him about this." Pollard and Bagby shook hands. (28.3)

A crowd was beginning to form near the street in front of the station. "Cluverius! There he is!" cries began.

"We will speak, Mr. Bagby. We will speak.", Pollard promised as he handed Bagby a business card and simultaneously nudged his client forward and through the doorway.

Chief Richardson sat in the center of a large table on the third floor of the Police Station. To his right was a young police clerk charged with keeping the volumes of paper work and files associated with these hearings in order for Chief Richardson. To the left of the Chief sat Captain Epps. Behind the table against the wall stood the dark imposing figure of Officer Grimes. Cluverius, his attorney, and their police escort walked brazenly into the room and sat at a small table opposite Chief Richardson. About thirty people, mostly newspaper men, pushed forward into the intimate surroundings of the Police Court, taking the few seats which lined the perimeter of the room. When the seats were filled, the remainder stood, all transfixed upon the chilling drama unfolding before them.

After a brief hesitation, Chief Richardson pounded a gavel on the table once and called the room to order. The loud constant hum in the room quickly tailed off. A few throats cleared and there was some brief shifting of chairs. Chief Richardson spoke again as the rest in the smoke-filled room fell silent.

"The Police Court of the City of Richmond, Commonwealth of Virginia, is called to order. Thomas Judson Cluverius, of King and Queen County, has been called to appear before this authority today to face an inquiry regarding the murder of Miss Fannie Lillian Madison, also of King and Queen County. The deceased's body was located within the city limits of Richmond, March 14, 1885. The Commonwealth Attorney's office has informed me that, due to the press of business within his office, this matter will not be taken up by that office until March 29th. Therefore, at my discretion, I have been asked to proceed with the dispensation of justice and make a recommendation to the grand jury. Mr. Cluverius, please rise."

T.J. Cluverius and his attorney, Henry Pollard rose. Cluverius coldly stared straight ahead at Chief Richardson, never once bowing his head; never turning to one side nor the other. The charge was repeated as the newsmen furiously scribbled in their notebooks.

"Thomas Judson Cluverius… This court has obtained evidence indicating that you were in the presence of the deceased just prior to her death. Were you with Fannie Lillian Madison on March 13th?"

"No, sir. I was in Richmond that day, but I did not see Miss Madison.", said Cluverius clearly without hesitation.

"Were you aware that Miss Madison was also in Richmond that day?"

"No, sir. I had no knowledge of her whereabouts that day.", said Cluverius with plain sincerity.

"Very well. Do we have a witness present who can place Mr. Cluverius in the company of Miss Madison in Richmond on or about March 13, 1885?"

Captain Epps stood and responded. "Yes, Chief. We do. We have a number of corroborating witnesses. Several of them are here today. Mr. Tyler, please address the Chief." Epps stood and reached out his hand, inviting a middle-aged colored man to stand.

Hat in hand, the dark black man cautiously sidestepped through the crowd to an open area near Chief Richardson. He nodded with gentle deference toward the Chief and other officials seated at the table.

"I am William Tylah, suh. Ise a portah at da 'Mercun Hotel."

"How long have you worked there, Mr. Tyler?"

"Oh, five-year o' so, Chief."

"And you can identify the man we have here today, Mr. Tyler?"

"Um, yessuh... Dat young man dar..", he pointed at Cluverius. "He was in an' out de hotel dat night."

"Which night was that, Mr. Tyler?", asked Chief Richardson

"Fridee befo' las', Missuh Chief. Ten days 'go. He was wif dat young woman who dey foun' in the rezwar... I sure he's da one, suh. I knows I seen 'im wif 'er."

"Would that have been Friday, March 13th, Mr. Tyler?"

"Yessuh, sho' nuff."

"That will be enough. Thank you, sir." Chief Richardson nodded at Tyler and the old porter melted back into the crowd. (28.4)

H.R. Pollard stood and addressed the chief. "Chief Richardson. I am H.R. Pollard and I am representing Mr. Cluverius at this hearing. I would like to question this witness."

"Denied. This is a preliminary hearing; not a trial. You will not be questioning any witnesses today, Mr. Pollard.", said the chief bluntly.

"But, chief!", Pollard began to protest.

The stern chief held up his hand. "Mr. Pollard, that is my decision. If you cannot abide by it, I will have you removed, and, if necessary, jailed." Chief Richardson leaned forward and stared Pollard in the eye, daring him to continue his disruptions. Pollard sank down heavily into his chair, clearly frustrated by the dictatorial constraints placed upon him and his client. "Who is the next witness, Captain Epps?"

"Mr. William Kidd, please come forward.", said Epps.

William Kidd stepped out from the crowd and stood before Richardson. "My name is William P. Kidd. I live o'er in Manchester. I am a nailer on Belle Isle – at the nail works. I've been there nearly thirty-one years. I'm in charge of seven machines. I worked my way up.", he offered.

'Mr. Kidd...", Chief Richardson began, "please tell us your recollections of March 13th."

"I saw a man and a woman come in through the west end door of the factory. I think it was just after noon. I thought it was odd that a man and woman would be there. They stood beside me while I fixed one of the machines. She looked solemn to me. But she was nice looking – as nice a looking lady as I would like to look at in my life. She had a red shawl wrapped around her or on her arm. I noticed her condition and remarked that she had better be at home. The gentleman looked at me and then laughed. The man had a light mustache – what I call a 'little fuzz'. Then they went back out of the west door toward the Manchester side of the island. When I read about the man's arrest, I went down to the jail. I recognized him immediately."

"Can you identify the man here today?", asked Chief Richardson.

"He is standing right there.", Kidd looked directly at T.J. Cluverius and pointed.

"Thank you, Mr. Kidd."

H.R. Pollard cleared his throat, wishing desperately for an opportunity to cross-examine.

"Thank you, Mr. Kidd. That will be all.", said Captain Epps. "Mr. Douglas Morton; please come forward."

Another man emerged from the crowd in the room and stood before Chief Richardson.

"Mr. Morton; please tell us why you are here.", said Richardson.

"My name is Douglas V. Morton. I have been a teller at the Planter's Bank for twelve years. I have known Mr. Cluverius for a few years. I do not know him well; but I know him. He came into the bank on March 13th and cashed a check for $5.00. It was sometime between eleven and one o'clock."

"Did you see a woman with him?", asked the chief.

"There was someone waiting outside the bank for him while he cashed the check. I only saw a glimpse of a figure. The person was shorter than Mr. Cluverius; but I cannot say who it was. I will say for certain that it was Mr. Cluverius who came in the bank that day." (28.4)

Chief Richardson excused Mr. Morton and then stated, "The court has reviewed the evidence collected regarding this case to this point and the court sees no reason to continue these proceedings. This court has a very full schedule and there is no advantage to presenting anything more. Mr. Cluverius, please rise again."

Cluverius stood perfectly erect with his hands at his sides.

"It is the decision of this authority that there is ample evidence to support referring this matter, in concert with the Commonwealth's Attorney, to a grand jury for a formal indictment.", declared Chief Richardson. "Mr. Cluverius will be remanded to jail until such time the Grand Jury of the Hustings Court has rendered a decision regarding a possible indictment. If the Grand Jury determines not to proceed with the indictment, Mr. Cluverius will be immediately released. If the grand jury returns an indictment, Mr. Cluverius will return once more to jail where he will await trial." Richardson struck the gavel soundly, then dismissed the prisoner.

Pollard leaned in and put his hand reassuringly on Cluverius shoulder as they rose from their seats. The noise level of the room increased with chatter. Their police escort appeared beside them and ushered the men from the room. The three men moved briskly through the halls. Cluverius kept his eyes straight head, never acknowledging the looks of suspicious condemnation and accusatory mutterings from the onlookers that lined the hall and stairways. As he emerged from the front doorway at the top steps of the Police Station, he paused curiously and finally turned his head to his left. He glanced downward into the crowd below. The impersonal glaze over his eyes suddenly sharpened as he focused in on the face of a middle-aged woman. Rachel MacDonald looked toward him with forlorn exhaustion. She shook her head slightly side to side then covered her face with her hands. The rush of people behind him forced Cluverius to look away as he lurched forward down a few steps. Once he regained his bearings he looked back to his left. Their contact had been brief, but as before, intriguing. He craned his neck a little more trying to find her in the background. He needed reassurance that their secret would be kept. Suddenly a small but forceful hand emerged from the crowd and clamped the top of his forearm. Cluverius' head snapped forward and down at the hand. The thin knobby fingers were pale blue with fingernails that were deep purple at their base and opaque yellow at their uneven ends. His eyes followed the arm into the crowd and found the face of the old woman it belonged to. His mouth opened in reflexive horror as he looked directly into the cold left eye of Annabelle Lumpkin. She updated and amended the words she had last said to him and their meaning came through with a chilling clarity that had been obscured the first time.

"*This,* will be your *last* trial; I will make sure of that! You are doomed!"

The demonic ecstasy of Annie's expression shook Cluverius to the core but through his own powers of self-control, no one else, but perhaps Suitcase Annie herself, knew it. The police escort's arm swiftly came down and broke Annie's grip on the accused. The guard firmly grabbed hold of Cluverius' arm and rushed him through the crowd and across the street to the waiting carriage.

Chapter 29   *The Horn Has Blowed For Dress Parade*

    A portly middle-aged gentleman pulled back the curtains and opened the window in the study at *Evergreen*. He breathed deeply and stroked his coarse graying beard as the cool morning air flowed in and rustled the papers on his desk. His wife quietly entered with a small teapot in one hand and a cup and saucer in the other. Under her arm she carried the folded morning newspaper. After setting the teapot, cup, and saucer on the cart beside his large desk, which dominated the room, she quietly laid the paper and the morning mail on the overstuffed chair near the window. "Thank you, dear Nellie. Now go rest awhile; you should leave these things to the servants." he said softly as he turned from the window. She smiled and poured a hot cup for him, adding two teaspoons of sugar; just as he preferred. Nellie was in the sixth month of her sixth pregnancy, but Fitz remained a priority for her.

    Weather and his schedule permitting, Fitzhugh Lee rode his horse for one hour each morning. Fitz was an accomplished rider, displaying unusual grace and agility in the saddle for a man of his size. He had just returned this morning and was looking forward to sipping tea and reading his newspaper. He picked up the paper and sat in his easy chair. It was immediately clear that he was not the first to read the paper that morning. "Ellen" he grumbled with exasperation to himself as he re-folded the April 7, 1885 edition of *The Gazette*. Ellen, his eldest living child, was eleven-and-one-half years of age; but her thirst for information and knowledge of current events far exceeded that of her peers. She had a natural inquisitiveness that endeared her greatly to her father, but simultaneously, it was a source of mild frustrations such as messy newspapers.

    Once he had gotten the paper back in order, General Lee perused the headlines. He intermittently reached over for his teacup, gently pressing the edge to his mouth below his mustache and sipping. He glanced over the pages, noting a few articles of interest to which he would return after going through his other mail.

    The first envelope he opened was thickly woven parchment of very high quality. Lee swelled with pride as he read the name on the return address. He carefully tore open the envelope and read the single handwritten page.

April 3, 1885

Dear Fitz,

    It is with the deepest gratitude that I write to thank you for your tireless personal dedication to my campaign. I understand the clamorous and well-deserved applause you received during the Inaugural Procession far out-distanced that of any other participant. It behooves my presidency to remain an ally of such a popular figure!

    Times in this wonderful country of ours are indeed changing for the better, but as you and I both understand, there is a great deal left to do to repair the old wounds of war. I will make it a priority of my administration to salve the old wounds but, at the same time, I will not unduly dwell upon them. It is the promise of a peaceful and prosperous future which shall do more to bring us back together than any recollection of the arduous and desperate past. I know you feel the same.

It is men such as Fitzhugh Lee that this country owes the greatest indebtedness; men who are willing to forgive the prejudices, suspicions, and misunderstandings of the past and work to regain hope and dignity for all Americans. The Commonwealth of Virginia and the Democrat Party are fortunate to have an ambassador such as yourself. It is my contention that there is no other Virginian, neither past nor present, who has any better understanding of what it means to be an American and the importance of overcoming our differences to create the land of opportunity our fathers envisioned. As you know, this places you in very lofty company; a position which holds both great honor and perhaps, even greater responsibility. I know you are up to any task which lay before you and I assure you that I shall remain steadfastly supportive of you, the Commonwealth of Virginia, and her children. I remain,

Sincerely yours,

Grover Cleveland
President, The United States of America

(29.1)

Fitz Lee blushed at the outpouring of compliments from his President, but he quickly balanced his ego by reaching over and lifting from his desktop a newspaper article his clipping service had sent a few weeks prior. From the March 18, 1885 edition of the *Indiana (Pennsylvania) Weekly Messenger* he read once again that paper's observations about his conduct in the Cleveland Inaugural Parade:

... In all the pageant I could not help noticing that General Beaver, who won fights in battles for the Union, rode with becoming dignity his old bay horse. That he had but one leg few knew. He sat in his saddle like an old soldier. As he passed along the line I did not hear one cheer come to him. In theatrical phrase, he did not get a hand.

How different it was when Fitzhugh Lee rode in front of the Confederate column. He was cheered to the echo.

Look at it here for a moment. Here, on one hand, is Beaver. He went into the Union Army, and in battle for the just cause of the United States was almost shot to death. He lost a leg in battle and he suffers from his wound every hour of his life.

Now Fitzhugh Lee comes in the procession - a nephew of the great Robert E. Lee. He is fat and about fifty, handsome in appearance and impressive in his manners. He rode a wonderfully beautiful horse and from the time he started from the Capitol he received cheers and wavings of flags and handkerchiefs most bewildering.

I do not know much of military matters, but still I cannot think that a great marshal at a great ceremony should bow right and left in acknowledgement of attention.

Yet Lee did this in a very silly manner.

All this goes to show is that with the new Administration "times have changed".

It also proves that the rebs are at the front and will try to run things. (29.2)

The General could not help but smile like an incorrigible schoolboy at the image of his irritated Yankee detractors; but he quickly regained the solemnity of a leader when he thought, as he knew he should, beyond his own personal delight. As he placed the clipping in the same envelope with the President's message, Lee softly remarked "Yes, Mr. President; there remains much work to do."

After fifteen minutes of solitude, his peace was broken. Ellen burst through the study doorway.

"Papa! Papa! Did you read the shocking news?", she squealed.

"Yes... Yes, I have...", he sighed and shook his head with feigned dejection. "General Tom Thumb must be turning in his grave knowing sweet Miss Lavinia has just remarried - and the groom has no pedigree - just a lowly Count! I was

Fitzhugh Lee
(Gilder Lehrman Institute of American History)

really hoping she would wait a few more years and marry one your brothers!", he winked and chuckled. "And, to think, the Astors and the Vanderbilts were in attendance; and not the Lees?! What has this world come to?! You do realize, dear Ellen, that Tom Thumb was one of the more gifted generals in the Union Army." Fitz Lee extended his index finger, "First, you had Grant..."; next extending his middle finger, "and then you had Sherman..."; counting out three on his ring finger, "then comes Sheridan..."; then finally closing those three fingers and extending his short, thick thumb upward, "and, of course, you had... Thumb!", he smiled with mischief. (29.3)

"Now, Papa! Please be serious! I am talking about the murder in Richmond. The Grand Jury has indicted him! It's right there in the paper!"

"Yes dear, well, justice shall be done.", said Lee in a more reserved tone.

"I cannot believe a man such as he could perform such a dastardly deed. He is so handsome! I believe he is innocent and so does mother."

"Ellen, do not foolishly underestimate the savagery of men. I do not know if this man is guilty, or not; but you should not be confused by his youth nor his beauty. I have seen boys of angelic appearance carry out some of the most brutal acts you can imagine."

Ellen groaned as she turned and left the study. Fitzhugh Lee's smile expressed the pride he felt watching his daughter become a vibrant and independent young woman; but it also masked trepidation and a sense of loss that she was no longer a small child and must be made ever more aware of the darker side of man. He quietly chuckled to himself as he turned back to his paper. Then, his thoughts drifted to his own youth.

      Lieutenant Colonel Fitzhugh Lee was at the head of a column of twenty-five horsemen of the First Virginia Cavalry. His broad-brim slouch hat rested firmly on his head and the attached black ostrich plume bounced with glorious confidence as the hooves pounded the road to Falls Church. Steam pulsed from the nostrils of the horses as they cut with determination through the late November dawn. About a quarter mile after passing the Federal pickets, Lee conspicuously raised his right hand. Lieutenant Frank Bond and eight troopers peeled off from the column and settled in at the base of a small hill. Bond's orders were to remain two hundred yards behind the lead forces and to be ready to support any retreat. Lee and the rest charged up the hill and confronted a group of red legged Zouaves from New York.

      Within seconds gunfire echoed through the skies and the pitched roar of the clashing men told Lt. Bond the battle was on. Bond became agitated as he waited for some sign to act. His mouth ran dry as his men sat nervously on their horses primed for battle. Bond wanted to follow orders, but the concerned impatience bombarding him through the wide-open eyes of his men demanded his disobedience. Three minutes passed and Bond finally decided that he must move forward and determine if his support was needed. He ordered his troops forward to the top of the hill. Once there, Bond found himself in the middle of the melee. Confusion reigned as bullets whizzed around him like swarming bees. Bond thought better of his decision to engage. He wheeled his men around and started back to his original position.

      "Halt and turn back!", a loud voice pierced the fury.

      Bond ignored the order, believing it was not directed at him.

      "Bond, halt and turn back!" demanded the voice. Bond glanced over his shoulder and saw the speaker was a short man on foot. Smoke and a dark muddy mask obscured his features.

      "Mind your own business! I know mine!", snapped an uncharacteristically edgy Bond.

      "You stupid son of a bitch!", the voice boomed. "I will plant my boot right up your ass if you do not obey my order!" The little man raised his fist and then wiped away the mud caked on his face revealing bared teeth and wolfen ice blue eyes. The gunfire began to subside as many of the surprised red legs lay dead, wounded, or had simply fled the field.

      Bond's jaw dropped as he realized that he had just sassed his commander. "Dear God…" he muttered to himself. He broke over immediately to Lt. Col. Fitz Lee.

"I was trying to obey orders, sir.", stammered Bond.

"Circumstances alter cases. Dash into that swamp, dismount, and capture the half dozen Yankees that have taken refuge. I want to put an end to this fight at once!" barked the frenzied commander. In the distance, a bugler blew the order to hold fire.

At that instant a squad of twelve men led by John Singleton Mosby rode up from the left flank. Mosby was readily identifiable by the bright scarlet lined cape that flowed around his shoulders and back as he approached. He and his Rangers, many of whom were barely more than schoolboys, pulled up alongside Bond and the horseless Lee.

Mosby smiled as he looked down upon the disheveled little man. "Colonel, the horn has blowed for dress parade.", he said in a mockingly pronounced drawl.

Lt. Col. Lee was in an atypically sour mood, but his wit was still rather sharp. "Sir, if I ever again hear you call that bugle a horn, I shall place you under arrest."

Mosby laughed and said, "I heard you were in the area, Colonel, and assumed you would be in need of assistance." John S. Mosby knew Federal troop movements better than anyone, even the Union generals themselves. Evidently, his knowledge of Confederate troop movement was of equal caliber.

"No, sir. These men have it well...", Fitz then changed his mind. He understood that the accomplished partisan fighter was well-suited for mopping up the battlefield and when possible, Fitz preferred to use Mosby's services rather than risk his own regulars. "No, go ahead, sir... A half-dozen red legs have made their way into that swamp. You and your men can go capture them and Bond will secure the rest of the field."

"With pleasure, colonel." Mosby whistled through his teeth and motioned toward the swamp. The twelve grey riders let out a rebel yell and disappeared into the wooded swamp like hounds on a coon hunt.

Lt. Colonel Fitzhugh Lee turned without any further word to Lt. Bond and walked thirty yards down the hill near a creek that fed the swamp. There, on its side lay his trusted bay horse, *Dixie*. *Dixie* was mortally wounded, having been shot out from under Fitz Lee. Her right leg was shattered and she had suffered a gunshot wound to her throat. Fitz knelt beside her placing his muddy hand on her head between her ears. He bowed down closer and seemed to be whispering words of consolation to the suffering beast. Lee pulled back and while still down on one knee he looked up toward the sky, then down again, closing his eyes in a silent prayer. After a few moments he stood, drew his pistol, and fired twice into the heart of *Dixie*.

Bond approached from behind and dismounted, reverently offering his reins to his commander. "Thus, the fate of *Dixie*.", said the distraught lieutenant colonel.

Mosby and his Rangers soon re-emerged from the swamps with five prisoners in tow. Their hands were bound and they were soundly battered from being dragged rapidly from the bowels of the swamp. Mosby pointed to a massive oak tree which stood one hundred yards across the field alongside an old turnpike. The horsemen dragged the struggling captives toward the tree and then circled them. The five helpless red-legs quivered with exhaustion as they awaited their fate. Mosby halted the proceedings. He pointed to one of the captives, a very small one. "You there; boy!" The boy looked up. "What is your age?", asked the ghostly warrior.

"Twelve years", shuddered the boy before dropping his chin to his chest.

Mosby turned to one of his troopers. "Munson, he's nothing more than a drummer boy. Release him. I will not inflict undue punishment upon this innocent child."

The trooper quickly entered the circle and pulled the boy to the side. "Give him some water and deliver him to a spot where he can safely reunite with his regiment; over by Taylor's Tavern. Take him now… there is no reason to subject him to this outcome." The trooper quickly mounted his horse and pulled the weary boy up behind him. The two galloped to the east toward a crossroads down Leesburg Pike.

Two young rangers, both barely twenty years of age, dismounted and pulled two ropes each from the back of their saddles. They furiously began tying nooses. One by one, the loose ends were thrown over a black sturdy branch that extended more than fifteen feet above the field. Four of Mosby's men vacated their saddles. Each of the bound prisoners was put backwards in a saddle as the horses underneath were formed into a tight row below the ominous branch. One of the young troopers reached up with an almost gleeful energy and tightened the noose around each man's head. The boy nodded to Mosby that everything was set. Mosby, without further delay, raised his right arm. "When you reach the gates of hell, you can inform the devil that it was your own command that sent you there…" He dropped his arm and each horse was slapped smartly on the rump and two pistols were fired in the air. The horses broke and three of the men instantly dropped three or four feet. The necks of three men broke cleanly bringing an immediate end to their lives. The fourth man's noose inexplicably unraveled and fell from around his neck as the horse he sat upon bolted back toward the swamp. In an amazing display of balance and coordination resembling Indian trick-riding, the man, with his hands still bound together, spun around in the saddle and righted himself. Mosby's men hesitated with astonishment. When their senses returned, they drew their pistols and fired several shots at the fleeing horseman. Two Rangers leapt onto their steeds to begin their pursuit when Colonel Mosby shouted, "Stop, boys! Do not follow that man! Halt!"

John S. Mosby and his Rangers – 43rd Battalion Virginia Cavalry
(Mosby Heritage Area)

The Rangers pulled up on their reins and turned toward their commander with concern, "But, Colonel…"

"Let him go…", Mosby wryly said. "Let him return to his comrades and report all that has happened here. He can relate in all the Yankee bastards' camps the experience he had with Mosby's men."

Mosby coolly drew a scrap of paper and a short pencil from his pocket and scribbled down a message:

These men have been hung in retaliation for an equal number of John Mosby's men. Measure for measure.

Mosby handed the note to one of the dismounted troopers who walked over and tacked it on one of the lifeless red legs.

From a distance Fitz Lee witnessed the grisly scene as the men's heads snapped and drooped to the side. He bolted toward the tree, but was too late to intervene. Lee screamed, "Mr. Mosby, what do you think you are doing! These men should have been taken prisoner! This is a travesty! I *will* have you held accountable for this!"

"Colonel, with all due respect; these prisoners, as you call them, participated in the unlawful hanging of four of my men. My men were afforded no mercy, no trial by these red-legs. They were hung like dogs under the spiteful eye of the Yankee command. You may bring charges against me if you like, but I suspect that it will not achieve your desired result. General Lee himself has authorized this action in order that we may curtail such treatment of our captured men by our desperate and bloodthirsty adversaries. This is war, Colonel; not a marching exercise at your beloved Academy!"

Lt. Col. Fitzhugh Lee was not yet twenty-seven years of age. No instruction at the United States Military Academy at West Point ever prepared him for situations such as this. In confused frustration Lee turned his back and said, "Mosby, you and your guerillas leave my sight!"

Mosby shot back, "You greatly err in thinking us merely guerillas, Colonel Lee. Every man of my command is a duly enlisted soldier. These are picked men, selected for their intelligence and courage. We plunder the enemy, as the rules of war clearly allow." (29.4)

Fitz understood that Mosby's Rangers, from a military command perspective, were nothing more than a freewheeling volunteer appendage to the First Virginia Cavalry. They were not an officially commissioned part of the Confederate Army and therefore very difficult to hold to all military standards. In some instances, that arrangement proved advantageous; at other times, it was very troublesome. Fitz Lee could count this episode as a victory in battle, but the charge levied upon his soul was an irretrievable loss.

Chapter 30 *A Loser's Bet*

Willie Cluverius sat quietly in the simple wood chair beside his brother's cot. He gently shook Tommie awake as his eyes peeled back to make sure the guard had left the area.

"Tommie… Tommie, wake up."

Thomas Cluverius sighed and rubbed his eyes as he threw his feet over the side of the cot and sat up.

"Good morning, brother. Do you have something for me?"

Willie deftly slid a gold watch chain from his pocket and held it in his fist. He grabbed his brother's hand and placed the chain in his palm. Thomas clutched the chain and smiled slightly.

"Very well, Willie. You have done good by me. I will not forget this."

Willie smiled with pride as he soaked in his brother's approval. Willie's momentary glee suddenly darkened.

"Tommie, I'm very worried. Everyone insists you are guilty and are very anxious to see you hang!"

"Oh, Willie. That's nonsense and you know it. Do not listen to people. They will never find me guilty. With your help, we will get through this. I am counting on you to help me but, more importantly, you must protect Aunt Jane from all of this. You both will hear all sorts of wild stories about me, but I promise you, they are all false. The police and the newspapers are so anxious to find the killer, they will stop at nothing to make it appear they have him, regardless of the truth. Remember that, brother." Tommie looked warmly into his brother's eyes.

"Very well, Tommie… You always know best."

"Listen, Willie. One more thing; go to Dr. Hatcher; tell him I need spiritual advisement."

"But, Tommie! I thought you said you were doing well?"

"I am, Willie. I am very well. I just need to speak with him."

"Anything you ask, Tommie.", pledged Willie.

An imposing darkly dressed man entered the Davis Hotel at 11:30 AM that same morning. He approached the front desk and cleared his throat. Mr. Vashon appeared from the small office behind the desk area.

"Ah, Mr. Jones... I did not expect a visit, today?" said Vashon with a smirk.

"Vashon, I'm not here for a social call. Let me see the hotel register.", the man demanded.

"I don't keep a registry; you know as much!"

"Mr. Vashon...", the brute exhaled deeply and tried to maintain his composure. "This is not a social call. You will hand over the register or I will tear this hotel apart until I find it. If I tear you apart in the process, so be it; and if I find one, I will make sure this hotel is run out of business... You know I can make it happen, Vashon. Now, for the final time, where is the register? Give it to me!"

Vashon hesitated. Jones quickly reached one hand across the front desk and throttled Vashon by the collar. He pulled the pudgy little man closer, forcing Vashon off balance and onto his toes. Vashon's hands leaned awkwardly on the desktop keeping him from completely tumbling over the desk. Jones reached his other hand outward and clutched a silver letter opener nearby. The powerful interrogator swiftly plunged the sharp point downward, burying it nearly half an inch into the small area of the wood desktop between Vashon's left thumb and forefinger. Vashon flinched and fell back quickly, clasping his hand to make sure it was all still there.

"Give me the damned register, Vashon!" Jones repeated the order. The veins in his neck and temple pulsed with anger as he moved to come around the desk.

Vashon's forehead was covered with sweat, but his throat was painfully dry. He struggled to get the words out. He held up one hand and stepped backward, begging Jones to desist. "Alright, Lieutenant... Alright... Stop!"

Jones watched closely as Mr. Vashon reached his hand far back under the desk. He slid out a thin black notebook. He handed it to Jones. "This is all I have, Grimes... That's who you are, today... right?", as Vashon regained his pithy composure.

A less than amused Lieutenant Grimes opened the notebook and ran his forefinger down each page, quickly reading the long list of names: judges, politicians, bank officers, merchants, ministers; it was like holding a case of nitroglycerin. Vashon usually entered the name provided by each client and the date they registered. If the client was personally known to Vashon, he would enter the real name in the last column of the ledger.

"How far back does this register cover, Vashon?" asked Grimes as he leafed through the pages.

"Oh, since the beginning of the year."

Without further editorial comment, Grimes closed the book and started out the door of the shabby Hotel.

"But, Lieutenant, my register?", asked Vashon helplessly.

"Start another one, Vashon.", said Grimes smartly.

Once outside, Grimes ducked into a nearby alley and leaned his back against a brick wall. He cracked open the black notebook once again. He smirked with menacing defiance as he ripped two pages from the book. He stuffed the loose leaves into his trouser pocket and tucked the book under his left arm before exiting the alley.

Grimes checked his watch. It was just past 4PM. The veteran policeman pursed his lips briefly while he considered his options. He looked up the street in the direction of the precinct, then turned his head the other way. Grimes bowed his head and grin slightly.

"Hell, it can all wait 'til tomorrow", Grimes muttered to himself. He checked his watch once more and continued down the street in the direction opposite the police precinct.

Ten minutes later, Grimes entered Ned Cummins' Bar on Broad Street near City Hall. As it was most afternoons, Ned's was full of patrons. Grimes sat at the far end of the bar. (30.1)

"Beer, bartender.", he muttered from the shadows.

The bartender put the glass and bar towel he had in hand down and wiped his hand across his dingy white apron. He nodded his head as he deftly switched his wooden toothpick from one side of his mouth to the other. He drew a large glass of beer from the middle tap and slid it down the bar a couple of feet to his left in the direction of Grimes.

"Nickel...", he mumbled in Grimes' direction. Grimes slapped a coin on the bar and slid it back toward the bartender. He raised the glass to his lips and took the first sip of the cool brew.

"That, is good...", he thought to himself. He exhaled through his nostrils and began to decompress. Just as his mind began to drift away from the pressures of his work, the voices of three men gathered at the table behind him caught his attention.

"I don't know, I think the evidence is too clear. He'll be convicted. Everyone I've talked to believes he did it!", said one man.

"Nah… You have it completely wrong.", protested another man loudly. "The evidence is just circumstantial. This man has the best lawyers in Richmond. They won't be able to prove it. Besides, who among us hasn't thought about doing the same to a bothersome woman!"

The trio erupted with laughter. Grimes turned his head slightly to glimpse at the table. His barstool creaked as he strained to look back over his shoulder. The three men fell silent and looked toward the eavesdropper. Grimes nodded slightly and lifted his mug as if to toast the men before turning back around.

After a moment's hesitation, the loud man continued, "I'll put good money on it! $1 he'll be found innocent. Any takers?"

"I'll take your bet, Goode!". One of the other men said.

"I'll take the same bet!", said the third.

"Very well! Then we have a bargain. $1 he's innocent with each of you. That's the easiest $2 I'll earn all year! Here's my money; let's give it to Harry for safekeeping. Goode collected a dollar from each of the other two men. He pulled two dollar bills from his own money clip and slapped the entire $4 on the bar.

"Harry, put that in the drawer, please!" The bartender nodded and scooped up the pile of cash. Goode grinned from ear to ear.

Grimes sipped his beer and in a low monotone said, "That's a loser's bet."

"What did you say?", asked Goode

"You will lose that bet, my friend." Grimes chuckled with condescension and took another sip.

"Would *you* like to wager, friend?", said Goode in an irritated manner.

"No, I don't place bets, either on fools or with 'em."

"What do you mean, friend? Are you trying to start a problem?"

Grimes coolly lifted his left lapel with one hand as he drew the mug to his lips again with the right. One of the few rays of afternoon sunlight that could reach this area of the bar glanced briefly off the silver police badge that he exposed. Goode's eyes widened as he stepped back.

"Are you?", asked Grimes.

The bar was silent for a brief moment. "Aww, it's no use...", Goode conceded as he waved off Grimes and turned back toward his table. Grimes smirked and shook his head slightly before finishing his beer.

"Two more.", Grimes ordered the barkeep. Grimes quickly drank the two glasses of beer; then two more. He reached in his pocket and recklessly pulled a fist-full of coins from his pocket. He counted out twenty-two cents. As he shifted and stood to put the rest of the change back in his pocket, two pieces of crumpled paper fell silently from his side and onto the barroom floor. The volatile officer tipped his cap toward Goode's table and strutted cockily out of Ned Cummins' Bar.

    A few minutes later, the bartender stepped out from behind the bar. He began to sweep the barroom floor when the crumpled papers caught his eye. He bent over and opened the papers. In the dim light he saw a list of names. The bartender shrugged his shoulders slightly and put the paper in the pocket in the front of his apron. He picked up the broom again and was about to begin sweeping again. His curiosity heightened as he looked around the room full of revelers. The barkeep discreetly went back behind the bar and sat on the low stool. He unfolded the papers and read through the list on the first page:

Name	Room	Date	In	Out
J. Bowman Lily	3	15/2	noon	12:45
Grimes Mary B.	2	15/2	2:00	2:55
Dr. Watts Loretta	3	15/2	4:00	4:20
F. Miller Lily	1	17/2	11:15	noon
J.L. Walters Lily	2	17/2	1:10	2:00
Foster Hannah	4	17/2	1:20	2:00
Deuring Hannah	2	18/2	3:10	3:55
Dr. Watts Loretta	3	18/2	4:00	4:25
S. Smith Mary L.	1	18/2	6:00	7:10

    At this point, less than midway down the page, the bartender broke into a cold sweat. "Hannah? ... Loretta? ... My God...", he muttered to himself. Harry Brazelton, a simple bartender and father of three was horrified at his discovery. He stuffed the papers in a drawer behind the bar and stood to resume his duties.

    Late that night Harry Brazelton turned his key and threw the top bolt on the door to Ned Cummins' Bar. He turned and flinched as he saw a large shadowy figure rush him and push him back against the door. He immediately recognized the assailant.

"What are you doing here?"

"Where are the papers?"

"What papers?", said Brazelton

"You know what I'm talking about!", demanded the voice.

"What is your name?" asked Brazelton.

"It doesn't matter." answered the figure.

"Is your name on the paper?", asked Brazelton.

Grimes tightened his grip on Brazelton's shirt and pushed his fist into the man's neck.

"Where are the papers?" Grimes insisted. A pause was followed by a stiff blow to Brazelton's stomach.

Brazelton gasped for air. I want.... your name, officer.... Either you can give it..." he strained and exhaled, "to me; or I can go down to the precinct tomorrow and find you there."

"Do not threaten me, you dog!"

"Do you want those papers back, officer? Then you better let me go and talk this over."

Grimes was frustrated but realized his physical prowess would not get him what he wanted this time.

"I'll give you those papers back under one condition."

"Yes, what is that?", asked Grimes.

"I know where that list is from. I know my name appears on other pages in that register. Get me the pages with my name on them and I'll give you the pages with yours."

"I will not!", reacted Grimes angrily.

"Then you will not get yours back."

Grimes thought for a moment then acquiesced. "Alright, alright! What's your name?"

"Brazelton…"

"When were you there? I need to know where to look."

"Many times."

"How many times *this* year. I only have the register for this year."

"Uh…twice in January and… once in February… no it was March! Bring me those pages and we'll trade."

"Brazelton… You better not cross me on this. I will make you pay!"

"You just hold up your end of the bargain, officer. I will keep my word."

Grimes clutched Brazelton one more time by the shoulders and shoved him back against the door of Ned Cummins' Bar. "Do not cross me.", he warned before disappearing around the corner.

Brazelton deeply exhaled and looked at his quivering hands. He rubbed them together and shook them, trying to regain some composure before beginning his long walk home. (30.2)

Chapter 31 *The Marshall House*

Francis A. Howell rolled over and opened his eyes. The soothing sounds of the pelting rain became increasingly unwelcome as his conscious reasoning overtook his illogical dreamy state and reminded him what would be in store for him that morning. The dawn had barely broken as he reluctantly crept from his warm bed toward his dresser. Howell put on his grey shirt and matching uniform pants. His wife Maria sat up in bed as he headed to the doorway as he tied his well-used leather shoes.

"Can I make you some coffee before you go, dear?", she softly asked.

"No, no thank you… I need to get to work. It's going to be a messy day, I'm afraid. You stay and rest. I want you to be well by the time I get home."

Mrs. Howell cleared her throat and blew her nose, "Alright dear, thank you."

Howell closed the door to the bedroom and walked downstairs. It was pitch dark as Howell descended the stairs, but he knew his home of nearly twenty years so well, it did not matter. In the kitchen he lit a lamp and poured himself a glass of water from the pitcher on the small worn table. He yawned as he reached into the cupboard and grabbed two small biscuits. He slathered them with some apple butter and quickly devoured both. Howell picked up his mailbag as he gulped the last few ounces of water. He wiped his sleeve across his mouth and headed toward the front room. With his wax hat and jacket on Francis Howell cursed the crashing sheets of water and stepped out into the mud on Pitt Street.

Francis Howell trudged three blocks to the south side of Prince Street and turned left. One block west sat an impressive granite palazzo which housed the Alexandria Customs House and Post Office. He wiped his feet and brushed some of the rain from his shoulders in the vestibule. He then opened the second doorway and encountered the familiar hum and conversation flowing from the rear end of the building where all the sorting was done. As has been the case most days over the last twenty years, the thirty-eight-year-old Howell was the first carrier to report that morning. He was greeted by the half dozen men who worked the night shift sorting packages and letters from all over the world bound for their final destinations in one of the four postal zones of the city.

Alexandria, Va Customs House and Post Office

Howell was doggedly loading his mailbag for the first leg of his route when another carrier, young Allen Green, entered the sorting area. He glided toward Howell and slapped him on the back, "Good day, old timer! That uniform still becomes you!", he chided.

Howell smiled at the gregarious youth. "I've only worn two uniforms in my life, boy; and they've both been grey!"

"When will you retire, Howell? I have my eye on your route, you know!"

"Well, Green, I don't know. Your father asked me the same question twenty years ago!". The room chuckled.

After a few moments, Howell's mailbag was packed and he moved toward the front of the building. He ducked his head back through the door and announced, "You do realize, Green, that, due to prudent investing and miserly saving practices, I need only work *another* twenty years!"

Green hooted and shook his head. "You're my hero, Howell!" The irrepressible young man turned to the rest of the room and said, *"That's* who I want to be when I grow up!" (31.1)

Daybreak had crept across the Potomac River and was slowly making its way up Prince Street. Howell slung his mailbag over his left shoulder. The pre-dawn rain had tapered off as he made his way through the waking city toward King Street.

Turning east on King Street, Howell passed the Marshall House. Though weathered and worn on its façade, the large brick Federal building stood firmly on its foundation, as it had for decades. Howell passed the old hotel each morning, and seldom did the sight of the structure fail to remind him of the tumultuous event that indelibly marked its place in the history of America.

Colonel Elmer E. Ellsworth, U.S.A. (Smithsonian Magazine)

On May 23, 1861, Virginia seceded from the Union. At daybreak on May 24, 1861, three long wooden steamboats docked at the wharf at the foot of King Street. Colonel Elmer E. Ellsworth and his 11th New York Volunteer "First Fire" Zouaves disembarked in an orderly fashion and formed three columns. Ellsworth smartly saluted the flag as the bearer moved to the front of the column. The colonel removed his kepis and bowed his head, mumbling a brief prayer to himself summoning God's righteous protection. He then returned his kepis to the top of his head and cocked it slightly to the right. Raising his sword, the gallant Ellsworth took his place at the head of the formation. The delicate fringe on his scarlet sash bounced with each movement as he barked the order to march westward up King Street. The troops shouldered their arms and began plodding their fateful course from the muddy shoreline of Alexandria toward destiny.

Alexandria lay less than eight miles down the Potomac from Washington, DC. After the attack of Fort Sumter, President Lincoln ordered that plans be drawn to send troops into Virginia to establish a perimeter defense of the City. If the Capital City were to fall in those tenuous first months of war, the Union certainly would be lost. In the event of such a catastrophe, the government would likely relocate to the north; but the fall of Washington would be a defeat to the morale of the Unionists; a defeat that Lincoln feared could never be reversed. In addition, Union war planners fully understood the symbolic significance of quickly conquering and occupying the hometown of Virginia's most favored sons, Washington and Lee.

Colonel Ellsworth strutted at the head of the fashionably attired regiment like a bantam rooster staking out territory in a new farmyard. Alexandrians knew the conflict would visit them at any moment, but no one envisioned the nonchalant audacity of a simple parade up King Street. As the early morning sun up-lit the backdrop to the City, Ellsworth continued his theatrical conquest through the slumbering waterfront warehouse district toward the top of the hill where Fairfax and King Streets intersected. Ellsworth's orders were to march through the center of the City and seize control of the telegraph office at the west end of town. When the column reached the hill's crest Ellsworth's eyelid twitched and his pulse quickened as he beheld a few blocks in the distance the *Stars and Bars* whipping defiantly in the face of the stiff northern wind. The young officer barely took note of City Hall to his right as he gritted his teeth, continuing his march with messianic determination toward the Marshall House. The Colonel raised his sword aloft and halted the columns directly in front of the building. He beckoned a junior officer to his side. He turned and ordered two troopers to break ranks. Fully understanding the publicity potential which lay before him, Ellsworth summoned Edward House of the *New York Tribune* to join the mission. Guns cocked and bayonets fixed, the five walked briskly into the second-rate hotel and, without further notice, stormed up four flights of stairs. Ellsworth ascended the narrow ladder at the top of the stair and forced open the trap door to the roof. He disappeared onto the roof as his escorts stood nervously by, wondering what type of reaction such aggressions may trigger.

After ten or fifteen seconds out of view, Ellsworth reappeared at the roof access and quickly descended the ladder with the rebel flag twisted irreverently around his left arm. Sword still drawn he ordered the small group to return to the street and continue securing the City. As the contingent rounded the stairs on the second floor landing, a doorway opened and one side of a double-barreled shotgun flashed and boomed from point blank range in the direction of the invaders. Through the loud concussion and blast of smoke, the twenty-four-year-old Ellsworth was instantly cut down. Private Francis Brownell quickly discharged his weapon in the direction of the mysterious rebel figure in the smoky stairwell. James W. Jackson, prominent secessionist and proprietor of the

The Marshall House, Alexandria VA

Marshall House Hotel, fell face forward to the floor. The final moments of his life passed as he lay bleeding from his forehead, sacrosanct in the belief that he was defending his property and his state's rights. Ears ringing, Private Brownell stepped toward the rebel and skewered him with a bayonet. The vengeful private planted his foot on the back of the fallen attacker, extracted the blade, and kicked the lifeless body of the southerner he viewed as nothing more than a common criminal down the stairs. The *Stars and Bars* had fallen helplessly to the floor, soaking in the blood of both North and South.

As additional Union occupation forces descended upon the City from the North, dozens of Alexandria men furiously assembled as planned with their firearms and the clothes on their backs at the Alexandria Lyceum at the intersection of Prince and Washington Streets. Rather than stand and fight against a more organized force which had gained an overwhelming advantage through surprise, the volunteer militias of more than 200 wisely decided to flee, sparing the town unnecessary destruction and securing for themselves a chance to fight another day under more favorable odds. The Alexandria Battalion, under the command of Colonel George W. Terrett, marched quickly a few blocks west on Duke Street to the roundhouse. Their rear was protected by thirty-five cavalrymen under Captain Mottram D. Ball as Union forces under Colonel Orlando B. Wilcox of the 1st Michigan Infantry closed within a few blocks. The secessionist infantrymen scurried aboard a train, narrowly making their escape to Manassas where they would join Lee's Army of Northern Virginia and enter the annals of Confederate lore as the 17th Virginia Infantry. (31.2)

Postman Francis A. Howell returned to the Alexandria Post Office at 3:30 PM. His deliveries were complete. His back was tired. As he walked through the front room toward the mail room young Allen Green called to him, "Howell! Did you see the board?"

Howell looked quizzically at the lad, then turned toward the large bulletin board hanging on the wall opposite the mail window. Amongst various public notices was a boldly printed new one. The notice was issued by the City of Richmond through the Circuit Court of Alexandria. It contained a list of fifty men, all citizens of Alexandria, who were being called to appear in Richmond in two days to serve as potential jurors for the trial of Thomas J. Cluverius, charged with the murder of Fannie L. Madison. Near the top of the list was the name, *Howell, F. A.*

"Damn!", Howell initially thought to himself. "I don't need this! Why do they need men from here?" Howell lowered his head and shook it slowly in dismay. Though he fully understood the disruption and hardship it would bring him, Howell, after a brief bout with selfish anxiety, willfully embraced his civic duty.

Green, sensing Howell's despair, offered, "Well, at least it should be case of great interest!"

Howell bit his bottom lip slightly and resolutely sought the bright side. "I haven't been to Richmond in many years. It will be good to see the city again."

Green lifted an eyebrow and nodded in agreement. Still trying to brighten spirits a bit, he added, "I promise, Howell; I won't steal your route - not yet!"

"Alright, Green", Howell smiled and made a valiant effort to maintain the levity.

"You may want to reconsider. I haven't missed one day of work in twenty years. This may be your only opportunity!" Both men chuckled but realized the joking had run its course, for now. "Boy, I shall see you upon my return." Howell simply tipped his hat and quietly left for home.

Chapter 32   *Opening Day*

Richmond Times Dispatch

    May 12, Richmond - After nearly one week, jury selection for the trial of Thomas J. Cluverius for the murder of Fannie Lillian Madison was finally completed yesterday. Five hundred men from the City of Richmond were called last week, but due to the pervasive notoriety of the case, only ten could be deemed eligible to serve. A call for fifty more venire men was sent to Alexandria. From this group, six more panelists were obtained. The defense was then allowed to strike any four from the jury. The twelve who remained were, as follows: Henry Keppler, W.H. Parker, John P. Heath, William D. Trice, Carter N. Harrison, and S. J. Davis from Richmond; R. J. Finch, J. T. Sherwood, W.T. Herrock, F.A. Howell, C.E. French, and W.H.P. Berkeley from Alexandria.

    Attorneys for both the prosecution and the defense, alike, found it exceedingly difficult to identify citizens who had not formed an opinion on the case. Interest in the mysterious case among the average citizen has reached pitched levels.

    Mr. Robert W. Larke of Richmond was initially approved to serve, but information soon came to light that disqualified him. The prosecution learned that Mr. Larke had been heard to say that "he could never convict anyone based upon circumstantial evidence". Since this case appears to be wholly circumstantial in nature, the prosecution immediately petitioned Judge T.S. Atkins, presiding over the Hustings Court proceedings, to dismiss Mr. Larke. Judge Atkins, after hearing witness testimony, agreed with the Commonwealth's prosecutors and disqualified Mr. Larke.

    Larke stated that he did not mean to say that he would "never" convict a man based upon circumstantial but rather that any conviction should require an "unbroken chain of circumstantial evidence that would have been fully proved". Based upon the conduct of the police investigation, this standard may prove difficult to attain. For this reason, the prosecution petitioned and to their good fortune, Mr. Larke was indeed dismissed.

    Mr. A.S. Goode was also dismissed from the panel of jurists after initial acceptance. His dismissal arose from revelations regarding multiple wagers he had made with associates regarding the outcome of the trial. Although the monetary amounts were a pittance, the Commonwealth's attorneys argued that he had acquired an interest in the outcome by betting that Cluverius would not be convicted. This, the prosecutors argued, would inevitably bias his opinions. After hearing corroborating testimony Judge Atkins agreed and dismissed the panelist.

    A doctor was called to the Exchange Hotel the night before last to attend to juror C. E. French who had taken ill and fallen into convulsions. The doctor has stated that Mr.

French has made a full recovery and the juror was present in court today.

The jury was photographed and sworn in. The trial was then adjourned for the day. Testimony will begin May 13. (32.1)

On May 13, 1885, Judge T. S. Atkins called the Hustings Court of the City of Richmond, Virginia to order. Thomas J. Cluverius quietly took his seat at the defendant's table. Flanking the accused on one side were three capable attorneys, Henry R. Pollard, A. Brown Evans, and the leading criminal defense attorney in the Commonwealth, Beverly T. Crump. On the other side, next to the center aisle was the defendant's brother, Willie Cluverius. (32.2)

At the opposite table were three distinguished criminal prosecutors: Rufus A. Ayers, Charles V. Meredith, and Col. William R. Aylett. (32.3)

Cluverius tilted his head backward, glancing upward toward the expansive ceiling more than twenty feet above his head. His mind wandered briefly from the proceedings before he was nudged back to the matter at hand when the gavel dropped twice, "The Hustings Court of the Commonwealth of Virginia will come to order. The case of the *Commonwealth of Virginia versus Thomas J. Cluverius* will commence. Bailiff, read the charges".

The bailiff nodded and cleared his throat. "Thomas J. Cluverius, of King and Queen County, has been charged with the murder of Fannie Lillian Madison, also of King and Queen County. The murder occurred March 13, 1885 in the City of Richmond. The accused entered a plea of "not guilty" in response to this charge on March 20, 1885 at the Police Court. Based upon evidence obtained and reviewed by the Grand Jury, an indictment was issued April 2, 1885. The Attorney's Office of the Commonwealth of Virginia has brought this indictment before this honorable court for trial by jury. A jury of twelve men has been lawfully assembled and sworn to dispatch its duty. The Defendant has waived his right to have legal representation provided by the Commonwealth and shall provide for his own defense."

"The Commonwealth shall call its first witness.", instructed Judge Atkins as he looked over his eyeglasses toward the prosecution's table.

Mr. Charles Meredith rose to his feet. He was an impressive gentlemanly figure standing six feet in height. His grey suit was impeccably pressed. His white collar was stiff. His hair was neatly combed to the side. With great confidence he stepped from behind the prosecutor's table and called a name, "Mr. Lysander W. Rose is called to the stand.".

L.W. Rose grunted as he stood from his seat near the rear of the gallery. He was wearing his work clothes, but they were clean. He held his hat in his hand as he made his way up the center aisle, favoring his troublesome knee. He placed his hat down, raised his right hand, placed his left on the Bible and swore an oath with God's help to tell the truth, the whole truth, and nothing but the truth. Rose side-stepped onto the stand, took his seat, and nodded deferentially to Judge Atkins.

"Good morning, sir.", said Mr. Meredith. "Please state your name and occupation for the record."

"Lysander W. Rose; Superintendent of the Marshall Reservoir", stated Rose.

"Mr. Rose. How long have you worked at the reservoir?"

"Well, I've worked for the waterworks for about eight years. I've been running the Marshall facility for about two and a half years."

"Can you describe for the court what you found at the reservoir the morning of March 14, 1885?"

"Yes sir.", replied Rose as he sat forward and tightened his grip on his hat with both hands. "I was making my inspection of the facility like I do every morning. When I got to the top of the embankment on the south side, I noticed a red glove laying on the ground. I…"

"Excuse me, Mr. Rose, please stop there for one moment." interrupted Meredith as he turned toward the prosecutor's table. Col. Aylett handed him something. Meredith turned back around and walked toward the witness, extending the item. "Is this the glove you found that morning.".

Rose stretched to get a closer look at the small garnet glove. "Yes, sir. I believe it is."

"The prosecution would like this entered into evidence for the jury. Note: a single red woman's glove found at the Old Marshall Reservoir by Mr. L.W. Rose, the morning of March 14, 1885. Please continue, Mr. Rose."

"Well, after I noticed the glove, I noticed there were some tracks in the pathway along the top of the bank. One set looked like they were made by a man's shoes and the other set appeared to be a woman's. It looked to me like there was some sort of struggle. The footsteps were all over the place. Then, I looked over into the reservoir and near the edge, I spotted something floating in the reservoir water. I called one of my men, Mr. Lucas, over. We got a long pole and when I pushed on it, it moved. It looked like a black blanket floating in the water. I lifted it with the end of the pole and we all saw a leg. That's when I left and went and got Dr. Taylor and told one of my men to go get the police."

"And for those on the jury who may not know him, who is Dr. Taylor?"

"Oh, he's the coroner here in Richmond.", said Rose

"Please continue.", said Meredith.

"Well, my men helped Dr. Taylor get the girl out of the reservoir. From there, we all went back about our business and let him and the police go about theirs.", he shrugged.

"No further questions, your honor.", said Meredith.

Beverly T. Crump stood and adjusted his waistline. Crump was perhaps the best-known defense attorney in the Commonwealth, having defended many wealthy clients with great success. Although he was gentle on the surface, his defense tactics were very aggressive. Rather than pursue an explanation for his clients' behavior he usually focused on a robust counterattack. The fifty-five-year-old cleared his throat loudly, commanding the court's full attention. Standing in place next to his seated client, Crump began the cross examination of L.W. Rose.

"Good day, Mr. Rose... You say you have worked for the municipal water works for nearly twenty years. Have you ever worked any other profession?"

"Before that, sir, I was in the navy - during the War."

"Very commendable. Do you have any experience with police investigation?"

"No, sir.", admitted Rose.

"What was the weather like the night of March 13?"

"As I recall, there was some rain and light snow." Rose was a little confused by the disjointed questions.

"Yes, you are right. Does weather like that usually make the footing around the reservoir embankments less stable?"

"I'm not sure I understand what you are asking, Mr. Crump."

"Did the weather that night make the pathways around the reservoir muddy?"

"Yes, most likely."

"Would this occurrence make average footprints deeper or larger; and perhaps more visible, lending the impression that the activity which caused them may be of a more extreme nature?"

"I still don't understand what you are asking me."

"Allow me to try a different line. You stated that there was a struggle at the top of the south embankment of the reservoir. On what basis are you drawing that conclusion?"

"I said it *appeared* that there was a struggle."

"Why do you think this?", pressed Crump

"It looked like there were different sets of footprints up there. They were going in all directions."

"Could these footprints have been made by playing children? Or boys from the College?"

"Well, yes, I suppose…"

"Could they have been made by any number of people? Perhaps you or your own employees?"

"Well, not very likely."

"Mr. Rose… Finding a dead person in the reservoir isn't very likely either, but it happened. Can you state with any level of certainty that these footprints were the result of a struggle?"

Rose turned pink and wrung his hat nervously. "No, sir. My guess is that it was a struggle; but, they could have been from something else."

Crump glanced down at his notes, then over at the jury before turning his attention back to the witness.

"Mr. Rose… Who found the red glove that's been entered into evidence?"

"I found it, sir."

"Where?"

"At the top of the embankment."

"Was this near the footprints you described earlier?"

"Yes, sir."

"How close, Mr. Rose?"

"It was right there among them."

"Did anyone else see it as you found it, Mr. Rose?"

"Well, no."

"No?", repeated Crump with emphasis.

"How could that be?"

"Well, I picked it up and put it in my pocket.", explained Rose.

"Do you make a habit of tampering with evidence, Mr. Rose?", struck Crump suddenly.

"I object, your honor!", blurted Charles Meredith.

"On what grounds, Mr. Meredith?", asked Judge Atkins.

"Mr. Rose should not be characterized in this manner during this proceeding. If Mr. Crump feels Mr. Rose did something illegal, he needs to bring proper charges in a separate proceeding."

"Objection sustained.", said the Judge. "Mr. Crump, you will refrain from judging Mr. Rose in such a manner. Rephrase your question."

"Yes sir, your honor. Mr. Rose. What did you do with the glove when you found it?"

A visibly angered L.W. Rose gritted his teeth and responded, "I have heard that you have the eye of an eagle and the appetite of a vulture, Mr. Crump…" Beverly Crump and the Judge alike ignored the comment. Rose continued, "When I first saw the glove, I… I picked it up… and put it in my pocket. I don't know why. As yet, I didn't know anything had gone wrong. I gave it to Detective Wren later that same day."

"So, you are the only person that saw the glove near the footprints? No one else can corroborate that claim?"

"Yes, that's correct.", he answered sternly.

"One last topic, Mr. Rose. The slope that runs down from the embankment to the water in the reservoir. How steep is it?"

"Oh, about forty-five degrees."

"What is it made of?", continued Crump.

"It's stone."

"It's lined with stone the entire distance from the bank to the water?", asked Crump looking for further clarification.

"Yes, sir.", replied Rose.

"Could a person leap from the top of the embankment and reach the water?"

"Maybe; when the water supply is full."

"What do you mean by that?", Crump squinted at the witness.

"Well, we had drawn off a significant amount of water to allow for repairs. The water level was about fifty inches below the waste water line."

"To be clear, Mr. Rose; would this mean that the distance from the top of the embankment to the surface of the water would have been a far greater distance than it would have been on a typical night?"

"Yes, on a typical day or night, the water level would have been much closer to the top of the embankment."

"On the date in question, could a person have leapt beyond the stones clear to the water?"

"No, sir."

"For clarity, Mr. Rose. If a young pregnant woman were to leap from the top of the embankment that night, she would have landed on the stones before tumbling into the water."

Rose paused and exhaled. "Yes, that would probably be the case."

"And how deep was the water where the body was found?"

"Oh, I would say eighteen inches to maybe two feet.", Rose answered.

"Thank you, Mr. Rose. No more questions." Crump said as he sat back down.

Thomas J. Cluverius subtly bit down on his lip with regret. "If that water had only been at the regular level, they would *never* have found her…", he surmised to himself.

Charles Meredith stood up for additional questioning. He walked out from behind the prosecutor's table as before.

"Mr. Rose; is there a fence around the reservoir?"

"Yes, sir; there is."

"Does this fence surround the facility in its entirety?"

"Yes, sir; it does."

"Can you describe this fence?"

"Yes, well… It's a standard wood picket fence… It's kept in good order by my men…"

"How high is this fence?", continued Meredith.

"Oh, I would say it's nearly four feet high."

"Very good, Mr. Rose. As a matter of fact, the prosecution has measured the fence. At no point is it lower than three feet three inches and at no point does it exceed three feet eleven inches. In order to leap into the reservoir, would someone, particularly someone of a size and physical state of the deceased, need to climb this fence first?"

"Oh, yes, sir.", assured Rose.

"Mr. Rose, when the deceased was retrieved from the reservoir. What was she wearing?"

Rose lifted his hand to his temple and scratched slightly as he tried to remember with complete accuracy. "I believe she was wearing a long black skirt; and a blue blouse; and shoes, of course."

"A *long* black skirt, eh?", repeated Meredith. "The shoes, Mr. Rose; can you describe them for the court?"

Rose was a little perplexed, but tried to translate his memory succinctly. "Well, sir, they were standard women's shoes; black; leather with laces."

"Did they have a high heel?"

"Yes, sir; they did.", Rose stated with certainty.

"Would a small woman; one with-child, dressed as you have described her, on a dark wet night, been capable of scaling the four-foot picket fence that encircled the reservoir without assistance?"

"It would be very difficult, I would think, Mr. Meredith." stated Rose.

"No further questions, your honor." Meredith returned to his table.

Crump stood and simply asked, "Are there any gateways through this fence, Mr. Rose?"

Hardening once again in the face of the cross exam, Rose curtly answered, "Yes, sir."

"How many and where are they located?"

"There are two; one at the north end and one at the south end."

"Are these gates locked, Mr. Rose?"

"No, sir, they have latches; but no locks."

"Are these simple latches, Mr. Rose; the type that any woman or child could readily operate?"

"Well, yes… I suppose."

"Thank you, Mr. Rose. No more questions."

Rose twitched slightly and squinted at the defense attorney.

Meredith paused briefly before standing once again. "Mr. Rose; were the gates closed and latched when you left the facility the evening of March 13, 1885?"

"Yes, sir."

"Were the gates latched the morning of the 14th when you returned?"

"Yes, sir."

"If opened, will the gates spring back and latch on their own?"

"No, sir; if left unlatched, they'd just blow with the breeze. I check them every night before I leave. I am sure they were closed that night when I left and I'm sure they were latched when I came back the next morning."

"No further questions, Judge Atkins.", Meredith stated as he sat down. Atkins looked back toward Crump and Crump shook his head, indicating he too was finished questioning the witness.

"Thank you, Mr. Rose. You may step down.", said Judge Atkins.

Prosecutor Meredith put on some magnifiers and looked down at his papers. After a moment he raised his head, removed his spectacles, and addressed the court.

"The prosecution calls Mr. Roland G. Lucas to the stand."

R.G. Lucas stood and cleared his throat. He walked quickly up the center aisle of the courtroom. Clean-shaven, he was dressed in his only suit with his hair combed neatly to one side. L.W. Rose's eyes widened at the first sight of Lucas that morning. It was not until Lucas raised his hand to swear in and Rose saw the familiar permanently grease-stained fingers which had worked so tirelessly turning wrenches that Rose could fully identify, without further hesitation, his most trusted workmate.

"Good morning, sir.", said Mr. Meredith. "Please state your full name and occupation for the record."

"Roland Garfield Lucas; Boss Workman at the Marshall Reservoir", said Lucas.

"Mr. Lucas. How long have you worked at the reservoir?"

"About ten years."

"And, in what capacity?"

"I came on as jus' a workman; but after the ol' boss left about two years 'go, Mr. Rose made me boss."

"Yes, very well.", said Meredith. "Can you describe the events of the morning in question?"

"Well, I was at the reservoir before dawn, along with Mr. Rose and Mr. Trainham. We drank our coffee like we always do. Then I went down to work on the #2 valve. It needed a new stem. Maybe thirty minutes later I hear Mr. Rose yell out from the other end of the reservoir. I know that when 'is voice raises, it's usually for good reason so I crawled out 'n run after 'im as fast as I could. When I got to 'im, he was on top of the south bank. He pointed down to the water and we saw somthin' floatin' in it. One of the men brought over a long pole. We nudged it and saw the leg. Mr. Rose told me to go get the police. So, I ran off. I come back later with some police men and I seen the body being pulled out of the water. Dr. Taylor was there…" Lucas paused and then shrugged a little. "That's all I saw."

"Thank you, Mr. Lucas." Meredith turned toward the defense and said, "Your witness, sir."

Crump rose to his feet and slowly moved from behind the table. He was not sure why Meredith did not seek more corroboration from Lucas, so he decided to.

"Mr. Lucas: did you see any evidence of a struggle on the embankment?"

"I seen footprints scattered in every direction up on top, sir."

"Could you identify them in any way? Did they belong to a man, or a woman?"

"Well, there was more 'n one pair up there, that I know for sure. Who they belonged to, I couldn't say…", Lucas looked down at his hands. Suddenly, he recalled something which he thought may be significant. "Dr. Taylor… Dr. Taylor did match one of the girl's shoes to a print on the ground."

"How did he do this?", asked a somewhat surprised Crump.

"Well, he took one o'er shoes off and got down on the ground an' put it right in a track an' it fit!"

"Mr. Lucas, are you saying that without any doubt, the deceased's shoes made some of those prints on the embankment?"

"Yes sir… Well, it looked like a fit to me."

"What about the other tracks? Could you identify those?"

"They looked like they belonged to a man."

"A single man? A few men? Many men?"

Lucas felt slightly intimidated. "At least one, Mr. Crump."

"But perhaps more?" Crump persisted.

"I don't know. I don't know."

"Did you, Mr. Lucas, see anyone walking on that embankment before you first went up there?

"Jus' Mr. Rose. Jus' that morning."

"Now wait, Mr. Lucas… That very morning was the first time you ever saw Mr. Rose walk up on that embankment?"

"Oh, no sir. Mr. Rose walks up there at leas' twice a day. Once in the mornin' and once in the evenin'."

"Did Mr. Rose walk up there the night before the body was discovered?"

"Yes, he did."

"What was the weather like that evening?"

"I believe it was startin' to rain a bit."

"So, the ground was softened?"

"Mos' likely."

"Could Mr. Rose have made some of those tracks that very morning or even the night before?"

"I suppose…"

"Could he have made all of them?", Crump prodded.

"No, I don't think so."

"Can you say that he did not make all of those tracks?" Lucas' mouth opened but nothing came out. "Mr. Lucas", Crump commanded, "Can you unequivocally state that those tracks you saw on the embankment, other than the ones which fit Miss Madison's shoe, belonged to any particular individual other than the only man you saw walking up there with your own eyes that morning and the prior evening?"

"No… No, I ain't completely sure; but I'm pretty sure."

"Thank you, Mr. Lucas. No more questions."

Meredith stood and almost began a redirect before deciding against it. "No further questions, your honor."

"You may step down, Mr. Lucas", said Judge Atkins. (32.4)

Chapter 33　　　　　*John Brown's Body*

"The prosecution calls Dr. William H. Taylor to the stand.", announced prosecutor Charles Meredith.

Dr. Taylor stood slowly and methodically walked up the center aisle to the stand. His bald head glared like a halo in the courtroom sun.

After swearing in, he calmly seated himself and awaited the first question.

"Dr. Taylor, please state your full name and occupation for the record."

"Dr. William H. Taylor, Medical Examiner for the City of Richmond."

After a pause, "I know you are a humble man, doctor, but it would be helpful if you further described your credentials to the court.", said Mr. Meredith.

Dr. Taylor cleared his throat and complied. "Well, after graduating from the Medical College of Virginia in '51, I took a position as professor at the 14th Street Medical College in New York. There I instructed in Principle and Practice of Surgery and Surgical Pathology. In 1859, I returned to Richmond and took a similar position at the Medical College here until the War came." (33.1)

The winds whipped through Charlestown, Virginia on December 2, 1859. Most of the observers were anxious to see the dispensation of justice, but, with a melancholy that was not entirely explicable, they sensed that the winds of change fueled this front. It would be a small momentary victory this morning. Ultimate victory could come only at the end of a very intense and dangerous struggle, one where the outcome, at this time, was wholly in doubt and the future, even if it held victory, would certainly render a very different world than the one they had always known.

Two hollow squares of military guards surrounded the gallows. The men in the outer square stood firmly with bayonets fixed at the ready. The inner square too had their bayonets fixed, but were present arms. The crowd of more than one thousand was quiet, not out of respect nor sympathy for the condemned, but rather from the befuddling moral apoplexy that surrounded the events. The soldiers' pant legs snapped as the winds ran roughshod across the hilltop. At the edge of the woods to the left of the gallows were a squad of mounted men. Flanking the gallows and formation of men were two howitzers, under the command of Major Thomas J. Jackson. Their weapons were drawn, ready for all contingencies. Six companies of riflemen surrounded the outer perimeter. Major General Richard Taliaferro with a staff of twenty-five officers looked on.

The rear of the hollow squares parted suddenly as a tall thin man with a thick shock of grey hair walked with determination toward the gallows. His arms tightly bound to his sides at the elbows, Brown was escorted by four men; Captain Willard Avis, the Jefferson County Jailer, and three deputies. Following a few steps behind was Fred Campbell, Sheriff of Jefferson County, Virginia.

John Brown looked strangely content for a man who was about to be hanged. He spoke comfortably to the guards as he passed and without hesitation ascended the stairway to the hanging platform. There was no religious ceremony, no final statement by the condemned. Brown's abolitionist message had been made clear in Kansas and Harper's Ferry; he felt no compulsion to make further peace with neither his Lord nor earthly judges. Here was a man who was unapologetic and prepared to die. Brown stepped forward and gazed down upon the curious crowd. His blue eyes burned through them. Even at the moment of his death the firebrand had the capacity to intimidate, inspire, and ultimately, to confound. It was impossible to bridge the chasm created when this just cause was embraced in such an unjust manner.

Sheriff Campbell placed a white muslin hood over Brown's head. He guided the blinded condemned into position over the trap door. The Sheriff then carefully tightened the noose. The command was given by the military officers to tighten the ranks around the gallows, to prevent any sudden rush from the crowd. The exercise extended Brown's lone blinded stance atop the platform for an additional five minutes. After the soldiers were settled in their defensive positions, Sheriff Campbell quietly asked Brown if he would like a handkerchief to drop, granting him the courtesy of deciding the exact moment of his demise.

"No, I do not care; I do not want you to keep me waiting unnecessarily.", Brown calmly responded.

Sheriff Campbell turned to the jailer and nodded. Captain Avis raised a hatchet aloft for a brief moment. Brown bid a quiet final farewell. Avis then quickly brought the hatchet down upon the rope which tautly secured the platform door. Less than one second later, the trap sprung and the insurgent felon plummeted into history. Brown's arms flew upward from the elbows as his body dropped. With the jerking stop at the rope's end, his arms fell back to his sides. His left arm twitched slightly and his knees drew up a few inches. Brown's red-slippered feet knocked spastically together two times. Within a few seconds, John Brown's body was limp and swung in a pendulum-like manner as the December wind persisted.

John Brown (1800-1859)

John Brown's body was placed in a black walnut coffin and handed over to his wife, Mary. Per a lucrative arrangement John Brown had made with members of the abolitionist movement prior to the execution, his body was placed on a train bound for Philadelphia and then, on to New York. Brown ensured that his wife would be paid handsomely for her compliance, for he had left her behind with many children, large debts, and no means of financial support. Once in Philadelphia, John Brown's coffin was unloaded from the train and paraded through the streets, engulfing much of the downtown in a vigorous celebration of the now legendary Northern hero. Handkerchiefs were waved, flowers were thrown, and speeches were delivered - all in the name of demagogic righteousness and social justice. Bars did a brisk business and as evening approached, all decorum was forgotten and opinions from all sides were easy to find. (33.2)

On December 7, 1859, Professor William H. Taylor, M.D. picked up a copy of the *New York Times*. A headline in the center column drew his immediate attention:

Medical Students Clash

Philadelphia - Students at the Philadelphia Medical College clashed on December 5 following a public parading of abolitionist John Brown's body around the city. Arguments erupted between students from Southern slave-holding states and their Northern peers.

Dozens of Southern lads organized a march through the streets declaring Brown a murderous insurgent who got exactly what he deserved. After the march they returned to the college and amid scorn and ridicule withdrew their enrollment, vowing to continue their studies in the friendly environs of colleges in the home states. It is understood that similar circumstances are present at other Pennsylvania colleges. It is safe to say that this trend may continue once the abolitionists reach New York with Brown's remains.

Ah, what fools these deputy saw-bones be! Philadelphia Medical College is among the finest institutions in the country and far superior to any college in the South. Had slave-holding fashions been imitated, they would have been driven back to their homes by a furious mob for daring to express their pro-slavery opinions. (33.3)

On December 14, 1859, Professor William H. Taylor, M.D. submitted his resignation to the administration of the 14th Street Medical College and boarded a train home to Richmond.

Dr. Taylor cleared his throat and continued to address the court, "During the War, I served over at Chimborazo (Hospital)." he pointed abstractly to his right. It was there that I, unavoidably, became familiar with our ultimate physical condition. Tens of thousands of men passed through that facility. Some left intact, or nearly so. Many others left with only their souls. My professional destiny had been revealed. At the War's end I applied for a position in the Richmond Medical Examiner's Office where I could further study this discipline and constructively apply my knowledge. There I have remained hence, serving as the chief coroner for nearly thirteen years."

"Are you expert in this field, Dr. Taylor?", asked Meredith.

"Yes, I may be considered such.", Taylor responded humbly.

"I don't believe there is any doubt about that, doctor. You are highly rated by all of your colleagues. Your reputation as a medical practitioner is stellar."

"Thank you, Mr. Meredith."

"Can describe what occurred that morning in question?"

"I was in my office preparing for the day ahead. Mr. Rose burst in unannounced and informed me that a body had been discovered in the Marshall Reservoir. I instructed him to return and do nothing until I arrived."

Dr. William H. Taylor, M.E.

Dr. Taylor calmly removed his spectacles and held them up to the sunlight. He squinted and pulled them closer to his nose. He reached in his coat pocket for a handkerchief as he continued, "I collected my medical bag and made my way to the reservoir. I arrived about 10AM and found Mr. Rose and a number of other men gathered near an embankment at one end of the reservoir. They informed me that there appeared to be struggle atop the embankment. The body was located in the water just below that embankment. I made an inspection of the site…"

"Excuse me for interrupting, doctor; but did you note your movements and findings that morning?"

As he wiped the thick lenses of his spectacles clean and returned them to his face, Taylor replied, "Yes, Mr. Meredith. I wrote notations at each point along the way. It is good practice for any Examiner, but especially one, well… one of my, shall I say, more advanced experience."

The courtroom chuckled lightly and most of the men, particularly those who had reached middle age, turned to one another in full understanding of the doctor's plight. Thomas Cluverius sat stiff and motionless, completely unaffected by the brief moment of levity.

"Let the record show…", Meredith boomed to refocus the proceedings, "that Dr. Taylor's note book, containing copious notes taken firsthand that very morning, has been entered into evidence." Meredith approached the bench and handed the worn leather-bound booklet to a bailiff.

Dr. Taylor's Notes from the morning of March 14, 1885 as entered into evidence:

14 March, 1885

8AM - Mr. Rose, reservoir superintendent, advises of possible dead body in reservoir, probably female

10AM - Arrive at reservoir to begin analysis - Superintendent Rose and others to assist.

On walkway top of embankment to the South saw many shoe tracks and scuff marks. Soil is soft here. Light rain and snow last evening. Tracks are fresh and are in area covering width of path for a stretch of six to eight feet. Tracks are numerous and confused. Two tracks of broad heels near picket fence facing reservoir. These are probably male tracks. Other footprints are much smaller and appear to be female.

10:15AM - Picket fence encircles reservoir. Fence approximately 3 and 1/2 feet high. Pickets are sharp and extend approximately 4 inches above top rail.

Stone embankment rather steep and conditions slippery. Body face down in water near edge of reservoir just below disturbed area. Arms are forward in front of head.

Reservoir near edge is about 18 inches deep. The floor appears very soft and silty. The men's feet sink 8 to 10 inches when walking along this part.

Men lift the body from the water. Cadaver hauled up the embankment face up. Fully clothed young adult female.

Removed left shoe and was able to match it to female footprints near embankment.

10:45 - Female body removed to reservoir office.

Age 20 to 25 years. Covered in mud. Approximately 4 feet 11 inches in height. Hair still pinned up.

Hands tightly clenched with mud still in them.

Blue Jersey has small tear inside left arm. Black skirt has some small rents. No jewelry.

Stiffening of the joints and muscles indicate death occurred at least six hours earlier. Exact time of death undetermined as of now.

Dead female in advanced stage of pregnancy, perhaps 8th month. (33.4)

"Now, Dr. Taylor, please continue."

"Well, after inspecting the embankment, I asked the men to retrieve the body. It was a young girl, fully dressed. As they raised her out, I stopped them and removed one of her shoes. I was able to match it directly with a footprint on the embankment."

Cluverius shook his head so slightly no one even noticed. He knew the good doctor had it wrong, but any attempt to quibble would only seal his own fate. Yes, those were indeed his tracks on the embankment; but the female tracks were not Fannie's, but rather Rachel McDonald's. It was pure coincidence that Fannie's shoes fit the tracks. "The doctor believes he is quite clever - ha!", Cluverius thought to himself. Cluverius closed his eyes as he prayed that other false assumptions would creep into the testimony; assumptions that could be refuted without damaging his defense.

Meredith continued, "Were there any other footprints, doctor?"

"Yes, there were many. Some appeared to be made by the deceased's shoes, others were of a different character altogether."

"How many distinctly different footprints were present, doctor?"

"Do you mean the total number of prints?"

"No doctor, how many of one type, or another."

"Well there were at least two different types of prints. One, as I stated, matched the shoes of the deceased. There was at least one other type with a broader heel. If these all belonged to the same person, or not, is difficult to say. Unless I had shoes with which to compare them, I cannot make that assumption. It was quite muddy up there and the shoe marks were confused. Time and weather had degraded the prints."

"I see, doctor. But, in your opinion, there were definitely more than one set of prints up there that appeared to be made at the same time as those made by the deceased's shoes."

"That would be a conclusion, but it is not the only conclusion."

"But is that *your* conclusion?"

"I cannot make that conclusion. It would be irresponsible without proper evidence. There were more than one set of prints up there. That is the most I can say without speculation."

"Very well." Meredith capitulated. The prosecutor was a bit frustrated with his own witness. He had hoped he could induce Dr. Taylor to opine and, and thereby exploit the doctor's good reputation and influence the jury; but alas, Meredith sensed that he could not wear down the stubbornly professional doctor and would no longer belabor the point, lest he give the impression that he is badgering his own witness. He respected Taylor's consistency and moved forward.

"Dr. Taylor, you mentioned the deceased was fully clothed. What was she wearing?"

"As I recall, Mr. Meredith, she wore a long black skirt and a blue jersey. Of course, she was wearing some undergarments and shoes."

"Was she wearing any jewelry?"

"No, sir."

"A wedding band?"

"No jewelry, sir."

Meredith reached into a small box sitting under the prosecutor's table. "Dr. Taylor, is this the skirt the deceased was wearing when you examined her?"

"Yes, it appears to be."

Meredith reached back into the box. "Is this the blue jersey she was wearing?"

Dr. Taylor nodded somberly, "Yes".

"And are these the shoes she was wearing?"

"Yes, they appear to be.", answered Taylor. Cluverius noticeably moved for the first time since the trial began. He shifted his weight in his chair, lightly cleared his throat and swallowed. As Meredith approached the bailiff to enter the garments into evidence, Cluverius looked down at his hands. He rubbed them together slowly and after a few moments, once the garments had been taken from view, he tilted his chin upward to the left. Cluverius' neck cracked, relieving some of the pressure. He then looked back up directly at the Judge Atkins.

"Let the record show that the clothing worn by the victim has been entered into evidence!"

"I object!", shouted defense attorney Beverly Crump.

"On what grounds, Mr. Crump?", asked Judge Atkins.

"The prosecution should refrain from referring to the deceased as "the victim". This type of characterization should be only allowed by the Court during final argument and should not be employed during testimony.", argued Crump.

"Yes, yes, Mr. Crump. Your point is well-taken. The prosecution will refrain from such characterizations.", advised Judge Atkins.

"Yes, your honor.", conceded Meredith while concealing his pleasure. Charles Meredith wasn't even sure that the jury would take note of such a characterization, but was delighted that the defense cast a clear light upon it. "Dr. Taylor,", Meredith cleared his throat lightly and continued, "Did you perform an autopsy on the body?"

"Yes, sir. The very next day."

"Let the record show the Dr. William H. Taylor, Medical Examiner of the City of Richmond, performed a complete autopsy on the deceased, Fannie L. Madison, on March 15, 1885. His official report is hereby entered into evidence."

Autopsy Report of Fannie L. Madison (unknown at the time) by Dr. William H. Taylor, M.E.

Date of Examination:	15 Mar 1885
Time of Examination:	7:20AM
Examination Procedure:	Post Mortem Autopsy
Place of Examination:	City of Richmond Coroner's Office
Name of Examiner:	William H. Taylor, M.E.
Subject Name:	Unknown
Subject Gender:	Female
Subject Age:	20 - 25 years
Subject Height:	4 feet 11 inches
Subject Weight:	120 pounds (approx)
Date of Death:	March 13 or 14, 1885
Time of Death:	Between 9pm on 13 Mar and 1am on 14 Mar
Cause of Death:	Drowning

Notes: Subject found in Old Marshall Reservoir, Richmond, on morning of March 14, 1885. Subject was face down in water's edge. Preliminary examination revealed subject to be in 7th or 8th month of pregnancy.

Body completely intact. Decomposition at time of examination is minimal.

Skull is intact. One large bruise approx. two inches wide directly above right eye near temple. No breaks in the skin in this area. Light scratches on right eyelid and on forehead. Another lighter bruise just below the bottom lip. Area beneath lower lip is slightly discolored in even distribution across two-and-one-half inch span. There is light blood vessel breakage on interior of lower lip.

The deceased retains fourteen lower teeth and thirteen upper teeth. First molar on the right side is missing and based upon condition of the gum, was removed at least thirty days prior to death. All teeth appear normal and of adequate condition.

No fractures inside skull. Brain appears normal and fully developed. On left top surface of brain an effusion one inch in diameter is observed.

Exterior of torso and extremities in excellent condition. No signs of bruising nor lacerations. There is some light elongated scarring from lower abdomen up to navel, due to rapid stretching of skin associated with advanced pregnancy.

Male fetus was well--formed and appeared normal and healthy. Weighed 4 pounds 5 ounces and 14 inches in length. Placenta was healthy.

No signs of internal injury nor bleeding. All organs appear of normal size, location, and outer appearance.

Lungs are normal size. There is unnatural redness on the interior lining and some small amounts of frothy water.

Stomach retains ten ounces of undigested food. Appears to be chicken or duck, green string beans and bread. No presence of the frothy water observed in the lungs. Otherwise, stomach appears normal and healthy.

The body was first examined at the Reservoir by this Examiner at 11 am on March 14, 1885. At that time this Examiner noted that based upon stiffness of the body and its general condition, it appeared the body had been dead for at least six hours prior to the examination. The presence of undigested food in the stomach indicates that the death probably occurred sometime before midnight on March 13, 1885. Assuming the victim ate her last meal sometime between 6 pm and 8 pm on March 13, 1885, this level of digestion would be consistent with food in the living and functioning stomach for a period of two to four hours.

The existence of the deep bruise above the right eye, coupled with the effused blood located on the left top of the brain, it is clear that a heavy blow was sustained.

The light bruising under the lower lip may have been caused by external pressure. The time of this bruising cannot be medically determined. It may have happened in conjunction with the bruising above the eye, or it may have happened sometime prior under completely different circumstances.

It is the Medical Examiner's opinion that the cause of death was drowning. It appears that the victim was knocked unconscious, but not killed, by a blunt blow to the head above the right eye and upon falling in the water in an unconscious state, was unable to breathe, thus causing distress in the lungs and accounting for the redness observed there. Though a large amount of water would generally be found in the lungs of a drowning victim, it is likely that the reduced breathing rate of the unconscious victim accounts for the reduced, but clear, presence of the frothy water in the lungs. It should be noted that at the initial inspection of the body, this Examiner noted that the victim's hands were clenched with mud inside them, lending further support to the idea that the victim entered the water in a living but somewhat incapacitated state and expired in the water.

In summation, the victim most likely received a solid blow to the head, then entered the water where she drowned sometime before midnight on March 13, 1885.

William H. Taylor, M.E.   15 March 1885   10:12 am   (33.5)

"Dr. Taylor, your report states that the deceased had a large bruise above the right eye. Would you please describe the injury in detail for the court?"

Dr. Taylor then removed a paper from his breast pocket. He unfolded it and held up in front of the courtroom. On it he had drawn a picture of a woman's head. He had clearly marked a couple of areas of interest to the court. He moved the paper to the side of his own head and pointed to it as if instructing his class. "The bruising above the right eye was approximately two inches wide. It is consistent with a blow to the head by a blunt object. The effusion that occurred on the surface of the brain directly beneath the bruise further supports the idea that her head was struck with a heavy force by a hard object.", explained Taylor. (33.6)

"Doctor, we are not medical experts and are not wholly familiar with some of your terms. Could you define "effusion"?

"Certainly, Mr. Meredith; an "effusion" is a concentration of blood in an area that is usually caused by a sharp blow. In this case, the deceased's head was struck so hard that blood "effused", or collected, or pooled in that area. It is a very normal reaction that our bodies have when injured. Blood flow encourages recovery to the damaged area, but also cause swelling and discoloration in these areas."

"Thank you, Dr. Taylor. Now, could this force have been a man's fist?"

"Well, based upon the severity of the blow, it would have to have been a large and very strong man. Certainly, anyone striking a skull that hard with his fist would most likely have suffered a serious break in the hand. It is possible that it was caused by someone striking the woman with a club of some sort, but this most likely would have cracked the skull. It is most likely that the injury came from the woman striking her head against a hard surface. This would explain the bruising on the exterior and the effusion on the brain; yet it also supports the fact that there were no breaks in the skull. You see, the woman's head most likely struck a broad hard surface with great force." Taylor held up his right fist and pressed against the open palm of his opposite hand. "But, because the blow was against a wide object, not a thin one, like a club; which would greatly concentrate force, the skull was able to hold up and not crack. But, the force was so strong that on the other side, the brain was pushed backward inside the skull and then rushed forward again and collided with the skull from the inside; causing the trauma and subsequent effusion."

"Dr. Taylor, your report also mentions a bruise under the deceased's lower lip. What would have caused that?"

"Once again, Mr. Meredith, none of this can be stated with absolute certainty. But, this type of light bruising usually occurs on delicate areas by means of some sort of pressure. One possible explanation is that someone grabbed the woman from behind around her mouth and pressed down, as if trying to subdue a scream. The pressure by the fingers may have caused the shape and depth of bruising I examined. This said, the bruising may have been caused at a time well before the fatal incident and under completely different circumstances."

"Dr. Taylor, your report lists the official cause of death as drowning. Is there any medical evidence that would indicate that this drowning was caused by any particular circumstances?"

"Mr. Meredith. I have given a great deal of thought to the circumstances surrounding this tragedy. Although I have personal opinions regarding the events in question, as a medical professional, which is the auspices under which I became involved with the matter and under which I am appearing today as a witness, I can draw no conclusion. I can state with relative certainty that the young woman drowned to death. Whether it was suicide, homicide, or a simple accidental occurrence, I cannot be sure based upon the evidence I have seen."

"Could you explain further?"

"I shall try.", said the old man. "Human impulse may tempt one to conclude that this was a homicide. It is certainly possible that the deceased was struck over the eye and thrown into the reservoir to perish. However, it should be noted that although the medical facts are not inconsistent with a homicide, based upon this Examiner's investigation of the Old Reservoir site and the location of the body, neither can they be deemed inconsistent with suicide. The deceased may have leapt from the edge of the reservoir embankment and as she tumbled down the steep stone -faced slope of the embankment toward the water below, she may have hit her head, rendering her unconscious upon entry into the water. Furthermore, it remains a possibility that she was simply walking recklessly and impetuously around the edge of the embankment and slipped and fell to her demise. The medical facts of this case cannot eliminate any of these possibilities."

"So, Doctor Taylor, is there any possibility which would be more likely than any other?"

"Mr. Meredith... I am a medical examiner, not an odds maker. If you would like a reference, I would gladly provide one; but not in the presence of law enforcement ..." The courtroom chuckled.

"No further questions, your honor." Meredith's frustration was not visible, but his abrupt silence clearly told the tale. Meredith sat down quietly knowing his own witness, under his own direct questioning, had given considerable hope to the defense.

A. Brown Evans, attorney for the defense, rose immediately. He gripped his lapels and tugged once, adjusting his jacket. Like a hyena the young self-assured attorney circled out from behind his table toward the stand, gauging the right moment to seize his aged and weakened prey. "Doctor Taylor" he began in an authoritative tone, "will you, without any quibbling, kindly tell this jury exactly how far you can see?"

Without delay, Taylor responded, "Ninety-six million miles..." A great collective gasp came from the courtroom. Evans smirked and rolled his eyes at the ridiculous statement. After a few tense moments of silence, Taylor explained, "I can see the sun, and scientists say it is that distance from the earth." The courtroom laughed. At first Evans joined in on the laugh and then, a degree of uncertainty entered his mind. After a few moments, it dawned upon the petulant defense lawyer that the joke was on him. From that moment forward, it mattered not how credible his inquisition may be, he had lost this witness. Brown tried to regain his bearings. He posited a few gratuitous questions reiterating the point that the doctor could not rule out death by suicide while he groped for a new strategy. Beverly Crump stood and motioned his colleague over to the defense table. Crump firmly clutched Brown's upper arm and drew him close, whispering in his ear. "End it, now!" Brown looked at Crump with defiant surprise, still eager to discredit Taylor. Crump squeezed Brown's arm. "End it!", he demanded through gritted teeth. (33.7)

A. Brown Evans cleared his throat and tugged at his lapels once more time. "No further questions, your honor."

Judge Atkins then looked toward the prosecution. Charles Meredith stood halfway from his seat shaking his head and quickly said, "No further questions, your honor."

"You may step down, Dr. Taylor.", said Judge Atkins.

The old doctor gently nodded, stood calmly, and left the stand. Crump bit his lip, tore a piece of paper from his notebook, and quickly scribbled a message. He slid the paper two chairs to his left where Brown was sitting. Brown glanced down and read the note,

"That was your last witness."   (33.8)

Chapter 34   *Heed Your Own Advice*

On May 14, 1885, The Hustings Court of Richmond was called to order. Judge T. S. Atkins was presiding. He nodded in the direction the prosecution, inviting them to call their first witness of the day.

Thomas J. Cluverius sat nearly motionless looking straight ahead. His hands were clasped in front of him. Occasionally, he would turn his head toward the prosecution or the bench. His controlled expression never changed. He breathed slowly and rhythmically through his nostrils, almost as if he were physically and emotionally detached from the proceedings. Observers failed to understand how even a completely innocent man could contain his emotions in this way, when so much was at risk.

Charles Meredith stood and said, "The prosecution calls Edgar J. Archer."

E. J. Archer stood with his ragged felt hat in hand. He pressed his greasy hair flat with his hand as he cleared his throat and walked to the stand. After reciting the oath, he took a seat.

"Mr. Archer, please state your name and occupation for the record."

"Edgar Jarvis Archer… I pre-fer E. J. Archer, though."

"And your occupation?"

"Oh… I'm da keeper at the Clark Spring Proper-tee."

"How long have you been doing that, sir?"

"Oh… nearin' 'leven yeas, now." Archer smiled and his tongue shot through the gap where his front teeth once were.

"Mr. Archer. Were you there when the police investigated the Marshall Reservoir and surrounding area on March 14th?"

"Yes, sir. I seen po-lice runnin' all over da area. I heard 'bout the body an' I figured I better give 'em the things I found that morning over by the da fence that run between the Clark proper-tee and the res'var."

"What were those items, exactly, Mr. Archer?"

"Well, I found a woman's veil and a, a red glove. I found 'em right near da fence."

Meredith turned and was handed a black veil and a garnet glove by Colonel Aylett.

"Were these the items you found that day, Mr. Archer?"

"Yessuh, they is."

"The prosecution would like to enter these two items into evidence. One, a woman's black veil, and the other; the mate to the garnet red glove entered into evidence prior which had been found at the embankment directly above the deceased. Both items were found on the Clark Spring Property, adjacent to the Marshall Reservoir, the morning of March 14, 1885."

"Thank you, Mr. Archer. No more questions."

Beverly Crump stood and removed his spectacles, laying them on the defense table.

"Mr. Archer. As the keeper of the Clark Spring Property, do you live on site?"

"Yessuh. I live in de small hoose der."

"Were you at home on March 13?"

"Yessuh, all night."

"Did you hear any disturbance coming from the reservoir the night of March 13?"

"No, suh."

"Have you ever heard any disturbances coming from the reservoir?"

"Well, I hear kids n' such over der sumtime'"

"Children, Mr. Archer?"

"Well, yes. When ders noise, it's use'ly kids. Mos'ly smaller ones, but sumtime dey bigger ones - come over from da college to swim in de res'var. It don't bother me none."

"Are the children just boys, or are there girls, too?"

"I'd say mos' of 'em is boys… But I guess I seen a 'casional girl, too."

"How do these children and young people access the reservoir grounds? Do they climb over the fence."

"Near as I know, dey go through da hole in da fence near my hoose. Mos' evry kid in da area knows it's der."

"So, if you didn't hear any disturbance the night of the 13th, does that mean that no one entered the property through the fence that night?"

"Well... Mos' likely... I guess.", Archer shrugged.

"No more questions."

Charles Meredith stood with reluctance. He didn't want to go in this direction, but he had to explain why Archer would not have heard much that particular evening.

"Mr. Archer. What night of the week was March 13?"

"I believe it was Fridee, Mr. Murdith."

"That's right, Mr. Archer."

"If I may ask a personal question; do you drink whiskey, Mr. Archer?"

"Oh, yes, Mr. Murdith. I don't mind sayin' I *like* whiskey.", Archer smiled and the courtroom chuckled.

"Were you drinking that Friday night?"

"Yessuh."

"How much do you figure you drank?"

"Oh, I don' know fer sure. But it was at leas' a bottle."

"An entire bottle, Mr. Archer?"

"Yessuh, that's my regler amount, 'speshly on Fridee. Hell, I may of even got on to a secon'", he smiled again with pride.

Although Meredith was somewhat discrediting his own witness, he was adhering to his priorities. This witness was not called to give eyewitness testimony regarding the crime itself, but rather to corroborate and identify the evidence collected from the site the following day. Therefore, he reasoned that he must undo the defense's attempt to make Mr. Archer a viable eyewitness of a non-event.

"What time do you think you stopped drinking, Mr. Archer?"

"Well, I git started pretty early. I probably fell 'sleep aroun' nine or ten 'clock."

"And when did you awake?"

"Oh, Mr. Murdith. After my bottle, I don' stir 'til mornin'. I git up 'bout 6 'clock or so that next mornin '.

"Thank you, Mr. Archer. No more questions."

Crump shook his head toward Judge Atkins, "No questions, sir."

Archer smiled broadly as he stood and acknowledged the judge. Clasping his hat in his hands in front, he made his way off the stand and back to his seat near the back of the room.

"The prosecution now calls Police Officer James J. Walton.", Meredith announced.

Young Officer Walton brushed the front of his uniform as he stood and walked to the stand. After taking the oath he sat in the witness stand. This was his first experience with trial testimony. He was nervous, but maintained a very professional demeanor.

"Good morning officer. Please state your name and position with the Richmond Police."

"I am Officer James Walton of the Richmond Police."

"And how long have you been a member with the police, sir?"

"It will be two years next week."

"And what is you relation to this case?", asked Meredith.

"I was the first policeman on the scene that morning… March 14th, sir. Mr. Lucas who works at the Old Reservoir came and found me. I joined and assisted Dr. Taylor, who was already there. When Detective Wren showed up shortly after, he asked some other officers and me to investigate the site and surrounding properties for possible physical evidence. So, a group of officers and I spread out and began to search. I found a black woman's hat on the floor of the "dead house" on the Clarke Spring property. It looked like the hat had been tossed through the open window facing Reservoir Street. Officer Stewart in our group found a red shawl hanging over a high wall on the Dunstan property a couple of blocks further up Reservoir Street."

Meredith brought forth a black straw hat with three ostrich feathers. "Is this the hat you discovered in the "dead house", Officer?"

Walton answered in the affirmative.

"Is this the red shawl found on the Dunstan property wall?"

"Yes, sir. It is."

"Objection, your honor!"

"Yes, Mr. Crump?", asked Judge Atkins

"There has been no chain of custody for these items established!"

Meredith spoke up, "Judge, may I ask the witness to elaborate?"

"Proceed, Mr. Meredith.", said the Judge.

"Officer Walton. Did you take physical custody of these items?"

"Yes, for a brief time. I soon turned them over to Detective Wren.", explained Walton.

"And, your honor,", continued Meredith, "they were in the custody of the Richmond Police from that time until they were turned over to my office, the Commonwealth's Attorney Office, until this time. There is your chain."

"Objection over-ruled.", said the Judge.

Meredith spoke once again, "The prosecution would like this hat and this shawl entered into evidence."

"I object!", cried Crump once more.

"On what grounds, Mr. Crump?", said Judge Atkins with a hint of exasperation.

"There is nothing to link these items to the deceased. These are just articles of clothing found in the vicinity. They could belong to any woman.", argued Crump.

Meredith responded, "Your honor, the prosecution will establish the significance and ownership of these articles with future testimony. We ask that the court please enter these items into evidence at this time. If for some reason the court becomes unconvinced of their veracity after the additional testimony; and wishes to remove them from the evidence, the prosecution will not object. But I contend that we have demonstrated that the time at which these articles were found and the locations at which they were found validate their entrance into evidence at this time."

"Agreed, Mr. Meredith. Objection over-ruled."

"No more questions, your honor."

Beverly Crump stood and stepped toward the witness stand. "Officer Walton. You say you have been with the Richmond Police for less than two years, correct?"

"Yes, sir."

"Have you ever been involved in an investigation and evidence collection of this type, Officer?"

"No, sir."

"Was collection of this type of evidence part of your training at the Police Academy?"

"Well, sir... I do recall discussions about it...", Walton hesitated.

Crump drilled down, "So, you say you really have *no experience* with this type of investigation?"

Walton, was unsure how to respond. He fell silent for three, four, five seconds... "I have been on the Richmond Police for nearly two years. I have done my job well. That is all I can say."

Crump smirked slightly. "No more questions, your honor."

Charles Meredith had been standing off to the side of the room with his arms crossed. He returned to the prosecution table and glanced down at his notes. "The prosecution calls Jackson J. Bolton to the stand."

Mr. Bolton stood in the second row and walked directly to the stand. After reciting the oath, he sat quietly.

"Please state your name and occupation.", asked Meredith.

"Jackson Bolton; Assistant City Engineer."

"How long have you held this position, Mr. Bolton?"

"Oh... nearly two-and-one half years."

"Where were you the morning of March 14th?"

"I was at the Marshall Reservoir."

"Why were you there, Mr. Bolton?"

"As an Assistant to the City Engineer, I oversee the operations of our municipal works facilities. Word that a body was found at Marshall reached my office around 10AM. Before 11AM, I was on site."

Meredith continued, "Would you please recount the events from that time forward."

"Yes sir. Upon my arrival I spoke with Detective Wren, who was conducting an investigation. His men were all over the area collecting evidence, mostly female clothing that was strewn across a large area."

"Did you personally witness any of the evidence collection directly?"

"I was present as Detective Wren inspected an opening in the fence on the east side of the property. I saw two sets of footprints going from the opening in the fence toward the embankment. One set appeared larger and heavier, like those of a man and the others were smaller with a narrow heel, like a woman's."

"Which direction were the prints headed?", asked Meredith.

"The male prints appeared to be heading in both directions, both toward the embankment and back from it. The female prints were only heading *toward* the embankment."

Cluverius sat with continued composure, but inside he was seething. "That's absolute bunk!", he screamed to himself. "This cannot be true! Rachel's tracks had to be going both directions, too! They are tailoring the evidence to suit my conviction!" He wanted to pound his fist on the table but knew, once again, any protestation would only tip his hand.

"Were you privy to any other evidence collection, Mr. Bolton?"

"Not directly, Mr. Meredith."

"No more questions, your honor."

Beverly Crump stood and leaned forward on the defense table. "What size were the supposed male tracks, Mr. Bolton?"

"I don't know. They were average size.", Bolton shrugged slightly.

"What size are Mr. Cluverius' shoes?"

"Well, I don't know." Bolton strained his neck to peak under the defense table.

"Do you have any indication that the tracks you saw belong to the accused?", asked Crump.

"No, sir.", admitted Bolton.

"Did these tracks belong to children, Mr. Bolton?"

"I doubt it, sir."

"But you don't know for sure?"

"Well... no. But they were rather large for a child."

"Perhaps.", said Crump. "As a boy, did you ever try on your father's shoes, Mr. Bolton?"

"Well, I may have. I don't recall."

"Well, would you say this is something many children do?"

"I object!", announced Mr. Meredith. "This has no bearing on these circumstances."

Judge Atkins held his hand up toward Meredith. He looked toward Crump for an explanation.

"Your honor. If the prosecution is going to use the evidence to create a set of circumstances that point toward the guilt of my client, am I not allowed to use that same evidence to reveal circumstances which exonerate him?"

"Not upon cross examination. Please save your circumstantial revelations for final argument, sir." ordered Judge Atkins

Crump nodded "Very well... Mr. Bolton; Mr. Archer has testified that he regularly witnesses students and female companions frolicking on the reservoir grounds. Could those tracks simply have been tracks made by playful young men and women?"

"Objection, your honor!", cried Meredith. "Mr. Crump is trying to elicit speculation from a man who has stated nothing more than he saw tracks. He has made no attempt to identify the people who left these tracks, whether they be children, students, or someone else!"

The Judge looked at Crump for a response. "Your honor. Quite the contrary. Mr. Bolton has already speculated that one set belonged to a man and another to a woman. How can that speculation be admissible and not any other?"

"Objection sustained.", said Judge Atkins. The defense will refrain from asking speculative questions of the witness and the witness will not be permitted to speculate on the source of the tracks."

"But, your honor. You have already allowed Mr. Bolton's speculation to enter the proceedings during Mr. Meredith's examination!", argued Crump.

"Perhaps *you* should have objected at the time, counselor." Slightly annoyed, but eager the set this straight, Judge Atkins turned to the court stenographer. "Please read back

Mr. Bolton's testimony regarding the tracks, Mr. Alexander."

H. H. Alexander furiously looked over his scribbles and cleared his throat (34.1):

"Mr. Meredith: 'Did you personally witness any of the evidence collection directly?'

Mr. Bolton: 'I was present as Detective Wren inspected the opening in the fence on the east side of the property. I saw two sets of footprints going from the opening in the fence toward the embankment. One set appeared larger and heavier, like those of a man and the others were smaller with a narrow heel, like a woman's.'

Mr. Meredith: 'Which direction were the prints heading?'.

Mr. Bolton: 'The male prints appeared to be heading in both directions, both toward the embankment and back from it. The female prints were only heading toward the embankment.'"

Judge Atkins nodded. "That testimony shall remain in the record. Mr. Bolton said the tracks '*appeared like* a man's, or '*like* a woman's. He made no speculative claim of the actual sources, Mr. Crump. Mr. Meredith's objection is sustained!"

Beverly Crump stood firm, "With all due respect, your honor, it is right there in the record. In the final sentence read, Mr. Bolton referred to them as "male prints" and "the female's" prints. He speculatively characterized them."

Meredith rejoined, "Your honor, that is a purposeful mischaracterization of Mr. Bolton's intent. Clearly, he opined on the prints' ***appearances*** at the beginning of the exchange. His later references were clearly truncated descriptions intended to avoid extraneous reiteration. These witnesses are speaking plainly and should be interpreted plainly by the court. I understand that attorneys such as Mr. Crump and myself live and die with nuanced wordsmithing; but let us not become preoccupied with the deconstruction of each and every witness statement. It is an impossible standard and does not serve the ultimate interests of the court and this proceeding."

Crump saw no value in continuing this debate. "Perhaps, Mr. Meredith should heed his own advice - plain language." A chuckle spread through the courtroom. "No more questions, your honor."

"No questions, your honor.", said Meredith.

"This court will recess for one hour. Proceedings will resume at 1:20 this afternoon." The judge banged his gavel. (34.2)

Chapter 35   *A Satchel and a Watch Key*

Judge T. S. Atkins sat behind the bench. He held his fist up to his mouth as he belched softly. He banged his gavel, "The court shall come to order and will continue the trial of Thomas J. Cluverius for the murder of Fannie L. Madison. Mr. Prosecutor, please continue."

Colonel William R. Aylett stood at the prosecution table. "The prosecution calls Mr. Aaron Watkins to the stand.

A wiry middle-aged colored man stood and approached the bench. After taking the oath he sat and awaited the questions. The prosecution was trying to counter some of the damage the defense had inflicted upon the testimony of Mr. Archer earlier that morning.

"Mr. Watkins, please state your name and occupation for the court.", said Aylett.

"I am Aaron Watkins. I shoe horses in the blacksmith shop at Tredegar. I also dig graves o'er at Hollywood Cemetery.

Yes, and where do you live, Mr. Watkins?"

I live on Cherry Street. Right across from Hollywood Cem'tery; near the res'var."

"Is that the Marshall Reservoir, sir?", Aylett asked for clarity.

"Yes, sir.", answered Watkins.

"How close to the Marshall Reservoir is your house?

"'Bout two hunderd fitty yard. Maybe less."

Aylett continued, "On the night of March 13th, did you hear anything unusual, Mr. Watkins?"

"Sometime aroun' 10:30 or 11 that night, I was headin' to da outhouse to do what I gotta do an' I hear a couple a squalls. One was just a yell. Sounded high; like a woman. The other I hear a woman yell out 'Oh Lawd!' I started to walk that way but after a minute or so, I didn't hear nothing else. So, I just went on back home."

In order to short circuit the defense Aylett asked, "Mr. Watkins. Had you anything to drink that evening? Any alcohol?"

"No, sir. I don't drink. I give that foolishness up when I was a younger man."

"Well done, Mr. Watkins. No more questions."

Beverly Crump stood and moved toward the witness. He grasped his left lapel with his left hand. "Mr. Watkins. Have you heard disturbances at night at the Marshall Reservoir before?"

"Well... Yes, sir. I have."

"Would you say you hear these types of disturbances on regular occasion?"

Watkins squinted and looked up toward the ceiling as he thought. "I would say I hear things o'er there maybe fo'or fi' time a year. Not regular; but ain't that unusual neither."

"We have heard reports that children and young people have been known to enter the reservoir grounds with some frequency. The noise you heard that evening; could it have been made by children, Mr. Watkins?"

"Well, sir. I s'pose that could be. But the noises I hear that night sounded a little diff'rent from ones I hear before. Just sounded more like a woman than a child; sounded more like somebody scared. Sometime I hear laughin' goin' on o'er there. There was no laughin' that night…"

Crump cut off the testimony, "Thank you, sir. No more questions, your honor."

Col. Aylett stood and announced, "The prosecution calls Mr. Joseph R. Mountcastle to the stand."

Joseph Mountcastle approached the bench and like all the witnesses before him, swore an oath of truthfulness. Colonel Aylett put his left hand in his trouser pocket as he stepped out from behind the table.

"Mr. Mountcastle, please state your full name and occupation for the record."

"Joseph R. Mountcastle; dock worker at the C&O Railroad wharf."

"Mr. Mountcastle, where is the C&O wharf located?"

"It's down on the river; below the City to the southeast."

"Will you describe for the court what you found the morning of March 14?"

"Well, a couple of other men and I were on the docks waiting for a barge to come in when I spotted a satchel floating in the water at the edge of the shore. I jumped down from the dock and fished it out of the water. Inside were some women's clothes. They were pretty wet, but not entirely. The other men and I took the clothes out and laid them on the dock to dry. There was also a little wood box with some sewing in it. The bag had initials on it."

"What were those initials, Mr. Montcastle?"

"F. L. M.", answered Mountcastle.

"Please note that the deceased has been identified as Fannie Lee Madison.", Aylett reminded the court. "Mr. Mountcastle", continued Aylett, "were initials found on any of the other items?"

"Yes sir. On one of the blouses. There were initials written in ink on the inside of the collar. They were a bit smeared because of the water, but they appeared to be "F.L.M., as well"

After a brief pause to let the connection sink in with the jury, Aylett went on, "Now, what happened next, Mr. Mountcastle?"

"I showed everything to my boss. He was suspicious and he told me I should take this to the Coroner; so I did."

Colonel Aylett turned back to the table. Mr. Meredith handed him a light brown satchel. "Is this the satchel you found that morning, Mr. Mountcastle?"

"Yes sir, it is." affirmed Mountcastle.

"The prosecution would like to enter this satchel and all of its contents into evidence.", declared Aylett.

"The defense objects, your honor!", cried Beverly Crump.

"On what grounds, Mr. Crump?", asked Judge Atkins.

"There is no direct evidence linking this satchel and its contents to the deceased. The link proposed by the prosecution is speculative in nature. It is the defense's position that only articles found on the deceased or on the site where the body was located be entered as evidence."

Aylett interceded, "Your honor, the initials which match those of the deceased and the female clothing should be sufficient. Future testimony with validate the evidence, your honor."

The Judge paused and thought for a moment. "Over-ruled; enter the evidence.", ordered the Judge. "The prosecution may continue."

No further questions, your honor.", said Aylett. "Thank you, Mr. Mountcastle." Colonel Aylett returned to his seat behind the prosecutor's table.

Beverly T. Crump stood. "Good afternoon, Mr. Mountcastle." he said with a disarming smile.

"Yes sir, good afternoon.", replied Mountcastle.

"How long have you been employed at the C&O Wharf, sir?"

"I'd say more than ten years."

"So, you're very familiar with the river, it's currents, and so forth?", asked Crump.

"Well, yes. I've spent a lot of time down there."

"Was there anything unusual about the current that morning, Mr. Mountcastle? Were the currents particularly fast, or slow?"

"Not that I recall.", answered a confused Mountcastle.

"So, you would say the current was running at its usual pace that morning?"

"Well, yes."

Crump paused for a moment and then continued. "You stated that the clothes were not completely wet. Is that right?"

"Yes. Some articles were wetter than others, but the contents were not entirely soaked."

"So, how long do you think the bag was in the water?", asked Crump.

"Oh, sir. I really have no way of knowing."

Crump continued, "What time was it when you found the satchel?"

"Oh… It was about 7 o'clock."

"In the morning, Mr. Mountcastle?"

"Yes, in the morning."

"How far is the C&O Wharf downriver from the Marshall Reservoir?"

"I'm not sure, Mr. Crump; two and one half or three miles?", Mountcastle shrugged.

"Actually, Mr. Mountcastle, it's closer to three-and-one-half miles. Would you say that it is unlikely that a simple canvass bag could stay afloat for at least six hours and traverse that distance down the James River and not become completely soaked, or even sink to the bottom?"

"I object!", cried Meredith. "This witness is not an expert on these questions."

Crump responded, "Your honor, if the prosecution or anyone else could find someone more "expert" on these particular matters, I'd be glad to question him." The courtroom chuckled at Crump's cheekiness. "Mr. Mountcastle works along the river every day. I am sure he sees all manner of things floating down the river. The satchel and contents he found have been entered into evidence. The defense is perfectly entitled to try and discover for this court how it could be possible that this evidence, if indeed it belonged to Miss Madison at all, ended up such a distance from the reservoir."

"Objection overruled. Please answer the question as best you can, Mr. Mountcastle.", instructed Judge Atkins.

"I honestly don't know the answer to that question, your honor.", said Mountcastle.

Judge Atkins looked toward Mr. Crump for a reaction.

"Very well, Mr. Mountcastle.", replied Beverly Crump.

Crump was not going to get greedy by pressing Mountcastle further. The intent of his question was simply to raise it, not necessarily to get an answer. He understood very well that it was unlikely that the satchel could have traveled very far through the rapids in that part of the James River and be discovered in the condition in which it was found. Although he was certain the prosecution would come up with an explanation at some point in the trial, the experienced defense lawyer had preemptively cast doubt upon the first logical assumption; that the satchel had been cast into the waters well up-river from the canal near the Marshall Reservoir.

Colonel Aylett stood to respond and redirect. "Mr. Mountcastle; to what point is the James River navigable?"

"Barges can reach Mayo's Bridge, but they never go that far. The canal and wharf area is as far as any craft go."

"How far up river from the C&O Wharf is Mayo's Bridge?", asked Aylett.

"Oh, about a mile and one half."

"And, what are conditions in the river like above Mayo's Bridge?"

"Well, there's a great number of rocks and small islands in the channel there."

"Does the river run smoothly through that area?"

"No, sir. It's very rough and choppy up that way. It would be difficult for any thing to get through there."

"But, below Mayo's Bridge, it runs smooth again?"

"Yes, Colonel Aylett."

"Now… When you discovered the satchel, was it traveling with the current downriver?"

"No sir. It had found its way to the banks and was bobbing in one spot just a few feet from shore. That's how I was able to reach it. The current runs strong out in the middle of the river. But, near the shore, there is no current."

"So, it could have been in that position for some time, even hours?"

"Yes, I suppose. When I first saw it, it was *right there*." He held his open hands parallel to one another pointing to an imaginary object just a few yards in front and below him. "I don't know how long it had been there."

"Thank you, Mr. Mountcastle, no more questions."

Judge Atkins looked toward the defense.

"No questions.", said Crump.

Colonel Aylett then called his next witness, "The prosecution calls Police Chief Justice D. C. Richardson to the stand.

After swearing in, Chief Richardson sat stoically and awaited the questioning. Meredith stood and walked in front of the witness. "Please state your name and occupation, sir."

"My name is David C. Richardson. I am the Police Chief Justice for the City of Richmond."

"Chief Richardson; how long have you held this position?"

"Just over five years, sir."

"And how long have you been in this line of work?"

"I was the clerk to the Police Chief Justice for ten years prior. I have been studying, enforcing, and applying the law for eighteen years."

Colonel Aylett immediately brought forth an envelope. "Chief Richardson, do you recognize this envelope?"

"Yes sir, I do. This is an envelope in which I personally placed some physical evidence provided to me."

"Did you seal the envelope, yourself, sir?"

"Yes, I did.", Richardson responded.

"Please open that envelope and describe its contents."

Chief Richardson pushed his forefinger into the top corner of the envelope and ran it across the top, tearing open the letter. Inside was a golden watch-key.

"I see the watch key which was found at the reservoir and a small link of chain which is attached to it."

"And this was in your possession from the moment you received it?"

"Yes, Colonel Aylett. It was in the possession of the Richmond Police until such time I turned it over to the Commonwealth Attorney's Office."

"Thank you. Chief. No more questions.", said Aylett.

Beverly Crump stood and simply held his hand aloft, "No questions, your honor."

After a few moments the prosecution called its next witness. Colonel Aylett stood and announced, "The prosecution calls John Williams to the stand."

A tall thin man of about forty stood in the back of the courtroom and looked nervously from side to side. Simultaneously, a young boy hopped up near the front and moved directly toward the stand. Colonel Aylett held up his hand to stop the man in the back. "I believe we have two John Williams present! Sir, the boy is the one we need." The stunned man let out an audible sigh of relief, bringing brief laughter to the court.

As he stood in front of the bench, Judge Atkins looked down upon the boy. "Boy, do you understand what it means to *take an oath*?"

"Yes sir, I do.", said the boy quickly.

"Explain for me what it means.", said Atkins

"Well, it means you promise to tell the truth. It's a promise to God to tell what you know."

"Very well; are you ready to take an oath; to tell the truth?"

"Yes, sir."

After the oath, Colonel Aylett asked the boy to state his name and age.

"John L. Williams; eleven years old.", answered the boy.

"Master Williams…", a grandfatherly Colonel Aylett began. "You look like a fine boy. Where were you on Sunday, March 15th?"

"Well, sir, um… Well, after services some friends 'n I went over to play at the reservoir."

"Was that the Marshall Reservoir?", asked Aylett seeking clarification.

"Yes, sir. We were going there to sail our boat 'n throw rocks in the water."

"Ah, yes…", said Aylett. "But, you know, you're really not supposed to go in there. How do you rascals get on to the grounds?"

"Yes sir, we knew that. But it's such wonderful fun there. There's a hole in the fence near the dead house. We just move a board aside and go right in."

"And what happened that day?"

Um, I was crawlin' through and I seen this sparkling' gold thing hangin' on the fence right there in the openin'! It was a watch-key with a little ring on it."

"What did you do with it?"

"Well, there was a man from the newspaper there and he asked me what I found. I showed it to him and he said I should turn that over to the police. He said he'd take me to the station. But, I thought my mother should know if I was goin' to do somethin' like that. He said that was fine, so he came back with me to my house and we showed my mother. She agreed with the man that we should take it to the police."

"Is this the watch-key you found that day?", Colonel Aylett pulled the small gold key and ring from his vest pocket and handed it to the boy. John Williams held it close to his face and studied it carefully.

"Yes, sir; that's it.", he said with confidence.

"The prosecution hereby enters this watch-key into evidence. Thank you, Master Williams. No further questions."

Beverly Crump stood and abruptly announced, "The defense has no questions, your honor." Crump likened cross-examinations of children to vaudeville animal acts: folly was nearly inevitable, danger was entirely possible, and reward was highly unlikely. (35.3)

"Alright Master Williams,", said Judge Atkins, "you may now return to your seat. Thank you." Judge Atkins then looked at his watch. "Let us adjourn these proceedings for today. The trial will continue at 9 o'clock tomorrow." He banged the gavel and departed the bench.

Chapter 36   *Burn It*

Peter Burton of the *Richmond Dispatch* tapped lightly on the door to Chief D. C. Richardson's office.

"Come in..", called the Chief from the other side.

"Ah, Mr. Burton. Thank you for coming in this afternoon." Burton sat uneasily in the chair in front of Chief Richardson's desk. "I'm sure you remember Lieutenant Grimes.", Richardson said smartly as he gestured to the corner behind Burton. The hairs on the back of the reporter's neck stood as he turned his head and caught a glimpse of the brute looming over his left shoulder.

"Yes, I know *all* about Lieutenant Grimes.", said Burton, pithily trying to mask his nerves.

"Well, it appears that Lieutenant Grimes - and I - know some things about you, as well.", said the Chief. "Mr. Burton, I am a reasonable man. I am trying to right a police force that has been maligned for years. This will continue. As I have said to you on other occasions, I will not allow your reporting to compromise my ability to reform the force. Criticism by your paper is fine, when warranted. Unfair criticism bordering on lies is never warranted."

"Wait one moment, Chief!", cried Burton. "I have not written any negative stories about the force in weeks!"

"That's right, Mr. Burton. And there will not be any such reports in the future.", said the Chief flatly.

"Chief Richardson, why are we having this conversation? Are you threatening me? All of my reporting has been based in fact!"

"Facts... Lieutenant..." The burly Grimes handed a black ledger book to Burton. "Have you ever been to the Davis Hotel, Mr. Burton?" The Chief paused and dipped his head to try and catch Burton's eye. "Do you know Hannah? I believe you do."

Burton's eyes widened as he looked up toward the Chief. "You, bastards!"

"Now, Mr. Burton. Surely you wouldn't deprive me of my right to report *facts*, would you?"

Burton stood and broke for the door, clutching the hotel registry to his chest. Before he could escape, Grimes blocked his path. The Lieutenant delivered one sharp blow to Burton's abdomen. As Burton dropped to one knee and gasped, Grimes plucked the ledger book from his weakened hands.

"It would be a shame if your wife and family learned of these 'facts', eh Mr. Burton?". Grimes smiled as he grabbed Burton by the back of his collar, opened the door to the Chiefs office, and flung the panting reporter into the hall.

A dark-haired man bit the tip of his cigar and spat it toward the gutter. He struck a match and began puffing as he continued east on Main Street. It was late afternoon and the streets of Richmond were starting to fill with people heading home for the evening.

A young boy was standing on the corner of Main and 15th Street fervently making his sales pitch for trading cards. "Pictures of Cluverius, the murderer! Pictures of his victim! Ten cents for the pair!", he cried. The boy held the small cart d' visite's in the air.

The man had a strangely stunned expression as he drew near the boy. "Would you like a pair, sir? Get a piece of the most sensational crime of the decade!"

The man took some of the cards from the boy's hand and studied them with amazement. One card had a very good likeness of Thomas J. Cluverius. Across the top were the words "Sensational Trial of 1885". On the bottom edge it said "Thomas J. Cluverius - The Accused". The other was clearly Fannie L. Madison. The bottom of her card read "Fannie L. Madison - The Deceased".

"Where did you get these?", the man asked with astonishment. "I've never seen anything like this!"

The boy was a sharp salesman and did not divulge his supplier. "I don't know where the pictures came from, sir; but rest assured, this is the only place to get them now!"

"How many have you sold?", asked the man.

"Oh dozens, sir. Everyone wants to own a piece if this history!", exclaimed the boy.

The man stuffed his hand into his trouser pocket and pulled out a handful of change. "He plucked out a single dime. There you are."

"Thank you, sir", said the boy, "And, if you need more, you know where to come! But, sir, I'd prefer two nickels if you have them"

The man smiled with his cigar pinched in the corner of his mouth. "Very well.". The two exchanged the dime for the two nickels. The boy put one nickel in his right trouser pocket and the other in his left. The man looked back at the cards, giggled to himself, and lightly shook his head in disbelief.

H.R. Pollard entered Thomas Cluverius' cell just after 5PM. The prisoner lay on his cot, hands behind his head. Pollard approached calmly and flipped two trading cards onto Cluverius' stomach.

"It appears you are becoming a franchise, Thomas. I was hoping you would autograph these for me!", he said with a smile.

"Where did you get these?", asked Cluverius.

"A boy on the street was selling them - a dime for the pair."

"Ten cents, eh?", said Cluverius coolly. He shrugged slightly, appearing somewhat unaffected.

"Are you alright, Thomas?"

"Yes, Henry, I am fine."

H. R. Pollard could see that Cluverius was not particularly interested in visiting. "Well, Crump asked me to stop in and make sure you…", Pollard halted at the sound of rattling keys and the cell door unlocking.

"Good afternoon, I am Reverend William Hatcher.", the man introduced himself and extended his hand to Pollard.

"Good afternoon, sir.", replied Pollard. "I am H.R. Pollard, one of the attorneys."

"Ah yes; well I'm here to spend some time with Mr. Cluverius… You see, I am his spiritual minister… back in King William."

"Oh…", said Pollard. "Then Thomas, I shall keep you no longer.". The attorney smiled at Cluverius and nodded to the reverend. "Good evening, gentlemen."

Hatcher was a tall slender man in his forties. Neatly dressed in all black with a white collar, Hatcher pulled up a chair alongside Cluverius' cot. "What are those?", asked Hatcher as he pointed to the cards in Cluverius' hand.

"Oh, nothing…. They're silly cards they are selling on the street - pictures of me and Lillie."

"Ah, Thomas. This attention is quite unwanted, isn't it?"

Cluverius' thoughts uttered "absolutely not" but his mouth answered, "Yes, Reverend. It is a terrible burden for me. It pains me more to see poor Lillie's name and image being sold like a carnival trinket; it is disgraceful."

"Yes, son. I understand. Let us pray." Cluverius and the Reverend bowed their heads and closed their eyes. As Hatcher began, Cluverius lifted his head slightly and opened one eye toward the cell door. There he saw the shadow of the guard on the wall opposite the cell door.

Cluverius boldly exclaimed "Amen" as Hatcher's prayer was completed. The guard listening in, Cluverius continued the performance. "Reverend, may we say a prayer for dear Lillie, and the rest of the family? They are all I have thought about throughout this ordeal."

"Yes, Thomas.", said Hatcher. The Reverend stayed for more than an hour, reading passages from the Bible and offering many prayers to the Almighty on behalf of the tragic Cluverius. Even as Hatcher left, Cluverius remained on his knees at the foot of his cot, summoning the strength to maintain his burden. Once the Reverend was clearly out of earshot, a snickering self-amused Cluverius immediately returned to his cot.

A few minutes later, Cluverius once again heard the rattle of the guard's keys as the cell door lock was thrown open. Willie Cluverius came in. As the guard closed the door, he reminded the men. "All visitors must be out of here in ten minutes."

Cluverius sat up on the cot and smiled as he looked over the pictures. "These look fine…", he said softly. "Pollard bought these today. He said he paid *ten cents* for the pair. What's going on, Willie?"

"I don't know, Tommie.", answered Willie nervously. "I told the boy five cents a pair!" Willie repeated, "Ten cents. Ten cents?" Tommie burst out in laughter. Willie laughed reflexively. It had been quite a while since he'd seen his brother laugh and, for Willie, this was a pleasure. However, as Tommie cackled on, Willie became confused. "What, Tommie? What is it?"

"I can't believe the audacity of that boy! Who does he think he is, trying to cheat me?" Tommie's demeanor changed in an instant as he pulled his brother closer. "Fix this Willie. Do not let that little thief cheat me out of another penny."

"I will put a stop to it, Tommie."

"Wait, Willie;", Cluverius paused while a thought came to him. "Let him keep selling them for ten cents. But when you go to collect, make sure you collect it all!"

"Do you want me to leave him with anything?"

"Maybe a bloody nose, but nothing more!" Cluverius' voice began to rise, but then he modulated it once again. "This guttersnipe needs to learn a lesson. He will not cross *me* again!"

"Yes… Tommie… Is everything going well with the trial? I get so confused by all of the back and forth…"

Once again, Tommie's demeanor changed. With a soothing assuredness he said, "I understand, Willie. It becomes confusing for me, as well. Have no worry, brother. I am innocent. But, Willie; we need to ensure the jury comes to that conclusion. I need you to find Emmett Rogers... He rode with me on the train to Richmond on the 12th. Give him this note." Tommie put a small sealed envelope in Willie's hand. "He must get this; and he must get it soon!"

"Alright, Tommie; I will be back home tomorrow...". Willie put the note in his coat pocket. "Is there anything more?"

"Yes, Willie. You saw the watch key they produced at trial?"

"Yes.", responded Willie.

"Well, I don't know where they got it. I really don't think it is mine, but they will do everything in their power to make it seem that way, brother. I know what these men are trying to do. I'm certain they've already found the jeweler and they will get him to say whatever they want him to say."

"What jeweler, Tommie?" Willie was confounded.

"Willie... Listen to me." Cluverius hushed his voice. "The jeweler in Centreville; you know who I mean, the one who has the case in Bland's store; the who comes to town every month..." Cluverius paused while he sifted his memory, "the German; Joel, that's his name... He will testify that he worked on that watch key. He will testify that he knows it belongs to me. I'm sure they've gotten to him...If they have not, they will."

"Who, Tommie?"

"Willie, you imbecile!", Cluverius raised his voice in frustration and just as quickly regained control. "Willie, I am sorry. But you have to listen and listen closely. Joel did indeed work on my watch some time back in January. I gave him the watch when I was here in Richmond. But I picked it up from him a couple of weeks afterward back in Centreville. I paid him then and he recorded it in his ledger. I've been thinking about this since they produced that damn watch-key... I remember that he wrote my name in that ledger; he keeps it somewhere in a drawer behind the counter. You must find that ledger! You know the Blands. Do what needs to be done. If Meredith can link me to the watch-key and the watch-key to Joel, they will seal my fate!"

"Is that really your watch-key, Tommie?"

"Of course, not... But Meredith wants it to be mine. Don't you see, Willie? They have someone to blame for Lillie's death and, whether it's true or not, they want desperately to make it so. That's why you have to help me. If they find Joel and bring him into the trial, it will be very bad for me."

"Alright, Tommie. I'll find it. But what should I do with it?", Willie embraced his brother.

Thomas pulled Willie closer and whispered firmly in his ear, "Burn it."

Willie Cluverius left the cell. Thomas turned to the canvas bag behind the head of his cot. It was full of letters, mostly from strangers. Many of the letters insisted upon his innocence; some were poorly constructed depositions demanding he defend himself; a few were harsh indictments upon his soul. Nearly all of them were written by women; some nothing more than school girl admonitions of a forbidden love. Cluverius chuckled and blushed as he read through them. The professions were clear and their desires, at times, pornographic. Their words titillated him as he imagined himself exerting his prowess upon them; but his feelings of power soon changed to frustration. Ultimately, he saw these women as nothing more than Jezebels; intent upon taunting him with sinful promiscuities that could never be fulfilled. Cluverius wanted to be with them, to control them; but he held no respect for any of them. In fact, he hated them and wanted to punish them with his singular pleasure.

Cluverius was about to cast the entire lot upon the floor when the name on one envelope caught his eye. "Rachel", he said to himself. He took a deep breath before opening the seal.

May 12, 1885

My Dear Mr. "M",

I hope you are well. I have been following the proceedings. I find myself thinking often of our time together and look forward to seeing you again at the earliest possible moment. I assure you that, for me, nothing has changed.

Please respond. I must know you are well and that you are thinking of me. If there is any service I may perform, please instruct me.

R.M.

"She is going to become a menace...", Cluverius' instincts told him. He balled up the letter and tossed it into the corner of his cell; neither giving it nor its writer another thought. (36.1)

Chapter 37   *Benny Havens, Oh!*

On August 31, 1862, Brigadier General Fitzhugh Lee rode at the head of regiment of the 1st Cavalry of Virginia. Confederate forces had out-maneuvered Union forces for a second time in Manassas, Virginia and were pursuing General Alexander Pope's Army of the Potomac back down Little River Turnpike toward Washington, D.C. Fitz was leading over five hundred troopers on a ride around Chantilly as darkness fell. Major Johann Heros von Borcke, a close aide to General J.E.B. Stuart, had joined him for the evening ride.

Von Borcke was a proud Prussian cavalry soldier who had resigned his commission in the Prussian Army and joined the Confederate Cavalry. He was able to slip the Union blockade of Charleston Harbor and join Stuart's command in May of 1862. In just a few short months, the burly six-foot-four-inch Prussian distinguished himself and by August was promoted to Major. He was a voracious student of cavalry tactics and came to America to gain new insight and hone his craft.

Fitz Lee knew that Union troops were still in the area. He looked east down the turnpike to his left and spotted a farmhouse. Fitz slowed and halted the column as a late summer evening breeze cooled the air. He pulled his field glasses from his pocket.

"I see three campfires in the field behind the house.", he said to von Borcke. "And lamps are lit in the house. There must be three dozen horses tied off in the yard. I don't think it could be more than one company. "

"I say ve take der position, Herr General.", von Borcke suggested.

"Ya-bul mein major!" Fitz gently ribbed. "Let's go see who we find over there." Captain Charles Minnegerode and Major James Ferguson rode up to Lee and von Borcke. "Gentlemen; take Companies C through F and circle back and take that field of Yankees. Be ready to come in from the tree line. In twenty minutes, Major von Borcke and I will take Companies A and B and go down the road. We will go directly in the front door of the house. When you see us dismount and step onto that front porch, charge the field and secure it. After you have secured the field, gentlemen, come find us in the house."

Brig. General Fitzhugh Lee, CSA, (Library of Congress)

Twenty minutes later Fitz Lee let Heros von Borcke blaze their path as they burst through the front door of the clapboard farmhouse. Von Borcke drew his large Solingen sabre as they turned to the right and found four Union officers just sitting down for a home-cooked meal. Two of the Yankees sprung from their seats and bolted toward a table in the corner for their weapons.

Fitzhugh Lee popped out from behind the *Grey Giant* and raised his right hand, "Now quit your foolishness, gentlemen! The house is surrounded by my men and escape is impossible. All will be lovely if you will quietly surrender. Please do me the kindness to leave your arms piled in that corner." Fitz laughed with hands on hips and declared, "Well, as I've captured the party ordering it, I suppose I've captured the dinner, also. I cordially invite you gentlemen to partake of it as my guests!" One of the seated officers craned his neck to look out the dining room window. He nodded at his fellow officers in verification of General Lee's claim. Fitz then looked at the officer seated on the left of the table who, to this moment, had gone unnoticed. "My God! Tom Hite! Now, this is some luck!"

Captain Tom Hite was attached to the 2nd Cavalry Dragoons under Pope. "Fitz Lee, you sneaky rascal! How long has it been?" Hite stood and shook Fitz's hand. They each made the guttural sound men often make when they see an old chum and decide a hug is in order. They wrapped their arms around each other and slapped each other's backs and shoulders.

"It's been since the Academy. '56, I guess." Fitz then looked at another officer seated at the table. His eyes blazed, "Sweetie! This is hard to imagine!" Fitz turned toward von Borcke, "Von, I taught ol' John Sweet here in '60 during my year as an instructor at the Academy. I taught this man everything he knows about horsemanship; and now he wants to ride over me! Gentlemen; sit, please!" Fitz and von Borcke each pulled a chair up to the table. "Two more of my officers will be joining us soon. They are outside making sure your men are well looked after.", Fitz winked at Hite.

Heros von Borcke sat quietly and observed. He stroked his thick walrus mustache and beard. He was amazed how easily these Americans could jettison all hostility. Men that were shooting to kill just hours before

Major Johann Heros von Borcke, CSA

now sat shoulder to shoulder; sharing food, wine, memories, and mutual respect. To him, this was the pinnacle of the professional warrior spirit. Incidents such as this illustrated the inherent contradictions present throughout the conflict. Personal loyalties were often in juxtaposition to loyalty to country and duty. The bonds forged by the rigors of the training at the United States Military Academy at West Point were difficult to sever; even by the sharpest implement of total war. (37.1)

As they were finishing the last bites of the meal, Tom Hite turned toward his old classmate, "Fitz, remember that night at Benny Havens'?"

"There were a few. But I know the one you mean. Never to be forgotten…", he chuckled. "If we are to speak of these events, we will need to open another bottle of wine! And those who weren't there are sworn to secrecy!"

In the winter of 1853 Cadet Third Class Fitzhugh Lee and four comrades crept through the midnight shadows. They discreetly approached a particularly low spot in the wall that surrounded the old Academy. The December winds whipped coldly through the treetops of West Point, New York. The boys were looking forward to warming themselves at Benny Havens' Tavern. A sentinel stood guard about one hundred fifty feet from the hallowed spot where a breach could be attained with the minimal effort and with the lowest risk of detection. The boys watched closely as the restless guard stepped into his small sentry box. Fitzhugh Lee tapped Tom Hite on the shoulder and whispered, "Let's go!". The tall, angular Hite was dressed in a dark suit of clothes and a brown false beard. The shorter Fitz quickly threw a faded yellow dress on over his uniform and donned a frayed lady's bonnet. A worn blue woolen shawl completed the disguise. He was somewhat believable as a woman, particularly under cover of night, but hardly attractive. "When Hite and I pass the sentinel, we will create a diversion and you three must jump the wall and head down the bluff. We'll meet you there in a few minutes"

Arm in arm, Fitz and Tom walked confidently toward the sentry post. When they were about ten yards from the guard, Fitz muttered, "Get ready..."

"Ready, dear...", smirked Tom.

It was very dark at this hour and the moon was but a sliver in the sky. As the couple walked past, Fitz let loose with a very loud high-pitched sneeze. Tom stopped abruptly and said in a deepened voice, "Oh dear, my that cold is persistent!" He pulled a handkerchief from his breast pocket. "Here, my darling, clean your nose." The guard squinted in their direction with curious amusement. On cue, the three boys by the wall quickly scaled it and were over the top without detection. "Oh, my dear,", continued the bearded gent, "you are particularly lovely tonight. I am the most fortunate man on earth!"

Fitz convincingly sneezed again then growled lowly between his clenched teeth. "Don't over-do this, Tom..."

Hite was ready to burst, but maintained his composure. "There dear, that's better. I must get you to bed!", he said as he bit his lip, took his "beloved" by the arm, and escorted him beyond the gate and down the road into the darkness. A hundred yards further they approached the treacherous path that led down the bluff to the foot of Buttermilk Falls and Benny Havens' Tavern.

The five boys rendezvoused at the base of the bluff. Fitz balled up his dress, shawl, and bonnet and tossed them aside. He proudly proclaimed,

"Tonight, gents, will be one to remember... I promise you that!" Fitz's brilliant blue eyes shone through the darkness as the boys broke into a cheer. Fitz quickly put his forefinger to his lips and moved his other hand down has if dunking someone's head under water. "Shhh...", he pleaded, "Not too loudly, boys... The less people that know we're in the area, the better!" The boys followed Fitz like four thirsty puppy dogs. He was small in stature, but clearly in command. Fitz's leadership was an intangible power that was characteristic, and, to some extent, expected, of a Lee; but his was one rooted more in charm than example. It was an intoxicant that was equally capable of leading his peers to victory or disaster; or, on rare occasions, both.

Benny Havens' Tavern, Buttermilk Falls, NY

The boys scurried like a pack of rats around the base of the bluff until they came upon Benny Havens' Tavern. Benny Havens and his wife, Letitia, had owned and operated the little frame tavern near West Point, NY for nearly thirty years. It was a two-story structure. The first floor was the barroom and upstairs were The Havens' quarters and two very small rooms where over-zealous patrons often flopped for the evening. Over the years the tavern had become a sanctuary for weary homesick cadets. It provided a familial comfort and opportunity for relaxation that could be found nowhere else at the Academy. Perhaps most inviting was Letitia's cooking. Renowned particularly for her oyster stew and buckwheat pancakes, the motherly Letitia was certainly the most nurturing figure near campus.

The two front windows of the tavern were caked with dirt, but like the eyes of a black cat in the darkness a greenish yellow glow was detectable.

"Is anyone in there?", asked Brock Jennings.

"Most assured, Jennings. Ye, of little faith!" Fitz stepped forward and rapped sharply two times on the heavy wood door. He paused for a moment then rapped three more times quickly. "The secret combination!" Fitz's eyes widened and the boys swelled with anticipation.

Suddenly, a bolt was thrown on the other side and the door cracked open. A voice from the back of the room called up toward the door. "Who is it, Maynard?"

"It's young Lee and some other rag-tag dogs!" called Maynard back over his shoulder.

"Let 'em in, Maynard.", said the voice.

"Good evening, Maynard; Cadet Third Class Lee at your service!" Fitz smiled and put his hand near his temple as he bowed his head with sarcastic deference.

"Come in, boys!", said Maynard.

"Fitz!", the roar went up as Lee strolled into the tavern. Tom Hite and James Hughes were fellow Third Classmen. They had accompanied Fitz on a couple of successful ventures to Benny Havens'. But the other two, Brock Jennings and John Sample, were Fourth Classmen who had never been off the academy grounds since their appointment started a few months earlier.

The five surrounded a small table against the back wall, drawing chairs and seating themselves.

"Will it be five hot flips?", Fitz asked the boys.

Everyone nodded in the affirmative. "I always buy the first one!", said Fitz with a wink.

"And that will be the last!", chided Hite.

"That's a pittance for showing you gents such a good evening!" Fitz slapped Cadet Sample on the back. "Right, Sample?" Sample knew all his money had just been spent for him, but he didn't give it a second thought. He would have paid three times that amount to be where he was at this moment.

When Fitz left for the bar, Sample asked, "What exactly *is* a 'hot flip'?" Hite and Hughes erupted with laughter. Jennings had no idea what a "hot flip" was either, but laughed at his friend anyway.

"It's Benny's famous drink. It's a meal unto itself, boys.", said a gleeful Hite. Sample and Jennings were a bit uneasy; their experience with drink was very limited. However, it was too late to equivocate; they had committed themselves to the mission and, like aspiring military men, they would see it through.

Fitz plopped a tray crammed with five large tankards on the small round table. "Ambrosia, my fellows… Ambrosia!", the sturdy little purveyor of merriment exclaimed as he rubbed his hands together and licked his lips. Following closely behind Fitz was Benny Havens. Cadet Sample reached out for a tankard.

"Ah…ah! Wait one moment!", scolded Benny as he brushed Sample's hand away. He turned to Fitz, "Lee, I hold you entirely responsible. You really should mold these greensticks before bringing them in here!"

Hite laughed and added, "They don't make 'em like they used to, Mr. Havens. The standards of the Academy have dropped mightily this past year!"

Benny Havens chuckled and shook his head as he turned away from the table toward the fireplace. He grabbed a rag and quickly wrapped it around his hand. The old tavern keeper reached into the fire and drew a red-hot iron from the flames. With one fluid motion he thrust the hot iron into one of the tankards. After a few seconds, he removed the iron from the tankard and put it in the next. The boys watched with amazement as Benny entertained them with his display of searing controlled violence. The tavern keeper continued until all five tankards had been satisfactorily skewered. "There you have your *hot flips*, gentlemen!" he announced as he spun back away from the table and returned the iron to the fire. The boys each grabbed a tank full of the warmed frothy mixture, held them aloft, touched them in the center. Fitz stood and broke into song;

> "Come, fill your glasses, fellows, and stand up in a row;
> To singing sentimentally we're for to go.
> In the army there's sobriety, promotions very slow;
> So, we'll sing our reminiscences of Benny Havens, Oh!
>
> To our kind old Alma Mater, our rock-bound Highland Home,
> We'll cast many a fond regret as o'er life's sea we roam;
> Until our last battle field, the light of heaven shall glow,
> We'll never fail to drink to her, and Benny Havens, Oh!
>
> Oh! Benny Havens, Oh!   Oh! Benny Havens, Oh!

(37.2)

All five cadets raised their tanks and took a drink. Fitz then continued;

> " 'Tis nary a spot where I'd rather be;
> If you think that I'm lying, my name isn't *Lee*!
> Benny Havens, Oh, Benny Havens Oh!"

The boys cheered and took a large gulp. Tom Hite cleared his throat;

> "There's no mentor more worthy, no tutor more skilled;
> No soldier who drills here, shall ever be killed!
> Benny Havens Oh, Benny Havens Oh!"

The boys cheered and gulped again in unison. Then, it was Jennings' turn. He paused for a moment;

> "It's an enjoyable place.... Uh... After I drink.... I... I'll be sure to wipe my face?
> Benny Havens ..."

The boys groaned. With a wince Fitz broke the news to Jennings, "Now, you have to empty that tankard, Jennings... That was truly a pitiful performance! Sorry, friend, but that's the rule!"

"I wish I'd known that at the start!", said Jennings.

"Yes, yes, Jennings... We know, we know", said Lee with feigned compassion.

"Now, enough excuses and finish the tank!", ordered Hite.

Jennings took a deep breath and closed his eyes tightly. He inverted the tankard and poured the heated contents down his throat. "Don't waste a drop, Jennings! Don't waste a drop!" warned the gregarious Fitz Lee. Jennings nearly gagged as a small drop ran back from the corner of his mouth toward his ear. He struggled but completed the punishment. When the empty tankard slammed down on the table, the hands of the boys followed closely behind creating a celebratory tremor throughout the bar.

"*Now*, you can wipe your face, Jennings!", Hite teased.

"What is in there?", Jennings queasily begged.

"You see, Benny takes a pint of ale and adds some beaten eggs, sugar, and some other things. Then he puts a red-hot iron right in it! There is nothing more satisfying - on that you can rely! Well done, Jennings! Mr. Havens!" hollered Lee, "Jennings wants to buy another round of *flips*! He'll be up to collect them in a moment. Now, it's your turn, Sample." The young men went around the table for another hour, trying ceaselessly to come up with fresh inspired poetry. After each man had bought a round, the idea of food finally surfaced.

"I'm hungry, boys.", said Hughes.

"Ah, Jim... Now that's enlightened... Dear Mr. Havens!", Fitz called, "Is Mrs. Havens still holding the kitchen?"

"Absolutely! She cooks until midnight.", said Benny from behind the bar. It was nearly 11 o'clock and Benny Havens' Tavern was still quite full. "What would you men care to eat?"

"Buckwheat cakes and sausages would be much appreciated, sir...", answered Fitz. "Is there any soup?"

"Beef stew; but it's nearly gone.", said Benny.

"Very well, sir, please bring us what remains. But, in the meantime, sir, another round of *flips* will suffice. Sample, here will be up for them in a moment!"

"Yes, Cadet Fitz... And I'll tell Mrs. Havens to prepare a room for you and your friends! It appears you're heading in that direction!" The entire bar laughed loudly at Fitz's expense.

Fitz smiled heartily and graciously absorbed the ridicule. And, as was his nature, he continued the joke. "You are a wise man, Mr. Havens... Perhaps Mrs. Havens should prepare the room *before* the meal... I may not hold up much longer!"

Benny Havens reached for his own tankard at that moment and raised it aloft. "To the health of the greatest men who ever lived - Saint Paul, Andrew Jackson, and A.E. Burnside!", toasted Benny Havens.

"Here, here!", responded the bar before taking a drink.

Benny raised his hand to quiet the room. He turned toward the table of cadets and raised his tankard once more, "Oh, a fine appointee is Cadet Fitz, if he continues his ways, I'll add his name to my list!" The entire barroom exploded in raucous applause, whistling, and the like. Benny had spent a lifetime bringing enjoyment to everyday people and, even at age sixty-six, nothing had changed.

Fitz again rose to his feet, raised his tank, placed his hand over his heart, and proudly announced, "To Benny and Letitia Havens and the Class of '56; backbone of the Academy!"

"Here, here!" the room responded as Cadet Fitz beckoned Benny Havens back over to their table. Fitz put his arm around the aged host and explained to his comrades.

"Boys… No finer host will you find than Benny Havens. It is worth ten-fold every risk assumed to partake in his gracious hospitality!" The boys nodded in agreement, slurping their flips.

"How did you extricate yourself, this time, Cadet Fitz?", asked old Benny.

"Ah, Mr. Havens, we used the man and wife routine again. It's been awhile and there's a new sentry at the gate. Besides, I constitute a most attractive lady.", smiled Fitz.

"Your face is indeed lovely, Cadet Fitz,", chided Benny, "but your figure…", Benny poked a finger into Fitz's side, winced, and shook his head in mock disappointment. The boys erupted in concurrence and Benny winked one of his sparkling eyes.

"Dear, Mr. Havens…", said Fitz as the boys quieted, "Tell the boys about that adventurous Derby fellow who used to come down from the Academy some years ago."

Benny turned and grabbed an empty chair that sat against the wall. He pulled it up alongside Fitz and sat.

"Well, gentlemen… and lady" he turned and bowed to Fitz. "Eight or nine years ago there was an ingenious cadet by the name of George Derby here at the Academy. Derby was in especial bad favor and was in desperate need of a trip to Benny Havens. Permits to leave the institution were scarce and Derby was certain that he could not obtain one through ordinary means. He also knew that another unauthorized trip outside the walls would mean running a frightful risk. His mind set to work, and in much the same way your devilish friend Cadet Fitz would, a scheme soon came to him…"

The boys sat silently and listened intently to the gruffly enchanting Mr. Havens.

"So, Derby, who had to this time, been an inattentive student, suddenly found repentance and made it quite clear throughout the institution that he had forever changed his ways. He was toiling in his geology studies, fearful of failing his final examination. He approached Professor Twiddle, that curious and bookish buffoon."

"I know him! I suffered through his course last year!", yelped Hite.

Havens continued, "Derby had tears in his eyes as he bemoaned his transgressions, swearing never again to waste his valuable time and opportunity at the Academy. He vowed to use his remaining time to fit himself for battle with the world, with particular attention to his geology studies. The innocent professor embraced Derby and congratulated him on his epiphany. For three days Derby arrived early for his geology class. He was well-prepared for each lesson, asking questions, answering others. He showed great interest in the subject-matter, winning glowing opinions from his professor."

Benny Havens (1787-1877)

The firelight flashed in Benny Havens' eyes as they danced around the table making contact with each of the entranced listeners. "On the fourth day, Cadet Derby stayed after class and approached Professor Twiddle once again. Derby informed the professor that one of the milkmen that supplied the Academy had spoken of an area up on the mountain where there were tremendous petrifactions." Havens twisted his torso and raised an arm in the direction of the nearby mountain. He turned back, scooted his chair closer to the table and resumed the story.

"Derby, having carefully posted himself by the books, spoke of fish from such and such an age; and bird tracks from this age and that era. The professor rubbed his hands with delight, hearing of the bony treasure trove. Derby concluded by stating that the milkman had offered to escort Derby to the site. "Yes, yes! You must go!", the professor told him. Derby explained that in his current circumstance, a permit to leave the grounds of the Academy was not practicable. The professor told Derby not to worry; that he would obtain the countersign and the permit. The next day the professor presented Derby with the permit and Derby made straight off for this fine establishment!" The old tavern keeper smiled with self-deprecating pride as the boys all looked at one another in acknowledged delight.

"As I recall, he was over in that chair before 10 that morning stuffing himself full of flips and cakes. By 5 o'clock he was prone on the small sofa in the other room. By 8 that evening he had reawakened and was back on the cider, drinking tankard after tankard, chewing plug, smoking pipes, engaging profusely in all sorts of indulgences until late into the evening when I dragged him upstairs and tucked him into bed!"

The boys howled at the rich familiarity of the image.

"I woke him early the next morn and he slipped into the fog and safely back over the wall and into his bed. He was nearly asleep once again when a shock befell him. He had no specimens to show the professor! He jumped from his bed and trekked down to the river. He retrieved a few stones from the shallow bed near the bank and returned to his room." The cadets knew exactly the spot Havens was describing.

"He scratched and carved some marks in the stones' surface with a chisel, creating a rather impressive bird track forgery. He rubbed his creation with some dirt giving an appearance that these marks were quite authentic. He then lay back down and slept for a time. After waking and eating breakfast, he paid Professor Twiddle a visit." Havens paused and leaned back in his chair. With a tantalizing grin, he pushed his thumbs into his waistband and adjusted his trousers. He then leaned forward again, clasped his leathery hands together on the tabletop, and continued his tale as if he were revealing an ancient secret.

"Derby explained to the professor that the milkman had not kept the appointment. But he, Derby that is, took it upon himself to find the specimens. He allowed that he was unsure whether or not he actually located the site, but he produced from his pocket the marked stone and presented it to Twiddle. Derby stated in lucid terms that he had found this curious stone and, in his amateur opinion, he believed it represented tracks made by some heretofore undiscovered species of antediluvian bird from a bygone age. To his surprise, the professor enthusiastically concurred. Twiddle took the stone and related Derby's wonderful discovery to the class that very day. The matter was for a few days, the talk of the class. But our scholar could not retain his secret and told one or two friends. The truth spread quickly through the college and the result was that our dear cadet Derby was suspended for the remainder of the session. Afterward, Derby always maintained that a good night at Benny Havens' was well worth the price!" (37.3)

Benny stood from his seat as the cadets erupted in applause. The old man held up one hand to quell the youthful exuberance as he slid back over toward the bar to continue his duties of proprietor of what was simultaneously the most popular and most reviled institution in West Point, including the academy itself.

By 1 o'clock the cadets were full of hot flips and buckwheat cakes. Mrs. Havens closed the kitchen, Benny turned off the taps, and the barroom was emptied. None of the five cadet revelers, most particularly Sample and Jennings, were in any condition to scale the bluff and enter the academy grounds without grave risk of detection. Though there were protestations and expected drunken hubris, Benny convinced the boys to heed his sage advice and to bed down for a while before heading back.

"I'll wake you by 4 o'clock, Lee… That should give you time to get back before the morning call.", whispered Benny Havens.

"Yes, yes, sir…", mumbled Fitz Lee as he collapsed onto the floor of an upstairs room at Benny Havens Tavern. "That would be, eeyup, er, fine, Mr. Havens… 4 o'clock…" he sighed, and fell fast asleep.

The table of officers shared many hearty laughs that evening. As the meal concluded, Captain Hite turned to Fitz Lee, "Fitz, will we be paroled this evening?"

"Tom, now that is a difficult question." Fitz sat back in his chair and thought for a moment. At this earlier point in the War, it was customary to parole captured officers at the end of a battle. But, in this instance, a general order had been issued that none of General Pope's officer corps were to be paroled at any time. As the War continued through 1863 and '64, parole policy would be altered by both sides. Federal forces, in particular, tightened policy, for they discovered that prisoner release and exchange were significant means by which the Confederacy was replenishing its forces; thus, extending the length of the conflict. Although the Confederacy endeavored to tighten their policy in response; the logistical and humanitarian toll this placed upon them, in light of their limited and declining resources, became untenable. "I cannot parole you now, Tom. You and your fellow officers will ride with me. I assure you will be well-treated. I will parole you at my earliest opportunity. But, for now, I must seize your weapons and obtain your oath that you will not attempt to escape."

Heros von Borcke then leaned over and whispered in Fitz's ear. Fitz nodded and said, "And, my large friend, Major von Borcke, here; he will need one of your freshest horses. Spoils of war, gentlemen!", he smiled.

"Very well, Fitz. If I have to be a prisoner, you are the jailer I would choose!" The other Union officers looked uneasily at one another. "Gentlemen; do not worry.", Hite continued. "Lee has given me his word that we shall be properly treated and paroled. That is good enough."

Three days later, General Fitzhugh Lee and his men entered the City of Fairfax. Captain Hite and the other three Union officers were granted parole, provided fresh horses, and allowed to continue further east to reunite with Federal forces in Alexandria.

Chapter 38   *He Certainly Resembles the Man*

On May 15, 1885, Judge T. S. Atkins once again called The Hustings Court of Richmond to order. "The prosecution will continue.", said the Judge.

Colonel Aylett stood and called the first witness for the prosecution. "The prosecution calls Mr. George Wright to the stand."

A tall, handsome young man came from the back of the courtroom and ascended the stand. After the oath, Colonel Aylett approached him.

"Please state your name and occupation, sir."

"George Wright; conductor on the Chesapeake and Ohio Railroad."

"Thank you, Mr. Wright. If I may ask, where were you on March 12."

"I was on the number 16 train from Cleveland to Richmond.", stated Wright.

"Does this line have a stop out in Bath County?", continued Aylett.

"Yes sir; at Millboro."

"Did it stop there on March 12?"

"Yes, sir. Stops in Millboro around noon."

"Do you recall seeing Miss Madison that day?"

"Absolutely, I remember her. The train was pretty empty when she boarded. I recall that she was wearing a black skirt and a red shawl."

"Did she tell you her business?"

"Well, yes she did. She told me she was on her way to Richmond and was going to meet someone at the station, or perhaps it was at the American Hotel."

"Did she get off the train in Richmond?"

"Yes, Colonel, she did."

"And what time was that?"

"Well, I believe we were running about an hour behind schedule, so, it was well after 2 AM."

"So, that would be early the morning of the 13th?"

"Yes, Colonel; that's right.", answered the conductor.

"Thank you, Mr. Wright."

Beverly Crump stood and put his hand to his forehead. He closed his eyes for a moment, then stepped out from behind the defense table.

"Mr. Wright. How did you learn the deceased's name?"

"Well, um... I believe she introduced herself to me.", answered Wright.

"And you remember her name from that one meeting; among all the people you meet as a conductor?", said Crump with a hint of incredulity.

"Well... Yes.", Wright paused. "Well, I mean... I read her name in the papers afterward and knew that was the name of the girl I'd met on the train."

"Yes, of course. Newspapers often help to clarify one's memory.", Crump deadpanned. Then, he continued, "Did she ever mention the name 'Cluverius'?"

"No, sir."

"Did she ever mention the name 'Merton'?"

"No, sir.", said Wright.

"Did you notice that she was pregnant?"

"No, sir."

"You did not notice a woman in her eighth month of pregnancy as being pregnant? Yet you remember all this other detail about her?"

"I did not notice, sir.", Wright shrugged.

"Mr. Wright. Did you notice anything unusual about Miss Madison's behavior that day? Was she extraordinarily nervous? Or, gloomy?"

George Wright pursed his lips together and tried to remember. "She did say one thing that I found to be odd. At one point, I suggested that we could speed up the train in order to get her to her destination more quickly. Her response was a bit strange. She said she hoped the train would speed up so that it would jump the track and kill her! I was surprised by that."

"Yes, outspoken thoughts of suicide are awkward, to say the least!", said Crump in a slick attempt to reinforce her emotional instability with the jury.

"No more questions, your honor."

Colonel Aylett stood and cleared his throat. "Mr. Wright. Granted, it was not particularly adroit, but could Miss Madison have been teasing when she spoke of a train accident and death?"

"Perhaps…"

"I object!", cried Crump. "This proceeding should deal with the statement and the statement alone. Mr. Wright should not be allowed to opine for the jury!"

Judge Atkins sat back and looked to Aylett. On cue, the Colonel responded. "Your honor, I believe we should allow Mr. Wright to fully describe the situation. He was the only one there and the context of a remark such as this can have serious implications."

"Over-ruled, Mr. Crump. Continue, Mr. Wright.", ordered the judge.

Wright nodded. "Well, it was difficult to tell what she meant. I was not prepared for such a statement, whether it was a joke, or not. All I can say is that, otherwise, she appeared to be in very good spirits."

"Thank you, Mr. Wright. No more questions." Aylett waited for Wright to vacate the stand before announcing his next witness. "The prosecution calls Mr. Henry Hunt to testify." (38.1)

A thin little colored boy stepped out into the center aisle and strode to the stand. He squirmed slightly and then remembered to button the top button of his shirt, just as his momma had instructed.

"Good morning, young man. Please state your name, age, and occupation for the Court."

"Henry Hunt. Ise fo'teen an' I work in da office at da 'Mercun Hotel.", he anxiously wiped his shirt sleeve across his mouth, then recalled that his momma said he wasn't supposed to fidget. He sat on both hands to control his urges.

"Were you there on March 13th, Henry?"

"Yessuh, I was."

"Can you describe for the court what happened that morning?'

"Yessuh. A messunja come an' say he got a note for a lady in Room 21. He give me da note an' I take it to Room 21. So, I goes up thar an' knock. The lady come to da doe an' I give her da' note. She was eatin' brekfess. She read it quick an' tol' me to wait to take back a ansuh. She writes some words on some paper an'puts it in a invelope an' hands it to me. Den, Ise run downstairs an' Missa Dodson tol' me da messunja was out front. I went out thar to look for 'em. I find 'em an' give 'em da note. He walked on up da street. A few minits later, he come back in da hotel. He say he couldn't fine no man now. So, he gives me da note back an' Ise give it tuh Missa Dodson."

"Do you know the name of the woman in Room 21?"

"Well, now I knows it; but den I didn't."

"Let the record show that the American Hotel registry states that Room 21 was taken under the name of "F. L. Merton" on March 13th.", announced Aylett.

"Henry, did you recall what time it was when this note passing occurred?"

"It was befo' lunch, but pretty late. Dat's why Ise rememba da woman eatin' brekfess. It was 'bout half past 'leven, I'd say.", said Hunt.

"Do you remember what the woman was wearing that day, Henry?"

"She was wearin' a black hat an' dress, an' a bright red shaw."

"Could you identify the woman if you saw her?"

"Yessuh. I did see 'er agin... at da Almshouse; layin' thar dead."

Judge Atkins looked toward the defense.

"No questions, your honor.", said Beverly Crump. (38.2)

Charles V. Meredith, the leading prosecutor, then stood and called William Martin to the stand.

A well-dressed gentleman in a dark grey suit stood from the fourth row and approached the stand.

"Good morning, sir. Please state your name and occupation for the record."

"William F. Martin. I am Justice of the Peace in Manchester."

"Where were you midday on March 13th?", asked Meredith.

"I was coming here to Richmond. More specifically, I was meeting a man on business at Tredegar. I left Manchester a little early that day, so I found I had time to stop on Belle Isle and have a look at the nail factory.

"Mr. Martin, can you describe what you witnessed that morning?", asked Meredith.

"Yes, sir. After visiting the factory out on the island, I was crossing the bridge to the the Richmond shore. As I crossed, there was a couple, a young man and a woman, coming toward me. I thought I knew the man to be Mr. Ingram, an attorney from Manchester. As I got closer, I discovered I was mistaken. The couple stopped yards before me and the man pushed the woman against the rail of the bridge. She was laughing as he forced himself against her. Then, just as I passed, she pushed him away and he brushed against me. She said, 'Why, cousin Tommie!' in an excited, but, um, a playful manner. I recall stopping and looking in their direction. They excused themselves and then I continued on, thinking little of it at the time."

"Do you recall approximately what time it was when this happened, Mr. Martin?"

"Well, I would say it had to be noon, perhaps slightly later."

"Can you describe the couple?", asked the prosecutor.

"Both of them looked to be twenty or twenty-five. The woman was short. She was wearing a dark dress and a red shawl. I clearly remember that. The man was taller and thin. He was wearing a hat and an overcoat."

"Thank you, Mr. Martin." Charles Meredith sat down.

Beverly Crump stood and addressed the witness. "Mr. Martin, at what point did you come to believe that you had interacted with the deceased?"

"Well, after several weeks as I read more and more about the murder, I realized that I may well have come into contact with the killer.", said Martin.

"So, you read extensively about the case, Mr. Martin?", asked Crump.

"Well, probably no more than most people; at least up until the point that I recalled the encounter. Then, naturally, my interest increased."

"Is there any chance that these newspaper articles may have influenced your memory, Mr. Martin? For instance, the newspapers went into great detail describing the clothes worn by the deceased. Could these descriptions have provided you details about the deceased that you otherwise would not have remembered?"

"I don't believe so.", said Martin.

"Mr. Martin, this is very serious business. A man's future depends on this. Belief is not enough. You have to know these things… Mr. Martin, is this the man you saw on the foot bridge from Belle Isle that day?", Crump pointed directly to Cluverius, who sat completely still and unmoved by the testimony.

"Well...", Martin hesitated.

Crump became very authoritative. "Can you positively identify that *this* is the man you saw that morning, Mr. Martin?" The experienced lawyer pointed once again at Cluverius.

"He certainly resembles the man in size and appearance.", said Martin.

"Resembles? Come now, Mr. Martin... You are a Justice of the Peace.", Crump shook his head in frustration. "Do you know how many men named Tommie there are in this city? Do you know how many of them have female cousins?" William Martin shrugged. Crump turned his head toward the judge. "No more questions, your honor."

The combative Meredith was eager to illustrate the disingenuousness of Crump's questions. He rose to his feet for redirect. "Mr. Martin, do you know how many young men named Tommie were with their soon-to-be-deceased female cousins in Richmond that very day?" The courtroom chuckled. Cluverius' left lower eyelid twitched slightly.

Martin was silent, having no idea how to answer.

"No further questions, your honor.", Meredith concluded. (38.3)

Judge Atkins dismissed William Martin and then called Meredith and Crump to the bench. The judge leaned forward to have a private word with the counselors. "Gentlemen,", he said in a very calm and hushed tone. "I have seen enough of your theatrics. You will respect the dignity of the courtroom and not turn this into a circus to celebrate your own egos. Please keep your questions factual and resist the rhetorical. I understand the temptations and the pressures in a case such as this are great. But, you both *will* maintain a professional approach."

"Understood.", growled Meredith.

"Yes, of course, your honor.", Crump agreed.

"Very well; call your next witness, Mr. Meredith.", said the judge.

Meredith walked back over to the prosecutor's table and called James Thompson to the stand. From the back of the room emerged Thompson. He was a black man over six feet in height. Even through his best shirt and pants his robust physique suggested that he was a working man. But, when the eye encountered his aging face, his workman status was confirmed.

After humbly accepting the oath, James Thompson sat cautiously and quietly folded his powerful calloused hands in his lap. Meredith cleared his throat and Thompson's eyes turned toward him.

"Please state your name and occupation for the court, sir."

"My name is James Thompson an' Ise a fire man' at da Ol' Duhminyin Nail Cumpnee." He wrung his hands slightly.

"And, Mr. Thompson, how long have you been there?", asked Meredith.

"Oh… many ye-ahs, Missuh Murdith; 'bout since '46, I'd say. A long time!"

"Were you at work the morning of March 13, Mr. Thompson?"

"Yessuh."

"Do you remember anything unusual about that morning?"

"Well, I was doin' mah reglar work, runnin' da whellbarra aroun' n', well, it gits mighty heavy. Once you git headed in a drexshin', you jes keep goin' dat way. I was makin' a run wif a load n' I brush up agin' da man. Da lady stept back as I was comin', but I don' think da man seen me. After I drop da load, I turn on back to say 'scuse me… dat's all.

"Can you describe the man and the woman."

"Well, da woman, she was short n' chunky. Huh face was rosy-red. I 'member thinkin' I don' know why she dar, the way she look."

"What do you mean, Mr. Thompson?"

"Well, tuh me, she look like she should be at home. She was gettin' ready tuh have a chile'."

"What was she wearing, Mr. Thompson?"

"Oh, I don' 'member all she was wearin'; but I do 'member a red shaw.", he shook his head.

"Did you go to the almshouse to identify the woman, Mr. Thompson?"

"Oh yessuh. I hear 'bout da dead guhl an' I went on over an' sho' nuff, it was da guhl I seen on Belle." Mr. Thompson swallowed. He shifted his weight and wrung his hands some more.

"How about the prisoner, Mr. Thompson? Is he the man you saw with the girl that day?"

"Yessuh, Ise pretty sure he is. 'Cept I believes 'e had a mustache, Mr. Murdith. He don' got one now, bud 'e had one den. An' his sunk-in eyes; I recknize 'em. I wen' down tuh da jail an' look at 'im 'mongst a group; an' I pick 'im right out."

"Thank you, Mr. Thompson. No more questions.", said Meredith.

Beverly Crump stood and cleared his throat. He stepped from behind the defense table. He smiled slightly at the witness.

"Mr. Thompson ... You said you *believe* the man you saw with the deceased had a mustache?"

Thompson sat up even straighter. His broad chest expanded as he breathed deeply in and took a moment to reflect. "Yessuh... Ise priddy sure he did."

"Well,", continued Crump, "this is the first we have heard of any mustache. How do you suppose the previous witnesses failed to mention that?"

"Objection!", cried Meredith. "The witness cannot possibly comment on another's testimony, your honor. If the defense wishes to find this out, they need to recall those witnesses when they make their case."

"Objection sustained.", declared Judge Atkins. "Mr. Crump, please try again."

"Yes, your honor." Crump lowered his head and put his right forefinger to his lip. James Thompson swallowed hard and awaited the next question. Crump then raised his head and asked, "Mr. Thompson, were there other people in the nail works that day; meaning, people other than workers... you see, visitors and the like?" Crump knew this was a risky question, but he had to try to inject the possibility that the man and woman seen by William Martin on the bridge and the man and woman seen by Thompson in the factory could be different pairs.

"No suh, we don' git many vizters out dar. "'Cayshin we do. But dat day, dem twos da only ones I seen dat I don' know."

Crump was deflated, but tried not to show it. "Did you see the previous witness, Mr. Martin, there that day?"

"No, suh.", replied Thompson.

"Well, Mr. Martin has testified that he visited the nail works that very day. So, it *is* possible that someone could visit the nail works and you would not see them at all?"

"Well, yessuh. Ise sure dey could. Alls I can say is dat da only vizters I seen dat day was dat man over dar an' da dead girl. I don' 'member seein' no one else."

"Thank you for your clarity, Mr. Thompson. No more questions." (38.4)

Chapter 39 Sergeant Haight

On the afternoon of May 15, 1885, Judge T.S. Atkins abruptly announced that the court had arranged for two omnibuses to carry a party to inspect two areas of the City which pertained to the facts of the trial of Thomas J. Cluverius. The party would include the accused, the judge, the complete jury, attorneys for both sides, a few reporters, and several armed police guards. The omnibuses would make two stops: one, at Belle Isle, and; two, at the Old Marshall Reservoir and adjacent Clark Spring property. (39.1)

"The purpose of this public excursion is to help all interested parties in this trial gain a broader understanding of the locations and timeline of events. It is not intended to advance either case, but rather is intended to supply some context for the events in question.", explained Judge Atkins. "Furthermore, there shall be no discussion among yourselves at any point while we are touring; and certainly, *any* attempt by the prosecution or the defense to have any conversation with any witness, juror, officer of the court, or any other persons in attendance shall not be tolerated and shall be punishable to the full extent of the law. This includes members of the press, who have been invited along to document the proceedings but are in no way authorized to interview anyone associated with the trial during these proceedings. The court has arranged all of this unannounced so that we may avoid a spectacle. The court is well aware of the interest this trial has generated with the public, and the court does not intend to exacerbate conditions. Mr. Meredith will be allowed to identify the pertinent locations to the party; but he shall be under strict instruction of this court not to opine."

Juror Francis Howell stepped down from the omnibus along with the others. He breathed deeply as he looked out across the James River at Belle Isle. The area remained familiar. Tredegar Iron Works stood proudly over his left shoulder. Back to the right was Hollywood Cemetery and a few hundred yards beyond that to the west, the Old Marshall Reservoir. Directly in front was the old railroad bridge which stretched tenuously over the fast waters of the James to the hauntingly primeval island. He bowed his head down toward his feet and closed his eyes, recalling the events he had witnessed here more than twenty years ago.

"Are you alright?", fellow juryman William Berkley quietly asked him.

After a brief pause, Howell whispered, "Yes... Yes, Bill; I am fine. I was here during the War and have not been back."

In the Summer of 1863, Francis Howell's regiment of Northern Virginians marched into Richmond. The men were battle-weary but heartened by the prospect of performing a new less dangerous duty, at least for a time, as prison guards at Belle Isle.

At the War's outset, Belle Isle was reserved for the internment of enlisted men. Officers were sequestered at nearby Libby Prison. As time passed and conditions worsened, policy was altered. Confederate commanders were no longer concerned with isolating Union soldiers from their officers, but with mitigating the spread of disease that was ravaging the prison population and threatened their keepers, as well. All sick prisoners were moved to Libby and all well men were incarcerated, officers and enlisted alike, at Belle Isle.

By 1863, conditions in the withering South had become so desperate that both prisons were full of nothing but sick and starving men. Men at Belle Isle were dying at a rate of twenty-five per day. Most of this was due to a lack of proper shelter, scant rations, poor sanitary conditions, and captors who were so hungry and desperate themselves that they became indifferent to the suffering of their prisoners.

Following the commands of their superiors, Private Howell and his company stepped up onto the railroad bridge. As he shouldered his rifle, he swallowed hard and stared across the bridge. Then, he turned his head down to his right. On the City shoreline below the bridge, hundreds of discolored Union bodies were piled as high as ten or twelve feet - arms, legs, swollen torsos; mouths gaping widely as the flies skipped from face to face; body to body; searching for sustenance. If not for their distinct human form and clothing, Howell would have thought he was looking at an animal rendering plant. A small barge was just pulling up to the City shore delivering yet another load of the ghastly byproduct of total war.

The heated stench pressed heavily against the men as they walked on toward the fortified gate at the end of the bridge to Belle Isle. Howell sensed that he was crossing the threshold to hell's kitchen; a kitchen replete with ovens that were fueled not only by Union men's bodies but by all men's souls. Howell and the others formed a single line of grey as they kept to the right side of the tracks and continued forward. Drifting in the opposite direction was a faded blue line with a grey guard at each end. These pitiful creatures were little more than half humans; shriveled apparitions that had already passed on in every sense except the purely physical. The degraded group was so thin, so tattered, so consumed by abject hopelessness that Howell felt that, if ordered to do so, they would gladly have gone and just laid down amongst the piles of their comrades rotting along the shoreline. There was no emotion in their expression; no fear; no timidity; just blank resignation. The fight was gone from them and only the most basic of human instincts kept them moving through time and space. Howell tried to catch the eye of one of the dozens that passed, but there was no acknowledgement. The young private cautiously nodded his head, even smiled slightly at a couple of the ghosts as they passed. There was no reaction. To them, he was as dead as they were.

Inside the stockade of Belle Isle Prison, Private Howell stood with a few members of his company and waited uneasily for the next order. Barely a word was passed between the men. Mosquitoes hovered above the company, striking with stealth and wicked determination.

A large burly man with a brilliant red beard emerged from a shabby tent near the east stockade wall. As he stepped from the tent's opening, he paused and turned to one side. He raised his right forefinger to his right nostril and pressed. He blew sharply, violently expelling a large hunk of mucus from his left nostril. The lummox snorted, wiped his nose on his sleeve, adjusted his sweat-saturated kepis, and carried on with his business. Howell cringed with queasiness as the unsavory man plodded toward them, scratching his backside. Following closely behind was a scraggly brown mutt, *Link*.

"I … am Sergeant Haight…" With his right hand, the man drew a large black club from the loop on his belt and smacked it into his open palm of his left. "I am the boss here. I am y'alls' boss, and I boss them chickens…", he said pointing with the club. Howell cut his eyes toward the barbed wire pen along the southern end of the stockade. Behind the wires stood hundreds of sickly silhouettes. Though they were silent, their desperation screamed at Howell.

"I give y'all work, I give y'all food, I give y'all rest, I give y'all reward, and I give y'all punishment. This is *my* world y'all have entered. Both prisoner and guard, alike; y'all answer to me!" *Link* yelped in timid concurrence.

Suddenly the boom of a cannon sounded in the distance.

"Take cover!", warned Sergeant Haight. The Confederate guards rushed out from the stockade area. Howell and the other fresh guards followed in a confused panic. The screech of a shell came directly overhead and a loud explosion ensued, raining a fiery mist down upon the cowering Union prisoners trapped in their cage. Another soon followed; then another. Each shell exploded with intimidating accuracy but mysteriously, there seemed to be no shrapnel. Men sought cover and held their ears tightly, but there was no carnage. Howell couldn't believe the yanks had crept so close to Richmond; nor could he believe they had developed a cannon that could fire such a great distance. Yet, for a few moments, the prison appeared to be under full assault. After more than one dozen shells had shook the skies above Belle Isle, silence fell. In the distance, Howell could hear faint cheering laughter. He turned to one of his mates with a look of complete fogginess.

"Git used to it, boys." grunted Sergeant Haight as he emerged from a shallow entrenchment. "Happens nearly ev'ryday 'bout this time." He paused to spit, nearly missing *Link*. "The boys o'er at Tredegar think it's real humorous. They shake us and quake us, but they'll never break us!" He chuckled to himself. "Besides, they're just testing the new cannon. There ain't any real grapeshot or nothin' like that in those shells anyhow. They're nothing more 'n over-sized firecrackers." He chuckled again and shook his head.

The men looked at one another with wide-eyed disbelief. Howell tried to wake himself but to no avail; the surreal nightmare would continue.

"Alright, six of you men, follow me. I've got more chickens to show y'all. The rest of y'all wait here for now; I'll be back.", ordered Haight. The rotund sergeant headed southwest toward the center of the island. The small column followed Haight as he breathlessly beat a path with his black club through the bank of trees that separated the stockade from the rest of the island. *Link* followed closely sniffing the ground and occasionally lifting a hind leg to water a sapling. The group emerged from the shade of the full-leaved trees to the open area in the center of the island that contained the primary prison encampment. There were more than two thousand dingy white tents crammed in the barren center. The ground below had been stamped into muck. Occupied to levels of four or five men per tent, the overcrowding and summer heat fostered an unsanitary environment rife with frustration and desperation. Tempers ran high as the newer inmates competed for the most basic of possessions, from drinking cups to blankets to scraps of stale bread. Those who had the misfortune to be there for longer periods could no longer concern themselves with such trivialities as food, water, and shelter. These hapless men were completely reliant upon the charity of their fellow inmates, which rarely shined upon them, or the merciful hand of death, which unrelentingly shadowed them.

Haight led the men around the perimeter of the campsite. As they neared the southernmost end of the site, Howell spotted some inmates stoking a fire that sat beneath a large metal pot. The thin leathered men were adding some small wild onions and roots to the broth. They paused and looked briefly over at Haight and the new guards then returned to their preparation. The ever-inquisitive *Link* straggled about twenty yards behind.

Once again, the party entered the tree line. Sergeant Haight blazed away with his club, knocking light branches and leaves in all directions. On the other side in a clearing at the south end of the island, fifty prisoners were constructing a masonry building.

"This is where we keep them chickens that can still do some work. If they're busy *layin'* bricks, they can't be *hatchin'* no escape plans." Haight chuckled and slobbered a bit, surprised by his own wit. "Y'all will be charged with guardin' this group. There's six of y'all; that should be plenty. Start time is sun up; quittin' time is sun down. It's that simple. If there are any problems, come find me. I'll be back by here in a few hours. Go tell those boys guardin' them chickens to come back with me now…I need a smoke." Sergeant Haight sat down against a tree and pulled half a cigar from his shirt pocket. He struck a match against the sole of his shoe and puffed three or four times on the tip of the cigar. He sat quietly for nearly thirty minutes until he finally mustered the energy to get back up.

"Any y'all seen *Link*?", he asked the few men nearby. "*Link*! *Link*! Where are ya, boy?"

Sergeant Haight disappeared back amongst the trees, working his way toward the central encampment. When the bullying sergeant resurfaced on the other side, he saw a large group of Yankee prisoners gathered around the campfire. They were louder and more festive than usual, raising some suspicion within the veteran prison guard. Haight pulled out his club and walked toward the group, numbering perhaps twenty-five men. The brutish sergeant forced his way through the crowd. As the men recognized the identity of the interloper, they quickly fell silent. A spit had replaced the large metal soup pot simmering over the campfire. There, roasting over the coals, was *Link*. Haight was devastated, seeing his only friend skewered from one end to the other. *Link's* blue tongue drooped from his open mouth. The entire left side of his carcass had been stripped and devoured by the ravenous prisoners. Haight's face turned from bright pink to purple. Suddenly he erupted and with a guttural scream began swinging his club with deadly precision. Man after man was struck down. Within seconds the ground was littered with bleeding men. A few prisoners tried to restrain Haight, but they were too weak to overcome a large man engulfed in such a rage.

Even the other guards were afraid to confront the unhinged gorilla. Like a mad devil, Sergeant Haight continued to swing, shove, kick, and bludgeon each man in the vicinity. And, once all were incapacitated, he looked to move on to others. If left unfettered, Haight surely would have killed each of the ten thousand men in the prison. The other Confederates grudgingly knew he must be stopped. Five guards rushed over to him. Four of them each seized a limb while the fifth ordered Haight to cease. The irate sergeant disregarded the command and continued the fight. The guard steadied his feet, drew his rifle back with both hands over his right shoulder, and delivered a solid blow with his rifle butt. Haight's forehead split wide open and as blood horrifically cascaded down his face, he only grew angrier. The enraged monster worked his right arm free and, still holding his club, cracked the amazed guard straight across the face, shattering his cheek. Three other guards jumped in and finally, after more than a dozen blows to his head and body, Haight was overcome. (39.2)

Francis Howell closed his eyes tightly as he stood near the spot where Haight's rampage occurred. "The hand of Death will always grip this place.", he muttered to himself.

Thomas J. Cluverius lightly loosened his black string tie as he stepped down from the omnibus. He was surrounded by four large officers of the Richmond Police. Cluverius looked straight ahead toward the James River. His movements were very slow and deliberate, as if he were calculating every one of them. Cluverius knew that not only the eyes of the police escort, but every person there at the scene; alas the whole City of Richmond; and perhaps, the eyes of an entire nation were closely watching; waiting for him to do something, anything, that would give them a glimpse into his state of being. Cluverius could barely contain himself as he plotted in the recesses of his mind. "What shall I do?" he asked himself. He decided to do nothing but coolly observe. He would allow the suspense to build some more.

The touring party silently stepped one by one upon the narrow bridge toward Belle Isle. At the midway point, Charles Meredith stopped and reminded the group that this is the location where Mr. William Martin had testified that he saw a young man and a young woman engaged in conversation at midday on March 13. The afternoon sun beamed down brightly, but a cool steady breeze was coming off the James River; temporarily sweeping away the moisture that emanated from the saturated marsh lands and the new generation of insects which were steadily repopulating the island. The party continued across the island and quietly approached the Old Dominion Nail Company. Once again, Mr. Meredith spoke up and reminded the attendees that it was inside here that Mr. James Thompson testified that he witnessed a young man, whom he clearly identified as the defendant, and a young woman, whom he clearly identified as the deceased, visiting the factory a few minutes later same day. Cluverius continued to look upon the group without the slightest outward emotion. "Meredith… what a fool!", he thought to himself. "I would carve him up in the courtroom. Such arrogance to think *he* is in charge here. Who is paying any attention to *him*? I am the axis upon which all these events turn! They are all simple fools!"

The entire group walked quietly back across Belle Isle and across the bridge to the omnibuses waiting for them. Each boarded and took their seat. Judge Atkins gave the drivers a signal to move on to the Old Marshall Reservoir.

Chapter 40   Mad King Ludwig

The omnibuses turned north on to Cherry Street and slowly plodded nine blocks before turning west on Cumberland. Three blocks further the train slowly turned south on to Reservoir Street. All thirty-two passengers sat completely silent until Charles Meredith tapped the lead driver on the shoulder and asked him to stop in front of the Dunstan Property. Meredith turned and faced the passengers. He pointed to his left and identified where Fannie Madison's red shawl had been found.

"Here we see the Dunstan Property; where the red shawl, which has been identified by various witnesses and entered into evidence as belonging to the deceased, was discovered draped atop that ten-foot wall."

Meredith signaled the driver to continue forward. A few blocks ahead the Reservoir Street came to a dead end at Ashland Street. Once the omnibuses came to a stop, Meredith jumped down and pointed to the old dilapidated house about eighty yards to the left.

"There, in that old abandoned dead house, the black hat identified by testimony as belonging to the deceased was discovered. I now ask that the entire party disembark and follow me along this fence between the Clark Spring Property and the Reservoir. It is there we will find the place where one of the gloves and a woman's veil, each identified as belonging to the deceased were located. We will also see the hole in the fence where the gold watch key was found by the Williams boy. We will then enter the grounds of the reservoir and you will have the opportunity to see where the body was located, where the matching glove was located, and other evidence of the crime scene."

T.J. Cluverius stepped off the omnibus. He placed both hands on the small of his back and stretched. Flanked by four police guards he waited patiently until all of the others in the party had begun to make their way down the fence line between the Clark Spring Property and the Old Marshall Reservoir. The young defendant slowly but confidently ambled toward the fence. He bent over and smartly plucked a buttercup that had sprouted just above the awakening Spring grass. He gazed out over the property toward the James River, briefly escaping the scene. He gently ran the buttercup along his lower lip. A smile nearly surfaced until he regained his focus.

Cluverius fully understood the seriousness of his situation. He knew full well that even the slightest slip in his demeanor could seal his fate. But his faith in his own ability to extract himself from all peril had yet to be shaken. Cluverius knew he was more adept at this game than the rest of them.

He clasped his right hand with his left behind his back and strolled toward the opening in the fence. "Let's see how close they get with this…" he thought to himself. "Even if they get all the facts right, which they certainly will not; I am certain none of it can be proved."

After pulling back the loose board to reveal the hole in the fence where the watch key was found dangling, Mr. Meredith led the party back around to the front gate of the Reservoir and methodically continued the tour. Cluverius decided to remain near the gate with his guards while the rest of the party followed Meredith. The prosecutor pointed out the embankment and the picket fence that surrounded the reservoir pool. He then led the group directly up the embankment for a closer look at the area where one of the woman's gloves had been found. The foot prints were long gone, but he identified the area where those were observed. From atop the embankment, Meredith pointed down toward the water to the area where the deceased was discovered.

Judge Atkins then signaled to Meredith that he thought they'd all seen enough. The party quietly turned back toward the front gate. There stood Cluverius with the guards. Just outside the gate, a small crowd had formed. It was mostly women and children, as most of men were still at work. Judge Atkins asked Mr. Meredith to get the party back to the omnibuses quickly in an attempt to avoid spectacle. It was certainly not in the interest of the court for the jurors to be seen by the general public investigating the crime scene. As the group exited the gate more and more people were collecting on the street, coming from every direction to get a glimpse of the accused. Cluverius calmly boarded the rear omnibus. Cries of "You're innocent!" and, "We love you!" could be heard popping off like distant firecrackers. The frequency and volume of the calls increased as the ever-growing crowd was closing in. Judge Atkins nervously implored all of the bystanders to stay back and allow the omnibuses to leave so the court could get back to business. A teenage girl broke from the crowd and threw three flowers in the direction of Cluverius. He caught one of them and immediately brought it to his nose.

T.J. Cluverius looked down upon the pretty young girl with a warm gaze which struck her with such seduction that, at that moment, she and he both knew she would do whatever he commanded. Another woman yelled, "Thomas! I am here." Cluverius' enrapturing gaze broke from the young girl as his eyes darted to his left only to find Rachel McDonald standing there. Her chest was heaving from the four-block run from her home. Rachel's expression ached for reassurance; but Cluverius simply sat down and turned his head away from her. The omnibus began to pull away. Rachel dropped to her knees and reached out toward him "Thomas, please! Look at me!" Cluverius averted his eyes from the pathetic Rachel and looked back in the direction of the younger, more enticing, flower girl. But, standing in her place was the old hag Annie Lumpkin. "Good luck, to you, Mr. Cluverius!", she beckoned as she pointed and chuckled. Cluverius looked straight down at the floor of the omnibus for a moment and then closed his eyes tightly for a few seconds. He couldn't resist and looked back once more toward Annie. There, in her place, again stood a young girl; head down with her back now turned. The girl slowly tilted her head upward as she rotated back around. Cradled in her arms was a limp baby soaked red with blood. Cluverius shuddered as his eyes locked with the teary eyes of the girl now standing there, cousin Lillie Madison. He quickly spun back around in his seat, clenched his eyes shut once again and exhaled. He slowly reopened one eye and glanced over at the guard sitting to his left on the omnibus. Cluverius began to wonder if anyone else had witnessed the changeling apparitions – apparently, no one did. The people, thoughts and images regularly haunting him were, much like his guilt, to be ignored.

Upon return to the Hustings Court, Judge Atkins called the courtroom to order and announced that court would adjourn until the following Monday, May 18, 1885. (40.1)

On August 28, 1870, in the midst of the Franco-Prussian War, Henrietta Joel secured two tickets for passage on the steamship *Ocean*. She had travelled for three days from her home in Schollkrippen in the Kingdom of Bavaria to the Port of Bremen near the northern coast of Germany. She broke down as she held her boys one last time. The distraught mother put the tickets in the hand of her older son, Hermann. "Dear Hermann", she pleaded, "You must be brave. You must take your brother and go to America. There is nothing here in our country for you boys. You must go to America, find work, and make a life for yourselves."

"But Mama, you are here… Solomon and I don't want to leave you!"

"You must! I will not allow Ludwig to take any more of my boys! He will never stop with his wars!"

In 1864, Maximillian II of Bavaria died unexpectedly of illness. His son was cast at age eighteen onto the throne becoming King Ludwig II of Bavaria. Amid rising tensions between the great powers to his north and south, Ludwig increased military conscriptions. Among those conscripts was Hermann Joel's oldest brother, Mathias. The terms of conscription demanded that each family with men of military age have at least one man serving in the Bavarian forces at all times.

Prussia under King Wilhelm I and foreign minister Otto von Bismarck had expanded its sphere of influence throughout northern Germany and was looking south. In June, 1866, Franz Joseph of Austria preemptively reacted to the threat and declared war on Prussia. Ludwig chose to ally with his Austrian neighbor to the south. Prussian forces immediately advanced southward and began seizing territory. On July 10, 1866, the Bavarian army retreated to the town of Kissingen in an attempt to stop the Prussian advance at the Saale River. Mathias Joel was one of over two hundred Bavarians who were cut down that day and buried in a mass grave at *Kappellenfriedhof* cemetery. The Austro-Prussian War raged just forty-two days. Prussia emerged as the victor, annexing large swaths of southern German principalities and effectively segregating the Austrian Empire from the rest of Germany. Although defeated on the field of battle, Bavaria, through skillful negotiations, was able to maintain a certain level of autonomy from the Prussian invaders. King Ludwig II joined the Confederation of Northern Germany but still kept his crown and his forces. In 1867, Adolphus Joel, younger brother of the deceased Mathias, was ordered to join Mad King Ludwig's army.

At ages fifteen and thirteen respectively, Hermann and Solomon Joel left their mother behind and fearfully boarded the steamship bound for the Port of Baltimore. They swore to their mother that they would stay together and protect one another. They swore to themselves that they would one day bring her to America.

After an apprenticeship with a jeweler in Baltimore, Hermann and Solomon moved to Richmond and established their own business in 1877 at 15th Street and East Main Street. After some successful years they expanded their operation to include the sub-letting of a small case in Bland & Bros. General Store in Centreville, King and Queen County. The third Saturday of each month Hermann would travel to Centreville to retrieve sales proceeds collected on his behalf by the Blands, replenish his stock, and take in or pick up any items brought by local customers for repair. (40.2)

On May 18, 1885 Hermann Joel placed a satchel on a stool behind a counter along the back wall of J.T. Bland & Bros. store. He pulled a ring of keys from his pocket and reached to open the top drawer of a bank of drawers located on the right back side of the counter. His eyes widened as he noticed that the drawer had been pried open. He pulled the drawer handle and it caught slightly on the strike plate on the top of the drawer jamb. He tugged a little harder and the drawer opened. The thin lock bolt was bent nearly to ninety degrees. A man had followed Joel into the store and stood with arms crossed on the other side of the counter. Hermann Joel furiously rifled through papers in the drawer and with a sense of panic looked up at the man.

"Officer... Der ledger is not here!", he said in his thick German accent. "I don't know vut has happen't! It is not here!". Joel then searched the open shelves next to the drawers. He turned and looked down on the floor. He swallowed hard as he looked back at the policeman still standing with arms folded.

"Mr. Joel. You need to find that ledger.", sternly ordered the officer.

"It should be right here!", exclaimed the jeweler as he pointed with all fingers of his extended hand. He put his hand to his forehead and then slid it down over his eyes. "Dis is not possible!" Joel turned his back and leaned back against the counter for support. He glanced through a doorway behind the counter and to the right. There, he caught sight of something in the small room beyond the doorway. "Officer... look at der vindow... Look!"

There was a small window with two over two sashes. The top right pane had been broken and the sash latch was unlocked. The officer flatly stated, "Looks like someone got here before we did, Mr. Joel. Who else would know about this ledger? The Commonwealth's Attorney will not be pleased, Mr. Joel."

"I don't know Herr Officer... I think many of my customers have seen it ven I record der sales unt repair verk."

At this moment Joseph Bland, proprietor, approached the two men. "Mr. Joel, is something wrong? Why are you here today?"

"It appears your store has had a break-in.", said the officer as he pointed toward the window.

"What!?", Bland balked. "I-I just locked that window a couple of days ago!"

"Well, somebody broke the glass…", the officer explained.

"I-I don't know how that happened. I didn't notice that.", said Bland a bit shaken.

"Is anything else missing, Mr. Joel?", the officer remained focused.

"I do not tink so.", said Joel as he walked back and looked in the countertop display case. "Der case is still lock't unt it looks like all the tings are there. I vill open der safe." Joel knelt down and located a skeleton key on the key ring. He inserted the key and opened a small cast iron safe which sat below the countertop on the left side. "I do not keep much in here. Most tings of value that are not kept in der case I take vith me and verk on dem in Richmond; unt bring back der next time.", he continued as he twisted the handle and drew the door open. "Ya, ya… Only a few rings unt vatch chains in here. I tink dat is all."

"Do you keep any cash on the premises?", asked the officer.

"No…I do not keep cash here." (40.3)

Chapter 41   *The Seduction of Miss Madison*

At 9AM, May 18, 1885, Charles Meredith called the first witness of the day. A tall thin man thirty-one years of age took the stand.

"Please state your name, place of residence, and your relation to the defendant, sir", said Meredith.

The man cleared his throat. "My name is John Walker of King William County. The accused is my cousin. My father and his mother were siblings."

"And what is your relation to the deceased, Ms. Madison?" She is my niece – my sister's daughter."

"How would you describe the relationship between the defendant and the deceased? Were they close?", asked Meredith.

"Objection, your honor!", interjected Beverly Crump. "His opinion of their relation is of no consequence to the court."

The Judge looked at Meredith. "To the contrary, your honor", responded Meredith. "The motive for the defendant to act in the manner of which he is accused hinges directly upon their personal relationship. Mr. Walker's testimony, and other evidence and witnesses to follow, will demonstrate this for the court."

"Objection over-ruled. Please continue Mr. Walker."

John Walker cleared his throat, "Well, we are a large but close family, I would say. I never noticed anything unusual about Thomas' and Lillie's relationship. They were loving family members just like you would find in any family."

"Did either of them ever come and visit you recently?", asked Meredith.

"I have lived with my parents for a few years now. My father is somewhat paralytic and my mother often needs help caring for him. Both Thomas and Lillie have stayed with us. Lillie was with us for an extended stay from last July until last October, prior to her leaving for Bath County. Tommie visited a few times during that period, as well."

"Can you recall the exact dates of Ms. Madison's stay?"

John Walker exhaled while he thought. "I remember that Tommie visited on July 10. That is my father's birthday. I believe Lillie had arrived a day or two prior. Then, as I said, she stayed with us until early October; maybe until October 10th."

"And this was this past year? July to October of 1884?", Meredith sought clarification.

"Yes, sir. 1884."

"You state the defendant came to visit on July 10; how long did he stay?"

"He only stayed one night, Mr. Meredith.", answered Walker.

"What were the sleeping arrangements?"

"Objection!", cried Crump.

"On what grounds, Mr. Crump?", asked Judge Atkins.

"The defense sees no value in these details. Neither should the court.", argued Crump.

Meredith jumped in, "Your honor, this line of questioning is intended to establish the intimacy of the relationship and ultimately, the seduction of Ms. Madison by the defendant. Once established, the court will have the motive to support the other evidence presented. The prosecution realizes that some of this is certainly uncomfortable to hear; and some testimony may even be considered unsavory; but it the opinion of the prosecution that a clear understanding of the relationship between the defendant and the deceased is critical to understanding how and why all of this occurred."

"Please proceed, Mr. Walker", ruled Judge Atkins. Crump frustratingly sat down heavily in his chair. Thomas Cluverius sat expressionless. He glanced occasionally in the direction of his elder cousin John, but never once made eye contact.

"Tommie slept in my room with me. Lillie slept in another bedroom on the opposite side of the house." Walker shifted in his chair, sensing more uncomfortable questions were going to follow.

"And, on the night of July 10, did Mr. Cluverius stay in his bed throughout the night?"

"I don't know. I slept through the night. I believe I arose between 8 and 9 in the morning to tend to some duties in the yard and left Tommie in the room. I did not see him nor Lillie again until later that afternoon."

Meredith continued, "Did the defendant come visit at any other points during this period of Ms. Madison's extended stay?"

"Yes", replied Walker, "As I recall he came again in August."

"Can you be more specific with the date?"

"I believe he visited August 25th."

"And how long was that stay?"

"It was just a single night.", recalled Walker.

"When the defendant came for these visits, did he spend time with Ms. Madison?"

"Yes."

"Were they ever alone for extended periods?"

"I believe he arrived before noon on August 25th. My mother and I were visiting a friend of hers that day. We had left early that morning. Lillie and my invalid father were the only ones at home. We returned that afternoon. After dinner, I remember Tommie and Lillie went for a long walk and did not return until sunset."

"Did the defendant sleep in your room that evening?", asked Meredith.

"Yes. He slept in my room during all of his visits."

"Did he leave the room at all the night of the August 25th?"

"Yes, he did. He said he was feeling ill around midnight and left the room."

"Did he describe the illness to you?", asked Meredith.

"He said his bowels were out of order. I asked if I could be of assistance and he declined any help. He then left the room."

"How long was the defendant out of the room?"

"I don't know. I fell right back asleep and did not wake again until morning. He was there in my room when I awoke. I asked him how he was feeling and he said much better."

"Did he ever leave the house that night? Did he go to the outhouse?" pressed Meredith.

"I don't know, sir. As I said, I fell quickly back asleep."

"During this period when Ms. Madison was staying with you, were there any other overnight visitors?"

"No sir. I believe Tommie was the only other visitor we had; save a few local daytime visitors who just stopped in for an hour or two; maybe three or four visitors of that nature over that time."

"Were any of those visitors ever alone with Ms. Madison?"

"No sir. I am not certain that any of them even saw her during those visits", said Walker.

"So, the defendant is the *only* additional person to stay overnight during this time?"

"Yes, sir"

"After the visit in August, did you see the defendant again before today?"

"Yes sir, I saw him at Aunt Jane Tunstall's home in late January or February. It was a brief visit – maybe two or three hours.", said Walker.

"And you understood that the defendant was living with Ms. Tunstall?"

"Yes. He was living with Aunt Jane."

Prosecutor Meredith returned to his table and Colonel Aylett handed him a postcard. Meredith presented it to Walker. "Is this a postcard you received last Summer?"

"Yes"., replied Walker

"And who sent it to you?"

"It came from Thomas."

"The defendant?", asked Meredith looking for clarification.

"Yes".

"And it is written in his hand?"

"Yes".

"One last question, Mr. Walker." Meredith, still holding the postcard, approached the evidence table and picked up the gold watch key. "Did you ever see the defendant wearing this?"

"Yes sir. He was wearing one very much like it when I last saw him at Aunt Jane's. We sat right next to each other at dinner. He looked at my watch chain and I at his. He mentioned that he had recently acquired it. I believe that is the one he was wearing that evening."

Meredith turned to the judge. "No more questions, your honor."

Beverly Crump rose to his feet and stepped out into the middle of the courtroom. "Mr. Walker. I am finding it difficult to understand how, if indeed Mr. Cluverius did leave the bedroom at all, you did not hear him. I assuming this is a relatively small room. Would you not feel him arise from the bed?"

"Actually, sir, that bedroom is rather large. There are two separate double beds in there. I slept in one and Tommie the other. And I do tend to sleep heavily. Always have."

Crump gritted his teeth and changed tack. "Mr. Walker. How many nights would you say Ms. Madison stayed in your parents' home during this period?"

"I believe she was there every night during that time, sir"

"And how many nights would you say that was? From July 10 to October 10? About ninety days, correct?'

"Yes sir."

"And during that period, how many nights were you in the house?", asked Crump.

Walker hesitated and stammered, "Maybe eight-five or eighty-six. I-I did leave for a few nights…"

Crump cut him off. "So, you spent eighty-six nights there. And for only two of those nights was Mr. Cluverius there, as well. So, there were eighty-four nights when it was just you, Ms. Madison, and your elderly parents in the house. Is that correct?"

"I suppose…"

"Did you spend time with Ms. Madison alone, Mr. Walker?"

"Well, yes… but not in the way…"

Crump cut him off again. "And, there was no one else who can possibly confirm what *YOU* and Ms. Madison were doing on *ANY* of those *EIGHTY-FOUR* evenings?"

"Objection! Your honor, this is badgering." Meredith stood. "Mr. Walker has not been charged by the court with any offense. He is not on trial."

"Objection sustained. Mr. Crump, no more questions of this nature for the witness", ordered the judge. "The court is concerned with the relations between the defendant and the deceased."

"Yes, your honor. No more questions." A contented Crump returned to his chair.

"No further questions", added Meredith.

"You may step down, Mr. Walker." (41.1)

Meredith checked his watch as he stood and called the next witness.

A young woman twenty years of age approached the stand and gently sat down. After the girl was sworn in, Mr. Meredith placed his watch in his vest pocket and walked toward the witness.

"Good morning, Miss. Please state your name, relation to the deceased, and your place of residence."

"My name is Ella Madison. Lillie and I were cousins; first cousins. I live here in the City of Richmond – on 27th Street with my parents."

"Did your cousin, the deceased, ever stay at the home of your mother?", asked Meredith

"Yes, she stayed with us a few days this October past and one other time a few years ago."

"What were the dates of her stay in October?"

"She arrived the evening of October 10th and left the morning of October 14th."

Meredith stroked his chin. "What was the purpose of her visit?"

"Well, she said she had taken a position as a schoolteacher in Bath County. She was to take the train out there from Richmond. "

"If she was on her way to Bath County, why did she stay in Richmond for nearly four full days?", asked Meredith

"Well sir, I think she thought train was going to Bath on the 12th, but it turned out that she had the dates wrong and it did not leave until the 14th. So, it was nice. She was able to visit a little longer."

"I see… Did anyone else ever visit the house during this time?"

"No sir, I don't recall any other visitors."

"Did the defendant ever visit your parents' home?"

"He may have visited a time or two. But I do not ever recall him staying overnight."

"Did he visit between October 10 and 14?"

"No sir."

"Has he visited your home at any time in this past year?"

"No sir. It has been at least a couple of years since I have seen Tommie." She looked over at Cluverius. He looked straight down at the table top in front of him. He remained absolutely expressionless, almost as if he was not hearing any of the proceedings. "I do not believe he has been to our house since he was at Richmond College.", she concluded.

Meredith paused for a moment. "Is it your impression that your cousin, the deceased, knew the environs of the City of Richmond?"

"I am not sure I understand the question.", said Ella.

"Did she know the City very well? Could she have found her way around the City with ease, or would it have been difficult for her?"

"Well sir, I don't believe she knew the area well. I remember her saying she had been to Richmond only a very few times at that point. She barely left the house while she was with us. I think we walked around the block once or twice".

Meredith honed in. "Do you believe she has ever been to Hollywood Cemetery or the Old Reservoir?"

"Oh, I very much doubt that, sir. Those places are very far out on the West end of the City. We rarely have reason to go out there. I would be surprised if she even knew of those places."

"Objection, your honor. This is speculative.", said Beverly Crump

"Sustained", said Judge Atkins.

"Please allow me to re-state the question. Miss Madison, do you know if your cousin, the deceased, had ever been to Hollywood Cemetery or The Old Reservoir during any of her visits to Richmond? Did she ever make mention of those places?"

"No, sir."

"Thank you, Miss Madison. No further questions." (41.2)

The defense declined to question the witness. Charles Meredith then called his next witness. A short, stout, middle-aged man rose to his feet and straightened his tie. The rims of his eyes were red with pronounced dark circles below.

After the oath was administered, Meredith spoke, "Please state your name, residence and relation to the deceased."

The man cleared his throat, "My name is Charles Madison of King William County. I am Lillie Madison's father."

The courtroom fell very silent. "Mr. Madison.", Meredith began, "please describe your relationship with your daughter over recent months and years."

"Well, sir; we were somewhat estranged. Lillie and I had not spoken over the last year and one half."

"Why was this so, Mr. Madison?"

"Lillie was always a bit stubborn. But, nothing unusual. But, about a year and one half ago our relationship became very troubled. It got to the point where she could no longer be in my house. I could not allow it."

"This is unfortunate and I am sure distressing. How did things devolve to this level?"

"Mostly, it came from her relations with Mr. Cluverius." Charles Madison looked directly at the defendant. Cluverius kept his eyes straight ahead. "I suspect that he had seduced my daughter nearly two years ago. I found some letters last summer. I don't read well but I read well enough to know that they were of a… a personal nature. Lillie found me looking at them and became very angry. She took them from me. I demanded she give them back and she burned them…" Charles Madison put his head down and sighed heavily. He lifted his head again and continued, "I was so angry; angrier than perhaps I should have been… I told her she had to go find somewhere else to live. It was then she went to live with the Walker family."

"Were you aware that the prisoner spent time at the Walker house?", asked Meredith.

"I cannot say that is a surprise. His mother is a Walker. So was my wife."

"Did you ever hear that Mr. Cluverius, specifically, had stayed with the Walkers?"

"No, sir."

"Did you know that Lillie had moved to Bath County?"

"Yes. I heard that last October."

"Did you know why she went to Bath?"

"No. Not as a certainty. But I suspect it had something to do with Mr. Cluverius.", the father answered with clear anguish on his face.

"Did you know she was with child, Mr. Madison?"

"No, sir."

"Did you have any direct contact or correspondence with Lillie after she left your home?"

"No, sir. Regrettably, no.", Charles Madison held his face in his hands for a moment.

"No more questions, your honor."

Beverly Crump stood and stayed behind the defense table. "Mr. Madison. Were you aware of any other male visitors to see your daughter either at your home or at the Walkers' home?"

"I have heard talk of other suitors over the last couple of months. But before my Lillie's death, I had heard no such thing. Mr. Cluverius is the only man with whom I thought she had any untoward involvement."

"Did you hear of any male visitors while she was in Bath County?"

"No."

"Did you hear of any of these visits to Richmond we have heard discussed?"

"No, sir. All of this was kept from me."

"Thank you. No more questions."

Charles Madison sighed once again very heavily as he left the stand and walked out of the courtroom. Judge Atkins banged his gavel and instructed the court to adjourn for lunch and return in one hour. (41.3)

Chapter 42   *On the Delaware*

Judge Atkins called the afternoon session to order on May 18, 1885. The courtroom was bursting at the seams with humanity and curiosity. The early Summer heat was beginning to take hold of Richmond. The windows of the courtroom were opened to capture any elusive breeze. Open windows also elicited a new outer-ring of viewership; young men and boys erected step ladders and stood precariously outside the windows to catch a glimpse or hear a snippet of the spectacle.

"Please continue, Mr. Meredith.", said the Judge as he wiped his brow with his handkerchief.

Charles Meredith nodded his head to a bailiff. The bailiff turned and knocked once on one of the doors behind the stand. It swung open and two other bailiffs emerged carrying a large trunk. The two men rounded the witness stand and placed the trunk directly in front of the Judge's bench. "Your honor, the prosecution recalls Police Chief Justice D.C. Richardson to the stand."

"Good day, Chief. I don't believe the court needs to remind you that you remain under oath." Chief Richardson smiled and nodded. Meredith continued, "Do you recognize that trunk sitting in front of the Judge?"

"Yes sir, Mr. Meredith. That is the trunk that once belonged to Fannie Lillian Madison. After her identification, we had it brought from Bath County, where she was living and working as a school teacher."

"When was it brought to you, Chief?"

"I believe it arrived on March 20; about five days after the deceased was identified."

"And who has maintained custody of the trunk since this time?", Meredith continued.

"I sent two officers to retrieve the trunk on March 19. They returned with it on the 20th. It has been either in my personal custody in my office or in the evidence room at Police Headquarters under the control of Sergeant Lee. There it has remained except for the articles which were removed from the trunk and provided to you sir, at the Commonwealth Attorney's office.

"Yes, yes… Can you give us a description of those contents?"

"There are dozens and dozens of articles in that trunk, sir. Many articles of clothing. Perhaps twenty-five or thirty pictures, and hundreds of pieces of letters, poems, and papers with writing on them, as you may imagine a young woman having in her possession. There was also a diary she kept while at the school."

"Would you be able to recognize any of these letters?", asked Meredith.

"Yes sir, I believe I would."

Meredith walked over to the prosecution's table. Col. Aylett handed Meredith a piece of paper. Meredith presented it to Chief Richardson.

"Do you recognize this letter, Chief?"

"Yes. I found that letter at the bottom of the trunk among several others."

"Who wrote this letter and when is it dated, sir?"

"It is addressed to Miss F. Lillie Madison and signed by T.J. Cluverius. It is dated September 14, 1884."

Meredith took the paper back to the table and exchanged it with Aylett for another. He walked back over to Richardson. "Do you recognize this piece of poetry?"

"Yes, Mr. Meredith, I do. It was found in the same the trunk as the other. It was hidden under newspaper which lined the bottom of the trunk"

Beverly Crump stood and interjected, "I would like the opportunity to read these papers!"

"I object to that, your honor.", said Meredith.

"On what grounds, Mr. Meredith?", asked Judge Atkins.

Meredith argued, "These papers have not been entered into evidence. I am only using it as identification of the trunk and its contents."

"Mr. Meredith. Could that be a distinction without a difference?", the Judge inquired.

Meredith had the court right where he wanted it. He had the defense, in effect, asking for what was the most salacious pieces of evidence in the trial, written in the prisoner's own hand, to be entered into evidence. "Perhaps, your honor." Meredith handed the poem to Crump, "You can read it if you want to."

Crump read the first two lines of the poem, *On the Delaware*, and knew he had been trapped. He knew that this piece of perverted gutter tripe could now be presented as evidence. He silently handed the letters back to Meredith. Meredith knew he now had an advantage, but decided not to press it just yet.

Mr. Crump then thought better of it and decided to engage. "Your honor, we claim the right to examine for ourselves the same depository from which these particular matters were culled, in order to see if there is anything else there."

"I simply ask the question of whether they want to make an examination now or after the court adjourns.", said Meredith.

Judge Atkins turned to Crump, "Do I understand Mr. Crump wants to make a private examination of these papers?"

"That, your honor, I ask you *not* to pass upon at present.", said Meredith.

Col. Aylett followed on, "Let them designate what particular papers they want."

Crump responded, "We are content to make an examination so as not to interfere with the regular trial of the case."

Judge Atkins concluded, "The court will have a decision on this matter in the morning. Let us continue."

"Thank you. Chief. I have no more questions.", said Meredith.

Beverly Crump stood and walked toward the witness. "Chief Richardson, where was this trunk first opened?"

"In my office, sir. The deceased's father provided a key which I have since turned over to Mr. Meredith's office.", replied the Chief.

"And what were you looking for in this trunk?"

"Evidence of the guilt of the murderer of Miss Fannie Lillian Madison.", said the Chief firmly.

"No further questions at this time, your honor", conceded Crump. (42.1)

The prosecution then called W. R. Quarles to the stand. "Mr. Quarles, please state your name and occupation for the court.", said Col. Aylett for the prosecution.

"My name is William R. Quarles. I am an owner of a banking house in the City, Warren & Quarles."

"How long have you been in the banking business?"

"Twenty years. I have been involved in banking in all capacities.", stated Quarles.

"Do you have or have you had any banking dealings with the prisoner?"

"Yes, sir. I have been dealing with the prisoner for nearly a year. We have completed several transactions."

"Can you identify the handwriting of the prisoner?", asked Aylett.

"Yes sir."

"Objection, your honor!", cried Beverly Crump. "This man is not an expert in handwriting analysis. He is a banker!"

Judge Atkins turned toward Aylett waiting for a response. "Your honor, it is the prosecution's contention that a man who has seen another man's handwriting many times would be able to identify the writing of said man. He may not be able to analyze the writings of strangers. But, he almost certainly could identify the writing of a man with whom he has conducted such a level of business."

"Continue, Mr. Aylett.", ordered the Judge.

"Exception!", blurted Crump.

Aylett came forward with the postcard previously identified by Mr. John Walker as having been written by Thomas Cluverius. "Is this written in the prisoner's hand?"

After a few moments of silence Quarles looked up from the paper and confidently stated, "This appears to be written by T. J. Cluverius."

Meredith turned toward the Judge and exclaimed, "Your honor, the prosecution would like to enter this postcard into evidence as an example of the defendant's handwriting. Two witnesses have now identified it as such."

Judge Atkins turned to the defense table. Cluverius sat quietly looking straight ahead. "Mr. Crump, does the defense concede that this postcard is indeed written by the defendant?"

"We concede it to be his handwriting.", answered Crump.

Col. Aylett then brought another postcard and a letter to the witness. "Mr. Quarles. Does the handwriting on these belong to the same man?"

"I would say they were written by one and the same man… T.J. Cluverius.", said Quarles.

"These letters were found in Miss Madison's trunk.", explained Aylett. "How about this poem, Mr. Quarles?"

Quarles read the poem and tried to hide his uneasiness with the content. "In my opinion, this was written by the same man. The word *night* is there in both the poem and the letter. The g-h-t is clearly the same. The capital *D* is in *Dear* in the letter and in *Delaware* in the poem. They are the same. Also, the *W* in *With regards* is the same as *Wisdom* in the poem. The poem has the general appearance of having been written by the prisoner."

"Objection, your honor. Pure speculation.", insisted Crump.

"Over-ruled.", Judge Atkins responded.

"An exception is taken, your honor.", stated Crump.

"No more questions.", said Col. Aylett.

Beverly Crump stood and stretched. "Mr. Quarles, how long have you been conducting business with Mr. Cluverius?"

"Since June of 1884. I believe it was in relation to a bond.", answered Quarles.

"And how many times have you examined Mr. Cluverius' writing?"

"I've received maybe three letters and…"

"Three letters? Just three, Mr. Quarles?", interrupted Crump.

"And he has filled out several slips for deposit.", added Quarles.

"These three letters, Mr. Quarles. What was their nature? What was their size?"

"They were of a business nature written upon small pieces of paper that would be used in ordinary business correspondence.", explained Quarles.

"That's vague, Mr. Quarles. I have no more idea of the size of the paper in ordinary business correspondence as I would the size of a cake of cheese.", said the deadpan Crump.

Quarles curled his lip as he lifted between his forefinger and thumb one of the pages of the letters that sat in front of him on the witness stand. He rolled his eyes as he slightly waved the page toward Crump in obvious dissatisfaction as the courtroom suppressed laughter.

"Exactly how can the handwriting of an individual be identified, Mr. Quarles?", taunted Crump. "By what method?"

"The only way I know is through direct comparison and determining similarity.", said Quarles.

"Not particularly conclusive.", jabbed Crump. "No more questions; nor *quarrels*, Mr. Quarles." The room snickered once again.

Col Aylett stood on redirect. "Suppose Mr. Crump would open an account…"

"We object to that!", exploded Crump.

"I will not finish the question.", Aylett quickly conceded. Just having the question and Crump's reaction on the record created the distraction he sought for the jury. (42.2)

"No further questions. The prosecution now calls Mr. James Craig."

A small balding man with spectacles approached the stand and was sworn in.

"Mr. Craig; please state your name and occupation.", said Col. Aylett

"James D. Craig; I work for the first auditor's office at a bank here in Richmond."

"Please expand on that, Mr. Craig."

"Well, I am charged with auditing the activities and records of the bank", explained Craig.

"Would this work require that you examine handwriting?", asked Aylett.

"Oh, yes sir. A large part of my work involves linking and reconciling transactions within the bank system. This often requires me to match handwriting on different records and papers in order to clarify said records. I may need to track several deposits or withdrawls to a particular bank floor officer; or a teller; in order to recreate a trail so the bank can understand how these transactions transpired. It requires me, at times, to compare and identify the handwriting of bank employees and customers alike. I perform this type of analysis with regularity."

"So, you would consider yourself expert in this area; in handwriting analysis?"

"Yes, sir. I believe I would."

Aylett cleared his throat. "Mr. Craig, please examine the postcard, the letter, and the poem before you. Let the record show these were the same papers inspected by the previous witness."

Mr. Craig removed his glasses and looked closely at each of the three samples. He held each very close to his nose. His eyes got very large as he scanned the material. The courtroom sat still waiting for his analysis. The high temperature in the room seemed to increase more rapidly with each soundless moment. A bead of sweat ran down Cluverius' forehead. He sat motionless as it travelled the contours of his cheek and jaw until it was absorbed near the base of his neck by his damp shirt collar. After nearly two minutes of silence Mr. Craig put the papers down and put his glasses back on. The courtroom exhaled as they awaited the auditor's rendering.

"There is an individuality in them all. The punctuation is the same on each. I have no doubt that the man who wrote one wrote the others."

Aylett quickly followed up, "Your honor, the prosecution would like to enter, this postcard, this letter, and this poem into evidence".

Crump erupted, "Objection, your honor! We object to that poem's entry into the evidence. It is not signed by anyone! Any attribution to the defendant is purely speculative!"

Col. Aylett jumped back in, "Your honor, two witnesses have matched the writer of the poem to articles which the defense concedes as having been written by the defendant."

"Col Aylett, please bring me this poem.", said the judge.

Judge Atkins read the poem to himself. His eyes widened and his cheeks flushed. After a moment of thought he said, "As I stated earlier, I will rule upon the admissibility of all of the papers in the trunk tomorrow. This will include this poem. But, under *no* circumstances will this poem be read aloud in this court. None of its contents nor its meaning will be discussed in court. It may only be discussed in the context of the handwriting, itself. If the court deems it admissible evidence, the court will make arrangements for the jury to review this evidence at an appropriate time."

"As you wish, your honor. No more questions, your honor.", said a contented Aylett.

The courtroom became agitated as the mysterious poem piqued the public's imagination. Whispers quickly turned to chatter. Judge Atkins struck the gavel twice. "Order, please! The gallery will be seen and not heard!" The crowd quickly hushed and the judge nodded to the defense.

Beverly Crump stood and approached the witness. "Mr. Craig; have you ever seen the handwriting of the accused?"

"No sir".

"Have you ever closely studied the handwriting of the accused under a microscope?"

"No sir, I have not."

"Do you have any personal knowledge of the accused's handwriting?", pressed Crump.

"I have no personal knowledge of his handwriting whatsoever."

"Mr. Craig, did you read that poem before?"

"Sir, I have never read that poem! It is a vile, vulgar composition; and…"

"Do not say what it is, Mr. Craig!" interjected Judge Atkins. "A description in open court is not appropriate and will not be tolerated."

Craig grew agitated. Crump continued, "Can you tell the jury the extent of the general difference in the handwriting on the letter and the general difference of the poem?"

"I consider that at the time the letter was written, the writer was a little tired and was at that same time engaged in a task that was not agreeable. He seemed to want to fill the paper and spread the words as far as possible. That shows a weariness in writing – the desire to get through with it. The poem is much more neatly written which indicates it was copied from a prior draft or perhaps another source."

"So, are you saying the writer of the letter was somewhat lazy?", Crump proposed.

"Well, perhaps lazy; perhaps rushed; perhaps distracted. He just wanted to complete the task."

Crump looked a little perplexed. "So, you actually believe that you can ascribe a characteristic such as *laziness* to someone based upon their handwriting?"

"That was your word; not mine, Mr. Crump."

Crump shook his head and chuckled, exhibiting for the jury his mistrust in such interpretive exercises.

"No more questions, your honor."

Chapter 43   *Sic Semper Tyrannus*

At 4 AM on May 19, 1885, a strong breeze blew through an open window on the west side of the Clerk's Office at the King William County Courthouse. The door to Records Room was always latched shut; but on this early morning it was opened wide. A small dark figure stood in the doorway and peered in. The room contained nearly all the legal records of the county dating back to 1787 when a fire destroyed most of the county records to that time. Thousands of files filled with tens of thousands of documents were neatly organized on rows of wooden shelves that stretched from the floor to the top of the twelve-foot ceiling. The history of a still young but vibrant society was kept there by the trusted clerk; providing an important road map from the past to the present.

She moved slowly and deliberately up and down a few rows of files. Her breathing steadily increased as her vengeful anticipation grew. The older woman scampered across the room to the east side of the building and opened another window. She then turned and picked up a five-gallon can of kerosene. The wooden plug was pulled from the spout and the contents began to spill on the floor of the westernmost row of files which sat near the base of the stairwell. She marched down one side of the row pouring to her right. At the end of the row, she spun one hundred eighty degrees and continued to pour; pacing like a stalking horse back to where she started. She looked at the can and determined about one gallon remained. She continued her pour across the front of each row of files until she reached the final row. She quietly sat the can down and reached into the pocket of her skirt and removed a large match. It was struck against the wooden shelf leg. The match burst into a single blue flame with a white tip. Not even the bright light of the match could bring warmth to her cold left eye.

"I told *all* of you that you were doomed. I will see to it! *Sic Semper Tyrannus*!", Annabelle Lumpkin muttered to herself as she cast the match forward into the pool of kerosene in the center of the aisle. The flame bolted in two directions toward the shelves on either side of the row. Within twenty seconds the entire row was consumed by flame. Suitcase Annie smiled widely, clenched up the empty can, and dashed through the front door of the Clerk's Office into the shadows of the night.

County Clerk Owen. M. Winston walked two miles to work each morning. This morning was no different except as first light was appearing, he saw a dark column of smoke rising above the tree line to the East. He quickened his pace. Fifty yards further he found himself running ever faster as it became increasingly clear that something was terribly wrong at the Courthouse.

Winston was completely out of breath as he rounded the last bend in the road and the Courthouse came into full view. Not only was it a fire he was fearing, but he was horrified to see his own office completely engulfed in flames. Since 1869 he had taken great pains to organize, catalogue, and protect the public record. Now in a single morning, all was lost. At twenty yards distance the heat and sound intensified. The distraught man dropped to his knees helplessly witnessing the vaporization of his cherished work. By 9 o'clock the fire burned out. All that remained was a smoldering Flemish Bond shell.

Later that same morning, Samuel Boulware entered an old farmhouse alone. He had toured much of the 207-acre property, inspecting broken fences and dilapidated outbuildings. It had been more than four years since he had last visited the old home in King William County he inherited from his aunt and passed on to his own son. The old farmer's emotions were a strange mix of melancholy and sanguinity. He mourned his son deeply, yet he was renewed with relieved optimism that he had wrested the family heirloom back from the dishonest Annabelle Lumpkin. His ultimate plans for the property were not yet clear in his mind, but he was determined to restore it in honor of his deceased loved ones and never again let it fall into such disrepair.

Boulware entered the dining room which was off the entry hall to the left. He drew back the dusty soiled curtains and let in some light. He looked up and beheld a ceiling full of cracks, water stains, and loose plaster. The large brass chandelier had separated from its mounting and clung precariously overhead. It was green with tarnish but remained in one piece. Boulware turned to look out the window into the sun-filled yard and was reminded of earlier times.

Aunt Piddy burst through the door and to the edge of the porch. "Dear sister! Welcome!", she boomed as she rushed the carriage.

Aunt Piddy was a stout woman with an equally powerful personality. She grinned broadly as she embraced her sister, Letitia Boulware.

"And dear Sam... My, how you have grown!", she said. She clutched the quiet boy and pulled him close to her bosom. Sam looked at his mother with a hint of embarrassment. "How old are you now, Sam? Fifteen? Sixteen?" Aunt Piddy winked at Letitia, well aware she was fawning.

"No ma'am, I'm twelve.", admitted Sam.

"Twelve! Well then, I know you're getting too old for hugs from Aunt Piddy; but I just can't help myself, Sam. You are so big and handsome!"

She chuckled as she reached out, grabbed each of them by the hand and led them into the house. Aunt Piddy's house was always meticulously maintained. The home sparkled inside and out with fresh paint; the furniture was carefully dusted and always positioned in its proper place. Young Sam was impressed with the orderliness of Aunt Piddy's household. Aunt Piddy had no children and had lost her husband ten years prior when he was thrown from a horse. However, she never spent a moment alone. She owned more than one dozen slaves, two of whom were full-time residents in her home. Fred, a friendly man fifty-years of age, took care of maintenance and repair around the main house and kitchen. He also spent much of the time caring for Aunt Piddy's horses and carriage.

Betty, a woman nearing forty, took care of all other matters regarding the operations within the main house. She cooked, cleaned, washed the clothes and linens; but most importantly, she kept Aunt Piddy company.

The rumble of thunder and sudden darkness overhead interrupted Boulware's daydream. Dark clouds rolled over the trees in the western distance and furiously approached.

"Yes, the chandelier...", he thought to himself.

The old man dragged the dining room table toward the wall out from under the dangling fixture. He went down to the cellar, recalling that Fred kept a step ladder down there. After a few minutes of fumbling through the damp dimly lit underground area, he located the old ladder and hauled it back up to the dining room. The hinges on the ladder were rusted tight, but with some effort, Boulware managed to open them. He positioned the ladder under the chandelier and cautiously ascended the ladder. By the fourth rung he was able to barely touch the top of the chandelier. He strained to reach a few inches higher but to no avail. He raised his right foot to step toward the top rung. A sudden bolt of lightning struck very near the home. The crackling piercing tone enveloped the room. He flinched and clasped both ears to block the deafening waves of sound, simultaneously trying to find a place for his suspended foot. He lost his balance as the entire ladder lurched to one side. Boulware desperately reached one hand out to steady the ladder. He leaned backward and over-compensated for the initial lurch. The horrible sound seemed to intensify as he was torn away from the ladder. The world fell dark and silent as Boulware's head crashed against the edge of the dining table. Sam struggled to call for Aunt Piddy. He closed his eyes tightly. He opened them one last time and there standing over him was the smiling Annabelle Lumpkin.

"Mr. Boulware, you really should not be in *my* house. You were not properly invited. Now, you will be leaving." She lowered her voice even more and said, "Good bye.", before delivering the definitive strike to his head. (43.1)

Chapter 44   *A Storm Is Coming*

Judge Atkins called the courtroom to order at 9 AM on May 19, 1885. Charles Meredith called the first witness of the day for the prosecution. "The prosecution calls Mary Dickinson."

Thomas J. Cluverius was seated calmly at the defendant's table as he had been for every moment of the trial. He slightly shifted his weight and turned his head to look out the window. He noticed the sky darkening in the distance off to the west. "A storm is coming.", he thought to himself.

A large woman straightened her back, pressed her shoulders against the back of her seat, and tipped herself on to her feet. She puffed as she squeezed her way to the center aisle of the courtroom and began to waddle toward the bench. She stopped after a few feet and breathed deeply. She moved slowly but her face displayed real vibrancy. A gentleman stood and offered to help her make her way to the stand. Mrs. Dickinson smiled and latched on to his arm. Her cheeks were flushed. The man looked as if he were dragging an over-sized blue urn planted with two large blooming red roses down the aisle toward the stand.

Mrs. Dickinson crawled up the step onto the witness stand. The gentleman escort returned to his seat. Mary Dickinson raised her right hand and took the oath.

Mr. Meredith walked toward her. "Good morning, madam. Please state your name, place of residence, and occupation for the court."

"Thank you very much, sir. My name is Mary Dickinson. I am from Bath County. I run a school there." Her voice was loud and clear but her smooth Virginia accent was quite pleasing to the ear.

"How long have you lived in Bath County?"

"I have lived there all of my life."

"And what is your relation to the deceased?"

"I knew Lillie Madison. She worked at my place, Mr. Meredith… She taught school.", said Mrs. Dickinson.

"How long has she been in your employ?"

"Since October 16th; this past October".

"When did you last see Miss Madison?"

"She left Bath on March 12[th.] I never saw her again.", replied Mrs. Dickinson as she audibly exhaled and patted her brow with a handkerchief. The finality had dawned upon her. "'Tis warm in here already."

Judge Atkins interrupted and instructed the bailiff to open more windows.

Meredith resumed, "Can you describe for the court the clothing that the deceased typically wore? What type of dresses, hats, jerseys, and so forth?"

"Lillie had a red crochet shawl … It was torn on the border and I mended it with yarn. She had a hat; it was black straw with three ostrich feather tips. It was lined with velvet. The trim outside was silk and velvet. I gave her the bungles for it … She had a blue veil. It had a hole in the end; made by my dog when she visited one day. She sometimes still thinks of herself as a pup. My dog, that is…" The courtroom briefly chuckled and Mary Dickinson continued, "I remember Lillie had a pair of brown gloves that she wore a good deal. She also had a pair of what I call, garnet gloves, which she did not wear as much."

Meredith brought forth a red shawl as Beverly Crump made a notation on his paper.

"Is this the shawl you have described?", asked Meredith.

Mary Dickinson took out a pair of spectacles and spread the temple arms wide to fit them around her broad face. She pushed the bridge into the crease between the fat of her brow and the bridge of her nose. She pulled the shawl closer to her face. "Yes, this is it. I positively identify the shawl. There's where I mended it; right there. She had an alpaca dress on the day before she left. Lillie also had a blue jersey she wore quite often; I think I could identify that."

"The court should note that this is the shawl which was discovered hanging over the wall at the Dunstan property by Officer Walton and his men; a short distance from the Marshall Reservoir." Meredith then produced a blue jersey. "Is this the blue jersey?"

"Yes, that is certainly it."

"Let the court note that this blue jersey was being worn by the deceased, Lillie Madison, when her body was recovered from the Marshall Reservoir by Dr. Taylor. Mrs. Dickinson; do you recognize this tan dress?"

"Yes, sir. This dress is the alpaca dress I mentioned. It belonged to Lillie Madison."

"Please note that this dress was found in the satchel which was discovered floating in the river near the C&O Railroad Wharf by Mr. Mountcastle.", said Meredith.

Charles Meredith then moved over and stood near the witness. "Mrs. Dickinson, do you know why Miss Madison left your school in March?"

"I know the reason she gave me, Mr. Meredith.", she replied as she removed her spectacles.

"Yes, and what was her reason.?"

"Well, Lillie showed me a letter from a friend of hers in Richmond. In the letter, the friend was beckoning Lillie to come to Richmond to help her with some sickly relatives. They needed to travel to Old Point, I believe, for treatment."

"Did she provide any other reason why she would want to go to Richmond at that time?"

"No, sir. That is the only reason she gave and it was good enough for me."

Meredith returned to the prosecution table and picked up a piece of paper. He presented it to Mary Dickinson. "Is this the letter she presented?"

Mrs. Dickinson once again put her glasses on and closely examined the paper. "Yes, sir. This is the letter she showed me. I read part of it. Lillie read the rest to me. I granted her permission to leave the school and attend to this business. That is the last time I saw her." Mrs. Dickinson wiped the sweat from her brow and then a tear from her eye.

Charles Meredith read the letter aloud to the court:

Richmond, VA, March 9, 1885

My Dear Lillie, It is on business of sad importance I must write you to-day, as you know, both mama and Aunt Mary have been in wretched health for a long time, and both have been getting worse for some time, and the doctors say if Aunt Mary doesn't leave here, and soon, she cannot stand it long; so they advise papa to take her to Old Point, in order that she can take those sun-baths, which are proving so beneficial to consumptives. But she will not agree to go unless I go with her, which of course is out of the question, as mama is too ill for me to leave her, so we have been trying to persuade her to let someone else accompany her. So, at last, she agrees that if we can get you to come down and go with her, she will consent to go. Of course, we told her you were teaching, but she begged we would try to get you with her just as company for her, as her nurse will go with her, who has been waiting on her all the time. She says the reason she wants you to be with her is on account of your being so quiet and gentle in your manners when you were visiting us, and she is so nervous she could not bear to have someone with her who is not so gentle and kind. She told me to beg you please to grant her this request, as it was her last resort for momentary relief of her sufferings, as of course, we know she can never be well. My dear Lillie, imagine how it is with me, my dear mama and aunt both so sick. Mama is rapidly declining, I think, and aunt worse, I think; but if she can get to Old Point we hope she will get better. She will only stay there one week, as in that time the doctors think she will be better, if it will benefit her at all, Lillie, please come. Ask Mrs. Dickinson, I say, please excuse you under these sad circumstances, just for a week, and she will do it, I know, as you wrote me she was so good and kind. Papa wishes me to say to you, if you will come and go with aunt, he will never forget your kindness, and, besides, he will pay all of your expenses *and $2 per day for every day you are with her. He is such a devoted brother to her he would do anything in his power. Lillie, don't get any dresses for the purpose, as you and I wear the same clothes, and as we wanted, if possible, to attend the exposition, I have made up alot of new clothes for that purpose, but, of course, now we can't go, but we were in hopes mama and aunt would get better, so we could go, but we have given it out now. Now, dear Lillie, we are in hopes of seeing you soon. If you will accompany aunt, come Thursday (12), either on mail or express; we shall send to meet you and please, dear Lillie, do not disappoint us, for you know there is nothing I would not do for you. If aunt should get too ill, we will telegraph to you, so you will get it before time for you to start the 12th. If you will ask the lady you teach for to excuse you for just a short time, she will do it I know. All send much love; aunt is very nervous to-day.*

Ever your loving schoolmate,

Laura M. Curtis

"The prosecution hereby moves at this time to enter this letter, along with all of the papers in the trunk, into evidence. Your honor stated that he would rule upon previous material presented this morning."

"I object, sir!", shouted Beverly Crump.

"On what grounds, sir?", Judge Atkins responded.

"Mrs. Dickinson is on the stand. This is a point of order, your honor. You cannot rule on entry of evidence that pertains not to this witness."

This is fine, your honor. Prosecution withdraws the submission at this time. No more questions,", said Meredith.

Mr. A. Brown Evans eagerly stood for the defense. He confidently walked toward the witness.

"Mrs. Dickinson", he smiled. "Where did Miss Madison live while she worked for you in Bath?"

"She lived in my home. I gave her one of my bedrooms to use."

"How was her demeanor and conduct during her stay?"

"Faultless, Mr. Evans."

"Was she ever visited by any gentlemen while at your house?", asked Evans

"Never was."

"Do you remember her ever being visited by someone who has been spoken of as a *city gent?*"

"I have no recollection, Mr. Evans".

"Did anyone else live in the home?", asked Evans.

"Just my son, Willie."

"What about your husband?"

"He passed five years ago. Before Lillie came it was just my son and myself."

"Yes; and what was the relationship between Miss Madison and your son?", asked Brown as he squinted at Mrs. Dickinson cupped his right elbow in his left hand and placed his right forefinger to his lips.

"Oh, they got along very well. They grew very close. They spent a great deal of time together."

"I see. Could there have been any romantic interest?"

"Mr. Brown... really?" Mary Dickinson began to laugh so hard her sides shook. After a few seconds she was able to catch her breath and blurted out, "My son is nine years old!"

Beverly Crump stood amongst the laughter and waved Brown back to the table. "Damn you, Brown! I give you another chance and you do it again! I am taking the rest of this!", he demanded.

Brown sheepishly sat back down at the defense table. Cluverius, who had sat motionless throughout the testimony, slightly shook his head and cut his eyes toward Evans in disgust. "Where could we find such a man?", he asked himself.

Beverly Crump and asked Mrs. Dickinson a single question. "Were you aware, Mrs. Dickinson, that Miss Madison was eight months with child when she died? Did you realize she was with child during her entire stay with you?"

Mary Dickinson's face dropped with a mix of sorrow and guilt. "Why, no. I had no idea. I probably should have noticed. I thought she was just adding weight because of my meals. If she had told me, I could have helped her."

"No further questions. Thank you". (44.1)

The prosecution then called Laura Curtis to the stand. A tall slender young woman rose and took the oath. Her long brassy hair was pulled back over her ears and held in place by a large clip. She was neatly dressed in a long black skirt with a matching short black jacket. She wore a simple tan blouse with a high lace collar. Thomas Cluverius had heard

Lillie speak of Laura on a few occasions. But he had never met her. Now, after seeing the comely figure she cut, he wished he had. The defendant gently gripped his new watch key between his thumb and forefinger as he focused his imaginative gaze upon the temptress.

"Good morning. Please state your name, including your middle initial", said Charles Meredith

"My name is Laura M. Curtis."

"Do you live in Richmond, Miss Curtis?"

"Yes, sir. I do."

"Where in Richmond, Miss Curtis?", asked Meredith.

"On Church Hill; on 29th Street.", replied the young lady.

"Did you know Miss Madison?"

"Yes."

"When and where did you become acquainted?"

"We met at Dr. Garlick's school in King and Queen County. That would have been in 1881."

"How long did you attend school together?"

"Just one session, Mr. Meredith."

"And when did you last see Miss Madison?"

"I've only seen her once since I left school after that session. She came and visited me in Richmond one time. I don't recall exactly, but it was sometime in 1883."

"And how long did this visit last, Miss Curtis?"

"It was not long. Perhaps half an hour."

"So, to be clear; since you left school in 1881, you have seen Miss Madison one time for only one-half hour?"

"That's correct, sir." Her posture, poise, and comportment were noteworthy, indeed.

Meredith then walked over to his table and plucked a letter from the top. He handed it to Laura Curtis. "Did you write this letter?"

"No sir, this is *not* my handwriting."

"We object your honor!", cried Crump

"Denied!", the judge smartly retorted. At that moment a mighty flash illuminated the entire courtroom followed a nanosecond later by a massive blast of thunder. Thomas Cluverius flinched and reflexively ripped the brass watch key he still pinched between his fingers off its chain. The entire building quivered as high winds began racing through the open windows. Papers were tossed from both the prosecution and defense tables as the temperature in the courtroom plummeted fifteen degrees. The sky opened up and sheets of rain began pounding the City of Richmond. Cluverius deftly placed the separated watch key in his vest pocket.

Judge Atkins quickly directed the bailiffs to close the windows. The entire room darkened. Attorneys for both sides scrambled on their hands and knees trying to reassemble their files. One of the prosecution's papers had blown over to Cluverius' feet. The defendant calmly leaned over and picked up the paper. After scanning it for a few moments he realized he was holding a brief outline for the prosecution's case. At the bottom in large block letters it read:

WILL SEEK DEATH PENALTY

Cluverius fully understood from the moment he was arrested that this would be the prosecution's goal. But to see it written in the prosecutor's own hand rendered it much more real to him than it had ever felt before. Prosecutor Charles Meredith approached the defense table with his hand out beckoning the paper's return. Still seated and still fully in control of his emotions, Cluverius simply handed the page over to him and gently said, "Good luck with your case, Mr. Meredith."

After five minutes the mayhem subsided and the storm moved east. Judge Atkins banged his gavel. "Ladies and gentlemen, let's resume."

Meredith picked up his questioning, "Is that your handwriting, Miss Curtis?"

"No, sir."

"When was the first time you saw this letter? Before or after her death?"

"After her death.", another bolt flashed, instantly followed by another mighty clap.

Meredith flinched and then resumed his questioning, "Did you correspond with Ms. Madison within the last year?"

"No, sir. I corresponded with her some the first year after I left school; but have not since."

"Miss Curtis, do you know the handwriting on that letter?"

"Do I know it? Yes. It looks like Lillian's."

"Are you able to say whether or not it is Lillian's?"

"No sir. I could not swear to it."

"I object your honor!", said Beverly Crump

Judge Atkins turned to the court stenographer, "Strike that question and answer, Mr. Alexander. Mr. Meredith, Please re-state the question.".

"Yes, your honor… Do you believe the handwriting on this letter is the handwriting of Miss Madison?"

"Yes, sir.", replied Laura.

"No more questions, your honor."

Beverly Crump stood and approached the witness. "Miss Curtis. You say that you only attended school with Miss Madison for one session in 1881."

"That's correct."

"And you further say that you only corresponded with her for as much as a year after you left school, correct?"

"Yes, Mr. Crump. That is correct.", replied Miss Curtis.

"So, it is nearly three years since you have seen her writing?"

"I suppose…"

"And before that, your relationship with her only went back another two years at most. Yet, you say you can recognize her handwriting? Handwriting you only saw perhaps several times three years ago?"

Laura Curtis' poise was faltering. "Well… Yes… Well…"

Crump then piled on, "Did you have opportunities to study her handwriting while you were at school?"

"Yes.", she replied meekly

"Yes? Exactly how many times?", Crump pounded away at the point.

"Well, I couldn't say exactly."

"But you are confident that this letter is written in Miss Madison's hand?"

Laura Curtis shrugged. Crump curtly announced, "No more questions."

Col Aylett stood for redirect. "Miss Curtis, were you and Miss Madison close friends at school?"

"Yes, sir.", she said with a slight tremble.

"Were you roommates?"

"Yes. We even shared the bed."

"So, you saw her doing school work, writing letters, and so on nearly every day?", Aylett asked reassuringly.

"Yes. We spent a great deal of time working together. I saw her handwriting every day for the entire session", she answered with returning confidence.

"Thank you, Miss Curtis. No more questions."

Judge Atkins banged the gavel and announced the midday recess. He declared that the afternoon session would resume at 1:00 but would be abbreviated. Proceedings would end for the day at 2:00 pm.   (44.2)

Chapter 45   *We Do What They Want*

Judge T.S. Atkins muffled a belch as he called the courtroom back to order after the midday recess. Although a strong storm had blown through earlier in the morning and cooled the room, the sun was now bright and the temperature was beginning to rise again.

"The prosecution calls Joseph Dodson to the stand.", said Col. William R. Aylett.

A young slender man stood, tugged slightly as his lapels, and ascended the witness stand. After swearing in he stated his name and occupation, "My name is Joseph Dodson. I am a clerk at the front desk of the American Hotel."

Col. Aylett began, "Mr. Dodson… How long have you been employed at the American Hotel?"

"Over two years, sir."

"And, were you working there the morning of March 13th?"

"Yes, sir. I was at the front desk from 6am until 3pm that day.", Dodson responded.

"Did you see Miss Lillian Madison at the hotel that day?"

"No sir, I did not.", replied the clerk

"Did you receive any correspondence from any of your guests or visitors to the hotel that morning?"

"Yes, sir. A courier delivered a note to the front desk the morning of March 13th. The name was written on the note. I matched it to our register and handed it to our porter to deliver to the assigned room."

"Do you recall the name and room number?", asked Col. Aylett

"Yes. It was addressed to F.L. Merton in Room 21.", answered Dodson.

"Did the person in Room 21 respond to this message?"

"Yes, sir. She did.", said Dodson.

"Objection your honor!", cried defense counsel Beverly Crump. "This is conjecture on the part of this witness. Did he ever see the occupant of Room 21 with his own eyes? How can he know if that occupant was a man or a woman?"

Judge Atkins looked at Col. Aylett for a response. Aylett again asked the witness. "Mr. Dodson, did the occupant of Room 21 respond to that message?"

Dodson carefully worded his response, "Yes, sir. The occupant of Room 21 responded."

"In what way, Mr. Dodson?"

"It is my understanding that the person in Room 21 gave a note to our porter to give to the courier in response.", Dodson explained. "The porter was unable to locate that courier, so he brought the note to me."

"And, what did you do with the note, Mr. Dodson?"

"I left it at our desk. But after a few hours, when no courier came for it, I tore the note and put it in the waste can at the front desk. A few days later Detective Wren came to the hotel. He asked to see our registry for the previous days. One of the guests had left without paying after a single-night stay on March 12th. That person was in Room 21. The register said the name of the person in that room was F.L. Merton. Detective Wren asked our porter if he had seen this person. That's when the porter identified the person in that room as a woman and told us of the note exchange. That is when I recalled disposing of the note. I went to the waste can and it was still in there."

"So, to be clear, Mr. Dodson. The note you pulled from the waste can was the note which was supposed to be given *back* to the courier?"

"Yes."

"And that note was sent by a woman in Room 21 who was registered under the name, *F.L. Merton*?"

"Yes, sir."

Col. Aylett retrieved a hardbound register from the prosecution table and handed it to the witness. "Mr. Dodson. Is this the hotel register from the American Hotel?"

"Yes."

"Please read for the court the name of the person registered to Room 21 the night of March 12th."

"It shows F.L. Merton of Virginia registered at 2:40 am that night.", said Dodson

"To be clear for the court; the guest registered at 2:40 in the morning which is actually March 13th?"

"Yes, sir. But it would still be entered for our purposes as the night of March 12."

"Your honor", said Aylett, "The prosecution would like to enter this registry into evidence." He continued, "Now, Mr. Dodson, what was the name addressed on the envelope?"

Dodson cleared his throat and glanced toward the defendant and then back at Col. Aylett. "The name written on the envelope was *T.J. Cluverius*."

Col. Aylett returned to the prosecutor's table and picked up a torn note and a torn envelope. "Is this the note and its envelope, Mr. Dodson?"

"Yes, it is.", answered Dodson confidently.

"Please read the note to the court, Mr. Dodson."

"It says: *I will be there as soon as possible; so do wait for me.*"

"Thank you, Mr. Dodson. No further questions."

Beverly Crump rose to his feet and stepped out from behind the defense table. "Mr. Dodson, how often do you empty the waste can at the front desk of your hotel?"

Dodson hesitated, "Um… no more than once week. Sometimes longer."

"Yes. How many notes are left at the front desk in a given week?"

"I don't keep a count, sir."

"Well, please give the court an idea. Could it be once a week? Twice? Ten times?

Dodson's neck turned red' "Could be any of those, Mr. Crump. It varies."

"Very well… How many did you receive between say, March 9 and March 16?

"Sir, I really could not say."

Crump began to clamp down, "When you took this note in question out of the waste can; how many other notes were in there?"

"I don't recall."

"But, were there others?"

"There certainly were other papers in there. I do not know what they were, exactly."

"Could some of those have been notes and envelopes similar to the one we have here?", Crump persisted.

"That is possible."

"And, you say, that waste can may have represented a week of refuse?"

"Perhaps, sir; perhaps less."

"Or, perhaps more, Mr. Dodson?"

"Yes."

"So, is it possible that this particular note was put in that waste can at some other time than you think you put it in there? Could it have been placed in there On March 9th, or maybe even March 16th just before you removed it for detective Wren?"

"I don't think so… I am very sure that is the note I put in there the afternoon of March 13th."

"Are you completely sure, Mr. Dodson?"

"Yes, I am certain.", Dodson held firm.

"Mr. Dodson. Did you ever see the deceased in your hotel?"

"No, sir."

"Did you ever see this F.L. Merton in your hotel", Crump asked in a mockingly dismissive manner as he raised his hand and backhanded the air.

"No."

"Did you ever see the defendant, Mr. Cluverius, in your hotel?"

"No, sir."

"Did you see any of them at any other point in the City of Richmond on or before March 13th"

"No."

Crump turned toward Judge Atkins, "Your honor, I submit that this man is not a material witness to this case. He makes no claim to have seen either the defendant or the deceased in the American Hotel nor at any other place in Richmond at this time. All he saw were pieces of paper! The defense requests that this testimony be stricken from the record."

Judge Atkins understood Crump's point but wanted to hear more before ruling. "The court will take that under advisement; but for now, we shall continue."

"Thank you. Your honor. No more questions." Crump was encouraged that his request was still in play while the prosecution was confident that additional testimony on the subject would confirm the relevance of Dodson's testimony. (45.1)

Col. Aylett recalled Henry Hunt to the stand. "Please understand, that you remain under oath, Mr. Hunt."

"Yessuh. I understan'", said Hunt still mindful of his mother's advice not to fidget.

"Please remind the court where you work."

"Ise work in da office at da 'Merican Hotel."

"Is that the same as a porter, Mr. Hunt.", asked Aylett.

"Well, yes. I do some porter things. I carry bags 'n cases. I does whatever dey want me to do."

"Yes. As you stated in prior testimony, you delivered a note which had been brought to the hotel by messenger the morning of March 13th to the addressed, F.L. Merton, in Room 21.

"Yessuh."

Aylett presented the note to Henry Hunt. "And you delivered that message to the lady in Room 21. You then waited as she wrote a return message which you were to deliver back to the messenger. Is that correct?"

"Yessuh"

"Is this the note you received from the person in Room 21, Mr. Hunt?"

Henry Hunt paused and then sheepishly stated, "Suh, it look like it could be. Ise only seen the envelope. Besides, I don' know howda read, Missuh."

"I see.", said a slightly embarrassed Col. Aylett. "Here is the envelope that note was in. Does this look like the envelope you handled that day?"

"Ta be honest, Missuh, I never look't dat close. It could be. It was white like dat one; an 'bout dat size. But I never look't at de name. Couldn't read it, no-how. I was jes' lookin' fo' da messunja dat bring da firss note. I went n' found him outside the hotel. He took it n' went to do look for the da man it was s'posed to get to. After a few minits, he brung it back to me. He say he couldn't find no man. So Ise give the note to Missuh Dodson."

Col. Aylett turned to Judge Atkins and said, "The prosecution would like to enter this note and envelope into evidence."

"The defense strongly objects, sir!" boomed Beverly Crump.

"State your grounds, Mr. Crump.", said the judge.

"This piece of evidence is damaged. It was retrieved amongst other refuse. It is very ordinary white paper. There may well have been other notes or envelopes among that waste. Who can say that this note belonged with this envelope? That entire waste can should have been collected by the investigators. One witness cannot verify the presence of either the deceased nor the defendant at the American Hotel at any time. The other cannot conclusively state that this is the actual note and envelope which he ostensibly received from the occupant of Room 21.

Your honor, what is the proposition? To introduce a paper without a signature annexed to it to indicate the party from whom the paper emanated; to introduce a paper without being addressed to any individual, to connect a person to whom that paper is addressed? The only connection to the defendant appears to be the superscription upon a torn envelope which cannot be conclusively matched with the note? According to law, to accept as evidence such a paper would be tantamount to accepting hearsay testimony and would be placing the life and liberty of every individual in the hands of a wanton profligate. In *Newcomb v. Bannister* it was clearly ruled that the party to whom a paper was addressed must receive and open the document before it could be entered into evidence against him. This note amounts to nothing more than a verbal declaration by the deceased in the open air out of earshot and out of the presence of the accused. Allowing this paper into evidence would be an affront to every principle of law."

Colonel Aylett stood to present his counter-argument. "Your honor, we have found the dead woman; we are now looking for the living murderer. We are marching up to him pace by pace and we have reached a point where the law almost has its grasp upon him. And, just at this point, our friends on the defense come in and say 'Stop'.

This paper is clearly part of the *res gestae*. It is entitled to be introduced on its own merits having been addressed to the defendant. Additionally, it should be introduced for the purpose of identifying the lady who registered at the hotel under the alias **Miss Merton** as, in truth, Miss Madison. With regard to *Newcomb v. Bannister*; it was a completely different case from this; the principles of law differ. The principle of law in that case was a question of admission. This widely differs from the principle here, which the prosecution contends, is *res gestae*."

Beverly Crump stood again to make a final point. "Your honor, it should be noted that the prosecution has not produced the messenger who ostensibly took the note from Mr. Hunt, sought to deliver it to the addressed, and returned it to the hotel clerk, Mr. Dodson. This is a gap in the proof."

Judge T.S. Atkins sat back in his chair and wiped his brow. After nearly thirty seconds of silent deliberation he addressed the courtroom. "I agree with the defense that there are some evidentiary flaws with this note and envelope. Therefore, it shall not be allowed into evidence. But, the testimony of both Mr. Dodson and Mr. Hunt shall remain in the record. Any further questions for the witness, Col. Aylett?" (45.2)

"No, sir. No more questions.", the colonel responded.

Beverly Crump announced, "No questions at this time, your honor." (45.3)

"The prosecution calls Clara Anderson to the stand", said Col. Aylett.

"Miss Anderson, please state your name and place of residence."

The young girl held her head low and kept her voice lower, "My name is Clara Anderson and I live in the rooming house behind Mrs. Goss' cigar store. On 15th Street."

Many in the court struggled to hear her, including Judge Atkins. "Miss Anderson, please project your voice for the court to hear", he instructed.

"Yes, sir... My name is Clara Anderson and I live in the rooming house behind Mrs. Goss' cigar store. That's on 15th Street." Several men in the court looked at one another, some with a sly wink or a slight grin.

"Yes, Miss Anderson...", Colonel Aylett continued, "and what is your age?"

"I am seventeen, sir.", she meekly responded.

"Have you ever seen the defendant at Mrs. Goss' cigar store? At her rooming house?"

"Yes. I have seen him there on several occasions."

"Do you know him, uh, personally?", asked Colonel Aylett with a hint of embarrassment.

"No, sir. I've never even spoken to him. But I have seen him.", her voice became a little stronger.

"Well, yes... And did you see him on March 13th?"

"Yes, I saw him there with a young lady that day."

"Did he always bring this young lady to the cigar store, Miss Anderson?"

"I know I have seen the both of them before. But there was a time or two when the lady was not with him."

"Were they there just to buy cigars on the 13th, Miss Anderson?"

"Well, no sir.", Clara hesitated and chose her words, "They also took a room in the rooming house."

"And how long did they stay in the room?", asked Colonel Aylett.

"Well... Mrs. Goss rents them by the hour. But I do not think they stayed more than thirty minutes."

"I see..." Aylett cleared his throat. "What time on the 13th did you see the defendant and the lady?"

"It was sometime near 1 o'clock.", answered the girl.

"Can you describe the woman who was with the defendant?"

Clara paused and squinted toward the courtroom ceiling. "She was rather short. And maybe a bit plump. I remember she was wearing a blue jersey and a red shawl that day."

"Had you seen this same woman with the defendant before?"

"Yes, sir. I believe they were at Mrs. Goss' a couple of months earlier. I think it was January."

"You also stated that the defendant appeared at the cigar store alone, a time or two?"

"No, sir. That's not correct. I said there was another time or two when I did not see him with **that lady**. But, every time I saw him, he was with **a lady**."

"I see. Could you identify these other ladies?"

"No, sir. I can only say they were not always the same lady."

"Thank you, Miss Anderson." Colonel Aylett turned toward the prosecution table as Beverly Crump stood to address the witness.

"Good afternoon, Miss Anderson." Crump put is thumbs in his waistband. "What are your duties at Mrs. Goss' establishment? What do you do to earn your keep?"

Clara's voice lowered again. "Well, I work in the cigar store..."

"Please speak up, Miss Anderson. For everyone to hear!", demanded Crump.

"I work in the store. I also help clean the rooms...", she stopped there.

"Do you provide any other, er, services, Miss Anderson?"

Clara lowered her head and sighed. Then she mustered the strength to answer. "I do what Mrs. Goss wants me to do."

"Please elaborate, Miss Anderson,"

The young girl looked toward the prosecution for some sort of support. Colonel Aylett just clenched his lips together and nodded slightly.

"I do what Mrs. Goss asks of me."

Crump paused while he calculated how much further to continue. As he looked at the distress on the face of the young woman, he decided his point had been made. He could continue to tear away at her reputation; but he suspected that could easily backfire. He changed the subject. "Miss Anderson... Did the defendant have a mustache when you say you saw him?"

Clara Anderson was relieved but still guarded. "I don't know. I don't recall. It is possible."

"So, you are certain you saw him but cannot say whether he had a mustache?"

"Well, sir. If he had one, it was not a thick one. There isn't much light in the rooming house."

"And, all you can say about the woman is that she was short and had a red shawl? No other distinguishing features?", pushed Crump.

"I did say she was wearing a blue jersey… and she was plump…", responded Clara.

"But no other description?"

Clara hesitated, "No, sir".

"No more questions, your honor.", said Crump.

Colonel Aylett offered, "No questions, sir." (45.4)

As Clara stepped down, Colonel Aylett called his next witness. "The prosecution now calls Miss Lulu Woodward."

Judge Atkins intervened. "The defense and prosecution should note this will be the final witness of the day."

Lulu Woodward approached the stand. Cluverius blushed as he turned his head away and looked down at the floor. Lulu was even more beautiful than the last time he saw her. She was a confidently statuesque twenty-nine-year-old woman. She wore a custom-tailored emerald green satin dress with a matching hat and parasol. Her bright red hair flashed as she passed down the aisle from afternoon shadow to afternoon light. Every man took delight watching her subtle feminine movements. Most women in attendance seethed.

Colonel Aylett approached the stand. "Hello, Miss Woodward. Please state your name and place of residence."

"Good afternoon, sir.", she smiled. "My name is Lulu Woodward. I live on 8th Street between Marshall and Clay Streets."

"Do you know the defendant?"

"Yes, sir. I absolutely know him."

"When did you first meet the defendant?"

"I met him first in 1882. He was then attending Richmond College."

"Can you describe that first meeting for the court?", Aylett asked.

"Well, he was introduced to me one afternoon. I believe it was in April. We spoke for a short while. And then he invited me to dinner. He first said his name was T.J. Merton. But later that evening, while at dinner, we came across some of his friends; and they called him Cluverius."

"Did it arouse suspicion that he had more than one name?'

"No, sir. Most men I meet have an additional name. Sometimes two or three!"

Several men in the courtroom began to laugh. They were slapping knees and slapping backs. The women were considering slapping faces. Judge Atkins banged his gavel three times. "Order please! Gentlemen, please!"

The courtroom quickly regained its dignity.

"Do you recall who introduced you?", Aylett continued.

"No, sir."

"Did you see Mr. Cluverius more than once?"

"Yes, sir. Several times during his time at the college. Maybe seven or eight times over the course of a few months. But I have not seen him since those months in 1882. Until recently, that is…during this trial", she smiled as she removed a small fan from her clutch purse and cooled her neck.

Even though he and every other man in the court had several more questions they wanted the enchanting witness to answer, Aylett controlled his base animal compulsions and asked only one. "Did Mr. Cluverius ever have a mustache when you knew him?"

"Well, yes, he did. I saw him both with and without a mustache."

"Can you describe his mustache? Was it heavy? Was it light?"

"Oh, very light, sir. I have to say, he had some very attractive qualities, but a burly mustache was not among them." Lulu Woodward looked over toward T.J. Cluverius. He avoided looking in her direction entirely. Calmly he kept his hands clasped together on the table in front of him while he soberly cursed himself for getting involved with such a woman. But, in the very next conflicted moment of thought, he imagined himself blissfully in her intoxicating company once again.

"No more questions, Miss Woodward."

Beverly Crump declined to cross-examine the witness. He recognized that her poised allure would overpower any discrediting argument he could put forth. "No questions, your honor." (45.5)

The courtroom sat silently fixated as Miss Lulu Woodward descended the stand and once again graced the center aisle. Judge T.S. Atkins even drifted into her aura for a brief moment until he swallowed, checked himself, and reclaimed his authority.

"As stated yesterday, the court has ruled upon the admissibility of the papers from Ms. Madison's trunk. The court will allow all pieces to be entered into evidence with one exception. The "poem" shall not be allowed into evidence. However, it shall be read aloud to the jury, members of the defense, members of the prosecution, and myself. All other persons in this court are hereby ordered to vacate the premises at this time. All windows in the court shall be closed while it is read aloud and there shall be no onlookers through said windows. Anyone found to be making an effort to hear the contents of this "poem" in defiance of my wishes shall be held in contempt and prosecuted to the fullest extent of the law. This, I can assure you. So, jurors, please remain seated. Prosecution and defense remain at your tables. A single bailiff shall stay and read the "poem" for the jury. There shall be no further public discussion of this "poem" by any of you who are entrusted with hearing the contents. The jury may discuss the contents among themselves at the time of deliberation. There shall be no discussion of this by any jurors in any other forum. The prosecution and the defense may only discuss the content of this "poem" in the confines of my chambers. This is final. Everyone else, please leave and go home! The court shall immediately adjourn after the reading and we will begin again at 9 AM tomorrow."

The letter from T.J. Cluverius to F. Lillie Madison dated September 14, 1884 was formally entered into evidence. The letter was torn in a few places and parts of the contents were missing or obscured.

Tappahannock, Va
September 14th, 1884

Dear Lille:

I feel really ashamed for not having written to you and I think you ought to feel more so for not having written to me, for you have nothing in the world to keep you from writing, and I am so busy I have not time to do any thing. I am just out of a spell of sickness that kept me from coming up to King William Friday; I certainly wanted to come as t   (torn section)   the 2nd Friday,   (torn section) your   (torn section)
ailing   (torn section)
just as soon as you get this and a long letter, &c. Miss Bell Bland has gotten very much better and I hope she will be entirely well very soon.
I reckon you will wonder what I am doing here. I got here this evening. This makes twice I have been here within the last two weeks. I went to Richmond yesterday week after Aunt Jane; did not stay but one night. I did wish so much you had been over there. What a time we would have had. The theater was open.
When do   (torn section)   pect to go   (torn section)
in our   (torn section)
sick   (torn section)
and Mrs. Bray were all sick in bed Sunday and yesterday. I don't know how they are to-day. John Abrahams came down on the boat last Thursday to see Aunt Jane; went back same day. You remember you have never written that letter you have been promising so long. Now, let's have it. I don't want to wait a single day

for a letter from you after you get this. Well, I must close this letter, as I am tired. Pen is very bad. Write soon.

Your fond friend,
T.J. Cluverius

P.S. When are you and that fellow going to be married? You know you told me it would be this winter. I think it would be the best thing for you; ***so do*** *this winter.*

Ten minutes later, the courtroom had been cleared of all but those ordered to stay by Judge Atkins. The tawdry poem, *On the Delaware*, was read one time, in its entirety, to the jury.
(45.6)

Chapter 46   *Twenty-One Days In May*

On May 19, 1885, Fitzhugh Lee entered his study at his home *Evergreen*. For over a week he had been reviewing in his mind the events which had taken place this same month in 1864. He was haunted by events which had thrust upon him great responsibility, great achievement, and ultimately, great sadness and great failure.

On May 4, 1864 Major General J.E.B. Stuart and his force of 3,000 cavalry were assembled southwest of Fredericksburg behind the lines as R.E. Lee's and U.S. Grant's armies squared off at Wilderness. Robert E. Lee knew his Army of Northern Virginia was on the defensive. Ulysses S. Grant had massed a major force for a push south to Richmond. Major General Stuart and Major General Fitzhugh Lee were responsible for thwarting General Philip Sheridan's cavalry. It was anticipated that Sheridan would eventually break loose from the lines and probe for weaknesses in Confederate defenses. The question was, where and when? As the battle raged a few miles to the north, Stuart and Fitz Lee circled the action desperately trying to anticipate enemy troop movements. At 5:30 that evening Fitz scribbled a message to Stuart informing him that he intended move west in the morning to track Union horsemen (46.1). An officer set out on horseback to hand-deliver the message. Following him out of the encampment were three other soldiers in a small horse-drawn ambulance.

Major General J.E.B. Stuart, CSA

General Stuart sat quietly in his tent the evening before the expected engagement with Union forces. His staff officers had met a few hours earlier and finalized their reconnaissance plan for the next day. As he sipped a glass of port wine, he listened to the sweet tinkling tones of the most popular banjo player in the Confederate Army. Sweeney was his name and his ability to soothe and entertain the men during the quiet hours was prolific. His service to the Confederate Army, and by extension, the entire Confederacy, was of vital importance. He lifted the boys' spirits, often reminding them of home and the people for whom they fought. Sweeney's music was often the last pleasing sound these men would hear before the tectonic crash of armies on the field snuffed out their peace and, with increasing routine, their very lives.

Sweeney had been travelling with Stuart and his men since the *Buckland Races* the previous Fall. At Buckland, Stuart and General Fitzhugh Lee's commands had literally chased Union cavalry from the field of battle. It was one of the great routs of the War and one of the last clear victories for the increasingly diminishing and retreating Confederate forces.

Prior to and throughout the Buckland victory, and the raucous celebration that ensued, Sweeney had been with Fitzhugh Lee's command. Stuart had long-coveted the services of the banjo player. As the party broke up late into the evening, Sweeney had played for hours and had been drinking for even more. As Stuart and his aides headed to their quarters, they found the musician asleep on his back clutching his five-string banjo to his chest. Sweeney was under an empty supply wagon, snoring loud enough for the enemy to hear.

"General, I do believe that is the banjo player Sweeney under there", exclaimed Captain Frayser.

"Captain, I believe you are right", said Stuart. "Let us load him in that wagon and take him with us. General Lee will not miss him. Fitz would not recognize fine music if it bit him in the arse!"

"Yes sir, General!"

Stuart smiled as he closed his eyes and listened to Sweeney play *Soldier's Dream*. He chuckled as he recalled his appropriation of the coveted banjo player. As the song ended, Stuart dozed. Sweeney got up, slung his banjo over his shoulder, and walked around the back of the tents to relieve himself in the dark. As Sweeney finished and closed up his trousers three men suddenly moved on him from behind. They stuffed a rag in his mouth and threw a sack over his head. One of the assailants cocked a pistol and held it to Sweeney's head. "Don't make a sound...", he warned.

"Harry, don't break the damn banjo!" one of them whispered.

They quickly bound Sweeney's hands and marched their hooded prisoner about fifty yards through some light woods to another clearing. There they tied him tightly to a stretcher and loaded him onto the ambulance. Two men climbed into the driver's seat and one man jumped in the back with Sweeney and his banjo.

"Just stay quiet if you know what's good for you."

Sweeney was terrified to have fallen into unfriendly hands.

At this same time, Captain Charles Minnegerode entered Stuart's tent and delivered Fitz's other message.

One hour later the wagon came to a stop in the middle of a military encampment. The three men grabbed Sweeney from the back, untied him, and rushed him into an officer's tent. There were two lamps fully lit inside the tent. Sweeney was forced onto his knees and the sack was ripped from his head. There, sitting nose to nose, not three inches away from him, was a man with a thick black beard and piercing blue eyes.

"Sweeney...", he whispered with a sharp maniacal emphasis. "Sweeney... Hello. Welcome home!", said a grinning General Fitz Lee.

Sweeney smiled nervously. He wasn't sure if Lee's blazing eyes meant he was angry.

"I-I- I'm real glad to be back, G-G-Gen'ral..", Sweeney stuttered.

"Good! Well, then here's a drink and now let's get to work!" said the jovial Fitz rather matter-of-factly. The General forced a cup of whiskey into Sweeney's left hand and put his banjo in his right. "We sure have missed you dearly around here all these months, Sweeney, old man!"

The befuddled banjoist staggered out of the tent. General Lee placed a hand on Sweeney's shoulder and pointed over to the right. "There's your tent. It's 9 o'clock now. Let's say we play for an hour. You remember *Jine the Cavalry*. You know I like that one! Fitz excitedly began to sing, "*If you want to have a good time-Jine the Cavalry*", Fitz placed his hands on his hips and demonstrated his familiar little two-step in anticipation of his most favored tune. "Thank you, Sweeney". (46.2)

Sweeney Playing the Banjo (in tent) by Frank Vizitelly for Illustrated London News

By May 10, 1864, Union and Confederate forces had clashed continuously for over one week, in actions large and small; offensive and defensive; in a rolling brawl tumbling southward from Fredericksburg to a few miles just north of Richmond. Fitz Lee's forces tracked Sheridan's movements on the western flank while Stuart stalked Sheridan from the east. Sheridan had recently captured a train at Beaver Dam Station on Virginia Central Railroad. Over 3,000 Union prisoners were liberated and over 1 million rations intended for Lee's starving army were seized. But, perhaps more importantly, Sheridan now had positioned a force of 12,000 just ten miles directly north of the capital. Confederate command understood that, at some point, they needed to get in front of Sheridan's advance and stop funneling him into downtown Richmond. A force of 5,000 Confederates prepared to engage Sheridan's much larger force at Yellow Tavern.

Earlier in the day Stuart had a chance to visit briefly with his wife, Flora, and their two small children. Stuart, just thirty-one years of age, maintained his youthful flamboyant image, but he had recently developed a fatalistic melancholy. He confided in one of his aides, Major Andrew Venable, that he did not expect to survive this War and if he were to lose his country, he did not want to. (46.3)

At noon on May 11, 1864, the two forces collided. Three gray regiments blocked Sheridan's advance southward on Telegraph Road while four more aligned on Sheridan's right, providing a flanking option for Confederate forces. The gunfire raged for two hours while the Confederates held firm against the superior Union numbers with superior Spencer rifle firepower. Union forces struck repeatedly at the forces on their right; time after time meeting stiff resistance. About 4pm, Sheridan changed tack and refocused his assault on the three regiments blocking the roadway. Sensing a weakening in those defensive forces, Stuart led a column of cavalry out to Sheridan's left. He was able to disrupt the advance of two Michigan regiments, forcing many of them to dismount and flee past Stuart and his men toward the east. Stuart emptied his revolver and demanded surrender as he pursued the fleeing men in blue. As one of the Michigander sharpshooters ran by, he stopped, drew his own Colt .44, and fired a single shot at the magnificent mounted officer in a plumed hat. The bullet hit its mark, passing through Stuart's left side and exiting to the right side of his spine. Stuart turned his charger and rode at full gallop one half mile to the rear. He pulled up on the reins, listed heavily in his saddle to the left, and began to slump over. Captain Dorsey ran to his aid and eased the general down from his mount.

"Lieutenant Hagan! General Fitz must know what has happened! Find him and tell him immediately! Locate Dr. Fontaine, as well!", Dorsey yelled. Hagan and another trooper rode off quickly to the west where Fitz Lee was desperately trying to hold Telegraph Road.

Upon hearing word from Lieutenant Hagan, Fitz Lee, perched atop *Nelly Gray*, looked through his field glasses nearly a mile up the road. He could see Union forces massing once again for a frontal assault on his position. "Damn it! Lieutenant…", as he pointed to the left, "Captain Minnegerode is about two hundred yards over there. You will stay here with him and hold this position to the last man!" General Fitz turned to the trooper. "You, take me to him."

"But, sir", said Hagan, "you will need to bring Dr. Fontaine, as well."

"Alright! God damn it!" Fitz paused for a moment and turned toward the trooper. "He's a half mile back that way. We will ride together and collect him. Then you will take us both to Stuart."

"Yes, sir.", said the trooper.

Thirty minutes later Fitz and Dr. Fontaine arrived at Stuart's side. The melee had subsided on this part of the field. Stuart's men had carried him a few dozen yards and placed on a stretcher near a field ambulance.

Stuart's face lit up with hope when he saw his friend approach. Understanding his certain fate, Stuart transferred his command, "Go ahead old fellow; I know you will do what is right." He grimaced as he reached his blood-covered right hand out to Fitz. Their eyes met as Fitz knelt and gripped Stuart's hand. They both knew what had to be done. Neither could muster the strength to express the emotions of the moment. Fitz swallowed his tears, saluted his superior, and left to assume his command.

As Fitz mounted *Nelly Gray* Dr. Fontaine began triage. A nearly delirious Stuart was carefully loaded in the wagon bound for the safe confines of Richmond. J.E.B. Stuart saw some Confederate boys abandoning the field of battle and implored them, "Go back! Go back! And do your duty as I have done mine and our country will be safe! Go back! Go back! I had rather die than be whipped!" (46.4)

Fitz Lee looked down and saw Stuart's dark maroon blood on the cuff of his grey tunic. Fitz smiled and teared simultaneously as he whispered to himself, "Right again, Beauty!" The young commander spurred *Nelly Gray* and took off at full gallop back toward Telegraph Road. As Fitz approached the action, he saw Confederate infantry arriving from the south to reinforce his men. He instantly knew his boys would hold the line. Sheridan and his troopers sensed the stiffening of the Confederate line and veered east to begin a long left-hook maneuver to the south of Richmond.

On May 20, 1864, Major General Fitzhugh Lee, along with the rest of the Confederate Cavalry Officer Corps, received the following message from Headquarters of the Army of Northern Virginia:

> *The Commanding General announces to the army with heartfelt sorrow the death of Major General J. E. B. Stuart, late Commander of the Cavalry Corps of the Army of Northern Virginia. Among the gallant soldiers who have fallen in this war, General Stuart was second to none in valor, in zeal, in unflinching devotion to his country. His achievements form a conspicuous part of the history of this army, with which his name and services will be for ever associated. To military capacity of a high order, and all the noble virtues of a soldier, he added the brighter graces of a pure life, sustained by the Christian's faith and hope. The mysterious hand of an all-wise God has removed him from the scene of usefulness and fame. His grateful countrymen will mourn his loss and cherish his memory. To his comrades in arms he left the proud recollection of his deeds, and inspiring influence of his example.*

R.E. Lee, General
(46.5)

The punching and counter-punching between Union and Confederate forces continued in the days that followed. The War was being executed at a frenetic rate as the concentration of men, materiel, and good summer weather wrought unimaginable death and devastation on Central Virginia. But, as always, politics too contributed to the destruction. Word had reached the Confederate capital that negro Union forces had seized territory along the James River near Wilson's Wharf in Charles City County, Virginia on May 5, 1864. Once the newspapers got wind of this, fear and panic gripped Richmond society. Tales of unspeakable atrocities in Charles City County at the hands of Wild's African Brigade spread quickly through the Commonwealth. Many citizens of Richmond frantically conjured images of the brutality should former slaves be unleashed upon their City. The hysterical public, fueled by a sensationalizing press, implored the politicians to take immediate action. In turn, vulnerable politicians looked to the military for a solution. General Braxton Bragg, military adviser to Jefferson Davis, personally ordered Maj. General Fitzhugh Lee to assemble a force and eliminate the negro threat. (46.6)

On May 24, 1864, after a forty-mile overnight ride, Major General Fitzhugh Lee arrived in Wilson's Wharf with a force of 2,500 men including elements of the 1st Virginia

Cavalry and the 5th South Carolina Cavalry.

On the edge of a wooded area nearly a mile from the newly constructed *Fort Pocahontas*, General Fitz Lee raised his field glasses. After panning the north side of the fort, Fitz lowered them and growled, "We have a problem, here. General Wickham, this fort is very well defended. The earthworks are solid and from what I can see, there are many more soldiers there than we were told. Perhaps triple the number. Look at the number of tents inside the fort; the many camp fires. And, see out there on the river; there's a damn gunboat! Can't make out the name; maybe the *Dawn*? Yes, I think that is it. We will have to negotiate that abatis and the creek. Quite an unenviable position…"

"You think there are twelve hundred men in there, General?"

"Yes, you have a look.", as he handed the much older, but lower-ranked, General W. Carter Wickham his binoculars.

"My God, Fitz. This will not be easy."

"Yes, and if we lose to these negroes it will be far worse. But, if we retreat to Richmond now, we may find yet greater danger among our own citizens! I see two pieces of cannon in the fort plus those on the boat! This is a fool's errand! Politicians be damned!"

"Sir, if we concentrate our attack, I believe we can penetrate. Once inside the fort, surely the negroes will surrender."

"Yes, General. I suspect that is the truth." Fitz Lee concealed his serious doubts about the situation. He closed his eyes while he decided between following his conscience and following his orders. "General Wickham; prepare the men for a noon attack."

The terrain and entrenchments eliminated any advantage a cavalry charge could provide. Twenty-five hundred troopers dismounted and tied their horses off one-half mile deep in the woods beyond the range of both the land-based and water-based Federal artillery. Fitz Lee led the troopers on a quiet march through the woods to the north shore of the James River. He instructed five hundred of his best sharpshooters to remain there in reserve and to cut off any communication between the fort and the gunboat. Lee realized he was in a precarious position between *Fort Pocahontas* and the *USS Dawn*. He reasoned that the men left behind would be protected by tree cover whilst the bulk of his forces would advance directly toward the fort. At least for the initial assault, the steamboat would not fire upon him, for fear of striking their own fort. But, there remained, of course, the two cannon in the fort itself. With a stirring *rebel yell*, the charge began. General Fitz came first into the opening. He raised his sword and waved 2,000 dismounted troopers into the field. At the sound of the famous Confederate cry and the eruption of rifle fire by the two small Federal companies stationed outside the fort on the perimeter, the black soldiers inside the fort quickly abandoned their noon meal and manned the parapets.

Brigadier General Edward A. Wild raised his only remaining arm and gave the initial order, "Hold your fire men until they are at one hundred paces. Let them get close and then rain hell upon them!"

The Southerners ran furiously across the field and came upon the abatis. The tangled web of felled trees with cragged limbs jutting upward into the air posed a serious obstacle. The charged slowed as men tried to navigate the menacing maze. The force stacked up three or four men deep across a fifty-yard section in front of the fort. Finally, General Wild decided the time was right and ordered his men to open fire on the pre-occupied rebels. Volley after volley of Federal gunfire hailed. The troops who had yet to reach the abatis formed two lines behind their ensnared mates. The front line knelt and the second stood behind. They began to return fire while the poor men in the abatis worked feverishly to extricate themselves and retreat to the open field. After nearly 20 minutes of constant fire back and forth a cannon shot was fired from the fort. With this development, Fitz Lee gave the order and the bugler blew a retreat signal. The Confederates ran back across the field to the woods from which they came. A mighty celebratory cheer could be heard emanating from *Fort Pocahontas*.

Brig. General Edward A. Wild, USA
(Brookline Historical Society)

General Fitz quickly circled with his officers to consider the next move. He fully understood that he did not have a military advantage. But, he still felt that his forces held a psychological edge over the raw negro brigade.

"Gentlemen", he addressed his staff, "here is what we will do next. I will write a message and we will deliver it to the fort under a white flag." Fitz reached into his breast pocket and removed his field notebook and pencil. "Do we know who is in command in there?"

"It's General Wild, sir.", responded the adroit Captain Minnegerode.

Dear General Wild, you are surrounded by a superior force. If you will surrender your position it is my solemn pledge that all of your negroes will be treated fairly as prisoners of war and remanded to Richmond. If we are compelled to fight our way into that fort, I will not be answerable to the consequences. You have until 2:00pm to offer your surrender.
Most respectfully,
Major General Fitzhugh Lee, CSA

Three gray troopers entered the clearing holding a white handkerchief aloft. They were armed only with pistols, which were holstered. They silently walked toward the western gate of *Fort Pocahontas*. When they reached a point approximately fifty yards from the gate the twosome stopped and announced they were there under a truce flag and wanted to deliver a message from their commander. After a five minute wait the west gate opened and three black soldiers walked silently out to meet the Confederates. They, too, were armed only with holstered pistols. The two parties stood still ten yards apart. A black Sergeant stepped forward midway and smartly saluted his Confederate counterpart. The Confederate corporal looked hesitantly into the eyes of the negro soldier and then turned his head back toward his two comrades. With a slight shrug and a raised eye brow he saluted and handed the negro Sergeant the note. No words were spoken as both parties turned and reassumed their battle positions.

General Edward Wild read the ultimatum to his staff officers. "Can you believe the arrogance of this man, Lee? I don't think these Southerners understand Union resolve! We all know what happened at *Fort Pillow*. (46.7) This is a trap! These black soldiers will be sent to Richmond, paraded through the streets, and summarily shot or hanged! These rebels do not keep negro prisoners." An enraged Wild sat down at a desk. He pulled an envelope from his coat pocket and tore a piece from it. Pulling a pencil from another pocket he scribbled:

We will try that. Take the fort if you can.
(46.8)

General Fitzhugh Lee received General Wild's response just before 2 pm. It was clear to him that, regrettably, the effort to take the fort must continue. At 2:30 Confederate troops reinitiated the assault. The 5th South Carolina troopers under the command of Colonel John Dunovant, began a full-frontal assault while General Wickham led an additional force leftward in a series of flanking movements. The two cannon inside the fort began to ring out. Exploding shells shook the ground and choked the field with smoke. The 5th South Carolina continued a valiant charge through the abatis and reached a point thirty feet from the parapet when the relentless withering gunfire from within the fort forced the Confederates to turn back. The retreat call sounded as Lee's men fell back once again to the woods.

At 3:30 pm General Fitz rallied his remaining force of 2,300 men for another charge. He ordered his 500 sharpshooters to stay back as before in reserve while 1,800 once again crossed the field toward the fort. Just as the action began the guns of the *USS Dawn* opened up and began to pound the wooded area, rendering what had been their battlefield sanctuary another harrowing field of fire. The five hundred sharpshooters turned their rifles on the boat and began firing back at the boat which sat in the river about two hundred yards away. Despite the hail of mini balls, the operators of the deck guns kept their composure and continued to blast away at the woods.

Once again, the charging Confederates were repelled at the fort earthworks. The weary gray troopers retreated to the center of the field and summoned the will to make one more rush at *Fort Pocahontas*. As that charge stalled fifty yards from the fort, General Fitz looked through the smoky fog down the James River. What he saw rendered his next command elementary. The troop transport *George Washington* was steaming up the James carrying Union reinforcements. "Must be three or four companies", Fitz muttered to himself as he saw the Federals massed on deck. He instructed the bugler to sound a full retreat. The troopers scurried into the woods and hastily retrieved their mounts. They retreated a few miles further through the woods to the northwest and bivouacked near Charles City Court House.

Brigadier General Edward Wild and his African Brigade erupted with glee as they watched the Confederates evacuate the field of battle entirely. It was a hard-won victory against a very experienced and battle-hardened force. But, because his brigade's own battlefield inexperience, Wild hesitated to pursue Lee's vulnerable forces. General Wild chose to rest his weary troops for a few hours rather than seize an opportunity to decapitate a large element of the Confederate Cavalry. That night, Wild sent a scouting party out of the fort to reconnoiter Lee's position. A follow-up attack was planned for morning. However, the savvy Confederate horsemen detected the scouts and rightly understood what it foreshadowed. At 3am on May 25, 1864, Fitzhugh Lee and his battered but not yet incapacitated force of approximately 2,200 men quietly slipped away from Charles City Court House back to Atlee just north of Richmond. (46.9)

Grant's Overland Campaign continued to rage through the early summer of 1864. By late June Union forces had crossed the James River south of Richmond and had settled in for what would become the Siege of Petersburg. Although Grant's Army had endured enormous casualties and had suffered many tactical defeats, the strategy was prevailing. Starving Confederate forces had lost nearly as many men as the Northern Aggressors. The supply of new men and supplies for the Federals seemed inexhaustible. For the wilting Confederacy, each man lost represented another step toward ultimate defeat. Leaders on both sides fully understood this reality but many in the South viewed loss to the Yankees through the same recalcitrant lens as Major General J.E.B. Stuart.

Fitzhugh Lee was leaning back in a comfortable overstuffed chair in his study. His short legs were extended and crossed at his ankles. He exhaled through his nose and tapped his forehead as he concluded his mental review of turbulent events in May twenty-one years prior. The battle at Wilson's Wharf not only weighed heavily on Fitz's personal military record, but, in retrospect, it exposed the inherent bigotry which he and Southern society at large harbored for negroes. Fitz Lee examined his own conscience, recalling how he had downplayed the failure of his white troops in the face of a valiant and competent colored opposition. Even in his formal reports he had refused to give credit where credit was due and place the blame where it belonged; with himself. "We certainly found a foe worthy of their steel", Fitz finally admitted to himself. (46.10) "Young arrogant men make mistakes... Old wiser men regret them... God-willing, dead men are forgiven them."

Chapter 47 *Better Than Being a Defendant*

Judge T.S. Atkins called the Hustings Court of Richmond to order at 9 AM on May 20, 1885. Charles Meredith rose to his feet and called Captain Charles H. Epps to the stand.

"Please state your name and occupation, sir.", Meredith began.

"I am Captain Charles Epps of the Richmond Police.",

"And please explain your involvement with the case."

"I was one of the arresting officers. I accompanied Deputy Sherriff Oliver and Officer Robbins to the Tunstall house to question and then arrest the defendant,"

"What date was that, Captain Epps?"

"March 18, 1885, sir."

"Please describe for the court how the arrest was conducted."

"Deputy Oliver, Officer Robbins, and I arrived at Mrs. Tunstall's home in the late afternoon. Mr. Cluverius had not returned home at this time, so we waited in Mrs. Tunstall's parlor. Mrs. Tunstall and the prisoner's brother, Willie Cluverius, sat with us. When the prisoner arrived, we stood and introduced ourselves. We then informed him that he was under arrest for murder."

"Did you specify for whose murder he was being arrested?", Meredith asked.

"No, sir. I simply told him he was under arrest for murder. And his reaction was quite odd. He paused for a moment and then asked us to stay for supper. He did not ask who was murdered, nor where this murder took place. The first question he asked concerned what evidence we may have against him so that he can begin to build his defense. I must say, I have conducted dozens of arrests; but I have never had anyone act so calmly and yet so resigned to the matter. It was as if he was expecting it; yet he proceeded as if he knew he could not be found responsible. Then, Officer Robbins read the arrest warrant. We did stay for supper. Afterward, Mr. Cluverius gathered some personal items and we took him into custody. Because the hour was late, we spent the night in King and Queen County Jail. The next morning, we arose early and escorted the prisoner to Richmond."

"Was the arrest your sole involvement with this matter?", asked Meredith.

"No, sir. Two weeks ago, we executed a search warrant at the home of Mrs. Tunstall. We were there to search for some items that have repeatedly been mentioned by witnesses which were interviewed in connection with this case. We were sent to find a slouch hat and a small watch-key chain. "

"Was the search successful?"

"Somewhat. We did locate the slouch hat but were unable to find the watch-key chain."

Meredith went to the prosecution table and picked up a large grey overcoat and a grey slouch hat.

"Captain Epps... Do you recognize this overcoat?"

"Yes, sir. It is the overcoat Mr. Cluverius wore when we arrested him."

"This hat, Captain; do you recognize it?"

"Yes", responded Epps. "That is the hat I found at the Tunstall house in relation to the search warrant."

"Did you ask the defendant if he had been in Richmond on March 13th?"

"Yes.", replied the captain, "He said he was in Richmond at that time but he vehemently denied ever seeing Miss Madison while there. He said he could prove where he was while in Richmond. He said he saw many people while he was there.

"Captain Epps... When you and the other officers arrested Mr. Cluverius, did you see any signs that he had been in any kind of physical struggle?"

"Yes. We all saw some scratches on the top of his right hand. They were not fresh. They looked like they were healing – as if they had occurred a day or two before."

"Thank you, sir. No more questions."

Beverly Crump stood and walked toward the witness. "Captain Epps... What is the basis for the search warrant?"

"Evidently, the defendant was seen by several individuals at different times and places wearing the hat. He was also seen by others at various places and times wearing a watch-key on his chain."

"Did you ever see Mr. Cluverius wear that hat?"

Epps thought carefully. "I saw him holding that hat when we placed him under arrest; but I never saw him wearing it."

"What do you mean, he was holding it?", asked Crump.

"When we were leaving Mrs. Tunstall's house to bring the prisoner back to Richmond, he pulled his overcoat and that slouch hat off the coat rack in her front hall. Then he put the hat back and chose another that was hanging there."

"So, he never put the hat on?"

"Not in my presence, sir.", answered the Captain.

"Therefore, it could have been a simple mistake. He may have inadvertently picked up that hat. It may not have been his hat. I am sure he may have been somewhat nervous under the circumstances. Is that possible?"

"Mr. Crump. He may have mistakenly picked up that hat, I suppose; but I am quite certain it was not because he was nervous. He was the most serene prisoner I have ever seen; especially in light of the charges against him."

"Yes, yes…" Crump interjected to change the subject. "You mentioned there was a watch-key chain that was also included in the search warrant. You say you did not find it?"

"That's correct, sir.", answered Epps

"Did you see Mr. Cluverius wearing a watch chain?", asked Crump

"Yes, sir. All of the arresting officers saw him wearing a gold watch chain on his vest while we were at Mrs. Tunstall's house. There was another small piece of chain dangling from the chain. We believe this is a piece that would have had a watch-key hanging on it. But there was none there. The next day, while we were on the way to Richmond, he no longer had that small piece dangling from the watch chain. He said he had given it to his brother."

"And,", Crump continued, "did the defendant not arrange for his brother to deliver that piece of chain to you?"

"Yes, the defendant's brother brought a small chain to the King and Queen Sheriff's Office on March 20."

"And where is that chain now, Captain?"

"It was turned over to the Richmond Police and it is still in our possession.", answered Epps.

"And why is that?", pressed Crump.

"It is my opinion and that of the both Deputy Oliver and Officer Robbins that this was not the small chain we saw the prisoner wearing the night of his arrest."

"Why would that be, Captain Epps?"

"The links on that chain are a different type of gold than the one on the watch key which was found at the Marshall Reservoir. We believe there was another watch-key chain. That is why we searched Mrs. Tunstall's house."

"But, no other watch-key chain was found, correct?"

"That is correct", answered Epps with some reservation.

"Captain, you mentioned that you saw scratches on the defendant's hand. Did you ask him how he got those?"

"No, sir. I just noticed them during the meal at Mrs. Tunstall's."

"So, you cannot say in any way, shape, manner, or form how or when he may have acquired those scratches?"

"No, sir.", admitted Epps.

"No more questions, your honor."

Charles Meredith stood for redirect. "Captain Epps… You mentioned that the defendant was quite calm when you made the arrest."

"Yes, sir. Very calm."

"Please explain for the court what you mean."

Epps cleared his throat. "From the moment Mr. Cluverius entered Mrs. Tunstall's home and found us there, he was quite composed. I stated our business immediately upon his entrance and it did not seem to concern him. In fact, it appeared as if he was expecting us. The first thing he did after I informed him that he was under arrest for murder was to invite us to stay for supper! Although it was nearing supper time, we were all quite surprised. We agreed to stay for the meal. His next comment was to ask what evidence we had against him! It was an odd reaction. He remained very calm and resolute through the evening. He led the prayer before we ate. The only thing that seemed to disturb him at all was the prospect of his aunt, Mrs. Tunstall, seeing him in wrist shackles."

"Thank you, Captain Epps. No more questions."

Crump stood, "No more questions, your honor." (47.1)

Charles Meredith called the next witness, "The prosecution calls Emmett Rogers."

A slender young man stood and walked toward. After taking the oath he sat and straightened his tie. T.J. Cluverius felt some sweat beads forming on his forehead as he looked blankly ahead and awaited the testimony of a friend of many years.

"Please state your name, occupation, and residence for the court.", asked Meredith.

"My name is Emmett Rogers. I am an insurance broker and I live in Little Plymouth in King and Queen County."

"Do you know the defendant?"

"Yes, sir. I have known him for nine years."

"Did you see him this past March 12th?"

"Yes, we travelled together that afternoon to Richmond on the Richmond and York River Railroad. We both had business matters to attend to in the city. We arrived in early evening and went to our hotel. We were both staying at the Davis Hotel that night."

"After you both registered at the Davis Hotel that evening, did you see Mr. Cluverius at any other time over the coming days?

"Well, after registering at the Davis Hotel, we both went to the barber shop below the American Hotel. We went there for a shave. There, we made plans to meet at Mozart Hall the following evening. However, I told him I may not be able to if called back home earlier. This turned out to be the case as I was recalled home and left Richmond Friday morning. We parted after our time at the barber and I have not seen him again until today."

"Which performance at Mozart Hall were you to attend?"

"The 2:30 show, I believe."

"Did Mr. Cluverius receive word that you had left Richmond and would not be meeting him at Mozart Hall?

"I did not have the opportunity to inform him. So, I would think he did not know I would not be attending."

"Do you know if Mr. Cluverius attended that showing?"

"Yes, sir."

"How do you know he attended the performance?", Meredith sensed an opening.

"Umm … I must not have understood the question. What was the question, sir?", Rogers' hands quivered as he drew them together.

"Do you know if Mr. Cluverius attended the 2:30 performance at Mozart Hall on March 13th?"

"No, sir. I do not know… Sorry for the misunderstanding."

Cluverius exhaled through his nose and continued to fix his gaze on the wall behind the judge. A small bead of sweat ran down the side of his face. He did not move.

"Did Mr. Cluverius speak of any other plans he had in Richmond? Did he tell you his reason for the visit?"

"No, sir; nothing in particular. He said he was in Richmond on business."

"Can you describe what Mr. Cluverius was wearing the day you were with him?", asked Meredith.

"Yes. He was wearing a grey overcoat and a slouch hat."

Meredith picked up the coat from the prosecution's table. "Is this the coat he was wearing?"

"It would appear to be. The one he was wearing was exactly like that.", Rogers answered as he glanced toward the defendant. Cluverius continued to sit perfectly still and made no acknowledgement of his associate.

"Is this the hat the defendant was wearing?"

"Yes.", Rogers stated.

"The prosecution would like to enter this overcoat and slouch hat into evidence, your honor. The defendant was seen wearing these items in multiple locations throughout the City on March 12th and 13th. Both items were in his possession at his place of residence upon his arrest on March 18th."

Meredith cleared his throat, "Mr. Rogers... Did Mr. Cluverius have a mustache when you travelled with him to Richmond that day?"

"Well, he needed a shave. He commented that it had been two or three days since his last shave. I was in need of a shave, as well."

"Was his shave complete? Did he have the barber shave his mustache? His lip?"

"I believe so.", Rogers' voiced cracked slightly.

"But can you state it for certain?", Meredith pressed.

"I am quite sure the shave was complete. I do not recollect Mr. Cluverius directing the barber to do anything other than shave him."

"Did you not see Mr. Cluverius after the shave was complete?"

"No, sir. I left him in the chair. I had an appointment. I shook his hand while he was still seated and I left", answered Rogers.

"Well, did he have a mustache then, or not?", asked Meredith with some slight exasperation.

"I did not see any mustache."

"Was there shaving cream on his lip?

"Not that I recall, sir."

Meredith sighed and put his head down for a moment. Then he raised it again and looked at the witness. "Have you seen him with a mustache at any other time?"

"No, sir. I have not."

Cluverius gritted his teeth and screamed to himself, "Why can't the man just do what I told him and say I was cleanshaven?! 'Tis so simple!"

Meredith concluded, "No more questions, your honor."

Beverly Crump stood for the defense and echoed, "No questions, your honor." (47.2)

As Crump sat back down T.J. Cluverius leaned over and whispered into Crump's ear, "We need him to clarify. He needs to say I was cleanshaven."

"Not now, Thomas… We will address it again during the defense." Cluverius' instincts were to face the issue head-on at this very moment. But, in deference to the seasoned Bev Crump, he relented.

"Very well. During the defense.", Cluverius confirmed.

Charles Meredith called his next witness, "The prosecution calls Judge John B. Foster to the stand."

Judge Foster stood and approached the stand. A courtroom was a familiar place for a man with more than thirty years of experience as an attorney and a judge. But, as a witness, this was unchartered waters for him. To his own surprise he found himself slightly unnerved to be a witness in a proceeding. "Better than being a defendant", he deadpanned to himself.

"Judge Foster… Welcome to the Hustings Court of Richmond, sir. Please state your name and occupation for the court."

"John B. Foster. Circuit Court Judge for King William County, Virginia."

"Judge, how long have you been on the bench?"

"Fifteen years."

"And, how do you know the defendant?"

"Mr. Cluverius is a young attorney. He has appeared before me on several occasions over the last few years,"

"How many times has he been in your court?", Meredith inquired.

"Oh… I would say, maybe five or six times over the last two years, or so."

"And when was the last time he appeared in your court?"

"He was there in March. Just before he was placed under arrest."

"That's correct, judge. He actually appeared before you the morning of his arrest."

"Did you ever notice if the defendant wore a watch chain in your court?", asked Meredith as he leaned against the prosecutors table.

"Yes. He did.", responded the judge.

"Did you ever notice a small watch-key dangling from the watch chain?"

Judge Foster exhaled and then explained, "Yes. Many attorneys have habitual mannerisms or gestures they employ during an argument – helps them maintain concentration. I haven't had time to determine if you have one, Mr. Meredith; but Mr. Cluverius was before me enough for me to take note of his. He would pinch a little watch key between his thumb and forefinger and rub it in a circular motion. I saw him do that just about every time he appeared – usually during his final argument."

"Well, Judge, I am not sure if I display such a habit. You have made me rather self-aware, I must say! Judge Atkins, have you noticed anything unusual?"

"No, sir", responded Judge Atkins, "but I will start to look for one!" The courtroom broke into gentle laughter as Charles Meredith turned to the evidence table and picked up the watch key. "Judge Foster, this watch key was found at the Marshall Reservoir and was entered into evidence a few days ago. Is this the watch key that Mr. Cluverius has worn in your courtroom, sir?"

Foster took hold of the watch key and looked closely. "It looks like this could be it. I never had occasion to look this closely; so, I cannot be completely certain. But I will say that he clearly wore one very similar to this in my courtroom."

"Thank you, Judge Foster. No more questions, your honor."

Beverly Crump stood and addressed Judge Foster. "Judge Foster… How would you characterize the defendant's demeanor while practicing in your courtroom?"

"Well, I would say he is respectful. He knows the law. And he does a workmanlike job for his clients. He is a good, young lawyer."

"Thank you, Judge. No more questions, you honor." (47.3)

Chapter 48 *The 6th of January*

The Hustings Court of Richmond was called to order at 1:15 PM on May 20, 1885. Judge T.S. Atkins instructed the prosecution to call their next witness. Charles Meredith stood and called Claggett Jones to the stand.

Claggett Jones was a forty-two-year-old attorney. The bulk of his practice was in King William County although he did occasionally practice in surrounding counties and the City of Richmond. After identifying himself for the court, Meredith asked his first question.

"Mr. Jones, where were you on this past January 6th?"

"I was here in Richmond, conducting business on behalf of a client."

"And, did you stay over in Richmond on the 6th?"

"No sir. I actually came to Richmond the day prior. I did stay the night of the 5th at the Exchange Hotel. On the morning of the 6th, I checked out at the clerk's desk. It is there and then that I saw Miss Lillian Madison."

"So, you saw Miss Madison in Richmond on January 6th; more than two months before she would visit again and meet her fate?"

"That is correct.", affirmed Jones.

"Please describe further, Mr. Jones."

"As I was approaching the desk, Miss Madison turned away from the desk. She had a piece of paper, a pencil, and envelope in her hand. I assume she had just obtained it from the clerk. I recognized her and nodded toward her. She then continued on into the hotel parlor. I conducted my business at the desk and left the hotel."

"What time of day did you leave the hotel?"

"This would have been about 11 o'clock in the morning."

"How did you know Miss Madison?", asked Meredith.

"It is my understanding that for a time she attended Dr. Garlick's school, which was near my family home. We attended the same church during that time. I saw her every Sunday for nine months."

"What was she wearing the day you saw her at the hotel?"

"I recall she had a red crochet shawl around her shoulders.", Jones answered.

Meredith picked up the shawl from the evidence table, "Is this the shawl you saw her wearing?"

"It was very similar; but I cannot swear to it."

"Did you see her at any other time that day?"

"No, sir."

"Have you seen her since that time?"

"No, sir."

"No more questions, your honor."

Beverly Crump stood to question the witness. He cleared his throat, "Mr. Jones… Do you know the accused?"

"I have seen him a couple of times at the courthouse; but I have never spoken to him.", Jones replied.

"Have you any professional dealings with the accused, Mr. Jones?"

"No, sir. None at all."

"Did you even know his name prior to these events?"

"No, sir."

"Did you see him at the Exchange Hotel on January 6th?"

"No, sir."

"Did you ever see him in the company of Miss Madison?"

"No, sir.", Claggett Jones squirmed knowing the simple questions would not continue.

Crump circled the defense table and moved closer to the witness. "When you saw the woman you *believe* to be Miss Madison that morning, did she acknowledge you?"

"No, sir. She did not."

"Did she even look in your direction?"

"I am not sure. She did not say anything to me. She seemed focused on something else."

"Yet, you say this is the woman you saw dozens of times in church. How many people attended these church services?", asked Crump.

"Well, sir. Of course, it would vary. But, in general, this is a small church. There may have been as many as two dozen people there. Sometimes more; sometimes less."

"I see, Mr. Jones. And you say that you did not speak to Miss Madison at the Exchange Hotel on January 6th; but I assume you had made acquaintance with her on occasion at church, correct?"

Claggett Jones blushed a little, "Well, actually sir, I had not made Miss Madison's acquaintance at any time."

"Well, why not, sir? Would your wife have disapproved?", Crump smirked.

Jones turned from pink to red as he dropped his eyes to the floor, "Well, no sir. I am not married. I never have been."

"All the more reason to strike up a conversation with a young lady, Mr. Jones! How long had it been since you had seen Miss Madison in church and the time you saw the young woman you believe to be Miss Madison at the Exchange Hotel?"

"It had been over a year and one half."

"Mr. Jones!" Crump boomed, "Is it possible that you mistook the lady you saw in the Exchange Hotel for Miss Madison? She **did not** seem to recognize you in any way.", Crump began to count on his fingers. "You **cannot** identify the shawl the prosecution has shown you as having belonged to the woman you saw. You **never** made Miss Madison's acquaintance. You **had not** seen Miss Madison in over one and one-half years. How can you be certain that this lady in the Exchange Hotel was indeed Miss Madison?"

"I-I-I just know it was her. I had seen her many times. I would not forget her!", he insisted with tears welling in his eyes.

"Perhaps you wanted it to be her and it simply was not, Mr. Jones.", Crump hypothesized.

"No, sir. I know I saw Miss Madison."

"No more questions, your honor." (48.1)

Charles Meredith stood and called the prosecution's next witness. "Please state your name and occupation."

"My name is Alfred W. Arbuckle. I am a clerk at the Exchange Hotel."

Meredith began, "Mr. Arbuckle, were you working at the Exchange Hotel this past January?"

"Yes, sir."

Charles Meredith handed Arbuckle a ledger book. "Mr. Arbuckle, is this the registry for the Exchange Hotel?

"Yes, it is.", replied Arbuckle.

"Is Lillian Madison listed as a guest for January 6?"

Arbuckle turned a couple of pages. "I do not see that name listed here."

Meredith had the courtroom's full attention as he had inexplicably called his own previous witness' testimony into question. He drove the point home, "Are you sure you do not see name *Lillian Madison* or *Fannie Madison* listed in the registry?"

"Yes, counselor. That name is not here."

"Did you see the prisoner at the Exchange Hotel on January 6th?", Meredith continued.

"Yes, to the best of my knowledge and belief, I saw Mr. Cluverius at the hotel that day. He came in the hotel and asked to see the register. He went through the names and asked to see the occupant of Room 66."

Meredith crossed his arms confidently. "Mr. Arbuckle, please look in the register and read the name of the person registered to Room 66 of the Exchange Hotel on January 6, 1885."

Arbuckle quickly scanned the page and placed his index finger firmly on a spot, "Here it is; *Miss F.L. Merton; Roanoke City*."

Meredith let the courtroom sit in silence for a moment. "When he called for the occupant of Room 66, did he see her?"

"No, sir. She was not in the room at that time."

"And what did the prisoner do then?"

"By his expression I could see he was very irritated that Miss Merton was not there. He turned and left without another word."

Beverly Crump stood and called for a motion. "Your honor, this witness testimony should be stricken from the proceeding. As should the testimony of Mr. Jones. The prosecution is attempting to precariously link two shreds of questionable testimony and create elements of a conspiracy amongst the defendant and the deceased which simply did not exist. There is no other way to describe this testimony as anything other than flimsy.

"Denied, Mr. Crump.", answered Judge Atkins.

"The defense takes exception, your honor.", Crump retorted.

"Yes, yes… Please continue, Mr. Meredith.", said the judge.

"No more questions, sir."

Beverly Crump stood and brushed his left sleeve twice with his right hand. "Mr. Arbuckle, have you seen the defendant since January 6?"

"Yes sir. I went to the city jail not long after his arrest with Mr. Burton of the *Dispatch*. There had been talk that the prisoner had stayed at different hotels in the City and I wanted to determine if I had seen him. Mr. Burton wanted to know if I had seen him."

"Yes… Did you describe the man you saw at the Exchange Hotel on January 6 to Mr. Burton before you went to the jail to see the defendant?"

"Yes, I believe I did."

"Yes, you did. I read about it in Mr. Burton's newspaper. You indicated that the man you saw on January 6th had a light mustache and light hair. You can plainly see that the defendant has no mustache and his hair is brown.", Crump held his palm toward the ceiling and gestured toward Cluverius.

"Mr. Burton got that wrong. I told him the man had a *slight* mustache. I do not recall what I said about his hair."

Crump leaned toward the witness and continued, "You also said he had a light-colored overcoat and a black slouch hat." Crump walked over to the evidence table. "This coat is clearly a moderate gray color. The hat is a little darker. But it is not black. Is this more inaccurate reporting by Mr. Burton?"

"I do not recall the conversation I had with Mr. Burton. But the man I saw in the jail was the man I saw that day at the Exchange Hotel.", said Arbuckle.

"And how can you be so sure, Mr. Arbuckle?"

"It was the indifferent air he demonstrated when he came and asked for the occupant of Room 66. That is what caused me to notice him as I did. It is that same indifference he shows here today."

Crump turned immediately toward Judge Atkins, "Sir, that statement should be stricken from the record. It is clearly an attempt to malign the defendant. This witness is not here to pass judgment on the defendant's courtroom appearance in any manner. This is not appropriate!"

Judge Atkins turned to the court stenographer, "Please strike that last sentence only from the witness statement… only the sentence where he opines on the defendant's demeanor here and now. The rest shall remain. Thank you."

"Thank you, your honor", said Crump, "no more questions."

Charles Meredith stood and walked over to the evidence table and picked up the overcoat. He put his arm in the right sleeve and pulled it inside out. He did the same to the left sleeve, flipped the collar over, and turned the coat completely inside out. It now became clear that this overcoat was designed to be reversible. He walked over to A.W. Arbuckle and held the coat up by the shoulders. "Is this the light-colored overcoat you saw Mr. Cluverius wearing on January 6th when he came to the Exchange Hotel and asked to see the occupant of Room 66?"

"Yes, sir. I believe that to be the coat. To the best of my knowledge and belief, the prisoner is the same man I saw at the Exchange Hotel in January."

"No more questions, your honor." (48.2)

"Then please call your next witness, Mr. Meredith."

'The prosecution calls Henrietta Wimbush to the stand.", said Charles Meredith.

A young working-class woman in a plain black skirt and light tan blouse briskly approached the witness stand and was administered the oath.

"Please state your name and occupation, miss." Charles Meredith said.

"My name is Henrietta Wimbush. I am a chambermaid at the Exchange Hotel". She sat very upright in her chair and spoke with great clarity and confidence.

"Miss Wimbush, have you seen the prisoner before?"

"Yes.", she replied. "The gentleman came to the hotel on the 6th of January. I was working upstairs that morning. He came upstairs and asked me if the lady in Room 66 was in. I went to the door and tapped. She called through the door asking who it was. The gentleman answered that it was he; The lady opened the door and I continued with my duties."

"Did he say his name?"

"No, sir. I don't believe he did. I believe he simply said, 'It's me'".

"How long was he there?", asked Meredith.

"They spoke for a moment and then he left."

"Did you hear any of this conversation?"

"No, sir."

"What time of day did he make this visit?"

"It was before eight o'clock in the morning."

"Did the defendant return at any point that day."

"Yes. About two hours later he passed by me again in the upstairs hall and tapped on the door. The lady opened it again. They stood there and spoke for some time; maybe fifteen minutes. I passed by the door three times, tending to duties in the surrounding rooms. The third time I passed he looked a little strangely at me. He then stepped inside the door and pulled it to, not tight. I could see his coat sleeve."

"What was he wearing?"

"He wore a light-colored overcoat and a dark slouch hat."

"Did you hear any of the conversation during this second visit?"

"No…They were speaking in hushed tones… Well… I did hear him tell the lady he would wait for her in the parlor. Then he went downstairs."

"Did you ever see the lady in Room 66?"

"No, sir. I caught a glimpse of her through the doorway when they were speaking. But I do not think I could identify her. She was not very tall…. I never saw her leave. But, later that evening, she was not in the room. The door was left slightly open and the gas in there was lit. I turned down the lamps. I don't believe she returned that night."

"When did you see the prisoner again?"

"I saw him at the police court. It was the same man except he no longer had a small mustache like he had when he was at the hotel." She turned directly toward Cluverius and with certitude declared, "*That* is the same man. I know it is."

Cluverius did not look toward the witness. He bowed his head and shook it slightly. He closed his red-rimmed eyes and sighed.

"Thank you, Miss Wimbush; no more questions."

Beverly Crump stood and put his hand on Cluverius' shoulder as he rounded the defense table and walked toward the witness.

"Miss Wimbush… You say that you could not identify the lady in Room 66, correct?"

"That is correct, sir."

"So, it could have been anyone. Is that right?"

"Well, sir. It was clearly a woman. I heard her speak. And I did see enough of her to know that it was a woman."

"Yes, yes…", Crump said somewhat dismissively. "But, it could have been just about any woman."

Henrietta Wimbush stood firm, "No sir, it was clearly a younger woman. I could see enough to know she was neither a young girl nor an older woman."

"Yes…I will try once more. So, it could be any woman between say, eighteen and thirty years of age, correct?"

"No sir. She's also rather short.", she declared raising a forefinger and cracking a smile.

"Yes, Miss Wimbush." Bev Crump said with some exhaustion in his voice. "It could have been any *short* woman between age eighteen and thirty."

Miss Wimbush responded with some satisfaction, "Yes, I suppose *that* is true."

"Miss Wimbush… Were there occupants of other rooms on that date?", Crump asked.

"Yes."

"Who were the occupants?", Crump continued.

"I cannot say, sir."

Crump leaned in toward the witness, "Were any of them ladies?"

Henrietta Wimbush leaned back toward Crump. Their noses were now less than one foot apart. "Yes."

"So, the gentleman you saw could have been speaking to one of those other ladies.", Crump posited.

"That man was clearly speaking with the lady in Room 66.", the chambermaid said with complete confidence.

Crump paused for a moment and then began again. "Miss Wimbush… You seem to be very sure of yourself. You also seem to be quite observant. How is it that you saw all of these things and remember all of these things, yet you cannot recall *any* of the conversation between the man and the lady in Room 66?"

"Mr. Crump…", mimicking her inquisitor, "I did not hear what was said because it was clear that the gentleman *did not want anyone* to hear what he was saying to the lady. They spoke very discreetly."

Crump turned away from the witness, "No more questions, your honor."

Meredith quickly followed, "No more questions." (48.3)

Chapter 49 *Cluverius, Inc.*

Thomas Cluverius had just completed his evening meal when his brother Willie appeared at his cell door. The guard opened the door.

"Mr. Cluverius, you have a visitor. It is 6:35. All visitors must leave at 7 o'clock."

"Thank you, guard.", said the prisoner.

Tommie stood and greeted his older brother with a hug. "Willie… Come sit down." They sat quietly for a moment on the cot until they were confident the guard was out of earshot.

"Willie…", Tommie began in a hushed tone, "we need to change strategy. Things are not going very well in that courtroom. I feel as if public opinion must be turning against me."

"What can be done, Tommie?"

"We must become more sympathetic. And it has to make it into the papers. To this point I have maintained a solid demeanor. I am no longer sure that is advantageous. Beginning tomorrow, we will act differently. I have already spoken with Pollard about it. He agrees with my assessment. Tomorrow I will appear more as a pathetic and destitute figure. It must appear that this trial is wearing down my resolve. I will not sleep tonight. I will not comb my hair as thoroughly. I will not show any, but I will look as though I am on the verge of tears. And you, must be there to support me. You must appear strong on my behalf. At the time of recess, you must come sit with me and express brotherly compassion."

"I don't understand, Tommie. Why?"

T.J. Cluverius remained patient with his brother. "Willie, if the public can be shown that I am faltering, they will become sympathetic and will come to believe that these proceedings are excessive and unjust."

"But, will they not think that guilt is overcoming you, instead?", asked Willie.

"Yes, there is a chance some may see it that way. But I believe others will see the truth and realize that this proceeding is trying to dictate the outcome the prosecution and the newspapers desire. The public must come to understand that an innocent man is being unfairly held to account."

"I will do what you say.", pledged Willie.

"I have also spoken with Pollard about your testimony. Since you are closest to me and the laws of the Commonwealth prohibit me from testifying in my own defense, we believe we must have you testify. You and Aunt Jane are to meet with Pollard and the others Saturday at Crump's office. They will discuss your testimony. You are to be there at 9 o'clock. Be prepared, it will likely require the entire day to get things right."

"Oh, Tommie...", Willie sighed.

"No fear, brother. You both will do well. Just do what they say. It is critical for my defense."

Willie nodded and Tommie changed the subject, "Did you get Joll's ledger book from Bland's shop?"

"Yes, Tommie. I burned it last night."

"Very well.", Tommie smiled with approval. "Something else we need to address; we must press Aunt Jane to pay Crump and Pollard. You must tell her they require $200 immediately. We cannot afford to lose their representation. You must make it clear to her how critical this is for me, Willie."

"I will."

"Have you collected any money from the little guttersnipe card salesman?", asked Tommie.

"I found him this morning. He still has over two hundred sets of cards left to sell.", said Willie.

"That means he's sold about four hundred pairs! That's forty dollars in sales. Very good. Give him time to sell the rest and then collect. Remember what I said to do about him. He has crossed us."

"Yes, Tommie; I will make sure he keeps only what he deserves."

"Willie... We will need to think more and more of how to raise the money we will need to continue my defense. I know Aunt Jane has some, but it may prove insufficient."

"Yes, Tommie." Willie then reached into his coat pocket. "Tommie... I almost forgot; a woman approached me outside. She handed me this note and said you needed to see this. She said she knows you."

"Who?", asked Tommie as he took the note from his brother's hand and began to open it.

"I have never seen the woman. She was older...", Willie explained.

"Rachel...", Tommie muttered as he read the note.

Cluverius read the first four lines of the letter. In angered shock, he refused to read further and crumpled the paper in his hand. He looked down at the floor and sighed heavily.

"Tommie, what is the matter?", asked Willie.

T.J. Cluverius quickly regained his composure and instantly formulated a plan. "Willie; you must listen and you must follow my direction. This woman. You have to find her. You must find her quickly and arrange for her demise!"

"But... T-Tommie!", Willie stuttered.

"Willie! Remember what I told you when this all began? You may have to do things to help me maintain my innocence. This is one of those things. This woman... I know her. I have known her in personal ways. She is threatening to come forward and say things about me. They are untrue; but, with my burdens, it could destroy my defense. You have to eliminate this problem for me."

"Tommie... I- I- I don't know!", Willie panicked and looked toward the cell door.

Tommie grabbed Willie by his coat lapel, "Willie, keep your voice low! This must be done! Find a man who has experience with these types of matters. I am sure you can find someone who deals this way. Her name is Rachel McDonald. She lives over near the reservoir on Jacquelin Street. Find a man! And, it must be soon. And, Willie, the same fate must meet Nellie Goss. I am told she is too ill to testify for the prosecution at this time. And, although I am not proud of it, Willie; I have been to her house and consorted with women. I have enough women testifying to such things and cannot afford to have others come forward." Tommie grabbed Willie's chin and locked eyes with him. "You must take care of both of these treacherous women. And, it must happen right away, brother! Pay whatever such a man may require."

At that moment they heard the rattle of keys and the cell door lock open. Reverend Hatcher entered Thomas Cluverius' cell for a short prayer session.

"Good evening, Thomas.", said Hatcher.

"Good evening Reverend. I believe you know my brother, Willie. He has come to pray with us.", Tommie grinned and winked at his brother.

"Very well. I am pleased to welcome Willie into our circle."

"Fifteen minutes, gentlemen.", reminded the guard.

Reverend Hatcher bowed his head, "Let us pray." (49.1)

Chapter 50   He Looks Scared

Private Detective Jack Wren sat at his breakfast table. His son Edward retrieved the morning paper from the front porch. Jack sipped his coffee and then looked that front page of the *Richmond Dispatch*.

The Richmond Dispatch
May 22, 1885

Cluverius Weakening – He Looks Scared and Nervous

Richmond, Va, May 21

A cool breeze, but a very damp one fanned the brows of judge, jury, lawyers, lookers on and reporters this morning when Judge Atkins took his seat on the bench. At this stage of the trial, its burdens and fatigues tell plainly on those who are compelled to be present daily. The jury look tired and homesick, and lounge rather than sit upright in their high back chairs. Counsel for defense are not as sprightly as at first – except Bev Crump – with his ever-exhausting "We object, sir." He is the oldest in years and the youngest in labor of the prisoner's counsel. H.R. Pollard and A. Brown Evans both look badly and will hardly hold out another week in that miserable courtroom. Mr. Meredith and Col. Aylett have not changed much in either looks or behavior since the first day of the trial. They knew then that they had a long chase before them, and they started at a pace that would last. They are cold water men and drink nothing but lemonade. (50.1)

Thomas Cluverius presented this morning a more broken-down appearance than ever before. He has paled and his nervousness is painfully apparent. It has been reported that he has been spending more time in his cell praying with his spiritual guide, Reverend Hatcher. During today's recess the prisoner became strangely agitated, so much so that his brother, Willie Cluverius, went to him, sat upon the arm of his chair, and braced him by leaning against him. The prisoner shook like an aspen leaf and struggled to conceal his real condition. His features were set, face-blanched, and an indefinable dread seemed to hang over his imagination. Frequently he looked up at his brother, and with one hand clung closely to him. The brother is devoted, and nothing can be more admirable than the firm stand he has taken by the prisoner's side in this hour of great need. This is tolling on him and there are those who are free to say that before the trial is over, Cluverius will break down and make a clear admission of the part he has played in this matter. (50.2)

Officer Logan Robbins of the Richmond Police was first called to the stand. He was present at the arrest of Cluverius at the home of Cluverius' aunt, Jane Tunstall of King and Queen County. Robbins described the strange behavior the prisoner exhibited at the time – his coolness and failure to deny the charges outright. He showed more immediate concern with preparing a defense. Officer Robbins also corroborated Captain Epps' testimony about the watch chain and the apparent disappearance of the small dangling watch-key chain which hung from it. Officer Robbins also corroborated Captain Epps' testimony regarding the prisoner's grey overcoat and slouch hat. The prisoner had first picked up a slouch hat similar to the one he had been seen wearing in many locations around Richmond, but then chose to wear a black derby for the transport to Richmond in custody. Both the gray overcoat and the slouch hat have been entered into evidence. Officer Robbins testified that the prisoner told him that he "could never have done Lillian any harm". The prisoner also said that he thought someone may have been impersonating him in Richmond. The prisoner indicated that he intended to employ detectives from St. Louis and Chicago to clear the matter up. The prisoner admitted that he had come to Richmond that day on the York River Railroad but had spent the evening at Mozart Hall and the Dime Museum.

Officer Charles Sweeney of the Third Police Station in Richmond was also called to testify. Officer Sweeney had a conversation with the prisoner shortly after his arrival at jail. Sweeney first saw Cluverius in the waiting room reading a newspaper. Sweeney remarked to the prisoner that it was a very serious charge against him. The Officer testified that he asked Cluverius if he had been to Richmond the week before. The prisoner responded that he "came up to Richmond Thursday and went home Saturday". The prisoner acknowledged that he knew Miss Madison very well but did not see her while in Richmond. Sweeney then testified that he noticed marks on the prisoner's hand and that it looked like a breaking out. The prisoner agreed that he may have had a kind of eruption. Sweeney then asked the prisoner if he ever frolicked with bad women. The prisoner told him, "Yes, I have done such things in my life." Sweeney asked Cluverius where he was the night of the tragedy between 8PM and midnight. The prisoner declined to answer that question.

Dr. James Beale, Physician for the City Jail, was then called. He performed a physical examination of the prisoner shortly after he was brought to the jail. The doctor said Cluverius appeared very healthy but he did have three umbilicated scratches on his right hand. One was between the index and middle finger; another between the third and fourth fingers; and a third on the little finger. There was a fourth found on the left hand between the thumb and forefinger. Dr. Beale asked the prisoner how he received those scratches and the prisoner said he recently scraped his hand on a fence. Dr. Beale further testified that the shape of the wounds indicated that they would have been made by something "scoop" shaped. The doctor did not think such marks could be made by striking against furniture or a fence. Dr. Beale said the marks appeared to have been healing for several days. The prosecution asked if they could have been made by finger nails. The doctor declared this was certainly possible. The doctor examined the prisoner's arms up to the elbows and found no other marks.

Mr. R. D. Wortham of Essex County has known Cluverius for a few years. He saw Cluverius shortly after his return home to King and Queen County from Richmond on

March 14. Wortham noticed scratches on Cluverius' hand and asked how he got them. Cluverius said he received them striking his hand against a car railing.

All indications are that the prosecution's case is nearing a close. It is expected that it should be complete on Friday. Then the defense will begin its work. (50.3)

After completing the article Detective Wren leafed quickly through the pages of *The Dispatch* until he reached the "wanted" advertisements. The stream of clients and cases required to support a burgeoning agency were not materializing. Doubts about continuing as a private detective were invading his thoughts. He tried to ignore the signs, but the increasing responsibility of a young and growing family was looming. The new baby would be coming in August.

Chapter 51   **The Prosecution Rests**

Judge T.S. Atkins called the Hustings Court of Richmond to order at 9:15 AM on May 22, 1885. "Mr. Meredith, please call your witness."

Charles Meredith stood, "The prosecution calls Mr. W. F. Dillard to the stand."

A very tall and thin man arose from near the rear of the courtroom and began walking toward the stand. His over-sized hands brushed against his pant legs as he methodically lurched forward. He sat uncomfortably in the witness chair as his knees pressed up against the rail balusters across the front of the stand.

Judge Atkins leaned over toward the witness, "Sir, you may move the chair back some to provide more leg room."

Dillard nodded and thanked the judge as he slid the chair back about six inches and re-settled himself.

"Please state your name and place of employment, sir.", said Meredith.

"My name is Waldo F. Dillard. I am the night watchman at the American Hotel."

"Mr. Dillard… Did you see the prisoner in your hotel the night of March 13th?"

"I saw a man whom I am quite sure was the prisoner.", Dillard replied.

"And can you describe his actions that evening?"

"He entered the hotel between eight o'clock and half past eight. He asked to see a lady in Room 21. I asked him if he had a calling card. He reached in his coat pocket and pulled one out. I gave the card to our porter and asked him to escort the gentleman to the parlor and deliver the calling card to Room 21. A few minutes later, I was in the hallway near the service stairs. I saw the gentleman there. He explained that the woman in Room 21 was not the woman he thought was there; that the woman he was looking for went to school with his sister, or something of that nature. He then went out a side door in the hallway and out into the alley. A few moments later I saw the woman in Room 21 in the lobby. An older gentleman had just escorted her to the hotel and then *he* also left the hotel. I offered to escort the lady to her room, Room 21. I told her that another younger gentleman had been there just before asking to see her. She just asked where he went and that she was supposed to see *him* earlier that day. She offered no further explanation. It was all getting quite odd, I must say." Dillard ran his long fingers through his hair. "Then, about ten or fifteen minutes later, the young man entered the hotel once again and asked to see the young lady in Room 21. I guided him once again to the parlor and had our porter go bring the lady."

"Did you see them at any point again that evening?", asked Meredith.

"About fifteen minutes after I left them in the parlor, the gentleman came to the front desk, purchased a stamp, placed it on an envelope, and then walked out the front door with the lady. I did not see them again.", explained Dillard.

"You said the gentleman had a calling card. Do you recall the name on the card? Was the name T.J. Cluverius?"

"I do not believe it was. I think I would have remembered an unusual name such as that. I am not sure what it was; but I believe it was a somewhat common name; maybe Jones, or Johnson, or Jackson."

"What was the gentleman wearing that evening, Mr. Dillard. You mentioned he pulled the calling card from his coat pocket."

"I object!", cried Beverly Crump, "The prosecution is leading the witness, your honor!"

"Your honor", Meredith coolly explained, "I believe the witness already testified, with no direction, that the calling card was indeed taken from a coat pocket…"

"Mr. Alexander, please read back the pertinent portion of the testimony", requested Judge Atkins.

I asked him if he had a calling card. He reached in his coat pocket and pulled one out.", the stenographer recited.

"Please answer the question, Mr. Dillard."

W. F. Dillard cleared his throat, "He was wearing a gray overcoat and a slouch hat."

"What was the lady wearing, Mr. Dillard?"

"She was wearing a black skirt and a red shawl."

"Did either of them have a small satchel when they left the hotel?", Meredith asked.

"Yes, the lady came down the stairs with a satchel. The gentleman took it and placed it under his arm. He was carrying it when they left the hotel."

"Thank you, Mr. Dillard. No more questions."

Beverly Crump tapped on the defense table as he collected his thoughts. "Mr. Dillard, you mentioned that Miss Madison was escorted into the hotel that evening by an older gentleman. Is that correct?"

"Yes, sir."

"Have you seen this gentleman before at the hotel? Could you identify him?"

"I do not recall seeing that gentleman before. I do not know him and I have not seen him since that night.", Dillard explained.

"Did you see any odd interaction between this older gentleman and the lady?"

"I am not sure I understand the question."

Crump cleared his throat, "Did the older gentleman and Miss Madison seem to know each other? Was there a noticeable intimacy between the two? Was there any physical contact?"

Dillard looked uncomfortable with the insinuation. "I did not see anything to give me that impression, sir. The gentleman may have been lightly holding her arm as they entered the hotel. But, I did not see any indication that their relationship was anything other than chaste."

"Did you see Miss Madison and the older gentleman engage in conversation?"

"Yes.", Dillard flatly responded.

"What was the nature of this conversation? Was there laughter? Did you hear what they said?"

"It appeared genial; I did not hear any of it; or if I did, I paid no attention to the content."

"Were they happy together? Did the conversation appear secretive? Playful?", Crump pressed.

"I saw no such indication. They were friendly; nothing more than that."

"Very well, Mr. Dillard.", Crump combined frustration with doubt. "You say that you do not recall the name on the calling card given to you by the younger man. But you also concede that it was clearly not the defendant's name. Is that correct?"

"Yes, that is correct.", answered Dillard.

"You say you believe the defendant is the man that gave you this card. Is there any possibility that the man you saw that night in the American Hotel is *not* the defendant?"

"Well... I am as sure as I can be that it was the defendant."

"Mr. Dillard. I will ask again. Is there any chance that the defendant *is not* the man you saw that night?"

Dillard paused, "If it were not the man, I would be very surprised."

"Thank you, Mr. Dillard. As I thought, you are not equipped to say with resolute certainty the defendant is the man who gave you a calling card with a name quite different from the defendant's name. No more questions, your honor." (51.1)

Meredith stood, "No questions, your honor. The prosecution calls Michael Delahanty."

A sturdy man with a slight limp approached the stand, took the oath and introduced himself. With a clear Irish accent, he stated, "Me name is Michael T. Delahanty. But I am known as Mick. I drive the tug-horse trolley. Been doing as much since I first landed in the states, nearly fahrty years ago. I live at 10 Elm Street. I own me own house!", he beamed with pride.

"Please describe what you were doing the night of March 13, Mr. Delahanty."

"Well, we started our route from Rocketts Street at 9:00 pm. We travelled up Main…"

"Excuse me, Mr. Delahanty,", Meredith interrupted, "but who is *we*? Were others with you at this point?"

"It was just meself and me horse *Mr. Bianconi*, of course. Oh, he's a fine lad!", Delahanty declared as he cocked his head and winked.

Mick Delahanty was born on a small farm near Thurles, County Tipperary, Ireland in 1832. At age twelve he began driving a jaunty car for Charles Bianconi. Mr. Bianconi, who had emigrated from Italy to Ireland as a very young man, became an innovator in Irish transportation. In 1815 he established a revolutionary business in Clonmel, Ireland transporting travelers, mail, and commodities via overland horse-drawn carriages throughout the region. Although Bianconi fares were higher than the alternative modes of transport (primarily by river or canal barge), he was able to deliver passengers and freight to their destinations in a more timely and efficient manner. This ultimately proved to be a cost savings for his customers. Bianconi created a prosperous system linking market towns; making use of local hotels and, ultimately, rail stations, as terminals.

By 1847, the Great Famine had taken a toll on much of southern Ireland. Tens of thousands were emigrating to America on a monthly basis to escape starvation. The Delahanty family was evicted from their poorly performing farm by their British landlords. The family had few options other than to use the money Mick had earned and saved to gain passage to America. Upon arrival in Baltimore, Mick and his family found themselves, like so many others, penniless and with no prospects for work. Young Mick Delahanty found continued inspiration in the sage words espoused by Charles Bianconi, "Money melts; but land holds while grass grows and water runs."

By 1848 the Delahanty family made their way to Richmond where they joined a small but growing community of Irish Catholic immigrants. Mick initially found employment driving a freight wagon for the Manchester Cotton and Woolen Manufacturing Company, where he stayed throughout the War. In 1866, he began driving a tug-horse trolley for the City of Richmond. In 1870, with great pride and in homage to his mentor, he purchased his own property. (51.2)

Mick Delahanty continued to address the courtroom, "A rider boarded at 18th Street and then anudder at Market bottom. We arrived at 15th in front of McGraw's store where we took up a lady and a gentleman. We then kept up Main. We added a few more passengers at 12th. Then at the Post Office I believe we took up anudder rider but udders stepped off. We dropped a passenger or two near 2nd. At Monroe Park, I turned back for a look and saw just a man and a lady. When we reached the turn table at Beach and Main, they stepped down. It was twenty-five minutes before 10:00 according to our railroad time. I remember the gentleman asking where Reservoir Street might be. I pointed, as its right near the turn around. He asked again and I assured him 'twas Reservoir."

"Did you see the woman clearly, Mr. Delahanty?", asked Meredith.

"No sir, I could not see her well. I am not even sure if she was a black or a white. She had a veil on her head and it was quite dark. But she was rather short and a bit round."

"Was she carrying a satchel?"

"This, I don't know. But your man was carrying a small one. I saw him more clearly. He had a light mustache and light hair. He was wearing a large coat and a slouch hat."

Meredith picked up the overcoat and the hat from the evidence table. "Is this the overcoat and hat the man was wearing that night, Mr. Delahanty?"

"Well… Ya know I have no way to know for sure. But, they strongly resemble what I saw him wear."

"Is this the man you saw that night, Mr. Delahanty?"

"This very much looks like your man. 'Tis hard for me to recognize the man and I would not like to swear that this is the same man I saw in my car unless I was sure of it, indeed. It does look like him; I would say to the best of me knowledge, this seems to be your man."

"No further questions, your honor."

Beverly Crump walked out from behind the defense table. He stroked his chin and then gripped his coat lapel in his left hand. "Mr. Delahanty … Do you drink spirits while you're driving the trolley?"

"Objection, your honor!'" Meredith protested. "This is not relevant …"

Mick Delahanty spoke up, "Now, gents… This question is no problem for a man like meself – none at all. I will answer the man. The answer is no; I do not take drink at work or anywhere else. I understand this may seem unusual for an Irishman like meself. But, I just don't like it; never have. Now, *Mr. Bianconi* is a different lad altogether. He has been known to take the stout on occasion! Copious amounts, if I dare say!" Mick put his right hand on the left side of his mouth, "But, please don't be tellin' his employer!" Mick Delahanty winked and smiled at Bev Crump.

"No more questions, your honor." Beverly Crump quietly returned to his seat.
(51.3)

Charles Meredith called Dr. Thomas Stratton to the stand. "Please state your name, occupation, and place of residence, sir."

"I am Dr. Thomas E. Stratton. I live in Henrico just inside the City Limits on Floyd Street. I practice medicine in both the City and the County."

"Please describe for the court what you did the night of March 13."

"I visited a friend the evening of March 13th. He lives on Cherry Street. I left my friend's home after 9pm and walked over to a cigar store on Main Street near Laurel. I lit my cigar and continued down Laurel Street and turned west on Cary toward home. As I crossed Reservoir, I passed a man and a woman briskly coming down Reservoir. In fact, the man and I almost collided. The man stopped and asked me the time in a somewhat… well… aggressive manner. I told him it was 9:40. He then asked what street they were on. He appeared annoyed that we had nearly collided. I identified both Cary Street and Reservoir Street. He thanked me and the two continued on their way."

"Did you see what the man was wearing?"

"He was wearing a long overcoat. The collar was turned up near his chin. He had a slouch hat pulled down over his eyes."

"Did he have a mustache?"

"Yes, he had a small mustache."

"What was his approximate age?"

"He appeared to be between twenty and thirty years of age."

"Did you see what the woman was wearing?", Meredith continued.

"The woman was wearing something around her head. I do not believe she had a cloak, which struck me as odd. I assumed she must have been a factory girl. She was carrying a small bundle under arm."

"Was she wearing a red shawl?"

"I cannot say. I did not look as closely at her. She did not speak to me. I focused more closely on the man."

"Is the man you saw that night the defendant we see here, today? Did you see Mr. Cluverius that night?", asked Meredith.

"I am very confident this is the same man."

"After this interaction, what did you then do?"

"I returned home for the rest of the evening.", Stratton responded.

"When you left the man and the woman, were they walking in the direction of the Old Marshall Reservoir?"

"Yes; and one other thing I found somewhat odd at the time. As they walked away from me, I heard the man tell the woman that he knew me but that I did not know him. After learning more about him, I suspect he recognized me from Richmond College. I have learned he was enrolled there a few years back and I was teaching classes there at that time."

"Thank you, Dr. Stratton. No more questions, your honor."

Beverly Crump stood and once again rounded the defense table and approached the witness stand. "Dr. Stratton... What was the nature of your visit to your friend's house, that evening?"

"Well, sir... I was simply invited to evening supper at a friend's house."

"And. Who is this friend, if I may ask?"

"His name is Randall Tyler. I have known him and his family for many years. A fine man."

"What was served at the meal, Dr. Stratton?"

Stratton looked quizzically at Crump. He shrugged slightly and answered, "I believe it was a pot roast with potatoes and carrots."

"Was wine served with the meal, Dr. Stratton?"

"Why, yes; it was."

"Do you recall how many glasses you took, doctor?"

"Two or three.", Stratton replied.

Crump then changed the subject, "Dr Stratton... You indicated it was quite dark when you encountered the lady and gentleman on Reservoir Street."

"That is correct, sir."

"You said you gave the man the time. Could you see your watch in the darkness, sir?", asked the wily Crump.

Stratton hesitated for a moment, "Well, in truth sir, I could not see my watch.", he admitted. "I took it from my pocket and, yes, it was too dark to read. However, I had looked at it moments earlier at the Tyler's house as I was leaving. It was about 9:35 at that time; so, I estimated for the gentleman on the street that it was nearly 9:40."

"So, to clarify...", Bev Crump began, "It was very dark when you encountered this man and woman. So dark, in fact, that you could not even see a watch face. But, you claim that you saw the face of the gentleman through this darkness to such a degree that you can sit here now and identify him as the defendant sitting before us today. Additionally, you were admittedly under the influence of wine. With these facts and circumstances laid before this court; can you unequivocally say that the defendant is the man you saw on Reservoir Street that night?"

"I have said I am very confident this is the man.", Stratton insisted.

"Unequivocally, Dr. Stratton? Would you stake your reputation on it?"

Stratton readjusted in his seat and sat forward placing his fist on the rail in front of the witness chair. "I would, sir."

"No more questions, your honor." (51.4)

"The prosecution calls Hermann Joel to the stand."

Hermann Joel sat and cleared his throat after reciting the oath.

"Please state your name and occupation.", Charles Meredith requested.

"My name is Hermann Joel. I am a jeweler."

"Mr. Joel, do you have a shop here in Richmond?"

"Yes. I have a shop here vith my brother. Ve also have smaller shops in Dinviddie County unt King unt Qveen County."

"Mr. Joel. Do you know the prisoner?"

"Yes. I have done verk for him on a few occasions."

"What kind of work, sir?", asked Merdith.

"I have done verk on some vatches unt vatch chains for him. I also believe he has brought me jewelry from his relatives or friends for me to verk on a few times."

"So how many times have you seen him?"

"I am not sure. Maybe four or five times over der last two or three years."

"Has the prisoner ever visited your shop in Richmond?"

"Yes. It vas last January. He came to my Richmond shop unt left a vatch to be cleaned unt adjusted. One of der vatch hands vas schticking"

Meredith squinted, "Do you recall a date in January, Mr. Joel?"

"I believe it was January 5 or 6. It vas certainly early that veeek. Later that veek I went to der Centerville shop. He vanted me to clean dis vatch unt bring it to Centerville unt he vould pick it up there."

"Is this what happened, Mr. Joel?"

"Yes. He picked it up in Centerville."

"Is that the only time he came to your Richmond shop?"

"Yes. I think so. Other times he came to see me in Centerville."

"Do you keep records of this activity?", Meredith continued.

"Yes. In general. Dis is vat I do. I record my verk in a ledger book."

"Do you carry this ledger book with you between your shop locations; or do you have more than one ledger book?"

"My brother unt I keep vun ledger book in Richmond. He keeps another in Dinviddie, unt I keep a third in Centerville."

"In which one would you have kept this transaction with the prisoner?"

"Dis vould be in der Centreville book. I record the verk ver it vas paid."

"Where is this ledger book, Mr. Joel?"

"Vell... I vent to Centerville get it vith a policeman four days ago; unt it vas gone. My shop had been broken into unt the book vas gone. Der policeman saw, too."

Charles Meredith went to the evidence table and picked up the watch key. He handed it to Hermann Joel., "Mr. Joel. This watch key was found at the Old Marshall Reservoir following the untimely death of Lillian Madison. Have you seen this watch key before?"

"Vell. sir... I verk on man, many pieces of jewelry. I have probably seen hundreds of vatch keys. This vun is not like most. It does appear to have been repaired. Unt, I may have done verk to it before. I cannot say for sure unless I can open it and look more closely. You see, ve jewelers vill leave marks ven ve verk on pieces. Der vould be scratches inside that vould help me be sure."

Meredith turned to the judge. "Your honor, the prosecution moves to allow Mr. Joel to open the watch key so that he may closely inspect for his marks."

"I object!", erupted Bev Crump. "This will destroy the evidence, your honor! It cannot be allowed!"

Meredith interrupted, "Your honor, this is a crucial piece of physical evidence. If Mr. Joll can expressly identify it as a piece he has worked on for the prisoner, it will serve to tie the prisoner to the crime scene."

"Your honor! The prosecution is flailing around in the dark with this request. The court cannot allow this piece of evidence to be altered. It may well prove the innocence of the accused just as easily as it could prove guilt. What if Mr. Joel were to take the watch key apart and then determine it is *not* a key he has worked upon? It may well make it impossible for any other jeweler to identify his own work and perhaps exonerate the accused; if the watch key has ever really been repaired at all. You cannot allow this to occur."

Judge Atkins sat back in his chair for a moment and put his hands together. He rested his elbows on the arms of his chair. The tips of his index fingers rested against the tip of his nose as his thumbs supported his chin. After a few moments of quiet he sat forward, "The prosecution's request is denied. The jeweler will not be permitted to take the key apart. He may look at it closely but he will not open it."

Meredith continued, "Mr. Joel; please look again at the watch key. Can you identify it as a watch key you have worked upon?"

Joel pulled a jeweler's loupe from his coat pocket and placed it over his right eye. He held the watch key in his hands and leaned in the direction of the sunlight coming through the courtroom windows. "I cannot say for certain that I have verked on dis vatch key. I does look like der tube ver der ring connects has been verked on. But vunce again; I cannot say vithout taking der vatch key apart."

Meredith exhaled in frustration, "No more questions, your honor."

Beverly Crump rose to his feet and addressed the witness. "Mr. Joel… You say that you have been doing work for the accused for two or three years. Do you have any way of demonstrating this?"

"If I could open der vatch key…"

Crump interrupted, "The judge has ruled upon that, Mr. Joel. This cannot happen.

Do you have any other way of demonstrating that Mr. Cluverius was your customer at any time over the last three years?"

Joel sat silent. "If I had der ledger…"

"Yes, but you don't have that. Somehow you have lost it or misplaced it.", Crump shot with sarcasm.

"I did not lose it… I was taken from me.", Joel responded.

"Yes, yes…", Crump dismissed. "Any other way to demonstrate your relationship with Mr. Cluverius? Did he ever come in your shop with anyone else? Did anyone else see him in your shop?"

"I cannot say this.", answered Joel.

"Are you certain that Mr. Cluverius is your customer at all? Are you sure he has ever visited your shop?"

"Yes, he has been in my shop."

"Have you ever known Mr. Cluverius to wear a mustache?"

"I do not remember any mustache."

"Mr. Joel; when you saw Mr. Cluverius in your shop on January 5th or 6th, did he have a mustache?"

"No… I don't believe he did.", responded Joel with some confusion.

"Interesting. Others who claim to have seen him that day say he *did* have a mustache. Somebody is clearly mistaken, Mr. Joel. Once again; are you certain that Mr. Cluverius has ever been in your shop/"

"Yes, yes!", Joel's voice began to crack.

"No more questions, your honor."

Charles Meredith decided not to redirect the witness. He and his team were confident they had presented a very convincing and comprehensive case. He did not wish to leave any further opening for the defense to discredit a witness who could conclusively link Cluverius to the crime scene. The judge's denial of the prosecution's request to open the watch key had dealt a large blow to this prospect. Meredith stood and announced, "The prosecution rests, your honor." (51.5)

Judge Atkins replied, "Very well. The court will adjourn until 9:00 Monday, May 25th. At that time the defense will present testimony." He banged his gavel once.

Chapter 52   *Loose Ends*

Rachel McDonald sat upright at her dressing table and studied herself in the mirror. Age was playing its dirty tricks on her, slowly smothering her youthful features in a pale wrinkled patchwork blanket. The bags under her eyes were darker than ever. Her hair was tangled and dull. She buried her hands in her face as her thoughts once again turned to Thomas Cluverius. She tried mightily to remove him from her mind; but to no avail. "Why does he reject me? Why will he not even acknowledge my being?" she moaned to herself. She placed her left hand into her lap and slowly ran it across her lower abdomen. She looked again into the mirror. Rachel's eyes welled as her hand scanned the growing curve in her waist. "He is in there.... He is in there. And when he comes out, I shall always have him. He shall not be able to deny me." she insisted.

At that moment there was a knock at the door. Rachel quickly placed a scarf over her head and wiped her eyes. She leaned her head out of her bedroom door and called down the stairwell toward the front door, "Just a moment.... I am coming." She wasn't expecting a visitor. She put on her shoes and scurried down the stairs.

When Rachel reached the door, she called out once more before opening it. "Who is it?" A deep voice from the other side answered, "I have a message from Cluverius." Rachel's senses tingled. Instantly she felt invigorated. She unlocked the door and pulled it open with a hopeful smile.

"Yes! And who are you, sir?"

"May I come in, ma'am? It's a private message. The man turned his head back over one shoulder, then the other. It was nearly 8:00PM and was getting dark that late May evening.

"Mr. Cluverius must have received my last message, is that right?"

"Oh yes, he certainly did, ma'am.", replied the tall imposing messenger with deadpan assuredness.

"And, what is the message, sir?"

"Um, well, would it be too much trouble to ask you for a drink of water, Miss McDonald? It's a bit warm out and my message may take a while to, er, deliver."

Rachel was struck with the oddity of the man's cryptic behavior. "Well, yes, of course! Where are my manners? Excuse me for a moment."

She left the man standing in the living room and headed into the kitchen. She had a pitcher of water sitting on a side table. She reached into the cupboard for a glass. Rachel walked back through the doorway into the living room and extended the glass out to give to the man. He wasn't where she had left him. She began to call out when his arm came slicing down and knocked the water from her hand. She spun around quickly and before she could scream, he clouted her in the jaw with his fist encased in brass knuckles. Rachel collapsed to the floor nearly unconscious. The man kicked a small tea table aside. He easily picked up the limp woman and flung her toward the loveseat. He turned her face down over the arm and took a position behind her. He tore the scarf from Rachel's head and yanked her skirt down around her ankles. He feverishly unbuttoned his trousers and began to deliver the message.

"Don't you make a sound, bitch! Don't make a god-damned sound!". Rachel was not sure what was happening was real. She stayed quiet just as he commanded. The deviant monster grabbed her hair at the base of her skull and controlled her as if he was riding a pony bare back. After nearly two minutes it stopped. He wiped himself on her skirt and then closed his trousers. "That message was from me, Miss McDonald. Now I will deliver a message from Cluverius." She opened her mouth but could not muster the wherewithal to speak. "Pull up you skirt!" he demanded. "Pull it up, dammit!" Rachel reached down and somehow found the waistband. She pulled the skirt up over her hips as she lay on her side and began to sob.

The man reached into his coat pocket and pulled out a straight razor. He returned once again to the sofa. The brute grabbed Rachel's right arm and wrenched it behind her back. He dragged her up to her feet. He reached around from behind her with the razor in hand and quickly stroked deeply from ear to ear across her neck. Rachel clutched her throat with her left hand. The man held her upright as they both watched her life pour down the front of her blouse and spill onto the floor. The last earthly words she heard were, "I don't think you understood who you were dealing with. You should have kept your distance, Miss McDonald." (52.1)

Six hours later the man entered Nellie Goss' cigar shop on Fifteenth Street. He walked silently but with resolute purpose to the back room. At this hour things were very quiet, even in a bawdy house. He had been here many times before and knew where to find Nellie. He discreetly approached the door to Nellie's quarters. The fiend slowly turned the knob and opened the unlocked door. In complete silence he crept toward Nellie's bedroom. There was a small oil lamp with a dim flame flickering on the small table beside her bed.

Nellie Goss had been suffering with a high fever for over two weeks. She had passed in and out of delirium for the last few days. The man carefully dislodged one of the pillows supporting her head. She mumbled and groaned. He gritted his teeth and put the pillow over her face. After about thirty seconds she twitched and shifted. Her weakened hands slapped helplessly at his burly forearms. Another two minutes passed before Nellie fell perfectly still. The man continued to hold the pillow forcefully in place for another five minutes. When he slowly lifted the pillow from her face, her eyes and mouth were motionless and opened wide. Even in the dim light he could see Nellie's complexion had become ashen. The man carefully returned the pillow to its original position under Nellie's head. He kissed her softly on her cooling forehead. "That's one way to break a fever.", he quipped to himself. He then slipped inaudibly out the window of her bedroom into an adjacent alley. (52.2)

Chapter 53 *The Defiant Mrs. Tunstall*

Judge T.S. Atkins called the Hustings Court of Richmond to order at 10am on Monday, May 25, 1885. The courtroom was filled to capacity in anticipation of a vigorous defense of Thomas J. Cluverius.

Henry R. Pollard stood and called the defense's first witness. "The defense calls Mrs. Jane Tunstall."

An aged woman stiffly rose to her feet and walked slowly toward the stand. Cluverius turned his head to see her. He had not seen her since the arrest. Although it was just over two months ago, she looked as if she had aged ten years. She was slower; her hair was whiter; her skin, more yellow. Dark circles under her eyes were now a dominant feature.

Pollard smiled and greeted Mrs. Tunstall, "Please state your name, residence, and relation to the defendant for the gentlemen of the jury."

"I am Jane Tunstall. I live in Little Plymouth, King and Queen County. Thomas is my nephew and he lives in my house."

"How long has the defendant lived in your home?'

"He and his brother moved to my house in 1874. Shortly after that my husband died. The two boys have stayed with me since."

"And, are you any relation to the deceased?"

"Yes, she was my grandniece.", said Mrs. Tunstall.

"Did the defendant live with you at all times between 1874 and his arrest?"

"Well, no sir. He was away for two years at Richmond College. That would have been in '81 and '82. When classes were in session he lived in Richmond."

"And, what about his brother, William?"

"Willie has been in the house that entire time."

"How would you describe the defendant's relationship with the deceased?", Pollard asked.

"They were just like any other family members. They cared for one another."

"But, Mrs. Tunstall; was there any romantic interaction between the two?"

"Oh, heavens no! Anyone who says that is dead wrong! Tommie was engaged to a girl named Nolie Bray."

"Did Lillie Madison know of this engagement?"

"Yes, she must have."

H.R. Pollard then turned to the evidence table and picked up the watch key found at the Marshall Reservoir. As he handed it to Mrs. Tunstall he asked, "Have you ever seen this watch key, madam?"

"No."

"Did the defendant ever wear a watch key?"

"Yes, he did. When my husband died, I gave Tommie his watch and a watch key. It certainly wasn't that one. Tommie wore the one I gave him. I never saw him wear that one."

Pollard then produced another key. "Is this the key you gave the defendant?"

"Yes, now that is a familiar key. That is the one I gave him.", she answered.

Henry Pollard then turned and retrieved the watch key found at the reservoir once again. He presented it again to Mrs. Tunstall, "And you have *never* seen this watch key before?"

"No. I've *never* seen that watch key before."

Pollard hesitated for a moment while he let that sink in with the jury. He then changed his line of questioning, "Did Lillian ever correspond with you?"

"Yes. And I wrote her two or three times a month."

Pollard picked up a piece of paper from the defense table and handed it to Mrs. Tunstall. "Did Lillie Madison write this letter to you?"

"Yes.", Aunt Jane responded

"Is this Lillian Madison's handwriting?"

"Yes, I believe so."

Understanding that Mrs. Tunstall did not read very well, Pollard took the letter back from her and addressed the court. "If it pleases the court, I would like to read this letter from the deceased to Mrs. Tunstall, your honor."

"Proceed.", said the judge.

My Dear Aunt Jane:

It is the 21st and I have just gotten your letter. They have abused you and me for everything that is inhuman. O! what a terror my life is! O! how I am struggling – struggling with my poor weak self tonight to keep my resolve. I have wept until tears are no relief. And O! my sad suffering; but I have Jesus to look to. He suffered too, even death, at the hands of merciless tormentors, and of course, He knows my suffering. It is my prayer to-night that the sun of to-morrow may shine on me a corpse. O! if suicide were not a sin, how soon the lingering spark of my life would vanish; but I will wait God's own time. I know He is just, and will see that you and me, too, shall be righted. You spoke of my being altered, but I reckon, dear aunt, you only wrote that to be seen, for surely you must know I am not changed, but the same Lillie I was the 9th of August, when we parted at Clifton. Dear, dear aunt, I will never change. I do not know where to direct this letter, as I reckon you are in Richmond ere this. O, to think of my school almost kills me. I got a letter from dear Nolie tonight. Good night, dear aunt.

Ever your devoted,

Lillie

As I can't find out your No. in Richmond, I am going to send this to Plymouth. You will get it sooner. (53.1)

Pollard paused and then asked Mrs. Tunstall, "What were the circumstances surrounding this letter? Why was the deceased contemplating such things?"

"Well, Mr. Pollard. Lillie was very upset. She had been living with me over nine months. I was paying for her schooling. Her parents not only could not afford to send her to school; but they were actually against her going at all! You see, they feared that she would learn things which would make her feel suited for a higher station in life. They believed she was dissatisfied with her humble home. Lillie became very distraught and even melancholy. I told her that I could no longer pay for her schooling in defiance of her parents. I told her that she must be reconciled to her life and remain with her parents until she was twenty-one. It was after she left my house that she wrote this letter."

"How long ago did she write this letter? It is undated.", Pollard asked

"It was about two years ago."

"Why did her parent's hold such resentment toward you, as Lillie indicates?"

"I believe they viewed me as an interloper in their family business. I was only trying to help Lillie improve herself and I had the means to do so. She had great potential; Dr. Garlick even said as much. They took offense, I suppose. They prohibited us from corresponding; but we did anyway."

"Did you send letters through the postal service?", asked Pollard.

"No, sir. We used various other means. I could never have sent them by post because she would most likely have not received them. We feared her parents would intercept them and it would only cause more problems for her. I would sometimes write to her aunt and would include a letter for Lillie; and her aunt would carry it to church and give it to Lillie. Sometimes she would send them to the court and somebody there would give them to Tommie and he would bring them to me."

H.R. Pollard then turned to Judge T.S. Atkins, "The defense would like to submit this letter into evidence."

Judge Atkins looked at Charles Meredith. "No objection, your honor.", said Meredith.

Pollard turned back to the witness, "Mrs. Tunstall; how late did you correspond with Miss Madison before her death?"

"I received a letter from her in early March. Then I did receive a letter she wrote after she came to Richmond; that Friday morning…"

"Objection, your honor!", Meredith blurted. "The witness should not speak of that letter. She should let us see the letter first!"

"I do not have the letter.", Jane Tunstall replied.

"Then the prisoner's counsel has it, I suspect.", returned Meredith.

Beverly Crump stood and handed the letter to Charles Meredith.

"Gentlemen,", Meredith announced after a few moments of perusal, "We have no objection to the introduction of this letter."

Pollard continued with the witness, "Will you look at that letter and see if you identify it as a letter you got from Miss Madison?"

"I do not think that is my writing.", said Mrs. Tunstall with confusion in her voice.

"No, not your writing, Mrs. Tunstall; but hers?", Pollard clarified.

"She sometimes wrote in a hurry and I couldn't say this is her handwriting. I would think it is her writing. I do not know anyone else who may have written it." Mrs. Tunstall suddenly felt weary. She turned to Judge Atkins. "Sir, may I have a glass of water. It is quite warm in here."

"Of course, madam.", answered the Judge as he signaled to one of the bailiffs.

Henry R. Pollard took the letter back from Charles Meredith and read it aloud to the jury.

Richmond, March 14th, 1885

My Dear Aunt Jane,

  I will drop you a few hurried lines this morning, as I want to go with a friend of mine on quite an unexpected little trip. As the weather is too bad up in the mountains either for me or the children to attend regularly, we thought proper to suspend for awhile, and so a friend of mine wants to go to Old Point for awhile and will pay all my expenses if I will go to be company for her. She is a nice and good lady, and it will be a nice little trip for me. Don't you think so? I have not time to say more, as it will be time to start soon. We came down on the train this morning. Love to all, and tell Tommie I will write to him real soon; but they must not count letters with me. You all need not write until you hear from me again. I will write as soon as I can. As I am in such a hurry I must stop. Love for all and lots for your dear self.

I remain, as always, yours,
Lillie   (53.2)

  Charles Meredith interjected, "Your honor, since the defense has read the letter, should they not read the envelope? They are introducing both together."

  Pollard responded immediately, "We will do that."

  Beverly Crump stood behind the defense table and handed the envelope to Pollard:

  Mrs. Jane F. Tunstall, Little Plymouth, King and Queen County, Va.

  H.R. Pollard then disclosed, "The postmark is from Richmond but the date is indistinct."

  "Is it time-stamped?", Meredith asked.

  "The time, too is indistinct,", Pollard explained, "but it does say "A.M." Pollard then turned to the witness, "When did you receive this letter, Mrs. Tunstall?"

  "I got it the Monday morning before I heard of her death. She was dead then, but I did not know it. I would not hear of her death for two more days."

  "Do you have any other letters from the deceased in your possession, Mrs. Tunstall?", Pollard asked.

  "No, sir. I believe you have all that I had."

  "But, you say you corresponded with her on a regular basis?"

  "Yes, I did. But I don't keep old letters. I usually burn them."

The bailiff returned with a glass of water for Jane Tunstall. She nodded and thanked the officer.

"Mrs. Tunstall; will you be kind enough to state how Tommie Cluverius, since you have knowledge of him, has borne himself towards you and how he has borne himself generally in the community?"

"Objection! Is that a legitimate question?", Meredith interposed. "The question of his character can be proved by his general reputation in the community in which he lives."

"Sir, I will put it in a more general way, and probably more satisfactory to you; Mrs. Tunstall, what character has the prisoner borne?"

"I think he has borne an excellent character. I have never heard any complaint of him, at all. Everybody in the neighborhood is fond of him."

"No more questions, your honor.", said Pollard.

Colonel William R. Aylett stood and approached the witness for cross-examination. "Mrs. Tunstall; other than Lillie Madison, did you correspond with others in the Madison family?"

"I wrote to Lillie's mother before she got mad at me." She took sip of water.

"And, this was a result of the situation with your paying for Lillie's schooling?"

"Yes.", said Tunstall. "I know of no other reason for her anger." She took another sip.

Aylett continued, "Did it ever occur to you that your assumption of this responsibility, without the consent of her parents, could lead to some resentment?"

"Well, I suppose…"

"And could you not see the natural effect on Lillie – fitting to make her disdainful of her own home and upbringing?"

Mrs. Tunstall cleared her throat, "Lillie brought the same opinion of her home to my house that she carried away."

"How did you know this, Mrs. Tunstall?"

"By what she told me."

"Did it not occur to you that you should eradicate that unfilial idea? Did you never tell her that it was improper for her to entertain such ideas of her parents?"

"I reckon I did.", she answered. "I have advised her every way I could whenever she would say anything. She spoke of suicide and I always wrote her word not to think of such a thing; that she must try her best and they, too, would do better. I always told her I was afraid she was partly at fault."

Aylett drilled down, "Is it not a fact that after she had experienced the sweets of education and a more exalted station in society, her humble home and her old parents became distasteful to her?

"No, sir. I don't think so, at all! It was the treatment she received that caused her…"

Colonel Aylett interrupted, "How do you know except from what she told you?"

"I heard her mother speak of problems; of Lillie's disobedience. But Lillie always wrote me that she did her best and that her parents refused to understand her."

"Didn't you have as big a row with Tommie's family as you did with Lillie's?", Aylett asked.

"No, sir."

"Mrs. Tunstall, didn't you have a big quarrel with Mr. and Mrs. Cluverius?"

"They had a quarrel with me; but not I with them.", she dryly answered.

"So, we have two families; one in King William and one in King and Queen, which have had furious quarrels with you - and *they* have done *all* the quarrelling; and not you?", Aylett circled closer to the witness. "Did Mr. and Mrs. Cluverius board with you at one point?"

"Yes, they were having some financial difficulty and lived with me for a while. The boys came at that time, too."

"Did you then separate from them?"

"Yes, sir. I could not live with them peaceably."

"So, you did furiously quarrel with them?"

"No, sir;", she said definitively, "I never quarreled. They did. I did right and I don't think they did right; so, I told them it was best that we separate."

"In what way did they do wrong?"

"I don't know how to tell you that. In many ways."

"Did Tommie take your side with you?"

"No, Tommie did not take a side."

"Did Tommie stay with you after his parents left?"

"Yes, he said he and Willie would stay and take care of me."

"But Mrs. Tunstall; you are a lady of means. What did he provide?"

"He had his education…"

"Which you provided for him!", Aylett interjected.

"Yes. But I still needed help."

"And he needed money, Mrs. Tunstall. What was the immediate cause of your quarrel with the Madison family?"

"I told you, I never had any quarrel.", said an increasingly indignant Jane Tunstall." They had a quarrel with me; they just got mad and would write. Lucy got mad and wrote me two very insulting letters; and so did Mr. Madison. "

Aylett sighed, "So, let us understand this; without any quarrel, you had angry correspondence. They got mad and furnished all the anger and you just took it!"

"I wrote a little; but nothing in it like a quarrel.", she conceded.

"When you wrote a little were you not striking at them over Lillie's shoulders?"

"No, sir; I don't think I did.", she said laughing.

"Why are you amused by that?", Aylett asked.

"It just sounds funny, The very idea, Colonel Aylett… really? I never tried to make Lillie disobedient to her parents. I always encouraged her to stay at home and do her best until she was twenty-one. If she couldn't live at home peaceably afterward, she could leave when she was of age."

"It seems she took your advice and left as soon as she was twenty-one…"

"Yes!", Mrs. Tunstall lashed back, "And she would have left years before had it not been for me."

"When she lived at your house, was she kind and attentive to you?"

"Yes, she was."

"And, you were very attached to her?"

"Yes, it made me very distraught to hear her family was mistreating her.", she finished her glass of water.

"Did you feel resentment toward the Madisons?"

"I did not. I had nothing to do with it; but she and her parents did."

Colonel Aylett was growing frustrated with the testimony. "So, what was the source of the quarrel with the Madison family?"

"I had no quarrel.", Mrs. Tunstall insisted.

"But they had one with you. Is it not true that Mrs. Madison had been spreading information; a pamphlet around the area about your sister and her purported abuse of children?"

"There was a pamphlet that some Yankees had put together a few years after the War accusing my sister of burning a colored girl with some hot coals. Mrs. Madison did tell me of the pamphlet. I never saw it. She encouraged me to attend church to show it to me. I told her that I do not spend time at church dealing with such matters; so, I just never went back to her church. I joined another. I told her that the pamphlet was certainly false. That may be why she got mad. I really do not know. I never said a word about any of it until now."

"How did your quarrel with the Cluverius family arise?"

"I don't know."

Aylett sighed again, "Did you accuse the Cluverius family of stealing your property?"

"Never.", she answered.

"Did you not have your cousin, John Walker, at your house and point to property in the distance and say that the Cluverius family took it?"

"No. I deny it."

"Mrs. Tunstall; did you not tell other members of your family that money was taken from under your mattress while the Cluverius family was living with you? Was this not the reason you asked them to leave?"

"I cannot tell you the reason that we could not maintain a peaceable existence; but it is not for the reasons you suggest. We simply could not live together any longer. I asked Tommie's parents to leave and was very grateful when Tommie and Willie decided to stay with me."

"How can it be that both the Cluverius family and the Madison family have difficulty with you, and yet the son of the Cluverius family and the daughter of the Madison family sided with you against their parents?"

"They did not side with me against them.", Jane Tunstall insisted. "Tommie would take his father's part now sooner than he would mine; but he still promised to stay with me."

"Have you ended all interaction with the Cluverius family?"

"No, indeed. They don't live more than a mile and a half from my house. They are at my house now. They came to my house the night of the arrest and have been coming all the time since. We are, after all, a family, sir."

Colonel Aylett grimaced and shook his head slightly. "No more questions, your honor."

Judge Atkins banged his gavel, "This court will reconvene at 1 o'clock." (53.3)

Chapter 54   *The Difference Between Doctors and*
                              Lawyers

Judge T.S. Atkins called the Hustings Court to order for the afternoon session on May 25, 1885. The afternoon heat and glare blasted through the large glass windows in the Hustings Court. The inhabitants sat still in their seats like potted plants in a hot house. "The defense will continue, please."

H.R. Pollard stood and called his next witness. The defense calls Reverend John W. Ryland to the stand."

Reverend Ryland approached the stand with a bible clutched closely to his chest. He sat his bible down on the witness chair as he placed his left hand upon the court's bible and raised his right hand to God. He then collected his bible from the chair, clutched it once again to his chest, and sat down.

"Reverend, please state your name and place of residence for the court.", Pollard requested.

"I am Reverend John Ryland. I am the pastor of Olivet Church two miles from Little Plymouth."

"How long have you been preaching at this church, sir?"

"I have been there since 1870."

"How long have you known the defendant?"

"I have known him for nearly nine years. I baptized him in 1876 and he has been a member of our congregation since."

"Can you speak to the character of the defendant?"

"Yes. He is of the highest moral character. His reputation in the community is spotless, as far as I know."

Pollard continued, "Did Mr. Cluverius have any official role in the church?"

"Yes, about two years ago I asked him to help as an assistant to the director of our Sunday School. In light of his clean character and his education, he appeared to be a very fine selection to tutor our youth regarding the mysteries of faith."

"And, did he perform these duties to your satisfaction?"

"Absolutely, sir. The children at the Sunday School were inspired by him."

"Was Sunday School held on Sunday, March 14th, Reverend?"

"Yes, sir."

"Did Mr. Cluverius teach any lesson to the children that Sunday?"

"Yes, sir; he did."

"Did you see him and speak to him that day?"

"Yes, sir."

"Did you happen to shake hands with him?", Pollard continued.

"I believe I did. I always shake hands with the congregants after the service. He was in attendance and would have instructed his class immediately after. I believe I would have shaken his hand out in front of the church that morning after the service, as I always do."

"Much has been made of some purported scratches on his hands at that time. Did you see any scratches on his hands that morning?"

"No, sir. I saw no scratches."

"Thank you, Reverend. No more questions, your honor."

Charles Meredith rose to cross examine. "Reverend Ryland; you say you shook hands with the prisoner that morning and you say you did not see any scratches, correct?"

"That is correct, sir."

"Can you state with absolute certainty that you inspected the prisoner's hands closely enough that you can unequivocally state without hesitation that he did *not* have any scratches on his hands? Can you affirm that there were inconclusively no scratches on his hands, at all?"

"No, sir. I cannot."

"Thank you, Reverend. No questions, your honor." (54.1)

H.R. Pollard then called Thomas Milby. A young man stood and walked up the aisle. He was wearing a blue work shirt, dark blue pants, and brown suspenders. He wore light brown leather lace-up half-boots. His clothes were clean, but clearly working-class. His sleeves were rolled up to the elbow exposing large powerful hands and lean but bulging forearms. His fingernails were short and ringed with black dirt.

"My name is Thomas Milby. I work in the blacksmith shop at Little Plymouth. I live near there with my folks."

"How old are you, sir?"

"Almos' twenty-two.", he answered.

"How long have you worked at the blacksmith shop?"

"Well, it's my Pa's shop. I been working there since I was five years old."

"Do you know the defendant?", asked Pollard.

"Who?", Milby asked.

"The defendant, sir. Mr. Cluverius. Do you know him?"

"Oh… Yes, sir. I known Tommie for eight or nine years."

"When was the last time you saw Mr. Cluverius?"

"I seen him March 14th. He was in the shop with his pa. They come in for a few minutes."

"Did Mr. Cluverius have a mustache?"

"No, sir. Can't say he did. I wasn't looking to see if he had one. I know I did not notice any."

"Have you ever known Mr. Cluverius to have a mustache? In all the years you've known him?"

"No, I never seen him with a mustache."

"Do you see Mr. Cluverius often?", asked Pollard

"Except when he was away at Richmond College, I probably seen him at least once every week or two - pretty regular."

"And, he has never had a mustache?"

"No, sir."

"Mr. Milby; it has been reported that Mr. Cluverius had some scratches or marks on his hands at the time of his arrest. Did you see any marks on his hands that day; March 14th?"

Milby shook his head, "No, sir. I didn't see nothing wrong with his hands."

"Did the people of Little Plymouth think highly of Mr. Cluverius?"

"Yes. His reputation was pretty good. Nobody I known had trouble with him."

"No more questions, your honor." (54.2)

The judge looked at Charles Meredith, "No questions, your honor."

H.R. Pollard then re-called Emmett Rogers. The judge reminded Rogers that he was still under oath as he took the stand.

"Mr. Rogers, please refresh the memory of the court regarding your relation to the defendant."

"I am Emmett Rogers. I live in Little Plymouth and have known Thomas Cluverius for about nine years. We both came to Richmond on March 12th on the York River Railroad. We sat next to one another. When we arrived in the city we went up to Davis House and registered for our stay. We then went to the barber shop under the American Hotel. We both were in the city on business but made tentative plans to meet at Mozart Hall the next evening. I was called home Friday morning so I did not attend the show."

"Did Mr. Cluverius have a mustache when you went to the barber shop?"

"We both had two or three days of growth on our faces."

"Did you leave the barber shop before Mr. Cluverius?"

"Yes."

"Were you cleanshaven when you left?"

"Yes,", Rogers answered flatly.

"Was Mr. Cluverius cleanshaven when you left the barber shop?"

"That is my recollection… Yes."

Pollard moved on to another subject, "Did you see Mr. Cluverius wearing a watch key that day?"

"No, sir."

"Have you ever known Mr. Cluverius to wear a watch key?"

"Yes, I have seen him wear one in the past.", answered Rogers as he wiped his sleeve across his brow.

Pollard then showed Emmett Rogers the watch key introduced by Jane Tunstall. "Is this they key you have seen Mr. Cluverius wearing?"

"If this is not the key, it looks mightily like it.", exclaimed Rogers.

H.R. Pollard loosened his tie and opened his collar. He then picked up another key from the evidence table. "Have you seen the defendant wearing this key?"

"No, sir. I have never seen that watch key."

Pollard turned toward the jury, "Please note that this is the key found at the Reservoir. The witness has **never** seen the defendant wearing such a key. No more questions, your honor."

Charles Meredith stood and walked toward the witness stand. "Mr. Rogers... are you also friends with the prisoner's brother, William Cluverius?"

"Yes."

"Have you spoken with William Cluverius since the arrest of his brother?"

"Yes."

"Were you aware that William Cluverius visits the prisoner in jail nearly every day?"

"Well... I know Willie has visited him..."

"Has William Cluverius discussed any of the meetings he has had with the prisoner with you?"

"Well, I suppose...", Rogers tried to begin an explanation.

Meredith cut him off, "Has William Cluverius transmitted any messages from the prisoner to you?"

Rogers began to blush a little, "Only salutations... There have been no discussions concerning these events."

"Are you sure?"

"Yes.", he wiped the beads from his brow again.

"Mr. Rogers... Witness tampering and perjury are very serious offenses against the Commonwealth. Now, again; has the prisoner instructed or informed you in any way that may influence your testimony here today?"

"No, sir."

Meredith smiled with suspicion. "Very well, Mr. Rogers. No more questions."
(54.3)

Pollard stood and quickly announced, "No more questions, your honor. The defense now calls Dr. Wendell C. Barker."

After taking the oath, Pollard approached the witness, "Please state your name, occupation, and place of residence for the court."

Dr. Barker cleared his throat, "My name is Dr. Wendell Barker. I am a medical doctor. I live and practice in Stafford County."

"What is your relation to the defendant?"

"He and I attended Richmond College together."

"Were you friends?"

"Yes... I would say we were good friends."

"Have you maintained this friendship?"

"Well. We have written to each other a few times since we left college' but I have only seen him once. That was very briefly in Richmond about a year and one half ago."

"Very well, doctor. How would you describe Mr. Cluverius' behavior and general character?"

"Objection, your honor!", cried Colonel Aylett. "The defense is asking the witness to talk about a man with whom he has had very little contact in recent years. The question needs to be narrowed to the time they spent together at Richmond College."

Judge Atkins looked at H.R. Pollard to elicit a reaction.

"I will narrow the question. Dr. Barker... how would you describe Mr. Cluverius' behavior and general character *while attending Richmond College*?"

"He was above reproach. I considered Mr. Cluverius a moral and pious individual. He paid close attention to his studies and did very well."

"Did he consort with women of low character?"

"No, sir.". Dr. Barker removed a handkerchief from his coat pocket and dabbed each of his temples.

"Did you ever know him to visit Miss Lulu Woodward?"

"No, I've never heard of this woman. No, sir."

"Thus, the difference between doctors and lawyers, I suppose!", quipped Pollard. "Thank you, doctor. No more questions, your honor."

Charles Meredith stood and approached the witness. "Dr. Barker. Are you familiar with the Old Marshall Reservoir?"

"Yes."

"Was it common for students to go on to the reservoir grounds to swim?"

"Well, yes. That has happened.", answered a wary Barker.

"Did you ever swim there, Dr. Barker?"

"Well... Yes, on a few occasions."

"So, it was a well-known activity for college students. Is that right, doctor?", Meredith pressed.

"Yes."

"Do you know if the prisoner ever went to swim there, Mr. Barker?"

"Yes, I believe he did. We all did."

"And, how did you typically gain access to the property? I assume this was mostly happening at night, correct?"

"Yes. At night…"

"Yes, I'm sure…" Meredith cracked a smile. "I have seen Mr. Rose and would not want to come across him under those circumstances, Dr. Barker."

Barker nodded in confusion. Meredith asked again, "How did you typically gain access to the property? It is fenced all the way around and I'm sure the gates are locked at night."

"There was a loose plank in the fence. On the Clark Spring side. We would crawl through that opening."

"That is interesting, Dr. Barker. Do you think Mr. Cluverius knew of this loose plank? Did he ever enter the property that way?"

"Well, yes. I am sure he did. The whole student body knew about it. There was no secret.", Barker admitted.

"Dr. Barker; did you share a room with Mr. Cluverius during your time at Richmond College?"

"No, sir."

"Did he share a room with other students?"

"Yes. I believe he roomed one session with Mr. Hawley and another with Mr. Courtney."

"So, for much of this time at Richmond College, you can give no account of Mr. Cluverius' activities or whereabouts, correct?"

"Well…not hour by hour…"

"Is it possible that Mr. Cluverius could have spent a great deal of time consorting with low women, including Miss Lulu Woodward, and you would be none-the-wiser?"

"I think I would have known, sir. We were friends."

"Yes, one would think as much. But that assumes that he truly was your friend. After all, a man can unequivocally state *he* is *someone else's* friend. But can a man unequivocally state that *someone else* is *his* friend? That is a much more difficult to ascertain, isn't it, doctor? Thus, *another* difference between doctors and lawyers, I'm afraid... No more questions, your honor."

"No more questions for the defense, your honor.", added Pollard. (54.4) H.R. Pollard then returned to the defense table and motioned to A. Brown Evans.

Evans moved from behind the defense table with a piece of paper in hand. "At this time, if it pleases the court, the defense would like to read a statement from Miss Nolie Bray, the prisoner's fiancée. She does not wish to testify in open court but has agreed to allow us to enter her statement for the record. The defense has already presented this statement to the prosecution and they have agreed to allow it to enter the record."

Judge Atkins looked at the defense table, "Is this so, Mr. Meredith?"

"Yes, it is agreed.", said Meredith.

"Very well, counselor. You may read it for the court. After you have finished, in light of this excessive temperature, we will adjourn until 9 o'clock tomorrow morning."

A. Brown Evans read the statement aloud:

Mr. Thomas Cluverius and myself had been engaged up to the time of his arrest for two years from last summer, with one intermission of three or four months about eighteen months ago. Miss Fannie Lillian Madison knew of our engagement from conversations with me up to September, 1883; she knew of our engagement up to June, 1884, for I received one letter from her in June, 1884, in which she made mention of it. I do not know of her knowledge of the engagement since then – since June, 1884. I have received two letters from her, but in neither of them did she make mention of it.

Nolie Bray (54.5)

Judge Atkins banged his gavel, "Court is adjourned."

Chapter 55　　　　　　　　*Who's the Bigger Man?*

Two young brothers quietly approached a simple wood cabin in King William County. Full darkness had yet to close-in as the late summer sun had set just twenty minutes before. They left their fishing poles leaning to the left of the front door and cracked the door open with trepidation. A small fire still burned in the fireplace to the right. The older brother entered first, spotting the shadowy figure of his father seated at the table, head down atop his crossed arms. An empty whiskey bottle sat nearby on the edge of the table. The boy cut his eyes toward the back wall and saw the familiar sight of his mother asleep on her back, her right arm draped across her face while the left hung limp over the side of the bench, her fingertips gently resting, as if caressing the cabin floor.

They slowly crept through the doorway, hoping to make it to their bed in the small loft on the left side of the house. The air was thick with the smell of alcohol, but the boys barely took note. The younger boy began to ascend the ladder; his brother following close behind.

"Where the hell you boys been?!", broke the silence and sent a shiver into the older boy's body.

"We were fishin'…", the older boy responded.

"I tol' you boys to be home 'fore dark! I tell you boys that all the time! Damn it, I'm tired of gettin' no respect from people!", he boomed as he rose to his feet. "Well, if I can't get respect from other people, I'm sure gonna get some respect from the two o' you an' I'm gettin' it right now! Git o'er here!"

The boys scrambled quickly across the room. They were wholly familiar with their father's volatility, especially after the drink had taken hold; but something seemed more desperate in this evening's hair-triggered reaction. The father clumsily stepped back from the table and slid his chair out into the middle of the room. He then took the other empty chair at the table and pushed it opposite the other, back to back. He stumbled forward and inadvertently jostled the table. The whiskey bottle toppled and shattered on the floor. Their mother remained helplessly comatose. "Look what you make me do! Time for a beatin'. You've earned it…" He drew his belt out from around his waist and doubled it up in his hand. "Both of you; on your knees!"

The boys looked sadly at each other. They each understood the dangerous futility of making any appeal when their father was in such a state. The older one reached over and touched his younger brother's sleeve seeking some reassurance. They dropped to their knees each facing a chair. They reached across the seats and gripped the base of the chair backs as they had done many times before. "You know how this works. You each get three; anybody cries or makes a sound, he get one more… Let's see who's the bigger man…"

The boys picked their heads up and looked at one another through the vertical spindles in the chair backs. They were inmates in a common cell block, looking helplessly through the bars of their private cells, forced to witness the suffering of the other as they girded for their own. The father drew his belt back and cracked the older brother with a solid strike. The older boy winced and put his head down. "Keep your eyes straight ahead!", the demon commanded as he circled to the other side. He delivered an equal blow to the younger brother. The younger boy's eye slightly twitched but he maintained a cool focus on his brother opposite him. The father drew back his belt once again. The thunderous clap seemed to shake the cabin, but the older boy bit firmly into his bottom lip and called upon all of his strength to silently endure. The father grunted to himself with a hint of surprised disappointment. He circled once more around and dealt another stinger to the younger boy. This time, the younger boy's resolve appeared even stronger. He barely blinked with the impact. Somewhat frustrated with himself, the father then upped the ante. "Pull them pants down...", he growled. The older brother's legs quivered as he stood and unbuttoned his trousers. The younger one stood firmly and calmly unbuttoned his own. Both boys then reassumed their positions on their knees in front of the chairs. The drunken sadist wound his belt even further behind his head and delivered a blistering blast to the older brother's bare hindquarters. The boy could no longer block the agony and reflexively cried out. He then descended into tears as he understood there would be yet one more strike to come; perhaps more. "I thought so.", the father taunted. The savage then smiled as he rounded the chairs once more and laid into the younger boy's naked backside. Once again, the younger brother did not faulter. With each withering blow endured the younger boy felt his internal power grow ever stronger. The father returned to the other side to mete out his deviant justice to the older brother. The older boy struggled back into position, trying desperately to swallow his tears and block the pain.

The father drew the belt back once more when the younger boy shouted, "Stop! I will take Willie's punishment!" The father paused and looked bewilderingly at Tommie.

"Is that really what you want?", Whitey Cluverius asked.

"Yes...", Tommie coldly confirmed.

"Alright then. It shall be.". He then delivered the hardest blow yet and still Tommie showed no sign of weakening. Willie watched in shameful amazement. To him, his brother was now akin to Christ, freely accepting a brutal punishment he did not deserve; but one that would spare another. Tommie thought self-satisfyingly to himself. He truly cared little about Willie's pain. But Tommie had proven to himself that he could easily absorb whatever punishment this flawed authority could muster; and it could never erode his belief in his own self-righteousness nor his power of self-control.

"I am impressed, Tommie. I tell you, Willie; Tommie is *my* son. You? I'm not so sure. Tommie even looks like me. Hell, I don' know who the hell you look like... You know that mother of yours over there...", he pointed toward the bench, "she was nothin' more'n a whore in a West Point saloon back then. She get with child and for some reason, I married 'er. She says I was the father. I coulda been. But probably ten others it coulda been, too. An' then Willie, you come out. Tommie, though; he's all mine. An' he showed it again here tonight. Willie, your father musta been a weak man. That's all I can say. Now, both of you, git to bed. No dinner here, anyhow."

Early the next morning Tommie and Willie awoke to the sound of their parents speaking. Willie's eyes were crusted with the tears which had flowed late into the night until he finally fell asleep.

"Git the boys up", Whitey Cluverius told Mary. "I wanna be out 'fore the Sheriffs git here."

"Yes, I know.", Mary Cluverius softly answered as her hangover competed with her depression to drive her toward complete debilitation.

"The wagon is in the front. I'll hitch the horse. Just bring clothes and bring me the money; *all* of it…", he warned. "Leave the rest to the Sheriff. You don't need anything else."

"What about my mother's china? It's only twelve pieces.", Mary begged.

"Alright, bring it." Whitey answered to Mary's relief. "I can sell it somewhere.", he continued to her sad disappointment. "When we get to the Tunstall's I will figure out the next stage. They've got everything we need, for now. If not, I will figure something else." (55.1)

T.J. Cluverius laid quietly in the cot in his cell with his hands crossed atop his chest as he recalled this event of his upbringing. Willie would be called to the stand later that morning and Tommie questioned if Willie could withstand the belting he was about to receive. "I am in no position to endure *this* punishment on his behalf. I just hope he is able to endure some part of it on mine.", Cluverius thought to himself. "If not, I will figure something else."

The Hustings Court of Richmond was called to order at 9am on May 26, 1885. Henry A. Pollard stepped forward and motioned the court for a change of venue to a better ventilated courtroom. Summer was bearing down on the City of Richmond. Afternoon sessions in court were increasingly unbearable. The prosecution did not object to the motion but felt that such a request should come directly from the prisoner. Judge T.S. Atkins stated that he wanted to review the laws that govern such matters and would render a decision the following day. "For now, we will continue to slog through, gentlemen. Please call your witness, Mr. Pollard."

"The defense calls Mr. William B. Cluverius to the stand.". Willie Cluverius stood and adjusted his neck tie. He was frightfully nervous but drew inspiration from his brother and walked confidently toward the stand. T.J. Cluverius turned and nodded deferentially toward his brother. He shifted his chair slightly so that, for the very first time during the entire trial, he was facing the witness.

After the Willie Cluverius was sworn in, H.R. Pollard opened the questioning. "Where do you reside, sir?"

"Little Plymouth, King and Queen County", Willie answered.

"What is your relation to the defendant?"

"He is my brother."

"Where exactly do you reside in Little Plymouth?"

"At my Aunt Jane's house; along with my brother."

"How long have you lived there?"

"I have lived there nearly eleven years."

"Has your brother resided there that entire time?"

"Yes, all but the two years he was at Richmond College.", Willie said.

"Which of you is older?"

"I am older. I am twenty-four and he is twenty-three."

"Do you and your brother share a bedroom at your aunt's home?"

"Yes, we do."

"Did you see him the morning of March 12th?"

"Yes, I was in bed. He arose early and got dressed in our room. He was to make the 8 o'clock train from West Point to Richmond."

"Do you know why your brother was travelling to Richmond that morning?". Pollard asked.

"I knew that he had business in Richmond."

"Objection!", Meredith interrupted, "Did he know this for a fact or is this what he was told?"

Pollard quickly parried, "You may cross-examine him in that regard. I haven't gotten to that point yet. If you will allow me, I will let the jury know how he knew it."

Judge Atkins turned to instruct the witness, "You must state it only from your own knowledge; not what you were told."

Pollard interjected, "We would like to be heard upon that point. We contend we have a right to put in his declarations and his motives as to coming to Richmond. That question has been settled in the case of the deceased, as to indicating what was her purpose in coming from Bath County to this place."

"Proceed", said the judge.

Pollard turned back to Willie Cluverius, "You say that you knew of your own knowledge of certain business…"

Meredith interrupted again, "No, he did not!"

Willie Cluverius reacted, "I do say so!"

Judge Atkins struck his gavel sharply, "Gentlemen!"

H.R. Pollard carefully constructed his question, "Mr. Cluverius; you stated that you knew, based upon your own knowledge, that your brother was called to Richmond on certain business. Please state it in your own language."

Willie took a deep breath, "I knew Tommie had a suit for some land sold in the bankruptcy court in Richmond for Mr. Bray, and that he had been to Richmond two or three times to see about it. There was to be a Trustee's Sale in connection. I had made copies of the sale advertisement for Tommie. Tommie was to take those and hang them in various courthouses."

"And you understood that this property was before the bankruptcy court?"

"Yes."

"And you heard your brother say he was coming over to Richmond to see about that land in the bankruptcy court?"

"Yes, I heard him say that on two or three occasions."

"Willie, did your brother wear a watch?"

"Yes."

"When did he acquire this watch?"

"My Aunt Jane gave it to him shortly after the death of her husband, Uncle Sam Tunstall."

"How many years ago was that?"

"Uncle Sam died a few months after we went to live with them; so, 1874 or 1875.", Willie explained.

"Did he wear a watch guard?"

"Yes, a leather one."

"And did Tommie wear a watch key on the watch guard?"

"Yes."

"What type of watch key did he wear?"

"Well, when he went to Richmond College Aunt Jane gave him a steel one."

Pollard reached for the watch key introduced during Jane Tunstall's testimony. He handed it to Willie, "Is this the watch key your aunt gave your brother?"

"Yes, that is the watch key Tommie always wore.", said Willie with confidence.

Pollard then picked up the watch key found at Marshall Reservoir. He showed it to Willie Cluverius. "Did you ever see Tommie wear this watch key?"

"I've never seen that watch key in my life, sir."

"Did your brother have one similar to this one?", Pollard asked.

"I have only seen the steel one you have here today. He has never had one anything like the one found at the reservoir."

"Willie, has your brother ever worn a mustache?"

"I have known my brother his entire life and I have never seen him wear a mustache; not once.", Willie put his fist down on the rail in front of the witness chair.

"Thank you, no more questions."

The defense chose to limit their questioning of Willie to three simple areas to best exculpate the defendant: his reason for travelling to Richmond; his physical appearance; and the one piece of physical evidence which could link him to the crime. Otherwise the defense would allow the prosecution stake out positions during the cross-examination and, if required, the defense would blunt them on redirect. The strategy was to keep the defense simple and not aid the prosecution by leading the witness into any areas the prosecution could easily exploit.

Colonel William R. Aylett stood and looked briefly down at some notes on the prosecution's table. He then approached the witness. "Mr. Cluverius; did you see what your brother, the prisoner, was wearing the morning of March 12th when he left for Richmond?"

"As I recall, he was wearing a dove-colored overcoat.", Willie replied.

"Dove-colored? Is that gray?"

"I would say it is a very light gray, sir."

Col. Aylett went over to the evidence table and picked up the reversible overcoat submitted days before into evidence. "Is this the overcoat your brother wore on March 12th?"

"No, sir. That coat is mine.", declared Willie Cluverius.

Aylett was surprised by the answer. "But, Mr. Cluverius, you are aware this is the overcoat your brother wore at the time of his arrest? And it is the same coat that several other witnesses have testified as having seen your brother wearing it about Richmond on March 12th and 13th."

"Yes, sir. I am aware of that. But it's not the overcoat he was wearing when he left Richmond on March 12th.", Willie repeated.

Colonel Aylett paused and placed his forefinger to his lips. "Mr. Cluverius; where were you when you last saw the prisoner on the 12th?"

"As I said, sir; I was still in bed. Tommie got dressed in our room that morning and left."

"How early was it when he left? Was there enough light for you to see him clearly?"

"It was before sunrise. But he lit a lamp while he got dressed. He was wearing the dove-colored overcoat.", Willie answered.

"But, Mr. Cluverius. The prosecution has demonstrated that the overcoat here in evidence is reversible. And, one side is clearly a lighter gray than the other. Is it possible that he was wearing this reversible coat and that the lighter side was facing out?"

"No, I don't believe so."

Aylett was growing both more frustrated and more curious. "Sir, is it possible that the prisoner left your room that morning, went downstairs, and changed into the overcoat we see here today?"

"That is not possible, sir.", said Willie with certainty.

"Why not?", asked Aylett

"I wore the reversible overcoat that Friday, the 13th, to a funeral." The courtroom rumbled as speculation grew. Tommie smiled ever-so-slightly at his brother's performance.

Judge Atkins immediately inserted himself, "Quiet in the courtroom, please."

"Did you meet with very many acquaintances at this funeral?

"Yes, very many.", Willie responded.

Aylett regrouped for a moment before continuing, "Your brother wore a Derby hat when he was arrested, is that correct?"

"Yes."

"Was that hat his, or someone else's?"

"That hat belongs to me."

"Why did he not take his own hat?"

"Well, when the officers were taking him, he mentioned his hat had a hole in it. He took mine, instead."

"Did he ask your permission to take your hat?", asked Aylett.

"Well, no...", Willie hesitated for a moment, "he did not."

"Is that unusual? Should he not have asked?"

"No, sir. Not at all. Tommie and I share clothes on a regular basis. We always have. We are brothers."

"So, you would be just as comfortable wearing his clothes as he would be wearing yours?"

"Yes.", Willie flatly answered.

"Is it possible that you wear each other's things with such frequency that you may not even notice when you do so?"

"I do not think..."

Aylett cut off the answer, "Is it possible that Tommie wore your reversible overcoat to Richmond and you wore his dove-colored overcoat to the funeral and, because you both exchange clothing with such regularity, you no longer even notice such details?"

"No... No... I don't believe that to be the case.", Willie's voice strained for the first time that morning.

"Mr. Cluverius... were *you* in Richmond March 12th and 13th? Because we have ample testimony that your reversible overcoat was.", Aylett snarked.

"Objection!", Beverly Crump erupted. "This is not a legitimate question, your honor! This is meant to ridicule the witness!"

"Your honor,", Aylett rebutted, "the witness has opened himself up to such inquiry. He has claimed here in open court that evidence duly admitted into this proceeding is flawed. He needs to answer the question."

"Objection over-ruled; the witness will answer the question", said Judge Atkins.

"I was not in Richmond March 12th or 13th. And neither was my overcoat.", Willie insisted.

"Very well… If, in fact, you were wearing the reversible coat we have here in evidence to that funeral on March 13th, were you wearing it with the light gray side showing, or the darker?"

Willie calculated the most logical answer. "I usually wear it with the light gray side showing."

"Which way did you wear it that day, Mr. Cluverius?", Aylett insisted.

"The light gray side was showing.", Willie stated.

"Mr. Cluverius… you have testified that the prisoner wore a leather watch-guard chain. Is that correct?"

"Yes."

"Is that the only watch-guard chain you have ever seen him wear?"

"Yes."

"Captain Epps and the other arresting officers have testified that the prisoner was wearing a gold watch-guard chain the day he was arrested at your Aunt's house. Were you present during his arrest?"

"Yes, I was there.", Willie acknowledged.

"Did you not see him wearing the gold watch-guard chain that day?"

"No, I did not."

"Did you see him wearing the leather one of which you have spoken?"

"No… I guess I did not notice his watch-guard chain. I have only known him to wear a leather watch guard."

Colonel Aylett scratched the top of his head in wonderment, "Is it possible, as close as the two of you are, that the prisoner could have owned a watch-guard chain which you never saw?"

"I do not believe that is likely.", Willie wobbled.

"Well, not only do we have testimony that the prisoner was wearing a gold watch-guard the night of his arrest; but we have recently obtained a receipt from Mr. Hermann Joel, the jeweler, demonstrating that he sold a gold watch-guard chain to the prisoner this past January for $3.50. This purchase was made in Mr. Joel's Richmond shop January 6th. It is clear that the prisoner owned a gold-watch chain."

"I never saw him wear anything but a leather watch-guard.", Willie asserted.

"Captain Epps has also stated that he and the other arresting officers saw another small chain dangling from the prisoner's watch-guard chain while they were interviewing the prisoner a Mrs. Tunstall's home. Yet, by the time he reached Richmond in their custody, that piece of chain was missing. The prisoner contended that he removed that piece of chain before leaving Mrs. Tunstall's and that you would bring it to Sheriff Oliver within two days. You did bring a piece of chain to Sheriff Oliver. However, we have heard testimony from Captain Epps that he believes the chain you brought to Sheriff Oliver was not the chain the prisoner was wearing the evening of the arrest. How do you account for this? How did you come into possession of the piece of chain you brought to Sherriff Oliver?"

"Tommie gave me the piece of chain before he left with Captain Epps and the others.", said Willie.

"When?", asked Aylett.

"Right before they left.", said Willie trying to keep his responses short and direct.

"Where did he give you the chain?"

"At Aunt Jane's."

"No, where in the house were you?"

"We were in the parlor."

"Please explain how this exchange occurred.", said Aylett.

"Tommie came down from upstairs with his satchel. He went into the parlor to get a few other items. There he put threw the bit of chain on a side table and asked me to take care of it for him."

"He *threw it* on the table?", asked Aylett with some skepticism.

"Well, he did not *throw* it. He was close to the side table and tossed it on to the table top. He was as close to the table." Willie flicked his right hand outward as if dealing a card.

"And then he told you to 'take care of it'?"

"Yes. He asked me to take care of it until he came back."

"Did he say this distinctly, so that anybody could hear?"

"Yes. He spoke normal; I mean, he did not shout it, or anything. He just said it plainly.", Willie explained.

"Was anyone else in the parlor besides you and him?"

"Yes, Officer Robbins was there. And perhaps Captain Epps."

"And, it is your contention that they could easily have heard this remark?"

"Yes."

"When did you retrieve it from this table?", Aylett squinted and turned his better ear toward the witness to hear the response.

"I picked it up later that night."

"Was it still on that table?"

"Yes, it was right where he left it."

"If your brother removed it from his watch-guard chain in your presence, how did you not see the gold watch-guard chain he was clearly wearing that evening?"

"I did not see him remove it. I only saw him place it on the table. I did not look at his watch-guard.", Willie remained cool.

"Why did you collect it that evening? What made you think he would even need it?", Aylett chipped away.

Willie took a breath. "As soon as I thought about the key, I thought about all, and I remembered all."

"Let us understand, Mr. Cluverius. When your brother had asked if you would take care of the watch-key chain, you determined to do so, but afterwards, when you heard about the watch-key, you decided to bring it to the sheriff?"

"I heard about the key before…"

"Then why did you not tell your brother to take it with him?"

"I did not think of these things until later that night. I brought the chain to Sheriff Oliver a day or two later."

Aylett was not satisfied but saw little point in belaboring it further. "Mr. Cluverius; were you aware of any romantic relations between the prisoner and the deceased?"

"No, sir. Absolutely not! Tommie and Lillie were friendly like most cousins. But there was nothing more than that."

"Were you aware that they had met on more than one occasion in Richmond over recent months?"

"I know nothing of these things, sir.", Willie said forcefully.

"Did you know Lillie was with child?"

"No, sir. I had not seen Lillie in over a year."

"And your brother never mentioned as much?"

"No, sir."

"Did you correspond with Lillie?"

"No, sir. I don't believe we have ever corresponded."

"Did you know the prisoner corresponded with Lillie?", Aylett continued to fire rapidly.

"No, sir. Tommie never made mention of any correspondence."

"Did you ever know your brother to visit bawdy houses?"

"No, sir. Tommie was above such things."

"Not even during his time at Richmond College?"

"I have no knowledge of these things.", Willie firmly stated.

"No more questions, your honor."

H.R. Pollard saw no need to engage in re-direct. Willie had done a workman-like job on his brother's behalf. There was no reason to expose him to additional questions from the prosecution. "The defense has no further questions, your honor." (55.2)

As Willie Cluverius left the stand, he locked eyes with the defendant. The tears in Tommie's eyes registered the approval Willie had always sought from his brother. Willie had stood courageously and faced down his brother's inquisitors. He hoped his convincing effort would be enough.

Chapter 56 *Welcome to Fendallsburg*

Ellen Lee slipped into her father's study at *Evergreen* early Friday morning. Amongst the pile of newspapers on his desk she located the latest available edition of the *Richmond Dispatch*. Richmond newspapers were always a day late arriving at her home in Northern Virginia. She knew it contained the most current and comprehensive information within her reach regarding the trial of the century.

Fitz Lee was out on his morning constitutional ride. Ellen knew she had at least thirty minutes to read for herself and formulate her own opinion without the annoyance of her hopelessly logical father's ennobled, moral piety. She settled into his large comfortable chair and began to read.

Richmond Dispatch
May 28, 1885

Trying to Save His Neck – Course of Cluverius Defense

Richmond, Va, May 27, 1885

The defense has been very weak up to this point. The line pursued has been to prove the good character of Cluverius so far as the witnesses know, but in each case came the trip hammer blow of Mr. Meredith and the prosecution. None could answer for Mr. Cluverius' conduct when out of their sight. Although the defense has done much to prove that the accused never wore a mustache, the jury will have to exercise their judgment as it is plain as can be that if the prisoner goes unshaven for two days that his upper lip, with its peculiar curl, will deceive any casual observer and leave the impression that there is a mustache. The witnesses for the defense all testify that they have never seen the prisoner wear a key exactly like the one found on the reservoir grounds. And none of them remember to have seen any scratches on his hands after his return from Richmond on the 13th of March. This is about the sum and substance of the evidence of the defense, and legal minds can see at once how shallow it all is.

The prisoner looked badly today. The great crowd and the bad air of the courtroom and the close confinement of the prisoner cell has told on him, and his appearance indicates his suffering. He no longer receives bouquets, not even from his own people; and he is now shunned by nearly all who see him. He has certainly been an unfortunate man. Judge Atkins ruled upon the defense's request to change the trial venue to a better ventilated location. The judge ruled that, at this advance stage of the proceedings, he would not allow for any change. It would prove a delay and a disruption which could compromise the integrity of the proceeding. He asked the defense how many more days they intended to continue the defense. The defense indicated that they had no specific timeline but that their case was more than halfway complete. In order to improve conditions in the courtroom, Judge Atkins issued an order excluding all visitors from the courtroom. None but officers of the court, lawyers, members of the press, and witnesses were admitted inside the courtroom. This had to be done on account of the uncomfortableness of the building. This exclusion of the curious made the courtroom much more pleasant. (56.1)

Mr. Thomas Bagby, of West Point, was one witness called who was able to introduce some testimony regarding the movements of the prisoner on that fateful day. He has known the prisoner for several years. He testified that he was in Richmond on March 13th and saw Cluverius at Mozart Hall at 2:30 o'clock. The witness said the Dime Museum company was performing "Chimes of Normandy". He saw the prisoner standing a few rows behind him and then saw the prisoner seat himself at the start of the performance. He looked toward the prisoner and nodded but was not sure if the prisoner saw him. Later, during the performance, he looked back and did not see the prisoner. He could not say whether the prisoner had changed seats or had left entirely. He has not seen the prisoner since that day. He said he did not believe the prisoner had a mustache. The witness said the prisoner was wearing a light grey overcoat. He did not see if the prisoner wore a hat, since they were indoors. Mr. Bagby, like many other defense witnesses, had known prisoner to wear a black leather watch guard. He never saw prisoner wearing a gold watch guard and never noticed any watch-key hanging from the guard.

Harry Dudley, of 528 Fifth Street, Richmond, also provided the court with additional information regarding Cluverius' time in Richmond. He told the defense that the prisoner, who was a relative of his wife, met him at his house on Thursday night, the 12th of March. He took tea there and left at 10 o'clock. He did not see the prisoner at any other time since. Dudley stated that the prisoner also visited the 5th or 6th of January. He came for tea one of those evenings, as well. Likewise, the prisoner left his home about 10 o'clock that night. The witness said the prisoner was in Richmond for the evangelist D.L. Moody meetings.

Mark Davis, owner of the Davis Hotel on Franklin Street, testified that Mr. Cluverius stayed at his hotel several times over the last two years. Most recently, he stayed there the 5th and 6th of January, 1885 and the 12th and 13th of March, 1885. He said that on both occasions Mr. Cluverius first arrived at the hotel at four or five o'clock in the evening. He left the hotel and returned at eleven or twelve o'clock each night. He would then leave the hotel early the next morning and would, once again, not return until after eleven o'clock. Davis said that he recalled Mr. Cluverius coming in about that time the night of March 13th. He remembered that they ate apples in the hotel lobby and that Mr. Cluverius' deportment was quiet and pleasant. He asked to be called at 5 o'clock in order to catch an early train back home. Davis was asked if he saw any mud on the prisoner's shoes. He testified that he did not. Cluverius then asked for a bottle of whiskey to be sent to his room.

Davis said he would have one sent up. Mr. Cluverius then paid his bill and went to bed. On cross-examination, Mr. Davis testified that when Mr. Cluverius entered the hotel that evening, he was carrying a small brown satchel.

Cary Madison was called to the stand. The counsel for the defense asked if he would give up certain letters written by Lillian to him and he refused. The prosecution then asked and he consented to do so in the afternoon session. Beverly Crump for the defense argued that the object in having these letters was to show that in the summer of 1884 Cary Madison, a distant cousin of Miss Madison, was the sole object of Lillian Madison's solicitous love. In the afternoon Mr. Madison was recalled. He was hesitant to go through with the disclosure of the letters, stating that the information contained within were very much of a personal nature. He wished not to have his private thoughts and feelings divulged in open court. After some time meeting in Judge Atkins' chambers, an agreement was reached and a statement was produced for the court. Mr. A. Brown Evans for the defense read the statement:

"It is agreed that it shall be admitted that Cary Madison was a suitor of Miss F. Lillian Madison from the spring of 1884 until the time of her death, but it is also admitted that the parties never met later than the summer of 1883. It is further admitted that on September 12, 1884, she wrote him a letter expressing her love for him as being stronger than for any one else; and asking him to meet her in Richmond in October, 1884; and that she did not care to go around with any other gentlemen, as she did not think it right, and signed the letter "Your true and loving Lillie"; and added in the postscript a verse of love poetry. That up to the time, her letters had only been of a cousinly nature. That Cary Madison asserts there was no actual engagement between them; that in no letter since Sept. 12th did she express her love for him, but did in one chide him for not continuing to love her. The above statements are gleaned from correspondence between them of nine or ten letters apiece, Cary Madison being unable to write had his written for him."

The court adjourned for the day. It certainly appears this trial will end in the next few days. (56.2)

Ellen continued to peruse the news of the day for the next several minutes until her father burst into the study and disturbed her sanctuary.

"Good morning, dear. I see you are familiarizing yourself with my newspapers again!", he smiled half-mockingly.

"Yes, Papa. I am still troubled by this trial in Richmond. Thomas is not being treated fairly!", she said

"***Thomas***, it is now.", Fitz Lee noted.

"It seems plain to me that much of the evidence against him is in question. Some who are in Richmond are trying to say he had a mustache; others who have known him for years say he did not have a mustache and never has. And then, there is the matter of this watch-key. Everyone who has known him for some time says that the watch-key found at the reservoir is not the one he wears. And, the girl had other suitors. Why haven't they been brought to trial?"

"Now dear, you have to let all of the evidence be presented. Then, you have to carefully consider it. And then, and only then, can you make the decision…"

"But Papa, the prosecutors are not doing that! They are trying to make the crime fit him; they are not being fair! You just believe them because they work for the beloved Commonwealth, don't you?"

"That is not the case, Ellen… I will withhold my opinion, should I ever even develop one, until the evidence is in." He looked at her and pointed, "You should do the same. And, hopefully, the jury will agree and justice shall have been served."

Ellen rolled her eyes and shook her head as she stormed from the study and up the hall toward the kitchen.

There she found her mother putting some clean china in the cabinet. "What is the matter, dear?", asked Mrs. Lee.

"Oh, nothing, mother.", answered Ellen unconvincingly. After a brief pause, she grumbled, "Well, Papa just knows *every* thing! Oh, but that's the Lee Family way, isn't it? They are all so sensible, so logical, so tedious… It's really sickening! These men never feel *anything*. They just claim to do right and move on! They act as if they are perfection! And, everyone tells them the same!", she exclaimed.

"Now, Ellen. This is quite enough. You mustn't be disrespectful.", Mrs. Lee warned. "There are many delightfully independent personalities in our family; your father among them. I believe you and he are very much the same."

"Oh, mother… That cannot be true!"

Fitzhugh Lee interjected on cue, "My dear Ellen. I know you prefer to think of me as a boring old curmudgeon, but I assure you that, particularly in my youth, I did not always behave as I ought to have. As a matter of fact, at times, to the great displeasure of the Lee Family, I was downright impetuous and mule-headed in nature."

Fitz Lee and his three cousins grew weary of the family gathering at the Fendall home on the corner Oronoco Street and Washington Street in Alexandria. The four boys informed their parents that they were going to explore the town on a Saturday afternoon. Two of his cousins were brothers. Willie Fendall was a year older than Fitz and Claude Fendall was a year younger. Rooney Lee, a son of Uncle Robert, was the youngest of the four; two years younger than Fitz.

The four boys stood out in front of the unusual telescopic-style clapboard home with their hands in their trouser pockets, deciding upon a course of action.

"Let's go down to the river!", Claude suggested as he kicked a stone into the street.

"Naw... we did that yesterday!", returned Willie.

"How about the church yard?", asked Rooney.

"That's no good...", said Willie. "Only time that's fun is at night."

They stood silent for a moment. "What do you say, Fitz?", Willie asked.

Fitz stroked his chin. Then he spread his legs assuming a wider stance and rubbed his round little tummy with both hands. "Cannndyy!", he said in a deepened monster-like tone.

The boys cheered in unison. "Yes!"

The four skipped, jumped, ran, shoved, and punched their way for four blocks south on Washington Street before they turned east on King Street. Three doors from the corner on the north side of the block was Mrs. Appich's Candy Shop. The boys scrambled to the storefront window and pressed their noses against it to see what was inside. Their eyes grew large and their mouths watered as they saw the treats on display: chocolate bon-bons, rock candy, lemon cakes, cinnamon twists, jujube paste! They stormed into the store and spread to the corners as if on a tactical maneuver. The colors and the smells of Mrs. Appich's store presented a confectionary carnival. The atmosphere alone was worthy of a visit; but the delightful sweets were of immeasurable value to boys of this age.

"Hello there, boys!", called the jovial Mrs. Appich. What can I do for the Lee Clan, today?

After a few moments, Fitz piped up, "I'd like two licorice whips and two pieces of toffee, my dear Mrs. Appich". Fitz batted his eyes.

"I'll have a lemon cake and some jujube paste!", cried Willie. "Please!", remembering his manners.

"Very well, and you two boys?"

"I would like two caramels and a lemon cake, too.", said Claude.

Rooney rounded out the order, "Two mint chocolates, a caramel, and a licorice whip! Thank you, Ma'am!"

Mrs. Appich filled the orders and then turned to her note pad, "Let's see... that will be twenty-four cents, boys."

The four boys looked at one another in horror. "Anybody have any money?", Willie winced as the other three shook their heads.

"We're sorry, Mrs. Appich. We forgot to bring money...", said Fitz sheepishly.

"We can run home and get some."

"No… no… you can pay next time you come in."

"I think my mother has an account here, doesn't she, Mrs. Appich?", asked Willie.

"You're Elizabeth Fendall's boy, right?"

"Yes, Ma'am, Mrs. Appich. Can you charge it to her account?"

"Fair enough… thank you, boys!"

The boys filed out the door and onto the sidewalk. King Street was bustling with traffic as it was all days other than Sundays. The foursome was laughing and enjoying the sweets when Letitia Alexander and Lizzie Herbert came around the corner. Willie's joyful demeanor changed instantly as he saw the girls approach. Letitia was reaching for the doorknob to enter Mrs. Appich's when Willie stuck out his tongue and greeted her with some raspberries. Letitia stopped and sternly looked at Willie, "Don't be so childish, William. If you wanted to say hello, just do so."

"You think you're so special, Letitia! Just because the town is named for your family!", Willie lashed.

"And so, it is.", Letitia coolly deflected.

"Well… you know… m-my family has Leesburg!", he flailed in desperation.

Letitia chortled lightly and said, "I don't even know where that is! Besides, your name is Fendall. Those other two are the Lees… Where, may I ask, is Fendallsburg?" Letitia and Lizzie laughed to one another and continued into the candy shop.

Willie was red with a mixture of rage and embarrassment. He would have clouted her if she weren't so pretty. "Don't listen to her.", Fitz consoled him. Then Fitz snapped his fingers, "I've got an idea!" Fitz reached into the pocket of his waist coat and produced two three-inch glass vials. He held each up between a thumb and forefinger.

"What are those?", asked Willie.

"Stench clouds…", Fitz grinned. "Eddie Leadbeater at the apothecary showed me how to make them. It's just match-heads and ammonia. You put those together in the vial and cork it shut. Then wait a few days. If we were to break these in there it would run everyone out of the store! It is a horrible smell; like rotten eggs and Rooney's feet!"

"Brilliant, cousin!", said Willie.

"I don't know…", Claude worried.

"Quiet, Claude!", ordered Willie. "Letitia needs to be shown her place!"

Rooney remained apprehensively silent as he crouched down and tried to smell his foot.

"Alright…", Fitz lowered his voice and huddled the boys together. "We will all go in there. I will place one on the floor near the back of the shop. Willie, you place the other near the front. Just act like you are looking for more candy. When the time is right, I will step on the vial and will send up a signal. Willie, you step on yours - then we get out! We should have a few seconds before they realize how bad it smells. We will be long-gone and the girls won't even want their candy!"

"What will be the signal?", Claude asked.

Fitz rubbed his chin as he thought, "Fendallsburg!"

The boys quietly re-entered the shop and casually moved into position. Letitia and Lizzie were at the sales counter still making choices. Fitz covertly sidled up near the girls. He dropped to one knee pretending to tie his shoe. He deftly laid the vile next to the front counter just behind Letitia.

After a few tense moments Fitz reached out with his right foot and crushed the vial. "Fendallsburg!", he announced. Willie instantly smashed the second olfactory attack device. Willie, Claude and Rooney barreled out the door, nearly stampeding a young woman who was just entering the store. Fitz was a few steps behind. As he rushed through the doorway, the irritated woman extended her foot. Fitz's foot hooked around hers and his momentum sent him careening across the sidewalk and into the gutter. The small bag with his remaining candy flew from his grip and landed in the middle of King Street. The quick-thinking young woman quickly pounced on Fitz and twisted his ear, "Get up, young man!", she demanded.

"Oww!", Fitz squealed as he feared his ear was being removed from his head.

"My name is Sarah Hooe. And whose acquaintance am I making?", she said with cynical chastisement. Fitz cut his eyes down King Street in time to see his cousins disappear around the corner onto St. Asaph Street.

"I can't remember, ma'am… Ouch! Ouch! Ouch!", he repeated as he rhythmically hopped on one foot. He paused his performance and took some solace as Letitia and Lizzie evacuated the store with tears in their eyes and handkerchiefs over their mouths. He strained to peer around Sarah Hooe to determine if the girls got their candy. He didn't see any bags in their hands and wryly smiled with self-satisfaction.

"What is your name, sir?", she twisted again.

"Oww!", his skinned knee was stinging almost as much as the vise grip on his ear.

Mrs. Appich came to the door, put her hands on her hips, and shook her head. "Don't come back to my store for six weeks, Fitz Lee!", she decreed as she smothered a smile.

"Now that we have your name, Master Fitz Lee; who are your parents?"

Fitz knew the jig was up, "Mr. and Mrs. Smith Lee, ma'am.", he conceded.

Miss Sarah Hooe tersely continued the interrogation, "Where are your parents now?"

"At the Fendall's home, ma'am."

"Good, then we shall have time to talk as we make the walk over there and tell them what you and the other scoundrels have wrought. I am sure a reparation will be in order, Master Lee."

"Yes ma'am... uhh... may I collect my bag of candy?"

"My God, man; you are an audacious one!", Sarah Hooe exploded. "Absolutely not! We shall leave that treat for the birds. Now, let's walk!"

"Yes, ma'am.", Fitz surrendered unconditionally.

Ellen Lee and her mother were giggling as Fitz Lee concluded the tale of his childhood hi-jinx. "And, dear Ellen; do you know who Miss Sarah Hooe became?" Ellen wasn't sure, but the name was familiar. Her father continued, "Well, she would have the good fortune to get married, go on to have a beautiful young daughter called Nellie and, perhaps most importantly, a handsome young son-in-law named Fitzhugh Lee!"

"You mean Nanny Fowle was Sarah Hooe?", Ellen opened her mouth in disbelief.

"Yes, she was and she is! And, she hasn't let go of my ear since!", Fitz chortled. "You see, my dear... I am a far distance from perfect."

"But, Uncle Robert... what about him?", Ellen asked.

"He is another matter altogether, dear. I don't know if he was perfect. The Lord makes these determinations. But he is the closest any Lee has come; and most likely will ever come."

"Poor Uncle Rooney.", Ellen empathized. "Poor, poor Uncle Rooney."

Fitz hugged her tightly. "Rooney didn't have it so bad, either.", he kissed her atop her head. "The Lees are blessed and therefore, must lead, Ellen. Be humble and remember that. I shall try to do the same."   (56.3)

Chapter 57   *Keys to the Case*

Charles V. Meredith and Colonel William R. Aylett arrived at the Hustings Court of Richmond just before 10 o'clock on May 28, 1885. Meredith reached for the large double door at the entrance to the courtroom when a muffled voice called from behind two large bouquets of flowers.

"Gentlemen... Mr. Meredith and Colonel Aylett... these flowers are for you."

Meredith and Aylett looked down at the pair of skinny legs behind the flowers. "What? For us?", Meredith asked.

"Yes," the delivery man replied, "it appears you are both admired and appreciated."

"Who sent these, sir?", asked Aylett as he stuck his nose into a carnation.

"They wish to remain anonymous, sir."

"Very well. Thank you very much, sir." Each of the attorneys placed a large bouquet under their arm and entered the courtroom. (57.1)

Thomas Cluverius was already seated at the defense table as the prosecution and their flowers came down the aisle. The newspaper men filled a dozen seats in the back half of the room. Cluverius scowled as he watched the confident prosecutors basking in their newfound celebrity. Inside he seethed at the by-product of his misfortune. Judge Atkins, too, was in his seat, reviewing some notes from the previous day's proceedings. He looked up and removed his spectacles, "Gentlemen... Let's get those potted and in some water. We have removed the curiosity crowd from the proceedings. That has certainly improved the pestiferous odor of the room. But, the scent from these bouquets will be welcome perfume! Bailiff, please find something for the flowers."

Beverly Crump and A. Brown Evans quietly entered the courtroom and sat by the prisoner. The jury entered shortly thereafter. Judge Atkins called the court to order. Beverly Crump stood and addressed the court, "Your honor, my colleague, Mr. Pollard, fell ill yesterday evening. He had to have some medicine in the form of morphine administered. And whilst he has recovered to some extent from his pains and the effects of the medicine, he remained quite dizzy this morning. He believes he shall be able to appear about 12 o'clock."

"Do you wish to take a recess until that time?", Judge Atkins asked.

"Yes, sir."

Atkins turned to Meredith and Aylett, "Do you gentlemen have any objection to that?"

"No, sir.", Meredith replied.

"Recess until 12 o'clock granted.", the judge banged his gavel.

At 12 o'clock, Judge T.S. Atkins returned to the bench and struck the Hustings Court back into session.

Beverly Crump rose to his feet and addressed the court. "Mr. Pollard remains ill, your honor; but the defense shall proceed. We thank the court for its consideration."

Just then a knock came to the large double doors at the rear of the courtroom. Judge Atkins looked around with puzzlement, "There are to be no others in this courtroom. Is someone missing? Perhaps it is Mr. Pollard. Bailiff, please answer the door."

The bailiff slowly opened the door. A procession of five deliverymen, each carrying a large bouquet, filed down the center aisle. The first man stopped near the defense table. "My apologies for the disturbance, sir. I have bouquets for four gentlemen.". He pulled a small card from his trouser pocket and read the names: "Mr. Beverley Crump; Mr. H.R. Pollard; Mr. A. Brown Evans; and *two* bouquets for Mr. Thomas J. Cluverius."

Charles Meredith turned to Colonel Aylett, "A desperate ruse, I say." Aylett nodded in agreement.

"And, who sent these flowers, sir.", asked the judge.

"I do not have names, sir. They come from a citizen group of admirers and supporters.", the deliveryman answered.

"Very well... Bailiff, do we have any other pots for these?"

The Bailiff shrugged and shook his head.

"Please rest them in front of the jury box, sir.", Atkins instructed. "The court will take it from there. Thank you and please leave the premises. We are in session and it is closed to the public." Judge Atkins glared at both teams of attorneys, "Will there be any further distractions, gentlemen?"

"No, sir.", both sides pledged.

"Defense counsel, please call your witness.", said the judge.

"The defense calls Joseph Bland.", said Bev Crump.

"Please state your name, residence, and occupation for the jury."

"My name is Joseph Bland. I live in Little Plymouth, King and Queen County. I work in Bland & Bros. store nearby in Centreville. I am the youngest of the brothers."

"How long have you worked there?"

"I finished school five years ago and have worked in the store ever since."

"Do you know Hermann Joel, the jeweler?"

"Yes, he rents a case in our store in the dry goods section.", the young man answered.

"How long has Mr. Joel had a case in your store?", asked Crump.

"I would say it's been at least two years… maybe a little longer."

"Do you see his customers?"

"Yes. I work that part of the store most of the time. Some of the time I am called to work outside and sometimes I am called away from the store entirely. But, most all of the time I would see any customers of Joel."

"How often does Mr. Joel come to your store?", Crump continued.

"He comes once a month. He comes to check his stock, or replenish it. He also comes to bring back and retrieve things which are brought to him for repair."

"So, when Mr. Joel is not there, who would collect these items on his behalf?"

"Most of the time, that would be my responsibility. If he sells something, I would collect the money and hold on his behalf; or if someone brings something in for repair, I would put it in his safe. Generally, I conduct these simple transactions on his behalf and he pays monthly for the space and that service."

"Do you know the defendant?"

"Yes, I have known him for several years."

"Has he ever been in your store?"

"Yes, I believe he has on a few occasions over the years."

"Do you know if he has ever conducted business with Mr. Joel?"

"I have never known of any business between the two."

"Has he ever brought anything in for Mr. Joel to repair for him?"

"Not as far as I know.", Bland replied.

"Has Mr. Cluverius ever come to you to transact any business with Mr. Joel?"

"No."

Crump honed in for clarification, "So, to your best knowledge, Mr. Cluverius has never conducted business with Mr. Joel either directly or indirectly?"

"That is correct, sir."

"Have you had any other association with Mr. Cluverius?"

"Well, I have seen him from time to time in Little Plymouth or Centreville. But I have never spoken directly with him other than to say hello when we have passed on the street."

"Thank you, Mr. Bland. No more questions, your honor."

Colonel Aylett stood for the cross-examination. "Mr. Bland; you say that the prisoner has been to your store several times in the past, correct?"

"Yes, sir."

"Did you see if he purchased any items on those occasions?"

"I cannot say.", said Bland.

"You mentioned that you work inside the store, outside the store, and are called away from the store at times."

"Yes."

"So, you are quite busy with many different things that happen at the store on a daily basis. Is that a fair statement?"

"Yes, sir."

Aylett moved a little closer to the witness. "Is it possible that Mr. Cluverius came into your store and conducted business with Mr. Joel, either directly or indirectly through another associate at the store? Is it possible? After all, you did not follow Mr. Cluverius at all times while he was in the store, did you?"

Bland hesitated for a moment, "I suppose it is possible; but I believe it would be very unlikely. You see, I am the only other person in the store who has keys to Mr. Joel's case and his safe."

"Ahh yes, the keys, Mr. Bland. We will get to those in a moment. Is it possible that Mr. Cluverius dealt directly with Mr. Joel at your store and you did not see it?"

Bland wiped his brow with his sleeve. "Yes, that could be possible. But I never saw the two of them together."

Aylett paused for a few moments. "Was your store broken into recently, Mr. Bland?"

"Yes."

"How did you learn of this break-in?"

Bland turned his head to the left and cracked his neck. "I learned of it the day when Mr. Joel came with a police officer to collect his ledger book."

"Why did Mr. Joel come, with a police man, to get this ledger book?", Aylett put his index finger up to his lips.

"Well, it is my understanding that Mr. Joel was looking to see what was recorded in the ledger in connection with any possible transactions with Mr. Cluverius."

"So! Mr. Joel seemed to think he had conducted business with Mr. Cluverius, in one way or another, either directly or indirectly, at your store. Is that correct?"

"Yes, I suppose…"

"When did this intrusion into your store occur?"

"It apparently happened the night before Mr. Joel and the officer came. Or perhaps it could have happened the night prior to that.", Bland contended.

"And, is true that the only disturbance that anyone could find that resulted from this intrusion was a drawer below Mr. Joel's case was forced open?"

"That is correct."

"Do you find that odd, Mr. Bland? After all, there was jewelry in the case right there above the drawer. And you have a large store full of valuable merchandise. Wouldn't you expect something else would have been taken?"

"Yes, sir… very odd.", Bland admitted and wiped his brow again.

"And it happened just before Mr. Joel was to come testify before this court – just days ago in the midst of this proceeding. Someone knew exactly what they were looking for, didn't they Mr. Bland?"

"I would agree that it is very strange."

"Do you have keys to your store?", Aylett moved closer again.

"Yes, of course."

"And you have keys to Mr. Joel's case, drawer, and even his safe, correct?"

"Yes."

"So, you were the only one to have complete unfettered access to that ledger book; any time; day or night?"

"I suppose.", Bland capitulated.

"Do you know the prisoner's brother, William Cluverius?"

"Yes."

"Do you know him better than you know the prisoner?"

"I would say so."

Aylett moved to within three feet of the witness stand and turned to face the jury. "Was William Cluverius ever employed by Bland & Brothers' store?"

"No.", Joseph Bland answered meekly.

"Did Mr. William Cluverius have any business relationship with Bland & Brothers store?"

"Yes. At one time he supplied the store with firewood. We would purchase loads from him for resale at the store."

"When and for how long?"

"That would have been in the fall and winter of 1883; for four or five months. I do not believe he continued in that business afterward."

"Did he have access to any keys?"

"No, sir."

"Did he know Mr. Joel?"

"I don't know, sir."

"Was there ever any business disagreement between anyone at Bland's and Mr. William Cluverius?", Aylett asked.

"Not that I am aware. He just informed us he was not going to supply firewood for us any longer. There was no particular problem as far as I know."

"Have you spoken with William Cluverius since this business ceased?"

"I have said 'hello' to him a few times when I have seen him in Centreville or Little Plymouth. But nothing more."

"Thank you, Mr. Bland. No more questions."

Beverly Crump stood for re-direct. "The prosecution, with this last line of questions, failed to make something clear. Yes, there was a breach several days ago at the Bland & Brothers store. In fact, a window in the rear of the building was broken and forced open. It is evident that the intruder entered unlawfully from the rear of the building. Mr.

Bland; you stated that you have keys to the both the store and to Mr. Joel's case, drawer, and safe."

"Yes.", Bland answered in a depressed tone.

"If you had reason to go into Mr. Joel's drawer, would you forcibly enter your own store in the middle of the night and pry open the drawer; or would you simply use your keys?"

"I assure you, sir; I would use the keys."

"Thank you. No more questions, your honor."   (57.2)

Chapter 58 *So, Be It*

The Hustings Court of Richmond was called to order at 10 o'clock on May 29, 2019. The defense began the fourth day of their presentation by calling Beverly W. Cluverius to the stand. Whitey Cluverius rose and walked purposefully toward the stand. He was wearing a new suit tailored from inexpensive brown broadcloth. His white beard was so long, a tie was not visible. For the first time since the trial began, Willie Cluverius was not in courtroom.

H.R. Pollard rose to his feet to resume his duties for the defense. After slowly making his away to the front of the defense table, he steadied himself with his right hand on the table top. The dark circles under his eyes and a clearly weakened conditioned brought his endurance, but not his dedication, into question. "Sir, please state your name for the jury."

"My name is Beverly Whiting Cluverius; but people call me Whitey."

"Are you related to the defendant?"

"I am his father."

"Where do you reside?"

"I live in King and Queen County, about a mile 'n a half below Lil' Plymouth."

"Have you been staying at your home since the arrest of your son?"

"No, I been staying at Jane Tunstall's house; lookin' after things for 'er while she 'n Willie have been here 'n Richmon'."

"Did you know your son was going to Richmond on March 12th?", Pollard shifted position and leaned his backside against the defense table.

"Yes. Tommie brought me his buggy that Tuesday b'fore he left. He said he'd be goin' on the train to Richmon' later 'n the week 'n would be back Saturdee. We agreed'a meet in Centerville on Saturdee; that was the 14th."

"What time did you meet your son?"

"It was 'bout 2 o'clock after noon.", Whitey Cluverius affirmed.

"Did you see any marks or bruises on your son when you met him; particularly on his hands?"

"Well, he hurt 'is hand on a fence right while I was drivin' up 'n the buggy to get'im. I seen'im fall right as I was getting close to'im. I was maybe fifteen feet away on the other side of the road. He was leanin' back against the fence like this…", the old man leaned back in the witness chair and extended his arms out from his sides, holding the position for a few moments in a Christ-like manner. "Then, all of a sudden he slip't and fall. I jumped from the buggy 'n took'im by the hands. I seen three or four scrapes on 'em; on his hands; little ones."

"So, you say he scratched his hands on the fence?"

"That is what I'm sayin'."

"Other than this accidental fall, did you notice any unusual behavior?"

"No, sir. No,sir. He was actin' like he always did. No difference."

"And, what happened the rest of that day, Mr. Cluverius?"

"Well, Tommie 'n I rode on back to my house 'n he leaves me there. Then, he said he was goin' on to Jane's."

"Did you see him again prior to his arrest?", Pollard asked as he started to work his way back around the defense table.

"No, sir."

Pollard pulled his chair out from under the table and glanced at the judge as he said, "No more questions, your honor."

Colonel William R. Aylett rose for the prosecution.

"Mr. Cluverius; you stated that you have been staying at Jane Tunstall's home since your son was arrested. Have you and Mrs. Tunstall reconciled your differences?"

"We have no diff'rences, sir.", Cluverius snapped.

"Mrs. Tunstall testified that there were differences between the two of you in years past. Are these differences the reason your sons have lived with her these last eleven years?"

Whitey Cluverius ran his fingers through his thick coarse head of gray hair, "Sir, I'm goin' to answer your question with a question. What business is this of yours?", his temper flared.

"Mr. Cluverius, I am here to interrogate *you*, not to answer *your* questions!", Aylett shot back with a smile.

"Please answer the question, Mr. Cluverius.", Judge Atkins intervened.

Whitey Cluverius snorted as he fought to contain his outrage, "Any diff'rences were family business. My boys stayed with Jane because she needed help. Her husband had just died. We all get on fine, now. That's all I have to say 'bout this!"

"Mr. Cluverius… did you ever take money from Jane Tunstall.", Aylett leaned in for the answer.

"I only take what she give.", he squinted in defiance.

"Where is your wife, Mr. Cluverius?"

"She's at my house."

"Has she stayed at Mrs. Tunstall's with you?"

"No, sir. She's been sick along time. I jus' leave'er at home."

Thomas Cluverius grunted to himself in resentful disgust, "Not sick…drunk."

Colonel Aylett continued, "Mr. Cluverius; it is your contention that the prisoner injured his hand when he fell near a fence. And, this happened right as you were driving up to meet him on Saturday, the 14th, correct?"

"Yes."

"What sort of fence is it?"

"'Tis a rail fence. The rails are mawled."

"Where is this fence located?"

"Along the road from Centerville to Lil' Plymouth. Just on the north side of Centerville."

Aylett wrapped his thumb and forefinger around his chin, "If I were to ride out there, would I still find this fence along the road?"

"Yes."

"Do you know what type of wood this fence is made from?"

"It's either ches'nut or oak."

"Please describe again for the court how this fall occurred. I am having trouble figuring how a man could injure his hands in such a way by leaning against a fence."

"Tommie fell as I was ridin' up. I did not see clearly how he fell. He had his arms out and elbows were restin' on the middle rail of the fence. He had one foot on the ground and the other was restin' on the bottom rail. The top rail was 'bout the same level as his head. I look away for a secon' or two; I guess lookin' at the horse pullin' the buggy. And, when I look back toward Tommie, he was already on the ground. That's when I stop and go on o'er to'im. I asked him what was the matter and he says he hurt his hands…"

Aylett interrupted, "Wait… So, you say he actually said his hands were hurt. You did not say this before, Mr. Cluverius."

"Yes, he said it...", Whitey Cluverius stared back at his tormentor. "I took hold o' his hands and I seen the skin on his hands was knocked off a little. I look at the fence 'n I seen a knot hole in the second rail with some little spears sticking up from it. I think he caught his hand on that."

"Mr. Cluverius. Did you see the position of the prisoner's hands as he fell?"

The old man paused for moment and tried to let his exasperation subside. "I did not see his hands before he fell an' I did not see his hands when he was recoverin' from the fall. I only seen his hands when I come o'er an' take hold of 'em."

"So, were you concerned for the prisoner's well-being after you helped him recover from this fall?"

"I don't understand what you're askin'; but if you're askin' if I care 'bout my children 'n worry about 'em when they get hurt; then, yes! I'm jus' as fond o' my boys as if they was still babies. Whenever they get hurt, I take notice 'n measures to make sure they're alright."

Colonel Aylett retrieved a blank sheet of paper and a pencil from the prosecution's table. He handed it to the witness. "Please sketch a diagram of this knot hole, Mr. Cluverius. I am having trouble picturing this in my mind's eye and suspect the rest of the court is having similar difficulty."

Whitey Cluverius rolled his eyes as he took the paper and turned to his right to sketch a picture on the small side table beside the witness chair. After a few moments he handed the paper back over to Aylett. Aylett moved the paper back in forth as if trying to place it in a field of focus. He then turned the page ninety degrees and paused again for a moment. "That looks more like an early rose potato than a knot hole!", he ridiculed.

"You can take it for either you please.", Cluverius seethed.

"I apologize, sir. I am teasing, Mr. Cluverius.", Aylett feigned repentance. "You seem to have taken greatly detailed note of this fence and the knot hole. And, you were only there with the prisoner for a few minutes. Have you been back to see this fence since the arrest of your son?"

"Yes. I visited the fence with Mr. Pollard 'n Mr. Evans. They wanted to see it when I told 'em what happened there."

"I see. Are you aware that other witnesses have testified that your son has given more than one explanation regarding these wounds on his hands?"

"No, sir.", the witness flatly answered.

Aylett explained further, "We have testimony from Officer Sweeney of the Richmond Police that your son told him these marks were skin eruptions. We have heard that the prisoner told Mr. Wortham of King and Queen County that he received the marks by striking his hands on a train car railing. Now, we have your testimony that the prisoner received them from a fall next to a rail fence. Do you find this strange, Mr. Cluverius?"

"I can only tell you what I know. My son's been asked many questions by many people since this all started. Maybe he's been confused sometimes? Maybe the people askin' questions are confused? I stand by what I have said. I stand by my son. He is innocent.", said Bill Cluverius as he looked directly at the jury.

Colonel Aylett exhaled and said, "No more questions, your honor."

An exhausted Pollard stood part way out of his chair, "No more questions."

The three defense attorneys quietly huddled around the table with their client. A few anxious minutes passed as the rest of the court awaited the next witness. The three lawyers nodded in agreement to one another and then turned as one and looked at T. J. Cluverius. The young prisoner pursed his lips and hesitated for a moment as the attorney's braced for his response. He nodded his head and whispered, "So, be it."

Beverly Crump stood and announced, "The defense rests, your honor."

Judge Atkins cleared his throat, "Then we shall adjourn for recess now. We will reconvene at 1 o'clock and the prosecution can present any rebuttal." (58.1)

The afternoon session was called back to order at 1 o'clock. A cold front had moved through, bringing clouds, showers, and some easing of the summer heat. Charles Meredith called Owen M. Winston to the stand.

"Please state your name, place of residence, and occupation, sir.", Meredith began.

"My name is Owen M. Winston of King William County. I am the Clerk of the Court for the Circuit Court of King William County."

"May I first express my sympathies regarding the horrific fire you recently suffered at the King William Courthouse."

"Thank you, sir;", Winston replied. "It has been devastating to the operation of the court; but we will recover."

"Mr. Winston; how long have you held this position with the clerk's office?"

"I was elected to the position in 1870.", Winston recalled.

"And, do you know the prisoner?"

"Yes, he practices law before the court in King William. I have seen him many times over the last few years."

"Have you ever known the prisoner to wear a mustache?", Meredith asked.

"Yes. I last saw him in late February. He had a light mustache. I remember noticing it for that very reason. He was in my office filing some motions. I noticed him pulling at the mustache with his fingers."

"Had you ever known him to wear a mustache prior to this time?"

"No, sir. I cannot say I have noticed one before. However, that may be the reason I clearly took note of the one he wore in February."

"Thank you, sir. No further questions.", said Meredith.

Judge Atkins looked at the defense. Beverly Crump shook his head, "No questions, your honor." (58.2)

Charles Meredith then called in rebuttal a succession of witnesses who knew the prisoner in various capacities ranging from: his appearances in different courthouses in the area; to old college classmates; to barkeepers in King William County. To a man, all testified that they had seen Thomas J. Cluverius wear a mustache at one time or another over the last few years. Several noted that they had seen him twirl his light mustache in his fingers. Charles Meredith felt that this question of a mustache was the one area where the defense had, to some degree, pierced the prosecution's case. Although he could not directly contradict the testimony of those who knew Cluverius well and stated they had never seen him wear a mustache, he felt that he had assembled a substantial and credible group of witnesses to suggest otherwise. The defense chose not to cross-examine any of these witnesses, seeing no value in extending the argument. (58.3)

Judge Atkins adjourned the proceedings for the day and informed the court that the jury would report Saturday, May 30 at 10 o'clock for instruction and that final arguments would commence Monday, June 1, 1885 at 9 o'clock.

Chapter 59 *Debt Collection*

Judge T.S. Atkins entered the courtroom at the Hustings Court of Richmond a few minutes before ten o'clock on Saturday, May 30, 1885. The jurors in the trial of Thomas Cluverius were already seated in the jury box. The judge handed twelve sheets of paper to the bailiff who distributed one to each juror. Judge Atkins kept one sheet for himself. "Gentlemen, here are my instructions as we finally are nearing the end of this proceeding. Monday you will begin to hear the final arguments for guilt or innocence. As you listen to these and perform your deliberation, there are some basic precepts to which you must adhere. This, is a criminal legal proceeding. Your judgment must be based in a legal framework. I have provided a list of six rules of instruction. Please review these and be prepared to apply them on Monday. Judge Atkins then read the instructions aloud.

1. *Before the jury can convict the accused they must be satisfied from the evidence that he is guilty of the offense charged in the indictment beyond reasonable doubt. It is not sufficient that they should believe his guilt probable only. No degree of probability merely with authorize a conviction, but the evidence must be of such character and tendency as to produce a moral certainty of the prisoner's guilt to the exclusion of a reasonable doubt.*
2. *Each fact which is necessary in the chain of circumstances to establish the guilt of the accused must be distinctly proved by competent legal evidence. And, if the jury have reasonable doubt as to the material fact necessary to be proved in order to support the hypothesis of the prisoner's guilt to the exclusion of every other reasonable hypothesis, they must find him not guilty.*
3. *If the jury are satisfied from the evidence that the accused is guilty of the offense charged in the indictment beyond reasonable doubt, and no rational hypothesis or explanation can be framed or given (upon the whole evidence in the case) consistent with the innocence of the accused, and at the same time consistent with the facts proved, they ought to find him guilty.*
4. *It is not essential to proof of guilt by circumstantial evidence that the facts and circumstances established should produce on the minds of the jury absolute and demonstrative certainty; but it is sufficient if they produce moral certainty of the commission of the offense charged to the exclusion of reasonable doubt.*
5. *The law presumes a prisoner to be always innocent of the charges alleged against him until he is proved to be guilty, and the burden rests upon the Commonwealth to prove the guilt of the accused beyond a reasonable doubt: no mere preponderance of the evidence will suffice as in the trial of a civil case : nor is it enough that by conjecture or speculation he may be supposed*

> to be guilty, but the jury must be satisfied by the evidence that he is guilty beyond a reasonable doubt.
> 6. If, upon the whole evidence in the case, the jury entertain a reasonable doubt as to whether the deceased came to her death by violence, committed by herself, or by the hands of someone other than the prisoner, they must find the prisoner not guilty. (59.1)

Terry McIlhenny stood on the corner of Ross Street and 13th Street across from the Virginia Governor's Mansion.

"Buy them while they last! Souvenir Cards from the Trial of the Century!", he called to passers-by. "Closing Arguments begin this week in the Trial of Cluverius! They say he'll be hanged! Souvenir Cards for sale! Cluverius and Lillie! Ten cents for the pair!"

A firm hand came down upon the boy's shoulder from behind. The boy spun around and looked straight into the chest of a very imposing figure. The man opened his coat slightly. A shiny police badge caught the boy's full attention. "It violates city ordinance to sell items on the street without permission, boy.". The policeman was not even sure if it was the truth; but that did not matter. "Come with me, now!", he commanded. The brute gripped the boy's jacket by the nape and dragged him east down Ross Street. A half block down he hurled the boy into an empty alley. "How many of those have you sold?"

The boy shook in fear as he scrambled to pick up his cap, "I don't know..."

"Don't lie to me! If you don't want to end up in jail today, you better give me my answers. And, it better be the truth!" The law man wrapped his powerful hand around the boy's throat. "How many?!", he demanded.

"Five Hundred Seventy-Five... or maybe Five Hundred Eighty...", the boy trembled.

The thug lifted the boy upward. The boy's face turned as red as the brick pavers his toes were barely scraping. McIlhenny clamped his fingers around the man's grip and tried to free a little space so he could catch his breath. "It's true!", he gurgled. "It's true!". The giant sat the boy back down and loosened his choke-hold.

"How much money have you made?", the man growled.

"Twenty-nine dollars...", the street urchin replied.

"Do you think I'm stupid, boy? Do you?!", as he applied pressure once again to the boy's throat.

Tears popped out of the corner of Terry's eyes, "Alright, alright… Fifty-eight dollars.", he confessed.

"Where is the money?"

"I don't have it all here!", the boy explained.

"How much have you here now? Empty your pockets!", the bully squeezed again.

The boy reached in his trouser pockets and pulled out a dozen dimes and another ten nickels and handed them over. "Dollar fifty, sixty - one dollar seventy… Where's the rest?", the man impatiently demanded. The boy stood silent. The ogre backhanded McIlhenny across the face, sending him tumbling into a stack of wooden crates in the alley. "Where's the rest?!" The assailant reached down and tore the shoes from the boy's feet. He checked the inner soles. Inside the left he found four five-dollar notes. In the right were a ten and four more fives. "That's fifty-one dollars and seventy cents. I need another six dollars…"

The boy whimpered and rubbed his sore cheek as he looked up at the mugger. "I don't have any more! That's all I have!"

The man noticed a golden ring on the boy's right middle finger. He reached down and forced it off the boy's hand. "This should make up for the rest…", he said.

Terry McIlhenny cried out in desperation, "No, my mother gave me that! She gave it to me before she died! Don't take that from me!", he begged.

"Well, that's good. Seems as though your mother is still looking after you.", the man said with emotionally-detached cruelty as he placed the ten-karat ring on his smallest finger. "I know you had six hundred of those cards at the outset; you can sell the rest and keep those proceeds. Maybe you should consider raising prices. Mr. Cluverius is finished with you now. If you try to argue any of this; I will find you. You don't want that!"

The boy pulled his knees up to his chest and wrapped his arms around them as he sat helplessly in the alley. He buried his face into the tops of his knees and mourned the loss of the last link he had to his mother. The man disappeared from the alley onto Ross Street.

Willie Cluverius entered Ned Cummin's Bar at 3 o'clock on Saturday afternoon. He spotted a large man seated alone in a snug near the back corner of the bar. Willie removed his hat, sat across from the man, and closed the narrow door to the snug.

"Did you talk to the boy?", Willie began.

"Yes. He didn't have it all.", Sergeant Charles Deuring of the Richmond Police responded.

"How much?", Willie continued.

"Thirty-seven dollars.", Deuring claimed as he gulped his beer.

"That's all?", Willie asked. "Tommie won't be happy about this. What are you going to do?"

"About the rest of the money?", Deuring asked in disbelief. "Nothing... he is a child. What would you have me do? The same fate as the ladies?"

Willie shook his head slightly. "No... But this is not good. Give me what you have.", Willie put his open palm across the table.

"No...", Deuring coldly declared. "Where is the remainder of *my* money? You and your brother owe me another five hundred for those ladies. And, I will need four hundred more if you want the case of Miss McDonald to be of no further concern. Remember, she lived in Henrico. It is your good fortune that I know both the Sheriff and the coroner over there. If you want their investigation to be favorable, well...there are costs."

Willie sighed, "You never mentioned this potential! How can you expect me to pay that kind of money?"

"How you do it is not my concern, Mr. Cluverius. *If* you do it, is my concern..."

"What about Nellie Goss?", Willie grimaced and braced himself for additional charges.

"She was already very ill. Her passing is not suspicious." Deuring drank again and sat the empty glass on the table.

Willie exhaled with relief. However, that feeling quickly abandoned him as he steeled himself and continued the conversation, "Look Deuring, we don't have the money yet."

Deuring tilted his head back and laughed. His smile dissipated as he leaned in toward Willie, "You don't have it? You sound like that boy. And you wouldn't want me to treat you the way I treated him."

"We will get it from my aunt. Have no worries.", Willie groped for a reassuring statement. "My aunt will go to the bank on Monday. I will get you the money Tuesday."

"I want nine hundred on Monday!", Deuring snapped as he slammed his fist on the table. Both Willie and the beer glass flinched and shuddered near the table's edge, "And, I will keep this thirty-seven from the boy, too. You and your brother need to understand the importance of paying debts when due. Do not cross me, Cluverius." Duering pushed open the door and abruptly exited the snug. (59.2)

Chapter 60   *The Dark Mantle of Midnight*

On June 1, 1885 Colonel William R. Aylett rose in front of the Hustings Court of Richmond to deliver the first closing argument for the prosecution in the trial of Thomas J. Cluverius. Judge Atkins had allowed the public back into the courtroom to witness the conclusion of a legal proceeding on a scale which had heretofore never been conducted in Virginia history. Colonel Aylett was determined to earnestly and eloquently deliver an impassioned argument in the tradition of his esteemed and celebrated great-grandfather, Patrick Henry.

"Little did I think two months ago that I would be here now, that faces that were then strange to me, through our long association, would become as familiar to me as those in my own household and will stay with me as long as life lasts.", he smiled with his hand over his heart.

"Little did I think, gentlemen, that when called upon at the invitation of the Commonwealth's Attorney Richmond Office, that the public voice of my county should blend with the public voice of the community in the presentation of this case. I cannot go further into the case without making certain acknowledgements, which I might otherwise forget.

My esteemed friend and associate, who was a comparative stranger to me when I entered here, has fought nobly, gallantly, and truthfully, and to Mr. Charles Meredith is due the credit of conception and organization of the plan of conducting the case." Aylett turned and nodded gently toward his colleague. Holding his right hand in the air and then closing it into a fist, he continued, "Mr. Meredith has seized this case with the grasp of a mastermind and soon, order grew out of chaos.

Nor, do I feel indebted to him alone, but to the noble body of men of the Richmond Police including, among many, Captain Charles Epps and Detective John Wren. But, not alone to these, gentlemen of the jury, but to the good men and women of Virginia everywhere who abhor crime and with ten thousand arms have held up the ideals of the Commonwealth.

Alas, little did I think that the cloud of guilt and accusation which hung over the prisoner's head; then no longer than a man's hand; would steadily increase until today, where it stands over his head ready to burst with destruction."

Aylett turned and looked directly at T.J. Cluverius, who sat motionless staring a thousand yards into the distance at the front wall of the court room, "Gentlemen of the jury, the prisoner is placed before you under a shield of innocence until a fair presumption of guilt comes in. If the facts drive the theory of suicide from the minds of the jury, then those facts in proof of guilt must evoke a verdict of guilty. The jury must convict, if they find no reasonable doubt of guilt, dark and bloody guilt, as proved by the evidence. Even if such evidence is circumstantial and unproved by ocular demonstration, if the jury can ascertain, with moral certainty, that there is no reasonable doubt of guilt, the jury must convict. Every man acts on circumstantial evidence. Witnesses may lie or be mistaken; but circumstances are unerring.

The first question we must answer is if the murder was on the 13th of March last. That faithful official, L.W. Rose, in his daily rounds at the Marshall Reservoir, sees afloat on the water a form of a female. The accomplished Coroner of the City, Dr. Taylor, comes immediately to the scene. The form is brought to shore, stark and cold. Facts were called from the tracks on the bank and from the evidence of a desperate struggle which utterly exploded the theory of suicide. To the Almshouse she was carried. The noble and sympathetic people of Richmond tenderly viewed the swollen lips and bruised temple of that poor girl who had been sent hurriedly to eternity.

The idea of suicide is utterly untenable and absurd. She would never have sought so wild and lonely a spot and carried a man's foot to imprint the grounds in order to commit suicide. A big satchel she must have thrown into the James River, a shawl here, a hat there. And, whence she throwed that satchel into the river, why not throw herself in, as well? Why would she have discarded the satchel in the rushing waters of the James, only to throw herself into the calm waters of the Marshall Reservoir? No! Gentlemen of the jury, she must have died by violence! Furthermore, it is a strange fact that the instinct of maternity makes a woman desire to live, even if that life be one of shame. If they feel like suicide for themselves, they do not want to crush the infant!", he pounded his right fist into his open left palm.

"No, gentlemen of the jury, the prisoner, after first ruining her life for his vile purposes, he then proceeded to take away her life in toto. He had first to dispose of the body, the gloves, the veil, and the satchel. They would float. They would not sink. Dazed and confused, perhaps by his crime, he drops the gloves. He catches his watch-key in the fence upon exiting the grounds of the reservoir. He flings away the hat in agitated remorse into the dead-house. He holds the shawl a little longer, with its crimson hue, until tossing it over a wall of the Dunstan home. Her good name was gone and he sought to affix her shame upon the heads of others. He then found a convenient point to discard of the satchel in the river.

Gentlemen of the jury, you must come to understand the thoughts of the prisoner. The circumstances of his life which could have driven him to murder. A pregnant woman is found dead. At once, the father of her unborn child would be suspected; and the lustful father of that child is the prisoner. He is engaged to be married to a woman of means. To consummate the marriage, the victim of his lust must be dispatched. Her betrayal traced to him, the affianced would have spurned him; the legal profession would have turned their back upon him. As an unworthy member of a noble profession he would have been hissed with scorn and condemned by those high and noble men belonging to a profession to whom the country owes everything; and of which Lord Bacon said "sparks of every science can be raked from its ashes."

It is clear the prisoner carefully planned the seduction, choosing time and place at the Walker home to conduct illicit intercourse. His room was near Lillian's. There were no locks on the doors. He was at the Walker home with Lillian eight months before the murder. Lillian was eight months with-child at the time of the murder. But, in the only letter from him found in her trunk dated September 14, 1884, he advises her to marry "that fellow". It is true that Cary Madison was in correspondence with Lillian. To Cary Madison the prisoner wished to cast the soiled dove, when she was in a position glad to seek shelter in the arms of any honest man and hide her shame. And, along with that letter we found the most atrocious paper that I have ever read. Of all the compositions that the English language has ever been made to speak or develop, that dirty piece – that poem, *On the Delaware*, exceeds anything I have ever seen! This single paper speaks to his true character more than the volumes of testimony the defense has presented in favor of his character. He ought to have been hung for writing that paper and sending it to a virtuous woman! When it was read, I noticed your countenances and the countenances of everyone who was compelled to listen to it; and you all looked as if you were in the presence of a corpse – so atrocious and horrible was it!", Aylett grimaced with disgust.

"If you recall the letter of September 14th. In the body he refers to a trip he made alone to Richmond and how he wished that Lillian were with him. His plan was to meet her as frequently as possible and seize upon and destroy her when the opportunity presented itself. He wanted her to feel comfortable coming to Richmond with him; all under a pretense for her demise. If you recall in the postscript of that same letter, he writes to her: *"You told me you were going to marry that fellow this winter. So do."*. This is demonstrative evidence that the prisoner desired to transfer his guilt and disgrace to other shoulders. When this failed to happen, he pursued other, more drastic, measures.

It is incumbent upon the jury to follow all of the evidence; to follow the prisoner's movements throughout Richmond on that fateful day. Mr. Meredith will outline in full detail the movements of the prisoner and the deceased; from their first meeting outside the American Hotel; to their clandestine tour of Belle Isle; to their fatal hours on the tug-horse trolley toward the Old Marshall Reservoir. No distinct piece of evidence or testimony in this case will directly point to the guilt or innocence of the prisoner. But, if viewed in their entirety as a single body of evidence, the finding of guilt shall be rendered an elementary exercise. Thank you, gentlemen."

Colonel Aylett gracefully nodded to the jury and took his seat at the prosecution table. (60.1)

Henry R. Pollard stood to deliver the first closing argument for the defense. He pulled at his lapels and ran his fingers through his hair before gathering his concentration and exhaling.

"Thomas J. Cluverius has led a life of high character and achievement. From the time he was a young boy, this has been evident. He and his brother moved in with Mr. and

Mrs. Samuel Tunstall, their uncle and aunt, in 1874. Shortly after their arrival, their poor uncle passed, leaving a vulnerable wife, Mrs. Jane Tunstall, with no children of her own. But the boys stood by her, helping to nurse their elder through good times and bad; helping her maintain her property. They became her sons. And Thomas, always loyal and caring, looked after her interests and well-being. Of course, Mrs. Tunstall showered the boys with love and attention in return. She sent them to school at Dr. Bland's; then to The Aberdeen Academy, and for Thomas, who was an excellent scholar, the halls of Richmond College. Upon graduating from the college, he began work in the noble profession of the law; of which, I feel authorized to say, he has been an honorable member.

You have heard the evidence that relates to his reputation and to his character in all the relations of life – professional, social, moral, religious, and I undertake to say, gentlemen of the jury, that no young man could have been introduced before you more highly than has been this young man, Thomas J. Cluverius. His panoply of decency protects him against suspicion. It is a suit of armor. His integrity and purity of conduct can only be assailed by indisputable proof. Suffice it to say that there is nothing that exists in the nature of the charge, nor of evidence, to convict. Up until the time of his arrest there is no account nor evidence of any improper intimacy or association with his cousin, Lillie Madison. And never was there a single word uttered detrimental to his character as far as the relations between himself and his cousin existed until after the tragedy at the reservoir on the night of the 13th of March.

You have heard evidence regarding two recent visits of his made to the City of Richmond; the first of these being the visit of January 6th. It is clear from witness testimony that none of the witnesses for the prosecution can claim to have seen the defendant and the deceased together on that day. It is clear that Mr. Cluverius was in Richmond at that time conducting business matters and, as part of his dedicated religious study, attending a gathering held by the famed evangelist, D. L. Moody, which attracted throngs of auditors. Mr. Cluverius also visited with a friend, Mr. Harry Dudley. The single witness who claimed to have identified Miss Madison in Richmond at the time, Mr. Claggett Jones, testified that he had not seen Miss Madison in at least one-and-one-half years prior and had never spoken directly with the young woman. Additionally, Mr. Jones testified that the woman he saw, whom he supposed to be Miss Madison, did not acknowledge him in the slightest. It would make one question how well Claggett Jones actually knew Miss Madison. It is entirely likely that this witness mistook some unknown stranger to be Miss Madison. Other than this confused testimony, we have no evidence indicating that Miss Madison travelled to Richmond in January.

The same must be said for the visit of the 13th of March. At no time has there been any testimony that definitively places Mr. Cluverius and Miss Madison in the company of one another. All testimony that has been given as to their whereabouts has been granted by people who were, up to this time, strangers to both of them. These strangers could easily have misidentified one or both. Not one of the witnesses brought forth by the prosecutors who claimed to have seen a couple resembling Mr. Cluverius and Miss Madison at that time in Richmond had any prior knowledge of either of them. The only witnesses who personally knew Mr. Cluverius and saw him in Richmond in March have been provided by the defense. These were Mr. Emmet Rogers, who travelled by train to Richmond with the accused on March 12th; Mr. Harry Dudley, who hosted the accused for tea the night of March 12th; Mr. Mark Davis, owner of the Davis Hotel, where the accused stayed in both January and March; and Mr. Thomas Bagby, a friend of the accused who saw him March 13th at the 2:30 performance at the Mozart Theater. To a man, none of these witnesses saw Miss Madison in Richmond that weekend, either in the company of the accused or not. Not one person who previously knew either of them have placed them in each other's company on those fateful days. This inability to conclusively place these two together in Richmond on those days leaves ample doubt for the jury.

Here, I will dwell upon the life of Lillie Madison. Here, I tread upon sacred ground. I am going to make reference to the life and character of the woman whose life and whose death has excited my sympathy. If tears of sorrow and condolence are to be dropped and would be received by counsel representing the defense in this case, I would gladly drop it and lay it alongside of the flowers upon her grave. Sad as the task may be, gentlemen, I am not going to attempt to draw that character in my own words. I am going to let her be her own artist, her own biographer, and I am to lift the veil into her life by recalling the letters that have been adduced in evidence in this court. What do these letters disclose? They disclose the fact that the relations between herself and her parents at home were such a character as to drive her to desperation. To her beloved Aunt Jane Tunstall, she communicated that death would be preferable; that she, herself, in moments of solitude and reflection, longed for death and contemplated suicide. It is proof from the lips her of her father that the poor girl was so restless that it became impossible for her to live under the parental roof. It is clear that as soon as she attained her legal majority, she left home; a home which, to her, was cruel and wretched. It may not have been an accurate perception on her part, but certainly existed and demonstrates the sadly confused state of desperation in which she endured the last few years.

Now, let me call your attention to the single undated letter from Lillie to Mrs. Tunstall, in which she alleged abuse of herself and Mrs. Tunstall by her parents. This memorializes her unhappiness and ideas of suicide. The jury has a view of this girl's history from the time she left home and entered the home of her grandfather, Mr. Walker. In October last she then goes to the county of Bath. There is a dreadful secret in her heart, known to her alone. She is deflowered and disgrace is her fate. She is found corresponding in love letters with her cousin, Cary Madison. By the 12th of March, she is fast hastening to maternity. Her parental home is closed to her. Disgrace stares her in the face. The future is full of horror to her. Her adopted home in Bath she cannot hold. What is she to do? She composes a letter to obtain permission from her employer to leave town. The letter was purely fabricated by Miss Madison. Mr. Cluverius, contrary to what the prosecution would have you believe, had no complicity in its composition. It provided Miss Madison an excuse that would not raise suspicion from her employer, Mrs. Dickinson. For the girl was so determined to meet her fate by her own hand, that she did not want anyone to suspect her intent and intervene in the decision she had made. From a rural home to a crowded city she would naturally come for the culmination of her shame. Sadly, she spent her last hours franticly pacing the streets near the reservoir, shedding clothing and casting it aside as the flames of self-destruction burned inside her. Upon breaching the fence which surrounded the reservoir property, she scaled the embankment, perhaps pacing with nervousness and final indecision before mustering the fortitude to throw herself from atop the embankment, tumbling down the stone face, and plunging herself into the watery abyss. The knock received on her head was enough to render her unconscious and bring a silent and still end to what had become a very disturbed and tumultuous existence. Perhaps some of those tracks found atop the embankment were her own. But, for those that appeared larger, these certainly were not; and there is no evidence that they belonged to the accused. Did they belong to the older gentleman who brought her to the American Hotel? He has never been accounted for. Did they belong to another man present at the time of her death? Were they left by another man entirely at some other point earlier in the day? There are many credible answers.

Could a man alone have lifted this poor woman over the fence which encircled the embankment?", Pollard squatted and put his arms in front as if picking up a heavy sack of flour and flung it atop his right shoulder. "That would have required a mighty effort. Now, gentlemen, I ask the question: what motive could possibly have prompted anybody else but Lillian Madison to have taken those gloves off her hands and to have dropped one on the parapet walk and one outside the fence on the Clark Spring property? What could have prompted a man to have gone to the dead-house and to throw therein a hat? Would a murderer have bothered to remove her gloves? Would a murderer have bothered to remove her other articles of clothing and have distributed them around the surrounding properties? This does not stand to reason. It is so unreasonable that only a person in the throes of hysteria, a person devoid of hope, would behave so erratically.

Additionally, why would a murderer have thrown the red shawl across the top of the wall of the Dunstan home? This, I cannot answer." He placed his forefinger over his lips pensively. Then, raising that same forefinger in the air he continued, "But what I can tell you is that there is a distinct possibility that Lillian Madison was familiar with the Dunstan home. You see, the very girl who first identified the body of Miss Madison at the Almshouse, is one Miss Melanie Dunstan. Miss Dunstan lives on Church Hill, far from the scene. But, Miss Dunstan's uncle lives at the property near the reservoir. Miss Dunstan and Miss Madison were well-acquainted. It is indeed possible that Miss Madison knew that this home belonged to her friend's uncle; and that the shawl was left as a farewell token for her friend."

Henry R. Pollard walked closer to the jury. "These occurrences are all a mystery to be solved, gentlemen. However, it does not rest upon the prisoner to solve it. Raising a fist in the air, he shook it rhythmically and concluded, "It does not devolve upon him to tear asunder the dark mantle of midnight and let light in upon that deed of darkness! Thank you, gentlemen of the jury."

Judge T.S. Atkins sat forward and grasped his gavel, "The proceedings will adjourn for the day. In light of the excessive heat, there will be no afternoon session. Final Arguments shall be completed tomorrow. We will begin at 10 o'clock." (60.2)

Chapter 61 *What He Deserves*

Judge T.S. Atkins called the Hustings Court of Richmond to order at 10 o'clock on June 2, 1885. Beverly T. Crump stood and bowed his head as he leaned over the defense table taking a few moments to gather his thoughts and ask his Maker to guide him through this final argument. Thomas J. Cluverius sat calmly with his hands folded in his lap. The courtroom was once again filled to capacity. Public opinion had decidedly turned against the defendant but the crowd still hoped that the respected Crump would mount a stout defense.

"Gentlemen of the jury,", Crump began, "they call these proceedings a trial for a reason. They are not easy. Your efforts are greatly appreciated by this court and indeed, by the prisoner himself. For, it is now your efforts to weigh the testimony upon which his life rests. It is incumbent upon both sides to put forth all of the evidence, in good faith, and to allow the wisdom of the jury to come to a conclusion. As you know, the case against the accused rests entirely upon circumstantial evidence. The prosecution has failed to deliver in several areas. Let us count them."

Holding up a single finger, Crump commenced, "One; the prosecution has failed to prove that a murder was committed. Good Dr. Taylor, through his expert analysis, has concluded himself that the death of Lillian Madison is not inconsistent with suicide. If this fact cannot be unassailably ascertained, then was there even a crime? If it cannot be said for certain that Miss Madison was murdered, then why are we even here? Perhaps she could be prosecuted posthumously for her own death? Or, for the death of her unborn child? When, during the prosecution's case, have they done more than speculate that her death was due to murderous acts? That's the first question you must ask yourself. Was this a murder?

As my colleague, Mr. Pollard, explained yesterday; Miss Madison had been in a very delicate state of mind for many months, if not years. She was pregnant with a child for whom no man would take responsibility. Her prospects for finding a proper husband and father for the child were in jeopardy and would become even more unlikely once the bastard was brought into the world. She spoke of unhappiness and thoughts of suicide in correspondence with her aunt. She even mentioned her hopes for a quick and easy death to the train conductor during her ill-fated trip from Bath to Richmond the night before her demise. The circumstantial evidence pointing to suicide are of equal, if not greater, strength to any evidence of foul play by another.

Two; if we were to assume that Lillian Madison was murdered, an assumption and an assumption only; what evidence connects Mr. Cluverius to the crime? The prosecution has presented a note from the deceased to the prisoner which was discovered in a waste basket at the American Hotel. Please remember this note is **unsigned**. There is a danger in relying on such documents. It was found in the waste basket several days later, torn in pieces. There is no clear evidence that Miss Madison even wrote this note. And, there is no evidence that Mr. Cluverius was at the American Hotel that morning. The defense unequivocally denies that Mr. Cluverius was at the American Hotel the morning of March 13th.

Three; the prosecution has produced several witnesses who claimed to have seen Mr. Cluverius and Miss Madison in various locations throughout Richmond on March 13th. Many of these witnesses were in conflict as to who they did exactly see. Some described him as tall, others say he was of average stature. Some say he had a mustache. Others say he did not. It is not clear that a couple could have made the trip that morning from the American Hotel to the foundry on Belle Isle in the time allotted by the prosecution, particularly in light of the consideration that Miss Madison was in an advanced stage of pregnancy. It is further seen in testimony that the lady purported to be Miss Madison was seen entering the American Hotel the evening of March 13th with an unknown older gentleman. What role could this man have played? What became of him? Was he yet another suitor seeking Miss Madison's attention? This being, if we of course, make the leap and assume that it was indeed Miss Madison at the hotel that evening. This man has yet to be identified and has yet to come forward. Has he something to hide?

The defense contends that the alleged parties, Miss Madison and the accused, were never together either at the American Hotel nor at Belle Isle. In fact, the letter dated March 14, 1885 from Lillian Madison to Jane Tunstall demonstrates quite the opposite. In that letter Miss Madison begs Mrs. Tunstall to tell Tommie that she, Lillian, will write him soon. This indicates that Lillian knew Mrs. Tunstall would see Mr. Cluverius before Lillian would see him again. It should also be noted that this letter is dated March 14, 1885. Logic informs us that Miss Madison wrote this letter sometime *after* midnight on the 13th. Of course, we have testimony from Mr. Davis of the Davis Hotel that Mr. Cluverius returned to his room the evening of the 13th prior to midnight and went directly to his room. Mr. Cluverius would be called in five hours for his return trip home. This suggests that Miss Madison wrote this letter after midnight and posted it that evening. Sometime between that occurrence and the discovery of her body at 7 o'clock the morning of the 14th, it would seem that Miss Madison made her way to the Old Marshall Reservoir where she met her fate most likely by her own hand. If, in the unlikely event, her death were caused by another; it could not have been by the hand of Mr. Cluverius. At the time that Miss Madison met her unfortunate demise, Mr. Cluverius was on the other side of Richmond asleep in his room at the Davis Hotel." Crump stopped and looked directly into the faces of the jurors. Pounding his left palm with his right fist he declared, "Mr. Cluverius *never* saw Miss Madison on March 12th or 13th.

Four; we have the matter of the watch key. You have heard testimony from several people that know Mr. Cluverius quite well that say he never wore a watch key like the one found at the reservoir. Some witnesses claim to have seen a man they believe to have been Mr. Cluverius wearing such a key. This, the defense insists, is insufficient testimony. The prosecution has clearly attempted to construct a fact pattern to fit a crime. But, as I said, if they cannot prove beyond reasonable doubt that the crime with which they charge the prisoner even occurred, then how can there be any faith in their evidence that it was he who ostensibly committed this supposed crime? This is pure fallacy and the jury should reject it as such.

And, of course, the newspapers have engaged in similar fallacious activity. In their fervent desire to sell newspapers, they have embraced the sensational claims of the prosecution and often provided further irresponsible speculation. They have never granted equal weight to the idea that Miss Madison ended her own life even though the medical testimony indicates an equal likelihood. As regrettable and dramatic as such occurrence may be, we all understand that a tragic suicide will never sell as many editions as a salacious murder.

Crump held his hand with all five fingers extended before the jury. "Five; the scratches on the back of the prisoner's hand. The prosecution simply failed to demonstrate that the small scratches seen by several witnesses on Mr. Cluverius' hands at the time of his arrest and following his arrest had any relation to the purported crime with which he has been charged. There is no evidence provided by the prosecution to indicate when he received these wounds. In fact, it is only the defense that has provided the time and the place when Mr. Cluverius was scratched. It was on a wood rail fence when he was collected by his father upon his return from Richmond on March 14th. All other testimony is speculative, especially that of the Doctor Beale. Although he is a medical professional and expert, expert testimony must be carefully considered. Jurors must remember that when an expert is called to testify, it is his nature to tailor circumstances to fit his expertise. Otherwise, he is of no value. A wise jury will remember that and review such testimony with appropriate scrutiny.

The issues of life and death will soon be in your hands. To you, is given to consign that man once more to the enjoyment of existence and the dignity of freedom, or to consign him to an ignominious death and brand upon his grave the awful epithet of a murderer. Gentlemen, mine has been as awful task. To violate the living temple which the Lord hath made, to quench the fire in this man's breast, is an awful and terrible responsibility, and when it is once pronounced, let me remind you, it is irrevocable. Remember that the laws of the Commonwealth do not allow the accused to take the stand in his own defense. As unfair as that may seem, it is the law. Thus, it has fallen upon myself, and the others representing him and testifying upon his behalf, to tell his story. We cannot pretend to convey his story with the eloquence with which he would himself, but we only hope that we have impressed enough upon the jurors to find in his favor. Speak not the words of your verdict lightly. Speak it not upon suspicion, however strong and apparently well-grounded, upon inference, upon doubt, or upon anything but the broad, clear, irresistible, noon-day conviction of the truth of what is alleged.

And now, gentlemen, having travelled through this case of mystery and darkness, my anxious, painful task is ended. But, gentlemen, yours is about to commence. I can only say may Almighty God guide you to a just conclusion. I speak to you in no hostile feeling; I speak to you as a brother and fellow Christian; and thus, remind you of your awful responsibility. I tell you that if you condemn that man lightly, or upon mere suspicion condemn him to an ignoble death, the recollection of the deed will never die within you. If you should pronounce your verdict without a deep conviction of guilt, your crime will be present with you for the rest of your lives. It will pursue with remorse like a shadow in a crowded walkway. It will render your own death-bed one of horror, and taking the form of that man's spirit, it will sink you before the judgment seat of your God. So, beware! I say, beware! Beware what you do!" (61.1)

Beverly Crump backed slowly away from the jury and lowered his head. He turned quietly and took his seat at the defense table. He placed his left hand on T.J. Cluverius' right shoulder and squeezed lightly in reassurance. Cluverius was impressed with his counsel's theatrics, but the cynic who dwelt within him wondered if Crump had perhaps taken it too far.

Charles V. Meredith then stood to make his final address. He straightened his tie as he approached the jury box. He smiled as he clasped his hands together.

"Gentlemen of the jury. The job of a prosecutor is to present the facts and the evidence in an orderly manner under the oversight of a judge and let you, the jury, render a decision. This is a case borne of tragedy; a case injected with a level of interest and sensationalism like none ever seen in our Commonwealth. It has heaped a large amount of attention and undue pressure upon all involved in these proceedings. It has engendered many opinions and an inordinate amount of emotion. All of this has served to distract all of us from the purpose of this proceeding. That purpose is simply to find the truth and to render judgement. I will lay out the facts of this case, based upon the evidence collected and the witness testimony, in a clear and fair manner. The emotions entangled in this case speak for themselves. I will endeavor not to add to that cacophony. I will begin by retracing the movements of Mr. Cluverius and Miss Madison in Richmond on March 13th.

Fannie Lillian Madison registered at the American Hotel early the morning of March 13, 1885. She registered under a false name, F.L. Merton and was given Room 21. At 11 o'clock a messenger brought a note to the hotel for Miss Madison. Henry Hunt, a boy working at the American Hotel, took the note to Room 21. Miss Madison read the note and quickly wrote a response, *I will be there in a minute, so do wait for me.* Hunt gave the return note to the messenger. It was addressed to ***T.J. Cluverius***. The messenger could not find Mr. Cluverius and returned the note to the hotel. It was kept at the front desk and later that day was torn and discarded. Shortly after, Miss Madison left the hotel.

At 11:30 that day, Mr. Martin testified that he saw a man and a woman fitting the descriptions of Thomas Cluverius and Lillie Madison on the footbridge linking the river shoreline to Belle Isle. He heard the woman refer to the man as ***cousin Tommie***. Minutes later several workers on Belle Isle at the Old Dominion Nail Works saw this same couple touring the nail works. They described the woman as short and stout and in a delicate condition. The man wore a hat similar to the one found in the prisoner's home by

Richmond Police officers. He was wearing a gray overcoat. Some of the men indicated he had a mustache.

At 12:00 Mr. Cluverius entered the Planter's Bank and cashed his check for $5.00 with the teller, Mr. Morton. Morton testified that he saw a smaller woman waiting outside the bank for Cluverius, but he could not identify her.

At 1:00, according to witness Clara Anderson, Mr. Cluverius and Miss Madison arrived at Mrs. Goss' house of ill fame on 15th Street. Here they rented a room for a short time. The woman was wearing a blue jersey, and a red shawl. Lillie Madison was wearing a blue jersey when she was discovered in the reservoir. Her red shawl was found on a wall of a nearby property – the Dunstan house. Miss Anderson testified that she also saw them at Mrs. Goss' the previous January.

After 2:30 Mr. Cluverius was seen at the Mozart Theater by Thomas Bagby. They did not speak and Mr. Bagby was not certain Mr. Cluverius saw him.

We have no information nor testimony regarding the movements of Mr. Cluverius nor Miss Madison for the next several hours. The next time they were seen was between 8 o'clock and 8:30 that evening in the lobby of the American Hotel. The night clerk at the hotel testified that the prisoner entered the hotel at that time and asked for the lady in Room 21, which was where Miss Madison was staying – although please recall that she was registered under the name of Merton. He sent up his calling card bearing an alias of his own and was escorted to the parlor. Mr. Cluverius was wearing a gray overcoat and a slouch hat, as he had been described wearing in multiple locations earlier in the day. As has been testified, Miss Madison was not at the hotel at that time. Mr. Cluverius appeared agitated by her absence. This would indicate he had a plan for the evening. A few minutes later Miss Madison appeared in the company of an older gentleman who asked the night clerk to get her a room. He was informed she was already registered, so the older gentleman left. Miss Madison retired to Room 21. At that time Mr. Cluverius returned to the hotel lobby and said once again he would like to see the lady in Room 21. It is apparent that he had seen her return but wished not to confront Miss Madison in the presence of the older man. This time she was brought to him in the parlor where they remained for a short while. Then, the couple left. On the way out of the hotel Mr. Cluverius purchased a stamp and attached it to an envelope. It is believed that this is the letter dated March 14, 1885 from Lillie Madison to Jane Tunstall. It is the prosecution's belief that Miss Madison and Mr. Cluverius composed this letter together in the parlor of the American Hotel in order to cover their romantic tryst. It is the prosecution's belief that this was a carefully conceived layered alibi for the prisoner. Not only would the mention of him in the letter provide deniability of a romantic meeting with Miss Madison at this time; but it would also provide him with an alibi should she meet an unwilling demise in Richmond. Mr. Cluverius was seen carrying a small satchel when they left the hotel.

Mr. Delahanty, driver of a tug horse trolley, testified that he dropped a man and a woman matching the descriptions of Mr. Cluverius and Miss Madison at the trolley turnaround near Monroe Park and the Old Marshall Reservoir at 9:35 that night. The man was wearing a gray overcoat and a slouch hat. He was also carrying a small satchel. Mr. Delahanty testified that he did not see the woman clearly, but she was short and stout.

At 9:40 the prisoner and Dr. Stratton nearly collided while passing on Reservoir Street. The prisoner asked the time and asked which street they were on. Dr. Stratton answered both questions. He said the man was wearing a long overcoat and a slouch hat. He also looked like he had a light mustache. He could not see the woman well. She had a shawl wrapped around her head and was carrying a small bundle or satchel.

After this time, Fannie Lillian Madison was not seen again until her body was discovered the next morning by the workers at the Marshall Reservoir. Mr. Cluverius returned to the Davis Hotel just before midnight on March 13th. Mr. Davis testified that he had a brief conversation with the prisoner. Mr. Cluverius asked to be called at 5 o'clock for his return trip home. Davis noted that Mr. Cluverius was carrying a small brown satchel. This was undoubtedly the satchel belonging to Miss Madison which was later found floating along the river shore below Mayo's Bridge.

It is between these hours of 9:40 and midnight, the evening of March 13th, when the act of murder was committed. The prisoner lured Miss Madison into the grounds of the Old Marshall Reservoir, a property with which he had familiarity since his days at Richmond College. The prisoner guided Miss Madison through a loose plank in the fencing on the Clark Spring side of the property. We have testimony from the prisoner's college friend, Dr. Barker, that this was a well-known access point to the property for college men looking for a swim. It is here, at the top of the embankment on the southern end that an argument and a subsequent struggle took place. We have testimony from a neighbor, Mr. Watkins, that he heard a woman's cries between 10:30 and 11 that night emanating from the reservoir grounds. The foot prints found by Dr. Taylor are consistent with a struggle. It is at this time the prisoner over-powered and rendered the young woman unconscious with a severe blow to the head. He then lifted her over the three-foot picket fence and lowered her body down to the water's edge where he most likely held her head submerged to ensure her demise. In his haste to leave the scene, Mr. Cluverius collected various pieces of Miss Madison's clothing which had fallen off during the struggle including two gloves, a veil, a hat, and her red shawl. Of course, one of the garnet gloves fell silently in the pitch darkness to the ground atop the embankment. He also collected her satchel and, with the armful of items, slithered back through the fence. It is at this point that his watch-key became snagged in the fencing and tore from his chain. As he hastily fled the old reservoir, he dropped a veil and the matching garnet glove in the field on the adjacent Clark Spring property. He passed the dead house on the same property and tossed her hat through an open window. Finally, a half mile down Reservoir Street, out of sheer panic, he tried to discard the last piece of clothing, the red shawl, over the wall of the Dunstan property. He then made his way undetected through the shadows back across Richmond to the Davis Hotel. When he left the hotel at 5 o'clock the following morning, still under cover of darkness, he headed toward the river and threw the satchel and its contents into the rushing waters of the James. It is most likely that he dropped the bag from Mayo's Bridge, as it washed ashore a mile and one half down river at the C&O Wharf, where it was found by Mr. Mountcastle. The prosecution contends that Mr. Cluverius purposely discarded the satchel such a distance from the reservoir as to preclude any connection of it to the body in the reservoir; should that body ever be discovered. You see, Mr. Cluverius surmised that if this body would be found, it would have decomposed to such a state as to render it unidentifiable; and, the contents of her satchel and personal belongings would have long washed far down the river and possibly out to sea.

It is undeniable that both the prisoner and Miss Madison were in Richmond on March 12th and 13th. Miss Madison came under false pretenses. She forged a letter to herself from a friend, Laura Curtis, which she provided to her employer in Bath County to obtain permission to leave for the weekend. Why would it be necessary for her to give Mrs. Dickinson an untrue reason for her absence? Would Mrs. Dickinson have been concerned whether Miss Madison were going to Richmond or, as the letter indicated, to Old Point? The answer is certainly '*no*'. Would it have mattered to Miss Madison if Mrs. Dickinson knew her true destination? Once again, the answer is '*no*'. The only person who needed to hide Miss Madison's presence in Richmond was the prisoner Cluverius. It is he, and he alone, who was compelled to hide her whereabouts. He sought to convince her to do something other than rely upon him for her care and the care of their child. And yes, it was certainly his child. She was in the eighth month. That meant that she became pregnant in July, 1884. We have heard testimony from Mr. Walker that Mr. Cluverius and Miss Madison were both staying in the Walker home on July 10th and again on August 25th. Mr. Cluverius left his room for several hours late at night on at least one occasion, and perhaps both, during those stays. Miss Madison's room was nearby. The opportunity was clearly there for him. We have also heard the testimony of Miss Madison's father, Charles Madison. It is his belief that his daughter and the prisoner had been having relations for quite some time. Letters he found in Lillian's possession two years ago indicated she had already been seduced by the prisoner.

Based upon the letter dated September 14, 1884 from Mr. Cluverius to Miss Madison, it would seem that Mr. Cluverius may have known of her condition at that time. At a minimum he concluded that he had no further use for Miss Madison and strongly suggested that she marry another man.

We have heard testimony that both Mr. Cluverius and Miss Madison met in Richmond on January 5th and 6th. By this time, Lillian certainly knew she was pregnant. If her condition were not known to Cluverius before this time, it would have certainly become clear to him. We have heard Clara Anderson's testimony that the couple spent time at Mrs. Goss' bawdy house during the January visit. A cursory understanding of what transpires in establishments such as that reveals to us all that Mr. Cluverius **must** have become aware of her condition. It is at this point that the prisoner must have been considering the ramifications of these circumstances and what must be done about them. In the midst of his formulation for her demise, the prisoner continued to manipulate Miss Madison; enticing her to return once again to Richmond on March 13th, where he would bring an end to his troubling circumstances.

We have heard testimony from dozens of witnesses placing a man and a woman fitting the descriptions of the prisoner and Miss Madison in various points around Richmond on March 12th and 13th. We know what Miss Madison was wearing while in Richmond. She was found in the Marshall Reservoir wearing her black long skirt and blue jersey. Her gloves, hat, veil, and red shawl were all found nearby. Her satchel was found washing down the James River. Inside were items known to belong to Miss Madison and verified by the testimony of Mrs. Dickinson. The man she was seen with at these varied locations fits the description of Mr. Cluverius. Some have said he wore a light mustache. Others said he did not. Still others could not be sure. But almost to a man, all agreed that he wore a long gray overcoat and a gray slouch hat. Articles of clothing matching these descriptions were located at the home of Mrs. Jane Tunstall, where Mr. Cluverius resides.

    A gold watch-key with a small piece of chain connected to it was found on the Old Marshall Reservoir fence. It was found near a loose plank, known to many in the area for many years as an access point to the grounds of the reservoir. Mr. Cluverius has been known by several witnesses to wear a watch-key such as this on his watch chain. Among those who have identified this watch key, or one very similar to it, as belonging to Mr. Cluverius are: the prisoner's uncle, Mr. John Walker; Judge John Foster, in front of whom the prisoner practiced law; and the jeweler Hermann Joel, who says with some certainty that he did some work on this watch key for the prisoner. Mr. Joel insists that he could unequivocally identify the watch-key as belonging to Mr. Cluverius if he were able to take it apart and examine the markings inside the piece. The court has decided not to allow this step to be taken for fear that it may permanently compromise the integrity of the evidence. The prosecution must accept this view of the court. However, despite this restriction on the presentation of this piece of evidence, based upon the credible testimony of the aforementioned, the prosecution is wholly satisfied that the watch-key in evidence does indeed belong to the prisoner.

    Captain Epps of the Richmond Police led the arrest party to the home of Mrs. Tunstall on March 18th. At this time, Captain Epps has testified that he saw a small piece of chain, with no key on the end, dangling from Mr. Cluverius' watch chain. By the time Mr. Cluverius arrived at the Richmond Jail, the small segment was no longer on the primary chain. When confronted by Captain Epps on this matter, Mr. Cluverius explained that he had removed the small piece of chain and given it to his brother. The prisoner had his brother provide a piece of chain to the police two days later. In the opinion of the arresting officers, this was not the same chain they had seen hanging from the prisoner's watch chain just a few days before. Thus, they searched for the chain in Mrs. Tunstall's home under the authority of a search warrant. The chain was never found. Why would the prisoner have removed this chain if he did not suspect that it may link him to the crime for which he had just been arrested? If the watch-key were an item immaterial to the case, why take such pre-emptive action? The arresting officers made no mention that this key had been discovered at the reservoir during the arrest. How would an innocent man have anticipated that this watch-key, and the chain from which it dangled, were of any interest to the investigation at all?

Gentlemen of the jury, the defense would have you believe that Miss Madison took her own life. They submit, based upon the March 14th dating of the letter from Miss Madison to Mrs. Tunstall, that Miss Madison wrote and posted the letter after midnight on the 13th. It is then that she made her way to the Marshall Reservoir and threw herself asunder. And, witness testimony places Mr. Cluverius at the Davis Hotel before midnight on the 13th, thereby precluding his involvement in her death. But, the defense would have you believe that Miss Madison was in a frantic state; tossing articles of clothing hither and yon. This begs the question, would a woman in this unstable state of mind have the awareness to carefully date her last letter before she was to leave the surly bounds of earth because it was presumably shortly after midnight? The esteemed Dr. Taylor testified that based upon his expert understanding of the dead, Lillian Madison perished between 9pm on March 13th and 1am on March 14th. This would leave little time to post a letter after midnight and still make it to the reservoir in time to end her own life within the hour. This, does not stand to reason. We must also recall that the tug-horse trolley ceases service at 10 o'clock. Thus, Lillian Madison would need to post her letter and, in all likelihood, walk several blocks to a neighborhood we have been told she would not recognize, to a facility no one believes she had ever visited before, climb through an obscure hole in the fence in the dark, scale a large embankment, hurdle a picket fence nearly as high as herself, and catapult herself into the unknown abyss; all while being in her eighth month of pregnancy. Furthermore, if Miss Madison were intending to commit suicide, why would she ask Mrs. Tunstall to tell Mr. Cluverius that she, Miss Madison, would be writing him soon? This was hardly a farewell letter. This, is pure folderol, gentlemen. It is an insult for the defense to think you wise men of the jury would accept this fiction.

To this point, I have recited the facts of the case and put forth where they lead. It is at this time I must ask for your forgiveness in advance; for I must now break a promise I made at the outset of my recitation. I promised that I would not further muddle the discussion with emotional oratory. Alas, this case, this case of the century, requires more than a simple factual discussion! It is here I humbly ask for your indulgence. The defense has deluged us with platitudinal speeches regarding the high character of the prisoner. They have held the prisoner aloft as a paragon of good works with an unyielding devotion to his family, to his profession, and to his God. Yea, the prosecution does not argue that the prisoner has hung a righteous visage upon his public character. Lo, it is what a man does in private which measures the true depth of his character. It would appear the prisoner is a man who will take from any woman what she has to offer; or perhaps more precisely, he will take from her what he wants. Whether his victim is the sad girl trapped in a life of depravity at a bawdy house, or a member of his own family, it is his own needs which must be satiated. You have heard testimony of his debauchery and lustfulness dating back to his days at Richmond College. These women were there to serve his dark needs and he availed himself of their lascivious attention on many, many, occasions. But even this deviant behavior was not reserved for strange women who would engage in such acts to make a living. But, this man would even pervert the mind of his own cousin; not for any natural love, but for one utterly unnatural. He so poisoned the flower known as Lillie that she relented to his villainous charm and accepted a state of sin in order to maintain his attention; attention she mistook for love. In reality, it is the basest form of contempt he had for her. A man who would treat his own cousin in this manner; lead her astray and continue to feed her sinfulness; a man who would deem to send her such a vile composition as *On the Delaware*; a man who would give her a child and then refuse all responsibility; such a man deserves no quarter! Even the women in his life whom he did not treat in such a physically demeaning manner; even these women were in his life to serve his purposes. They, too, are debased. Whether it was the financial support his aunt, Mrs. Jane Tunstall, which she continues to provide to this very day; or the elevated social status Miss Nolie Bray could provide for his burgeoning legal career; *he takes what he wants*.

Now, gentlemen, as you prepare to deliberate and determine the fate of this man, I ask that you carefully consider all of the facts brought before this court and that he no longer *takes what he wants*, but rather that *he gets what he deserves*. The jury must find Thomas J. Cluverius guilty of murder in the first degree!"

Charles Meredith nodded with respect to the jury and then turned nodded to Judge Atkins with equal reverence. The awestruck courtroom seemed to freeze in time for a few moments. In the back of the courtroom an old woman raised her hands in front of her face and slowly brought them together. She brought her hands together again… and again, with accelerating rhythm. Annabelle Lumpkin's eyes blazed and she smiled gleefully while dozens of onlookers turned in her direction. Then, a few at a time, more and more joined in until the entire courtroom was in full applause. Charles Meredith sat quietly in his chair as the thunderous clamor shook the room. Judge Atkins started banging his gavel forcibly. After ten seconds the noise had finally subsided enough to a level where his persistent pounding was finally becoming audible. A few more seconds passed until his voice, too, was finally able to pierce the curtain of sound which had descended upon the room, "Order! Quiet in the court! Quiet, I say!" Finally, the crowd complied. Judge Atkins turned to the jury with exasperation, "Gentlemen, it is time to deliberate. Please choose a foreman to lead your discussions. Please take whatever time is necessary. When a verdict has been reached, please inform the bailiff and we will re-adjourn within thirty minutes of your decision." (61.2)

Chapter 62   *Step Forward, Mr. Cluverius*

The jurors in the trial of Thomas J. Cluverius filed into the jury room and sat around a long table with twelve chairs. Carter Harrison seated himself at the head of the table. "Gentlemen, I propose we first decide upon a foreman. Are there any nominations?", he asked as he looked at Mr. Henry Keppler.

Keppler cleared his throat, "Oh, um, yes... I nominate Mr. Harrison of Richmond."

"Thank you, Mr. Keppler. I accept. Will there be any others?"

"I nominate William Trice of Richmond.", announced John Heath.

Carter Harrison looked mildly annoyed as he asked again, "Any other nominations?"

After a moment of silence, William Berkeley spoke up, "Francis Howell."

Howell snapped his head in the direction of Berkeley in surprise. Carter Harrison asked once more for nominations. No further names were put forth. William Berkeley spoke again, "How shall we conduct this election? I propose a simple vote and a simple majority."

Carter Harrison quickly responded, "No, no, sir... That will not suffice. Since there are three nominees, I propose that we hold a vote. The top two finishers will then be voted on again. Unless, of course, one of the candidates receives more than six votes; there would be no need for additional votes; that man would be the foreman.", Harrison smiled with confidence. After a moment he continued, "Are we agreed, gentlemen?" All twelve agreed upon the process.

A hat was passed around the table and each man placed a piece of paper in the hat with the name of one of the candidates. Harrison took the hat last and dropped his slip of paper in. He then held the hat out and invited Keppler to pull the slips and read the names. Francis Howell received the votes of all six jurors from Alexandria; Carter Harrison received four votes; and, Mr. Trice received two votes.

"Very well, gentlemen; we will vote again on Mr. Howell and myself.", declared Harrison, his smile now erased. Henry Keppler once again tallied the vote. "Mr. Howell received eight votes. Mr. Harrison, four." Carter Harrison gritted his teeth. His open right hand turned into a fist.

"Mr. Howell should take the seat at the head of the table.", William Berkeley suggested. Howell stood and quietly walked around the table. The taller Harrison stood and looked down at the new foreman, "Congratulations, Mr. Howell.", he grudgingly uttered as he turned away and took Howell's vacated chair.

"Well... perhaps the first thing to do is to take an initial vote.", Francis Howell began. "Unless, any of you see a reason to do otherwise." Howell scanned the others and saw no objection. "Very well; we will simply go around the table. Please indicate your finding. Mr. Berkeley, I ask that you tally the vote." Howell turned to the first man on his left, Mr. Finch.

"Guilty.", Finch declared. Howell turned his head to the next man.

"Guilty.", Mr. Sherwood echoed; as did the next three jurors. At the opposite end of the table was Carter Harrison.

"*Not* guilty.", Harrison stated with self-assurance.

The next five men all expressed a finding of "Guilty". Francis Howell was the last to vote. He joined with the majority in a "Guilty" finding. "It appears we do not have the necessary unanimity to convict. Mr. Harrison, would you like to discuss the case in any way? Is there anything that could convince you to come into agreement with the rest of the jury?"

"Most assuredly, not.", Harrison replied dismissively.

"Very well, let us send our report to the judge in that form. You are willing to take the responsibility of your opinion, Mr. Harrison, I suppose; and we are no less so."

Harrison swallowed and cleared his throat as eleven sets of eyes trained intently upon him. "If a single man hangs this jury, will the rest agree to keep his name secret?"

"No, sir; we cannot make that assurance.", Howell began to rise from his seat. "Let us report to the judge."

"Hold on!", Harrison interjected, "Let us think about this!"

"We have thought for five weeks, Mr. Harrison,", said Howell turning up the pressure. "And, *we* know our proper verdict as well as *you* do."

Harrison deflated in his chair, "Well, perhaps you do..."   (62.1)

A squad of twelve officers from the Richmond Police pushed through the large crowd gathered outside the Hustings Court and entered the courthouse. The sea of curious onlookers parted in the hallway as the officers, with nightsticks drawn, ordered the crowd to make room for their passage. Two rows of six officers smartly descended the center aisle of the courtroom until reaching the rail which bisected the room behind the prosecution and defense tables. One line turned to its left and the other two the right until the tail ends met and formed a single line of dark blue behind the tables. Thomas J. Cluverius and his attorneys quietly emerged from a small ante-room in the back, left corner of the courtroom. They briskly made their way down the left side aisle of the courtroom and seated themselves at the defense table. Charles Meredith and Col. Aylett walked down the center aisle and stood behind the prosecution table.

City Sergeant See, the head bailiff, entered the room from a doorway behind the bench. "All rise.", he announced as Judge Atkins entered from his chambers and stood behind the bench. Atkins then nodded in See's direction. The sergeant stepped over and opened the door leading to the jury room. The twelve jurors emerged and took their seats. Francis Howell assumed, for the first time throughout the proceedings, the seat in the front right of the jury box. As the jury was seated, nearly every muscle stilled in every person in the courtroom, save the hundreds of eyes which dashed about with a quantum randomness; bouncing from the accused, to the judge, to the prosecution, to the jury; until Atkins banged his gavel. "Gentlemen of the jury, have you reached a verdict?"

Francis Howell stood and cleared his throat, "We have, your honor."

"The accused will rise.", the judge ordered. Thomas J. Cluverius stood and stared straight ahead, seemingly void of emotion and concern. The glare of the courtroom trained upon him once again to no distinguishable effect. The judge continued, "Gentlemen of the jury, what say you; is the prisoner guilty or not guilty of the felony charged in the indictment."

Without hesitation Foreman Howell responded, "Guilty." Howell then handed a note to Sergeant See who transferred it to Judge Atkins.

Judge T.S. Atkins read the note aloud, "We the jury, find Thomas Judson Cluverius guilty of the murder of Fannie Lillian Madison in the first degree, as charged in the indictment."

Although the verdict was as expected, the reaction of the crowded courtroom was unexpectedly muted. The weight of the finding had suddenly set in amongst the citizenry as the circus atmosphere which had surrounded much of the proceedings became a tragic reality.

"Does the defense have any further motion?", Judge Atkins asked.

Beverly Crump humbly replied, "We respectfully request that the court adjourn until tomorrow, so that we might have time to consider a course of action."

"Granted", said the judge. "Court adjourned until tomorrow at 10 o'clock." With the judges gavel the courtroom erupted with the hum of conversation. (62.2)

Thomas Cluverius defiantly squared his jaw and stood. Four policemen surrounded him and escorted him up the left side aisle of the courtroom toward the small ante-room. The group moved as one as they hastily passed through the ante room and through another doorway. They scurried down a short hallway leading to a side exit onto a narrow alley. The prisoner was quickly shuttled into a black covered carriage. The driver cracked his reins and carriage accelerated forward. Cluverius was relieved that he had managed to avoid the crush of the mob as the carriage turned sharply onto Broad Street. A few blocks east the carriage turned south on 14th Street as it had done every day of the trial. At the intersection with Main Street, the carriage came unexpectedly to a full halt as a funeral procession passed. A simple infant's casket, resting atop a small flatbed hearse with a single driver, moved slowly through the intersection. A lone woman veiled in black walked forlornly behind the casket. Cluverius tilted his head toward the carriage window to see the pathetic figure as she approached holding a bouquet of bright white flowers. She raised and turned her head toward him. Cluverius gasped and turned away from the figure of Lillie Madison. He immediately turned back and squinted; mystified to see prosecutor Charles Meredith stepping down from the hearse driver's seat. Meredith lifted the casket lid open and beckoned Cluverius to come look. Cluverius lowered his head and closed his eyes. He was compelled to open them and look once more in the direction of Lillie. Her flowers wilted, draping limply down over her clenched fists. Cluverius' eyes shot upward as Lillie's face transformed into Rachel McDonald's. His mouth opened as he held a hand forward trying desperately to call a stop to the nightmare. Once again, Charles Meredith motioned him to come see the inside of the tiny casket lined with blood-red silk. Cluverius refused, covering his eyes with his arm. A woman's sobbing echoed, obliging him to look again. Rachel had put her head down and had buried her face in the stiffly browned bouquet. She slowly raised her head revealing a third disturbing transformation. Aunt Jane Tunstall stood in Rachel's place. Tears poured down both cheeks as she silently implored him to explain himself. Meredith persistently called a third time for Cluverius to approach. The casket had now grown to a full size. Cluverius vehemently shook his head in defiance of the call. He leaned out of the window and ordered his own driver to start the carriage. The driver was a portly older man with a white mustache and beard. Cluverius had never seen him before but still felt an odd familiarity with the man. "Driver, please move forward! You are the only one who can rescue me from this!", he begged.

The driver simply shook his head and lifted his chin in the direction of the casket. "You must face this alone. I will not help you." Cluverius did not fully comprehend but, for some reason, felt he must do exactly as the driver instructed. Cluverius stepped from the carriage and began a trepid approach toward the casket. He looked up to the hearse driver who had inexplicably morphed into a police sergeant. The smiling sergeant invited him to step up on the hearse's running board to look inside. Cluverius braced himself on the side of the casket, finally mustering the courage to pull himself up and peer inside.

"Step forward, Mr. Cluverius… We have prepared this is for you.", the policeman solicited with macabre warmth.

Thomas Cluverius gasped for air and suddenly sat up in his cot. His head and neck were soaked in sweat. He sat on the edge of the cot and looked at his dank surroundings.

The prisoner chuckled lightly with relief as he thought to himself how amenable these accommodations felt compared to the inside of that casket. Cluverius turned his head as he heard the jingling of keys at his cell door.

"You have twenty minutes, Mr. Cluverius.", the guard said.

"Willie!", Tommie exclaimed as he rose to greet his brother.

Willie was surprised to find his brother in good humor. "Tommie, are you alright?"

"Well, I've certainly been better, brother. However, we will appeal the decision. Crump and Pollard are preparing the motion." Tommie put his hand on his brother's shoulder and guided him away from the door. "What happened to Mr. Harrison?", he whispered.

"I do not know, Tommie. I have yet to speak with him; but I will."

"You haven't paid him anything, have you?"

"Not one cent.", Willie replied.

"Good... He is a disappointment... I could see the weakness in him as he sat with the jury. And, you say he boasts too much; a sure sign of frailty. That said, he can still be of use. You must speak to him. Offer to pay him to go to the newspapers and recant his vote. We must do whatever we can to discredit the process. It could result in a mistrial. At a minimum, it would aid public opinion."

Willie looked down and shook his head, "I don't know..."

"Willie! You cannot give up now! I need you now as much as ever! This is not the end!" Tommie grabbed hold of both his brother's shoulders and looked him in the eye. "This is **not** the end." (62.3)

The Daily Index-Appeal
Petersburg, VA
June 19, 1885

Cluverius Sentenced – Judge Atkins' Solemn Address

Today Cluverius was brought up from jail as usual. The deferred motion for the arrest of judgment in his case was to be considered. That is, counsel for the defense has been trying hard to stave off the death sentence and had succeeded in doing so up to today. Beverly Crump and A. Brown Evans were in court as counsel for Cluverius. Mr. Pollard was absent. A large crowd gathered about the hustings courtroom and awaited the decision of the court, and when it was known that Judge Atkins had overruled the motion for arrest of judgment the feeling evidenced outside was one of satisfaction.

Cluverius now goes into solitary confinement and the horizon of his hope is narrowing to a small sphere. There are those who pity him, but it is a fact, that fewer people doubt as to the righteousness of the verdict than have ever been known in any case of similar character.

A carriage wheeled away from the City Jail this morning at ten minutes past ten, and in five minutes afterwards it stopped at the little alley-way that leads from Tenth Street into the City Hall. A hand touched the handle. The carriage door flew open and Deputy Sargeants Lovenstein and Allen, who had in their custody Thomas J, Cluverius, the convicted murderer of the poor unfortunate Lillian Madison, stepped out upon the pavement and hurriedly walked into the courtroom.

As soon as the carriage reached the top of Broad Street hill, coming up from the jail, a dozen voices in the crowd near the courthouse simultaneously exclaimed, "There they come!" These persons crowded around the carriage when it stopped at the little alley, and there was intense desire expressed by each individual to get a look at Cluverius. Each man and woman in the crowd eyed the prisoner as closely as possible, and he in turn glanced first to the right and then to the left, neither bowing nor speaking to a single individual. The courtroom was soon reached, and in he walked, with a quick and steady step to his accustomed seat inside the bar. For a while he sat alone but soon Mr. Evans, one of his counsel, walked in and took a seat next to him. The usual handshaking followed and afterwards the two engaged in a low conversation regarding the case. There was no change in the prisoner's appearance. He bore the same stern look which has attracted the attention and evoked wonderment of so many persons who have closely noticed him during the long and tedious hours of his trial. His eyes wandered around the courtroom, and he glanced first at one person and then another. His left elbow rested upon the arm of his chair, and his clear-cut chin hid itself in the palm of a soft, white hand, while his finger stroked a clean-shaven lip. Close to him were lawyers, reporters, preachers, and policemen; and beyond the railing a cosmopolitan crowd leaned forward to get a glance at the celebrated criminal. The judge ascended the bench and the sergeant cried out, "Order on the court. No man in that crowd must say a word."

Order was restored. The almost inaudible whisperings of the crowd were heard, but they did not amount to confusion and the sergeant was not again called upon to command silence, until a moment or two before the adjournment of court.

Beverly Crump, the prisoner's senior counsel, asked a further continuation of the motion for arrest of judgment until tomorrow. Mr. Charles Meredith of the prosecution objected because he did not see wherein the prisoner could be benefited. Mr. Evans followed Mr. Meredith, and in the course of his remarks said that if the bills of exceptions are not ready to be signed tomorrow, the court could not proceed to pronounce the sentence. Judge Atkins agreed with Mr. Meredith.

A deep silence followed the decision of the court, and after this pause, Clerk William P. Lawton said, "Thomas J. Cluverius, stand up. You have been indicted, tried and now stand convicted of murder in the first degree. Have you anything to say why the court should not now proceed to pronounce sentence of death upon you, according to law?"

The prisoner arose and leaned lightly against the railing in front of the bar. Every ear in the courtroom turned to catch whatever he might say. Some expected that he would speak out and tell what he knows about the murder of his cousin, Lillian. At first he hesitated, and seemed a little confused. His face flushed a little, and contortions of the facial muscles, lasting only a moment, were perceptible to those who sat within several feet of him. In a clear voice not loud enough to be heard all over the court, Cluverius said, "I will say, sir, that you are pronouncing sentence on an innocent man. That is all I have to say, sir."

He did not call Lillian's name or have one word to say about his relationship with her. The diary of that day on which Lillian was murdered was not read by the prisoner. He advanced no theory, nor did he attempt to account for those "fatal hours", as Col. Aylett called them, between 8 and 12 o'clock.

"Thomas J. Cluverius," said Judge Atkins, "you have been indicted for the willful, deliberate, and premeditated murder of Fannie Lillian Madison, your companion and cousin, whom you had, betraying her confidence, treacherously seduced. Twelve of your fellow-men, selected for their intelligence and impartiality, have patiently and attentively listened to the evidence in this case. Witness after witness has been examined, and day after day consumed in an endeavor to find the truth, the whole truth, and nothing but the truth of this charge. Exceedingly able counsel has done all that learning, eloquence, skill, and experience could accomplish in your behalf; you have had a fair, and I may say, a liberal, trial. And, finally the jury, in faithful discharge of their duty, has pronounced you guilty, and that verdict has been approved by the court.

I shall not harrow your feelings by referring at length to the enormity of your crime, every step in the perpetration of which must be deeply engraved upon your memory. To a man of your intelligence no good could be accomplished by doing so. I commend you to the suggestions of your own better thoughts. Nor is it necessary to comment upon it in the interest of society; the public press fully inculcates upon the people the lessons to be drawn from such events.

I do not deem it my duty, therefore, to do more than to pronounce upon you the sentence which the law affixes to the crime of murder of which you stand convicted; which sentence is, that you, Thomas J. Cluverius, shall be taken hence to the jail of this city, and there securely kept until the 20th day of November next on which day, between the hours of 9 in the morning and 6 in the evening, you shall be taken to some convenient place of execution at or near said jail, and in the presence only of such officers of the law as may be necessary to see that this sentence is properly carried into effect, be there hanged by the neck until you are dead. And may God, of His infinite goodness, have mercy on your soul."

The prisoner looked Judge Atkins squarely in the face. His eyes sparkled, his lips were firmly pressed together, and that strange and peculiar smile, which has often played over his face and lit up his countenance in some of the darkest hours of his trial, had gone from him. He stood there pale, but not nervous nor excited. His calmness and his self-control did not forsake him, but he listened to the sentence with a calmness and an imperturbability no less interesting than striking. Every eye in the courtroom was upon *him, and he knew it. Men and youths with bated breath caught the words of the death sentence as they tremulously fell from the lips of the court. Silence, solemn silence, reigned even in the crowds around the windows and at the doors of the courtroom while the fate of the prisoner was being announced.*

Soon after the sentence was pronounced the court adjourned, and the condemned man was taken back to jail and placed in solitary confinement in the murderer's cell. An effort will be made by counsel for the defense to get a new trial through the supreme court, which meets in Richmond the 5th of November. Should the court refuse Cluverius a new trial, the condemned man's only recourse would be an appeal to the new Governor of Virginia. Whomever that may be shall be determined on November 3rd. (62.4)

Chapter 63   *Give Them Their Waterloo*

Fitzhugh Lee sat quietly on his front porch smoking one of his favored cigars. The afternoon summer sun was beating down on *Evergreen*. Fitz rocked easily in shirtsleeves as he puffed away, relieved to be resting in the shade. Sons Fitz, Jr. and George tied their ponies up in the yard and lay their wooden cutlasses on the grass. The boys sighed and wiped their sweaty brows as they staggered through the heat up onto the porch.

"Which battle did you fight today?", asked the elder Fitz.

"Crooked Creek.", answered Fitz, Jr.

"Ah... Comanches... It's definitely as hot as Texas today!", Fitz exclaimed.

"Papa, I was you, of course", said the proud ten-year old. "George was that dastardly Comanche you killed!"

"I assure you both, that Comanche nearly killed me, as well. It was a very dear situation.", said the elder Fitz, wanting to keep the record straight. "You understand, I was face to face with that Comanche, barely ten paces apart. He fired his arrow at the same moment I fired my pistol. Each of us hit the mark, only I aimed between his eyes and he aimed at my chest. His arrow went clean through me! Feathers were sticking out of my chest and an arrow head poked out my back. If not for the good army surgeon, that savage would not have been the only one dead!"

Fitz, Jr.'s eyes widened. He lifted his forefinger, cocked his thumb, and aimed at George. Once again, he re-enacted the deadly exchange, "Bang!"

George began to well with tears of guilt, "But Papa, I did not know that... I would never try to kill you - Fitz made me be the Indian!" Fitz, Jr. rolled his eyes at his baby brother.

"George... George... shh...", said Papa as he pulled the seven-year old closer. "There is no shame in playing the role of the Comanche. They were very brave and the finest horsemen I ever saw. They were a bit filthy in their habits, but quite admirable foes. It's alright, George. I understand it is all a game, and you should, as well. In a few short years you shall have ol' Sydney to play the fearless Comanche to your undaunted Lieutenant Lee!" (63.1)

George sniffled and wiped his nose on his shirt sleeve. He felt better. "Now boys, go on to the parlor. I'm sure there's a fresh pitcher of lemonade in there." The boys bolted through the doorway and down the hall.

Fitz Lee smiled as he sat back in his porch rocker and got reacquainted with his cigar. After a few minutes of quiet, he saw a man on a horse coming up the long front driveway to *Evergreen*.

Fitz stood as the rider approached and dismounted. The young man bowed his head.

"General Lee?"

"Yes sir."

"I have a special delivery for you from the telegraph office."

Fitz Lee extended his hand and the young man placed an envelope in it. Lee reached in his pocket and handed the deliveryman a quarter dollar.

"Thank you, General. Thank you!" The man tipped his hat and mounted his horse. Fitz turned and sat back down. Fitz carefully opened the envelope and removed the telegraph transcription.

July 25, 1885
Hudson, NY

Dear General Lee,

It is with a remorseful heart that the I inform you of the death of my husband, President Ulysses S. Grant, on July 23, 1885. Our family wishes to extend an invitation to you to attend his funeral ceremonies on August 8, 1885 in New York City. It is with utmost respect that my family makes this request. You and your honorable family represent his most worthy adversaries during the War. Though those were terrible times which almost put our nation asunder, it was a defining period of his worthy life and certainly brought forth his greatest qualities, as it did your own. We would be honored if you would accept this invitation and it is my personal belief that your presence will further the cause of reunification for which he fought many years and which you embody today.

Sincerely,
Mrs. Julia D. Grant

Fitz Lee repaired immediately to his study where he crafted an acceptance of the invitation. Though his schedule over the coming weeks would potentially be very full, he could think of no more important activity than the opportunity to represent his family, his people, and his state at General Grant's funeral.

July 27, 1885

Dear Mrs. Grant,

It is with deep sympathy that I learn of the President's death. I assure you that although we were once mortal foes, my feelings have softened greatly as the years have passed - I believe his did, as well. You are correct in stating that the goal of this country's reunification ultimately brought us together. It is my solemn intent to carry forth his noble desire for this country's complete reconciliation.

It would be my distinct honor to attend the services and I pray that I may be worthy of shouldering the mantel you place upon me.

If there is any other service my family or I may provide in your time of sadness and remembrance, all you need do is ask.

With Deepest Respect,

Fitzhugh Lee   (63.2)

At noon on July 29, 1885, The Honorable John S. Barbour, Chairman of the State Democrat Party of Virginia, slowly walked on the stage of the Richmond Opera House and called the Democratic State Convention to order. After a warm applause had subsided, Barbour began:

"For the first time since 1856, the Democrats of the nation have elected their President!"

The crowd erupted in loud cheers and applause.

"And, the Executive Departments at Washington are filled with the men of their choice. The power of the Federal Government will be no longer administered for the oppression of our people; and our rights and liberties will now receive that protection and recognition to which we are entitled under The Constitution and the laws of the land!"

Barbour paused and stepped back from the edge of the stage and coughed lightly into his hand as the crowd applauded profusely. He then stepped forward again as the crowd noise subsided.

"Not only do we realize the operation of these important facts, but there is every reason to indicate that the advent of the National Democratic Party to power will be continuous and permanent. The Democrats have control and possession of the government; and have come to stay! The wise and prudent man who now directs the operations of the government will, in my judgment, meet all the requirements of his

position; and give full and just satisfaction in the discharge of his high office. He will give us honest government, reduce expenditures, and lighten the burdens of taxation. In a word, he will restore government of our fathers!

There is nothing about the nominations of the other side to cause alarm. We know well who these Republican Mahone Men are and what they are worth. With all the odds against us we beat them in 1883; repeated our victory in 1884; and with the charged conditions which now exist in our favor, we must win! Fully as I am impressed with these views of our prospects for success, it would be unwise to underrate the strength of the enemy or shut our eyes to the fact that a campaign of unusual vigor and bitterness will be inaugurated on his part. The violent denunciation and inflammatory appeals to the lowest passions of their followers permeate nearly every paragraph of that remarkable paper put forth as their platform.

That we can defeat them, there is no doubt; but it will require wisdom and labor. They have selected their own battleground. They will make the campaign in Southwest Virginia. They have thrown down the gauntlet; we have picked it up. Our clans are marshalling for conflict. Our beacon-fires are burning from the tops of the mountains; our bugles sound from the valleys. We are eager for the battle of ballots. The contest is nearing. Let it come! In 1884 we gave the enemy their Trafalgar; and in this good year of 1885, we will give them their Waterloo!

This morning we confirmed a new President of our Organization Committee. Let us welcome to the stage this new president; Mr. Henry R. Pollard of King and Queen County."

H. R. Pollard proudly walked on to the stage. He energetically shook Barbour's hand and turned to the hundreds of loyal party men in the crowd. Although his defense of Thomas J. Cluverius had ended unsuccessfully, the Democrat Party had taken note of his strong performance in the spotlight. This, combined with his youth, made him an attractive candidate for promotion within the party.

"Gentlemen of the Convention; it is my distinct honor to be named President of the Organization Committee. I will embrace its duties with the utmost sincerity and commitment. As you know, the Republicans held their convention in this very building a mere two weeks ago. Boss Mahone has chosen Mr. Wise to run for Governor and Mr. Blair for Attorney General. The railing, the ranting, and the whining of the apostates who lately filled these halls are as powerless to dim the lustre of Virginia's fair name as they will be to deceive the people. If they are representatives, then Virginia has lost pre-eminence. We are here to equip ourselves with leaders worthy to bear our standards to victory on the third of November. The contest is to be one of momentous importance; the lines are to be drawn sharply against the malign Mahoneism; an influence that advocates hate instead of peace; that has sought in the halls and committee rooms of Congress to blast the good names and blot the pages of history with foul libels against our people; seeking by lying artifice to secure from Northern Republicans sympathy and soap, with which to debase the ballot. The lines are drawn against corruption in high places, against participation in politics by judges, against partisan decisions by the courts, against oath-bound legislators, and last, but not least, against the interference of federal judges in the levy and collection of revenues of this Commonwealth. The apostles of hate and sectional strife; the Mahones, the Wise's and the Blairs, are to be relegated to private life!" (63.3)

After a rousing cheer, Chairman Pollard announced, "We will now open the floor for nominations for the Office of Governor!"

On August 6, 1885, Fitz Lee returned from his morning ride and entered the familiar surroundings of his office at *Evergreen*. His morning newspapers were stacked neatly on his desk. "Good! For once, I shall know the day's news before Ellen!", he thought to himself. The first paper he picked up was the August 4th edition of *The Boston Weekly Globe*. With some reservation, he gritted his teeth and scanned the headlines until a bold one caught his eye.

GENERAL FITZHUGH LEE – Nominated for Governor of Virginia – A Black Eye for Senator Mahone

Richmond, Va, July 29 - The nomination of Fitzhugh Lee gives great satisfaction. Lee, whilst not an eloquent orator, is a graceful speaker, and his record is irreproachable. He cannot be bulldozed by Wise, Mahone's candidate for the same place. General Lee will take the stump and surround himself with the most enthusiastic following of any candidate Virginia ever had. He is popular all over the State. His popularity was shown by the strength he developed in the convention, when he was nominated on the first ballot against all other candidates in nomination. Of all other candidates that could have been nominated the Mahoneites feared Lee the most. Tomorrow the convention will select for Attorney General and Lieutenant Governor. The convention will adopt a platform which will arraign Mahone for the many frauds committed by his party. It will show the hollowness of the claim that the Democrats are responsible for the election frauds charged against them. (63.4)

Fitz Lee grinned with self-satisfaction. He was a bit surprised that any publication above the Mason Dixon Line, much less one in Boston, would look so favorably upon his candidacy.
Fitz dug further through the stack and discovered *The National Republican*, which was published in Washington, D.C. "Hmmm… This could be of interest.", he dead-panned to himself.

JOHN S. WISE FOR GOVERNOR OF VIRGINIA – Democrats Run a Rebel

Washington, D.C., August 5 - There are two classes of men in the South who took part in the effort to destroy the Union and set up a Southern Confederacy. Those of one class accepted the issues of the war as settled and have since formed political affinities according to their ideas of tariff, reform, temperance, progression, and questions of State polity. They have not accepted terms at the hands of the Republican Party, and then sought to repudiate their bargains, and make hatred of the Republican Party the impelling motive of their political lives. They fought honestly and bravely for an idea. They submitted the question to the arbitration of the sword, and they abide by its decision. They accepted the terms that slavery should be abolished, that the freedmen should have civil rights, and that they should have a free ballot. In a few words, they have accepted the situation and transferred their allegiance and good will from the Confederacy to the United States Government. Of this class are General Longstreet, General Mosby, General Mahone, and John S. Wise, the Republican Nominee for Governor of Virginia. These men, it is true, were hard fighters for the rebel cause. But we honor their bravery while we condemn their cause. Had they come dragging the putrid corpse of secession and States' Rights back with them into the Union, they would deserve no more consideration from lovers of the Union than they did while they were fighting against it. We have no feeling of disrespect or hate for any man because he fought for the South, unless he carries some part of the Confederacy's carcass as a souvenir about his clothes. We do not think Mr. Wise is unworthy of Republican support because he was a rebel soldier. If we were in Virginia, we would give him our hearty support.

  The Democrat Party places rebels in office that have not accepted the situation and who are still loyal to the lost cause; or refuse to carry out, in good faith, the terms of surrender. They refuse to give the black man his rights and they cheat him out of the ballot. They love the lost cause still, and exalt it above the Union. They vote the Democratic ticket because they know that Democratic success will enable them to honor the lost cause. They hate the Republican Party because it conquered and destroyed their Confederacy. They do not differ from the Republican Party on tariff, or temperance, or civil service, or honest money; but simply on questions at issue during the war and created by the war. They overlook all issues and rally around the Confederate flag, as it were. They hold their noses when they pass the American flag, but carry the rotten carcass of the Confederacy wrapped near their hearts. Of this class are Jeff Davis, Lucius Lamar, and Fitzhugh Lee, the Democratic candidate for Governor of Virginia, who, on a recent visit with a company of Confederate soldiers to the North, boasted that they had no American flag and never had one; but wore, each man on his breast a miniature rebel flag, under the lapel of his coat.

  There is a vast difference between a rebel soldier who has honestly surrendered and one who is daily violating his parole; and only willful partisan blindness can keep anyone from seeing it. (63.5)

  Fitzhugh Lee's heart sank. He knew the characterization was inaccurate and unfair; but it stung nonetheless. He resolved that he would continue the work of reunification he had started many years before. His time as a gubernatorial candidate would emphasize his own and his state's desire to wholly rejoin the Union and patiently allow earnest deeds to overcome heated rhetoric. There would always be detractors, particularly Northern detractors. Fitz wondered if, at times, it was actually these unforgiving Northerners who sought to continue the conflict. His goal was to minimize the detractors; but never at the expense of the proud citizens of Virginia.

Chapter 64   *Appomattox to New York*

By April 8, 1865 Union forces under General Ulysses S. Grant had overrun Petersburg and were continuing their dogged pursuit of Lee's Army of Northern Virginia to Farmville. The Confederate Army was secreting a horrific trail of flesh and blood as it parlously crawled westward. Man, mule, and horse fell prey to the ungodly torture of starvation, sleeplessness, and misery. The roads were choked with Confederate supply wagons, purposely set ablaze to deprive the ubiquitous Federal Army of every possible trophy. Shells and ammunition repeatedly exploded as the flames touched them, expectorating large billows of black smoke toward the heavens; scripting the obituary of a nation. General Robert E. Lee ordered his troops to cross the Appomattox River and destroy all the bridges in their wake in a desperate attempt to place time and distance between the exhausted and depleted Confederate forces and the ever-emboldened Federal Army. By late that afternoon the harried Confederates had failed to carry out the bridge demolitions but continued a hasty retreat west toward Appomattox Court House. Defeat was a certainty; the only decisions which remained were where, when, and how to accept it.

Major General Fitzhugh Lee entered his commanding general's simple field tent just before sundown. He had been riding with his force of 2,400 cavalrymen since dawn; continuing to duel with his familiar foe, General Philip Sheridan. Fitz pushed aside the tent flap and saw dear Uncle Robert laying in his cot. Robert's gray uniform coat was hanging on a rack in the corner. His boots were still shined and stood tightly next to one another below. Robert E. Lee remained the consummate soldier. Lieutenant General James Longstreet and Major General John B. Gordon were each seated with legs outstretched. Longstreet had his arms folded comfortably across his chest. Gordon had his right arm resting on a small end table while holding a tin cup of water in his left hand.

"General Lee... please have a seat.", beckoned the elder General Lee. Fitz sat quietly, rather awestruck by the surreal calm and informality inside that small tent whilst all the world raged uncontrollably around them.

The elder Lee interlocked his fingers, placed his hands behind his head, and crossed his socked feet at the ankles. General Fitz paused and looked closely at his uncle for the first time in months, perhaps years. He was taken with how aged Robert's appearance had become. The stark whiteness of his beard; the deep lines in his face; the strain had nearly broken him. Fitz looked down at his own hand. He made a fist and then opened it once again, spotting a few white hairs atop his own wrist. The weight of responsibility bearing down on that small white tent was crushing, even for the greatest Virginian Fitz had ever known.

"Gentlemen...", General R.E. Lee began "it is clear to see that we have some decisions to undertake. If you step outside that tent you can see that the Yankees are all around us. The glow of their campfires emanates from all directions. There may be a small path to the north we could take; but the risk of having our forces divided with such an action is high. General Grant and I have exchanged correspondence today. Each of us is seeking a way to stop the flow of blood." General Lee swung his legs over the edge of his cot and sat up. He looked directly at his lieutenants. "I would like to hear what you gentlemen have to say about this."

"Gentlemen, our forces are clearly tired. I know our army's numbers have been cut in half these last few days and many men are too weak to carry a musket.", said General Longstreet, "But we are not defeated! There is a chance we can get to Lynchburg. There we can regroup our forces and prepare a march to meet up with Johnston in North Carolina. We should be able to access supplies from points south and west once there."

General John B. Gordon took a sip from his cup, placed it on the table, and sat forward in his seat. "I am in agreement with General Longstreet. These boys are not ready to quit, General Lee. If we move to the west, we should be able to better fortify a position and hold it for a time. The Yankees will not be able to cut off supplies from the Valley."

"Fitz, will you be able to create the opening required to break for Lynchburg?", asked Longstreet.

"Absolutely, General. We still have enough good men and horses. Keeping the horses rested, watered, and fed is the primary concern."

"This is understood, Fitz;", said General R.E. Lee, "but that luxury may not be afforded until we reach Lynchburg… Well then… we are in agreement: we will make one more try to break through to Lynchburg. It is our duty, gentlemen. I think Ol' Pete" (a nickname Longstreet had earned at West Point) "has the proper thoughts.", said Lee with a friendly informality Fitz had rarely witnessed from his uncle. Robert put on his boots and stood. He stepped over to the end table and laid out a small map of the area. "Fitz will open the attack. John's force will follow and you both will swing to the left and open a corridor.", his finger tracing the maneuver on the map. "We believe the west is manned only by Sheridan's cavalry. If Fitz can run them off, we should have time to pass through to Lynchburg. All the wagons and what artillery that remains must follow closely while Pete, you must defend the rear. Ordnance wagons shall remain with Pete's forces to keep his men supplied. We must then press on to Lynchburg as a single determined force."

Despite the calm delivery of the battle plan, General Fitzhugh Lee recognized the resigned desperation. Although Fitz longed to maintain some confidence that the plan could work, his instincts told him that he needed to have a contingency plan in place. Fitz's forces would be out ahead of the rest, therefore most isolated from command if circumstances devolved. "General Lee,", he addressed his uncle, "should it become evident that we will be unsuccessful; I ask for advance permission to peel the cavalry off and join up with Joe Johnston. I respectfully choose not to avail the cavalry of a cessation of hostilities pending the existence of a flag of truce, sir."

"Permission granted.", General R.E. Lee responded. "And, if such occurs, gentlemen; I shall immediately surrender the Army of Northern Virginia to General Grant under his terms. I will not force any further spilling of blood." Fitz understood that this decision would be the most difficult one of the War for his uncle. But Fitz strangely sensed relief in the old man as the terrible words of possible surrender breached his lips. All four generals understood that should the Confederate force be blinded by the total separation from its cavalry component, there would be no military miracle which could prevent total annihilation. Surrender would be the only option.

After shaking hands and saluting, Lee's three generals left the tent and returned to their own encampments to instruct their aides. Fitz Lee met first with Captain Charles Minnegerode.

"Captain...", he began, "I fear that I just attended the last council of war for the Army of Northern Virginia,"

"What do you mean, sir?"

"Well... as you know... our circumstances are very difficult right now. Dear General Lee is trying to weigh the balance between honor and insanity. I think we may be nearer the latter." General Fitz Lee's lip uncharacteristically quivered. Minnegerode saw the anguish on his face. Fitz sighed and continued, "We have agreed to make one last push to break away and move to Lynchburg. The hope is that we will be able to regroup, re-supply, and rest for a few days. Then we will move to unite with Johnston. As much as I would like it to be, Charlie, I don't feel it can happen. This Federal force is enormous and seems to grow more each day." Fitz paused hoping Minnegerode would have something to say to brighten his outlook. After a few futile moments of silence Fitz gave the order, "We shall lead the attack tomorrow. Gather the rest and we will prepare for duty."

At 5AM on April 9, 1865, General Fitz Lee and General John B. Gordon followed the plan and began the assault on the Union forces west of Appomattox Court House. They moved toward the Lynchburg Road. Initially they found success, briefly opening a corridor as they chased Sheridan, apprehended two artillery pieces, and captured dozens of prisoners. But just as their hopes began to rise, Fitz spotted Union General Ord approaching with two infantry corps. Sheridan's cavalry quickly stiffened with the arrival of support. The field was overshadowed by an impending blue tidal wave. A union counter-attack commenced with heavy incoming fire. General Fitz Lee sat helplessly on his horse and watched his diminishing force scatter. General Gordon's men tried to return fire as the situation rapidly deteriorated. Fitz turned to Captain Minnegerode, "I don't wish to be included in the surrender. Come, let us go."

At that moment Minnegerode let out a cry and tumbled forward across the neck of his horse to the ground.

"Dr. Randolph!" Fitz shouted. "Dr. Randolph!" The sturdy little general leapt down from his horse and knelt over a face-down Captain Minnegerode. Fitz took hold of his trusted aide and turned his shoulders and held him in his lap. "Charlie! Charlie! Say something!", he begged.

Minnegerode groaned as he opened his eyes. "I'm hit, General. Finish me... Please just shoot me!"

"Nonsense, Captain! Dr. Randolph! Come quickly!", he waved the doctor over. By the time Dr, Randolph reached the General and his wounded aide, Charles Minnegerode had closed his eyes again and was unresponsive. Fitz desperately patted his cheek. He shook him; to no avail.

"General Lee, this man is dead.", said the doctor.

"Good Lord, No! Not now!", Fitz cried as the mini balls continued to screech overhead. Fitz Lee reached inside his uniform and pulled out his notebook. He tore a page from it and quickly wrote some instructions:

This is the body of Captain Charles Minnegerode of General Fitzhugh Lee's staff. Whoever finds it will confer a great favor by seeing that it is properly cared for and that his father, the Reverend Doctor Minnegerode of Richmond, receives the information.

Gen. Fitzhugh Lee

With tears welling in his eyes and rolling down his cheeks, Fitz Lee pinned the note to Captain Minnegerode's uniform. Another aide approached and informed the general. "Sir, the Yankees are moving this way fast! We need to go now!"

Fitz Lee wiped his sleeve across his face, quickly mounted *Nelly Gray,* and followed a handful of officers west toward Lynchburg. Their ultimate goal was to avoid Union lines, turn south and still meet up with Joe Johnston's forces in North Carolina. Talk of unleashing a protracted guerilla war on the Northern occupiers had been circulating through the Confederate officer corps for months. Now, it was under full consideration.

Captain Charles Minnegerode, CSA and Major General Fitzhugh Lee, CSA
(Encyclopedia Virginia)

Hours later, along the Lynchburg Road, a lone rebel soldier was heading east toward Appomattox. General Fitz Lee pulled up on his reins and stopped beside the man. "Soldier, where are you headed?"

"I'm going back to join my company. I've been on furlough, sir."

"Well… You should know that General Lee has surrendered. The fight is over. You should go home."

The soldier shook his head and kicked the dirt, "Must have been that damned Fitz Lee! Rob Lee would never surrender!" (64.1)

Fitz and the four other officers chuckled for the first time in days, "You are most probably correct, soldier; that damned Fitz Lee!", Fitz exclaimed as he shook his fist in comic defiance at the sky. Just as quickly as the light of humor had reappeared in his midst, so it rapidly retreated as the darkness of guilty thoughts of Captain Minnegerode advanced and overran his mind.

House Where Maj. General Fitzhugh Lee, CSA and Staff Stayed During Surrender at Appomattox

Two days later, Fitzhugh Lee and his remaining staff officers had reconsidered their plan to continue the fight. Concerned about complicating the generous terms his uncle was afforded by Grant, Fitz and his men returned to Appomattox, rode into the Federal lines, and offered their unconditional surrender. Per General Grant's instruction, the entire Army of Northern Virginia had been paroled, ordered to lay down their firearms, and encouraged to return peacefully to their homes. There would be no imprisonments, no executions; the War was over and they were all to be joined as Americans once again. Grant wisely enabled the ex-confederates to take a first step toward rebuilding their shattered agrarian society by, at General R. E. Lee's personal request, allowing them to return home with their horses. On April 11, 1865, Major General Fitzhugh Lee became something he had not been for his entire adult life - a private citizen.

On August 7, 1885 the Democrat nominee for Governor of Virginia boarded a train in Washington, D.C. bound for New York City. Fitzhugh Lee would proudly represent the old Confederacy and the new Virginia at the funeral ceremony for onetime mortal foe, General Ulysses S. Grant. Fitz's days and nights had been consumed by Virginia politics for the last few weeks. Even though he was off for a somewhat somber occasion, he was glad to be getting a brief respite from his intensifying schedule. He fully understood that the months of campaigning ahead would demand his full energy and attention. The candidate excused his staff and asked that he be given this time on the train to relax. He sat in his private Pullman car and quietly watched as the train pulled away from the Baltimore and Potomac Station and the scenery began to move by. Fitz drifted back to his last visit to New York, just over two years earlier.

Fitzhugh Lee was seated in a private box at the Casino Theater on Broadway and West 39th. The orchestra was warming up for the afternoon matinee production of *Queen's Lace Handkerchief*. The Casino Theater had completed construction less than one year earlier in 1882. It was a state-of-the-art elegant Moorish Revival structure with colorful interior arches and arcades. Fitz sat admiring the fine Arabesque carvings which adorned the box. He was there at the invitation of Colonel John S. Austin of the Thirteenth Volunteers of New York. Also in attendance were Colonel John A, McCaull and Quartermaster Albert Ackerman, both of the Brooklyn Thirteenth. As part of his work as an officer with the Virginia National Guard, Fitz sought to cultivate relationships with

National Guard regiments from other states. Most particularly Fitz focused on establishing ties with regiments in northern states. Invariably, the commanding officers of these Guard units were Civil War veterans like himself. Some served alongside Fitz prior to the War and still others were classmates at The United States Military Academy at West Point. With some regularity, Fitz came across units he had directly engaged on the battlefields of Virginia, Maryland, and Pennsylvania. Fitz's purpose was to convert these former foes into friends with common experiences and now, a common goal of complete unification; all contributing to the ultimate enrichment of his home state and his country. The officers with the Brooklyn Thirteenth afforded Fitz another opportunity to heal the wounds of war and bind the nation back together.

Casino Theater, New York

Fitzhugh Lee, with the permission of his hosts, invited another officer who had served directly under him with the 1st Virginia Cavalry. This particular gentleman was on an extended visit to New York and Fitz had not seen his old friend in several years. Just minutes before the performance was to start, a slender man entered the box at the Casino Theater. Fitz rose to his feet, "My old friend! Welcome!" The two men warmly shook hands and embraced. Fitz continued, "Gentlemen, this is Captain Charles Minnegerode, perhaps the finest staff officer I ever had. He is simply wonderful! Charlie, please meet Colonels Austin and McCaull. And this gentleman is Quartermaster Ackerman – all fine members of the Thirteenth New York. Charlie, I believe we came up against them in a few places - Sharpsburg and Fredericksburg, among others.

Fitz and Charlie had just taken their seats when an usher entered the box. "Excuse me, gentlemen,", said the usher, "a gentleman is here to see Captain Minnegerode." As Charlie stood the usher held open the burgundy velvet curtain at the rear of the box. A short, powerful man nearing sixty years of age entered with a large smile. Captain Minnegerode moved toward the rear to meet the visitor. Fitz nudged Colonel Austin on the shoulder and pointed toward the two men.

"You do not remember me?", the visitor queried Minnegerode.

Minnegerode turned back toward Fitz for a clue and then turned again and faced the man, "There is something about your face, sir, that tells me I *do* know you."

"You were left for dead on the field at Appomattox, and…"

A bolt of recognition struck Minnegerode, "Yes, yes!"

"I am Doctor Cornelius Carter."

"My God, sir, you are the man that saved my life!" Charles Minnegerode grabbed hold of the Yankee doctor and hugged him. After an extended moment, Charles pulled back but still held the good doctor by the shoulders. He turned back toward Fitz, "General, this gentleman saved my life, undoubtedly! He discovered me on the field and personally carried me over his shoulder to his field hospital!"

Fitz Lee approached the doctor to greet him. The doctor smiled, "Yes, and I took the bullet out, as well!" as he shook Fitz's hand.

"And here is the bullet!", beamed Minnegerode as he removed the slug from his pocket and held it up between his thumb and forefinger. "It was the act of an angel. I am forever indebted to you, Dr. Carter."

The show had begun but the small band of brothers were more interested in the lovely real-life drama unfolding before them in the little theater box.

The celebration continued after the show as the group of officers, including Minnegerode and Doctor Carter, made their way to the Fifth Avenue Hotel. There, the Brooklyn Thirteenth Regiment turned out in full force to honor General Lee with a five-course meal. Toward the end of the evening, Colonel John Austin rose to his feet and toasted the health of their esteemed guest from Virginia. Amidst a rousing cheer and the clinking of glasses, General Fitz Lee stood and offered a few remarks.

This meeting of soldiers of the two sections has a far more significant meaning than mere friendship. It means that all sections of the land are united, happy, prosperous, and peaceful; and that hereafter the sections shall walk side by side to the music of the Union. The days of abuse have passed, and henceforth, we can declare that these United States are bounded on the North by ice and on the South by bananas. And, anybody or any nation that attempts an uninvited entrance (or exit!) will surely slip up!

Fitz allowed a moment for the chuckling to subside.

Leaving joking aside… There is no longer any separate section in this land, North, South, East, and West - all are Americans with a common flag, a common country, a common destiny. I have seen the dawn of that paternity which must spread until it embraces all States, and thus shall the great destiny of this Republic be fulfilled. Time is a great healer and the South and North now understand each other better; and now the South is watching the welfare of the Union. Virginia and her sons here tonight are ready to respond now. And, if New York will raise the National Anthem, the Old Dominion will take it up, send it along the mountain tops, make it reverberate through the sky, and touch the stars; until it shakes every State from pillar to post! The Star-spangled banner, long may it wave, O'er the land of the free, and the home of the brave! Thank you, fine soldiers of the Brooklyn Thirteenth!" (64.2)

The silence was shattered with thunderous applause. Fitz turned and embraced trusty Captain Minnegerode, "We have made it back, Charlie. We've done our duty once again; and I could not have done mine without you."

"Thank you, General.", said Charlie smiling with tears welling in his eyes. "It has always been my honor, sir. 'Tis a far better method for taking New York!"

Fitz then beckoned Charlie to step away from the table with him and walk toward the door of the large dining room. For the next hour and one half, General Fitzhugh Lee and Captain Charles Minnegerode stood, exchange some kind words, and shook the hand of each member of the Brooklyn Thirteenth.

On August 10, 1885 Fitzhugh Lee descended the main stairwell of the St. James Hotel in New York City. He was to breakfast with John B. Gordon before boarding a train home to Virginia. Fitz briskly crossed the main lobby and shook hands with his old friend. Before the two old generals could complete their greetings, two newspaper reporters approached.

"General Lee… John Nuland of the *New York Herald*… May I ask a few questions?"

Fitz smiled and turned to the reporter as he warmly put his arm around Gordon, "Of course, General Gordon and I would be happy to entertain you for a few moments!"

Grant's Funeral Procession, August 8, 1885, New York City (PBS.org)

"Sir,", Nuland began, "first and foremost, congratulations on your nomination for the Governorship of Virginia. As a former military adversary and now a candidate for high office, we would like to hear your impressions on General Grant's funeral."

"Thank you, sir. Words will not allow me to express the warm reception given my fellow Southerners and myself at the hands of the North. It was a glorious procession worthy of a great general and statesman. I am told the procession was seven miles in length! It was truly an honor. I was filled with emotion when we passed the large portrait of General Grant with the inscription below. 'Let them have their horses; they will need them for their crops.' That line brought Appomattox back to me like some sad dream. It was a touching coincidence. General Gordon and I were two of the three remaining corps commanders who were with General Lee when Grant gave utterance to that magnanimous sentiment. General Gordon saw the inscription that same moment that I did and our eyes instinctively met as we rode by. I don't know exactly what General Gordon felt; but I was ready to use my handkerchief." Gordon nodded in solemn agreement as Fitz Lee continued, "You cannot imagine what those words implied. In the Confederate Army every man had to supply his own horse; within the Union Army everything was supplied by the government."

"General, what do you think this funeral demonstration means?", the reporter asked.

"It means the Union is now more firmly and inseparably united than it was even twenty years before the Buchanan administration. The War was the inevitable culmination of differences that had to be settled by blood. Before the War there was always talk of breaking up the Union and secession whenever any issue was brought forward for national arbitration; and the South would invariably threaten secession if her whims were not gratified. Of course, immediately after the War, wounds were fresh and there was little show of any disposition for reconciliation. But, notwithstanding this fact, a reconciliation would have been effected had it not been for the policy of the administration succeeding Mr. Lincoln's. The government then sent men down south to rule us; men who were unprincipled and unfair; and the colored man was placed in our legislatures to make laws for us. This was too severe a transformation, and the South felt that she was being belittled. It was putting the bottom rail of the fence on top. The people got so they took no interest in the government nor the country. Any insignificant little carpet-bagger would be sent down there and boosted into Congress, and our own men would be thrust into the shade. I am a strong Democrat and talk strong Democratic principles; and I am going to add that this was done for no other purpose than to perpetuate the Republican Party in power.

But now; God be praised, all that is gone by. That was the work of the politicians, and the South has discovered that the people of the North – the body of the people, I mean – had no hand in it. Old issues are eradicated in the South now. The colored man is no longer regarded as a usurper; and he knows he will not be returned to slavery. We don't want men to represent us who will constantly wave the bloody shirt. The people of the South have come to love the people of the North for the grand, magnanimous, fraternal treatment they have received since the War; and they have been longing for this grand opportunity, which has at last been afforded, to express their hearty good will for the Union. No man has done more, and neither has any circumstance, nor series of circumstances, to propitiate the feelings of the South and bring about this grand millennium, than General Grant. The sufferings of General Grant awakened the sympathies of the whole South, and the whole South is now glorying in the treatment its old commanders are receiving. Just think of it. Here are General Simon Buckner, General Joe Johnston, General Wade Hampton, General Gordon, and myself; all rebel leaders being made lions of your city, and we are all over-flowing with gratitude in return. We came here to make up. The South sent us here to make up. There is no divided North and South now. It is the Union forever. The South feels that it is part of the country once more, and takes an interest in the prosperity of the whole undivided land. The South is already reviving!"

"General Lee… Hiram Smith of *The New York Sun*. I had the opportunity to recently interview Mr. Robert Toombs, former Secretary of State of the Confederacy. He stated that Jefferson Davis ruined the Southern Cause by letting West Point men, like yourself, control the policy of the Confederacy. Do you have a comment?"

"Yes, I read that article.", Fitz replied with clear tone of indignation. "There was scarcely a soldier of renown on either side who was **not** a West Point graduate. Toombs contradicts himself by saying that West Point ideas of martial discipline throttled the South and then, going on to state that Albert Sidney Johnston or Joe Johnston could have saved the Confederacy. Both of these generals were West Point men! Lee, Jackson, Beauregard, Stuart; all men of the school on the Hudson. Now, had he argued for the leadership of General Gordon here", placing his hand upon Gordon's shoulder, "it would be a different matter altogether. I would accede to the general's exemplary leadership abilities despite the fact he is **not** a product of West Point!"

"How about Toombs' claim that he was offered the Confederate presidency?", Smith followed up.

"I never heard anything of it and I do not know who could have tendered Toombs such an offer. As I remember it, Jeff Davis and Toombs were candidates in 1861; and Davis was elected. We elected Davis because he was able and pure; two essential qualifications in statesmanship and private life; and we believed that his military education at West Point would be of great value to the president of a nation plunging into a war of independence." Fitz Lee smiled again and grabbed Gordon by the elbow. "Now, gentlemen; please excuse us. General Gordon and I must get our breakfast." (64.3)

As the two generals made their way to the dining room of the St James Hotel, Gordon exclaimed, "Dear Fitz, I believe you are even more agile on your feet as a politician than you were on your horse as a cavalry commander!"

"You are right, John. I have to be! The incoming fire a politician receives is far deadlier!"

Chapter 65   *The Readjusters*

Republican Gubernatorial Nominee John Sergeant Wise sat comfortably in an over-stuffed chair in the main lobby of The Homestead in Bath County, Va. As he gazed through a front window the afternoon sun lit the treetops as they swayed gracefully in a gentle late summer wind. His campaign was in the midst of a two-week-long trip down the Shenandoah Valley toward the western panhandle of the Commonwealth. Wise spent that morning in the nearby Jefferson Pools, soaking in the rejuvenating properties of the warm mineral baths. After a few quiet moments a gentleman approached.

"Mr. Wise; Peter Burton of the *Richmond Dispatch*.", as he extended his hand.

John Wise rose to his feet. He gripped Burton's elbow with his left hand while firmly shaking with his right. "Mr. Burton… Welcome to The Homestead. It's a lovely afternoon. Shall we step out onto the porch?"

"Yes, sir. That would be fine."

The two gentlemen walked through the front door and turned right, passing the towering Ionic colonnade and continuing onto the long adjacent veranda. The candidate and the reporter each sat in tall-back wooden rockers and breathed in the mountain air. Mr. Wise's assistant followed several steps behind and sat nearby; not too close but certainly within earshot.

The Homestead, Bath County, VA

"I want to be elected.", John Wise offered as Peter Burton removed a pencil and notebook from his breast pocket. "To tell you the truth, it's the only office I ever really did want. I ran for Congress once and was beaten. I ran again and was elected. I didn't care a fig about the result in either race – comparatively speaking, I mean. But I am in this fight with my whole soul, and I mean to win it if I can."

"Are you not running as a Readjuster, backed by Republicans?", asked Burton.

"No sir, I am the nominee of the Republicans and of nobody else. We will have a square fight between Republicans and Democrats this time."

"But sir; you were clearly nominated with William Mahone's validation. The Readjusters have dominated the Republican Party in Virginia for many years. Some would say that the Readjusters and the Virginia Republican Party have become nothing more than the *Mahone Machine*. How can you separate yourself from that impression?"

"It is true that General Mahone waged his campaign for the U.S. Senate on the issue of readjusting the State debt; and he was able to effect a coalition with the Republican

Party. And I, as a Republican, have been part of that coalition. The victories that have been achieved by Republican leadership, not only on the debt readjustment, but also in the areas of public education and negro suffrage, are undeniable. Those are **Republican** priorities."

"But, sir;", Burton persisted, "it is also undeniable that Senator Mahone was formerly a Democrat; albeit a somewhat disaffected Democrat. Many contend that he aligned his Readjuster movement with Republicans for purely self-serving reasons. There is an argument to be made that he sought power in Virginia and in Washington to advance his railroad interests."

"Mr. Burton, the Readjuster movement and the Virginia Republican Party have common objectives. The Commonwealth of Virginia was largely Democratic just after the Reconstruction. In order to break the grip the Democrats held on Virginia politics, consensus had to be built among the opposition. This included Readjusters, Republicans, and, as you say, disaffected Democrats. Maybe we should now call those Democrats, *Wise Democrats*?", the candidate winked and smiled. "Joking aside, it is as simple as that – a consensus."

"Yes, Mr. Wise. But as you know, once General Mahone went to Washington as Senator Mahone, he found himself, as a third party Readjuster, in an enviable position. The Senate was evenly split with thirty-seven Democrats and thirty-seven Republicans. Two third-party senators, Mahone being one of them, held all of the power. The one gentleman caucused with the Democrats while Mahone, in exchange for many concessions, including the chairmanship of the powerful Agricultural Committee, caucused with the Republicans. This, in effect, handed the Republicans control of the Senate because Vice President Arthur would cast the tie-breaking votes. This, of course, has been viewed by many, as a corrupt bargain. Especially since we have all seen the federal Republican appointments which have subsequently flowed into many influential positions in Virginia. And, of course, these appointments have all been "Mahone men". Does the appearance of "bossism" on the part of Senator Mahone taint the rest of the Virginia Republican Party?"

U.S. Sen. William T. "Boss" Mahone

Wise adjusted in his seat and cleared his throat. "I can assure you that my governorship would be a Republican governorship. I will govern in the interests of the citizens of Virginia, employing Virginia Republican ideals and principles. My administration will not be subject to the "bossism" of any one man."

"What is *the* issue in this campaign?"

"There are many. We are going to make it hot for the Democrats on several lines. They have got us all in trouble over the State debt again. The Readjuster Party rose up and gained control of Virginia because it represented the popular idea on the debt question. We enacted such laws as would have settled the question fairly and finally; and would have saved the people from the unjust burdens which the funders were trying to impose upon them. Much of this debt preceded the War. The *Riddleberger Bill* we passed assigned one third of the $30 million debt to counties that now comprise West Virginia. The bill fixed Virginia's debt at $21 million. New bonds were offered to repay this debt. The interest rate on the re-issued bonds is one half the rate of the old original bonds. Additionally, any interest accumulated on those old instruments during the War was cancelled. All was moving along beautifully when in came the Democratic Legislature in 1884 and forced on us a lot of statutes to cooperate with those we had already passed! The Democrats had come over to *our* platform on the debt question and were trying to rob us of the glory of its successful solution! What they actually did was complicate and encumber the situation. Once elected, I will work to repeal those add-on pieces of legislation and return to the pure form of the *Riddleberger Bill*."

"What other issues will you raise?"

"The partisanship and corruption of the Democratic Legislature. They turned out seventeen members without the shadow of law or justice in order to obtain a two-thirds majority and render Governor Cameron powerless. They passed a bill designed for the perpetration of the boldest election frauds. They robbed the Governor of every prerogative he had relative to elections, and saddles upon us the worst returning board ever trumped up in this country. There were bare-faced frauds in our local elections last Spring. We will find enough to make the Democrats answer for."

"Are the Democrats in Virginia united?"

John Wise gasped, "They are worse divided now than I ever knew them to be. There are jealousies among their leaders; and factions among their masses."

"How do they like the Cleveland administration?"

Wise shook his head, "President Cleveland has made sad havoc among them. At first they abused him for not making appointments and now they abuse him for those he has made! He has struck some bad material in Virginia and the real active element in his party there is truly disaffected. I don't know a man among all the presidential appointments in Virginia who represents the best and most valuable element in the Democratic Party of the State. The people are sick of this business!"

John Sergeant Wise

"Are the Readjusters and Republicans completely welded into one party?"

"They are. We will carry the bulk of the old Readjusters and all of the Republicans are solidly with us."

"What about the negroes?"

"They never were as solidly Republican as they are now. There are not 200 Democrats among 128,000 negro voters in Virginia; and the Democrats can't buy and bulldoze more than 5,000 of them!"

"Do you think you will be elected, Mr. Wise?"

"I do. I firmly believe I will be elected. As I said, there are 128,000 negro voters in Virginia. And, there are 210,000 white voters. I will get 120,000 negro votes and between 50,000 and 60,000 white votes. If you recall, the Democrats carried Virginia for Cleveland by only 4,000 votes; and they are much more solid on national than State issues."

"It is stated that you intend to make a thorough canvass of the State."

"I am going all over it. I am going into every county in the State; and all through every one of them. I would like to have the Democratic Nominee go along with me, but I doubt there is another man in Virginia who can stand the program I have laid out. When I defeated Parson Massey for Congress, I traveled 7,200 miles and made seventy-two speeches in one hundred days. That was pretty good work!"

"You mentioned the Democratic Nominee. How do you feel about General Lee?"

Wise sat forward in his rocker and rubbed his hands together. "That is just what I wanted. It is the weakest nomination the Democrats could have made, and I am more confident of my election than before."

"Is not General Lee very popular?", Burton proposed.

John Wise snickered and looked off to his left. He turned back and composed himself. "He is a very nice gentleman and has many friends; but if his name had been Fitzhugh Smith he would never have been heard of as a candidate for Governor. He is a nephew of his uncle. He bears the same relation to Robert E. Lee that Napoleon III bore to Napoleon Bonaparte. General Lee will enter the campaign with a whoop and a dash, in glorious, yet predictable, cavalry style. He will exit the campaign with a whimper and a crash. I, on the other hand, as a proud cadet from the Virginia Military Institute; one that proudly participated in the charge at New Market; assert that General Lee will find that the common infantrymen are in large majority in Virginia and his elite cavalry is a minority. I truly believe the Democrats could have nominated a much stronger candidate. However, it just suits me as it is!"

"What is General Lee's political record?"

"He has very little. The only prominent feature in what you might call his political record is a letter which he wrote in 1877, taking the most extreme possible view of the State debt question. He advocated the payment of the debt in full, and a little more too. That letter won't go over well in Virginia and the General will have difficulty explaining it. Yes, he suits me, exactly." (65.1)

Chapter 66 *Small Compensation*

Democrat Gubernatorial Candidate Fitzhugh Lee grunted as he climbed into his carriage. His personal aide Tom Stockton climbed in behind. Stockton knocked on the carriage ceiling to signal the driver. The carriage headed east on Cary Street. After a few blocks it passed Mayo's Bridge. Fitz looked out toward the Kanawha Canal. A crowd of men and boys were gathered in the middle of 15th Street. The banks of the James River were swollen from the heavy rains the previous evening. Water had crept up 15th Street to a point just one half a block from Cary Street.

"Stockton, let's stop.", said Lee. "Let us see what is bringing this excitement."

Stockton rapped on the carriage ceiling and the driver immediately pulled up on the reins. Fitz bounded from the carriage, placed his derby firmly upon his head, and approached the group. A dozen young men and boys stood looking down at the encroaching tide. There was much laughter and chatter as money changed hands.

"One quarter he doesn't wake up before the tide takes him!", said one man.

"A half dollar he does!", another responded.

An aged man in a long black coat tried to pierce the wall of onlookers. "Stop this! This man needs help; not mockery!"

"Shut up, you old drunkard!", one of the tormentors bellowed as he turned and firmly shoved the old man, sending him tumbling backward across the sidewalk. Laughter erupted as the street thug taunted further, "I think I saw some pennies on the street over there, Cap'n Billy. Might help you buy that next bottle. Don't say I never help the indigent!"

Fitz pushed through to the front of the group. "What is this!?"

"Just some drunk taking a nap!", one hooligan snidely remarked.

The unconscious man laid parallel to the gutter; face-up, head pointed downhill toward the canal. The water was slowly rising around him. His shoulders and chest were four inches deep and water was beginning to lap at his cheeks. In another ten minutes, his head would certainly have been submerged.

"Who is this man?", asked Fitz. Fitz bent over at the waist to get a good look at him. He was wearing a decent suit. His bowler hat had floated about ten feet away to a nearby doorway.

"Are you certain this man is drunk? He could be sick or injured.", Fitz said with growing concern. "How long has he been here?"

"Nobody knows for certain, sir… But…", the man pointed toward a near-empty bottle of whiskey sitting on the sidewalk nearby.

"Disgraceful! Stockton, reach in the jacket and see if he has a billfold."

Stockton knelt down on the sidewalk beside the gutter and reached in the man's breast pocket. He looked up at Fitz as he struck pay dirt and produced a wallet.

"Good work. Please give that to me." Fitz opened the billfold. There was no money. There were several business cards and a small lapel pin inside. Fitz pulled the wallet up near his nose to look closely at the inscription on the pin. **RPD**

Captain Billy Pierce had struggled to his feet but kept his distance from the mob. "Sir, that man is up-standing. He doesn't belong here. Please help him."

"Stockton, we need to put this man in the carriage. We will take him to the hotel suite. He needs assistance. These dogs would have left him to drown!"

"No, sir… We were going to move him if the water covered his face.", explained one of the men.

Fitz assumed full command. "No! You are going to move him right now!", Four of you men; each grab a limb and take him immediately to my carriage!"

The men did not know who this older portly gentleman was; but they innately understood that he was not to be trifled with. Fitz grabbed a boy by the arm. "And you! Bring me the man's hat!"

Fitz Lee approached Captain Billy. "Thank you, sir, for trying to aid this man…" Fitz looked closely at the decrepit character before him. "Sir, in turn, I would like to be of assistance to you. Please come with me in my carriage. I should like to get you a hot meal."

"Oh, no sir, General Lee. That will not be necessary…", Pierce respectfully replied.

"Well, it seems that you know who I am. And, whose acquaintance am I making?"

"My name is Billy Pierce, sir."

"These men called you 'Captain'. Why would that be?", sensing from the man's age that there was history attached to the moniker.

"Well, sir…", Pierce hesitated before deciding to come clean, "I was the captain of a blockade-runner during the War… In fact, I once delivered some precious cargo which you would know."

"And, how is that, Captain?", Fitz Lee's curiosity was piqued.

"The Prussian, Heros von Borcke, sir... I delivered him through the blockade from Nassau to Charleston in '62.", Billy divulged with a sense of long-forgotten pride. (66.1)

"Dear man; I am certain there were others, but that, in and of itself, was a heroic deed for the Confederacy! Had he been born in Fairfax County instead of Prussia; there could have been no soldier more loyal to the Army of Northern Virginia than von Borcke.", Fitz grabbed Billy's filthy hand and shook it vigorously. "On behalf of Major von Borcke and the entire Confederate command, I thank you!". Fitz stood back and saluted Captain Billy. Billy beamed a smile, exposing, for one of the very few instances, his sparse yellow teeth. He proudly returned the salute. Fitz Lee quickly put his hand in his trouser pocket. He stepped forward once more and shook Billy's hand, discreetly leaving a ten-dollar bill in Billy's palm. Fitz winked, "Small compensation... for a job well-done. Thank you, Captain Pierce." Fitz turned to Stockton. "Let us go, Stockton!"

Fitz Lee sat and studied the comatose man reclining on a small sofa opposite him. He shook his head in wonderment as he formulated a hypothesis. The drunk man slowly cracked his eyes open. His vision was bleary as he slowly rotated his head to the left, stretching a very sore neck. He breathed heavily as a pounding headache quickly took the lead on his slow return to consciousness. He shaded his eyes with his hand as he looked with bewilderment at the short, stocky man seated in a wing chair across from him.

"Welcome to the Fitz Lee Suite!", the man announced with an understanding grin. "I am Fitz Lee."

"Sir, where am I?", asked the man trying to make some sense of things.

"Well, sir... I recently found you in the gutter. Now you are in the Ballard House Hotel. Let us begin with your name.", Fitz suggested as he leaned forward placing his elbows on his knees and clasping his hands together.

Still not certain he wasn't hallucinating, the man answered, "Jack... Jack Wren."

"There is a pitcher of water.", said Fitz pointing to the small table in front of the sofa. "Please tell me what happened, Mr. Wren."

EXCHANGE HOTEL & BALLARD HOUSE, RICHMOND, VA

"With all due respect, sir... I would prefer not to. It's quite an embarrassment."

"Mr. Wren. I found that pin in your wallet. I know you are with the police department. Behavior like yours is not becoming of a police officer. But, I understand from a reliable source that you are an up-standing man; so I sense there is something wrong here. And, I wish to help you."

"Please, sir…", Wren held his hand up, simultaneously realizing that he was wearing only his under clothes.

"Mr. Wren… I want to know what happened.", Fitz firmly stated.

Wren ran his fingers through his hair and across his brow. He was humiliated to be in such a circumstance in the presence of a great and popular figure such as General Fitzhugh Lee. Wren trembled and blushed as the shameful feelings he felt the last time he was half-dressed before a superior instantly rose from the depths of his memory to the surface of his skin. He looked at Lee's smile and instead of Captain Morse's mocking disdain, he sensed compassionate sincerity. Wren reached and poured a glass of water as Fitz patiently waited. Wren took two large gulps and wiped his forearm across his mouth. He took a deep breath and exhaled. He began, "General Lee. I am no longer on the police force. I was terminated several months ago… I have since established my own detective agency; to little success. I am under severe financial strain. I cannot support my family…" Wren paused and took another deep breath. He heaved as grief began to overtake his emotions. The broken man sobbed outwardly for a moment as Fitz Lee sat still and waited. "I had three children… I have two sons. My daughter…", he sobbed some more. "My only daughter… She was just four weeks old. Miranda was lovely…She was taken by fever two weeks past…" Wren looked across again at Fitz Lee. Lee's sincerity had turned to remorse. Tears welled in the General's eyes.

"Mr. Wren… I, too, have lost a child recently. My youngest boy, Sydney; less than one month ago. He was just six weeks in age. It is the darkest of days when we lose a child. However, we must stay strong for those that remain. For a time, I felt I would abandon the campaign. I soon realized that is not the solution. It is not a solution for you, either. You are a strong man; I can see that in you. You will recover and you will move forward in honor of your Miranda. You will perform for her as if she were here now. And, when you see her again, you will know you have done your duty for her and her family… You must draw upon your faith and believe this, too, is part of God's design. You are being tested and you will not fail!" Fitz stood and walked across to Wren. He placed his hand on Wren's shoulder. "You are a detective, eh? You know, I am embarking upon a campaign tour for the next several weeks. I could use a good, experienced man to head my security. Might you be that man?"

Jack Wren was stunned by the twist of fate. "I…I am not sure what to say, General."

"Yes, will suffice!", said Fitz with a smile instantly returning to his face.

Tom Stockton entered the room, "Excuse me, General. Time to leave for supper."

"Yes, yes… Fundraising…" Fitz muttered. "Tom Stockton; this is Detective Jack Wren. He will be heading up our security."

Stockton looked quizzically at Lee, "Very well, sir."

"And Tom, please have the carriage take Detective Wren home. I will cross over to the Exchange and wait in the lobby for our supper guests. We are to meet in the lobby of the Exchange Hotel at 6 o'clock, correct?"

"Yes, sir.", said Stockton.

Fitz Lee then turned toward Wren. "Detective Wren, please report here tomorrow morning at nine o'clock and we can review the campaign schedule moving forward. We are heading west in two days. Your family should prepare for your regular absence over the coming weeks."

"Yes, sir. Thank you, sir.", said Wren still reeling from the sudden and wholly unexpected reversal of fortune. "But sir, where is my suit?", Wren sheepishly asked as his eyes darted about the room.

"Ah, yes...", Fitz Lee smiled once again. "I had the valet take it to be dried and pressed. Mr. Stockton, please retrieve Detective Wren's suit for him, as well." (66.2)

Chapter 67 *The Fight for His Life*

A hulking locomotive screeched and belched as it came to a halt. The red, white and blue buntings swayed with the crosswinds but remained firmly anchored along the guardrail at the rear of the caboose.

The mid-October afternoon sun was breaking through the clouds releasing the promise of fair weather ahead. A stout, bearded little man hopped down from the club car. He placed his hands emphatically on his hips as he spun back around and looked adoringly at the train. Tethered along the side of the car was a large light grey banner. Thirteen blue stars and fifteen red ones were sprinkled across the edges of the banner. In the center were three bold letters "**LEE**".

Fitzhugh Lee really was the Democratic Party nominee for Governor of Virginia. He breathed in the fresh air of Staunton as he marveled at the thought. He shuddered only slightly as he reminded himself of the potential responsibilities that lay before him.

His aide, Tom Stockton, approached his side, equally impressed. "Have three simple letters ever spoken such volumes, General?" Stockton answered his own question, "**USA**, perhaps?"

Lee cut his eyes over to his aide, "Others may argue, **CSA**, Mr. Stockton!". The General devilishly winked.

"Right again, sir!", said Stockton with a broadening smile.

"But you have to wonder, Stockton;", Fitz postulated, "should they all not stand for the same thing, now?"

Another man emerged from across the street and held out his hand to Lee. "Ah, welcome, General Lee! The town of Staunton is honored to have you come! My name is Henry Wigart. I am your precinct captain here."

"Yes, of course, Mr. Wigart; it is very kind of you to have me! We truly appreciate all of your efforts in the campaign. It has been some time since I was here in Staunton. It is a lovely spot!"

"Thank you, sir.", responded Wigart. "We have a grand stage erected on Captain Ranson's property just a mile from here. There is a large crowd assembling there, now."

Lee looked at his pocket watch. "It is 1:10, Mr. Stockton. What happens next?"

Stockton looked at Lee and then at Wigart. "General Lee will arrive on stage at 2 o'clock and will deliver his address, Mr. Wigart."

"Very well, we will be waiting." At that moment, a crowd of one hundred or more appeared from the narrow street that dead ended at the station. The crowd was jubilant as they caught sight of their candidate. They cheered and rushed toward the train trying to get close to the man in whom they were investing so much hope for the future.

As the crush drew near, Fitz Lee skipped up onto the second step of the club car. The chants of "Lee! Lee! Lee!" were beginning to heighten, forming almost seismic reverberations as they bounced back and forth between the broad side of the train and the sturdy brick warehouses across the street from the depot. "Lee! Lee! Lee!", they thundered. Fitz clasped his hands above his head and thanked them for nearly thirty seconds. Then, his hands came apart and he drew his open palms down slowly, imploring them to cease with the applause.

"Now, I understand the power of the citizens of Staunton!", he cried, eliciting another thunderous ovation. After about ten seconds, he quelled them once more. "No, thank you... Thank you for the welcome. But, dear Virginians, please give us thirty minutes to unpack our things. Then, we shall all have a nice visit, I assure you!"

Wigart spoke up. "Yes, everyone... Please meet us at Captain Ranson's property. We must grant our distinguished guest a proper forum. Your enthusiasm is much appreciated, but certainly it can be contained until our candidate has had a few moments to prepare. Thank you."

The crowd, without a hint of disappointment, quickly regained order and withdrew from the train.

"Thank you, Mr. Wigart.", said Lee. "I only hope my speech can match their vitality."

"Oh, dear General; there is little doubt among us. You are the man for these times and everyone here senses as much.", replied Wigart.

Two cars ahead a wonderful black stallion was led down a ramp. Fitz's eyes lit up as he saw the powerful steed. Fitz turned to Stockton, "What is the name of that fine animal?"

"I believe they call him *Mars*, sir."

"*Mars... Mars...*", Fitz repeated to himself. "God of War...I like the name; but it's not quite appropriate... Let's call him *Pax*, instead. Yes, *Pax*...Much more indicative of our mission."

Thirty minutes later *Pax* was led to the head of a column of two hundred horsemen who had assembled near the passenger depot. Fitzhugh Lee approached and put his hand on the saddle which now sat upon *Pax*; the very saddle which had once rested upon *Traveler*, the warhorse ridden by the estimable General Robert E. Lee throughout the War.

Fitz bowed his head for a moment of reverence before lifting his foot into the stirrup and sweeping aboard. Although he was dressed in civilian clothing, Lee still retained the authority and mannerisms of a Major General. He raised his arm and whistled. The bugler sounded and the large contingent of former members of the 1st Virginia Cavalry proudly rode west on Augusta Street.

Just behind Fitz Lee two horsemen rode in tandem, one carrying a bright new Star-Spangled Banner and the other carrying the faded, tattered, bullet-ridden Confederate battle flag which led Pickett's Charge at Gettysburg; symbolizing the line which Fitz Lee sought to walk; balancing the prideful heritage of Old South with the eager rapprochement of the New South. Augusta Street was lined with cheering well-wishers, shouting words of encouragement to their candidate and the noble men following him. Fitz Lee turned left into the Ranson property and spurred *Pax* into a canter. The audience erupted in celebration when *Pax* briefly accelerated into a gallop as he and Lee passed in front of the stage which had been erected for the speech. A rifle team composed of veteran members of the 5th Regiment, Co. G, Staunton Rifles fired three volleys into the air. Immediately after the echoes of the rifle fire had subsided, the Stonewall Brigade Band played a rousing rendition of *Jine the Cavalry*. The throngs poured on to the grassy field as Fitz Lee circled behind the stage and dismounted.

Fitzhugh Lee allowed the anticipation to grow for a few more moments as he quickly reviewed his notes one last time. He then took a deep breath and climbed the steps backstage and walked through the curtain.

Thank you, citizens! Thank you, citizens of Staunton! I am Fitzhugh Lee and I am running for Governor! It is my pleasure to be here and my campaign is very humbled by your support and hospitality.

Virginia is getting back to business!

Fitz paused as the crowd whistled and cheered.

Last year we elected a Democrat Legislature! This year we will elect a Democrat Governor, a Democrat Lieutenant Governor, and a Democrat Attorney General! You have seen the progress the legislature has made in a very short period. Once we have secured the other levers of power, Virginia will return to form as one of the leading states in the nation!

We have the ardent and steadfast backing of our Democrat President! We have the strong backing of our National Democrat Party! And, we will earn the most important backing of all; we will earn the backing of our people!

We Democrats will eschew the politics of our rivals. The Republican-Mahone alliance has led to detestable corruption. They do not work for the people. They work for their own interests. And, I say we have seen enough!

The multitudes roared with approval.

There will be no increase in taxes. We seek the abolishment of the Republican-

imposed Internal Revenue System.

We accept the settlement of the public debt known as the "Riddleberger Bill". However, there remains the need to protect the State from further harassment by creditors. We pledge to enact legislation toward this end. We appeal to the people to refuse wholly to pay any tax in coupons and thus, at once, by their own united patriotism and sovereign will, to rid the Commonwealth of this long and baneful controversy. The question of the State debt has ceased to be one of dollars and cents. It has become one of State sovereignty. The question is whether the Commonwealth of Virginia shall be arraigned before the Federal courts, controlled by Republican judges, adjudicating upon this question to all men, irrespective of party, and invite them to unite with us in defending the imperiled rights of Virginia.

It is the cherished purpose of the Democratic Party to labor in the sacred work of public enlightenment until country and town alike enjoy the full advantages of free education. We will continue to support public education until every child in the Commonwealth, of whatever race or color, might secure the benefits of free education. To this end, we favor the furnishing of free books to the pupils of free schools and an appropriation for the benefit of the common school system from the surplus revenues of the Federal Government, by what is known as the Blair Bill. Over the last two years, under Democrat legislation, $275,000 for arrearages to the school fund have been paid. In addition to all regular appropriations, we have funded the establishment of a female normal school at Farmville. We have also granted liberal annuities to all of our institutions of learning.

The Democratic Legislature has enacted legislation to care for our disabled Confederate soldiers. We will continue to address their needs, both for the mind and body and we will follow up with further provisions for their care. All proper aid should be given those disabled veterans who have gone without the government support but have forever consecrated the soil of Virginia by their dauntless valor and devotion.

The Democrat Party of Virginia has always been foremost to exalt and dignify every function of State Government. It has created the vast network of railroads and turnpikes which have developed our resources. It has been the steadfast friend of labor, and it has never neglected the just and ordered rights of property; frowning upon all class distinctions in all efforts to array one portion of the community against another on issues. It recognizes and will maintain all classes of the Commonwealth in their civil and political rights. It will be my mission to continue development and progress on all fronts!

You have heard my Republican opponent deride my candidacy. Mr. Wise has claimed that had my name been Smith, none of you would have heard of me. To him, I am only the nephew of my uncle.

The din of "boos" and "hisses" gathered above the crowd.

I do not think, fellow citizens, that I ought to be blamed for being the nephew of my uncle, for I had nothing whatever to do with that arrangement! It is true that I was present on the occasion of my birth...but I had nothing whatever to do with my lineage. Fellow citizens, has the time come in Virginia when it must be held as an unpardonable crime against a man that he is the nephew of Robert Edward Lee?

But, truly, this ridicule does not belittle me. I have never yet seen the day when I was ashamed of being the nephew of Robert E. Lee!

Fellow Virginians! I proclaim my allegiance to the Constitution and the Union of the States; and to the National Democratic Party as their interpreter and defender. The maintenance of the principles of local self-government administered by the States; the limitations on the imperial power entrusted to Federal administration; these are the charges of our Democratic Party. These are the principles I will fight for as your governor. I humbly ask for your vote! (67.1)

The resounding applause of the crowd gave way to chants of "Put him in! Put him in!" Citizens of all ages came forward to the edge of the stage and reached out to Fitz Lee. He moved forward and dropped to knee, energetically shaking hand after hand as the Stonewall Brigade Band broke into *Carry Me Back, to Ol' Virginny*.

After stops in Lexington and Lynchburg the following day, Fitz Lee's campaign locomotive continued on to Roanoke. Lee awoke to the sound of the train pulling in to the freight depot. After dressing he walked to the dining car. There, waiting for him at his table, was his morning coffee and a stack of recent newspaper articles culled from various publications throughout the country. Fitz looked at his pocket watch. He had over two hours before his scheduled stump speech.

The Lynchburg Virginian:

This is in all respects a superb candidacy. Gallant and glorious Fitz - a Bayard "sans peur et sans reproche"; in war and in peace, as soldier and citizen, everywhere and always, a model man, every inch of him from the crown of his head to the sole of his feet. We can proudly put Fitz Lee against John Wise and say with Hamlet, "Look here upon this picture, and on this".

The Philadelphia Press:

The man whose presence in the inaugural procession of President Cleveland last March prompted the rebel yell from the Southern spectators who crowded Pennsylvania Avenue in Washington has been chosen to lead the Virginia Democrats in the campaign for Governor. Fitzhugh Lee has nothing to recommend him to his fellow Democrats except the fact that he was a leader in the Confederate Army. He has on no occasion shown any adaptability for civil affairs. Compared with John S. Wise, the Republican candidate, the weakness of Lee becomes easily conspicuous. The former has been prominent for years in State affairs. He ranks as one of the ablest debaters in Virginia; whilst the candidacy of Lee arouses, as it was intended it should, nothing but Confederate war spirit. Neither the candidate put forth nor the platform adopted at this first Democratic State Convention held since the inauguration of President Cleveland encourage the hope that liberal politics are making progress in the party in that section.

The Alexandria Gazette:

The people have been allowed their way and Fitz Lee is our candidate for Governor; the people will see he is elected. Triumphant over the politicians with their ifs and buts, he will be equally successful in routing the discomfited hosts of Mahoneism. From the Atlantic to the Alleghanies, Virginia rejoices. Her gallant son, dear to her for his deeds of war, has become equally so for his works in peace. Among the first who realized that the contest was really over, his energies have been ever bent towards a solid and sincere reconciliation. And, probably no man in the South stands higher in the esteem of Northern people. When November's blasts shall bear to the country the tidings of his greatest victory, "Well done!" will be the echo from west to east. (67.2)

Fitz Lee chuckled to himself, "If I am the Southerner held in highest regard in the North, what a lowly state of affairs there be! Evidently the *Gazette* editors do not read the Northern papers…" Fitz then reached for the next paper in the stack.

The Baltimore Sun
October 10, 1885

LOGAN ON THE RAMPAGE

Eutaw House Hotel, Baltimore. MD

General John A. Logan distinguished himself in a speech made on Friday night at a banquet given in his honor at the Eutaw House in this city. General Logan's characteristic way of speaking in public and in the Senate is well known. He is a partisan of partisans, a man of rude and not always grammatical utterances, and of narrow ideas. There is one thing about him – he is never dull. His blunders, his exaggerations, and his gross assumptions, although not humorous, are amusing. He says the most irrelevant things in such a positive and dogmatic way. His Eutaw speech was Loganism throughout. It consisted of two parts, sometimes separated, sometimes blended and mixed inextricably together. On the one hand his purpose appeared to exalt the Republican as the best and greatest party the world ever saw; on the other, to denounce the Democratic Party for all that is bad, and to flaunt once more "the bloody shirt". He has gone one better than Senator John Sherman by *adding to the "bloody shirt" the "bloody saddle".*

General Logan is indignant that General Fitzhugh Lee should be riding about Virginia with a horse "caparisoned with his Uncle Robert E. Lee's saddle and bridle"; and, by a bold slander, General Logan asserts that riding on that saddle "makes Fitzhugh Lee feel as though he were in command of a great army, fighting for the destruction of his country". According to Logan, "the blood-stained saddle appears to be the leading card in the Virginia campaign," and the man who rides upon it a nobody. "If it makes the young man feel happy to mount and wobble about in his uncle's saddle", says Logan with a feeble attempt at facetiousness, "let him do it!" Then, rising to the height of his great argument, he exclaimed: "Have you ever heard of a Republican prancing over the country on some old saddle that was used by some other general or even by himself in the Union Army to help himself through a political contest?"

And all this "bosh" comes from the lips of a man who was a good soldier and professes to be a statesman. With the inconsequence that is so characteristic of General Logan's speeches he wanted to know "why cannot the facts of the War be stated in a public speech without raising the cry of a bloody shirt?" If we were to answer we should say it is because he is one of the Republican Bourbons "who learn nothing an forget nothing," who imagine that the passions and the bitterness of a quarter of a century ago are the passions and bitterness of today; whose idea of the South is "once in rebellion always in rebellion"; and always to be kept under Republican domination. He would have the Southern States turned over again to the intolerant and feudatory rule of carpet-baggers. Like Mr. Sherman, he deliberately declines to believe that peace prevails in all parts of the South; that the colored people are well-treated and prosperous according to the measure of their industry and ability; and that the profession of loyalty to the old Union and the old flag is other than a mere sham. He even sees in the saddle of General Lee – that "bloody saddle", as he calls it – the symbol of a new rebellion.

It is dreadful to Logan to find "the Democratic Party of the North and that of the South reunited in one harmonious band of brothers, advocating the same propositions, standing upon the same platform, and voting for the same measures.". His besetting notion is that the Republican Party has a lien upon the government for all time to come; that the Democrats are trespassers on the Republican bailiwick, and that the only way to oust them is to revive at the North the old passions and hates against the South. It is a shallow device. The Southern Republicans who, it is intended to help are themselves frightened by it. The "Richmond Whig", the organ of Mahone, no later than Wednesday last asks mournfully: "Why will Northern Republicans and their organs prejudice their righteous cause (which is even more the cause of Southern and Virginia Republicans) by always lugging in phrases or considerations that invoke or provoke feelings of race and color, or of section, or of the late War Between the States? The issues", it declares, "are not sectional, nor of race, nor even

John A. Logan, US Senate, Illinois

of party."

Will General Logan and Senator Sherman heed this despairing cry of their Southern Republican friends? Will they believe that all their talk about the solid South, the oppressed negro, the bloody shirt and the bloody saddle, is pure and unadulterated, as the "Whig" puts it, "slosh"? We fear they will not, even though it comes from men who are of the South, who understand the South, and who know and feel that such utterances are not justified by any facts, and that they are truly "slosh". With such men as Logan in power there would be an end to progress in the South and harmony between the sections. (67.3)

Jack Wren entered the dining car just as Fitzhugh Lee was laying down the *Baltimore Sun*. "Good morning, General."

Fitz Lee shifted his weight in his chair sighed. "Good morning, Jack."

"Is there a problem, sir?"

"No, no… Just perusing some of the opinion columns." Fitz Lee looked up and could see the man standing there with his arms crossed was doubtful. "Well Jack, we're in for a fight.", Fitz admitted, "But, I knew that was the case. Nevertheless, it is disheartening to hear all the negative ideas which swirl about us."

"Well, from what I have read, it does appear that most of the Virginia papers are leaning heavily in your direction, sir. That should be a good sign. It is the Governorship of Virginia which you seek; not the Presidency.", Wren rationalized.

"This is true.", Fitz replied with a hint of despondency. "But, I did believe that my candidacy would bring more hope and clarity to the other sections of the country with regard to our intentions."

Jack Wren smiled as he sought to reassure the candidate. "Sir, this is a fight for your life; but it's only a political fight for your life. You have survived and overcome far more! And, you will prevail in this instance, as well"

Fitz Lee looked up at Wren, "Thank you, Jack. I will be ready to go in one half hour." Lee adjusted his weight in his chair once more and looked out the train car window.

On January 13, 1860, Lieutenant Fitzhugh Lee and twelve members of Company B, 2nd U.S. Cavalry were tracking a hostile Indian party. Amidst a gale force winter snowstorm, Comanches had been spotted moving a band of rustled horses and mules through an area several miles from *Fort Colorado* near Austin, Texas. It was well-understood by U.S. Army forces that the any appearance by any Indians in that area would be solely for the purposes of murder and plunder. Lieutenant Lee and his men painstakingly pursued the party; carefully interpreting horse and mule tracks which had been obscured by the natural elements and Comanche trickery, alike.

After more than eighteen hours of vigorous yet frigid pursuit, the soldiers came upon a partially cooked and devoured colt; indication that they were on the right path and the savages were not far ahead. The storm had finally moved off and, although it remained cold, the emergence of the sun had begun to melt the tracks, making the hunt increasingly straightforward. The tracks led them to the edge of a cedar forest and then turned north. After a few miles one of the troopers pointed into the trees, "There's something in there!".

Fitz Lee halted the column. As he pulled his hat low over his brow to reduce the glare, he peeled his eyes. "Corporal Hayes; go see what that is.", he ordered.

Hayes swallowed and responded, 'Yes, sir.", before making a slow advance into the cedars.

Five minutes later Hayes came crashing urgently back through the woods toward the rest of the men. "Lieutenant! I saw them… They are just a half mile ahead. I saw them disappear just over that hill!", as he pointed to the northeast.

"But what was that we saw in the woods, corporal?", Lee asked.

"Oh… That was just a loose pony."

"Did they see you?"

"No, sir. I don't believe so."

"Men, drop your blankets, overcoats, and knapsacks here. Prepare your weapons. We are going to ride over that hill and engage those heathens.", Lieutenant Lee ordered.

**Lieutenant Fitzhugh Lee,
2nd US Cavalry
(The Kansas State Historical Society)**

The cavalrymen reached the top of the hill and began to accelerate on the downside. The Comanches were less than one mile in front of them; with heavy blankets wrapped around them from head to toe, muffling the sounds of the approaching hooves. When the soldiers reached a point about two hundred yards from the party, the men drew their pistols. One trooper's pistol misfired, sending a late but clear signal to the Indians of the U.S. Army's arrival. Lieutenant Lee immediately yelled "Charge!" as the soldiers broke into full gallop. The Indian party had no time to mount a defense and simply scattered in several directions, leaving the harras of horses adrift like a rudderless ship.

Two Comanches on horseback bolted toward the cedar trees. Lieutenant Lee, Corporal Hayes, and Private Maxwell followed. Maxwell closed to within fifty yards of one of them before pulling up and neatly squeezing off a shot. The red warrior instantly dropped from his saddle as his horse continued unabated toward the trees. The other brave reached the tree line and with an unexpected audacity turned and fired four successive arrows back in the direction of his three tormenters. Pausing their chase, Fitz

Lee pulled a muzzle-loading carbine from its holster in his saddle and fired a shot, missing the fleet Indian as he was swallowed by the forest.

"We are going after that bastard!", Fitz insisted. The three troopers followed the horse tracks about two hundred yards into the trees before seeing them once again turn north. After more than seven miles the wooded ridge spilled into a large ravine; and beyond that was open prairie. Fitz sensed that the Indian was running out of time and could not continue much longer. Fresh tracks led into the center of the ravine.

"Private Maxwell; you will go up the left side of the ravine. I will go right. Corporal Hayes, you will continue to follow the tracks up the middle."

After a few hundred yards, Hayes heard the snapping of branches. He quickly looked behind him and to his right. The Indian was now on foot and scampered up the side of the ravine and over a small hill beyond. "There he goes, Lieutenant!", Hayes shouted. Fitz Lee spun around just in time to see the brave's head disappear over the hill.

"Damn it!", Fitz let cry. The three troopers immediately turned their horses and galloped toward the hill. "Where is he? Anybody see him?", Fitz breathlessly asked. The three men dismounted. Hayes looked down and spotted moccasin tracks leading further down the hill toward a thicket patch.

"Private; you stay here with horses. Corporal Hayes and I will continue the chase."

Fitz threw his cape over his right shoulder, picking up his carbine in one hand and drawing his Colt .44 pistol with the other. Hayes drew just a pistol and the two began their cautious breach of the thicket wall. They advanced abreast about thirty yards apart, carefully listening and looking for any sign of movement.

"Jack, keep a good look out now; for he is not far off.", Fitz warned in hushed tones. "Here is his blanket."

Fitz draped the blanket over his left arm, hiding his carbine from view. At that moment, the Indian rose up from a small rock formation just ahead, let out a treacherous yell, and let fly an arrow directly at Fitz's breast. Fitz quickly raised his left arm as he twisted in that same direction. The arrow passed through the blanket and struck the stock of Fitz's carbine, knocking it from his grasp and splitting it on two. Fitz aimed his pistol as the brave lunged toward him. Before Fitz could squeeze the trigger, the Indian had gripped the barrel, turning it to the side. The pistol discharged, the bullet flying harmlessly out of sight as the pistol dropped to the ground. The enraged Comanche drew his knife and slashed at Lieutenant Lee. "Corporal! Do something, damn it!" Hayes awoke from his paralysis and drew his own pistol. By this time the larger and stronger Indian had negotiated a position behind Lee, holding him around the neck and placing the Lieutenant between himself and Corporal Hayes. Hayes cocked his pistol and tried to steady his hand for a clean shot. At this moment of mutual hesitation Fitz Lee quickly moved and hurled the Indian to the ground, falling on top of him. As Fitz suddenly seized the advantage, he was able to reach for his fallen pistol. In a singular motion he cocked the pistol and fired it into the cheek of the Comanche. He then repositioned the pistol in the middle of the Indian's forehead and fired a final shot.

Fitz freed himself from the dead man's embrace and stood to check himself for wounds. He had several slashes and punctures in his heavy wool coat, but nothing broke his skin. The lieutenant bent over and put his hands on his knees, trying to catch his breath.

"You had a pretty close call with that Indian", Hayes remarked.

Fitz stood up and extended his arms to the sides, "Yes, he was a big fellow.," Fitz said while still breathing heavily. "But I was only getting my muscle up with him! Now I feel I could get away with a half dozen just like him!"

"How did you throw him?", Hayes asked still in disbelief over what he had just witnessed.

"He was very strong, as far as brute strength went.", Fitz explained. "But he knew nothing of the science of wrestling. For a time, I thought he would get me; when I happened to think of a trick in wrestling which I learned during my school days in Virginia. It was known as the *Virginia Back Heel*. I tried it and I *fotched* him!", he declared with great satisfaction. "Now, let us go find the others and collect up those stolen horses." (67.4)

Fitz Lee continued to look out the window of the dining car. His confidence in his campaign and its meaning had been renewed. "Yes, it is nothing but a political fight for my life… and I am fit for it."

Chapter 68 *Mud Splattering in the Homestretch*

Fitzhugh Lee awoke just before sunrise the morning of November 3, 1885. He quietly dressed and descended the stairs and crept toward his office at *Evergreen*. He looked out his office window as the first beams of light were scaling the treetops in the east. He held the back of his hand against a pane and felt the coolness. He lifted the lower sash to confirm his impression that it was a very mild morning. The tireless candidate plucked a sweater from a side chair with his left hand as he scooped a handful of newspaper clippings from his desk. Fitz softly walked through the foyer and unlatched the front door. He stepped onto the porch and sat in the rocker to his right.

The Atlanta Constitution

> *The campaign in Virginia is the most picturesque political fight that the country has ever witnessed. Fitzhugh Lee has the best of it in spectacular effects. His cavalcades of gallant cavaliers and black-eyed mountain maidens glittering in semi-military finery, make a dazzling show. On the other hand, John Wise's fervid appeals to negroes and the lower orders of society, remind one of the reckless methods of the French Revolution.*
>
> *Mingled with the lurid lights and shadows playing over the scene, are certain bizarre and grotesque points and incidents. In this remarkable contest some of the most serious questions, from the Virginia point of view, present a humorous aspect to the outside world. One feature of the fight is the comparison of pedigrees. Wise in his speeches insists that his ancestors came to this country two hundred and fifty years ago, long before a Lee set foot on the soil of Virginia. Naturally, this ringing boast wakes up the Lees and their friends. One of them rushes into print that Wise is mistaken, as Captain Charles Lee landed in this country in 1593 and again in 1597. Among the members of the Virginia Company of London, the founders of the colony, were Sir Francis Lee, Sir Robert Lee, Mr. Henry Lee,*

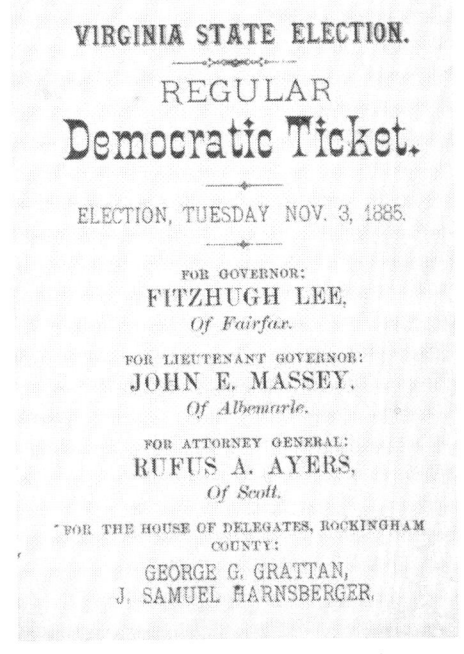

Democratic Election Day Flyer, Rockingham Co.

and Mr. Richard Lee. Mr. Henry Lee landed in Virginia in 1608 and died there during the following winter. At least three of the Lees came to Virginia prior to 1624 and at least ten of the name came to Virginia in 1635, the same year the Mr. John Wise sailed from London.

Both are descended from Generals and Governors. But here, too, Fitzhugh Lee would seem to hold the edge. Lee is the grandson of a Revolutionary General and Governor. He is the son of a naval Commander. And, of course, he is the nephew of his uncle. Wise has but his own father to claim such military and statesman lineage – although impressively, just as Lee's grandfather, Wise's father held both prominent positions.

This would seem to settle the pedigree question in favor of the Lees, but the correspondent referred to clinches the matter by saying: "The old Wises, too were Virginians, and they were always true as steel to their old mother; they never gave the slightest aid or comfort to the slanderers of Virginia. Therefore, I cannot understand many of the reported sayings and acts of some of the family in the present generation. Are they full-blooded Virginians?"

The awful doubt here suggested would kill Wise, even if he could survive his own suicidal policy and methods. Outsiders may fail to understand the full import of the question, "Are they full-blooded Virginians?". But the sons of the Old Dominion understand it, and that is enough. The bare possibility that in some remote generation, one of the Wises took to his bosom a wife from Pennsylvania, Maryland, or North Carolina, thus causing his descendants to fall out of line of "full-blooded Virginians", will send a thrill of horror in zig-zag ripple from the Potomac to the Tennessee border.

Fate and pedigree are both against Mahone's Johnny. It is safe to put him down as a dead duck.

The Savannah Times

John Wise says that if General Lee's name had been Fitz Smith instead of Fitz Lee he never would have been heard of. But suppose Wise's name had been John Smith? Would he have been Mahone's man for governor? It is very doubtful.

The Philadelphia Times

Advices from Virginia indicate that while the Democrats have been indulging themselves in a noisy brass band campaign for the governorship, Mahone has been carrying on a still hunt for the legislature and through it, of course, to senatorship to succeed himself. Careful correspondents are even inclined to concede that Fitzhugh Lee will be elected governor, but that the legislature may be carried by Mahone. If this should be the net result of all the noise which has been coming up from the Old Dominion for the past three weeks the Democrats would not be so enthusiastic, but they certainly would be wiser. To the country at large the defeat of Mahone for senator is a very important matter. While the governorship would concern only Virginia and Virginians, the presence of Mahone in the U.S. Senate is a positive disgrace to the entire country which ought to be rendered impossible after March 4, 1887 at all hazards. A little less chivalry and a little more work would ensure this and not interfere in the least with the election of General lee as governor – something which Virginians have evidently set their hearts on.

The Louisville Courier Journal

To the Democrats and all other decent people of Virginia; Wise is bad enough but Mahone is worse. Better have ten Wises for governor than one Mahone for senator. Don't forget this in your enthusiasm for Fitzhugh Lee!

(68.1)

The Muscatine Iowa Daily Journal

They are having lots of fun in the Virginia campaign, particularly the Republicans, who appear to be laughing General Lee out of the canvass by reason of his claims of being the nephew of his uncle and riding on his uncle's old saddle. A local poet gets off the following hit, which has somewhat the flavor of a Pinafore:

> Look at me!
> Don't you see
> I'm a Lee?
> I'm the nephew of my uncle, Robert E.
> And my uncle Robert E. left to me,
> And I claim
> His great name
> And his fame.

"Uncle Robert's saddle" bids fair to become historical in Virginia, the fun about him being uneasing. Republicans have also made note of "Uncle Robert's saddle's" poor standing in his class at West Point – finishing forty-fifth of forty-nine. Another poet gets off this:

> Though it was not my luck to inherit the brains
> Of my uncle, he left me the bridle and reins,
> And also his beautiful saddle –
> The beautiful saddle astraddle
> And though I don't make a nice show on the stump
> You will admit I'm a regular trump
> Astraddle this beautiful saddle,
> This beautiful saddle astraddle.

(68.2)

The National Republican

The people of Rome elected a horse as Consul; it appears the people of Virginia may elect a saddle as Governor! (68.3)

Fitz grinned at the absurdity. He well-understood that the barrage of late personal attacks indicated that Republican arguments had failed. He was more confident than ever that if his voters turned out, the Wise campaign would be overwhelmed. He pulled his pocket watch out from under his sweater, "Time for this 'saddle' to get polished and ready to go to the polls!"

Fitzhugh Lee entered Mrs. Appich's Candy Shop on King Street in Alexandria just before 4 o'clock on Election Day. The smell of confections and cakes made his stomach growl as his eyes widened.

"Well, if it isn't Fitz Lee!", Mrs. Appich beamed. "Welcome home, my boy! And, my word, you have Master Rooney with you!", the old woman struggled off her stool and made her way around the counter.

Fitz stepped forward and embraced her, deftly placing his right hand behind her waist, giving proper support; gently grasping her right with his left before leading her in a short waltz ending with a delicate spin. Fitz stepped back releasing her hand and bowed in princely fashion. Mrs. Appich blushed and curtsied as Rooney applauded.

"It is so nice to see you again, Mrs. Appich. You look very well! And, the shop is as enticing as ever!"

"Thank you, General. I am glad you have come by. For, I will be closing the store next month. As you may know, Mr. Appich passed nearly one year ago. And, I am tired."

"Yes, I had heard that news. My condolences, Mrs. Appich. He was a fine man.", Fitz said with concern.

"Yes, Mrs. Appich. You and your husband were a stalwart fixture for us; and so many children in town.", Rooney added.

"Thank you, both. Well, Fitz. It appears to me that you may be moving to Richmond very soon!", she said with a wink. "Of course, if it were my station to do so,", she demurred with a pinch of sarcasm, "I would vote to send you there! And, I have been unafraid to make this known through the town."

"You have my thanks, but we do not know as of yet … anything to get me to leave Alexandria, eh Mrs. Appich?!", Fitz winked.

"Oh, you are so full of things, Fitz... always have been. I suppose you will need to find another candy shop in Richmond."

"If I can, it will certainly pale in comparison, my dear. Now, I have four hungry children in need of candy this evening.", Fitz began to scour the glass cases.

"And what about you, Master Rooney? Any candy for your children?"

"Oh, no thank you ma'am; my boys are a little older..."

"Nonsense! You are never too old for candy!", she insisted.

"Yes, Mrs. Appich... very well...I suppose you are correct.", Rooney smiled.

Richmond Dispatch – FITZ LEE ELECTED GOVERNOR and a DEMOCRATIC LEGISLATURE in BOTH BRANCHES

Richmond, Va., Nov. 3. – Returns received here up to ten o'clock tonight from the election in this State indicate that the Democrats have carried the State for Lee and the whole State ticket and secured both branches of the Legislature. These returns and other information received show a fair proportion of the colored vote in the back counties was cast for the Democratic candidates.

The Richmond Dispatch, democratic, tonight feels warranted in making the claims indicated in this dispatch. There was no contest over the State Senate and the Democrats have carried that body, according to the figures now received, by a large majority, possible two-thirds. The estimates now are that the Democrats will have the Legislature by between 20 and 25 on joint ballot and will elect a Democratic successor of Mahone in the Senate of the United States. The Democrats fix Lee's majority at over twenty thousand.

Mr. John S. Wise, the Republican candidate for Governor, has been in the city all day. He visited several of the large colored precincts to look after his interests. Tonight, he is at the office of "The Whig", Mahone's organ here. He said: "If the returns received are correct, I am defeated. General Lee, though, unless he has resigned his place as a member of the Board of Visitors to the West Point Military Academy, a federal office, is ineligible to hold the place of Governor." The Mahoneite alluded to this point earlier today and seemed to be saving it in reserve. It is not regarded as anything by the Democrats and is laughed at by them.

About 10:30 P.M. General Fitzhugh Lee, the Governor-elect, came to the Alexandria telegraph office, where the Democratic Committee, with many of his friends, had gathered. He was very warmly received, one of the assembled taking the new Governor in his arms and giving him a hearty hugging, which the General took in good part. He remained in the telegraph office seeing how his friends enjoyed the welcome news, which came with each pulsation of the wire, and did not leave until a late hour.

The overwhelming defeat which Mahone met in this State today it is believed has doomed all his future political aspirations, and those of his associates. It is believed that his defeat is, in some measure, attributable to the disgust for him engendered by the methods he has resorted to to keep himself in power. Governor Cameron, General Groner, Riddleberger, and many other Republican leaders gave Mahone little assistance in the campaign. Many of the Republican leaders who supported Mahone candidates did so with half-heartedness. (68.4)

Chapter 69   Mugwumps and Warhorses

A young man helped an older lady walk down the steep incline of Jail Alley. An early morning rain had slickened the surface. The rain had ended but the November skies remained dark with cloud cover. The woman clutched tightly to the young man's arm as he patiently led her to the main entrance of the Richmond Jail on Marshall Street. The young man raised his head, removed his hat, and addressed the two officers at the guard post.

"Good morning; William Cluverius and Jane Tunstall to see Thomas Cluverius."

It was somewhat a formality, for Willie and Aunt Jane had been visiting the prisoner, both together and separately, several times a week for the last eight months. The guards silently nodded and stood to the side, allowing the couple to pass through. The guards had barely spoken to either of them at any time over the previous months, but knew them well enough to immediately sense that this visit had a different tenor than any of the others.

Richmond City Jail from Jail Alley

Mrs. Tunstall sighed as she slowly moved forward; fighting against both her physical deterioration and her emotional exhaustion. She and Willie followed a narrow dimly lit hallway, taking a turn to the right and then another back to the left. At the end of the hallway was a large steel door which accessed a block of single cells. Another guard met them at this point and escorted them to Tommie's cell.

The guard reached for his keys as he announced, "Thomas Cluverius... your brother and your aunt are here to see you." He unlocked and swung the heavy oak cell door open.

Tommie stood from his cot as Willie and Aunt Jane entered. He shook his brother's hand and then warmly embraced Aunt Jane. He cupped the sides of her face in his hands and looked into her gray eyes surrounded by rings of darkness. "My dear Aunt Jane; thank you for coming again."

"Yes, Tommie...", she whispered with a forlornness. She clasped his hands and removed them from her cheeks; bringing them together within her own. "This shall be my final visit. I will not be witness to Friday..." Jane Tunstall began to weep.

Tommie smiled, "Oh, Aunt Jane... Do not worry, Pollard and Crump say there is a very good chance the Supreme Court will take the case under review; they meet today in Staunton and I am hoping to hear of their decision today or tomorrow. I am confident they will choose to review and over-turn the case."

"Do you really think so?", Willie asked.

"Yes. Our procedural grounds are strong.", Tommie assured.

Jane Tunstall shook her head slightly. Her eyes rolled in dejection. "Tommie, my boy... I am old and I am tired. I am also out of money. We owe the lawyers thousands! Also, I just received a letter from that nasty Mr. Deuring. He says I owe him over eight hundred dollars! Whatever could he have done on our behalf where he could charge that kind of money?"

Tommie's eyes cut briefly to his brother. "He provided assistance collecting information from witnesses, Aunt Jane. Willie and I will figure out how to get him paid. Please do not think of him for another moment!"

"But I do worry, Tommie!", she whimpered and wiped her nose on her sleeve. "I have no way to earn money. And without you, it is a lot for Willie to undertake on my behalf." Jane turned away from Tommie and Willie, rubbing her hands together and mumbling to herself, "I could sell the fifty acres in King William; or maybe I could get a mortgage? Oh, that's probably not a good idea..."

"Aunt Jane... Aunt Jane! Please! Willie and I will take care of you. I am not going anywhere. In a few months I will be free... You must continue to believe. It may require some more sacrifice; but we will endure!"

"I don't know what to do... I don't know what to do...", the old woman repeated to herself as she stared blankly rocking back and forth.

"I should take Aunt Jane away, Tommie. I will return her home and be back here tomorrow. I will get Maybelle to come and stay with her while I'm gone.

"When you return, we will discuss how to pay Deuring.", said Tommie

Willie nodded at his brother and turned to their aunt, "Come now, Aunt Jane; we should be going.", Willie whispered as he grabbed her hands.

Tommie approached and reached toward his aunt. She looked directly in his eyes, "Tommie; did you hurt Lillie?"

Tommie smiled and looked back at her. "Now Aunt Jane, I believe you know the answer to that question. We all do."

She shook her head slightly, "Yes, I do… Good bye, my love." (69.1)

On November 30, 1885, Willie Cluverius entered Tommie's cell at the Richmond City Jail. Tommie was seated in a comfortable upholstered chair in the middle of his cell under a reading lamp. On a table beneath the window at the far end of the cell, sat two potted geranium plants. On the floor next to the table were piles of newspapers and a stack of books. Tommie laid the newspaper he was reading in his lap as Willie rushed to his side and knelt.

"Tommie!", he excitedly whispered, "I did it! I have gotten the money to pay Deuring – and then some!"

"How did you do it? Did you go to the fights like I said?"

"Yes; I can't believe it actually worked!", Willie's eyes grew large as he explained further.

Willie Cluverius entered a saloon on King William Road in West Point, VA. A few patrons sat quietly in the barroom, passing the late Fall afternoon. Willie removed his hat and nodded in their direction as he walked through a doorway in the back-left corner of the room. He walked across the small back yard toward a frame outbuilding which sat near the rear of the lot. He noticed six or seven crates covered in blankets to the right of the building's doorway. The sound of men clamoring and cheering grew louder as he approached the doorway. Willie slowly opened the door. The smell of smoke overwhelmed him as he entered and saw perhaps three dozen men crowded around a ring, leaning in with cigars or pipes in one hand, and bank notes clenched in the other. Fists were raised, admonishing the combatants to fight harder. The afternoon sun provided the primary lighting but several lit torches hanging on the four walls which surrounded the crowd and the octagonal ring enhanced the view. Above was a large chandelier with sixteen large candles, further illuminating the fighting surface. Four brass spittoons leaned against every other exterior side of the octagon.

Willie pushed closer to lean over the ring and watch the action. A thin bearded man was holding his right arm aloft. He suddenly dropped it, signaling for the action to start. A *Spangled Mugwump* was dropped to the floor by his negro handler. At the opposite side, a *Whitehackle* was simultaneously released. The combatants furiously screeched, charged one another, and raised their heels. The *Mugwump* flapped his wings, elevated above his opponent and circled to the right, delivering the first blows to the back of the *Whithackle's* neck. The *Mugwump* deftly bounded beyond his foe, then spun and slashed with his gaffs across the chest of the *Whithackle*. The wounded fowl stumbled backward. The *Mugwump* quickly pressed his initiative, wading into his opponent with talon, gaff and beak. The *Whitehackle* fell back against the boards of the cockpit and began to painfully squawk. The *Mugwump* pursued with deadly efficiency, delivering several kicks to the chest and throat of the disoriented *Whithackle*. Blood spattered onto the ground and side boards as the flailing continued for a few more moments. The *Whitehackle* fell over on his side with labored breathing as the *Mugwump* moved in and furiously pecked at its eyes. The *Whitehackle's* handler, with the referee's permission, stepped forward and snatched his severely wounded bird from the floor.

Willie Cluverius breathed a sigh of relief that the contest appeared to be ended. To his surprise, the handler simply blew several times on the fowl's face as he tapped its head. After a few moments, the bird regained consciousness. The handler dropped the *Whitehackle* back in the center of the cockpit. The negro handler released his bloodthirsty warrior from his grasp. The *Mugwump* immediately seized upon his hapless opponent once more, delivering several hard kicks to the side and back. The gaffs penetrated two inches deep, puncturing the lungs. The *Whitehackle* cried out as blood began to trickle from its beak, creating a pathetic rattle for mercy as the relentless *Mugwump* stood atop, delivering blow after blow. After thirty more seconds of stomping and pecking, the *Whitehackle* fell limp. The referee raised his arm, signaling an end to the fight. The negro handler smiled broadly as he collected his champion. He walked the victorious *Mugwump* over to a man in a spotless white coat with brown piping. The man grinned as he bit down on his cigar. He patted the handler on his back as the bookmaker approached and handed the man his victor's purse of $25.00. The bookmaker then approached the handler for the vanquished *Whitehackle*; handing over the loser's take. The defeated handler stuffed the $5 note in his pocket with his left hand as he swooped down and plucked up his dead *Whitehackle* by the talons. He quickly removed the metal gaffs, walked over to the rear window of the room, and tossed the bloody carcass out into the yard. The bookmaker walked around the room, making his payouts to the successful bettors. This included a $125.00 payoff to the man in the white coat, who had placed a bet of $100.00 on his own gamecock.

The man in the white coat was named Bertram Sinclair. He was a well-known successful gamecock breeder, fighter, and gambler from Macon, Georgia. Each year he travelled through the Carolinas, Virginia, and Maryland with two dozen of his best battle cocks.

Willie Cluverius turned to a man standing beside him, "How many fights have there been so far?"

"That was the fourth one. Sinclair's fowls have won 'em all. An' they say his best cock ain't even fought yet! His name is *Hannibal* an' he's up next!"

"Who is he fighting?", Willie asked desperately trying to educate himself on a topic of which he knew little.

"He's fightin' some bird some fella brought from out west. I think from Lynchburg area. I don't think it matters. Nobody gonna beat Sinclair's best…"

The negro handler returned from outside holding a large bird beneath a red velvet cock-bag. Another handler entered the room carrying his fowl in a simple brown linen bag. The bookmaker stepped into the center of the cockpit.

"Gentlemen: bout number five will feature a *Bronze-back Mugwump* called *Hannibal*; owned by Mr. Sinclair and handled by his man, Phil… versus a *Warhorse* called *Lord Botetourt*; owned and handled by Mr. Atwill." Phil removed the velvet bag and revealed a large impressive black gamecock with a striking bronze streak of feathers running from its shoulders down to the base of its white tail feathers. The well-conditioned gladiator exuded strength and vibrancy. *Hannibal* flapped his wings and stretched his head upwards, letting out a great crow and brandishing his heels; seemingly playing to the crowd.

Mr. Atwill then removed the linen bag from *Lord Botetourt*. The crowd barely took note of the rather unremarkable *Warhorse*. *Lord Botetourt* displayed no memorable identifying features other than his drab ordinariness. He was barely larger than a bantam and seemed rather sedate in the arms of his owner.

"Place your bets, gentlemen!", the bookmaker cried.

Bertram Sinclair stepped confidently into the pit and handed the bookmaker five $100 notes. The bookmaker's eyes popped as he announced, "$500 from Mr. Sinclair on *Hannibal!*"

Over a dozen men crowded into the pit, anxiously laying down bet after bet on the invincible *Hannibal*. The bookmaker was collecting wads of cash and furiously making notes, failing to realize that he had nary collected a single bet on *Lord Botetourt*. This finally dawning upon him, he raised his hand and halted the betting. "Is there anyone willing to bet on Atwill's *Warhorse*?" After a moment of silence, Willie Cluverius stepped forward and held out a $10 note. The crowd of men all turned toward Willie. Many laughed while others placed their hands on his shoulder and offered their condolences. After a minute of calculation, the bookmaker informed Willie that his odds were 100 to 1. Willie turned red with embarrassment; but he had done exactly as Tommie suggested; waiting for a match with long odds and putting it all on the underdog. Willie glanced over at Mr. Atwill and his bird. Atwill nodded slightly and reassured Willie with a wry wink.

The anticipation grew within Willie as the combatants entered the cockpit. The referee raised his hand and the entire room fell silent. As his arm fell, the eruption of cheers and boisterous entreaties made Willie flinch. *Hannibal* burst across the cockpit as if shot from a canon. *Lord Botetourt* stood still as if he had not noticed what was about to happen. Willie cringed as he braced for the expected disastrous result. When *Hannibal* was less than one foot away, *Lord Botetourt* suddenly leapt from his standstill position and thrust both legs outward. As *Botetourt*'s 3-inch gaffs reached full extension, *Hannibal* could not control his forward momentum. Both of *Botetourt*'s gaffs skewered *Hannibal*'s skull. *Lord Botetourt* withdrew his legs and landed back on his feet. *Hannibal* flopped forward and to the left, sprawling uncontrollably until landing motionless and silent. The crowd fell equally motionless and silent as disbelief swelled within the room. Bertram Sinclair's cigar dropped from his mouth as he saw his prize cock lifeless in the pit.

A man turned to Willie Cluverius and slapped him on the back, "Good Lord, man… You've just won $1,000! I've never seen a cockfight end so quickly!"

Tommie Cluverius laughed aloud. "That is magnificent, Willie! We have done it! Now, take care of Deuring and give the rest to Aunt Jane."

"Yes, Tommie. It is good to hear you laugh again, Tommie. But what about the lawyers? How will we ever pay them?"

"I have thought of that, Willie. I will write my story and we will sell it. The proceeds will be used to pay the lawyers and to repay Aunt Jane. And, if that is not enough; then it will all have to wait until I am once again free." (69.2)

Chapter 70 *A Riot in Baltimore*

Governor Fitzhugh Lee awoke early on January 2, 1886, his first full day in office. He quietly dressed, descended the stairs at the Virginia Governor's Mansion, and entered his office. Daybreak was dimly lighting the room as he assumed his place behind the large Governor's desk. His thoughts turned to the last Lee to have served as Virginia's Governor, Henry Lee, III. It dawned upon Fitz there were many similarities he shared with his grandfather, a man he had never had the pleasure to meet, but still felt he knew as well as he knew himself. From the time he was a young boy, Fitz had heard of his grandfather's love of horses and his unsurpassed ease in the saddle. Harry Lee had distinguished himself as a brash cavalry officer during the Revolution, earning the admiration, confidence, and trust of General Washington as he rose to the rank of Major General. By 1790, Harry had so distinguished himself as to secure the nomination of the Federalist Party for Governor of Virginia and ultimately, the official validation of the public for that very position (1791-1794). Perhaps "Light Horse" Harry's highest honor was his eulogizing of the great Washington in 1799; his utterance of the phrase by which the humble national commander would forever be epitomized; "first in war, first in peace, and first in the hearts of his countrymen." The parallels so struck Fitz at that moment that he wondered to himself if the arc of his life may continue to mirror that of his grandfather as the years advanced.

On June 18, 1812, President James Madison signed a declaration of war against Great Britain into law. For several years Great Britain had blockaded trade between the United States and Napoleonic France. Over five hundred American merchant ships had been forcibly boarded and more than fifteen thousand seamen had been impressed into duty aboard British ships. Great Britain considered support of France, economic or otherwise, through trade or other means, an act of aggression. British leaders considered themselves the last, best hope to defeat the ever-expanding tyrannical French empire and would not countenance American support of the French on any level. France took a similar view of any nation which attempted to trade with Great Britain. Although French actions against American shipping interests were not as numerous nor pervasive as the British, incidents of similar French aggression exceeded two hundred.

The Federalist Party staunchly opposed Madison and his Democrat-Republican Party's march to war. Although the impressment of American sailors was of very serious concern, the Federalists did not believe it warranted a full-scale declaration of war which, in their view, would potentially bankrupt the fledgling U.S. Treasury and imperil the continued existence of a weak and vulnerable democracy still reeling from the costs of the Revolution. The Federalists viewed post-revolutionary France as an equal, if not greater, threat to American Democracy. Although it was undeniable that Britain was conducting hostile acts and hampering the ability for America to conduct free trade, the prospect of a globe dominated by the French regime was even more fearsome. It was the party's position that war with the British would serve only the French, who themselves had repeatedly displayed a penchant for duplicity with American diplomats surrounding these issues for nearly ten years. The Federalists were not advocating for the United States to take either side in this clash of titans; but rather that America sit still and allow the conflict between the superpowers to continue and, hopefully, come to a relatively speedy conclusion in favor of the British.

Democrat-Republican (later to become the Democrat Party) members of Congress, led by *War Hawk* House Speaker and Henry Clay and South Carolina Representative John C. Calhoun, argued that American unwillingness to stand and combat these British interdiction and impressment actions would severely hobble America on the world stage. American inaction would only invite continued abusive action with accelerating regularity by Great Britain and other nations across the globe. Increasingly, much of the American citizenry and their Democrat-Republican representation became deafened by the reverberating drum beat of war. The rift between those who believed the burgeoning democracy was compelled to project power and influence abroad and those who were more concerned with stabilizing a very tenuous economy on the home front grew ever more broad, fractious, and disharmonious.

British interests in Canada, in anticipation of American retaliation for the maritime seizures, were interested in exploiting the growing political rift between the Federalists and the Democrat-Republicans. In 1809, Sir James Craig, the Governor-General of Canada, engaged the services of a spy, John Henry, to report on disaffection amongst the Federalist-dominated area of New England. The Governor-General believed that the potential existed, should the Democrat-Republican administration headed by Madison declare war on Britain, for the New England states to establish a northern pro-British confederacy which may ally itself with Britain. In exchange for this information, Craig promised Henry a position in Canadian government. Henry wrote several letters to Craig over a three-month period in 1809. Governor-General Craig died in January, 1812, ending Henry's prospects for the Canadian position. After a chance meeting with an agent of France, Henry contacted James Madison and offered to sell him the highly questionable intelligence for $50,000. In his desperate desire to promote the war and to discredit Federalist opposition, Madison purchased the tendentious documents, sight unseen, in February, 1812. Subsequently, President Madison publicly presented the information to Congress, effectively tarring his Federalist opposition as pro-British traitors to America. (70.1)

On June 22, 1812, a pro-war Democrat-Republican mob invaded the offices of the anti-war *Federalist-Republican* newspaper located on Gay Street in Baltimore. The Mayor, Judge of the Criminal Court, and several magistrates and police officers stood by while the mob crashed into the offices and destroyed the entire printing apparatus. The ruffians chased the employees from the building, threatening assassination and other horrible circumstances. Alexander Contee Hanson, proprietor of the *Federalist-Republican*, was notified the next day at his home in Rockville, Maryland. Hanson formulated a plan

Alexander Contee Hanson, Publisher

to immediately recommence distribution of his paper in Baltimore. He informed his closest associates of the affront; beckoning their assistance. Eight men: General James Lingan, Captain Richard Crabb, Dr. Peregrine Warfield, John Thomson, Otho Sprigg, Esq., Ephraim Gaither, John Howard Payne, and General "Light Horse" Harry Lee volunteered to accompany Hanson back to Baltimore in defense of the rights of person, property, freedom of speech, and the liberty of the press.

One month later, Hanson had re-established a printing office in Georgetown, MD (later to become part of Washington, D.C.). He had also received permission from his partner in Baltimore, Mr. Garrett Wagner, to use his home at 45 South Charles Street as a Baltimore distribution point. Wagner, under the continued threat of the mob, had evacuated the home and moved his family to an undisclosed location. On July 26th, Alexander Hanson, his eight loyal compatriots, and a dozen other supporters occupied the large brick house on Charles Street. They brought along a cache of small weaponry in anticipation of a boisterous, and perhaps fierce, resistance. The following day they recommenced the dangerous distribution of the *Federalist-Republican*.

As the sun closed-in on the horizon on July 27th, an agitated group assembled in front of the house on Charles Street. Shouts began to echo among the brick buildings lining both sides of the street. Alexander Hanson looked at the other men with a mixture of profound disappointment and trepidation.

"Gentlemen, I fear that the confrontation is upon us even sooner than expected. I already regret that I have brought you to these circumstances", he grimaced.

"Alexander, dear friend,", began Harry Lee, "I am sure I speak for General Lingan, and I may even speak for the others among us; we are here to defend your honor and that of your family. Your father served alongside us to procure a hard-fought independence from the British. From that struggle our Constitution was birthed. It is the tenets of that Constitution which are under threat by the rabble outside these walls. It is our honor to defend your right, and the right of all men, to freely and peaceably speak, print, and disseminate political opinion."

At that instant a large stone blasted through the upper sash of one of the front windows. Alexander Hanson darted to the front door and opened it. He stepped out onto the front stoop and raised his hands in the air and looked out at the angry mob populated largely by young men and boys. "Gentlemen! Gentlemen, please!", Hanson called, "I implore you to consider what you are doing! All we seek to do is publish a newspaper. We ask that you disperse. We mean none of you harm. However, you must understand…", he hesitated as a bead of sweat ran down the side of his face. "The men in here are armed and this building will be defended!" Another rock hit the building façade just feet above Hanson's head. He flinched, cowered, stepped back through the door, and bolted it.

"Gentlemen, prepare your weapons. We must gird for an assault!", Harry Lee warned.

The crowd outside continued to grow as the sun disappeared. The shouts became more frequent and increasingly threatening. "We will root you out, Tory bastards! We will drink your blood!" Two more large stones shattered windows on the first floor.

"Mr. Gaither, take two men and go upstairs.", ordered General Lee. "Fire two shots each out of the windows over the heads of the crowd. It is my hope that will encourage them to disperse." Lee carefully moved toward one of the downstairs windows and gently slid the curtain slightly to the side to watch. A few moments later a succession of six shots rang out. The men in the street quickly broke and scrambled in opposite directions up and down Charles Street. The men inside waited quietly. With each minute that passed, hope that the crowd had given up the assault edged toward belief. But, after five minutes, any belief proved unfounded as the horde re-assembled in larger and more intemperate numbers. An order was barked in the street and a barrage of stones rained on the front of the house. Stone after stone came crashing through, obliterating every pane of glass in the structure. Several others exploded through the rear windows, informing the occupants that the structure was surrounded and there would be no escape. Fists were felt pounding on the front door. Henry Lee, now gray and fifty-six years of age, had not experienced the adrenal forces of battle in over twenty years. As a shoulder slammed heavily against the door, his instincts took hold. He grabbed a musket and fired a shot through one of the windows and into the street. Hanson chose a pistol and two other men picked up and aimed muskets. Three more shots hurtled into the darkness, at least two hitting a mark. Screams were heard from the street. The assault on the front door ceased as the crowd retreated down Charles street a few dozen yards and regrouped to discuss their next move. Inside the house, the defenders furiously piled furniture in front of the doors. They abandoned the first floor, and retreated upstairs. Four men waited with two firearms apiece to defend the stairwell. A fifth stood ready to greet any intruder with the blast of a blunderbuss. The remainder assumed positions in the upstairs windows, waiting to lay down enough fire to suppress any charge originating in the street below. After two hours of intermittent action, the mob organized for a large focused assault on the house. By this time, several men in the crowd had muskets of their own. At 2 AM several shots were fired from the street and rocks once again pelted the façade. Gaither leaned out the center window and squeezed off a shot at a group of men storming toward the door. It hit home and a man in front dropped quickly to the street. Seconds later fire was returned and hit Gaither. He immediately coiled on the floor clamping a hand over his neck. Two men rushed him to a rear bedroom where Dr. Warfield began administering to the wound. The sound of a drum was heard circling the neighborhood, calling more men to the streets to punish the Federalist anti-government seditionists.

Gen. Henry "Light Horse Harry" Lee

The quake of trampling hooves induced immediate paralysis in the street. The crowd parted as twelve horsemen led by Major Charles Barney of the Maryland National Guard approached the house on Charles Street.

"Citizens,", the Major announced, "we are here to protect person and property; and to prevent violence. I assure you that I am here as your personal and political friend. I ask that you disperse so that we can secure the party in the house."

"Under whose authority?", a figure in the crowd asked.

"Brigadier General Stricker.", Barney responded.

"Then show us the order!", the man demanded.

Major Barney removed a piece of paper from his pocket, dismounted, and beckoned a rioter he knew to follow him around the corner and into an alley. "Mr. Mumma, There is no written order from General Stricker.", Major Barney explained. "However, we now must restore the peace."

"We want those men, Major. They are sowing the seeds of sedition. These Federalists are no more than Tories! The disgusting opinions that man publishes lend aid and comfort to our enemy. The President has declared war and these men still look to subvert him! The men of Baltimore will not stand for this!"

"Mr. Mumma, we will take them to jail and allow the civil authorities to prosecute this matter. They will stand trial."

"You may take them to the jail, Major. But it is only a short delay; for we will take them out of the jail. And we will put them to death!"

"Mumma, do not impede my men! We intend to remove these men to the jail. What happens afterward will be between you, them, and the civilian authority."

"Do what you will.", snarled Mumma.

As Major Barney emerged from the alley a cannon was being trained upon the brick Federalist stronghold. Barney bolted over and leapt atop the field piece. "This cannon shall not be fired! My men will stand guard across the street. Should it be fired, it shall be fired upon friends! You must now disperse and leave the dispensation of justice to the civil authority!"

"They must die! These Federalist Tories must die!", came shouts from the crowd. Barney crossed the street and mounted his horse. His men lined up alongside him forming an equine barrier between the mob and the house. A tense standoff ensued until just after sunrise when Brigadier General Stricker and Mayor Edward Johnson appeared at the house. Major Barney allowed the two officials to pass his line and approach the door. Mayor Johnson knocked and announced their presence.

"Mr. Hanson. We are here to negotiate an end to this. Please open the door and allow General Stricker and myself to enter. We mean no harm and wish to resolve the matter." A few moments later the sound of furniture sliding across the floor was followed by the sounds of two bolts disengaging and a lock being thrown open. The door opened slightly.

The mob pressed forward. The horsemen stood firm. "Stay back! Stay back!", Major Barney warned.

"Gentlemen, please come in.", General James Lingan said softly as the door swung open. The mayor and General Stricker entered the front hallway and closed the door behind them.

"Gentlemen,", Mayor Johnson began, "you must recognize the great peril those men in the streets represent for you. The General and I do not believe that we can contain them. We are impressed with the belief that a civil war is inevitable and I consider this the commencement of it. The opinions presented in Mr. Hanson's publication are dangerous. And, the implication of the government in this dispute between the parties and the paper has been noticed…"

Alexander Hanson interrupted, "Mr. Mayor, this is not the time nor the place to enter a dispute over politics. I have a right to defend this house, and my person; both of which have come under felonious assault! It is your duty to protect these rights by disbanding that mob!", pointing toward the street. "If you will not perform your duty, then I assure you the men here are competent in their own defense!"

"Mr. Hanson, General Stricker and I are simply not capable of protecting you here from the men outside. We suggest that you and all the men here surrender yourselves into the hands of the civil authority. We will provide an effectual escort for all of you to the jail where we will station an equally effectual guard to protect your persons until such time a bail has been posted."

"To jail! To jail for what?!", Hanson erupted in angry disgust. "If you cannot disband the mob here, you will not protect us to jail; nor after we are in jail!"

General Henry Lee sensed his young friend had lost his poise. "Alexander; allow me to speak with these gentlemen in the parlor for a moment." Lee grabbed hold of the young publisher's arm and looked in his eyes to project reassurance. "General Lingan, you and the others please escort Mr. Hanson to the back room for a moment. I would like to discuss terms with the Mayor and General Stricker." Hanson nodded in agreement as he took a deep breath and tried to lower his temperature.

"Gentlemen, I am General Henry Lee. Please understand…", he began. "Mr. Hanson is at risk of losing everything. He retains the impetuousness of youth. However, his requests for our safety should be honored. You, gentlemen, are sworn to protect the rights of all citizens. We have done nothing more than defend our rights against a criminal mob. If we agree to go with you to the jail, we would like to bring our arms for our own defense. We would ask that you provide horses or carriages for our safe and unimpeded transport. With your assurance that once we reach the jail, our safety will be guaranteed and we will be safely handed over to the civil authority, we will comply. One of our compatriots is wounded. We would ask that he and the attending doctor be transported to the hospital."

"General Lee, I must first beg the question: why are you here?", Mayor Johnson asked.

"Sir, I am here in defense of a friend; in defense of our American rights.", Lee replied.

"General, I understand your position and appreciate your service to this country;

but you must see that this situation is untenable. As a general you must see the futility of continuing the fight. As a governor, you must understand the will of the people is sometimes impossible to deny." Lee could see the helpless disappointment in the Mayor's eyes. "That is a large and volatile force outside and we are not confident in our ability to protect you. General Stricker and I must go speak with these men and negotiate your passage to the jail. I will ask them to consider your terms."

"Very well, Mayor. And I will speak with Mr. Hanson." Harry Lee escorted the two officials to the front door. As the door cracked open, he glanced outside and saw Maryland Attorney General John Montgomery speaking with members of the mob. "They are all Democrats and are all in this together...", the old general muttered to himself.

General Lee called to all the occupants of the house to gather once again upstairs. He quickly explained the terms he had proposed to secure safe passage to the jail. Mr. Hanson again erupted in emotion, "General! We must stay and fight! 'Tis better to die here with our arms in our hands than to be led through the streets like malefactors! It will be a massacre! You see how timid these officials be! They will not protect us! Their crimes will go unredressed!"

"Alexander!", Harry Lee strained, "You must see the impracticability of our defense. There are over one thousand ruffians out there. And, they are armed, as well. We have no provisions. We are low on ammunition; food; water. We are all fatigued. If we stand and fight, we will certainly all die. We cannot prevail! All we can do is hope to survive. I believe a move to the jail and the protection afforded by the civil authority should be satisfactory to quell the passions of the bloodthirsty gang."

Alexander Hanson held both fists up to his eyes and took a deep breath. "Very well, General Lee.", he capitulated.

After ten more uncomfortable minutes Mayor Johnson, General Stricker, and Attorney General Montgomery approached the front door. Alexander Hanson and elder Generals Lee and Lingan descended the stairs and let them in.

Mayor Johnson cleared his throat, "We have discussed this matter with the leaders of the mob. They have agreed to allow your passage under the escort of General Stricker to the jail. General Stricker has sent for additional cavalry and local militia to bolster the escort party. They have rejected all other terms suggested by General Lee. You will leave your weapons here and you will travel to the jail on foot. There, you will be turned over to the civil authority. Attorney General Montgomery will have you arraigned as soon as possible. General Stricker and his men will stand guard outside the jail until your bail can be met.

"What are the charges?", Hanson demanded.

"Those have not been specified, as yet.", the Attorney General responded. "We will discuss these matters at the jail. You do understand that you shot dead one of the men in the street?" Alexander Hanson looked with angered concern at Lee and Lingan. General Lee held his palm up, imploring Hanson to maintain composure.

"What about our wounded? Will he be taken to a hospital?", asked Harry Lee.

"Is he able to walk under his own power?", General Stricker inquired.

"No...", Lee began before a shout from the stairwell interrupted him.

"Yes! I am able to walk. I will go with the rest to the jail!", bravely announced Ephraim Gaither.

At eight-thirty that morning, the group of twenty men walked out the door of the house on Charles Street. General Stricker's cavalrymen formed two columns surrounding the Federalists. A foot guard of forty men then encircled the horsemen, creating an outer ring of defense. General Stricker pulled to the head of the columns and gave the order to march. They had not travelled one-half block before the first stone sailed over the horsemen and struck near Alexander Hanson. General Stricker immediately halted the column, drew his pistol, and fired a shot into the air. "There will be no more projectiles cast upon this party! Any man that dares to defy this order shall be met with deadly retribution!"

There arose a great clamor among the mob. A shout came soon filled the air, "This is but a temporary condition! These men will die!". This was followed by a chorus of death threats; a vile performance that continued for the next seven blocks as the prisoners made their way through the streets of Baltimore to the jail.

Once at the jail the Hanson and the others were marched up the long front staircase of the building and escorted by the jailer down a dark hallway to a large holding cell. The size of the mob had decreased in size, many resigned to the belief that the civilian authority now controlled the outcome. However, a steadfast group nearing one hundred strong gathered out front of the jail and continued to hurl insult after insult, threat after threat, at the exhausted group of twenty. After several hours Mayor Johnson, General Stricker, and Attorney General Montgomery appeared at the jail. They were curiously accompanied by three prominent members of the mob, Mr. Mumma among them. As the three officials continued to grant their assurances of safety and lawful treatment, Mumma and the others stood behind them silently studying the faces of each of the twenty prisoners. The brief conversation ended and the six men exited the jail. A moment later the jailer appeared and unlocked the large iron cell door. He then turned and left the jail, taking the keys with him. Mayor Johnson addressed the mob, "Gentlemen, the prisoners are safely within the jail. The Attorney General and I would like your assurances that these men will remain safe until their bail is received tomorrow."

Mr. Mumma stepped forward, "You have our word, Mr. Mayor."

"Very well.", the Mayor replied. He then nodded to General Stricker who proceeded to dismiss the militia. "The Attorney General and I are satisfied with your assurances. This is settled. Please disperse and return to your families." As General Stricker and his cavalry rode off to the east, Johnson and Montgomery calmly walked to the west and disappeared around the corner.

Thirty men armed with knives and clubs stormed through the front doors of the Baltimore jail. Shouts of death and destruction rang through the dark hallways as the monsters descended upon the holding cell. They ripped open the large cell door and grabbed Alexander Hanson. He was quickly funneled down the dark hallway. John Thomson was next taken; then General Lingan; then General Lee. Lee was punched, shoved, and spat upon as he raced through the hallway. He looked up briefly as he stumbled toward the light of the front doorway. He gathered his balance as he crossed the threshold. There in front of him was the angry mob numbering over one hundred. Hanson, Thomson, and Lingan were all near the bottom of the staircase. Each was surrounded by a half a dozen men with clubs. The retribution had begun. "Light Horse" Harry was suddenly struck from behind by the blow of a club, propelling him head first down the long stone staircase. The jeers of the ravenous crowd intensified as he tumbled to the bottom. Six men instantly preyed upon him, delivering multiple club blows to his head, back, arms, and legs. Their laughter and taunts punctuated each blow. Lee desperately rose onto a knee, raising his arm to protect his head he tried to beg for relief but was unable to get a word out before another club cracked behind his ear pushing him face down into the street.

Man, after man was plucked from the cell and hurtled down into a medieval slaughter pit which had re-emerged from the bowels of history into the heart of what purported to be a civil society. Seemingly decent working men; sons, husbands, and fathers alike had been zealously overtaken by an irresistible drive to maim and kill; like satanic changelings, the wolfpack had risen and seized upon their rivals to rip them limb from limb. The months and years of suspicion, fear-mongering, and falsehood, which had been injected into their hearts and minds, had unleashed an irrational and needless reprisal against their own brethren. The humane instinct which compelled men to protect their families and neighbors was twisted by raw politics into a shamefully inhumane desire to viciously destroy in summary judgement.

A bloodied General Lingan rose to his knees, "I am old and infirm! I fought for your liberties in The Revolution!". One of the barbarians stepped forward and kicked the old general in the groin before unleashing a backhand across his face. Lingan raised a quivering hand as a silent plea for mercy. Another enraged man came forward and shoved General Lingan onto his back and proceeded to stomp more than a half-dozen times on his chest. Blood over-flowed from the old hero's mouth as a third assassin lurched forward and delivered a *coup de grace*, plunging a dirk into Lingan's chest. "That old rascal is hard dying!", the killer declared with fiendish delight. "Tory bastard!"

John Thomson had been beaten with equal severity. After more than a dozen club blows to his skull and an iron bar having been rapped across his legs, he was dragged about thirty yards from the crowd to a small cart. Two brutes tore his shirt from his body. Another reached in the cart and removed a bucket of hot tar and dumped it atop his head and bare torso. A fourth demon applied the complimentary feathers. Thomson fell to his back as the hot tar burned through the surface of his skin. One of the men reached down and tried to gouge out Thomson's eyes, but the thick tar, though damaging in and of itself, provided a shield. Two men lifted Thomson to his feet as another black-hearted thug struck a match and set the tar on Thomson's back ablaze. Thomson dropped quickly and writhed on the ground to the stinging laughter and delight of the mob. He found the strength to call out, "For God's sake, be not worse than savages! If you want my life; take it by shooting or stabbing!"

General Harry Lee stayed on his feet as long as he could, desperately trying to block and deflect the seemingly endless barrage of cudgelings. As he spun in an exhausted stupor, trapped on a merry-go-round of death, he caught alternating glimpses of his battered comrades and his possessed tormenters. He dropped to one knee as the sounds of wood pounding flesh echoed all around him. A boy of no more than fifteen came from behind and grabbed Lee around the head with one arm as he put a knife to the bridge of Lee's nose. The boy began to dig in. Lee reflexively pulled away as the sharp edge slid down the side of his nose, taking with it several layers of skin and a nostril. General Lee struggled briefly to his feet before the fist of a large man landed between his eyes and catapulted him onto his back. The boy again appeared with the knife, trying to plunge it into the old man's eye. Lee, once again, reacted quickly as the knife point caught his cheek and sliced another three inches down the side of his face. Two others then descended upon the helpless old patriot. One held Lee's head steady whilst the other malicious lout poured hot candle oil into his eyes. The general screamed in agony as the degenerate firmly pressed his thumbs on Lee's eyelids. The blinded beaten man rolled on to his side as the pack of devil-dogs seized again upon him, clouting him a dozen times with clubs. Lee sensed his soul exiting his body. The pain was dulled as his mind travelled home to his wife and young family. As yet another blow crashed down upon his head, he fell, comatose.

The limp and broken bodies of eight men were collected and stacked near the foot of the jail stairs. A few boys circled the pile, sticking pins and pen knives into the bodies, probing for life. Lee awoke as a pen knife penetrated the top of his left hand. Somehow, he summoned the presence of mind to control the impulse to move; realizing that appearing dead would be his only hope for survival. Suddenly Alexander Hanson's desecrated body landed beside him. Hanson's unrecognizable face rested upon Lee's chest. Blood poured from his scalp and quickly saturated Lee's shirt. Mr. Mumma, who had reserved Hanson's punishment for himself, chuckled, "These Tory traitors will never forget this day. See? Hanson's brains are upon his breast!"

At that moment five angels of mercy appeared near the bodies. Five doctors who adhered to their oaths above any political belief implored the mob leaders to allow them to tend to the dead bodies. The doctors deftly suggested a return of the battered corpses to the jail and that the final dispensation could continue the following day.

"Very well. It has been a long day. We will return in the morning.", said Mumma with psychotic pragmatism. "We intend to hang these traitors to ensure their deaths." Mumma then took the stick in his hand and jabbed Hanson firmly in the privates. "*This one*, will be dissected!", he fiendishly proclaimed.

"Understood.", one doctor flatly replied as he smothered his temper.

As the crowd cleared the street in front of the jail, the doctors hastily removed the eight bodies back to the jail. To their surprise, seven of the eight were still alive; only poor General Lingan having succumbed to the perverse brutality. After the administering of drinks and opiates, the doctors called for carriages to transport the survivors to undisclosed locations. Alexander Hanson and two others were taken to a family friend's home in Anne Arundel County, Maryland. Three others were transported to Ellicott's Mills twenty-four miles outside of Baltimore. General Henry Lee and John Thomson were escorted to an associate's home in York, Pennsylvania. General James Lingan's body was brought to his home, Georgetown, for burial. Through divine intervention twelve other defenders of the house on Charles Street were able to blend into the crowds as the melee at Baltimore jail ensued and escape relatively unharmed.

Although there were some public hearings in the State of Maryland decrying the travesty of the Baltimore Riot, no legal action was taken against any of the mob; nor any of the politicians, military commanders, and civil authorities who chose to coldly turn a blind eye to the base criminality perpetrated upon the Federalist defenders of liberty. State-wide outrage over this incident and a general dismay over the course of *Mr. Madison's War* led to the unseating of the Democrat-Republican Governor of Maryland in the next election in favor of a Federalist. However, the City of Baltimore would remain firmly in the grasp of the Democrat-Republican machine for many years to come. (70.2)

The remaining four-and-one-half years of General Henry Lee's life were spent in a vain attempt to recover from the multitude of debilitating injuries suffered in Baltimore. "Light Horse" Harry died in 1818 at age sixty-two.

Governor Fitzhugh Lee shook his head in disgust as he considered the irony of his grandfather's tragic fate. The idea that a mob of Democrat-Republicans had so egregiously violated the sacred rights first codified by Lee's own maternal great-grandfather, George Mason, in the *Virginia Declaration of Rights* and then permanently enshrined for the nation by James Madison in the *U.S. Constitution* seemed impossibly absurd. Furthermore, to think it required a member of the Federalist opposition to stand in support of rights proudly espoused by the Democrat-Republican Madison; rights which, in practice, this same man clearly ignored! For Governor Lee it further illustrated the poisonous effect that a lust for power and the practice of vengeful politics can have on any man's soul. Lee reaffirmed to himself that his leadership would be different; he would resist the temptations that cloud men's judgment; whether in the favor of his allies or the defeat of his adversaries, the precepts of fairness and honesty, and the adherence to the rights of the individual, would navigate his course. He reconciled that yes, the arc of his life would indeed continue to mimic that of "Light Horse" Harry Lee; whether the defense of freedom, liberty, and the rule of law would bring him glorious victory and comfort or whether it would cast doom and tragedy upon him, he chose to forge a principled path.

Chapter 71   ***The Right to Testify***

  Beverly T. Crump sat at his desk and read a copy of the new law signed by Governor Fitzhugh Lee the previous day.

AN ACT TO ALLOW PERSONS CHARGED WITH CRIME TO TESTIFY IN THEIR OWN BEHALF   January 21, 1887

1. Be it enacted by the General Assembly of Virginia, That in any case of felony or misdemeanor the accused may be sworn and examined in his own behalf, and be subject to cross-examination as any other witness; but his failure to testify shall create no presumption against him, nor be the subject of any comment before the court or jury by the prosecuting attorney.

2. This act shall be in force from its passage.   (71.1)

  Crump turned and looked out his third-story window onto 9th Street. He caught a glimpse of H.R. Pollard crossing the street toward his building. Crump looked at his pocket watch, "Right on time.", he thought. A few moments later, Beverly Crump's clerk escorted H. R. Pollard into his office.

  "Good morning, Henry."

  "Hello, Bev.", Pollard replied.

  "Have you seen a copy of the new law?", Crump asked as he handed Pollard the sheet of paper.

  "I've heard about it; but I've not seen the language. I believe it's the right thing to do."

  "I am not so certain. I see potential problems. It is not a necessity; and I believe it will encourage perjury. The results will not be good."

  "I tend to disagree.", said Pollard. "I've been reading up on this. I believe Virginia is the thirty-eighth state to enact this type of legislation. Judge Appleton, of the Supreme Court in Maine, wrote rather extensively on this many years ago. He asserted that the exclusion of any testimony, even that of an accused, is improper. He contends that exclusion results in insufficient proof; and that impunity is the result of insufficient proof. Partial exclusion, which is exactly what the law used to demand, results in partial impunity."   (71.2)

"That may have some theoretical merit; but I believe, in practice, this will have an adverse effect on the proceedings. If the accused is guilty, he will simply obfuscate and tell falsehoods. If the accused is innocent, aggressive prosecution will intimidate the witness and perhaps compel an otherwise innocent person to commit perjury; thus, creating a crime where none previously existed."

"This could happen; but I feel more often than not, it will shed further light on the matter in question. It will allow the jury to hear the accused in his own words; to read his emotions, his vocal inflections, his mannerisms. You and I both understand that this business is very unscientific. Witness credibility is an important consideration. Besides, it is written into the law that the accused has the right to testify; but he is not compelled to do so. The accused also maintains the right to stay silent. I believe we are in an era where the rights of the individual are expanding, Bev. And, I don't mean just those of the negroes; but of all men. The time has arrived. There is an awakening, of sorts, and it is my belief, that in a just few years, we will have grown to believe that a reinstatement of the denial of a man's right to testify in his own behalf would be as distasteful and unimaginable as a return to slavery."

"Yes, this may be true; but you cannot deny that in many instances when an accused would decline to take the stand, it will infer guilt to the jury. No matter how much a judge instructs a jury not to make this type of inference; it will still happen. As you said, this business is not scientific."

"Point taken.", Pollard conceded, "But you must also realize that until this time, the guiltiest of criminals could, with impunity, shield themselves behind the law and a lawyer's eloquence." (71.3)

Bev Crump nodded, "Perhaps… which leads me to the question before us. Should the Supreme Court vacate the decision of the Hustings Court and order a new trial; what will we do with our accused?"

"That is a troubling question, Bev. Obviously, Thomas would be a very calm and credible witness. I have no doubt that he would effectively state his case in open court. And, it is my contention that should a jury have the opportunity to *hear* directly from Thomas, his case would be made effectively. If this opportunity never materializes, we will be left with a situation where the court and the Governor will have only the opportunity to *read* our petitions. This would have a much smaller chance of achieving the desired effect. (71.4)

This said, should he be granted an opportunity to testify in a new trial, I still believe that corroborating his story would prove the most difficult task for us. There are several people he says that he saw that day in Richmond. And, very few of them are willing to come forward and speak of it under oath – we know this. Whether they cannot recall times and events as he recalls them; or whether they are just hesitant to get involved with such a well-known trial – there is near-unanimous resistance. I believe that the public, in general, is so tainted by the press reportage and the raucous proceedings, that none of these potential exculpatory witnesses want to be the witness who "sets a guilty man free". I believe many of them are fearful of the backlash – and I am not certain that any of their testimony would be convincing enough to sway the negative general public opinion."

"Yes, I believe you are correct. The public opinion is definitely our largest barrier. I suppose that if we are granted another trial, we would then approach each of the potential witnesses and perhaps we will then be able to persuade them to freely come forward. If the Supreme Court were to demand a new trial; this possibly would swing opinion back in our direction. I believe the longer we can maintain these proceedings, the more likely the rage of the mob will subside and Mr. Cluverius will begin to be viewed as a man, rather than a monster."

Chapter 72 *Toddies at The Willard*

Three older gentlemen entered the barbershop adjacent to The Willard Hotel in Washington, D.C. All four barber chairs were occupied so the gentlemen took seats along the side wall and continued their conversation.

"Gentlemen, after we have our shave, we should retire next door and see what spirits the hotel has to offer.", said one man.

"The Willard is known for *Mint Juleps*; but I believe I'm looking forward to a toddy.", said another.

"Ah, yes... I like a good toddy! They always remind me of the time at Catlett's Station during the War. I was attached to Pope's command at the time. Colonel Marshall and I were mixing glasses of toddy in his tent. It was late August as I recall... A thunderstorm had just blown through and it was pitch dark. We were adding small quantities of sugar, nutmeg, and the like; tuning them perfectly to our taste with just the right amount of ice... When, like another crack of thunder, we heard that terrible sound; the sound to make any man in Lincoln's army shudder with dread – that damned *Rebel Yell*! And this one, in particular, was unnerving as it sounded as if 10,000 Confederate bastards had hit that screeching note in unison just outside our tents. Gunfire rang out immediately, soon followed by the pounding hooves of Stuart's cavalry. And I declare to you gentlemen, that I never remembered, and cannot tell to this day, whether we drank those toddies, or not! I do know that we scurried through the back of that tent and escaped into the woods in the darkness with just the clothes on our backs!"

The Willard Hotel, Washington, D.C.

A man in the barber chair directly beside them began to chuckle. He was in full recline with a warm towel over his face, listening all the while to the conversation amongst the Yankee strangers. His large belly tremored as his laughter began to erupt. He grunted and guffawed as he struggled to raise his head up. After finally sitting up, he removed the towel with his left hand, exposing a red face, a white trimmed goatee, and bright blue eyes. "Excuse me, gentlemen, for interrupting your conversation; but it so happens that I can supply the information about which that gentleman seems in doubt. **They *did not*** drink those toddies. I drank one myself and a member of my staff drank the other!" The three gentlemen looked at the pugnacious little man with bemused astonishment. He continued, "Coming up to that tent after it had just been vacated, we found two glasses of toddy and had sufficient confidence that they had not been poisoned. We desired to test their quality.

And, I can testify that this gentleman and my beloved first cousin, Colonel Louis Marshall, *know very well how to make toddies!*" (72.1)

The four men enjoyed a round of laughter. "Well, who might this pilferer of toddies be?", asked one of the men.

"My name is Fitzhugh Lee of the 1st Virginia Cavalry."

The men stood wide-eyed as one of them said, "And now you are Governor of Virginia!"

"One in the same.", said Fitz.

"Well, it is an honor, sir. I am Bill McBurney of the 1st Ohio Cavalry. These men are Jim Laughlin and John Cannan; both also from the 1st Ohio."

Fitz Lee checked his pocket watch. "Gentlemen… I still have nearly an hour before I have to be at a meeting; perhaps you could postpone your shave and join me next door for a toddy?"

The three men looked at one another. Bill McBurney responded, "Our pleasure, Governor."

Fitzhugh Lee and his three new friends crossed through the lobby of The Willard Hotel and entered the lounge. They seated themselves near the fireplace in some lovely stuffed chairs which surrounded a low table. A waiter quickly approached. "Four toddies, gentlemen?", Governor Lee asked.

"Nothing else would seem appropriate.", said Bill.

"Four toddies, it is!", Fitz informed the waiter. "So, Bill,", Fitz began. "how is it you were there at Catlett's Station?"

"Well, I was part of the Quartermaster Corps under Pope at that time. Jim was a cavalry officer. John, here was a surgeon; but they never came east. Most of our unit stayed in the west. We are here for a small reunion. There's probably thirty members of the 1st Ohio here."

"Ah, yes. And what was the name of that Quartermaster?", asked Fitz.

"Frankeberger, Colonel John Frankeberger.", Bill McBurney replied. (72.2)

"That's it. I think that's the one. I never met him but I know of a great tale involving him. It happened that same night – the night I captured the toddies."

"He was captured, too…", said McBurney.

"Yes, and so he was…", replied Fitz.

On August 22, 1862 the skies of Virginia opened up as thunderstorms rolled over the Blue Ridge and flowed east. The driving rains converted the narrow roadways to fast-running streams and the creeks to raging river torrents. Major General J.E.B. Stuart determined, that although conditions were miserable, it afforded his forces an opportunity to strike at General John Pope's growing Army of Virginia. Catlett's Station sat at the junction of the Orange and Alexandria Railroad and a spur running west to Warrenton. By striking there, Stuart hoped to disrupt Union supply lines from Washington and capture Pope's headquarters (and perhaps Pope, himself); sowing confusion and fear in preparation for a full- scale assault by Robert E. Lee's Confederate forces near Manassas.

General Stuart led nearly 2,000 men on an undetected ride around the right flank of the Federal forces encamped near Catlett's Station. At 11 o'clock that night a shattering *Rebel Yell* pierced the darkness as Stuart's forces fanned out and overran Pope's camp, taking over four hundred prisoners, over five hundred horses, and supplies and equipment of all sorts. The Confederates also seized over $500,000 in greenbacks and $20,000 in gold. But, perhaps most important, Stuart captured General Pope's personal baggage, official papers, and a treasure trove of intelligence detailing the plans of the entire Federal campaign.

Early the following morning Stuart dispatched his trusted aide, Major Heros von Borcke, to ride back to the rear column of their forces and deliver additional orders. As von Borcke road down the lonely narrow pike nearing Warrenton he glanced over at a small farmhouse and spotted what appeared to be a Federal soldier quickly closing a curtain. The observant *Grey Giant* smartly dismounted and knocked upon the door.

"Open dis door, at vunce!", the Prussian commanded.

He turned his ear to the door hearing tables and chairs being dragged across the floor to barricade the door. He hurled his shoulder, with his full two-hundred twenty-five pounds behind it, against the door. The door exploded open, blowing the Yankee and the furniture backwards into the parlor. Von Borcke lunged through the doorway, but before he could get his powerful hands on the terrified unarmed soldier, a very pretty woman appeared carrying a tray with a bottle of wine and refreshments. "Welcome, sir. May I offer you something to eat and drink?", she smiled.

"Was zum Teufel?!", von Borcke blurted out as his eyes cut back and forth between the nervous Union officer and the delightful young woman. After a moment the major regained his wits and his manners. "Tank you for der hoospitality. I vill be ready to accept after I do my duty." Von Borcke stepped to his right. The woman stepped to her left. He stepped back to his left; and she back to the right; maintaining a mirroring obstacle between the potential combatants. The Union officer glanced over at an open back doorway. Sensing the panting man was about to break, the Prussian drew his pistol and aimed it at the man's chest. "My dear madam, if you cannot bear separation from der enemy of your country, I vill leave him vith you; but I vill *not* leave him alive."

The young woman backed away. She set the tray on a table in the parlor and buried her hands in her face. Von Borcke looked at the soldier with confusion. "My name is Lieutenant Sullivan with the 2nd West Virginia. This woman is to be my wife."

Major von Borcke rolled his eyes and shook his head in disbelief. "Now you must come vith me." He looked over at the young woman, "I am sorry madam, but dis is my duty."

Later that afternoon, a momentary lull in the action enabled von Borcke to stop in the town of Warrenton and rest for a brief time. His uniform was still damp as he approached a field kitchen set up near Main Street and Alexandria Pike. He removed his coat and hung it on a chair back before sitting down. He rubbed his eyes with the heels of his hands and took a few deep breaths. Then he heard the sound of a familiar angelic voice, "Welcome sir. May I offer you something to eat and drink?" He looked up and saw the same lovely woman he had encountered at the farmhouse just hours before. She stood before him with a tray of coffee and some biscuits.

"Madam. I do not know vut to say. I am sorry…"

"Please, sir. As you said; you were performing your duty. And now, I am performing mine." Von Borcke's face expressed confusion. "I am very conflicted by loyalties with this war.", she explained. "So, I have decided that I can only help all soldiers on both sides with the hope that, one day, this will all be resolved and peace will return to my country."

At that moment a young captain walked up and asked for some more coffee. He turned to Heros von Borcke, "Major, it appears we acquired a great amount of Yankee supplies last night. We captured their Quartermaster's store and the Quartermaster, himself!"

The young woman began to laugh. "Madam, vy do you laugh?", von Borcke asked.

"That Quartermaster, Colonel Frankeberger, was staying at our house just a few days ago. He boasted that he would be in Richmond by the end of the month. I wagered him a bottle of champagne that he would not. It appears that I have now lost the bet; for he will almost certainly be in Richmond very soon! Albeit, under far different circumstances than he imagined."

A bit smitten, and perhaps tamed, by a woman who possessed an alluring combination of comeliness, bravery, compassion, and humor, the large grey beast longed to find some small way to please his beauty. "I vill talk vith General Stuart. I vill help you pay dis bet.", Major von Borcke pledged with a smile.

A few hours later, the 1st Virginia Cavalry formed a column and began marching from Warrenton. Heros von Borcke rode out ahead with a bottle of champagne, directly from General Stuart's own stock. He stopped at the little farmhouse on the edge of town. Von Borcke and the young woman waited in front of the house on the side of the road. As Colonel Frankeberger rode by with a group of captured Union officers, the young woman dashed toward them with the bottle in hand. "Colonel Frankeberger! I am here to pay my debt! You will certainly reach Richmond before the end of the month after all!"

Frankeberger tilted his head back for a good laugh. Graciously accepting the bottle, he held it aloft, and declared, "I shall always be happy to drink to the health of so charming a person!"

The young woman curtsied before Frankeberger and walked back toward a satisfied Major von Borcke. She beckoned her Heros to lean over before kissing him softly on the cheek.

"Thank you for your chivalry, sir. I shall never forget this day."

A blushing von Borcke bowed his knightly head and softly said, "Danke, meine schone junge dame. It is my honor. My hope is your young man returns to you vun day and der is peace in your country." (72.3)

Tom Stockton finally located Governor Lee in the lounge of The Willard Hotel. "Excuse me, Governor…", he breathlessly interrupted, "President Cleveland will expect you in ten minutes."

"Yes, yes, Tom. Thank you. Gentlemen, I have enjoyed the toddies and the conversation; but now, unfortunately, I must leave you.", finishing his toddy as he stood.

"Certainly, a visit with the President is more fortuitous than any number of toddies with the likes of us, Governor!", exclaimed Bill McBurney.

"Likely not.", Fitz Lee retorted. "But, as dear ol' Von said: ***dis*** is my duty!"

Chapter 73 *Incoming Fire from All Directions*

Governor Fitzhugh Lee stopped just short of the doorway to his office at the Governor's Mansion. He peeked carefully around the door jamb. Fitz, Jr. and George were seated on the oriental rug in front of the Governor's desk.

"I'll see your two cat's eyes and raise you a swirly!", young Fitz exclaimed.

George looked suspiciously at his brother and then looked down into the five cards in his little hand. He looked again at his brother, this time with blank confusion.

"Come now, George! Place your bet!", said the impatient older brother circling for the kill.

George hesitated, reached into his dwindling pile of marbles, and pulled out his last swirly. Fitz, Jr.'s eyes lit up as George flipped it into the betting pile.

"Aren't you going to raise me?", greedy Fitz, Jr. prodded.

George shook his head. "Very well,", said Fitz Jr., "Show me your hand!"

"Show me yours first!", George demanded.

Ellen lowered her newspaper as she took her feet off her father's desk. She removed an unlit cigar from her mouth and spit a little bit of tobacco leaf onto the floor. Holding it between her first two fingers, she pointing the stogie at her little brothers, "Can't you two fools take your game in the other room?! I am trying to do some reading!"

Sensing things were getting ready to boil over, Fitz Lee moved into the doorway putting his hands on his hips, "I've seen more savory characters in a San Antonio saloon!"

Ellen quickly sat up straight and tried to discreetly lay down the cigar, "Sorry, Papa… I was just reading. These two…"

"…are gambling in the Governor's office!", Fitz Lee yelped as he raised his finger. "Ellen, if we aren't careful, you'll be reading about *this* scandal in tomorrow's paper!", he smiled. "But dear," lowering his voice sternly, "I do not want to see the cigars anymore. Those are not for young ladies."

Ellen thought of a sharp reply; then tactically retreated, "Yes, Papa." She then deftly maneuvered to a new subject and launched a counter-offensive, "Papa, I've been reading in the paper that Willie Cluverius is circulating a petition that he intends to present to you. He will ask you for clemency and for you to commute his brother's death sentence. You must commute Tommie's sentence!"

Governor Lee rolled his eyes and ignored Ellen's imagined familiarity. He, too, was choosing his battles. "Ellen, this is really not …".

"What is clemency, Papa?". Fitz, Jr. broke in.

The Governor exhaled through his nose and closed his eyes for a moment, "Fitz, it is rude behavior to interrupt an elder while he is speaking. Manners are important.

"I am sorry, Papa."

"Now, clemency is the power I have as governor to pardon someone of their crime. Or, as governor, I can change the sentence."

"So, will you pardon this man?", Fitz, Jr. followed up as George rolled a marble across the rug.

Governor Fitzhugh Lee on Stairway in Richmond c. 1886

"I have not made that decision.", Fitz squirmed a little. "These are important matters and it is my duty to study them very closely. If I believe this man has been wrongly convicted and sentenced, then I may act. But this is not something which can be done lightly. It is a very serious action for a governor to over-rule the decision of the court. It is imperative that a governor not let his own feelings enter into the decision. A governor must respect the findings of the jury and of the judiciary; and should act to overturn their decisions only in very extreme circumstances."

"Well, Papa," Ellen said, "there appears to me to be ample reason to overturn the decision: the evidence against Tommie was all circumstantial; he has never been availed of the right to testify in his own behalf; and, the Supreme Court decision was not unanimous."

"I think you should kill Tommie!", Fitz, Jr. erupted.

"Quiet, Fitz! You don't understand anything!", Ellen screeched.

"Enough!", Governor Lee roared. "This is not a topic of discussion in which we will engage! This is a very consequential matter for me, as Governor, to contemplate. And I will not discuss it any further with any of you! Nor will you discuss it with anyone else! You are free to think what you will; but you will not make mention of this again! Perhaps when the matter has been resolved we may speak of it. But, until that time, with regard to this matter, or any matters of State, I shall be considered your Governor; not your father. If you want to discuss matters of State with your Governor, you may seek an appointment like any other citizen. Please understand, the Governor's schedule is quite full. So, I wouldn't expect a hearing if I were you. However, if you wish to visit with your father, you may do so at any time – no appointment is necessary."

"Papa…", George spoke up. "If the man is killed; are you the one who will do it?"

"Well, George… No. The State has decided to kill him and it is the State which would do such. I can either allow the State to kill him, or, under very unusual circumstances, I can tell the State that they cannot kill him."

Ellen threw the newspaper down and stood. "Is there a difference? It's wrong for the State to kill anyone!"

Ellen angrily marched out of the office. Governor Lee turned to his boys, "I think the two of you should take your card game elsewhere. I have a busy day of work ahead." Fitz picked up a file sitting atop his desk and sat down. He opened the file and began to review a collection of newspaper articles and letters contained therein.

The Baltimore Sun
CLUVERIUS MUST HANG – A New Hearing Refused Him – The Case Remanded to Richmond
October 1, 1886

Richmond, Va., Sep 30 -   This morning the Supreme Court of Virginia, sitting at Staunton, handed down the papers in the Case of T.J. Cluverius, who stands convicted of the murder of Lillian Madison at the old reservoir, in this city, with the endorsement that the petition for a rehearing is denied. This remands the case to The Hustings Court of Richmond, by which time will be fixed for the death penalty by hanging unless executive clemency interposes.

It is not considered at all probable that the executive will interfere with the sentence of the court. As soon as the record in the case is certified by the Court of Appeals down to the Hustings Court, the latter tribunal will re-sentence the doomed man.

Soon after the announcement of the action of the Court of Appeals today Cluverius was visited in his cell by the newspaper reporters. He seemed to be enjoying excellent health and appeared quite cheerful. After discussing the prisoner's situation, a reporter asked him if he would not make a full statement of his connection with this affair before his sentence was executed. "Yes,", said he, "At the proper time I will make a statement, and it will implicate some"-   Here, Cluverius stopped short, and added: "I was about to tell too much." "Oh, continue.", pressed the interviewer. "No, I had better not say anything until my counsel decide what steps they will take next. That will probably be in a few days, and the I will give you a statement of the whole affair." "Of course, you will tell where you were on the night of the murder?" "Yes, I will." – Here the prisoner again hesitated, laughed, and said: "But I am talking too fast; I think I had better hold up." Before the reporters left Cluverius promised one of them to give a full story of this case within the next three days.

The Supreme Court of Appeals, in May last, decided by four to one, that the conviction of Thomas J. Cluverius of murder in the first degree of Fannie Lillian Madison, by the Hustings Court, was warranted by the evidence, and that no defect in the trial could be found to warrant giving a new trial. Judge Fauntleroy read the opinion. The opinion of the court rejecting Cluverius' appeal rejected all of the bills of exception presented by his counsel. There were nine of them. One, because a juryman was rejected because he had made a bet on the result of the trial; one because of the rejection of a juror for having expressed an opinion about circumstantial evidence; one as to the manner of impaneling the jury; one because the torn note written by Lillian and addressed to T.J. Cluverius had been admitted as evidence; another because the "Laura Curtis" letter had been admitted, and four others of not great importance. In the opinion, Judges Fauntleroy and Lewis fully concurred, Judges Richardson and Lacey concurred as to the result, and only Judge Hinton dissented. The following are the closing paragraphs of the opinion:

"We have reviewed this most voluminous record of the proceedings of the Hustings Court in this protracted and difficult trial, and we find no error of law or of fact which would justify this appellate court in interfering with the verdict of the jury or the judgment of the court.

The prisoner has had a fair and impartial trial. He has been defended both in the Hustings Court and in this court of review by able, experienced, and most faithful counsel, and the law has been vindicated in the result.

Justice to the prisoner and mercy to all the innocent public, whom the impunity and second offense of the prisoner would 'after gall' alike demand that he shall now pay the penalty of his crime, and, answering with his life for his foul deed, live not to act another. The judgment of the Hustings Court is affirmed." (73.1)

The Richmond Whig
October 10, 1886

CLUVERIUS CONDEMNED – Date of Death Fixed at December 10th

Cluverius, about whom so much has been written, on account of the murder of his cousin, Fannie Lillian Madison, saw sky-light once again yesterday. It was a sad day for him, however, for he was to brought before the Hustings Court of the City of Richmond to be sentenced to death for the murder of his cousin. Once before Cluverius underwent this ordeal. It was the 19th of June, 1885. He stood up boldly and heard the sentence coolly. He had a hope in the action of the appellate court. He is a lawyer, and thought that the intricacies involved in the large number of questions appealed would give him a chance for life.

From that time on, until the present, the prisoner has been confined closely. A guard has watched his movements all the time, and in his cell he has had ample opportunity to reflect upon passing events. He has seen an entire year pass since Judge Atkins, of the Hustings Court, pronounced the sentence of death on him the first time. It is a matter that no one can even fathom, what Cluverius' thoughts were during these twelve long months. Cluverius has changed since his last appearance in the Hustings Court room. He does not wear that indifferent stolid look, and to the close observer it is perfectly apparent that he is more keenly sensitive to the appalling consequences of the situation than ever before. His bearing was not, however, cringing- He took his seat and turned half way in his chair and gazed fixedly in one direction. The talk in the court room went on, and Cluverius stood the gaze of the battery of eyes in an unflinching way. He kept his eyes steadily in one direction, turning them neither left nor right. It was plain that he did this by a strong mental effort, and that in so doing he disclosed the fact that he was possessed of strong nerves.

Just before 2 o'clock, Beverly T. Crump came in and spoke to Cluverius. The salutation was brief, and the prisoner spoke only a few words. At 2 o'clock promptly Judge Atkins entered the courtroom from the side door of his office. Mr. C. V. Meredith, who represented the Commonwealth in the prosecution of Cluverius, was in his seat. Judge Atkins ordered the clerk to read the decision of the Supreme Court of Appeals and the certification back to the Hustings Court before saying: "Thomas J. Cluverius, the Supreme Court having overruled application for a new trial and affirmed the judgment of this court of June 19, 1885, it becomes my duty to fix a day for the execution of that judgment. Have you anything to say?"

Cluverius replied, "No, sir;", and then halting only for a second, he added, "Nothing but what I have said before."

Judge Atkins then sentenced him to death with the following words: "It is considered by the Court that you, Thomas J. Cluverius, shall be taken hence to the jail of this city and there securely kept until the 10th day of December next, on which day, between the hours of 9 in the morning and 6 in the evening, you shall be taken to some convenient place of execution, at or near said jail, and in the presence only of such officers of the law as may be necessary to see that this sentence is properly carried in to effect, be there hanged by the neck until you are dead. And may the Lord have mercy on you." (73.2)

The Massillon Independent
December 1, 1886

A STARTLING CONFESSION – Cluverius to Make Statement About the Celebrated Murder Case

Richmond, Va, Nov 29 - What may be a revelation in one of the most mysterious and interesting murder cases that ever occurred in Virginia, it is believed, will be made here soon. For the past eighteen months Thomas J. Cluverius, a young lawyer, has been confined in the city jail awaiting death upon the scaffold for the murder of his pretty cousin, Miss Fannie Lillian Madison. The girl met her death at the old reservoir, in the western part of the city, on the night of March 13, 1885. The prisoner was arrested, and after a long and tedious trial, was convicted on strong circumstantial evidence. Finding all attempts to obtain a new trial in vain, the prisoner and his friends have recently endeavored to arouse the sympathy of the public in his favor and secure a pardon or commutation of the sentence. Several thousand names have been obtained to petitions. Most of those who signed them were induced to do so because of what was considered the insufficient evidence upon which the young man was convicted. One of the most damaging circumstances against Cluverius was his and his counsel's refusal to give a full account of his movements on the night Miss Madison met her death. During the trial and at frequent intervals since, Cluverius has invariably declined to give the explanation.

      At the request of the doomed man, Mr. F. A. Howell, of Alexandria, who served on the jury that convicted him, visited Cluverius in his cell at the city jail. During the interview the prisoner asked his visitor if it would make any difference if he made a statement accounting for his movements from the time of his arrival in Richmond on the day before the murder of Miss Madison until he was arrested several days later. Mr. Howell said that every member of the jury hoped that he could prove his innocence. It is stated by the brother of Cluverius that such a paper will be presented. It is believed it is already in the hands of Cluverius' counsel, and will be submitted for a pardon or commutation of the prisoner's sentence from death to life in the penitentiary. (73.3)

Statement Presented to Governor Fitzhugh Lee by William B. Cluverius on Behalf of Thomas J. Cluverius

December 3, 1886

The statement of my movements in Richmond during the day and night of March 13, 1885, is this:

      I left the Davis House about 9 o'clock in the morning and went on Main Street. I saw Mr. H.R. Pollard, and after about 5 to 10 minutes' talk with him I went to Morgan Sterns on Broad Street between Fourth and Fifth Streets to get breakfast. I came back to Ninth and Bank Streets a little after 10, and went into the bankrupt court office and met a gentleman. I did not know who told me the clerk was not in. I went then up to the state library, as the most convenient place to get a city directory, to try to find the address of two gentlemen (William Wood and R.W. Barker) who had an interest in a tract of land in my county that Mr. Bray wanted to buy, he thinking that they lived here. Coming out on the steps of the capitol, I got into a casual conversation with one of the guards, who told me of Governor Cameron's losing a horse a short time before, etc. This was about 11 o'clock. I went from there to Grigg's shoe store, to Eighth and Main Streets, to get a pair of shoes, and my aunt carried my shoes to my room at the Davis House. I got there about 11:30 and went to my room and put the shoes in my satchel. After I came to the reading room I stayed there awhile. I wrote a check on the Planter's National Bank for $2 (the amount of the due bill at the Davis House). I left about 12 o'clock and went to the bank and got the money. I went from there to the bankrupt court again. This is the time I saw the porter who told me that the clerk was sick and that he had the office key and knew nothing about the papers. I went then to the money order department in the post office (about 12;15 or 12;30) to see if I could get a money order to Ayletts (Va). I had to wait for two persons before me to get there, and then I examined the books and found that Ayletts was not a money order office. As I was leaving the office (between 12:30 and 1 o'clock) I met and spoke to Mr. B.W. Henly. I went from there to Lumsden & Ford's jewelers between Eighth and Ninth Streets, on Main, to call for a breastpin I had brought over for Mrs. Dr. J.E. Bland and left there to have fixed. Coming back I met a college mate named Harrison, attorney at law, about 1 o'clock, on the north corner of Eleventh and Main Streets. We went together into Schoen's and had a glass of mineral water and a smoke. We stayed there nearly half an hour, talking over college days, etc. Parting there I went to a restaurant, next to the Dispatch office. There I met Mr. Lipscomb of King William county, in company with Dr. Whiting, of West Point, and got dinner. I left there between 1:30 and 2 o'clock and went to the Dime Museum, where I saw T. P. Bagly. I left there about 5 or 5:30 at the close of the performance, and went up 7th Street above Broad to a barber shop and got shaved. Coming back, I bought a copy of the States on the street. I came to the Davis Hotel and went in the dining room. I read also the New York papers; went to my room and brushed my hair. I came down and got supper and left at 8 o'clock. I went to Ford's Hotel to see if Pollard was there. I wanted to see him, as he was looking after some papers in the bankrupt court that I wanted. He was not stopping there. I went to the St. Clair Hotel to find him, knowing he had stopped at both hotels while in the legislature. Not finding him, I went around to the Dime Museum. I got there after the performance began and stayed until its close, as I was passing out in the crowd, I saw Bernard Henly with another young man. I spoke to Henly, but did not shake hands, my attention being drawn just then to the falling of a little child in the crowd. I went from there to Morganstein's. I had fried oysters, also a box of fried oysters fixed up for lunch. Next morning I came back to Davis House between 11;30 and 12 o'clock. I ate an apple with Davis, paid my bill, and went to bed. I was called after 5 o'clock the next morning. I left the hotel for the depot about 6 o'clock. There I met Captain A. Bagley, a Dr. Whitney and others and left the city with them about 7 o'clock.

This is the statement of my movements during the day and night of the 13th of March, 1885. With the people that I saw I am willing to stand on it; for believing that some day, be it early or be it late, I must stand before the judgment throne of Almighty God, I can say my hands are clean and my conscience clear.

THOMAS JUDSON CLUVERIUS   (73.4)

The Richmond State
December 4, 1886

THE "OLD MAN'S" STATEMENT

Mr. William H. Chiles, the "old man" of the Cluverius case, has sent the following to the Richmond State:

"To the best of my knowledge and belief I met a lady on Bank Street; somewhere between 10th and 11th Streets; between the hours of 6 and 8 o'clock P.M. on the 12th day of March, 1885. She stopped me and said: "Will you be kind enough sir, to tell me where The American Hotel is?' I said to her, 'Certainly, I will, it is not very far from here; I will go with you if you wish me to do so.' She said, 'I will be very glad if you will do so.' I remember she had a small travelling bag in her hand and I said to her: 'Give me your satchel and I will take it', to which she readily consented. I asked her if she was acquainted with the city. Her reply was, 'Only slightly.'. She was acquainted with Miss or Mrs. Curtis on Church Hill. She also mentioned that she was a schoolteacher and that she was from Roanoke – she also excused herself to me by saying she expected a friend or friends to meet her on her arrival in the city, and by some means they failed to meet her at the train. I did not ask her name, nor neither did she give it to me. She was a chunky looking woman and looked tired from travelling, etc. I went with her to the American Hotel, at the Main Street ladies' entrance; went up the steps to the parlor. She went up to the hating register and warmed her hands and as I thought, struck the bell, as the parlor boy soon came in the door, and I understood her to say s wished to go to her room. She told me on the way to the hotel that she had be there before, but it was in the daytime, and she had difficulty finding the hotel at night, and from the way she acted at the hotel I had every reason to believe what she said to be true. It was quite cold on that night. The boy took her satchel upstairs to her room, as I thought. I bade her good night. She thanked me very kindly for my trouble and I came out of the hotel, went home, and told my wife about it. After we read in the papers Sunday morning about finding the body, I mentioned my meeting the lady to several of my friends and none of them thought it would help the case one way or the other, so I have never thought much more about the matter. I will further state, that I did not know her, though from her appearance I thought she was a stranger in the city." (73.5)

Manquin Post Office
King William County, VA
December 4, 1886

My Dear Governor:

Please, my dear Governor, let the law take its course with that wretch Cluverius, who has caused a father, mother, and eight brothers and sisters to see so much trouble. Only, if possible, hasten all such on as quick as possible for all the other poor mothers and innocent females. Please, for the sake of a mother whose heart and mind has been nearly crazed with grief and distress, let the judgment of the court stay as it is, is the prayer of the mother he has caused so much trouble. Much more, dear Governor, I would say but leave it all to your tender parental heart. Please, I pray, grant me this one petition, is the prayer of your humble and respectful fellow creature.

LUCINE T. MADISON   (73.6)

On December 6, 1886, Mr. Hermann Joel entered the Virginia Governor's Mansion. He was escorted directly to the Governor's office. He removed his hat as he walked through the double paneled doors and approached the sturdy little man seated at the desk.

"Welcome, Mr. Joel. Please; remove your coat and hand it to Mr. Stockton."

"Dank you, Herr Governor." Joel was visibly quivering as he removed his coat and turned it over, along with his hat, to Stockton. He noticed another gentleman seated behind the governor against the wall.

"This man, Mr. Joel, is Mr. Wren. He is familiar with this matter and will be here to assist with the interview." Joel's eyes widened and his throat went dry as he tried to determine what exactly the governor meant by "assist".

"Ah, yes…", he acknowledged as his imagination began to explore some unpleasant interpretations. Jack Wren's knuckle-cracking only inflamed Joel's suspicions.

"Mr. Joel. I'm sure you know why you are here. It's this Cluverius matter. An appeal has been made for clemency. To my thinking, this is a case based largely upon circumstantial evidence. This begs a question: is it proper to sentence a man to death for a crime where the preponderance of the evidence is circumstantial in nature? How do you feel about that?"

"Vell, sir… I really do not know…"

"Mr. Joel… You must have some thoughts on this, particularly since you are a critical witness in the matter."

"I do not support wiolence in most cases. But dis is for somevun else to decide."

"I agree. And that someone is me. But, you see, I will not intervene in the decision of a jury under ordinary circumstances. And, Mr. Joel, if you were able to confirm whether or not that the watch-key found at the Marshall Reservoir is indeed the one you repaired for Mr. Cluverius, it would certainly inform my decision.

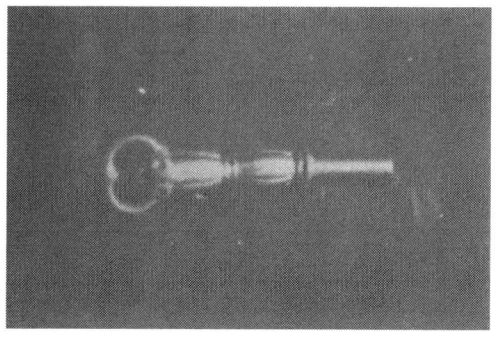

"I vould be glad to assist, Mr. Governor… But der court vould not let me open der vatch-key. Unt dis is der only vay I can be certain."

"I understand that, Mr. Joel. That's why we are going to crack that watch-key open here and now; and you will tell me if you have worked on it."

"Herr Governor… You do understand that der court vould not let me open der vatch-key because der judge said it vould destroy der evidence?"

Believed to be the watch-key found at the Marshall Reservoir (from *Virginia Trooper*, Nov, 1952, No. 18)

"Yes, Mr. Joel. I understand this. But the possibility of any more trials or hearings has been foreclosed. I am the only person who can look at the evidence and act upon any new finding. If we open the watch-key and find nothing, it may or may not have an impact on what course I take. If we open it and we do find something, it certainly will." Fitz Lee opened a small envelope and poured the golden key onto his desktop. "Jack, please bring that spirit lamp over here."

Jack Wren placed the lamp on the Governor's desk. He reached into his pocket for a match and lit the wick.

Governor Lee cleared his throat, "Mr. Joel. Do you know Mr. Cluverius well enough to pick him out of a crowd of a hundred?"

"Governor. I know him vell enough to pick him from a crowd of five thousand!" Joel picked up the key with a pair of tweezers and held it over the small flame. He slowly rotated the key with his left hand, allowing the heat to evenly spread and expand the thin metal shell. He took another pair of tweezers in his right hand and carefully removed the shell, exposing the interior skeleton of the watch-key. The jeweler placed the tweezers in his right hand down on the desk and lifted his jeweler's loop to his eye. He held the watch key near the light for a few moments. "You see here, it is just as I thought it vould be if it vuzz my verk; der is a soft solder here, and there are marks of der file here."

"Yes, I see it!", exclaimed the bespectacled Governor. "Is that the key you mended?"

"Yes, dat is der key I mended. I vill svear to it!"

"Are you absolutely sure, Mr. Joel?"

"Governor. A jeweler knows der marks of his file as vell as another man vould know his signature in his own handwriting..."

"Excellent Mr. Joel! You know, I haven't heard English like yours since Heros von Borcke. Do you know who he was?"

"No, sir."

"He was a fine Prussian soldier. Are you Prussian, Mr. Joel?"

"No, sir. I am from Bavaria. A Prussian soldier killed my brother.", Joel revealed with a sudden distance.

"Oh, my apologies, Mr. Joel. Please forgive me!" Hermann Joel's demeanor further deteriorated as he sat down and looked at his hands as he furiously wrung them. Fitz Lee leaned forward over his desk. "Mr. Joel... Please... I am very sorry for the insensitive remark."

"No, it is not dat; it is fine. I take no offense. It is some-ting else. You see Governor... A man came into my shop dis morning. He vuzz a large man. Somehow, he knew dat I vuzz coming to see you today."

"What do you mean, Mr. Joel? Jack, are you hearing this?"

"Yes, sir.", Jack Wren snapped to attention.

"Please continue, Mr. Joel.", said Lee.

"Der man picked out a vatch from my case. He asked me der price. It vuzz $4.50. He grabbed my wrist qvite firmly. Den he put $35 in my hand unt said he knew I vuzz coming to see der Governor unt that 'dis is business', unt ven I go to der Governor I am not bound to remember every-ting vich I know. He also said dat ven he hears dat I have not told der Governor der things I know, I vould receive another $65 for his new vatch. I asked him ver der money vould come from. He said *he* did not have ten cents, but people behind him vould provide der rest of der money."

"Vut… I mean… *What*, is this man's name?", an entranced Fitz asked.

"His name is Deuring."

"Deuring!", Wren interjected as he started to chuckle. "Governor, he is easily the most corrupt officer on the Richmond police force!"

"Herr Governor. Dis man is dangerous. I vorry vut vill happen if he finds out dat my memory is so good."

"Yes, Mr. Joel. Do not worry. We will protect you. Mr. Wren here will see to your safety until we have dealt with this man, Deuring. And, we *will* deal with him. You have my assurances." The Governor extended his hand. "Thank you, Mr. Joel. You have performed a vital service to the justice system and to society at large."

"Dank you, Herr Governor." (73.7)

On the morning of December 7, 1886, Governor Fitzhugh Lee called Jack Wren into his office.

"Good morning, Jack.", the Governor welcomed him with a smile. Lee then gestured with his left hand to one of the seats in front of his desk. "Please, sit down."

"Good morning, sir. Thank you.", Wren responded as he took his seat.

"Jack, I assume you have had time to review the Cluverius file, as I have asked?"

"Yes, sir."

"Well, I have formed an opinion on a course of action; but before I do anything, I would like to hear your impressions. Especially in light of the fact that you have a great amount of familiarity with this matter from its outset."

"Yes, sir. I would be honored to give you my thoughts; of which I have many."

"Most particularly, Jack; I would like to hear what you think of the prisoner's recent statement regarding his movements that day." Governor Lee turned his better ear slightly toward Wren and peeled his eyes to listen carefully.

"Well, Your Excellency; there can be no doubt that Cluverius has presented a detailed and somewhat plausible account of his movements. However, it is the timing of this disclosure which I find most troubling. It seems clear to me that he is trying to use the rules and procedures to his advantage and has little interest in getting the truth out to you or the public. During the trial, he and his counsel used his incompetency as a witness in his own defense, as prescribed by the law, to obscure his true desire to say little in his own defense. They insisted that he wanted to testify on his own behalf; but the law sealed his lips; thus, conveniently providing a reason to withhold *any* account of his movements. All the while, the prisoner was able to say that, should the law be changed and should he be granted another trial; he would gladly provide the details. Of course, the statute was indeed changed and you, yourself, signed it into law; but alas, the Supreme Court did not grant him a new trial. This allowed the prisoner to continue to insist that he would eagerly mount a defense of himself but for the constraints of the legal system. It is only since the time that your executive powers of clemency have become his lone avenue, and that his sentence has become imminent, that he has put forth a recitation of his actions that day. In all honesty, Governor, I find this a repulsive and cynical act. Cluverius is clearly relying on the pressure he can bring to bear upon a single man to overturn the proceedings; rather than allow a proper hearing and examination of his claims by a judge and jury of his peers. Cluverius knows that none of these claims can be challenged in court; none of his witnesses can be put under oath and cross-examined. He understands better than anyone that his story could not stand up to the scrutiny of a full court proceeding; so, he is attempting to exploit the emotions of a fair-minded man as yourself, at this late and desperate moment, to callously achieve what he knows the legal system would not provide him. He is attempting to use the sensational and emotional pleas of the press and other sympathetic people and organizations to place you in an untenable position. I find this despicable.

And, if I may add, Governor; regarding the Deuring bribe. I believe that confirms the guilt of Cluverius. Who else would have any interest in thwarting the testimony of the jeweler? If Mr. Joel had not worked on that watch-key, they would have nothing to fear and no reason to try to influence his testimony. Mr. Cluverius and his family are the only ones who could benefit from such an obstruction of justice.

I have suspected Cluverius' guilt from the moment of his arrest; and there is nothing which has occurred since that time which softens that impression. In fact, I find his manipulations of the system and of those around him to have further incriminated him. Whatever you decide, sir; I, as your servant, will support the outcome. But I would not consider myself your true servant if I did not make my honest opinions clear to you."

Jack Wren stood and firmly placed his right fist down upon the Governor's desk. Leaning in toward one another, Governor Lee thought he saw tears welling in his aide's eyes. "Your Excellency,", Wren began, "justice can be a very bitter medicine. Governors, officers, and fathers must honorably apportion and administer it; citizens, soldiers, and sons must humbly accept it. If not, all civilization shall be lost."

Fitz Lee stood and firmly shook hands with Jack Wren. "Thank you, Jack. You have certainly thought capably about this matter. I appreciate that. You have been very helpful – just as I knew you would."

As Jack Wren left the office, Governor Lee pulled a sheet of paper from his desk drawer and began to write:

Commonwealth of Virginia
Governor's Office
Richmond, Va.
December 7, 1886

To: Messrs. B. T. Crump, H. R. Pollard, and A. Brown Evans, counsel for Thomas J. Cluverius

Gentlemen:

I have the honor to say that I have given to your statements and to the papers and petitions presented by you, the prisoner, and others for the exercise of executive clemency to Thomas J. Cluverius, the careful examination and considerate attention which their importance and the distinguished character and learning of his counsel imperatively demanded.

The prisoner came from the judicial to the executive department of the government marked "guilty" by judges and jury; starting at that point, therefore, I have been diligently studying the record while industriously seeking information and evidence from all other sources which might conclusively prove to my mind that the verdict of the court was an error, and that therefore the sentence pronounced by the court of Hustings and affirmed by Virginia's highest court must be set aside or commuted; with an earnest desire to faithfully execute, without fear or favor, the laws of the state impartially to all.; with most profound sympathy for those upon whose hearts this blow must fall; with a clear conscience that I am discharging my duty to the people of my state as God has given me strength to see it. I now write you to inform you that I have not been able to reach a different conclusion from that held by the courts and, therefore, the case of Thomas J. Cluverius is not one in my opinion to call for executive interference either by the exercise of the pardoning power or commutation of sentence.

I am, gentlemen, with great respect, your obedient servant,

FITZHUGH LEE

(73.8)

Late on the afternoon of December 8, 1886, Tom Stockton knocked lightly on the Governor's office door. "Come in.", came a muffled voice from the other side.

"Excuse me, Governor. There is a Reverend Hatcher here to see you. He is the spiritual adviser for Thomas Cluverius."

Fitz Lee wanted nothing more than turn him away at this late hour, but he succumbed to his godlier instincts. "Tell the Reverend I will see him now."

After a few moments, the tall slender man in black humbly crossed the threshold into the Governor's office. "Forgive me, your Excellency, for intruding at this late hour. I come with a petition from Thomas Cluverius. As you know, he is scheduled to meet his sentence on Wednesday and he has asked me to respectfully represent him and deliver a request for a short reprieve so that he may get his final affairs in order." The Reverend removed a small envelope from his breast pocket and presented it to the Governor.

Governor Fitz Lee put his reading spectacles on and opened the envelope. He read the brief but poignant request.

Richmond, Va.
Dec 8*th* 1886

To Gov. Fitzhugh Lee

I hereby present to you my humble and last petition that you will grant to me a reprieve for a term of 60 days that I may have a suitable time to prepare for my inevitable end. This I solemnly feel is most needful and important for me in my present sad condition, all earthly hope being now cut off.

THOMAS J. CLUVERIUS

Thoughts of his dear Ellen crossed Lee's mind as he mustered the courage to bestow mercy. He knew the City of Richmond had grown weary of the grinding march toward justice and was primed for its dispensation in just two days. But, as Governor, Fitz Lee understood that although he had a legal duty to carry forward, he also had a duty to demonstrate humanity, even toward the most discredited and reviled among the citizenry.

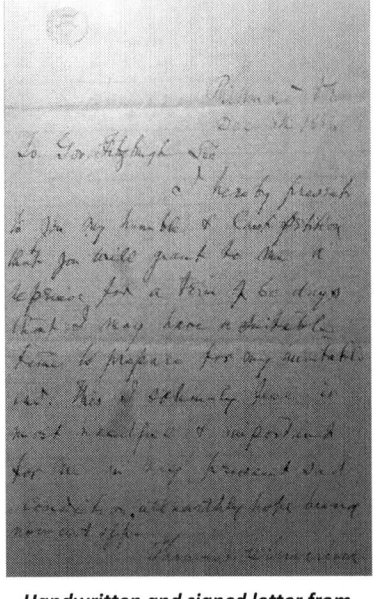

Handwritten and signed letter from Thomas J. Cluverius to Gov. Fitzhugh Lee.

"Reverend Hatcher,", he began. "Mr. Cluverius has requested a sixty-day reprieve. I am amenable to a reprieve but I feel five weeks is an adequate amount of time for Mr. Cluverius to finalize his affairs. I will order his execution to be delayed until January 14, 1887. You may tell Mr. Cluverius, as much."

"Thank you, Governor Lee. Your kindness toward a doomed and desperate young man will be a comfort. Shall we pray?"

"Yes, Reverend; I would like that. Let us pray." (73.9)

Chapter 74   *Coming Over to Your Side*

Richmond, Va
Jan 12th 1887

His Excellency
Fitzhugh Lee
Governor of Va

Dear Governor:

    I have sent you a petition by Mr. Crump asking Your Excellency for mercy, but I cannot stop there. I must ask you to bear with me while I make an attempt to say something to try to save the life of one dearer to me than my own. Your Excellency has brothers and more than one, and it is natural to suppose that a brother's love when divided between two or three is never so strong as when there are only two – Dear Governor, no brother could feel stronger love than that existing between my brother and myself.
    Ever since we were old enough to know each other, we have only been separated only for a short period. We slept side by side when life was bright and no sorrows to cast a sad and gloom over our life.
    Every joy and sorrow were equally shared between us. Today I solemnly declare before you that I am willing to share his fate be it what it may. Will you not hear a brother's plea? Will you not allow him a chance that his life may be saved? There are not one thousand men in Va capable of judging who can say that my brother has had a fair and impartial trial, with that fact in view will you not allow the reprieve issued for when there can be no harm done to the course of justice and might save an innocent life – Your Excellency can readily see the mystery with which this case is surrounding and will it be a violation of the Laws of Va to give an opportunity clear away such mysteries? Every day there coming to light new facts that could not have been gotten before. Is it not likely that in the near future the truth might come <u>out</u>?
    For these reasons and others, I can and will give Your Excellency, will you not hear our pleading? I have an aged mother, father, and dear aunt whose days will be but few if my dear brother's life is taken.
    Dear Governor, begging you not to turn our petition aside, but give us a chance to have this wrong corrected. I must leave my brother's life in your hands, praying you to have mercy, and hoping that God may guide your actions in this behalf

I am your humble servant,
W. B. Cluverius   (74.1)

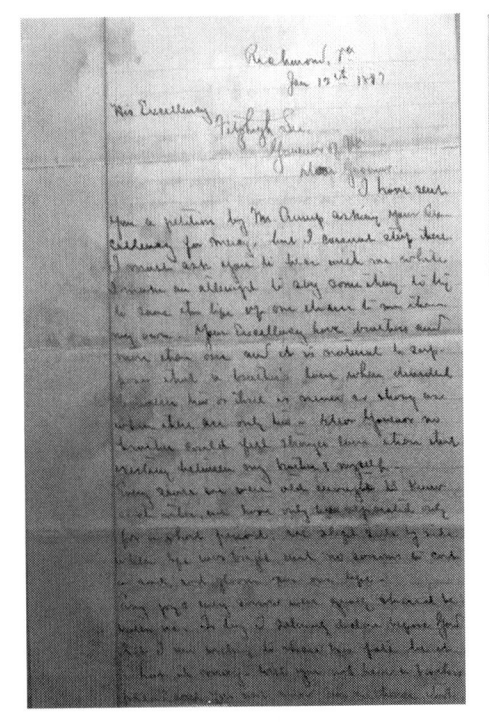

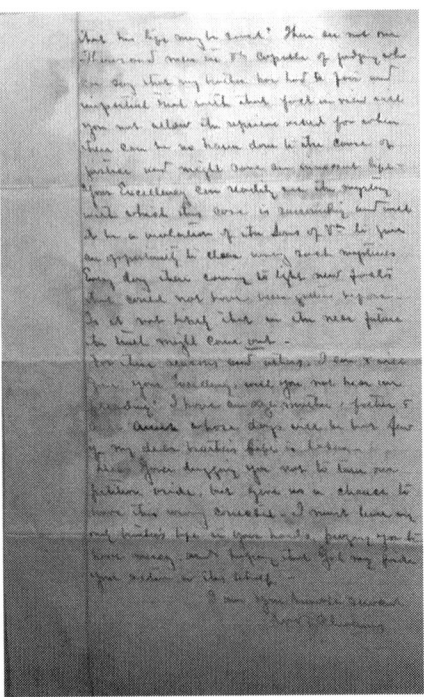

Original Handwritten and Signed January 12, 1887 Letter to Governor Lee from Willie Cluverius

    Governor Fitzhugh Lee laid the letter down upon his desk. He put his hands behind his head and stretched as he leaned back in his chair. He closed his eyes as pangs of empathy collided with his call to duty. Lee had extensive experience with sending young men to their deaths; but this was different. Battlefield casualties were ultimately left in the hands of God. Lee knew that orders he gave during the War would result in death; but it was never personal; and the fruits of the sacrifice could be imagined. Additionally, he was there beside his men, in the line of fire; knowing full well that his actions could result in his own death; he fully shared the risk. The weight of the decision with which he was now faced, though similar in result, presented a very different moral quandary. Although it was just a single life he now held in his hands, the outcome of his decision would be certain; and he, as the arbiter of this young boy's existence, would have the luxury of returning to a normal and happy life; whilst this man would be gone forever, never to experience the slightest joy that even a lifetime behind bars could, at times, feed to the human soul. Self-doubt crept in as Fitz realized that the deaths of the brave boys during the War were largely beyond his control; part of a situation which would persist despite his participation; and perhaps, under lesser leadership, would have resulted in even more deaths. The death of Cluverius, however, was completely within his singular power to decide.

Tom Stockton entered the Governor's office and handed the Governor another letter which had just arrived. "This is from one of the jurors…", Stockton said.

Lee cut his eyes over his reading glasses and up to Stockton, "What, now?", he asked with a hint of exasperation.

Tom Stockton shrugged, "I have not read it, Governor. Mr. Crenshaw and Reverend King will be here within the hour to meet with you, sir. General Wickham will be in attendance, as well."

"Very well, Tom. When they have all arrived, please show them in." Fitz Lee opened the envelope Stockton had just placed before him.

Richmond, Va
January 8, 1887

Fitzhugh Lee
Governor of Virginia

Dear Governor Lee:

I am writing in my capacity as a member of the jury in the trial of Thomas J. Cluverius. As you are well aware, it was a very long and arduous process. A great deal of evidence of a circumstantial nature was presented and reviewed. The proceedings were also highly scrutinized and, in my humble opinion, sensationalized, by a voracious national press. The pressure brought to bear upon the jury was prolific and, in my opinion, resulted in a flawed result. It had been my sincere hope that the Court of Appeals would see fit to declare a new trial for the condemned. It should be understood that at the time of this appeal, the case had yet to be freed from the manufacturers of evidence. When the appeal failed, it was my hope that you, as a fair-minded and experienced man, would, as Governor, commute the sentence. But alas, it appears that you, in your official capacity, have decided not to intervene on behalf of the condemned. Therefore, it is now incumbent upon me, as a member of the jury, to make some facts known to you concerning the conduct of the proceeding, which I hope, in all sincerity and with utmost respect for your office, that you see fit to remedy at this late hour before the irreversible execution of the sentence is carried out.

I will admit that I, like other jurymen, fell prey to the relentless pressure of the bloodthirsty rabble; it is a failing of my character which I have continued to regret since the fateful day a decision was reached. The trial and conviction of Mr. Cluverius was a horrible and ghastly farce, revolting in every way tending to bring dishonor and shame upon the jurisprudence of the Commonwealth. You have received my previous appeal for commutation, which was simply an attempt to frame a document acceptable to the largest number of jurors. I was able to procure two members from Alexandria to agree to the petition – Messrs French and Sherwood. All others were too beholden to public opinion, which threatened the characters and the very lives of these men, particularly those who reside here in Richmond. Unfortunately for the furtherance of the ends of justice and the maintenance of a just and uninfluenced administration of the law, they have perhaps a somewhat too profound regard for public opinion.

As a result of my recantation, it should be noted that I have received relentless abuse; insulting and cowardly messages through the mails from dastards and cravens all over the land.

It should also be understood by you, dear Governor, that one of the members of the jury is a known perjurer and inebriate. Reputable citizens of Alexandria have substantiated that Mr. Howell has a long history of dishonesty and inebriation; and he is a man which certainly should never have qualified to serve on the jury, much less as the foreman for that body. Please understand that I refer not to the guilt or innocence of Mr. Cluverius; I refer to the flawed process which resulted in the guilty rendering and ultimately, to his sentence of death. Mr. Cluverius had a right to be tried by twelve of his peers. This was not done, unless Cluverius is himself an inebriate and subject to all the mental disorders superinduced by inebriety. If the Governor has doubts of my contention, please consult Dr. Cabell, who was called to the Exchange Hotel several times during the trial to administer to Mr. Howell and other inebriated jurors.

Lastly, Governor, it has come forth that you have interviewed the itinerant keymaker, Mr. Joel. It is reported that you instructed Mr. Joel to open the key from the reservoir for your inspection. I humbly submit that this action was ex parte. This was new evidence and, in my opinion, as a member of the jury, is evidence which should have been brought before the jury.

While I fully understand that this matter rests solely in your hands, it is my sincerest hope, as a concerned citizen of Richmond and the Commonwealth of Virginia, that you re-consider your position and grant Mr. Cluverius an immediate commutation.

Respectfully your servant,
Carter N. Harrison
(74.2)

Governor Fitzhugh Lee shook his head. It was all very unpleasant but he understood that he must step outside of his own person and continue to approach these matters with measured balance. "Emotions matter; but facts matter more.", he told himself. He glanced down at his desktop and a newspaper headline diverted his attention.

Accomac Peninsula Enterprise
January 8, 1887

ILLINOIS SENATOR LOGAN DEAD

    Senator John A. Logan, Republican candidate for Vice President on the ticket with James G. Blaine, in 1884, is dead. For many years he was a prominent figure in our country and his record contains much that is creditable to him, but he cannot be classed among the "great men" of the United States, nor can any Southern man consider him faultless, who remembers his efforts to degrade and humiliate them, in securing adoption of Reconstruction measures. That he possessed many noble traits of character every one concedes, but that his bitter partisanship tarnished to some extent his good reputation is also equally true. That he was not entirely just to the Southern people no one denies, but that he sinned against them believing he was right, no one perhaps, doubts. His military record was a fine one, his services as an office holder are strictly, we believe, in accord with his notions of right. In private and public life he was incorruptible, we believe - a fact which can hardly be doubted, as with all opportunities he had to enrich himself, he died poor. His record is a good one, but had he been more charitable to the Southern people, would have been better. (74.3)

    Governor Fitzhugh Lee chuckled to himself as he reflected about a lifetime foe. Although Fitz never developed a personal fondness for the irascible General Logan as he had acquired for the likes of Grant and even Sheridan, he agreed that Logan was a respectable, albeit very partisan, fellow who acted in accord with his beliefs, as inflammatory and misguided as they may have been; and Fitz could not fault his sincerity. Fitz Lee understood that if it were not for men like Logan, his own ascension to the Governorship of Virginia would not have been possible. Interestingly, the bitter conflicts on the fields of battle, both military and political, create the opportunities for men like Lee and Logan to excel. Fitz wondered where his life would be were it not for these great conflicts between ordinary men; conflicts which often brought forth the best – and sometimes the worst – in such men; pushing them to achieve things that extraordinary men in ordinary circumstances could only imagine.

    Tom Stockton poked his head through the door to the Governor's office. "The gentlemen are here, sir."

    Fitz nodded and stood. As he made his way around his desk, the three gentlemen entered the room. Governor Lee smiled and graciously extended his hand, "Welcome. Gentlemen."

    "Governor Lee. I am Reverend John Crenshaw; this is Reverend Rufus King."

    "Nice to meet you gentlemen."

"And, Governor, I assume you know State Senator Wickham.", Crenshaw said with a wink.

Fitz laughed, "Yes, yes… Senator Wickham and I often start out on opposite sides of the issue; then end up together! It's been that way since before the War, hasn't it, Carter?" (74.4)

Wickham smiled and graciously bowed his head, "I have never held your impetuous youth and inexperience against you – even as I humbly serve you, Governor!"

Fitz laughed again, "Now, please have a seat. What brings you gentlemen to my office, today?"

"Well, Governor Lee; it is the matter of Thomas Cluverius which brings us all here.", Reverend Crenshaw began. "As you fully understand, Quaker beliefs hold capital punishment in contempt. But, putting our religious beliefs aside, there is increasing evidence that from a legal enforcement standpoint, capital punishment is ineffective. In Michigan, capital punishment has been abolished for thirty-five years; and official statistics show that murders have decreased, relative to the population, by thirty percent. There are many states and counties which have tried the question both ways – that is to say, they have abolished capital punishment for a period of years and then restored it. They have almost unanimously found that as soon as hanging was restored, murders increased; prompting them to once again abolish the practice. This seems to me to be a peculiarly propitious time to bring the subject of hanging afresh before our people, while the whole community is so stirred by the Cluverius case."

Reverend King then interjected, "We all know, sir, that every good government endeavors to enact laws for the protection of its citizens, and now that we have in the history of hanging an accumulation of evidence showing that so far from being a protection, the example of the state taking vengeance on the murderer by hanging educates the citizens in a like spirit, one towards another, and causes an increase in murders. Let us unite in abolishing it and leave vengeance to Him who hath said, 'Vengeance is mine. I will repay.'"

Governor Lee sat quietly and somewhat expressionless as Reverend Crenshaw spoke again, "In the special case before us some of the ablest lawyers of this state, among them our friend John W. Daniel, have stated that they could not have brought forth a verdict for hanging on the evidence before the jury. Many have expressed the conviction that if guilty, it was not proven, and therefore there is justifiable grounds for executive clemency to commute the punishment from the death penalty to imprisonment for life. We are here to plead with thee most earnestly to at least extend the time until after the legislature shall have met again, whether it be two months or twelve months, to afford those, who like ourselves believe capital punishment is against the spirit of our holy religion, the opportunity to make the effort before the legislature for the abolition of the death penalty in this state. We are promising to devote ourselves to the accumulation of evidence in detail from various states and governments on this continent in relation to this important question.

Governor, no harm can come from a delay and we feel much good will come of it whatever may be the final result."

Governor Lee cleared his throat, "Gentlemen... I thank you for coming here today and making your beliefs known. Believe me when I say that I have not taken this matter lightly. It is among the most important decisions a Governor can make. This said, you must also understand that my decision will be guided by the Laws of Virginia as they exist; not by how any of us may wish they existed. My duty is to execute the laws as they are written. And, unless I see some clear and grievous misapplication of these laws by a judge or jury, I am compelled to follow them. As sound and heartfelt as your petition may be, it should be brought before the Virginia Legislature and not the Executive." Governor Lee then looked at Senator Wickham.

"Yes gentlemen,", Wickham began, "as much as I agree with your sentiments regarding capital punishment, it is a matter which should be debated by the General Assembly and not left to the Executive to legislate. Governor Lee must follow the law as it exists."

"But, Governor; can you not delay the execution until the General Assembly has time to review the matter?", Rufus King implored.

"Reverend,", Fitz Lee tried to empathize, "I am in full agreement that this is a very difficult situation. There is a legal maxim put forth by William Penn, a prominent Quaker like yourselves; ***to delay justice is injustice***. We must weigh the impact a further delay may have upon the family of Lillie Madison. They have been waiting nearly two years for justice to be served. I, as Governor, have a duty to ensure that the justice system has worked for them. It would be unconscionable for a verdict and sentence to be reached in defense of Miss Madison; only to delay the dispensation of said justice in the interest of retroactively changing the law to suit an alternative desired outcome; whether that outcome is sought by the party found guilty of the offense or by any other party which may be acting in a manner which accrues to the benefit of the guilty. That, would not be justice. If you wish to encourage members of the Legislature to draft legislation to change our laws regarding capital punishment for future cases; I would be glad to review such legislation, assuming it passes through the Legislature; and should it be compelling enough, I may even sign it into law. But I refuse to circumvent that process. That simply is not the role of the Executive in our system. I thank you once again for coming to see me; and I encourage you to continue to fight for the changes in which you believe. However, I cannot help you at this time."

The three gentlemen quietly stood and thanked the Governor for his time. They shook hands and began to walk toward the doorway. "Senator Wickham; may I have a moment with you?", Governor Lee called.

Senator Wickham closed the door to the office after Reverends Crenshaw and King left and turned back toward the Governor.

"Yes, Fitz?"

"Carter, I know you are disappointed. But, truly, this is the role I must play. I hope you understand."

"Dear Governor… say no more.", Wickham raised his palm. "I fully understand. Once again, I have come over to your side."

Governor Lee smiled and shook his old friend's hand, "Thank you, Carter…thank you." (74.5)

Chapter 75   *All's for the Best*

Soon after sunrise on January 14, 1887, the citizens of Richmond began to assemble on the corner of Marshall and 15th Streets. Warmer air was moving across the city, breaking a freeze which had persisted for over one week. A scaffold measuring eight feet square had been erected the previous day in the white prisoners' yard on the east side of the Richmond Jail. The platform sat eleven-and-one-half feet above the yard surface. A trap door three-and-one-half feet square had been installed in the center of the platform. Rising an additional seven feet above the platform was solid wood crossbar. Dangling from the crossbar was a silk rope, composed of four brightly colored strands of orange, claret, purple, and white.

As 9 o'clock approached, the crowd had swelled to more than four hundred. A contingent of twenty-five Richmond uniformed police officers arrived to maintain order. Other officers wore citizen's clothing and dispersed among the growing numbers. Six uniformed officers guarded the gate on Jail Alley and two others stood guard at the Marshall Street gate. Police Sergeant Smith appeared in front of the jail. "Attention citizens of Richmond. Today we will be conducting the execution of Thomas J. Cluverius, barring any additional reprieve from the Governor. Two hundred citizens will be granted access to the jail yard to witness the proceedings. I will hand out tickets to gain access. No one without a ticket will be allowed inside the jail walls." Smith removed a large roll of tickets from his trouser pocket. "Please form a line and I will hand them out. It will be one ticket per person. If you are not here, you will not receive a ticket!"

At this same time, Thomas Cluverius was waking in his cell. He had spent much of the previous evening speaking with visitors and praying with Reverend Dr. William E. Hatcher until 6 AM. The breakfast he requested was brought to his cell just after 9 o'clock. Beef tenderloin, mushrooms, and an egg omelette were placed on the small table near the window. Cluverius quietly took a few bites before rising and walking over toward a pile of papers he had left on the upholstered chair in the center of the cell. One by one, Cluverius began to tear letter after letter, paper after paper, document after document; shredding them to such a degree that no one could reconstitute them. After ten minutes of this activity, he sighed lightly and went back to pick over his breakfast plate.

Sheriff Southard of Henrico County arrived at the jail at 9:45. Two officers from the Richmond police carried a one-hundred-pound bag of sawdust up the stairs to the scaffolding. They carefully placed the sack immediately atop the trap door. Sheriff Southard, having experience with hangings, tied the silken rope through the handles on the sack. He raised his hand and signaled another officer to spring the trap door. The door flung downward and toward the rear of the platform, making a squeak followed by a crack as the bottom side of the door struck against the framing below. The sack dropped four feet and stretched nearly to the brick-paved surface below. It recoiled upward before settling into a slow spinning pendulum swing approximately three feet above the ground. Southard pursed his lips and decided to increase the distance of the drop from four feet to the maximum eight feet, creating enough distance and speed to ensure a sharp neck-snap.

Willie Cluverius and Aunt Jane Tunstall arrived at Tommie's cell at 10:15 that morning. Aunt Jane had not seen Tommie in forty-five days. Tommie smiled as he approached his aunt, holding his arms open and taking hold of her. "Dearest Aunt Jane. I cannot tell you how happy it makes me to see you again. I am so glad you have come."

"Tommie,", she began to cry. "You and Willie are sons to me. I could not forgive myself if I had missed this chance to say...", she then moaned and nearly collapsed. Willie quickly grabbed her arm and supported her as she crept toward a chair in the cell.

"I know, Aunt Jane. And you are like our mother. I appreciate all you have to done to support me throughout my life. And I am thankful that there shall remain Willie to stand in my stead on your behalf. I only wish this had not cost you so much. But Willie has been working to remedy this." Tommie then turned to his brother, "Willie, have you delivered my manuscript to the publisher?"

"Yes, Tommie. Dudley over on Main will print 10,000 copies next week. All proceeds will go to Aunt Jane."

"I don't want that money! If you try to give it to me, I will not accept it! Willie, you will pay the remaining expenses and keep the rest."

"But, Aunt Jane... you will need your money back!", Tommie implored. "It is my wish."

Aunt Jane fell silent and then looked directly at her condemned nephew, "Tommie... A part of me will die today. And it is that part of me which has a dying wish, as well. Willie shall keep the money."

"As you wish, dearest Aunt Jane.", he cupped her cheeks and kissed her on the forehead. (75.1)

Sherriff Southard climbed a ladder which leaned against the crossbar of the gallows. He placed a towel in the center of the crossbar and wrapped the oiled silk rope around it. This would prevent the sharp edges of the wooden crossbar from cutting the rope. He then measured out enough length to allow for the contemplated eight-foot drop. The sheriff descended the ladder and took the opposite end of the rope and methodically tied the hang-man's noose. Southard called Deputy Sergeant Allen over to him to instruct Allen how to place the noose around the prisoner's neck.

At 12:00 Willie Cluverius arrived at his brother's cell carrying a new black suit of clothes. As Willie was entering the cell, Beverly T. Crump was exiting. Crump simply shook his head, looked downward, and walked down the hallway toward the exit. Willie thought he was prepared for the final answer, but as his eyes met Tommie's, the reality that he had less than one hour to remain with his brother crashed upon him. Willie sighed heavily as his eyes welled with tears.

"The Governor will not intervene, Willie.", said Tommie. "Crump was with him for two hours this morning, and alas, I am finished. I have been praying with Reverend Hatcher; praying for one last reprieve for the past hour before Crump came with the news. The Reverend left but will return just before 1 o'clock. Then, all the prayers of ten thousand people shall be answered."

Willie placed the suit of clothes on Tommie's cot and then collapsed into the upholstered chair. He put his head in his palms and began to heave with sadness.

Tommie Cluverius came and silently placed his hand on Willie's shoulder. After a few moments, Willie felt Tommie's hand lift from him; but Willie could not bring himself to raise his head and look. Tommie calmly removed the gray suit he had worn since his arrest nearly two years prior, laying it neatly upon his bed. Slowly, he began to change into his black wardrobe for the final act.

Willie struggled to control his crying, finally asking, "Tommie… did you kill Lillie?"

Tommie smiled slightly. "Willie, you know my answer to that question. If I said I did, would there be any difference?"

At 12:55 Sergeant Smith and two deputies arrived at Thomas Cluverius' cell door. They paused for a few moments when they heard Reverend Hatcher's voice, "And I will avenge their blood which I have not avenged. Say those with fearful hearts, 'Be strong, do not fear; your God will come.' He will come with vengeance; with divine retribution, He will come to save you… Amen." (75.2)

Seargeant Smith cleared his throat as he entered the cell, "It is time, Mr. Cluverius."

The prisoner stood and walked over to the small table beside his upholstered chair. He opened a book of poetry and tore a single page from it. He picked up a pencil and wrote a few words on the top of the page. Thomas Cluverius then crumpled the page in his left fist, "I am ready to go with you."

Reverend Hatcher stood and escorted Cluverius out of the cell. Sergeant Smith nodded toward one of the deputies. Deputy Sergeant Allen stepped forward, "Please hold your hands out and make fists." Cluverius followed the instruction. The deputy took a short piece of rope and wound it tightly around Cluverius' wrists. Deputy Macon then stepped forward and pulled a long black cloak over Cluverius' head; covering him entirely from neck to ankles. Sergeant Smith led the procession followed by Deputy Allen, then Cluverius, then Deputy Macon, and lastly, Reverend Hatcher. Hatcher opened his Bible and began to read Psalm 23.

The Lord is my shepherd; I shall not want,

He maketh me to lie down in green pastures: He leadeth me beside the still waters.

He restoreth my soul: He leadeth me in paths of righteousness for His name's sake.

Yea, though I walk through the valley of the shadow of death, I will fear no evil: for Thou art with me; Thy rod and Thy staff they comfort me.

Thou preparest a table before me in the presence of mine enemies: Thou anointest my head with oil; my cup runneth over.

Surely goodness and mercy shall follow me all the days of my life: and I will dwell in the house of the Lord forever.

As the procession neared the jail yard a cheer went up from a crowd which had formed on a nearby rooftops, a vantage which allowed them to see over the imposing thirty-foot walls. "Yonder, he is!" echoed into the yard. Trees and telegraph lines alike were scaled, young boys desperate to catch a glimpse of sudden death. The enormous crowd of thousands outside the walls on Marshall Street imagined the scene and broke into their own cheers. Inmates from the negro cell block crowded in their small windows, trying to catch sight of the condemned. *Wade in the Water* echoed from the block, mournfully beckoning God's grace through the troubled waters ahead. As the five men walked through the gateway into the yard, the two hundred observers inside let out a cacophonous roar, filling the streets of Richmond with bloodthirsty reverberations. Richmond police pushed the crowd back from the gallows, opening up a lane for the prisoner to pass. Thomas Cluverius held his head high and although somewhat pale and thin, his demeanor looked no different from his first appearance in the Hustings Court.

A few inside the yard hurtled insults, "Time to meet your Maker, Cluverius!" or "This is for Lillie!", were some of the common calls. Most maintained decorum, looking on with intense, if morbid, interest. Others were melancholy, still in disbelief that the tragedy of one death was soon to be compounded by another. Cluverius steadily climbed the stairs to the top of the scaffold. He walked with self-assurance to the trap door in the center of the platform. He looked out over the tops of the heads of the crowd inside the yard, picking a point on the yard wall behind them to transfix his gaze. Sergeant Smith stood beside him on the platform. Pulling a piece of paper from his coat he read:

Thomas Judson Cluverius. You have been convicted by the Hustings Court of Richmond of the crime of murder of Fannie Lillian Madison. You have been duly sentenced to be hanged by the neck until dead. The Supreme Court of Virginia has affirmed the conviction and the Governor of Virginia, His Excellency Fitzhugh Lee, has refused all petitions to intervene in the judgment of the jury and judges. Therefore, your sentence shall be carried out at this time, on this day, January 14, 1887.

He continued, "Thomas Judson Cluverius, have you anything to say for yourself?"

For the first time, Cluverius showed a hint of hesitation. His voice cracked and was barely audible as he said, "No, sir; nothing at all."

Reverend Hatcher then dropped to his knees on the top step of the gallows. He bowed his head in silent prayer for a few moments before rising and whispering in Cluverius' ear. Cluverius whispered back to the Reverend who nodded his head and stepped to the edge of the platform to address the crowd, "I am requested by the prisoner to utter one word for him, and that is that in the moment of death he carries to the grave no ill-will towards any man on earth." Hatcher then turned, held his hand to his quivering mouth, descended the stair, and left the yard.

Deputy Allen stepped forward, reached under the cloak, and tied the prisoner's knees tightly together. He then wound another rope tightly around the prisoner's cloak, pinning his arms underneath against his own body. The deputy looped the noose over Cluverius' head and then tightened the hangman's knot, adjusting it, as instructed, directly behind Cluverius' right ear. As Allen reached for the black hood, Cluverius cut his eyes down into the crowd. The faces were a blurred mass on an impressionist's canvas, save one particular face near the front which was all too clear. He looked into the old woman's cold left eye. Annabelle Lumpkin's mouth moved; and although he could not hear her words, they rattled clearly within in his own head, "It won't be long, but still longer than you think, Mr. Cluverius." The world went black as the deputy pulled the hood over Cluverius' face. His own labored breathing and accelerating heart was all that he heard.

Deputy Macon stepped from behind Cluverius and dropped a handkerchief. A third deputy, C. M. Johnson, was stationed in a room directly across from the gallows. At 1:09 PM Johnson jerked on a string and the trap door sprung. The door clanged after opening and Cluverius dropped eight feet. The silk rope began to stretch. Cluverius' feet twitched as they slowly descended closer to the brick surface below. All was quiet for a moment before the sound of heavy breathing began emanating from under the hood. The twitching of his feet and legs progressed into full spasm as the demonic sounds of gurgling and choking bounced off the walls of the jail yard. The crowd fell into shocked silence as the policemen began to look at one another with helpless panic. Sheriff Southard rushed under the gallows to get a closer look. Sergeant Smith followed close behind. After walking behind the struggling man in the excruciating throes of death, Southard reported to Smith, "The knot hasn't slipped. I don't think we need to re-hang him. His neck should be broken. He's not touching the ground. I don't understand it."

"Well, what shall we do?", Smith asked.

"Let him be.", Southard concluded.

After three minutes of spasms and stertorous breathing, Dr. W. T. Oppenheimer approached the prisoner and checked his pulse. It registered 96 beats per minute. The sound of the negro spirituals wafted into the yard as the stunned crowd remained catatonic, adding a sorrowful backdrop to a most unfortunate scene. After another three painfully tedious minutes, Oppenheimer again checked Cluverius' pulse. To his dismay, it had increased to 130. "This is unconscionable, gentlemen!", the doctor remarked.

Sheriff Southard stepped forward, 'Well what would you have us do? Re-hang him?!, Shoot him?!"

The crowd filled with restless concern as Cluverius' dreadful demise continued. Shouts of "Do something!" began to ring. Cluverius heard none of it. As his fitful panic drifted into resigned delirium, conflicting images ran through his mind: the softness of a woman's touch, the sting of his father's belt; the sweet smell of perfumed hair, the dank stench of the City Jail; the hopeful warm sunrise at Aunt Jane's farm, the dreary cold midnight at the Old Marshall Reservoir; the senses of his subconscious were completely in balance whilst his physical faculties progressively dimmed.

Sergeant Smith turned to the crowd, raised his arms, then lowered them, imploring the crowd to maintain composure. After three additional minutes, Dr. Oppenheimer once again checked for a pulse. It was very faint but still registering 30 beats per minute. Oppenheimer sighed in ironic relief as he saw that the patient was finally dying. Cluverius' movements slowed over the next minute, gradually tapering off to an occasional twitch and a shallow exhale. Sixteen minutes after dropping from the platform, at 1:25 PM, Thomas J. Cluverius was pronounced dead. (75.2)

Deputy Allen and Deputy Macon approached the body to cut it down from the gallows twenty minutes after it had plunged through the trap door. Allen noticed a small crumpled piece of paper laying below the dead man's feet. He picked it up and read it:

I believe this to be true (Hand-written in pencil atop the page)

ALL'S FOR THE BEST

All's for the best! Be sanguine and cheerful,

Trouble and sorrow are friends in disguise,

Nothing but folly goes faithless and fearful,

Courage forever is happy and wise:

All for the best, - if a man would but know it,

Providence wishes us all to be blest,

This is no dream of the pundit or poet,

Heaven is gracious, and – All's for the best!

All for the best! Set this on your standard,
Soldier of sadness, or pilgrim of love,
Who to the shores of Despair may have wander'd,
A waywearied swallow, or heart-stricken dove:
All for the best! – be a man but confiding,
Providence tenderly governs the rest,
And the frail bark of His creature is guiding
Wisely and warily all for the best.

All for the best! Then fling away terrors,
Meet all your fears and foes in the van,
And in the midst of your dangers or errors
Trust like a child while you strive like a man:
All's for the best! – unbiass'd, unbounded,
Providence reigns from the East to the West;
And, by both wisdom and mercy surrounded,
Hope and be happy that All's for the best!

MARTIN FARQUAR TUPPER

(75.3)

EPILOGUE

Thomas J. Cluverius

Richmond State
January 15, 1887

THE END OF IT ALL – *Cluverius' Body Sent Home*

The body of Thomas J. Cluverius was taken down to the York River depot about half past six o'clock by Mr. L.T. Christian, the undertaker, who had the remains placed on the coach attached to the freight train which left Richmond at ten minutes after seven o'clock.

Those who accompanied the remains were W. B. Cluverius, brother of the dead man; W. B. Walker, a relative; W. R. McGeorge, Fairfax Montague, of Richmond, formerly of King and Queen County; W. S. Courtney, commissioner of the revenue for King and Queen County, and Dr. J. E. Courtney, with whom the prisoner had an office. Mrs. Tunstall, the aunt of the dead man, was not seen on the train. The party purchased tickets for Romancoke, at which place the body was to be taken from the train and carried to the place of burial – the old family burying ground at Mrs. Tunstall's.

The body looked very natural, the art of the undertaker had concealed the bruised neck, and the features looked almost as natural as they did in life. The brother of the dead man was deeply affected. His eyes were filled with tears and he sobbed aloud when the coffin was being placed on the train.

The scaffold upon which the murderer of poor Lillian Madison had paid the penalty of his crime was removed shortly after the execution took place. It was taken to pieces and carried away from the jail. The rope used in the hanging was, it is said, given back to Mr. Brown, who made it. What final disposition will be made of this "rope of many colors" the "(Richmond) State" does not know. There is a report in circulation that the rope will be cut into pieces and sold. This report, however, could not be verified.

About the hour Cluverius was executed someone placed a handful of flowers upon the grave of Lillian Madison in Oakwood (Cemetery).

The trunk, clothing, and other articles that belonged to the poor girl, which were shown at the trial, are still in the Sergeant's Office at City Hall. The Commonwealth no longer has any use for them, and they will, if the dead girl's mother desires it, be sent to Mrs. Madison. The trunk has been closed for nearly two years.

Thomas J. Cluverius' effects will be distributed as he requested. The cell in which he was so long confined still contains many of his effects, such as clothing, flowers, and books borrowed from friends. An examination of the effects left by him in the jail is yet to be made. Some persons believe that Cluverius, notwithstanding the fact that he asserted his innocence up to the very last, has left a written confession. If it is in his cell it will soon be forthcoming, but officers do not expect to find such a document.

COMMENTS of the PRESS

Alexandria Gazette
January 15, 1887

  Richmond Va, Jan 14 - Cluverius was hanged today for the alleged murder of Miss Madison, protesting his innocence in the face of death and eternity. It is hoped no mistake has been made.

Richmond Times
January 15, 1887

  The execution of Cluverius closed yesterday one of the most painful records of a criminal case, about which there has been entirely too much sensation. The public will feel a great relief.

Norfolk Virginian
January 15, 1887

  We have not one word of comment, at this time, in regard to the execution of Cluverius, except to say that even presumable infidelity to a woman can never find endorsement in a Virginia jury box.

Wilmington Star
January 15, 1887

  The young murderer has paid the sad penalty of crime. He made no sign dying that he was guilty, and yet, if innocent, as he claimed, he was Christ-like enough to have no grudge against any one. A most remarkable scoundrel from first to last. If the high moral qualities had been his and opportunity had offered, what a hero he would have been. The death of poor Lillian Madison is avenged as far as law can do so.

Raleigh News-Observer
January 15, 1887

  Whether innocent or guilty, the awful fate before him would seem to have shaken his composure at times, at least; but his stolidity has remained fixed at every turn of his affairs, and he died in the firm silence he has maintained from the first. There is satisfaction in the thought that the chain of evidence against him was reasonably complete, and that, in any event, he was morally if not legally guilty of the death of Miss Madison. He could not have died an innocent man.

Baltimore Sun
January 15, 1887

    It is at all times painful duty to pass upon the life of a man, and in this case of Cluverius – convicted of murder after betraying his cousin - a certain amount of mystery has surrounded the crime from the first to leave doubts in some intelligent minds as to whether he was guilty of the crime and that the verdict of the jury and the affirmation of the Court of Appeals – one member of the court dissenting – declared him to have been.
    From the day of his arrest up to the hour of his execution Cluverius persisted in asserting his innocence of a crime for which he was to suffer the last penalty. His firmness throughout was remarkable. His conversation with those who visited him in prison was easy and unaffected, and showed at no time any signs of irritation or bravado. He went to his death with his lips sealed, so far as any confession of his guilt is concerned, and whatever there was of mystery about the case remains a mystery still. (E1)

Fitzhugh Lee

Norfolk Landmark
January 15, 1887

    A great deal of morbid sensibility was displayed by people scattered through the state, and the attempt to manufacture public opinion was persistent; but we are convinced that the sentimental view of the case really had no existence in the minds of the great mass of the people. During this time Governor Lee was harassed by a great sense of responsibility. He examined the case with care and intelligence, and the result of his investigation is already known to our readers. His decision rests upon the finding of the jury, the opinion of the judge that tried, and the attorney who prosecuted the case; and also on the ruling of the Supreme Court of Appeals of Virginia. He was fortified as to the facts and the law, and as the executive head of the State he decided the matter in the interests of justice, and public morality. That he acted wisely, as far as human understanding is concerned, admits of little debate; and this will be the judgment within the State and beyond her borders.

Lynchburg Virginian
January 15, 1887

    We had hoped and believed that the Governor would, at least for the present, suspend the execution of the sentence. We hoped this because of the unquestioned fact that a large proportion of those who had carefully read the testimony arrived at the conclusion that the case was not made beyond a reasonable doubt. We are not, of course, going into the details of the testimony. Much less would we for a moment intimate that Governor Lee has not acted from a high and conscientious sense of duty. He was perfectly satisfied of the guilt of the accused. But then we think he ought to have reflected that there were very many other persons whose judgment he knew to be as good as his own, who also believed there was doubt about it.

We repeat that no one should, for a moment, doubt the entire conscientiousness of Governor Lee. But nevertheless, we think he has made a mistake. It is human to err, and he is not exempt from error of judgment notwithstanding he is a true and noble man. He was in an atmosphere of such thick prejudice that it was next to impossible to hold his judgment in dispassionate equipoise. We can but feel that our friends of the Richmond press did much – more than they ought to have done – to create this prejudice. We trust they will, upon sober reflection, see the matter in this light and draw from it a salutary lesson for the future.

Richmond State
January 15, 1887

The cool demeanor of the doomed man, his protestations of innocence, and his conviction on circumstantial evidence have raised doubts in the minds of many who a few months ago were convinced of his guilt, and who then thought he should pay the dread penalty. When we look for any other basis upon which the change of opinion on the part of this class is founded, we fail to find it, and therefore we come to the conclusion that the refusal of Cluverius to confess is the only reason some people have for thinking him innocent. His friends have produced really no new evidence since the review of his case by the Court of Appeals, and though they were naturally persistent in their appeals to Gov. Lee and he gave the case exhaustive examination up to the very hour of the execution, he had absolutely nothing to act upon unless he allowed sympathy for the distressed relatives of the condemned to over-ride his duty as the upholder of the laws of the State. Gov. Lee did his duty, a painful duty indeed, but nevertheless, his duty.

Baltimore Herald
January 15, 1887

Governor Lee did his duty, and he will be honored for it by all sober-minded and law-abiding citizens. Capital punishment is a terrible thing, but it is better than the farce of repeated respites or commutations of sentence, both of which enables scheming politicians to turn human tigers loose upon the community. (E2)

Governor Fitzhugh Lee would serve out the remaining years of his gubernatorial term with dignity and distinction. He largely avoided political squabbles, leaving such matters to the General Assembly. Instead he focused on the intended role of the Executive. His early experience with the Cluverius case clearly had an effect upon the remainder of his governorship. Governor Lee took great and intense interest in the plight of prisoners, seeking to address problems with over-crowding in the state penitentiary. He also opposed the convict-hire system, which provided cheap labor to railroads and other infrastructure projects. The General Assembly, however, failed to address the shortcomings of the system, an indication that the railroad lobby still wielded heavy influence in Virginia politics. Lee also proposed the establishment of a reformative school for youthful offenders, seeking to separate them from older, more hardened criminals. Although no reform school was established during his term, Fitz's spotlight brought the issue to the fore, resulting in the opening of the Commonwealth's first reform school in Powhatan County in 1892. Governor Lee continued to take his pardoning powers very seriously, spending long hours reviewing the cases of convicted prisoners. He also continued to serve as an effective ambassador for Virginia. Working tirelessly to promote economic and industrial progress in the State, he attracted an estimated $100 million of new capital to the Commonwealth by the time his term ended in January, 1890. Fitz Lee was also on the cutting edge of technology, introducing both the telephone and the typewriter to the Governor's office.

Although Fitzhugh Lee flirted with a possible appointment to fill a vacancy in the U.S. Senate in 1893, he largely retired from electoral politics after his term as Governor. He dabbled in business ventures to little success but found great satisfaction as the author of *General Lee*, a biography of his famed Uncle Robert. At this same time, he was pressed into duty at the behest of his old friend, President Grover Cleveland. Cleveland initiated and the United States Senate confirmed Fitz's appointment as Consul-General of Cuba in 1896. When the USS Maine was destroyed in Havana in 1898, triggering the Spanish-American War, Fitzhugh Lee applied to re-enter the United States Army. President McKinley accepted his application, commissioning him as commander of the 7th U.S. Army Corps. After the war quickly concluded, Brigadier General Fitzhugh Lee, USA, was named Military Governor of Havana and Pinar del Rio, a position he held until November, 1900. General Lee retired from the US Army shortly thereafter.

In 1902, Fitz Lee accepted the position of President of the Jamestown Exposition Company, an organization established to prepare for the coming 300th anniversary (1907) of the first permanent English settlement in America at Jamestown, Virginia. As he did with any task he undertook, Fitz worked tirelessly to make the celebration a rousing success, travelling all over the country to promote the endeavor. On April 27, 1905 Fitz was travelling home from Boston by train from a meeting related to the Jamestown Exposition. Near New York, he suffered a heart attack, followed by a severe paralyzing stroke. His Pullman Car was diverted directly to Washington D.C. Lee was rushed to Providence Hospital where he died thirteen hours later on April 28, 1905 at age 69. Fitzhugh Lee was buried in Hollywood Cemetery in Richmond, adjacent to the Clarke Spring property and the Old Marshall Reservoir.

Fannie Lillian Madison

On March 20, 1885, Fannie Lillian Madison's family placed her body in a "handsome coffin" adorned with a silver plaque which said "At Rest". The remains were then moved from the small chapel at the Almshouse (where her body had been identified) to Oakwood Cemetery in Richmond, where she was interred for eternity. It was a very small funeral procession, consisting of her father, Charles Madison, and a few other friends and members of the family. Mr. Madison had decided to have her remains laid to rest in Richmond instead of their home in King William County in order to spare his wife and their other nine children the pain of facing her remains in person. (E3)

Ellen Lee

Ellen Bernard Lee grew up and married General James Rhea of the 7th Cavalry, USA. She would have four children (two surviving to adulthood) and four grandchildren. One grandson, Fitzhugh Lee Rhea Opie (1930-2000), was a friend of the author and provided the author with the initial information on the Cluverius matter. Although the interaction between Ellen and her father is dramatized, Mr. Opie informed the author that Ellen, as a child, was adamant about Cluverius' innocence and not pleased with her father's decision to not intervene. She became a family curator, of sorts, falling heir to, among other historically significant family items, the famed "Lee Saddle". Ellen died in 1959 at age 86 and was buried at sea near San Diego, CA. A memorial plaque of her burial is in the Fitzhugh Lee family plot at Hollywood Cemetery in Richmond.

Jack Wren

Although Jack Wren is a significant character in the story, he is highly fictionalized. The actual John "Jack" Wren's family came to America c. 1844 when he was four years old. The family initially lived in Baltimore, where Jack would spend his childhood. When the War broke out, he joined the Confederate Army and served with the Elliott Greys of Manchester. After the War, Wren stayed in Richmond and became active in conservative politics. He joined the Richmond Police force and became a detective. When the detective branch was abolished, he started an independent detective agency, The National Police Detective Agency (prior to the Cluverius matter). Contrary to the story, this agency was quite successful and Detective Wren was involved in many high-profile investigations in Richmond, the death of Lillian Madison among them. There is no evidence that Wren ever had any direct contact with Fitzhugh Lee. Wren became very well-known throughout Richmond for both his brash detective skills and his dapper appearance. He married in 1889 at age 48. He contracted pneumonia and died just a year later in 1890 at age 49. He left no children. (E4)

Jane Tunstall

Jane Walker Tunstall returned to her home in Little Plymouth, Virginia. She passed away May 7, or 12, 1892 at age 76. (E5)

Willie Cluverius

William B. Cluverius returned home to Little Plymouth, Virginia. It is unclear whether he continued to live with his Aunt Jane Tunstall until her death; but he did stay in Little Plymouth for the rest of his life. He married Bessie Hurst in 1887. They had one child in 1888. Bessie died in 1889. Willie remarried (Ula Jane Hurst) in 1890. They went on to have an additional 8 children. Willie died at age 81 on June 14, 1940 after an illness of several months. He was buried in the family cemetery where his brother, Thomas J. Cluverius, was buried. (E6)

Peter J. Burton

Peter J. Burton's character is highly fictionalized. The author has presented him as a rather devious, hard-nosed, bordering-on-corrupt reporter. From what the author can gather about the true Peter J. Burton, the opposite is true. Evidently, he was a very affable character who would never do harm to any man. Burton was clearly credited as one of the early reporters on the scene at the Old Marshall Reservoir the morning Lillie Madison's body was discovered and he was the first to pose a murder theory in the press. Shortly after the election of Fitzhugh Lee as Governor, Burton left *The Richmond Dispatch* and became editor of *The Richmond Whig*, where he enjoyed a long and successful career. It is also interesting to note that by act of the Virginia Assembly in 1886, The Erin Hunting Club of Henrico and Hanover Counties was organized and stock subscriptions were opened. Among the named directors of the club were: Peter J. Burton; Edward ("Ned") Cummins, (the bar owner); Beverly T. Crump, (Cluverius' defense attorney); and Samuel B. Witt, the Commonwealth's Attorney (who recused himself from the prosecution of Cluverius because they were related). These men evidently all knew each other quite well. (E7)

Charles H. F. Deuring

The author portrays Charles Deuring as a current officer on the Richmond Police. In truth, by the time of the Cluverius matter, he was an ex-policeman. After learning of Deuring's bribery attempt of Hermann Joel, Governor Lee immediately informed Charles V. Meredith and instructed him to open an investigation. When Deuring returned to Joel's shop to pay the remainder of the bribe, an officer from the Richmond Police was secreted below the store counter. Deuring, being of German extract himself, began to speak to Joel in German. Joel knew that the policeman did not understand German and, with great presence of mind, asked Deuring to speak in English so that Joel's wife, who spoke no English and was nearby, would not understand the illicit discussion. Deuring complied, and thus, incriminated himself before a reliable witness. Deuring was arrested on December 8, 1886 for attempting to impede justice by bribing Hermann Joel to make a false affidavit before Governor Lee. His trial was postponed until sometime after February 20, 1887, the last time he appeared in the Hustings Court of Richmond. It was speculated that Governor Lee, himself may have to testify in the Deuring trial. The author was unable to locate any further information on Deuring or the final disposition of his trial. (E8)

Hermann Joel

The author could not find any further information on Hermann Joel subsequent to the Cluverius matter other than evidence of his arrest for drunkenness. He appeared at the Richmond Police Court on June 20, 1887 and was fined $5 plus court costs. (E9)

Dr. William H. Taylor

Dr. Taylor is certainly one of the more interesting characters involved with the case. He was indeed a highly intelligent man of science with a sharp mind and a sharper tongue. He was named Medical Examiner of Richmond in 1872 and held that position until his death in 1917. He taught thousands of students over that same period at The Medical College of Virginia and Richmond High School. He was an expert witness in many trials, becoming one of the most revered doctors and scientists in the state. An excerpt from one of his lectures, Science and the Soul, published in *The Old Dominion Journal of Medicine and Surgery* grants some insight into the man. The paper addresses the age-old conflict between men of science and men of the cloth. Taylor expounds on the persecution he had endured from "ecclesiastic" clergy, who had condemned him as an "atheist". He wore it as a badge of honor:

"It was not without some feeling of satisfaction that I received the last epithet, which put me in the glorious company of worthies whose line extends from Socrates to Herbert Spencer. Where is the self-respecting man who, finding himself involuntarily thrust into even the humblest place among these kings and prophets of his race, would not feel infinitely more ennobled than he could ever feel though towering the most conspicuous among the horde of pygmies squeaking "atheist" at them?"

However, it is clear that the label also stung. At the close of his prefatory for the lecture, Taylor states:

"... It would give me sincere sorrow to believe that religion is so poor a thing as to stand in need of false science for its development and support. For the man of science can deeply feel for himself not only, but for his fellow man as well, though it is sometimes strangely said that he regards nothing that he cannot weigh or measure, or somehow test in his laboratory. If this description of him were true he would be a monster. But it is not true. He is of like fashion with others, sharing their strength and their weakness, their virtues and their vices. He feels as they do the inspiration of music, of art, of poetry, and is equally with them responsive to all forms of beauty. His interests are the common interests of all mankind. His religion, if it not be in subjection to conventional formulas, yet is as pure and practical as any that is set forth in creeds, and his system of morals is as exalted and as faithfully observed as that of any other man's. He has his joys and his sorrows as the rest of the world have theirs. He partakes the happiness of social and domestic communion, and he, too, weeps bitter tears when he sees his loved one sink into the grave. Nor is he, in that dark hour, without hope – hope, it may be, that is as consoling as is the hope of some who superciliously condemn, or others who generously pity him for what they think is his error. He is altogether human, and makes his pilgrimage to the ultimate goal of human kind guided on his way, as each of his companions is, by such light as has been vouchsafed him."

But just as he was viewed with a jaundiced eye by the clergy, so Taylor held contempt for women. One of his lectures on this subject stated:

"Woman is inferior physically, mentally, and morally to man."; her qualities "require us to class her as infantine," and that "she has not succeeded in obscuring her descent from the ape to the extent that her brother has done." He further described woman as "squatty and fatty, and is built up with a variety of exaggerated spheres, cones, and cylinders strung together."

Not surprisingly, Dr. Taylor was a lifetime bachelor. Dr. William H. Taylor died April 14, 1917 at age 81. He served the City of Richmond for over 45 years. He is buried in Hollywood Cemetery in Richmond, Virginia. (E10)

Heros von Borcke

Johann Heinrich August Heros von Borcke served the Confederate Army with distinction throughout the Civil War, ultimately rising to the rank of Lieutenant Colonel. He fought valiantly alongside J.E.B. Stuart during the Northern Virginia Campaign in the Summer of 1862, the Maryland Campaign in the Fall of 1862, and the Battle of Fredericksburg in December, 1862. In 1863, he fought at The Wilderness, The Battle of Chancellorsville, and The Battle of Brandy Station. During the early stages of the Gettysburg Campaign of 1863, von Borcke received a near fatal bullet wound to the neck at the Battle of Middleburg on June 19, 1863. He was rushed from the battlefield to Dr. Talcott Eliason's house where he was cared for by the doctor's family. In an opium induced trance, von Borcke lay awake but unable to move as his comrades came to pay final respects.

"At last Stuart himself came, and, bending over me, he kissed my forehead and I felt two tears drop upon my cheek as I heard him say, 'Poor fellow, your fate is a sad one, and it was for me that you received this mortal wound.' I would have given anything to have had the power of grasping my friend's hand, and pronouncing a few words of thankfulness for his heartfelt sympathy; and when, in later times, I stood by his own deathbed, these friendly words came vividly before my recollection."

Heros von Borcke would recover and return to duty, albeit it in a support role. He was dispatched to England on a diplomatic mission in February, 1865, and therefore was "saved the grief of being an eyewitness of the rapid collapse of the Confederacy, and the downfall of a just and noble cause."

Von Borcke returned to his homeland and served in the Prussian Army during the brief Austro-Prussian War in 1866, receiving the *Order of the Red Eagle* for his gallantry. He retired from the Prussian Army in 1867, returning to his family castle in Giesenbrugge. The bullet which entered von Borcke's body that day in Middleburg lodged in his lung and was never removed. It was a constant source of discomfort and illness, culminating in his death from sepsis in 1895 at age 59. (E11)

Francis A. Howell

Francis A. Howell returned to Alexandria, VA. He served in Co. A, 1st Washington, DC Volunteers in the Spanish American War. The author could not determine Mr. Howell's occupation. But, a small advertisement in the June 10, 1885 edition of the *Alexandria Gazette* indicates that Mrs. F. A. Howell ran a millinery shop at 104 King Street at that time. Francis A. Howell died February 19, 1919 at age 72. He is buried at Arlington National Cemetery. (E12)

APPENDIX

List of Witnesses: The Commonwealth of Virginia v. Thomas J. Cluverius

For the Prosecution

L. W. Rose	W.R. Quarles	Charles Madison
R.G. Lucas	Jas. D. Craig	Morgan Treat
J.W. Trainham	A.B. Cauthorn	Alfred R. James
Wm. Hutcheson	Mrs. Margaret	W.F. Dillard
Dr. W.H. Taylor	Dickinson	Wm. Tyler (recalled)
R.G. Lucas (recalled)	J. L. Oliver	William H. Gratton
Jackson Bolton	Emmett Richardson	William Tucker
A.W. Hargrove	Jas. M. Guthrie	John T. Williams
R.R. Dunstan	Willie Dickinson	Dr. Thomas E. Stratton
E.J. Archer	John D. Foster	Herman Joel
J.J. Walton	W.H. Madison	Aaron Watkins
C.W. Saunders	Miss Laura M. Curtis	Dr. James Beale
John Williams	R.H. Curtis	Dr. J.G. Cabell
Isaac Williams	Jos. H. Dodson	Charles H. Epps
Chs. Williams	D.C. Richardson	James Estis
William Thurston	(recalled)	Edward Pierce
Jos. R. Mountcastle	Hunter Hunt	Jos. H. Dodson
John B. Childress	C.J. Madison	(recalled)
J.D. Redwood	Hunter Hunt (recalled)	R.T. Dillard
Ro. J. Waddell	Wm. Tyler	Logan S. Robinson
Mrs. Anna Williams	E. Cuthbert	John L. Oliver (recalled)
Walter Hill	Geo. Wright	John R.J. Vaughan
B.P. Owen	Wm. Martin	Joel J. Bland
Sam'l B. Witt	D.V. Morton	Charles H. Sweeney
M. Gatewood	Benj. Earp	Loula V. Woodward
John Wren	Wm. Kidd	Hunter Hunt (recalled)
Claggett Jones	T.A. Spencer	Jos. H. Dodson
A.W. Archer	Jas. Thompson	(recalled)
Henrietta Wimbush	Thos. E. Bethel	R.D. Wortham
Miss Ella Madison	Joseph Perkins	Robert Caruther
E.C. Jones	Mary Curtis	
D.C. Richardson	Clara Anderson	

For the Defense

Mrs. Jane Tunstall
John W. Ryland
J.H. Atkins
Thomas Milby
Dr. W.H. Taylor (recalled)
George W. Minter
Emmett S. Richardson
Dr. W.C. Barker
B.W. Henley
Statement of Miss Nolie Bray
William B. Cluverius
William S. Courtney
D.C. Richardson (recalled)
John B. Yarrington
James F. Bland
Dr. F.M. Bland
Dr. A.C. Grubbs
Wm. T. Roane
Claggett Jones (recalled)
James T. Bland
D.C. Richardson (recalled)
H.H. Harris
William A. Edwards
Beverly Anderson
Dr. J.E. Courtney
Harry Dudley
J.C. Council
R.H. Spencer
T.N. Walker
Robert Todd
R.L. Savage
Monroe Morris
Alex. F. Bagby
Thos. P. Bagby
George R. Bagby
Miles Turpin
S.C. Greenhow

Dr. J.B. Bland
Ed. D. Pollard
Mark Davis
Charles B. Dodson
B.W. Vashon
A.F. Bagby
Hunter Hunt (recalled)
Jno. Thomas Williams
William Tyler (recalled)
John S. Dodson
Jos. Bland
J.J. Walton (recalled)
B.W. Cluverius
J.J. Cordle
G.W. Quicke
Capt. Epps (recalled)
Calvert Harris
Wm. P. Wall
Thomas P. Bagby (recalled)
C.W. Saunders (recalled)
O.M. Winston
William A. Spiller
L.B. Robinson
Magruder Puller
A.B. Hill
John H. Haw
Orvin T. Stearns
J.B. Simon
Herman Joel (recalled)
D.C. Richardson (recalled)
R.B. Kasey
F.A. Farland
Augustus Diggs
H.W. Flournoy
Dr. J.E. Courtney
Edgar E. Montague
J.T. Redd

BIBLIOGRAPHY

Anonymous, THOMAS J. CLUVERIUS vs COMMONWEALTH OF VIRGINIA, Johns and Goolsby, Richmond, VA, c. 1885 – "Making of Modern Law" Print Edition

Booker, George A. TRIAL and CONVICTION of THOMAS J. CLUVERIUS, for the MURDER of LILLIAN MADISON, MARCH 13, 1885, Johns and Goolsby, Richmond, VA, c. 1885 – "Making of Modern Law" Print Edition

Cluverius, Thomas J., CLUVERIUS. MY LIFE, TRIAL, and CONVICTION, S.J. Dudley, Richmond, VA, 1887 – "Making of Modern Law" Print Edition

Dabney, Virginius, RICHMOND: THE STORY of a CITY, University of Virginia Press, Charlottesville and London, 1990

Ezekiel, Herbert T., THE RECOLLECTIONS of a VIRGINIA NEWSPAPER MAN, Herbert T. Ezekiel, Printer and Publisher, Richmond, VA, 1920

Jackson, Mary Anna, *LIFE and LETTERS of GENERAL THOMAS J JACKSON (STONEWALL JACKSON)*, Harper Brothers, New York, 1892

Jones, J. William, VIRGINIA'S NEXT GOVERNOR, GENERAL FITZHUGH LEE, N.Y. Cheap Publishing Co., New York, 1885, Scholar Select Reprint

Jones, Virgil Carrington, RANGER MOSBY, The University of North Carolina Press, Chapel Hill, NC, 1944

Kinsley, Ardyce, et al THE FITZHUGH LEE SAMPLER, Brandylane Publishers, Lively, VA, 1992

Nichols, James L., GENERAL FITZHUGH LEE, a BIOGRAPHY, H.E. Howard, Inc., Lynchburg, VA, 1989

Powell, Mary G., THE HISTORY of OLD VIRGINIA from JULY 13, 1749 to MAY 24, 1861, William Byrd Press, Inc, Richmond, Va., Copyright, 1928, Mary G. Powell

Rhea, Gordon C., TO the NORTH ANNA RIVER: GRANT and LEE, MAY 13-25, 1864, Louisiana State University Press, Baton Rouge, LA, 2000

Thomson, John, AN EXACT and AUTHENTIC NARRATIVE, of the EVENTS WHICH TOOK PLACE in BALTIMORE, on the 27th and 28th of JULY LAST, Printed for the Purchasers, September 1, 1812, Classic Reprint Series - Forgotten Books, 2017

Von Borcke, Heros, MEMOIRS of the CONFEDERATE WAR for INDEPENDENCE, 1867, Arcadia Press Print Edition, 2017

Wise, George THE HISTORY of the SEVENTEENTH VIRGINIA INFANTRY, CSA, 1870, Kell, Piet and Company, Baltimore, and entered by Act of Congress by George Wise, 1870

VIRGINIA SUPREME COURT OF APPEALS OPINIONS

Cluverius vs. The Commonwealth of Virginia, Vol. LXXXI, 100-107, Richmond, May 6, 1886, Opinion - Judge J. Fauntleroy

Cluverius vs. The Commonwealth of Virginia, Vol. LXXXI, 107-110, Richmond, May 6, 1886, Concurring Opinion - Judge P. Lewis, Judge J. Richardson, Judge J. Lacy

Cluverius vs. The Commonwealth of Virginia, Vol. LXXXI, 110-112, Richmond, May 6, 1886 Dissenting Opinion – Judge J. Hinton

ACTS OF THE VIRGINIA ASSEMBLY

Acts and Joint Resolutions Passed by the General Assembly of the State of Virginia During the Session of 1885-86, Richmond, Va, A.R. Micou, Superintendent of Public Printing, 1886

PERIODICALS

NEWSPAPER ARTICLES

The Daily Index-Appeal, Petersburg, Virginia (29)

"A Corpse in a City Reservoir", *Daily Index Appeal*, Petersburg VA, March 16, 1885

"Richmond's Sensation: The Body of the Woman Found in the Reservoir Identified – Murder Suspected", *The Daily Index-Appeal*, Petersburg, VA, March 18, 1885

"Fannie Madison's Fate: Trying to Unravel the Mystery", *The Daily Index-Appeal*, Petersburg, Va,, March 24, 1885

"Trying to Lift the Veil Off Lillie Madison's Murderer", *The Daily Index-Appeal*, Petersburg, Va,, March 28, 1885

"Lillian Madison's Death: Cluverius Trial Well Started", *The Daily Index-Appeal*, Petersburg, Va,, May 14, 1885

"The Reservoir Tragedy: Important Testimony Given In", *The Daily Index-Appeal*, Petersburg, Va,, May 15, 1885

"Link by Link: A Chain of Evidence is Forged", *The Daily Index-Appeal*, Petersburg, Va,, May 16, 1885

"Lillian and Her Lover: Story of Their Intimacy Told", *The Daily Index-Appeal*, Petersburg, Va,, May 18, 1885

"Lillian's Letters: A Trunk Full of Them in Court", *The Daily Index-Appeal*, Petersburg, Va,, May 19, 1885

"Step by Step Cluverius Counsel Bar the Way", *The Daily Index-Appeal*, Petersburg, Va,, May 20, 1885

"Lillian's Last Journey: The Letter That Caused It", *The Daily Index-Appeal,* Petersburg, Va,, May 21, 1885

"Strand by Strand: The Net of Guilt is Woven", *The Daily Index-Appeal,* Petersburg, Va,, May 22, 1885

"Trifles Light as Air: Prove a Burden to Cluverius", *The Daily Index-Appeal,* Petersburg, Va,, May 23, 1885

"Cluverius Weakening: He Looks Scared and Nervous", *The Daily Index-Appeal*, Petersburg, Va,, May 26, 1885

"Cluverius' Defense: Another Watchkey Produced", *The Daily Index-Appeal,* Petersburg, Va,, May 27, 1885

"Cluverius' Brother: On the Stand for Many Hours", *The Daily Index-Appeal,* Petersburg, Va,, May 28, 1885

"Trying to Save His Neck: Course of Cluverius' Defence", *The Daily Index-Appeal,* Petersburg, Va,, May 29, 1885

"The Trial nearly Ended: Cluverius Father on the Stand",*The Daily Index-Appeal,* Petersburg, Va,, May 30, 1885

"Talking to the Jury: Argument in Cluverius' Case", *The Daily Index-Appeal,* Petersburg, Va,, June 2, 1885

"Pleading for Cluverius: Argument of Hon. A. B. Evans", *The Daily Index-Appeal,* Petersburg, Va,, June 3, 1885

"Cluverius Sentenced: Judge Atkins' Solemn Address", *The Daily Index-Appeal,* Petersburg, Va,, June 20, 1885

"The Capital City", *The Daily Index-Appeal,* Petersburg, Va,, August 8, 1885

"Fitz Lee's Tribute: The South Sends Us to Make Up", *The Daily Index-Appeal,* Petersburg, Va,, August 11, 1885

"State Capital Topics", *The Daily Index-Appeal,* Petersburg, Va,, September 15, 1885

"The Campaign: Points and Paragraphs Gathered from All Sources", *The Daily Index-Appeal,* Petersburg, Va,, October 21, 1885

"Startling Rumors About the Cluverius Case", *The Daily Index-Appeal*, Petersburg, VA, April 10, 1886

"Three Days Before His Death: Cluverius Appears Unshaken", *The Daily Index-Appeal,* Petersburg, Va,, January 12, 1887

"The End Drawing Nigh", The *Daily Index Appeal,* Petersburg VA January 13, 1887

"The End of it All: Cluverius' Body Sent Home", *The Daily Index-Appeal,* Petersburg, Va,, January 17, 1887

New York Times, **New York (12)**

"Medical Students Clash", *New York Times*, December 7, 1859

"Lillian Madison Buried: The Young Lawyer, Her Alleged Murderer, Still in Custody", *New York Times,* March 21, 1885

"The Cluverius Trial", *New York Times,* May 8, 1885

"Still Without a Jury", *New York Times,* May 9, 1885

"A Jury Secured for Cluverius", *New York Times,* May 12, 1885

"The Murder of Miss Madison: Evidence Showing That a Struggle with a Man Preceded Her Death", *New York Times,* May 14, 1885

"The Murder of Miss Madison: Continuation of the Evidence by the Prosecution", *New York Times,* May 15, 1885

"T.J. Cluverius on Trial: To Unravel the Mystery of Miss Madison's Death", *New York Times,* May 16, 1885

"The Cluverius Trial: Testimony in Support of the Theory of the Prosecution", *New York Times,* May 19, 1885

"The Cluverius Murder: Still Hearing Evidence to Sustain Prosecution", *New York Times,* May 20, 1885

"The Cluverius Murder Trial: Trying to Connect the Prisoner with the Murdered Woman", *New York Times,* May 21, 1885

"The Cluverius Murder Trial: Testimony for the Prosecution Drawing to a Close", *New York Times,* May 22, 1885

The Rockingham Register, **Harrisonburg, Virginia (6)**

"Murder Most Foul: The Sad Fate of a Young Virginia Girl", *The Rockingham Register*, Harrisonburg, Va., March 26, 1885

The Rockingham Register, Harrisonburg, Va, June 11, 1885.

The Rockingham Register, Harrisonburg, Va., January 28, 1886

"Cluverius Condemned: Date of Death Fixed at December 10th (from *Richmond Whig-October 10, 1886)*", *The Rockingham Register*, Harrisonburg, Va., October 14, 1886

"The "Old Man's" Statement (from *The Richmond State*)", *The Rockingham Register*, Harrisonburg, Va., December 23, 1886

"Cluverius Executed: He Dies Without Confessing; His Wonderful Nerve to the Last", *The Rockingham Register*, January 20, 1887

The Daily Times, Richmond, Virginia (6)

"No Pardon: Letter of Governor Lee Declining to Intervene with the Judgment of the Courts in the Cluverius Case", *The Daily Times*, Richmond, Va., December 8, 1886

"The Respite: Cluverius Allowed Five Weeks for Final Preparations", *The Daily Times*, Richmond, Va., December 9, 1886

"The Latest Sensation", *The Daily Times*, Richmond, Va., December 14, 1886

"Death Penalty: The Last Sad Act in the Reservoir Tragedy", *The Daily Times*, Richmond, Va., January 15, 1887

"Deuring's Trial Postponed", *The Daily Times*, Richmond, Va., February 20, 1887

"Detective Wren Dead: Pneumonia Puts an End to an Eventful and Exciting Career", *The Daily Times*, Richmond, Va., March 5, 1890

The Baltimore Sun, Baltimore, Maryland (5)

"The Virginia Democrats: State Convention in Session", *The Baltimore Sun,* Baltimore, Md, July 30, 1885

"Virginia Politics: Hon. John S. Wise Interviewed – Comments on Democratic Nominations", *The Baltimore Sun,* Baltimore, Md., August 1, 1885

"Logan on the Rampage", *The Baltimore Sun,* Baltimore, Md, October 10, 1885

"Virginia Democratic: Fitz Lee Elected Governor and a Democratic Legislature in Both Branches", *(Special Dispatch to the Baltimore Sun from the Richmond Dispatch), The Baltimore Sun,* Baltimore, Md, November 4, 1885

"Cluverius Must Hang: a New Hearing Refused Him; the Case Remanded to Richmond", *The Baltimore Sun, Supplement*, October 1, 1886

The Peninsula Enterprise, Accomac, Virginia (4)

"Platform of the Democratic Party of Virginia", *The Peninsula Enterprise,* Accomac Courthouse, Va,, August 8, 1885

"Virginia News", *The Peninsula Enterprise,* Accomac Courthouse, Va,, August 22, 1885

"Cluverius: Juror Harrison Says His Trial Was "A Horrible and Ghastly Farce"", *The Peninsula Enterprise,* Accomac Courthouse, Va,, January 8, 1887

"Cluverius", *The Peninsula Enterprise,* Accomac Courthouse, Va,, January 15, 1887

The Daily News, **Frederick, Maryland (3)**

"The Richmond Murder Mystery, Young Cluverius Denies All Knowledge of the Death of Miss Madison", *The Daily News,* Frederick, Md., March 21, 1885

"Did She Kill Herself? Rachel McDonald's Terrible Death Near Richmond, VA", *The Daily News,* Frederick, MD, December 5, 1885.

"Cluverius Ill in Prison", *The Daily News,* Frederick, Md., December 21, 1885

The Philadelphia Inquirer, **Philadelphia, Pennsylvania (3)**

"The War in Virginia...Lee Retreats During the Night", *The Philadelphia Inquirer,* May 26, 1864

"The Cluverius Trial: Taking of Testimony for the Commonwealth Began", *The Philadelphia Inquirer,* May 14, 1885

"Condensed News", *The Philadelphia Inquirer,* January 21, 1886

The Philadelphia Times, **Philadelphia, Pennsylvania (2)**

"The Reservoir Mystery: A Witness Who Heard Screams on the Night of the Tragedy", *The Philadelphia Times,* May 24, 1885

"The Cluverius Case: Verdict of Murder in the First Degree", *The Philadelphia Times,* Philadelphia, Pa, June 5, 1885

The Virginia State Journal, **Richmond, Virginia (2)**

"INSURANCE COMPANIES – Universal Life (NY) – L.W. Rose, Agent. 1113 Main Street", *The Virginia State Journal,* November 27, 1872

"VIRGINIA NURSERY AND WINE CO. – L.W. Rose, Treasurer. Corner of 13th and Cary Streets", *The Virginia State Journal,* November 27, 1872

The Richmond Dispatch, **Richmond, Virginia (2)**

"Dry Goods – SPECIAL ANNOUNCEMENT", *Richmond Dispatch,* January 28, 1876

"Bankruptcy Notice - L.W. Rose, Eastern District of Virginia", *Richmond Dispatch,* September 28, 1877

The Boston Globe, **Boston, Massachusetts (2)**

"Sick- A Cluverius Juror", *Boston Daily Globe,* May 12, 1885

"General Fitzhugh Lee: Nominated for Governor – a Black Eye for Senator Mahone", *The Boston Weekly Globe,* Boston, Ma, August 4, 1885

Other Newspaper Articles (26)

"The Hanging of John Brown", *The Warren Mail*, Warren, PA, December 10, 1859

"The Execution of Old John Brown!", *The North Carolinian*, Fayetteville, NC, December 10, 1859

"The Story of a Soldier: Two Brave Veterans Who Reached a Happy Drama of Life", *The Evening Light,* San Antonio, TX, February 19, 1883

The Indiana Weekly Messenger, March 18, 1885

"Charged with Murder: Counselor Cluverius Consigned to a Cell", *Piqua Daily Call*, Piqua, Ohio, March 22, 1885

"Marriage of Count Primo Magri and Mrs. Tom Thumb", *Evening Observer*, Dunkirk, NY, April 7, 1885

"John Phoenix: His Wonderful Fossil Discoveries at West Point", *The Indiana Democrat*, Indiana, PA, April 23, 1885

"The Cluverius Trial: Judge Atkins Refuses to Admit Torn Note in Evidence", *The Sunday Eagle*, Brooklyn, NY, May 24, 1885

"Trial of Cluverius: Work of Taking Testimony About Completed", *Columbus Sunday Enquirer,* Columbus, GA, May 31, 1885

"Cluverius' Crime: Declared Guilty of Lillian Madison's Murder", *The Lebanon Daily News,* Lebanon, Pa, June 5, 1885

"Virginia Politics", *The Newark Daily Advocate,* Newark, Ohio, September 1, 1885

The Muscatine Daily Journal, October 12, 1885

"Virginia Bankrupt", *The Marion Star*, Marion, SC, January 20, 1886

"Solomon Joel, Dealer in Watches, Clocks, Jewelry, &c; Repairing a Specialty. 1503 E. Main St, Richmond", *The Richmond Labor Herald*, June 12, 1886

"A Startling Confession: Cluverius to Make a Statement About the Celebrated Murder Case", *The Massillon Independent*, Massillon, Ohio, December 3, 1886

"Thomas Judson Cluverius: His Long Looked-for Statement Comes Out", *The Columbus Enquirer-Sun*, Columbus, Ga., December 5, 1886

"An Appeal for Vengeance: Prays for the Death of Her Daughter's Alleged Murderer", *The Evening Gazette*, Monmouth, IL., December 8, 1886

"Arrested for an Attempt to Bribe a Witness in Behalf of Cluverius", *The Staunton Spectator*, Staunton, Va., December 15, 1886

"With Silken Rope, Thomas J. Cluverius is Hung by the Neck", *The Weekly Constitution*, Atlanta, Ga., January 18, 1887

"Cluverius Hanged", *The Advertiser-Courier*, Hermann, Mo., January 19, 1887

"The Penalty Paid: Cluverius Executed-He Dies Without Confessing-Wonderful Nerve to the Last", *The Salem Times-Register,* Salem, Va., January 21, 1887

"Police Court", *The Evening Truth*, Richmond, Va., June 21, 1887

The Landmark, Statesville, NC., May 26, 1892

"Belle Isle Revisited: A Loudoun Ranger Taken in the Spot Where He Starved and Suffered", *The National Tribune*, Washington, DC, November 10, 1892

"Benny Havens, Oh!", *The Rock Valley Bee,* Rock Valley, IA,, March 29, 1929

Ezekiel, Herbert T., "Covers Story in 1887, and Rewrites Story in 1937", *The Richmond News Leader*, January 8, 1937

MAGAZINE/JOURNAL ARTICLES (5)

Taylor, William H., M.D., "Science and the Soul: A Lecture to the Class in Medical Jurisprudence of the Medical College of Virginia", *The Old Dominion Journal of Medicine and Surgery*, Vol. IV, No. 5, October, 1905

Pearson, C. C., "The Readjuster Movement in Virginia"*,* *The American Historical Review,* Vol. 21, No. 4, Oxford University Press, July, 1916, pp. 734-749

Robert Popper, , Vol. 1962, No. 4, "History and Development of the Accused's Right to Testify", *WASHINGTON UNIVERSITY LAW QUARTERLY,* December, 1962

Hudson, Leonne, "Valor at Wilson's Wharf", *Civil War Times Illustrated*, March, 1998

Trotti, Michael Ayers, "Murder Made Real:A Visual Revolution of the Halftone", *The Virginia Magazine of History and Biography*, Vol. 111, Number 4, 2003, p.381

ONLINE ARTICLES/SOURCES (15)

Strother, David Hunter, "John Brown's Death and Last Words", December, 1859 – written for *Harper's Weekly*, it is a first-hand account which, for political reasons, was not published until *American Heritage*, February, 1955, Volume 6, Issue 2. The author found the article americanheritage.com https://www.americanheritage.com/eyewitness-describes-hanging-john-brown

Igoe, Brian, "Charles Bianconi and The Transport Revolution", *The Irish Story: Irish History Online*, December 14, 2012 http://www.theirishstory.com/2012/12/14/charles-bianconi-and-the-transport-revolution-1800-1875/#.XO8bfYhKiUl

January 23, 2014 blog post on The Civil War Picket http://civil-war-picket.blogspot.com/2014/01/jeb-stuarts-banjo-player-and-famous.html

Harry Kollatz, Jr. "Hauling Washington: How the Statue Made It to Capitol Square", *Richmondmag.com*, November 20, 2014 https://richmondmagazine.com/news/richmond-history/richmond-capitol-square-statue/

Blumberg, Arnold, "Death of Legendary Confederate General J.E.B. Stuart", , *Warfare History Network*, November 4, 2016 https://warfarehistorynetwork.com/daily/civil-war/death-of-legendary-confederate-general-j-e-b-stuart/

John B. Hoey, "Federalist Opposition to the War of 1812", Archiving Early America -Varsity Tutors, 2007-2019, https://www.varsitytutors.com/earlyamerica/early-america-review/volume-4/federalist-opposition-to-the-war-of-1812

Peace, Roger. "The War of 1812." United States Foreign Policy History and Resource Guide website, 2016, http://peacehistory-usfp.org/the-war-of-1812

Timar-Wilcox, Estelle, "Legend of Civil War Era "Hangman's Tree" Lives On", *Falls Church News-Press.com*, June 29, 2018 https://fcnp.com/2018/06/29/legend-civil-war-era-hangmans-tree-lives/

Censusdiggers.com link on Belle Isle Civil War Prison
http://www.censusdiggins.com/prison_bellisle.html

Census Information on appalachianaristocracy.com for Beverly Whiting Cluverius
http://www.appalachianaristocracy.com/getperson.php?personID=I5892&tree=01

Census Information on appalachianaristocracy.com for Jane Frances Walker Tunstall
http://www.appalachianaristocracy.com/getperson.php?personID=I5922&tree=01

Census Information on appalachianaristocracy.com for William B. Cluverius
http://www.appalachianaristocracy.com/getperson.php?personID=I5871&tree=01

17th Virginia Infantry, CSA, Co. H, Old Dominion Rifles - Roster
http://stevegibson0.tripod.com/co_h.htm

1st Ohio Cavalry, USA – Roster
https://civilwarindex.com/armyoh/rosters/1st_oh_cavalry_roster.pdf

1st Ohio Cavalry, Companies A and C served under General Pope in August/September, 1862
http://civilwarintheeast.com/us-regiments-batteries/ohio/1st-ohio-cavalry/

OTHER SOURCES (3)

Carbon copy of typed "Memorandum" from a November 30, 1886 meeting between Hermann Joel and Governor Fitzhugh Lee regarding the infamous Cluverius watch-key

Original Letter Dated December 8, 1886 from Thomas J. Cluverius to Governor Fitzhugh Lee

Original Letter Dated January 12, 1887 from William B. Cluverius to Governor Fitzhugh Lee

NOTES

(1.1) This entire court case and some of the characters involved, including Annabelle Lumpkin and Samuel Boulware, are fictional. This case never existed, though Thomas J. Cluverius was, in fact, a practicing attorney and did appear before Judge John D. Foster in Court in King William County on more than one occasion.

Cluverius vs. The Commonwealth of Virginia, May 6, 1886, Vol. LXXXI - 106, p. 841-842 Opinion - J. Fauntleroy.

"The Cluverius Murder Trial: Still Hearing Evidence to Sustain the Prosecution", *New York Times,* May 20, 1885, where Foster is (errantly) referred to as "of King and Queen County".

(1.2) Captain Epps and Officer Robbins of the Richmond Police and Deputy Oliver of King and Queen County were the three arresting officers.

Cluverius vs. The Commonwealth of Virginia, May 6, 1886, Vol. LXXXI - 106, p. 843-844 Opinion - J. Fauntleroy.

(2.1) L.W. Rose was indeed the superintendent of the Marshall Reservoir during this period. Although the C.S.S. Torch was an actual Confederate warship, Rose's wartime activities are unknown. There is evidence that an L.W. Rose of Henrico County and Richmond served as a Treasurer of the Virginia Nursey and Wine Co and also ran an insurance agency associated with Universal Life of NY in the 1870's. L. Rose also ran dry goods store in Richmond called L. Rose & Co during this period. He took out an advertisement in the Richmond Dispatch stating that the contents of his entire store were for sale at below cost, indicating his business was failing. There are also several notices in the local papers in 1875 indicating foreclosure sales of property associated with Rose and advertisements placed by Rose to rent properties. There is also a notice of an Eastern District Bankruptcy Filing for L.W. Rose dated August 16, 1877.

Cluverius vs. The Commonwealth of Virginia, May 6, 1886, Vol. LXXXI - 103, p. 817-818, Opinion - J. Fauntleroy

"INSURANCE COMPANIES – Universal Life (NY) – L.W. Rose, Agent. 1113 Main Street", *The Virginia State Journal,* November 27, 1872

"VIRGINIA NURSERY AND WINE CO. – L.W. Rose, Treasurer. Corner of 13th and Cary Streets", *The Virginia State Journal,* November 27, 1872

"Dry Goods – SPECIAL ANNOUNCEMENT", *Richmond Dispatch,* January 28, 1876

"Bankruptcy Notice - L.W. Rose, Eastern District of Virginia", *Richmond Dispatch,* September 28, 1877

(2.2) As for R.G. Lucas, W. Trainham, and Wm. Hutcheson; the names are real and their involvements with this incident are somewhat factual, but their characters and prior actions, as described by the author, are fictional.

(2.3) *Cluverius vs. The Commonwealth of Virginia,* May 6, 1886, Vol. LXXXI - 103, p. 817-818,

Opinion - J. Fauntleroy

"A Corpse in a City Reservoir", *Daily Index Appeal,* Petersburg VA, March 16, 1885

Anonymous, <u>THOMAS J. CLUVERIUS vs COMMONWEALTH OF VIRGINIA,</u> Johns and Goolsby, Richmond, VA, c. 1885 – "Making of Modern Law" Print Edition., p.59

Cluverius vs. The Commonwealth of Virginia, May 6, 1886, Vol. LXXXI - 103, p. 818, Opinion - J. Fauntleroy

(3.1) This is a verbatim transcription of the "Laura Curtis Letter"

Cluverius vs. The Commonwealth of Virginia, May 6, 1886, Vol. LXXXI - 111, p. 888-889, Dissenting Opinion - J. Hinton.

(3.2) "The Cluverius Murder Trial: Trying to Connect the Prisoner with the Murdered Woman", *New York Times,* May 21, 1885

(4.1) The American Hotel was located on the corner of 12th and Bank Streets, across from Capitol Square in Richmond. Lillie Madison actually stayed in Room 21. The account of the hotel's history is fictional.

"The Cluverius Murder Trial: Trying to Connect the Prisoner with the Murdered Woman", *New York Times,* May 21, 1885

(4.2) The basic facts surrounding Miss Madison's stay at The American Hotel including her time of arrival, room assignment, ordering of breakfast, the exchange of notes via a delivery boy, and her exit from the Hotel and subsequent meeting with a gentleman outside the hotel are accurate.

Cluverius vs. The Commonwealth of Virginia, May 6, 1886, Vol. LXXXI - 103, p. 821, Opinion - J. Fauntleroy.

The remaining details of her stay to this point are fictionalized.

(5.1) All entries in Dr. William H. Taylor's notebook are composed by the author but are based upon actual testimony of the doctor and others as they appeared in various *New York Times* articles and the written opinions of the Appeals Court.

Cluverius vs. The Commonwealth of Virginia, May 6, 1886, Vol. LXXXI - 103, p. 818-825, Opinion - J. Fauntleroy

Taylor's personal history and biography are fictionalized.

(6.1) There was contradictory testimony regarding whether the man seen with Lillie Madison had a mustache or not; whether T.J. Cluverius had ever had a mustache in the past or not. Various sources indicated that Cluverius had very recently grown a mustache.

(6.2) Miss Madison and Mr. Cluverius were seen at a bawdy house on 15th Street between 12 noon and 2pm on March 13, 1885

Cluverius vs. The Commonwealth of Virginia, May 6, 1886, Vol. LXXXI - 105, p. 835, Opinion - J. Fauntleroy

Nellie Goss operated a cigar store with a bawdy house in the rear on 15th Street.

"The End Drawing Nigh", The *Daily Index Appeal,* Petersburg VA January 13, 1887

All other bawdy house patrons are fictional.

(7.1) Detective Wren, Officer Walton, and Jackson Bolton were all part of the investigation of the Old Reservoir. All personal details about their lives are fictionalized. Joseph Mountcastle did, in fact, deliver the canvas satchel to Dr. Taylor.

Cluverius vs. The Commonwealth of Virginia, May 6, 1886, Vol. LXXXI - 103, p. 820-821, Opinion - J. Fauntleroy

(7.2) All the information on the evidence collected and the locations they were found is corroborated by trial testimony as reported in newspapers.

"Trying to Lift the Veil Off Lillie Madison's Murderer", *The Daily Index-Appeal,* Petersburg, Va,, March 28, 1885

Cluverius vs. The Commonwealth of Virginia, May 6, 1886, Vol. LXXXI - 103, p. 820-821, Opinion - J. Fauntleroy

(8.1) This entire sequence is fictionalized. The author has found no evidence that Jack Wren or Jackson Bolton served during the Civil War. Captain Morse, Will Rollings, and Major Angle are fictional characters.

(9.1) All the information on the evidence collected and the locations they were found is corroborated by trial testimony as reported in the *New York Times*

Cluverius vs. The Commonwealth of Virginia Vol. LXXXI - 106, p. 820-821, May 6, 1886 Opinion - J. Fauntleroy

(10.1) Rachel McDonald was a middle-aged woman living just outside the Richmond City Limits (Henrico Co) at this time. Although she was suspected of being an abortionist, there is no conclusive evidence to that effect. There is also no evidence that she and Cluverius ever met.

"Startling Rumors About the Cluverius Case", *The Daily Index-Appeal*, Petersburg, VA, April 10, 1886

(11.1) Dr. William H. Taylor was known to regularly tell his students to "Swing on to it."

Ezekiel, Herbert T., THE RECOLLECTIONS of a VIRGINIA NEWSPAPER MAN, Herbert T. Ezekiel, Printer and Publisher, Richmond, VA, 1920, *Dr. William H. Taylor,* p.93

(11.2) This report is completely fictional but is based upon the following:

Cluverius vs. The Commonwealth of Virginia, Vol. LXXXI Va. - 103, p. 819-820, May 6, 1886, Opinion - Judge Fauntleroy

John Bellows is a fictional character, as are Hubert Gibson and Velma Howard.

(12.1) This *Richmond Dispatch* article is complete fiction. Although it was a real newspaper in Richmond and Peter J. Burton was a leading reporter there at that time, this has been created by the author to summarize events in the story.

(12.2) Wren's family, as portrayed here, is purely fictional

(13.1) Fannie Mays was an actual young Richmond girl who was mistaken for the deceased girl. The Richmond Chief of Police personally cleared up this question. The entire scene at St. Mark's Church and the characters there (aside from Ms. Mays) are fictional.

"Richmond's Sensation: The Body of the Woman Found in the Reservoir Identified – Murder Suspected", *The Daily Index-Appeal*, Petersburg, VA, March 18, 1885

(14.1) "Richmond's Sensation: The Body of the Woman Found in the Reservoir Identified – Murder Suspected", *The Daily Index-Appeal*, Petersburg, VA, March 18, 1885

(14.2) Captain Billy Pierce and his story are fictional.

(15.1) This confusing sequence at the American Hotel actually occurred. A letter to this effect was actually written by Lillie Madison at some point on the 13th (though dated the 14th), though it is not clear that it happened in the parlor at this time as the author suggests.

Cluverius vs. The Commonwealth of Virginia, Vol. LXXXI Va. - 105, p. 836-838, May 6, 1886, Opinion - Judge Fauntleroy

(15.2) *Cluverius vs. The Commonwealth of Virginia*, Vol. LXXXI Va. - 105, p. 838, May 6, 1886, Opinion - Judge Fauntleroy

(16.1) "Richmond's Sensation: The Body of the Woman Found in the Reservoir Identified – Murder Suspected", *The Daily Index-Appeal*, Petersburg, VA, March 18, 1885

(17.1) Jack Wren's parents and brother are purely fictional. Although the Union assault on Fort Gregg did occur and was an extremely intense battle, there is no historical account of a one-legged Confederate hero.

(19.1) Anonymous, THOMAS J. CLUVERIUS vs COMMONWEALTH OF VIRGINIA, Johns and Goolsby, Richmond, VA, c. 1885 – "Making of Modern Law" Print Edition., p. 156-177

(19.2) Anonymous, THOMAS J. CLUVERIUS vs COMMONWEALTH OF VIRGINIA, Johns and Goolsby, Richmond, VA, c. 1885 – "Making of Modern Law" Print Edition., p. 178-194

"Trifles Light as Air: Prove a Burden to Cluverius", *The Daily Index-Appeal,* Petersburg, Va,, May 23, 1885

(19.3) "Startling Rumors About the Cluverius Case", *The Daily Index-Appeal*, Petersburg, VA, April 10, 1886

(20.1) This *Richmond Dispatch* article has been created by the author to summarize events in the story. It is based upon actual newspaper accounts and CHECK OPINIONS

(20.2) D.C. Richardson was the Police Chief Justice of Richmond at this time. Charles H. Deuring was a police officer/detective with involvement in the case. Lieutenant Grimes, Detective Hanson, and other elements of this chapter are fictional.

(23.1) Harry Kollatz, Jr. "Hauling Washington: How the Statue Made It to Capitol Square", *Richmondmag.com*, November 20, 2014 – referencing quote from *Richmond Daily Dispatch*, c. November 3, 1857

https://richmondmagazine.com/news/richmond-history/richmond-capitol-square-statue/

(23.2) Harry Kollatz, Jr. "Hauling Washington: How the Statue Made It to Capitol Square", *Richmondmag.com*, November 20, 2014

https://richmondmagazine.com/news/richmond-history/richmond-capitol-square-statue/

(25.1) *Cluverius vs. The Commonwealth of Virginia*, Vol. LXXXI Va. - 106, p. 843-846, May 6, 1886, Opinion - Judge Fauntleroy

Anonymous, THOMAS J. CLUVERIUS vs COMMONWEALTH OF VIRGINIA, Johns and Goolsby, Richmond, VA, c. 1885 – "Making of Modern Law" Print Edition., p.221-266

(26.1) Cluverius and the arrest party did spend the night in King and Queen County Jail before heading to Richmond. But the dream sequence is, of course, fictional.

Anonymous, THOMAS J. CLUVERIUS vs COMMONWEALTH OF VIRGINIA, Johns and Goolsby, Richmond, VA, c. 1885 – "Making of Modern Law" Print Edition., p.221-266

(26.2) *Cluverius vs. The Commonwealth of Virginia*, Vol. LXXXI Va. - 106, p. 843-844, May 6, 1886, Opinion - Judge Fauntleroy

Anonymous, THOMAS J. CLUVERIUS vs COMMONWEALTH OF VIRGINIA, Johns and Goolsby, Richmond, VA, c. 1885 – "Making of Modern Law" Print Edition., p.221-266

(28.1) This *Richmond Dispatch* article has been created by the author to summarize events in the story. It is based upon actual newspaper accounts

"The Richmond Murder Mystery, Young Cluverius Denies All Knowledge of the Death of Miss Madison", *The Daily News,* Frederick, Md., March 21, 1885

"Charged with Murder: Counselor Cluverius Consigned to a Cell", *Piqua Daily Call*, Piqua, Ohio, March 22, 1885

"Fannie Madison's Fate: Trying to Unravel the Mystery", *The Daily Index-Appeal,* Petersburg, Va,, March 24, 1885

"Trying to Lift the Veil Off Lillie Madison's Murderer", *The Daily Index-Appeal,* Petersburg, Va,, March 28, 1885

(28.2) Dr. James Beale and another doctor, Dr. Cabell, performed a cursory medical exam on Thomas Cluverius in his cell at the Richmond City Jail on March 20, 1885

Anonymous, THOMAS J. CLUVERIUS vs COMMONWEALTH OF VIRGINIA, Johns and Goolsby, Richmond, VA, c. 1885 – "Making of Modern Law" Print Edition., p.220

(28.3) This exchange between Cluverius and Bagby actually occurred outside the police court.

Anonymous, THOMAS J. CLUVERIUS vs COMMONWEALTH OF VIRGINIA, Johns and Goolsby, Richmond, VA, c. 1885 – "Making of Modern Law" Print Edition., p.366

(28.4) This "hearing" is a combination of the Police Court Arraignment (March 20, 1885) and the Coroner's Inquest (March 23, 1885). Several witnesses appeared at these hearings. William Tyler appeared at the Coroner's Inquest and his preliminary testimony was determined to be among the most compelling linking Mr. Cluverius to Miss Madison.

"Lillian Madison Buried: The Young Lawyer, Her Alleged Murderer, Still in Custody", *New York Times,* March 21, 1885

"Fannie Madison's Fate: Trying to Unravel the Mystery", *The Daily Index-Appeal,* Petersburg, Va,, March 24, 1885

The other two witnesses (William Kidd and Douglas Morton) who appear at this hearing in the story did not actually appear at either the Coroner's Inquest (March 23, 1885) nor the Arraignment. They did both testify at the trial; but in the interest of the story-telling, the author placed their witness testimony at these two preliminary events.

Anonymous, THOMAS J. CLUVERIUS vs COMMONWEALTH OF VIRGINIA, Johns and Goolsby, Richmond, VA, c. 1885 – "Making of Modern Law" Print Edition., p.97-98

Cluverius vs. The Commonwealth of Virginia, Vol. LXXXI Va. - 106, p. 843-844, May 6, 1886, Opinion - Judge Fauntleroy

(29.1) Fitzhugh Lee did appear in President Cleveland's First Inaugural Procession on March 4, 1885. The letter from President Cleveland is fictional.

(29.2) Excerpt from *The Indiana Weekly Messenger*, March 18, 1885

(29.3) "Marriage of Count Primo Magri and Mrs. Tom Thumb", *Evening Observer*, Dunkirk, NY, April 7, 1885

(29.4) This scene is a combination of different incidents from multiple sources.

Lt. Col. Fitzhugh Lee, CSA did lead an action in Falls Church, VA and the exchange between Lt. Bond and him did occur; as did the putting down of the horse, *Dixie*.

Kinsley, Ardyce et al THE FITZHUGH LEE SAMPLER, *Frank Bond Remembers Minding His Own Business*, p. 47-49

Col. John S. Mosby was not present at this action, but the animosity between Mosby and Fitz is documented.

Jones, Virgil Carrington, RANGER MOSBY, p. 57

Col. Mosby did indeed hang several Union troops in retaliation for a similar action by Custer in 1864 in Rectortown, VA.

Jones, Virgil Carrington, RANGER MOSBY, p. 226-227

It has been long- rumored that Mosby performed a similar hanging of Union troops from the "Hangman's Tree" which stood beside Leesburg Pike near Taylor's Tavern in Falls Church, Va.

Timar-Wilcox, Estelle, "Legend of Civil War Era "Hangman's Tree" Lives On", *Falls Church News-Press.com*, June 29, 2018

https://fcnp.com/2018/06/29/legend-civil-war-era-hangmans-tree-lives/

(30.1) Ned Cummins' Bar "on Broad Street two doors above City Hall", Richmond.

Herbert T. Ezekiel, THE RECOLLECTIONS of a VIRGINIA NEWSPAPER MAN, Herbert T. Ezekiel, Printer and Publisher Richmond, VA *Peter J. Burton- a Sketch*, Page 106

(30.2) This chapter is fictional. Bruce Vashon was a clerk at the Davis Hotel. There is no evidence that anything was done to hide or alter the hotel registry. Harry Brazelton is a fictional character. All of the names which appear on the "registry" (except for "Deuring" – see 20.2) are completely fictional. A.S. Goode was called to be part of the jury for the Trial of Cluverius, but was disqualified when it was discovered that he had placed bets on the outcome. – though there is no indication that the betting occurred at Ned Cummins' Bar.

(31.1) Francis Asbury Howell was one of the Alexandria jurors selected for service in the Cluverius trial. He did serve in the 17th Virginia Infantry, CSA during the War. Otherwise, his biography is completely fictional. Indications are he did not join Company H ("Old Dominion Rifles" – men from Alexandria) until 1864. He is listed in the muster roll of *The History of the Seventeenth Virginia Infantry, CSA*, Publisher Kell, Piet and Company, Baltimore, and entered by Act of Congress by George Wise, 1870, Page 299, under the name Asbury Howell. It appears he had an older relative (Emory Howell), who did muster into Company H in 1861 and performed "detached service in Richmond", Ibid, Page 297. Francis Asbury Howell is buried at Arlington Cemetery, one of 482 Confederates buried there. Francis A. Howell's post war occupation as a postman and his fellow postal workers are fictional.

Howell, Francis Asbury is also listed on website below for 17th Virginia Infantry, CSA, Co. H, Old Dominion Rifles

http://stevegibson0.tripod.com/co_h.htm

(31.2) Information from an account by Edward House, reporter for the *New York Tribune*, who was by Ellsworth's side when he was killed.

(32.1) This article from the *Richmond Dispatch* is actually a composite of four newspaper articles spanning five days consolidated into one article by the author:

"The Cluverius Trial", *New York Times*, May 8, 1885

"Still Without a Jury", *New York Times*, May 9, 1885

"A Jury Secured for Cluverius", *New York Times*, May 12, 1885

"Sick- A Cluverius Juror", *Boston Daily Globe*, May 12, 1885

(32.2) Cluverius was actually represented by four attorneys: Henry R. Pollard, A. Brown Evans, Beverly T. Crump, and Beverly Crump's father, Judge William W. Crump. Judge Crump was a very prominent figure in Richmond law at this time. In the interest simplification and in order to avoid confusion between the two Crumps and Judge T.S. Atkins (the presiding "judge" in the case), I have combined the two Crumps into one and given the character the son's name. That said, the character is based much more heavily on Judge Crump, who was the lead criminal defense attorney and handled most of the courtroom examinations.

(32.3) These were the three attorneys present for the prosecution at the outset of the trial. However, it appears that Mr. Ayers had very little involvement in the remainder of the trial, at least from a courtroom perspective. It would stand to reason that Mr. Ayers became too distracted by state politics to be a full-time member of the prosecution. Six months after the outset of the trial, in November, 1885, Ayers would be elected Attorney General of Virginia.

Charles V. Meredith was technically the acting Commonwealth's Attorney for this proceeding, as the actual Commonwealth's Attorney, Mr. Samuel B. Witt, had to recuse himself from the case because he was related to Thomas J. Cluverius. Mr. Witt did testify in the case, as he did initially receive the watch-key found at the Marshall reservoir from Detective Jack Wren. This testimony, being somewhat brief and insignificant, was presented to illustrate the chain of custody of the evidence and was, therefore, not included in the story. Once Cluverius had been identified as the suspect and arrested, Witt recused himself and turned the watch-key over to Police Justice D.C. Richardson.

"T.J. Cluverius on Trial: To Unravel the Mystery of Miss Madison's Death", *New York Times*, May 16, 1885

(32.4) - TESTIMONIES of L.W. ROSE and R.T. LUCAS

Anonymous, THOMAS J. CLUVERIUS vs COMMONWEALTH OF VIRGINIA, Johns and Goolsby, Richmond, VA, c. 1885 – "Making of Modern Law" Print Edition, p. 57

Cluverius vs. The Commonwealth of Virginia, Vol. LXXXI Va. - 103, p. 817-819, May 6, 1886, Opinion - Judge Fauntleroy

"Lillian Madison's Death: Cluverius Trial Well Started", *The Daily Index-Appeal,* Petersburg, Va,, May 14, 1885

"The Murder of Miss Madison: Evidence Showing That a Struggle with a Man Preceded Her Death", *New York Times,* May 14, 1885

"The Cluverius Trial: Taking of Testimony for the Commonwealth Began", *The Philadelphia Inquirer,* May 14, 1885

(33.1)   TESTIMONY of WILLIAM H. TAYLOR

This account of Dr. Taylor's life prior to the trial is fictional. He was the Coroner/Medical Examiner of Richmond from 1872 until his death in 1917. He taught at Richmond High School and at the Medical College of Virginia. There is no evidence he ever taught in New York.

(33.2)   Sources consulted for hanging of John Brown:

Strother, David Hunter, "John Brown's Death and Last Words", December, 1859 – written for *Harper's Weekly*, it is a first-hand account which, for political reasons, was not published until *American Heritage*, February, 1955, Volume 6, Issue 2. The author found the article americanheritage.com

https://www.americanheritage.com/eyewitness-describes-hanging-john-brown

Jackson, Mary Anna, *LIFE and LETTERS of GENERAL THOMAS J JACKSON (STONEWALL JACKSON)*, Harper Brothers, New York, 1892, *Letter dated December 2, 1859*, p.130-132

"The Hanging of John Brown", *The Warren Mail*, Warren, PA, December 10, 1859

"The Execution of Old John Brown!", *The North Carolinian*, Fayetteville, NC, December 10, 1859

(33.3) Excerpt from: "Medical Students Clash", *New York Times*, December 7, 1859

(33.4)   There is no evidence that Dr. Taylor compiled notes nor were any entered into evidence as near as the author can determine. These "Notes" were compiled by the author to condense the information offered in Dr. Taylor's testimony

(33.5)   Like the "Notes" taken at the crime scene, this "Autopsy Report" was compiled by the author to illustrate Dr. Taylor's oral explanation of the autopsy he performed on Lillian Madison.

(33.6)   Dr. Taylor did present such a visual aid sketch at trial.

"Lillian Madison's Death: Cluverius Trial Well Started", *The Daily Index-Appeal,* Petersburg, Va,, May 14, 1885

(33.7)   Dr. Taylor did actually make the "Ninety-six million miles" response to the question regarding his famously poor eyesight (and equally famous sense of humor) and it did elicit considerable laughter in the courtroom. However, there is no evidence that the questioning attorney (who the author designated as A. Brown Evans) was criticized and censured by the rest of the defense team for this blunder.

Ezekiel, Herbert T., "Covers Story in 1887, and Rewrites Story in 1937", *The Richmond News Leader*, January 8, 1937

(33.8) Anonymous, THOMAS J. CLUVERIUS vs COMMONWEALTH OF VIRGINIA, Johns and Goolsby, Richmond, VA, c. 1885 – "Making of Modern Law" Print Edition., p.60

Cluverius vs. The Commonwealth of Virginia, Vol. LXXXI Va. - 103, p. 819-820, May 6, 1886, Opinion - Judge Fauntleroy

Ezekiel, Herbert T., THE RECOLLECTIONS of a VIRGINIA NEWSPAPER MAN, Herbert T. Ezekiel, Printer and Publisher, Richmond, VA, 1920, *Dr. William H. Taylor*, p.93-97

"The Murder of Miss Madison: Evidence Showing That a Struggle with a Man Preceded Her Death", *New York Times*, May 14, 1885

(34.1) H. H. Alexander was the court stenographer. He was brought in from Washington DC and was considered one of the top stenographers in the country. Once transcribed 60,000 words in one day of the trial. He received high praise for his work on the Cluverius Trial.

NO HEADLINE - *Rockingham Register*, Harrisonburg, Va, June 11, 1885.

Unfortunately, due to a lack of funds in the Virginia State coffers, Alexander was, at best, very delayed in receiving payment for his work.

"Virginia Bankrupt", *The Marion Star*, Marion, SC, January 20, 1886

(34.2) The TESTIMONIES of E.J. ARCHER, J.J. WALTON, and JACKSON BOLTON

Anonymous, THOMAS J. CLUVERIUS vs COMMONWEALTH OF VIRGINIA, Johns and Goolsby, Richmond, VA, c. 1885 – "Making of Modern Law" Print Edition., p.62-64

Cluverius vs. The Commonwealth of Virginia, Vol. LXXXI Va. - 103, p. 820, May 6, 1886, Opinion - Judge Fauntleroy

"The Murder of Miss Madison: Continuation of the Evidence by the Prosecution", *New York Times*, May 15, 1885

(35.1) TESTIMONY of AARON WATKINS

Cluverius vs. The Commonwealth of Virginia, Vol. LXXXI Va. - 103, p. 822, May 6, 1886, Opinion - Judge Fauntleroy

Anonymous, THOMAS J. CLUVERIUS vs COMMONWEALTH OF VIRGINIA, Johns and Goolsby, Richmond, VA, c. 1885 – "Making of Modern Law" Print Edition., p.220

"The Reservoir Mystery: A Witness Who Heard Screams on the Night of the Tragedy", *The Philadelphia Times,* May 24, 1885

(35.2) TESTIMONIES of JOSEPH MOUNTCASTLE and JOHN WILLIAMS

Anonymous, THOMAS J. CLUVERIUS vs COMMONWEALTH OF VIRGINIA, Johns and Goolsby, Richmond, VA, c. 1885 – "Making of Modern Law" Print Edition., p.64-65,66

"The Murder of Miss Madison: Continuation of the Evidence by the Prosecution", *New York Times,* May 15, 1885

"The Reservoir Tragedy: Important Testimony Given In", *The Daily Index-Appeal,* Petersburg, Va,, May 15, 1885

(35.3) Judge Crump actually did cross-examine young John Williams. The questioning essentially regarded the chain of custody of the watch-key between the time that Williams found it at The Marshall Reservoir and it finally getting into the hands of Detective Wren.

"The Reservoir Tragedy: Important Testimony Given In", *The Daily Index-Appeal,* Petersburg, Va,, May 15, 1885

(36.1) This chapter is entirely fictional except that somebody did sell carte d'visites with Thomas Cluverius' and Lillian Madison's likenesses on the streets of Richmond.

Trotti, Michael Ayers, "Murder Made Real:A Visual Revolution of the Halftone", *The Virginia Magazine of History and Biography*, Vol. 111, Number 4, 2003, p.381

(37.1) This chapter blends a few incidents in Fitzhugh Lee's life. Following a clear victory at the Second Battle of Manassas,on August 31, 1862, Fitz Lee teamed up with Heros von Borcke to lead a dusk raid upon a farmhouse in Chantilly, VA. They did, in fact, burst through the door in spectacular fashion and capture four Union officers as they were just sitting down to dinner. Fitzhugh Lee did find a friend or two from The United States Military Academy at West Point among the captured officers and they did indeed enjoy a celebratory reunion dinner before officially taking them prisoner. One of the captured friends was a Federal officer named Tom Hight. The author has changed the spelling of his name to "Hite" to avoid confusion with another character in the story, Sergeant Haight. The men did, among other things, sing a chorus or two of "Benny Havens, Oh", in homage to the Academy and Benny Havens, the famed Buttermilk Falls tavern keeper near West Point.

Von Borcke, Heros, MEMOIRS of the CONFEDERATE WAR for INDEPENDENCE, 1867, Arcadia Press Print Edition, 2017, p.56

Kinsley, Ardyce et al THE FITZHUGH LEE SAMPLER, *A Meal Interrupted,* p.59

"A Meal Interrupted" is a letter by a former Union officer describing Fitz Lee's exploits that evening in Chantilly. The author remained unnamed to avoid "further embarrassment"; but cross-referencing with other sources indicates there is a good chance the author of the letter was Tom Hight ("Hite").

Nichols, James L., GENERAL FITZHUGH LEE, A BIOGRAPHY, H.E. Howard, Inc., Lynchburg, VA, 1989, p.38

(37.2) It should be noted that although Tom Hight did attend West Point at the same time as Fitzhugh Lee, he was not one of the four cadets involved in the Fitz Lee-led breaching of the Academy walls and subsequent adventure at Benny Havens Tavern.

Kinsley, Ardyce et al, THE FITZHUGH LEE SAMPLER, *Arthur Cunningham Remembers the West Point Follies*, p.8-11

"Benny Havens, Oh!", *The Rock Valley Bee,* Rock Valley, Iowa, March 29, 1929

(37.3) "John Phoenix: His Wonderful Fossil Discoveries at West Point", *The Indiana Democrat*, Indiana, PA, April 23, 1885, a story told to the newspaper reporter by General William T. Sherman.

(38.1) TESTIMONY of GEORGE WRIGHT

Cluverius vs. The Commonwealth of Virginia, Vol. LXXXI Va. - 104, p. 826, May 6, 1886, Opinion - Judge Fauntleroy

Anonymous, THOMAS J. CLUVERIUS vs COMMONWEALTH OF VIRGINIA, Johns and Goolsby, Richmond, VA, c. 1885 – "Making of Modern Law" Print Edition., p.95-96

"The Cluverius Murder Trial: Trying to Connect the Prisoner with the Murdered Woman", *New York Times,* May 21, 1885

(38.2) TESTIMONY of HENRY HUNT

Cluverius vs. The Commonwealth of Virginia, Vol. LXXXI Va. - 105, p. 833, May 6, 1886, Opinion - Judge Fauntleroy

Anonymous, THOMAS J. CLUVERIUS vs COMMONWEALTH OF VIRGINIA, Johns and Goolsby, Richmond, VA, c. 1885 – "Making of Modern Law" Print Edition., p.93-95

"The Cluverius Murder Trial: Trying to Connect the Prisoner with the Murdered Woman", *New York Times,* May 21, 1885

(38.3) TESTIMONY of WILLIAM MARTIN

Cluverius vs. The Commonwealth of Virginia, Vol. LXXXI Va. - 105, p. 833-834, May 6, 1886, Opinion - Judge Fauntleroy

Anonymous, THOMAS J. CLUVERIUS vs COMMONWEALTH OF VIRGINIA, Johns and Goolsby, Richmond, VA, c. 1885 – "Making of Modern Law" Print Edition., p.96

"The Cluverius Murder Trial: Trying to Connect the Prisoner with the Murdered Woman", *New York Times,* May 21, 1885

(38.4) TESTIMONY of JAMES THOMPSON

James Thompson's testimony is a composite of the testimonies of six employees of the Old Dominion Iron and Nail Works located on Belle Isle. Thompson, Charles Isaacs, Benjamin Earp, Thomas Bethel, Joseph Perkins, and William Kidd all testified at the trial on May 20-21, 1885 regarding the movements of Thomas Cluverius and Lillian Madison on the island on March 13, 1885. All told a very similar story. "Testimony" from William Kidd also appears in Chapter 28 at the arraignment hearing before Police Justice D.C. Richardson.

Cluverius vs. The Commonwealth of Virginia, Vol. LXXXI Va. - 105, p. 834-835, May 6, 1886, Opinion - Judge Fauntleroy

Anonymous, THOMAS J. CLUVERIUS vs COMMONWEALTH OF VIRGINIA, Johns and Goolsby, Richmond, VA, c. 1885 – "Making of Modern Law" Print Edition., p.96-99

"The Cluverius Murder Trial: Trying to Connect the Prisoner with the Murdered Woman", *New York Times,* May 21, 1885

"The Cluverius Murder Trial: Testimony for the Prosecution Drawing to a Close", *New York Times,* May 22, 1885

"Strand by Strand: The Net of Guilt is Woven", *The Daily Index-Appeal,* Petersburg, Va,, May 22, 1885

(39.1) "T.J. Cluverius On Trial: To Unravel the Mystery of Miss Madison's Death", *New York Times,* May 16, 1885

(39.2) Belle Isle Revisited: A Loudoun Ranger Taken in the Spot Where He Starved and Suffered, *The National Tribune*, Washington, DC, November 10, 1892

Censusdiggers.com link on Belle Isle Civil War Prison

http://www.censusdiggins.com/prison_bellisle.html

(40.1) "T.J. Cluverius On Trial: To Unravel the Mystery of Miss Madison's Death", *New York Times,* May 16, 1885

"Link by Link: A Chain of Evidence is Forged", *The Daily Index-Appeal,* Petersburg, Va,, May 16, 1885

(40.2) The story of the Joel brothers is completely fictional. Hermann Joel (also spelled "Joll") was a watch-maker/jeweler who did work in the Richmond area. There is no evidence that he had any brothers, but there are advertisements which appear in Richmond publications of the time which may be a relative.

Advertisement – "Solomon Joel, Dealer in Watches, Clocks, Jewelry, &c; Repairing a Specialty. 1503 E. Main St, Richmond", *The Richmond Labor Herald*, June 12, 1886

According to testimony, Herman Joel was actually from Galicia, Austria, not Bavaria. The entire story of his childhood emigration to America is fictional, although there was a *Battle of Kissengen* in Bavaria during the Austro-Prussian War in 1866 where many Bavarian soldiers were killed and subsequently buried en masse at Kappellenfriedof Cemetery. Herman Joel's testimony indicated that he had only been in America for about four-and-one-half years at the time of the trial. but it does say that he had a case and repair. His testimony also indicated he actually first landed in New York and then came straight to Richmond.

(40.3) There is no evidence that Mr. Joel was escorted by the police to his shop at J.T. Bland & Bros store to look for his ledger. However, his testimony indicates that he did keep a case there and a small work table near a window.

Anonymous, THOMAS J. CLUVERIUS vs COMMONWEALTH OF VIRGINIA, Johns and Goolsby, Richmond, VA, c. 1885 – "Making of Modern Law" Print Edition., p.201

Hermann Joel testified that he had a "book" in which he kept names and account/repair information. It is unclear from the testimony where he kept the book most of the time, but when it was presented to investigators, he testified that he had it sent up to him from Bland & Bros store and when he received the book some pages had been torn out. He testified that he expected to find Mr. Cluverius' name in the book, but the pages where that name (and others) would have been written had been torn from the book.

Anonymous, THOMAS J. CLUVERIUS vs COMMONWEALTH OF VIRGINIA, Johns and Goolsby, Richmond, VA, c. 1885 – "Making of Modern Law" Print Edition., p.204-206

(41.1) TESTIMONY of JOHN WALKER

Anonymous, THOMAS J. CLUVERIUS vs COMMONWEALTH OF VIRGINIA, Johns and Goolsby, Richmond, VA, c. 1885 – "Making of Modern Law" Print Edition., p.68-73

"T.J. Cluverius On Trial: To Unravel the Mystery of Miss Madison's Death", *New York Times,* May 16, 1885

"Link by Link: A Chain of Evidence is Forged", *The Daily Index-Appeal,* Petersburg, Va,, May 16, 1885

"Lillian and Her Lover: Story of Their Intimacy Told", *The Daily Index-Appeal,* Petersburg, Va,, May 18, 1885

(41.2) TESTIMONY of ELLA MADISON

Anonymous, THOMAS J. CLUVERIUS vs COMMONWEALTH OF VIRGINIA, Johns and Goolsby, Richmond, VA, c. 1885 – "Making of Modern Law" Print Edition., p. 78

"The Cluverius Trial: Testimony in Support of the Theory of the Prosecution", *New York Times,* May 19, 1885

"Lillian's Letters: A Trunk Full of Them in Court", *The Daily Index-Appeal,* Petersburg, Va,, May 19, 1885

(41.3) TESTIMONY of CHARLES MADISON

Charles Madison was first called to testify on May 18, 1885. That testimony related only to identification of Lillie Madison's handwriting on some letters and also to identify a photograph of her. His most consequential testimony came when he was recalled a few days later. That is the testimony which is dramatized in this chapter.

"The Cluverius Murder Trial: Testimony for the Prosecution Drawing to a Close", *New York Times,* May 22, 1885

"Strand by Strand The Net of Guilt is Woven", *The Daily Index-Appeal,* Petersburg, Va,, May 22, 1885

(42.1) Anonymous, THOMAS J. CLUVERIUS vs COMMONWEALTH OF VIRGINIA, Johns and Goolsby, Richmond, VA, c. 1885 – "Making of Modern Law" Print Edition., p. 78-79

"The Cluverius Trial: Testimony in Support of the Theory of the Prosecution", *New York Times,* May 19, 1885

"Lillian's Letters: A Trunk Full of Them in Court", *The Daily Index-Appeal,* Petersburg, Va,, May 19, 1885

(42.2) TESTIMONY of POLICE CHIEF JUSTICE D.C. RICHARDSON

Anonymous, THOMAS J. CLUVERIUS vs COMMONWEALTH OF VIRGINIA, Johns and Goolsby, Richmond, VA, c. 1885 – "Making of Modern Law" Print Edition., p. 79-80

"The Cluverius Trial: Testimony in Support of the Theory of the Prosecution", *New York Times,* May 19, 1885

"Lillian's Letters: A Trunk Full of Them in Court", *The Daily Index-Appeal,* Petersburg, Va,, May 19, 1885

(42.3) TESTIMONY of WILLIAM R. QUARLES

Anonymous, THOMAS J. CLUVERIUS vs COMMONWEALTH OF VIRGINIA, Johns and Goolsby, Richmond, VA, c. 1885 – "Making of Modern Law" Print Edition., p. 80

"The Cluverius Trial: Testimony in Support of the Theory of the Prosecution", *New York Times,* May 19, 1885

"Lillian's Letters: A Trunk Full of Them in Court", *The Daily Index-Appeal,* Petersburg, Va,, May 19, 1885

(43.1) This chapter is almost entirely fictional, even nearly all of the characters. Owen M. Winston was the County Clerk of King William County at this time. And, the Clerk's Office did indeed burn, destroying most of the county records; but the fire occurred January 18, 1885, a full four months prior to the episode described in this chapter.

(44.1) TESTIMONY of MARY DICKINSON

Anonymous, THOMAS J. CLUVERIUS vs COMMONWEALTH OF VIRGINIA, Johns and Goolsby, Richmond, VA, c. 1885 – "Making of Modern Law" Print Edition., p. 80-89

Cluverius vs. The Commonwealth of Virginia, Vol. LXXXI Va. - 105, p. 837-838, May 6, 1886, Opinion - Judge Fauntleroy

"The Cluverius Trial: Testimony in Support of the Theory of the Prosecution", *New York Times,* May 19, 1885

"The Cluverius Murder: Still Hearing Evidence to Sustain Prosecution", *New York Times,* May 20, 1885

"Lillian's Letters: A Trunk Full of Them in Court", *The Daily Index-Appeal,* Petersburg, Va,, May 19, 1885

"Step by Step Cluverius Counsel Bar the Way", *The Daily Index-Appeal,* Petersburg, Va,, May 20, 1885

"Lillian's Last Journey: The Letter That Caused It", *The Daily Index-Appeal,* Petersburg, Va,, May 21, 1885

(44.2) TESTIMONY of LAURA CURTIS

Anonymous, THOMAS J. CLUVERIUS vs COMMONWEALTH OF VIRGINIA, Johns and Goolsby, Richmond, VA, c. 1885 – "Making of Modern Law" Print Edition., p. 91

"Lillian's Last Journey: The Letter That Caused It", *The Daily Index-Appeal,* Petersburg, Va,, May 21, 1885

The storm interruption is fictional.

(45.1) TESTIMONY of JOSEPH DODSON

Anonymous, THOMAS J. CLUVERIUS vs COMMONWEALTH OF VIRGINIA, Johns and Goolsby, Richmond, VA, c. 1885 – "Making of Modern Law" Print Edition., p. 92-93

"Lillian's Last Journey: The Letter That Caused It", *The Daily Index-Appeal,* Petersburg, Va,, May 21, 1885

(45.2) The motion to enter the "Torn Note" into evidence and the subsequent argument over its was actually made a day after Dodson testified.

"Strand by Strand The Net of Guilt is Woven", *The Daily Index-Appeal,* Petersburg, Va,, May 22, 1885

Judge Atkins did not rule upon the admissibility of the "Torn Note" until May 23, 1885

"The Cluverius Trial: Judge Atkins Refuses to Admit Torn Note in Evidence", *The Sunday Eagle*, Brooklyn, NY, May 24, 1885

(45.3)   TESTIMONY of HENRY HUNT (Recalled)

Henry Hunt is recalled to the stand. The author, for continuity and simplification purposes, altered Hunt's testimony.

Anonymous, THOMAS J. CLUVERIUS vs COMMONWEALTH OF VIRGINIA, Johns and Goolsby, Richmond, VA, c. 1885 – "Making of Modern Law" Print Edition., p. 93-94

"The Cluverius Murder Trial: Trying to Connect the Prisoner with the Murdered Woman", *New York Times,* May 21, 1885

(45.4)   TESTIMONY of CLARA ANDERSON

Clara Anderson and another girl who was not included in the story (Mary Curtis) testified regarding Mr. Cluverius' and Miss Madison's visit to Mrs. Goss' cigar store on March 13, 1885. Miss Anderson's testimony also recounted another visit the two made in January, 1885. Miss Curtis also gave extensive testimony regarding a visit Mr. Cluverius' made to another bawdy house (Lizzie Bank's) in 1883.

Anonymous, THOMAS J. CLUVERIUS vs COMMONWEALTH OF VIRGINIA, Johns and Goolsby, Richmond, VA, c. 1885 – "Making of Modern Law" Print Edition., p. 100-119

(45.5)   TESTIMONY of LULU WOODWARD

Anonymous, THOMAS J. CLUVERIUS vs COMMONWEALTH OF VIRGINIA, Johns and Goolsby, Richmond, VA, c. 1885 – "Making of Modern Law" Print Edition., p. 278

"Cluverius Weakening: He Looks Scared and Nervous", *The Daily Index-Appeal*, Petersburg, Va,, May 26, 1885

(45.6)   Anonymous, THOMAS J. CLUVERIUS vs COMMONWEALTH OF VIRGINIA, Johns and Goolsby, Richmond, VA, c. 1885 – "Making of Modern Law" Print Edition., p. 99-100

"Strand by Strand The Net of Guilt is Woven", *The Daily Index-Appeal,* Petersburg, Va,, May 22, 1885

(46.1)   Nichols, James L., GENERAL FITZHUGH LEE, A BIOGRAPHY, H.E. Howard, Inc., Lynchburg, VA, 1989, p.65

(46.2) This incident regarding the kidnapping of the banjo player Sweeney is fictional. That said, Fitzhugh Lee Opie (great grandson of Fitzhugh Lee and grandson of Ellen Lee) told the author many years ago that his grandmother had told him of the rivalry between Stuart and Fitz Lee for the services of Sweeney. Each had claimed to have "discovered" the gifted banjo player and they did "borrow" him from one another on occasion; usually without seeking permission. Additional information on Sweeney can be found on the January 23, 2014 blog post on The Civil War Picket

http://civil-war-picket.blogspot.com/2014/01/jeb-stuarts-banjo-player-and-famous.html

Jine the Cavalry was Fitzhugh Lee's favorite banjo tune.

Nichols, James L., GENERAL FITZHUGH LEE, A BIOGRAPHY, H.E. Howard, Inc., Lynchburg, VA, 1989, p.74

(46.3) Blumberg, Arnold, "Death of Legendary Confederate General J.E.B. Stuart", *Warfare History Network*, November 4, 2016

https://warfarehistorynetwork.com/daily/civil-war/death-of-legendary-confederate-general-j-e-b-stuart/

(46.4) Nichols, James L., GENERAL FITZHUGH LEE, A BIOGRAPHY, H.E. Howard, Inc., Lynchburg, VA, 1989, p.68-69

(46.5) Von Borcke, Heros, MEMOIRS of the CONFEDERATE WAR for INDEPENDENCE, 1867, Arcadia Press Print Edition, 2017, p.192-193

(46.6) Rhea, Gordon C., TO the NORTH ANNA RIVER: GRANT and LEE, MAY 13-25, 1864, Louisiana State University Press, Baton Rouge, LA, 2000, p. 362-367

Hudson, Leonne, "Valor at Wilson's Wharf", *Civil War Times Illustrated*, March, 1998

(46.7) Just six weeks prior to the action at Fort Pocahontas, in April, 1864 Confederate forces under Nathan Bedford Forrest had overrun *Fort Pillow* in Tennessee and reportedly massacred over two hundred captured black Union soldiers. This incident, of course, became a rallying cry to Union forces and was clearly fresh upon the minds of commanders of black units, such as Wild.

Hudson, Leonne, "Valor at Wilson's Wharf", *Civil War Times Illustrated*, March, 1998

(46.8) This is a combination of reported responses from Wild to Fitzhugh Lee's demand for surrender of the fort.

"The War in Virginia…Lee Retreats During the Night", *The Philadelphia Inquirer*, May 26, 1864

Rhea, Gordon C., TO the NORTH ANNA RIVER: GRANT and LEE, MAY 13-25, 1864, Louisiana State University Press, Baton Rouge, LA, 2000, p. 364-365

(46.9) Nichols, James L., GENERAL FITZHUGH LEE, A BIOGRAPHY, H.E. Howard, Inc., Lynchburg, VA, 1989, p.70-71

Rhea, Gordon C., TO the NORTH ANNA RIVER: GRANT and LEE, MAY 13-25, 1864, Louisiana State University Press, Baton Rouge, LA, 2000, p. 362-367

(46.10)   Hudson, Leonne, "Valor at Wilson's Wharf", *Civil War Times Illustrated*, March, 1998

Rhea, Gordon C., TO the NORTH ANNA RIVER: GRANT and LEE, MAY 13-25, 1864, Louisiana State University Press, Baton Rouge, LA, 2000, p. 362-367

(47.1)   TESTIMONY of CAPTAIN CHARLES EPPS

Cluverius vs. The Commonwealth of Virginia, Vol. LXXXI Va. - 106, p. 843-846, May 6, 1886, Opinion - Judge Fauntleroy

Anonymous, THOMAS J. CLUVERIUS vs COMMONWEALTH OF VIRGINIA, Johns and Goolsby, Richmond, VA, c. 1885 – "Making of Modern Law" Print Edition., p. 221-266

"The Cluverius Trial: Judge Atkins Refuses to Admit Torn Note in Evidence", *The Sunday Eagle*, Brooklyn, NY, May 24, 1885

(47.2)   TESTIMONY of EMMET RODGERS

The name of this witness was actually Emmet Richardson. The author changed it to Emmet "Rodgers" to avoid confusion with Police Chief Justice Richardson. His testimony is actually a combination of two appearances on the stand; once for the prosecution and once for the defense.

Anonymous, THOMAS J. CLUVERIUS vs COMMONWEALTH OF VIRGINIA, Johns and Goolsby, Richmond, VA, c. 1885 – "Making of Modern Law" Print Edition., p. 90, 328

"Step by Step Cluverius Counsel Bar the Way", *The Daily Index-Appeal*, Petersburg, Va,, May 20, 1885

(47.3)   TESTIMONY of JUDGE JOHN D. FOSTER

Anonymous, THOMAS J. CLUVERIUS vs COMMONWEALTH OF VIRGINIA, Johns and Goolsby, Richmond, VA, c. 1885 – "Making of Modern Law" Print Edition., p. 91

"Step by Step Cluverius Counsel Bar the Way", *The Daily Index-Appeal*, Petersburg, Va,, May 20, 1885

(48.1)   TESTIMONY of CLAGGETT JONES

Admittedly, the author highly dramatized Claggett Jones' testimony.

Anonymous, THOMAS J. CLUVERIUS vs COMMONWEALTH OF VIRGINIA, Johns and Goolsby, Richmond, VA, c. 1885 – "Making of Modern Law" Print Edition., p. 74-75

(48.2)   TESTIMONY of A.W. ARBUCKLE

The name of this witness was actually A.W. Archer. The author changed it to A.W. "Arbuckle" to avoid confusion with another witness, E.J. Archer.

Anonymous, <u>THOMAS J. CLUVERIUS vs COMMONWEALTH OF VIRGINIA,</u> Johns and Goolsby, Richmond, VA, c. 1885 – "Making of Modern Law" Print Edition., p. 75-76

"Lillian and Her Lover: Story of Their Intimacy Told", *The Daily Index-Appeal,* Petersburg, Va,, May 18, 1885

Regarding Reversible Overcoat – which was not really part of Arbuckle's (Archer's) testimony:

"Fannie Madison's Fate: Trying to Unravel the Mystery", *The Daily Index-Appeal,* Petersburg, Va,, March 24, 1885

(48.3)   TESTIMONY of HENRIETTA WIMBUSH

Anonymous, <u>THOMAS J. CLUVERIUS vs COMMONWEALTH OF VIRGINIA,</u> Johns and Goolsby, Richmond, VA, c. 1885 – "Making of Modern Law" Print Edition., p. 77-78

"Lillian and Her Lover: Story of Their Intimacy Told", *The Daily Index-Appeal,* Petersburg, Va,, May 18, 1885

(49.1)   This chapter is entirely fictional, but is based on innuendo surrounding the case.

(50.1)   This *Richmond Dispatch* article is really a compilation of two articles from the *Daily Index Appeal*

"Trifles Light as Air: Prove a Burden to Cluverius", *The Daily Index-Appeal,* Petersburg, Va,, May 23, 1885- Opening Paragraph

(50.2)   "Cluverius Weakening: He Looks Scared and Nervous", *The Daily Index-Appeal,* Petersburg, Va,, May 26, 1885 – Opening Paragraph

(50.3)   TESTIMONIES of LOGAN ROBBINS, CHARLES SWEENEY, DR. JAMES BEALE, and R.D. WORTHAM

Anonymous, <u>THOMAS J. CLUVERIUS vs COMMONWEALTH OF VIRGINIA,</u> Johns and Goolsby, Richmond, VA, c. 1885 – "Making of Modern Law" Print Edition., p. 220, 277, 284

"Cluverius Weakening: He Looks Scared and Nervous", *The Daily Index-Appeal,* Petersburg, Va,, May 26, 1885

(51.1)   TESTIMONY of W.F. DILLARD

Anonymous, <u>THOMAS J. CLUVERIUS vs COMMONWEALTH OF VIRGINIA,</u> Johns and Goolsby, Richmond, VA, c. 1885 – "Making of Modern Law" Print Edition., p. 133-155

"Trifles Light as Air: Prove a Burden to Cluverius", *The Daily Index-Appeal,* Petersburg, Va,, May 23, 1885

(51.2) Igoe, Brian, "Charles Bianconi and The Transport Revolution", *The Irish Story: Irish History Online*, December 14, 2012

http://www.theirishstory.com/2012/12/14/charles-bianconi-and-the-transport-revolution-1800-1875/#.XO8bfYhKiUl

(51.3) TESTIMONY of MICK DELAHANTY

Mick Delahanty is a completely fictional character. His testimony is loosely based upon two other drivers (William Tucker and John T. Williams) who did actually testify in the case.

Anonymous, THOMAS J. CLUVERIUS vs COMMONWEALTH OF VIRGINIA, Johns and Goolsby, Richmond, VA, c. 1885 – "Making of Modern Law" Print Edition., p. 156-177

"Trifles Light as Air: Prove a Burden to Cluverius", *The Daily Index-Appeal,* Petersburg, Va,, May 23, 1885

(51.4) TESTIMONY of DR. THOMAS E. STRATTON

Anonymous, THOMAS J. CLUVERIUS vs COMMONWEALTH OF VIRGINIA, Johns and Goolsby, Richmond, VA, c. 1885 – "Making of Modern Law" Print Edition., p. 178-194

"Trifles Light as Air: Prove a Burden to Cluverius", *The Daily Index-Appeal,* Petersburg, Va,, May 23, 1885

(51.5) TESTIMONY of HERMANN JOLL

Anonymous, THOMAS J. CLUVERIUS vs COMMONWEALTH OF VIRGINIA, Johns and Goolsby, Richmond, VA, c. 1885 – "Making of Modern Law" Print Edition., p. 194-219

"Trifles Light as Air: Prove a Burden to Cluverius", *The Daily Index-Appeal,* Petersburg, Va,, May 23, 1885

(52.1) "Did She Kill Herself? Rachel McDonald's Terrible Death Near Richmond, VA", *The Daily News*, Frederick, MD, December 5, 1885.

"Startling Rumors About the Cluverius Case", *The Daily Index-Appeal,* Petersburg, Va,, April 10, 1886

(52.2) Although Nellie Goss was the owner of the cigar store and bawdy house frequented by Thomas Cluverius and Lillie Madison, she was never called to testify in the trial (two girls that lived and worked with her did – Clara Anderson and Mary Curtis). The author does not know what became of her. Her murder, unlike Rachel McDonald's, is fictional.

(53.1) Letter Presented during TESTIMONY of JANE TUNSTALL

Anonymous, THOMAS J. CLUVERIUS vs COMMONWEALTH OF VIRGINIA, Johns and Goolsby, Richmond, VA, c. 1885 – "Making of Modern Law" Print Edition., p. 298

(53.2) Letter Presented during TESTIMONY of JANE TUNSTALL

Anonymous, THOMAS J. CLUVERIUS vs COMMONWEALTH OF VIRGINIA, Johns and Goolsby, Richmond, VA, c. 1885 – "Making of Modern Law" Print Edition., p. 288

(53.3) Anonymous, THOMAS J. CLUVERIUS vs COMMONWEALTH OF VIRGINIA, Johns and Goolsby, Richmond, VA, c. 1885 – "Making of Modern Law" Print Edition., p. 284-325

"Cluverius' Defense: Another Watchkey Produced", *The Daily Index-Appeal,* Petersburg, Va,, May 27, 1885

(54.1) TESTIMONY of Rev. JOHN W. RYLAND

Anonymous, THOMAS J. CLUVERIUS vs COMMONWEALTH OF VIRGINIA, Johns and Goolsby, Richmond, VA, c. 1885 – "Making of Modern Law" Print Edition., p. 325

"Cluverius' Defense: Another Watchkey Produced", *The Daily Index-Appeal,* Petersburg, Va,, May 27, 1885

(54.2) TESTIMONY of THOMAS MILBY

Anonymous, THOMAS J. CLUVERIUS vs COMMONWEALTH OF VIRGINIA, Johns and Goolsby, Richmond, VA, c. 1885 – "Making of Modern Law" Print Edition., p. 325-326

"Cluverius' Defense: Another Watchkey Produced", *The Daily Index-Appeal,* Petersburg, Va,, May 27, 1885

(54.3) TESTIMONY of EMMETT RODGERS (RICHARDSON) - Recalled

Anonymous, THOMAS J. CLUVERIUS vs COMMONWEALTH OF VIRGINIA, Johns and Goolsby, Richmond, VA, c. 1885 – "Making of Modern Law" Print Edition., p. 328

"Cluverius' Defense: Another Watchkey Produced", *The Daily Index-Appeal,* Petersburg, Va,, May 27, 1885

(54.4) TESTIMONY Dr. W. C. BARKER

Anonymous, THOMAS J. CLUVERIUS vs COMMONWEALTH OF VIRGINIA, Johns and Goolsby, Richmond, VA, c. 1885 – "Making of Modern Law" Print Edition., p. 328

(54.5) Statement of NOLIE BRAY presented to the court by A. Brown Evans

Anonymous, THOMAS J. CLUVERIUS vs COMMONWEALTH OF VIRGINIA, Johns and Goolsby, Richmond, VA, c. 1885 – "Making of Modern Law" Print Edition., p. 329

(55.1) This account of Tommie and Willie's childhood is complete fiction. However, it is clear from testimony that there were personal conflicts within the family. It should be noted that Thomas and William Cluverius had an older brother (John) who apparently died as a child sometime between the Census of 1860, where he was listed as age 4 in the Beverly Whiting Cluverius household (their father), and the Census of 1870.

http://www.appalachianaristocracy.com/getperson.php?personID=I5892&tree=01

(55.2) TESTIMONY of WILLIAM B. CLUVERIUS

Anonymous, THOMAS J. CLUVERIUS vs COMMONWEALTH OF VIRGINIA, Johns and Goolsby, Richmond, VA, c. 1885 – "Making of Modern Law" Print Edition., p. 329-357

"Cluverius' Brother: On the Stand for Many Hours", *The Daily Index-Appeal,* Petersburg, Va,, May 28, 1885

(56.1) The opening of the "*Dispatch*" article is a near- verbatim transcription of the opening paragraphs of:

"Trying to Save His Neck: Course of Cluverius' Defence", *The Daily Index-Appeal,* Petersburg, Va,, May 29, 1885

(56.2) TESTIMONIES of THOMAS BAGBY, HARRY DUDLEY, and MARK DAVIS. WRITTEN STATEMENT of CARY MADISON

It should be noted that the testimony of Harry Dudley was actually based upon the testimony of George Bagby. The author changed the name of George Bagby to avoid confusion with the previous witness, Thomas Bagby. Dudley was a witness, as well, but his testimony is not included in the story.

Anonymous, THOMAS J. CLUVERIUS vs COMMONWEALTH OF VIRGINIA, Johns and Goolsby, Richmond, VA, c. 1885 – "Making of Modern Law" Print Edition., p. 366-368

"Trying to Save His Neck: Course of Cluverius' Defence", *The Daily Index-Appeal,* Petersburg, Va,, May 29, 1885

(56.3) This episode is fictitious. Although the four boys involved (Fitz Lee, Rooney Lee, Willie Fendall, and Claude Fendall) were actually contemporaries and cousins, there is no evidence of such an adventure at the candy store. It should also be noted that the Fendall family had actually moved from the home on Oronoco Street by this time. The names of Alexander, Burke, and Leadbeater were all those of prominent Alexandria families, but these particular characters are fictional. Sarah Hooe Fowle was Fitz's mother-in-law and was from a prominent family in Alexandria, as well. Mrs. Appich did indeed run a candy store in this King Street location and there is evidence that Fitz Lee frequented it.

Powell, Mary G., THE HISTORY of OLD VIRGINIA from JULY 13, 1749 to MAY 24, 1861, William Byrd Press, Inc, Richmond, Va., Copyright, 1928, Mary G. Powell

(57.1) Flowers were sent to the prosecution during the trial

"The Trial nearly Ended: Cluverius Father on the Stand", *The Daily Index-Appeal,* Petersburg, Va,, May 30, 1885

(57.2) TESTIMONY of JOSEPH BLAND

Anonymous, THOMAS J. CLUVERIUS vs COMMONWEALTH OF VIRGINIA, Johns and Goolsby, Richmond, VA, c. 1885 – "Making of Modern Law" Print Edition., p. 374

"The Trial nearly Ended: Cluverius Father on the Stand", *The Daily Index-Appeal,* Petersburg, Va,, May 30, 1885

(58.1) TESTIMONY of BEVERLY WHITING CLUVERIUS

Anonymous, THOMAS J. CLUVERIUS vs COMMONWEALTH OF VIRGINIA, Johns and Goolsby, Richmond, VA, c. 1885 – "Making of Modern Law" Print Edition., p. 374-375

"The Trial nearly Ended: Cluverius Father on the Stand", *The Daily Index-Appeal,* Petersburg, Va,, May 30, 1885

(58.2) TESTIMONY of OWEN B. WINSTON

Anonymous, THOMAS J. CLUVERIUS vs COMMONWEALTH OF VIRGINIA, Johns and Goolsby, Richmond, VA, c. 1885 – "Making of Modern Law" Print Edition., p. 377

"Trial of Cluverius: Work of Taking Testimony About Completed", *Columbus Sunday Enquirer,* Columbus, GA, May 31, 1885

(58.3) FINAL TESTIMONIES

Anonymous, THOMAS J. CLUVERIUS vs COMMONWEALTH OF VIRGINIA, Johns and Goolsby, Richmond, VA, c. 1885 – "Making of Modern Law" Print Edition., p. 378

"Trial of Cluverius: Work of Taking Testimony About Completed", *Columbus Sunday Enquirer,* Columbus, GA, May 31, 1885

(59.1) Jury Instructions Provided by Judge Atkins on Saturday, May 30, 1885

"Talking to the Jury: Argument in Cluverius' Case", *The Daily Index-Appeal,* Petersburg, Va,, June 2, 1885

(59.2) Terry McIlhenny is a fictional character. His meeting with C.H. Deuring is fictional. Deuring's meeting with Willie Cluverius at Ned Cummins' Bar is also fictional, though there is evidence that Charles Deuring was doing private investigative work for Cluverius and there were issues with payment for his services.

"The Capital City", *The Daily Index-Appeal,* Petersburg, Va,, August 8, 1885

"Virginia News", *The Peninsula Enterprise,* Accomac Courthouse, Va,, August 22, 1885

There are also indications that the death of Rachel McDonald and the subsequent investigation were suspicious. The death of Nellie Goss is fictional.

"Did She Kill Herself? Rachel McDonald's Terrible Death Near Richmond, VA", *The Daily News*, Frederick, MD, December 5, 1885.

"Startling Rumors About the Cluverius Case", *The Daily Index-Appeal*, Petersburg, VA, April 10, 1886

(60.1)   COL. WILLIAM R. AYLETT – PROSECUTION FINAL ARGUMENT #1

This closing argument lasted approximately five hours. The author has based this rendition on reporting appearing in *The Daily Index-Appeal*, which, of course, greatly condensed the oratory. Much of what appears in the story is a direct quotation of the quotes appearing in *The Daily Index-Appeal*

"Talking to the Jury: Argument in Cluverius' Case", *The Daily Index-Appeal,* Petersburg, Va,, June 2, 1885

(60.2)   HENRY R. POLLARD – DEFENSE FINAL ARGUMENT #1

The initial closing argument for the defense was actually conducted by A. Brown Evans and lasted over four hours. The author has chosen to substitute Pollard, but the elements and many of the quotations of the argument, which were documented in *The Daily Index-Appeal*, remain.

"Pleading for Cluverius: Argument of Hon. A. B. Evans", *The Daily Index-Appeal,* Petersburg, Va,, June 3, 1885

(61.1)   BEVERLY T. CRUMP – DEFENSE FINAL ARGUMENT #2

The second closing argument for the defense was actually conducted by Henry R. Pollard and lasted over four hours, as well. The author has chosen to substitute Crump (neither Crump participated in the final arguments). This argument is based more heavily upon Evans' argument, as well. These arguments were all very long and there was a great deal of repetition.

"Pleading for Cluverius: Argument of Hon. A. B. Evans", *The Daily Index-Appeal,* Petersburg, Va,, June 3, 1885

(61.2)   CHARLES V. MEREDITH – PROSECUTION FINAL ARGUMENT #2

Mr. Meredith's argument lasted nearly nine hours. Interestingly, the author could not find any extensive reporting/transcription of the actual argument. This could be because after the completion of his argument, the decision went immediately to the jury, which returned a verdict within forty minutes. The announcement of the verdict seemed to dominate the news reporting the following day. It should be noted, the most detailed reporting the author has consulted for the trial came from *The Daily Index-Appeal*. The author could not locate the June 5, 1885 edition of that newspaper. Therefore, the argument presented is essentially a fabrication of the author, based, of course, upon the facts and testimony surrounding the trial.

"The Cluverius Case: Verdict of Murder in the First Degree", *The Philadelphia Times,* Philadelphia, Pa, June 5, 1885

"Cluverius' Crime: Declared Guilty of Lillian Madison's Murder", *The Lebanon Daily News,* Lebanon, Pa, June 5, 1885

(62.1) The facts surrounding the proceedings in the jury deliberation are largely unknown. This has been fictionalized. Henry Keppler was actually named the Jury Foreman, not F.A. Howell.

"Cluverius' Crime: Declared Guilty of Lillian Madison's Murder", *The Lebanon Daily News,* Lebanon, Pa, June 5, 1885

"Cluverius: Juror Harrison Says His Trial Was "A Horrible and Ghastly Farce"", *The Peninsula Enterprise,* Accomac Courthouse, Va,, January 8, 1887

(62.2) "Cluverius' Crime: Declared Guilty of Lillian Madison's Murder", *The Lebanon Daily News,* Lebanon, Pa, June 5, 1885

(62.3) The post-verdict sequence is fictional

(62.4) This is a verbatim transcription of a newspaper article (except the name of W.W. Crump was removed by the author) The final two sentences were added by the author for the benefit of the reader:

"Cluverius Sentenced: Judge Atkins' Solemn Address", *The Daily Index-Appeal,* Petersburg, Va,, June 20, 1885

(63.1)   Kinsley, Ardyce et al <u>THE FITZHUGH LEE SAMPLER</u>, *Jack Hayes Remembers the Battle at Crooked Creek*, p.23-27

(63.2) Although Fitzhugh Lee was clearly invited to attend and participate in the funeral of Ulysses S. Grant, this correspondence between Fitz Lee and Mrs. Grant is fabricated by the author.

(63.3) THE DEMOCRATIC STATE CONVENTION, JULY 29, 1885

Excerpts from the speeches of John S. Barbour and Henry R. Pollard with some slight modifications

"The Virginia Democrats: State Convention in Session", *The Baltimore Sun,* Baltimore, Md, July 30, 1885

(63.4) As stated in the chapter, this is an excerpt from:

"General Fitzhugh Lee: Nominated for Governor – a Black Eye for Senator Mahone", *The Boston Weekly Globe,* Boston, Ma, August 4, 1885

(63.5) This is a slightly modified excerpt from *The Van Wert Weekly Bulletin,* Van Wert, Ohio., August 7, 1885. It is actually a printing of an opinion, according to the citation in the paper, from *The*

Bellefontaine Republican, Bellefontaine, Ohio. The author attributed it to *The National Republican* for simplicity.

(64.1) This is a dramatized version of the Confederate Army's "Final War Council" based upon:

Nichols, James L., GENERAL FITZHUGH LEE, a BIOGRAPHY, H.E. Howard, Inc., Lynchburg, VA, 1989, p. 86-89

(64.2) "The Story of a Soldier: Two Brave Veterans Who Reached a Happy Drama of Life", *The Evening Light,* San Antonio, TX, February 19, 1883

(64.3) "Fitz Lee's Tribute: The South Sends Us to Make Up", *The Daily Index-Appeal,* Petersburg, Va,, August 11, 1885

(65.1) This interview was actually conducted in Atlanta, Georgia by a reporter from the *New York Times*. The printing the author found appeared in:

"Virginia Politics: Hon. John S. Wise Interviewed – Comments on Democratic Nominations", *The Baltimore Sun,* Baltimore, Md., August 1, 1885

The author incorporated some background on the Readjuster Movement into the "interview". Information on this can be found in:

Pearson, C. C., "The Readjuster Movement in Virginia", *The American Historical Review,* Vol. 21, No. 4, Oxford University Press, July, 1916, pp. 734-749

(66.1) Heros von Borcke was smuggled in to Charleston, SC on a blockade runner (*The Kate*); but, of course, it was not on a boat captained by Billy Pierce.

Von Borcke, Heros, MEMOIRS of the CONFEDERATE WAR for INDEPENDENCE, 1867, Arcadia Press Print Edition, 2017, p.11-12

(66.2) This chapter is fictional

(67.1) The campaign event is fictional but is based upon information about several of Fitz Lee's campaign events

Kinsley, Ardyce et al THE FITZHUGH LEE SAMPLER, *John Daniels Remembers Some Campaign Highlights*, p.115-119

Jones, J. William, VIRGINIA'S NEXT GOVERNOR, GENERAL FITZHUGH LEE, N.Y. Cheap Publishing Co., New York, 1885, Scholar Select Reprint

"State Capital Topics", *The Daily Index-Appeal,* Petersburg, Va,, September 15, 1885

"Virginia Politics", *The Newark Daily Advocate,* Newark, Ohio, September 1, 1885

Fitz's speech is fictional but is primarily based upon the official Democrat Party of Virginia's Platform as stated in:

"Platform of the Democratic Party of Virginia", *The Peninsula Enterprise,* Accomac Courthouse, Va,, August 8, 1885

(67.2)　The commentary from these various outlets was compiled and printed in:

"Virginia Politics: Hon. John S. Wise Interviewed – Comments on Democratic Nominations", *The Baltimore Sun,* Baltimore, Md., August 1, 1885

(67.3)　This is a verbatim transcription of an article which appeared in:

"Logan on the Rampage", *The Baltimore Sun,* Baltimore, Md, October 10, 1885

(67.4)　Kinsley, Ardyce et al THE FITZHUGH LEE SAMPLER, *Jack Hayes Remembers How to "Fotch" and Indian,* p.28-32

(68.1)　All of these snippets were found in:

"The Campaign: Points and Paragraphs Gathered from All Sources", *The Daily Index-Appeal,* Petersburg, Va,, October 21, 1885

(68.2)　*The Muscatine Daily Journal,* October 12, 1885

(68.3)　Kinsley, Ardyce et al THE FITZHUGH LEE SAMPLER, *John Daniels Remembers Some Campaign Highlights,* p.117

(68.4)　Excerpted from: "Virginia Democratic: Fitz Lee Elected Governor and a Democratic Legislature in Both Branches", *(Special Dispatch to the Baltimore Sun from the Richmond Dispatch), The Baltimore Sun,* Baltimore, Md, November 4, 1885

(69.1)　Jane Tunstall apparently owed C. H. Deuring a significant amount of money at some point. He sued her for $840

"Virginia News", *The Peninsula Enterprise,* Accomac Courthouse, Va,, August 22, 1885

Jane Tunstall did eventually "give up" and go home, after spending over six months in Richmond trying to help Thomas Cluverius. It appears she left Richmond in late December, 1885. In the story, the author has her leaving nearly one year later.

"The Capital City", *The Daily Index-Appeal,* Petersburg, Va,, August 8, 1885

"Cluverius Ill in Prison", *The Daily News,* Frederick, Md., December 21, 1885

(69.2)　This episode is fictional. There is no evidence that Willie Cluverius attended a cockfight during this period. However, it is apparent that raising funds for Thomas Cluverius' defense was on the family's minds.

(70.1) John B. Hoey, "Federalist Opposition to the War of 1812", Archiving Early America -Varsity Tutors, 2007-2019,

https://www.varsitytutors.com/earlyamerica/early-america-review/volume-4/federalist-opposition-to-the-war-of-1812

Roger Peace, "The War of 1812," United States Foreign Policy History and Resource Guide website, 2016,

http://peacehistory-usfp.org/the-war-of-1812.

(70.2) Thomson, John, AN EXACT and AUTHENTIC NARRATIVE, of the EVENTS WHICH TOOK PLACE in BALTIMORE, on the 27th and 28th of JULY LAST, Printed for the Purchasers, September 1, 1812, Classic Reprint Series - Forgotten Books, 2017

(71.1) The legislation as it appeared in:

Acts and Joint Resolutions Passed by the General Assembly of the State of Virginia During the Session of 1885-86, Richmond, Va, A.R. Micou, Superintendent of Public Printing, 1886, Chap. 39, p.41

The Rockingham Register, Harrisonburg, Va., January 28, 1886

(71.2) Robert Popper, "History and Development of the Accused's Right to Testify", *WASHINGTON UNIVERSITY LAW QUARTERLY*, Vol. 1962, No. 4, December, 1962, p. 461

(71.3) Robert Popper, "History and Development of the Accused's Right to Testify", *WASHINGTON UNIVERSITY LAW QUARTERLY*, Vol. 1962, No. 4, December, 1962, p. 470-471

(71.4) Cluverius, Thomas J., CLUVERIUS. MY LIFE, TRIAL, and CONVICTION, S.J. Dudley, Richmond, VA, 1887 – "Making of Modern Law" Print Edition, p.88

(72.1) An episode similar to this actually happened in the lobby of the Willard Hotel sometime after the war. Fitz was seated reading a newspaper in the lobby when he overheard the conversation about the toddies at Catlett's Station. Colonel Louis Marshall, USA was actually Fitz Lee's first cousin. Marshall's mother, Anne Kinloch Lee, was the older sister of Robert E. Lee and Sydney Smith Lee. Marshall fought for the Union.

Kinsley, Ardyce et al THE FITZHUGH LEE SAMPLER, *JEB Stuart Remembers His Second in Command*, p.54

(72.2) These men (McBurney, Laughlin, and Cannan) were actually members of the 1st Ohio Cavalry, but this reunion and chance meeting with Governor Lee is fictional.

1st Ohio Cavalry, USA - Roster

https://civilwarindex.com/armyoh/rosters/1st_oh_cavalry_roster.pdf

Companies A and C served under General Pope in August/September, 1862

http://civilwarintheeast.com/us-regiments-batteries/ohio/1st-ohio-cavalry/

(72.3) Von Borcke, Heros, MEMOIRS of the CONFEDERATE WAR for INDEPENDENCE, 1867, Arcadia Press Print Edition, 2017, p. 44-46

John C. Frankeberger was a Quartermaster for the 1st Ohio Cavalry – but the author is not certain he is the captured quartermaster referenced in Heros von Borcke's book.

(73.1) Excerpted from: "Cluverius Must Hang: a New Hearing Refused Him; the Case Remanded to Richmond", *The Baltimore Sun, Supplement*, October 1, 1886

(73.2) Excerpted and lightly altered: "Cluverius Condemned: Date of Death Fixed at December 10th (from *Richmond Whig-October 10, 1886)"*, *The Rockingham Register*, Harrisonburg, Va., October 14, 1886

(73.3) Verbatim transcription A Startling Confession: "Cluverius to Make a Statement About the Celebrated Murder Case", *The Massillon Independent*, Massillon, Ohio, December 3, 1886

(73.4) "Thomas Judson Cluverius: His Long Looked-for Statement Comes Out", *The Columbus Enquirer-Sun*, Columbus, Ga., December 5, 1886

Cluverius, Thomas J., CLUVERIUS. MY LIFE, TRIAL, and CONVICTION, S.J. Dudley, Richmond, VA, 1887 – "Making of Modern Law" Print Edition, p.90-93

(73.5) It should be noted that Mr. Chiles' statement says he had the chance meeting with Lillie Madison on the 12th of March. The other testimony in the case would indicate that he was mistaken and that this meeting actually occurred on the 13th of March.

"The "Old Man's" Statement (from *The Richmond State*)", *The Rockingham Register*, Harrisonburg, Va., December 23, 1886

"The Latest Sensation", *The Daily Times*, Richmond, Va., December 14, 1886

(73.6) "An Appeal for Vengeance: Prays for the Death of Her Daughter's Alleged Murderer", *The Evening Gazette*, Monmouth, IL., December 8, 1886

(73.7) This interview with Hermann Joel is based upon a carbon copy of a typewritten "Memorandum" of the interview Governor Lee conducted of Joel on November 30, 1886 which is in the author's personal collection

(73.8) "No Pardon: Letter of Governor Lee Declining to Intervene with the Judgment of the Courts in the Cluverius Case", *The Daily Times*, Richmond, Va., December 8, 1886

(73.9) This original letter from Thomas J. Cluverius to Governor Fitzhugh Lee dated December 8, 1886 is part of the author's collection. It also was printed in the newspaper

"The Respite: Cluverius Allowed Five Weeks for Final Preparations", *The Daily Times*, Richmond, Va., December 9, 1886

(74.1)   This original letter from William B. Cluverius to Governor Fitzhugh Lee is part of the author's collection.

(74.2)   This letter is composed by the author but based upon newspaper reporting of Carter Harrison's appeal to Governor Lee

"Cluverius: Juror Harrison Says His Trial Was "A Horrible and Ghastly Farce"", *The Peninsula Enterprise,* Accomac Courthouse, Va,, January 8, 1887

(74.3)   Death of Senator John A. Logan

The Peninsula Enterprise, Accomac Courthouse, Va,, January 8, 1887

(74.4)   Williams Carter Wickham was a cousin of Fitzhugh Lee. Although he was against secession, once Virginia left the Union, Wickham went with his state and served in the Confederate Cavalry, rising to the rank of Brigadier General. He was under Fitzhugh Lee's command at various actions, including Yellow Tavern and Wilson's Wharf (See Chapter 46). He would go on to become a Republican State Senator, where he and his dear cousin Fitz would continue to be on opposite sides of many issues. However, there is no indication that this damaged their affection for one another. The author informally refers to Wickham as "Carter". This is an assumption and could be in error.

(74.5)   "Three Days Before His Death: Cluverius Appears Unshaken", *The Daily Index-Appeal,* Petersburg, Va,, January 12, 1887

(75.1)   "Cluverius", *The Peninsula Enterprise,* Accomac Courthouse, Va,, January 15, 1887

(75.2)   Reverend Hatcher was overheard reading scripture pertaining to "blood guiltiness" to Cluverius the night before the execution

Ezekiel, Herbert T., THE RECOLLECTIONS of a VIRGINIA NEWSPAPER MAN, Herbert T. Ezekiel, Printer and Publisher, Richmond, VA, 1920, p.45

(75.3)   "Death Penalty: The Last Sad Act in the Reservoir Tragedy", *The Daily Times*, Richmond, Va., January 15, 1887

"With Silken Rope, Thomas J. Cluverius is Hung by the Neck", *The Weekly Constitution*, Atlanta, Ga., January 18, 1887

"Cluverius Hanged", *The Advertiser-Courier*, Hermann, Mo., January 19, 1887

"Cluverius Executed: He Dies Without Confessing; His Wonderful Nerve to the Last, *The Rockingham Register*, January 20, 1887

"The Penalty Paid: Cluverius Executed-He Dies Without Confessing-Wonderful Nerve to the Last", *The Salem Times-Register,* Salem, Va., January 21, 1887

(75.3) This poem, *All's for the Best* by Tupper (and the inscription in pencil) was actually found in the pocket of Thomas Cluverius when he was first arrested and brought to the Richmond City Jail.

"The Cluverius Trial: Judge Atkins Refuses to Admit Torn Note in Evidence", *The Sunday Eagle*, Brooklyn, NY, May 24, 1885

(E1) "The End of it All: Cluverius' Body Sent Home", *The Daily Index-Appeal*, Petersburg, Va,, January 17, 1887

(E2) "The End of it All: Cluverius' Body Sent Home", *The Daily Index-Appeal*, Petersburg, Va,, January 17, 1887

(E3) "Murder Most Foul: The Sad Fate of a Young Virginia Girl", *The Rockingham Register*, Harrisonburg, Va., March 26, 1885

(E4) Anonymous, THOMAS J. CLUVERIUS vs COMMONWEALTH OF VIRGINIA, Johns and Goolsby, Richmond, VA, c. 1885 – "Making of Modern Law" Print Edition., p. 74

"Detective Wren Dead: Pneumonia Puts an End to an Eventful and Exciting Career", *The Daily Times*, Richmond, Va., March 5, 1890

(E5) Census Information on appalachianaristocracy.com for Jane Frances Walker Tunstall
http://www.appalachianaristocracy.com/getperson.php?personID=I5922&tree=01

JANE TUNSTALL DEATH NOTICE - *The Landmark*, Statesville, NC., May 26, 1892

(E6) Census Information on appalachianaristocracy.com for William B. Cluverius
http://www.appalachianaristocracy.com/getperson.php?personID=I5871&tree=01

(E7) Ezekiel, Herbert T., THE RECOLLECTIONS of a VIRGINIA NEWSPAPER MAN, Herbert T. Ezekiel, Printer and Publisher, Richmond, VA, 1920, *Peter J. Burton*, p.104-106

"Condensed News", *The Philadelphia Inquirer*, January 21, 1886

Acts and Joint Resolutions Passed by the General Assembly of the State of Virginia During the Session of 1885-86, Richmond, Va., A.R. Micou, Superintendent of Public Printing, 1886, Chap 447, p. 505

(E8) "The Respite: Cluverius Allowed Five Weeks for Final Preparations", *The Daily Times*, Richmond, Va., December 9, 1886

"Arrested for an Attempt to Bribe a Witness in Behalf of Cluverius", *The Staunton Spectator*, Staunton, Va., December 15, 1886

"Deuring's Trial Postponed", *The Daily Times*, Richmond, Va., February 20, 1887

(E9) "Police Court", *The Evening Truth*, Richmond, Va., June 21, 1887

(E10) Ezekiel, Herbert T., THE RECOLLECTIONS of a VIRGINIA NEWSPAPER MAN, Herbert T. Ezekiel, Printer and Publisher, Richmond, VA, 1920, *Dr. William H. Taylor*, p. 93-97

Taylor, William H., M.D., Science and the Soul: A Lecture to the Class in Medical Jurisprudence of the Medical College of Virginia, *The Old Dominion Journal of Medicine and Surgery*, Vol. IV, No. 5, October, 1905, p. 186-198

Dabney, Virginius, RICHMOND: THE STORY of a CITY, University of Virginia Press, Charlottesville and London, 1990, p. 252

(E11)   Von Borcke, Heros, MEMOIRS of the CONFEDERATE WAR for INDEPENDENCE, 1867, Arcadia Press Print Edition, 2017, p. 187, 193

(E12)   17th Virginia Infantry, CSA, Co. H, Old Dominion Rifles
http://stevegibson0.tripod.com/co_h.htm

Made in the
USA
Middletown, DE